# The Cherry Cola Book Club

Center Point
Large Print

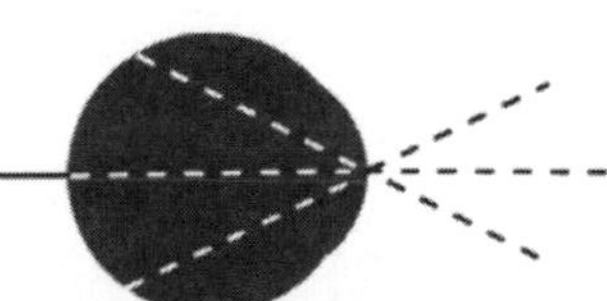

# The Cherry Cola Book Club

## ASHTON LEE



CENTER POINT LARGE PRINT
THORNDIKE, MAINE

This Center Point Large Print edition
is published in the year 2013 by arrangement with
Kensington Publishing Corp.



The text of this Large Print edition is unabridged.
In other aspects, this book may vary
from the original edition.
Printed in the United States of America
on permanent paper.
Set in 16-point Times New Roman type.

ISBN: 978-1-61173-713-4

Library of Congress Cataloging-in-Publication Data

Lee, Ashton.
The Cherry Cola Book Club / Ashton Lee. — Center Point Large Print edition.
pages cm
ISBN 978-1-61173-713-4 (Library binding : alk. paper)
1. Librarians—Mississippi—Fiction.
2. Library users—Mississippi—Fiction.
3. Book clubs (Discussion groups)—Fiction.
4. Library outreach programs—Fiction. 5. Mississippi—Fiction.
6. Large type books. I. Title.
PS3612.E34253C44 2013
813′.6—dc23

2013002153

For Weesie and Bob, beloved parents

# Acknowledgments

My creation of the Cherico, Mississippi, universe would not have been possible without the help and advice of so many friends, professionals, and family members. I must begin with my superb agents, Christina Hogrebe and Meg Ruley, of the Jane Rotrosen Agency, who matched me up with John Scognamiglio of Kensington Books. John makes the editor-author relationship a seamless one.

Next, I owe a great deal to my aunt, Abigail Jenkins Healy, for rounding up and certifying a number of delicious Southern dishes for the recipe section at the back of the book. These dishes appear in the plot, and I thought it would be a homey touch to allow readers to experience these dishes themselves.

Many librarians have contributed to this novel with their encouragement and factual input. Among them: Susan Cassagne, Marianne Raley, Deb Mitchell, Catherine Nathan, Jennifer Smith, Lesa Holstine, Regina Cooper, Susan Delmas, Judy Clark, Jackie Warfield, Derek Schaaf, Alice Shands, the staff of St. Mary Parish Library, in Franklin, Louisiana, Larie Myers, and Angelle Deshoutelles.

Many thanks also to Jerry Seaman for his fishing lure lessons, which I trust I learned well. And to my many Facebook followers at facebook.com/ashtonlee.net, I have appreciated your comments and support more than you know.

# The Cherry Cola Book Club

# 1

# Books versus Bulldozers

Maura Beth Mayhew shut her sky blue eyes and let the unsettling words that had just been thrown her way sink in for a few tense moments. When she finally opened them, she flipped her whiskey-colored curls defiantly at Councilman Durden Sparks and his two underlings seated at the other end of the meeting room table. Their only distinction was their nicknames—as in "Chunky" Badham, who had not missed many meals along the way, and "Gopher Joe" Martin, the consummate "yes man" if ever there was one. Colorful monikers aside, Maura Beth had no intention of letting any of them roll over her with those bulldozers they kept on romancing as if they were the secret to unlocking the universe.

"You actually think the citizens of Cherico are going to stand for this?" she said, her voice trembling noticeably as the stress crept into her face.

Councilman Sparks flashed his matinee idol eyes and prominent white teeth—the source of his ongoing popularity with many female voters—and leaned toward the town's pretty young librarian of six years standing. "Miz Mayhew," he began, "don't panic. This won't happen tomorrow. We'll give you up until our budget approval at the end of November to rev up that library of yours. Use the next five months to show this Council why we should continue to fund it in lieu of other, more beneficial projects such as our proposed Cherico Industrial Park."

Maura Beth had her response at the ready. "Interesting that you call it *my* library, now that you don't think it has any value. Or maybe you never did."

"Perhaps you're right," he answered, nodding her way. "I remember when I was eight years old and I wanted to participate in summer reading like some of my classmates were doing. They were getting blue ribbons for finishing a certain number of books, and that got my competitive juices flowing. I asked my mother if I could sign up, and I'll never forget how she rambled on about it. She described The Cherico Library as a burden for the taxpayers and told me that the librarian at the time, Miz Annie Scott, did nothing all day but read her favorite novels and try to get in good with all the wealthy families so she could wangle donations. Mom believed it was no coincidence that their children were the ones that always got the ribbons and that I could make much better use of my time playing sports and getting good grades. So that's what I did."

The shock clearly showed on Maura Beth's face. "I had no idea you had such a jaundiced view of the library. But you actually think that grading that tract of glorified cow pasture on the north end of town will pay dividends for Cherico?"

"We're not flying by the seat of our pants here. We've commissioned a study," he answered, brandishing a thin bound volume in the process. "We believe several viable companies would locate here if we prepare the land for them properly. That would bring jobs to our struggling little community. It would mean growth for us in this stagnant economy."

Well, there it was. The broken record of the current crop of local politicians who had gotten re-elected to office in Cherico, Mississippi, two years ago in the fall of 2010. They had won because they had campaigned with the same stale bumper stickers, but now that they'd gotten in once again, their mantra had suddenly morphed into growth and change. Even if she knew—and Durden Sparks, Chunky Badham, and Gopher Joe Martin also knew damned good and well—that Cherico was not the type of town that wanted to get busier with traffic and attract a lot of those copycat, big-box franchises that advertised on television all the time. It did not even have a daily newspaper anymore—only one of those weekly shopping guides full of coupons, discounts, and special sales gimmicks on certain days of the week.

No, Cherico was small and parochial, even

xenophobic at times. It had never taken full advantage of its picturesque location on Lake Cherico, which itself was a finger of the Tennessee River System in the extreme northeast corner of Mississippi. The town was not actually old enough to be called antebellum; indeed, it barely qualified for the Victorian Era with a smattering of homes in the Queen Anne or Swiss Chalet style here and there. Overall, the architecture was muddled and mundane.

Mostly, though, Cherico was full of people who wanted to be left alone, particularly the newer citizens who had built their ritzy vacation retreats and boathouses out on the lake and were therefore not even year-round residents. When they dropped in on the environs during warmer weather for some fishing and skiing, it was only for a few weeks at a time, maybe as long as a month, and they stayed out of local politics as a result.

"What you cannot deny, Miz Mayhew," Councilman Sparks continued after a healthy sip from his water glass, "is that your circulation figures have steadily declined over the past three years, and they weren't going gangbusters before you came here, either. By your own admission, your only regular patrons are Miss Voncille Nettles and the Crumpton sisters, who gather in your meeting room once a month."

"That's an exaggeration," Maura Beth said, her eyes flashing. "We have our regulars who check out books and DVDs. And just for the record, we also have the very respectable Mr. Locke Linwood attending 'Who's Who in Cherico?' His wife, Pamela, was also a regular before her untimely passing, as I'm sure you recall."

"Yes, I do. It was a most unfortunate event. Very well, then. I stand corrected. Three spinsters and a widower attend these utterly fascinating meetings." Councilman Sparks loudly cleared his throat and continued, "At any rate, they gather to run on about their fabled family trees. As if who begat whom is going to change from week to week. Hey, the bottom line is, you're stuck with your genes—good, bad, or something in between—and no amount of flowery window dressing will make any difference, to my way of thinking."

" 'Who's Who in Cherico?' has been the benchmark for genealogical research for many years," Maura Beth proclaimed. "Miss Voncille Nettles spends countless hours researching deeds and such at the courthouse for accuracy. She knows everything about everybody, as well as all sorts of historical nuggets about this town."

Councilman Sparks pursed his lips as if he had just taken a swallow of sour milk. "Tell me about it. I think sometimes we should just set up a cot for the darling lady in the archives and lock her in for the night. Maybe throw in a pitcher of water and a chamber pot for good measure. But Miss Voncille and her followers could just as easily meet in someone's living room as your library. They'd certainly have more space, and I bet she and her little crowd would enjoy a libation or two while they gossip about their dear, dead relatives. Unless you've changed the policy without my knowledge, I don't believe the library allows the consumption of adult beverages, if you will, on its premises. Why, that little bunch could leave you high and dry if they decided they'd had enough of teetotaling all these years. Face it, Miz Mayhew, they're now your only viable claim to fame!"

Chunky and Gopher Joe snickered, winked at each other, and nodded their heads knowingly while Maura Beth did her best to suppress her disgust. She knew those two would never carry on in such a disrespectful manner anywhere other than this special budget session she was being forced to endure without benefit of a single witness. It was clear that as far as they were concerned, she fit the definition of the proverbial redheaded stepchild.

"May I quote you on all that, Councilman Sparks?" Maura Beth said.

"It would be a 'he said, she said' at best, I'm afraid. You'll be gravely disappointed if you try to rally the public, because it's my belief that almost nobody out there really gives a damn about the library. It's my job as a politician to read the tea leaves on all the issues, and I don't think I'm wrong about this one."

Maura Beth shot him a skeptical glance and decided to stay on the attack as long as she could. "I'm curious. Why don't you just close down the library right now? Why wait until you approve the new budget?"

After a particularly patronizing grin and an overly dramatic pause, Councilman Sparks said, "Because we wouldn't want to be accused of not giving you one last chance to turn it all around. Even though we're all supremely confident that you won't be able to, of course."

"Well, I have to admit you've done absolutely nothing to help me up to this point."

"And how's that? I don't profess to know anything about running a library, except the cost efficiency."

Maura Beth allowed herself to roll her eyes as she exhaled. "I'm referring to the fact that this Council has consistently refused my requests to fund a couple of computer terminals so the patrons can come in and access the Internet. That would have bolstered library use considerably over the past several years. It's what knowledgeable patrons all over the country have come to expect. But I guess that didn't suit your long-range agenda."

"There, I have to put my foot down," he said, making a fist of his right hand and pounding it twice on the table like a gavel. "The public can buy their own computers. Everybody I know has one—not to mention all the other electronic gadgets people use now to keep in touch no matter where they are." He cut his eyes first at Chunky, then at Gopher Joe.

"Matter of fact, that reminds me of a joke going around. Stop me if you've heard it. Seems this fella walks into a doctor's office complaining of a peculiar growth on his ear, and now he's constantly hearing bells and loud voices. He's been really worried about it for a while and finally decides to get a medical opinion. 'Do ya think it might be a tumor, or am I going crazy, Doc?' the man says. Whereupon the doc flicks on his flashlight, squints real hard looking around, and finally answers, 'Nope, you're fine. It's just your cell phone.' "

The guffawing from Chunky and Gopher Joe was devastating for Maura Beth. She felt as if they were laughing at her and the joke was their cover. When it had all finally died down, she found herself staring at their wrinkled, solemn faces and wondering if these lackeys had ever in their lives read anything that had not been required for their high-school book reports light-years ago. In fact, she had strong anecdotal evidence to that effect when at a previous meeting, Chunky had rambled on about "all those snooty books in the library like *'Silence' Marner* that nobody likes to read." Even so, she knew she was up against it big-time, and that it would do her no good to continue to aggravate this powerful, privileged trio.

"Very funny joke. But I still have about five months to turn things around," she managed, quickly recovering from her unpleasant mental review. "And if I do so, you'll continue the library's funding?"

Councilman Sparks took his time, casting his eyes toward the whirring ceiling fan as he considered. "I wish I could give you a guarantee, Miz Mayhew. But if you do nothing to change the status quo, The Cherico Library is history. We can't justify the expense any longer. If you should impress us enough, maybe we'll be willing to work something out. Just remember, though—you'll need more than Miss Voncille beating the drum on your behalf. The fact is, there's no millage specifically dedicated to the library, and we think the time has come to stop pretending that we're getting good value for our money in this particular line item of the budget."

Meager as that peace offering was, it was still a vestige of hope from the powers-that-be. Maura Beth caught herself smirking faintly as the session came to an end and she rose from her seat without fanfare. "Please, gentlemen," she told them, nodding in their general direction. "By all means, don't bother to get up. I know you really don't want to."

Alone among the three, Councilman Sparks stood and executed a hurried little bow.

As she made her way down the hall, memories

of library science school at LSU suddenly flashed into Maura Beth's head. There had been no course titled "Dealing with Politicians 101," nor even something along the lines of "Elementary Schmoozing." There should have been, though. Some wise professor should have stood before her and the other innocent young library students taking lecture notes and warned them that the political aspects of librarianship were going to be the most difficult to maneuver. That libraries and their scant millages would usually find themselves first to be cut and last to be restored. It always seemed to be easier for politicians to favor the sound of bulldozers in motion over the static silence of the printed word.

Maura Beth walked down the steps of Cherico City Hall and out onto Commerce Street as if she had just been handed a prison sentence. Five months to get cracking. Her shoulders were slumped, and the blazing June sun glinting off the asphalt made them slump even more. It was just past three in the afternoon, and even though she had skipped lunch, she had no appetite at all. What she needed was a big helping of solace, not sustenance. So she made her way deliberately past the familiar lineup of one-story brick and wooden storefronts: Audra Neely's Antiques; Cherico Ace Hardware; Vernon Dotrice Insurance Agency; and Curtis L. Trickett, Attorney at Law, among others.

Finally, she reached the shade of the big blue-and-white awning dotted with silver stars belonging to The Twinkle, Twinkle Café. Inside, she knew she would find its owner and the woman who had become her sounding board since her move to Cherico half a dozen years ago—Periwinkle Lattimore.

"Maura Beth, you get your cute little redheaded self in here before you wilt like my famous warm spinach salad!" Periwinkle called out the second she spotted her friend sighing at the delicious blast of air-conditioned relief that greeted her just inside the door. The place was empty, being right in the middle of the no-man's-land between the lunch and dinner crowds, but the welcoming fragrance of spices and herbs lingered over the dozen or so tables with their blue-and-white tablecloths and delicate votive candles. Periwinkle quickly pointed to a corner two-seater beneath a mobile sporting an elaborate array of gold and silver metallic stars. "Right over there, honey! I'll wait on ya myself!"

"Oh, I didn't come to eat," Maura Beth said. "Just some much-needed talking and listening."

Periwinkle laughed brightly and headed over to the table with a complimentary glass of sweet tea. "Aha! Deep-fried talking and braised listening—my house specials!"

"And I've come for my fix. Sit with me until someone comes in."

Maura Beth had long ago concluded that the key to the success of The Twinkle, as many locals affectionately now called it, was Periwinkle's willingness to stop at nothing to keep it going. Not just ordering the food and supplies, but doing a major share of the cooking and even helping her waitress serve when the place got overwhelmed. The woman remained lean and indefatigable but somehow never seemed to break a sweat. Her blond hair with its stubborn dark roots was always styled attractively, never disheveled, even if she was seldom without the unsophisticated touch of a wad of Juicy Fruit gum in her mouth.

"So what's on your mind?" Periwinkle said, settling into her chair. "I can tell you're upset about something."

Maura Beth took a sip of her tea, breathed deeply, and then unloaded, covering every detail of the ordeal she had just endured at the hands of Cherico's three heavy-handed councilmen.

"Those . . . so-and-sos!" Periwinkle exclaimed, managing to restrain herself. "You mean you might lose your job? After all this time?"

"It's a distinct possibility."

Periwinkle put her elbows on the table, resting her fists under her chin as she contemplated. "Tell me true—do you think they would be taking you more seriously if you were a man?"

Maura Beth managed an ironic little chuckle. "Maybe, maybe not. In this case, I just think they're all about shuffling the budget around to suit themselves."

"I don't doubt it. But I wonder if they'd be as willing to bulldoze you—using your words here, honey—if you had a pair. Listen, we women have to fight for everything we get. Do you think I would have gotten the seed money to start this restaurant if I'd pulled my punches in my divorce settlement with Harlan Lattimore? Hell, he wanted to ditch me high and dry, but I bowed up and said, 'No, sir, you won't! Not after thirteen years of marriage, and my salad days are in my rear-view mirror. I helped you make a success of The Marina Bar and Grill, working hard as your secretary day and night, and I'll be damned if you'll leave me out in the middle of the water without a paddle!' "

There was a touch of envy in Maura Beth's quiet little sigh. "You certainly know how to stand up for yourself. Of course I know I can't let these men intimidate me. That's exactly what they want. But I can't force people to come to the library, either. I just don't know if there's a way out of this."

"You gotta have you a gimmick," Periwinkle replied, leaning in while furiously working her gum. "Listen to this. When I was trying to come up with a name for my restaurant, I realized that it wouldn't matter what I called it if my food was no good. I know how to put together a delicious meal, though, so that part didn't worry me. But I thought to myself that a catchy name might just get 'em in the door the first time, and then they'd be hooked. Did I ever tell you that I originally wanted to call this place Twinkle, Twinkle, Periwinkle's?"

They both laughed heartily, and Maura Beth said, "No. So why didn't you? I just love that!"

"Well, I thought it might be a bit too cutesy. So I ran it past my mother over in Corinth, and she said, 'Peri, honey, that sounds like you're running one a' those baby boutiques. You know—where they sell bassinets and cradles and that kinda stuff.' And after I thought about it for a while, I knew she was right on the money. So I put the café part in there so people would know it was definitely a new place to eat. Since then, of course, everyone's shortened it to The Twinkle. It's all worked out, but you need to come up with something that'll get people into your library pronto so you can fend off those fat cats."

Just then, a somewhat plump but still appealing middle-aged woman wearing big bouffant hair and a busy floral muumuu flounced through the front door, waving and smiling expectantly all the way. "Periwinkle," she said, slightly out of breath, "I finally found the time to pick up those tomato aspics I ordered this morning. I've been running behind all day with my errands."

Periwinkle stood up and offered her hand as the

woman reached their table. “They’re in the fridge, cool as a cucumber. I’ll run go get ’em for ya.” She quickly made a half turn toward the kitchen, but stopped just as suddenly in her tracks. “Now, where are my manners? Let me introduce you two. Maura Beth Mayhew, this is one of my newest customers, Connie McShay. She and her husband just moved here from Nashville about a month ago.” Periwinkle paused for a quick breath. “Connie, I’m sure you’ll be interested to hear that Maura Beth runs our library. I don’t have much time for books myself since The Twinkle takes up every minute of my day, but I’m sure Maura Beth’ll welcome a new patron with open arms, won’tcha, honey?”

“I most certainly will!” Maura Beth exclaimed, rising from her seat to shake hands and exchange further pleasantries while Periwinkle hurried off to retrieve the aspics.

“I’ve been meaning to drop by your library, you know,” Connie continued with an authentic warmth in her voice. “My husband, Douglas, and I have been so busy settling into our lodge on the lake, though. We’ve popped in only a week or two every year, but now we’re here for good. We still have so many boxes to unpack. I could swear those cardboard creatures somehow managed to reproduce in that moving van on the way down. Anyway, I’m a *huge* reader, and I even belonged to a wonderful book club up in Nashville. We called ourselves The Music City Page Turners."

Maura Beth brightened considerably. "And that's music to my ears. You simply must get your card soon and pick out a couple of the new best sellers we've just gotten in. I use every last cent the library has to keep up with all the popular reads. What's your genre, by the way?"

"I'm the ultimate mystery buff. But I only like the polite kind where they figure out everything over tea and buttered scones. No bloody, gory, true crime forensics for me. When Agatha Christie died, I went into literary mourning for months. No more Miss Marple padding around the village of St. Mary Mead stumbling onto murders committed by the landed gentry, what ho! Or Hercule Poirot waxing his mustache, for that matter."

Maura Beth laughed and was about to reply when Periwinkle reappeared with a small paper bag and handed it over to Connie. "Your aspics are just as snug as oysters in the shell in their little plastic containers in there. Just don't brake for any squirrels on the way home, and they should hold their shape nicely."

"Here's seven bucks, and keep the change as usual," Connie said, chuckling while she proffered a bill she had just retrieved from her purse.

"Much appreciated again, honey," Periwinkle replied, tucking the money into her apron pocket.

Then Connie leaned into Maura Beth as if they

had been the best of friends for the longest time. "Don't you just love these tomato aspics? I was hooked the first time I bit into one and got a mouthful of that sinful cream cheese that was hiding in the middle. Douglas makes me get them now practically every other night for our dinner. That's all we seem to eat these days—aspic and whatever fish he catches that day out on the lake. That I end up cleaning, by the way. Some retirement—I've spent most of it so far with stringers and fish scalers. Maybe I need to put my foot down."

"I don't know about that, but you've single-handedly turned tomato aspic into my biggest seller," Periwinkle added. Suddenly, she began giggling and couldn't seem to stop. "I'm sorry," she continued finally, "but I just thought of what a difficult time I had selling my aspic when I first opened up. No one would ever order it, and I couldn't figure out why. I knew there was nothing wrong with my recipe. It was my mother's, and everybody in the family always raved about it. Then one day the mystery was solved when one of my customers, a very polite older man visiting down here from somewhere in Ohio, complimented me on the food on the way out. But he also said, 'Just to satisfy my curiosity, could you tell me what *icepick* salad is? Your waitress recommended it as an appetizer, but it sounded pretty dangerous to me, so I passed on it. I've just spent a fortune having most of my teeth capped.' "

Both Maura Beth and Connie looked halfway between amused and bewildered as Periwinkle caught her breath once again.

"I know, ladies. I had that same expression on my face when that dear little man asked me that question. The deal is, there's a certain type of Southern accent where people pronounce words like nasty as 'nicety,' glass becomes 'glice,' cancer turns into 'kindsuh,' and, of course, aspic winds up as 'icepick.' Maybe you've run into somebody who does that. Anyway, my waitress at the time, Bonnie Lee Fentress, was the sweetest little thing, but that's the way she spoke, and she had no idea she was scaring people to death when she mentioned that item on the menu and left it at that. So I sat down with her and straightened out her diction, and lo and behold, my aspic was reborn. The rest is delicious history."

"I most certainly agree with that," Connie said while glancing at her watch. "Oh, I still have a million things to do, ladies. Let me run now. So nice visiting with you both."

"Don't forget about your library card!" Maura Beth called out as Connie exited as quickly as she had entered, hurling a muffled, "Will do!" from out on the sidewalk.

"I really like her," Periwinkle said as she and Maura Beth resumed their seats. "She may be living high on the hog out on the lake, but she's the salt of the earth—just my type."

Maura Beth was gazing at her tea in silence and let a few awkward moments go by. "Oh, yes, I know she'll be a welcome addition to Cherico, particularly since she's a reader," she finally offered, coming to. "I must track her down if she doesn't keep her word and come by for that card. She's given me an idea that might help the library out. It came to me just this second."

"Shoot!"

"That book club she said she belonged to," Maura Beth explained. "I need to pick her brain about that. Maybe we could get something like that going here in Cherico. You know, get people into the library to review books and socialize with each other. Maybe that's the type of gimmick you were talking about earlier that I could use to put the library back on the map."

Periwinkle looked particularly thoughtful and then nodded. "Couldn't hurt. I think you need to get on it right away, though."

"I knew I did the right thing coming in here to talk things over with you," Maura Beth added. "That shoulder of yours has come in handy quite a few times over the past several years."

Periwinkle reached across and patted her hand affectionately. "Hey, what are girlfriends for?"

# 2

# Turn That Page

The Cherico Library wasn't much to look at, and it was even harder to find. Tucked away on a little-used side street at the sinister-sounding address of 12 Shadow Alley, it had originally been a corrugated iron, farm implement warehouse seventy-something years ago. A decade later, a few wealthy matrons who decided it was time to improve the town had come up with the idea of starting a library and had even donated some of their inherited money to get one going. The City Council back then had been as indifferent as the current one was, however, and had done as little as possible in converting the warehouse into a suitable facility. The unproven rumor was that the lion's share of the funds had been cleverly pocketed by a couple of the politicians, including Durden Sparks's father. It seemed that Cherico had never suffered from an excess of integrity.

A few unimpressive improvements had followed over the years, consisting chiefly of tacking a couple of flimsy white columns onto a pedestrian portico and creating a cramped meeting room inside. There was no loading dock—just a back door—no off-street parking, and the building contained only a stingy 3,500 square feet of space for the librarian's office and shelving the entire collection. Although the fiction was more current, the nonfiction needed weeding for the more topical issues—but Maura Beth barely had enough of a budget to keep the patrons in best sellers, newspapers, and periodicals. It even made her feel guilty to endorse her own paycheck, which was far from what anyone would have called generous.

Oh, sure, it was enough for her to shop for groceries at The Cherico Market, pay the apartment rental, manage the note on her little Prius, and get her hair curled the way she liked at Cherico Tresses. But putting anything aside for the future—such as for a wedding, provided she could ever meet the right guy—was completely out of the question; and she was genuinely embarrassed by what was left in the coffers to pay the two circulation desk clerks that alternated workdays.

"I feel like a missionary in a foreign land sometimes," Maura Beth had confessed to Periwinkle shortly after they had first met. "I'm bound and determined to make everyone here in Cherico understand what a library is for and that they need to take advantage of it. Of course, I'm the first to admit that I got this job straight out of library school—right after my big booster shot of idealism that came with my diploma."

"Don't ever lose that kind of dedication, honey,"

Periwinkle had advised her back then. "No matter what happens. Because things'll bear down on ya both sooner and later. I speak from experience."

One week after the latest disheartening session with the City Council—another bona-fide example of "things bearing down"—Maura Beth was leaning back in her office chair and reflecting upon that memorable conversation with Periwinkle nearly six years earlier. Momentarily, Renette Posey, her Monday, Wednesday, and Friday front desk clerk, knocked on her door and popped her head in.

"There's a Mrs. Connie McShay here to see you. I just finished fixing her up with a library card," she said in the disarmingly sweet and girlish voice that had become her trademark. It was the main reason Maura Beth had hired the inexperienced eighteen-year-old permanently. She was, in fact, surprisingly good with the public—diplomatic beyond her years, even—and the library needed all the help it could get.

Maura Beth was hardly able to restrain herself, snapping to attention. "Yes! Show her in!" She'd been anticipating this meeting for the last five days, hoping that it would turn out to be the kickoff for holding on to her job and keeping the library open.

"Thanks so much for chatting with me over the phone and working this into your schedule," Maura Beth continued, as the two women shook hands and took their seats across from each other.

"Oh, it's my pleasure," Connie replied, quickly surveying Maura Beth's tiny, windowless office cluttered with book carts, uncrated boxes from wholesalers, and stacks of review journals. "Well, you weren't kidding about the lack of space here and the library being an afterthought with your politicians."

"Yes, I have to do practically everything around here. Order the books, process them, pay the invoices, even check things out when my clerks take their lunch break. I have no children's librarian, and no one in reference or technical services. It's a wonder that I even have this computer." Then she leaned in and lowered her voice. "Not to mention the lengths I go to in order to keep the collection safe. For instance, there's a supply of peanut butter crackers behind the front desk for Mr. Barnes Putzel. He's getting on up there, and his younger sister takes care of him. When he first started coming in, he'd spend all his time in reference and would eventually end up banging volumes of the encyclopedia together like a pair of cymbals. We had no choice but to ask him to put them down and leave. Then, his sister came in one day and suggested we offer him a couple of peanut butter crackers on the sly before he headed over to reference. She said they always calmed him down at home. So, I followed her advice, and we've had no trouble with him ever since. He's in heaven poring over the encyclopedias in blessed silence with no wear and tear on the bindings. The worst we have to deal with now is his peanut butter breath when he comes over to say good-bye."

"I have a thing for peanut butter crackers myself," Connie remarked, nodding with an appreciative grin.

"Yes, well, keeping the reference material safe with crackers is only a part of the reality of the small-town library with practically no funding. You have the patrons who don't understand why we don't have every best seller on the shelves yesterday, but don't bother to bring their books back because 'they've already paid for them with their taxes, so why not keep them?' Would they take a jackhammer and remove a piece of Shadow Alley out in front of the library because they'd paid for the streets and sidewalks? Not to mention the ones that show up with several boxes of moldy books from the turn of the century—not the millennium, but 1900, or even earlier—that they've just found in the attic and want to donate to us. 'If you'll pay for the fumigation,' is what I want to say to them, but instead we just end up having to smile politely and dispose of them as soon as they've left. You wouldn't believe how many people there are who think libraries don't take money to run and that everything gets on the shelves with the wave of a magic wand."

Connie was frowning and shaking her head now. "Is it really that bad here?"

"I wish I could say I was exaggerating."

"I can tell you're not," Connie continued, "because I'm still shocked by that ultimatum those councilmen gave you. I nearly dropped the receiver on the floor when you told me that. Nobody could get away with that sort of thing in Nashville."

Maura Beth pounded her fist on the desk for emphasis. "But Nashville, this isn't! That's why we've got to put our heads together and see if we can get a book club going. We've got to get more warm bodies in here and boost our circulation figures. I need your input as to how The Music City Page Turners worked, and we'll go from there."

Connie patted her well-sprayed and therefore inert bouffant hairdo and then settled back in her chair. "We had nearly thirty people in our club, mostly women, but there were a few men who showed up eventually. And you wouldn't believe what a fuss some of the divorced and widowed women made over them. They acted like high-school coeds. But that's another story for another day." She chuckled richly and cleared her throat. "We didn't start out with thirty, of course. Originally, we were just a group of seven and built from there. We concentrated on popular Southern writers, either classic or newcomers that had hit the big time. We'd meet quarterly, allowing six or seven weeks for all the members to read the selection for that particular quarter. So we ended up reviewing four books a year."

Maura Beth nodded approvingly. "Southern writers—I like that. I think that would work here. Faulkner, Richard Wright, Winston Groom, Willie Morris, Larry Brown—"

"Oh, we eventually got around to most of those men you mentioned and many more, of course," Connie interrupted. "But, oddly enough, we started out with Southern female writers like Margaret Mitchell, Eudora Welty, and Harper Lee—icons like that. I know our core of women really appreciated it, from the way they dug deep into the discussions. I like to say that it was probably all about heeding voices with estrogen in those early days."

"I've never heard it put quite like that," Maura Beth said, her laughter reflecting her surprise. "But there's no reason why we shouldn't go with that approach here. We could even call ourselves The Cherico Page Turners."

"Sounds good. It's not like we had a copyright on the page-turning concept."

"So, anything else I need to know about your club?"

Connie thought for a while, then perked up. "Well, I kept the books when we got big enough. I was always good with figures. Oh, and I almost forgot. We eventually brought our favorite dishes to these affairs—casseroles, layered salads, lemon and chocolate cake squares, just to name a few—and we learned to do our reviews fully sated after a few mishaps. When there were only seven of us starting out, we sat together in fairly close quarters. That's when we discovered that it's pretty distracting having someone's stomach growling loudly just when you're trying to make a serious literary point. You feel like you're being criticized right that instant."

"That's too funny!" Maura Beth exclaimed. "But it sounds like you ladies got past all that and literally made a delicious time of it."

"Not only that, but hardly anyone ever missed a meeting. Why, you practically had to be hospitalized with the swine flu or recovering from an auto accident not to show up."

A look of determination gripped Maura Beth's face as she set her jaw firmly. "And that sort of loyalty is exactly what we need to jump-start this library again. Only I was thinking that since we have just about five months to work with, we ought to shorten the reading time for our selections. We need to try to squeeze at least two meetings into our agenda before the deadline. I don't think one would be enough to gather any momentum and impress anybody, much less that bunch running City Hall. But once we're good and established, we can try a more leisurely pace the way you did in Nashville." She brought herself up short, flashing a grin. "Listen to me, going on as if we've got this thing in the bag."

"There's nothing wrong with that. You should definitely act like it's a done deal."

Maura Beth nodded enthusiastically and busied herself making notes, leaving Connie to mull things over during the ensuing silence. "Have you thought about how you're going to advertise the club, Maura Beth?" she finally said. "We printed up tons of flyers for our meetings and distributed them to all the branches in Davidson County, plus we found lots of restaurants downtown that let us tack them up for their lunch crowds."

"Flyers would absolutely work," Maura Beth answered, looking up and momentarily putting down her pen. "I know how to do that, and I could get Periwinkle to hand them out to all her customers at The Twinkle. I could also put a sign-up sheet on our bulletin board here for people who might be interested. Maybe we should have an organizational meeting first to see if we can even get this thing off the ground. I wish there were some way I could get the rest of those Music City Page Turners to follow you down here."

Connie smiled warmly. "I'd love the familiar company, but I'm afraid I have no following to speak of. Actually, Douglas and I weren't planning to move into our lake house for five more years, when we'll both turn sixty-five. We still feel like newcomers to Cherico. So even I shouldn't be here. But we sat down one night by the fire over a good bottle of Chianti, and Douglas told me he'd finally had his fill of trial lawyering for one lifetime. All the legal loopholes and angles were just wearing him down. He said all he really wanted at this stage of his life was to indulge his better nature and drift in the middle of Lake Cherico, sip beer, and catch a few fish. Then he asked me if I'd be willing to give up my job at the hospital so we could just move. You see, I'd been an ICU nurse since I graduated from college, and we'd both been socking away a good bit for our retirement."

"I've always admired you folks in the medical profession," Maura Beth offered. "I'm afraid I faint at the sight of blood, but I'm glad there are people who don't or the rest of us would be in big trouble."

"Frankly, I wondered if I would miss it," Connie added. "Especially the reality that I was always taking care of people on the brink. There was nothing more distressing to me than seeing somebody flatline. Oh, the finality of that monotonous sound, and the sorrow and trauma that it represented—I never did get used to it! On the other hand, I got such a kick out of seeing my patients recover and get on with their lives. That made it all worthwhile. I guess that's why I don't have trouble gutting all those fish Douglas catches. I'm not the least bit squeamish—I've seen it all." Then she suddenly leaned forward. "Do I have on too much perfume?"

Maura Beth cocked an ear and blinked twice. "What?"

"Sorry," Connie said, retreating slightly. "I just finished an entire stringer of perch before coming here. I was afraid my hands might smell too fishy no matter how many times I washed them. So I spritzed on some of my Estée Lauder for good measure. Too strong?"

Now that she was being asked to focus on it, Maura Beth actually thought that Connie had overdone it a tad. But she had no intention of saying so, as her best public servant instincts rose to the occasion. "I hardly even noticed it."

"Good," Connie replied, allowing herself to relax. "So, what's our next step?"

Maura Beth handed over the notes she had been making, and Connie scanned them quickly, suggesting a few changes. The two of them went back and forth a couple of times and finally came up with a suitable plan: Maura Beth would design and produce the flyer, but Connie would pay for everything out of her "mad money," as the library simply lacked the funds to pull it off; they would allow a period of two weeks for people to sign up for the club; then Maura Beth would call an organizational meeting at the library and officially get things under way.

"I only hope somebody else will show up," Maura Beth observed, arching her eyebrows dramatically.

Exactly when Maura Beth had come up with the idea of hand-delivering one of her flyers to Councilman Sparks, she could not recall. But she had run it past both Periwinkle and Connie before acting on it, and the three of them had decided that an aggressive approach was the best one to take. She needed to let the councilmen know she meant business about proving the library's worth and would be pursuing that goal immediately.

At the moment, she was standing in front of City Hall with its massive, three-story Corinthian columns—indeed, the ornate building dominated the otherwise low skyline of the town—while she summoned the courage to mount the steps and walk in to have her say. At all costs she must shrug off the lingering traces of intimidation that innumerable sessions with these politicians had produced.

Five minutes later, she found herself sitting in the councilman's outer office, staring uncomfortably at his personality-free secretary, Nora Duddney. In all the visits she had paid over the years, Maura Beth was quite certain that she had never seen the woman come close to registering an emotion of any kind.

"Miz Mayhew! You're looking lovely as ever!"

Councilman Sparks exclaimed, bursting through the door unannounced after a tedious ten minutes had passed. "So sorry to keep you waiting, but I have the City of Cherico to run, you know. So many departments, so little time. But do come in and tell me what's on your mind!" He gestured gracefully toward his inner office, turning on his bankable charm full-bore, but Maura Beth couldn't help but notice that Nora Duddney was as charmless as ever, blankly typing things onto her computer screen.

"So, what brings you in this morning?" he began just after they had settled comfortably into their sumptuous leather chairs. Whatever financial problems the City of Cherico might be having, they were clearly not reflected in the opulent décor of the head honcho's office. It had the aura of one of those upscale designer showrooms with Persian rugs covering the floor, as distinguished-looking as the touch of gray at Councilman Sparks's temples.

Maura Beth drew a deep breath as she leaned forward and handed over the flyer. "I'd appreciate it very much if you would read this, please. It will explain everything to you."

He quickly accepted the paper and commented immediately. "My, my! Is this color supposed to be some shade of gold?"

"The printer called it goldenrod, I believe."

"Cutesy name. But a little loud, I think."

"The other choice was bubble gum pink. I don't know what happened to everyday white."

"Aha! You were caught between a rock and a hard place! In that case, you chose wisely. Color is such an intriguing part of life. Myself, I'm partial to bright, flaming red."

After making quite a production of holding up the flyer and thumping it noisily a couple of times, Councilman Sparks chose to read out loud, his tone deliberate but managing to impart a hint of mockery at the same time:

> Announcing the organizational meeting of The Cherico Page Turners Book Club! Be one of the first in town to review classic Southern literature and sample delicious potluck dishes with your friends and neighbors. Circle the date. Friday, July 17, 2012, at 7 p.m. in The Cherico Library Meeting Room. Let us know you're coming by signing up today at the library or at The Twinkle, Twinkle Café on Commerce Street. We hope to see many of you there.
>
> Sincerely,
> Maura Beth Mayhew, Librarian,
> and the Rest of Your Friendly
> Cherico Library Staff

"I'd like for you to attend," Maura Beth said the instant he stopped reading. "And the other councilmen, too, if they'd like. You don't actually have to sign up and participate. Just drop by and see what we're trying to accomplish."

He patiently began folding the flyer several times until it had been reduced to a small square of paper, which he then pressed between his thumb and index finger for an awkward length of time. "Well, first, I'd like to say that the way you capitalized the line about the staff there at the end really made an impression on me," he began at last. "Just imagine how much more forceful it would have been to have used all caps. I do question whether three people is a staff, however."

Maura Beth managed to force a smile, refusing to let him get to her. "I'd like to have more personnel, of course. I'd even like to have a whole new library, for that matter. But it all takes money, as you well know."

"Yes, that appears to be the crux of the matter between us, doesn't it?" Then he abruptly switched subjects. "As for your invitation to the other councilmen, I think Chunky would definitely show up for the free food. He'd be the first one in line. But I know he wouldn't sit still for the rest of it. There are times I could swear he can't even read his utility bill. But he comes in handy with bringing certain voters into the fold. As for Gopher Joe, he'd come if I told him he had to, but you wouldn't get a peep out of him all evening. No, I think maybe I'd better make this a solo appearance on behalf of the Council. Just call it an executive decision."

"Then you'll come?"

"I enjoy keeping an eye on you, though I have to admit, I didn't expect something like this to pop up. You've been a busy little honeybee since we last got together, haven't you? Doing your frantic little dance to show the way to the pollen, it appears to me."

Maura Beth was feeling emboldened now and pressed on. "According to what you've told me, I have nothing to lose except my job."

"You have spirit, Miz Mayhew. I like the way you stand up for yourself. It's a very attractive quality among so many."

"Thank you for saying so. Oh, and you don't have to bring a dish with you, by the way."

"I assure you, I hadn't planned to. I can't boil water, and my wife's not much better. Evie and I eat out as often as we can. But I do appreciate you giving me a heads-up about this club of yours. The truth is, I detest surprises of any kind, especially successful ones." Then he rose quickly and said, "If there's nothing else, then, I'll be seeing you on July 17th at the library. I know you really don't believe it, but this office is and always has been open to you."

After she'd left and was heading down the hall, Maura Beth began to get an uneasy feeling about the exchange she'd just had with the man who had hired her. It would be beyond foolish to trust his slick, wolfish demeanor when she imagined him viewing her as Little Redheaded Riding Hood just ripe for the waylaying. He had been far too compliant about everything, and she ended up wondering if she really wanted him there as an observer after all.

# 3

# Missing in Action

The July session of "Who's Who in Cherico?" was well under way in the library's drab little meeting room with Miss Voncille Nettles holding forth in her inimitable fashion.

". . . and this is a photo of the Doak Leonard Winchester Family showing off the brand-new First Farmers' Bank of Cherico building," she was saying. "I'll now pass it around for your perusal. Note especially the big white bows in the ladies' hair. That was all the rage around the turn of the twentieth century. I know that from my research, of course, not because I was actually there."

Everyone laughed and began eagerly inspecting the picture, while Miss Voncille looked on approvingly. Though approaching seventy, she projected the vigor of someone ten to fifteen years younger. Especially impressive was the resonance of her voice, even though she was not a large person. Whenever she made genealogical and historical pronouncements as she was now to her handful of followers, they always lapped them up as the gospel truth. Criticisms or disagreements quickly brought out the sharpness of her tongue, enabling her to live up to her prickly surname. Despite the short fuse, however, there were still traces in her face and in the way she carefully arranged her salt-and-pepper hair of the great beauty she had once been, making people all the more curious about her perennial spinster status. If nothing else, she remained the town's most impeccably dressed woman with no place to go.

On this particular evening, Maura Beth had decided to join Miss Voncille and her loyal members—the Crumpton sisters and widower Locke Linwood—with the deliberate intention of recruiting for her book club. It would be easy enough, she reasoned, to chat with each of them over the fruit punch out of a can and store-bought sugar cookies they routinely trotted out for refreshments. In fact, she had already put a self-serving word in edgewise while ladling a plastic cup for Miss Voncille and was fully counting on closing the deal immediately after the adjournment.

All of a sudden, Mamie Crumpton was shouting about something, and Maura Beth was yanked out of the thoughtful review of her evening agenda.

"Why, Voncille Nettles, you take that back this instant. You simply must retract that outrageous statement. It is most certainly the lie of all time!"

As the older and decidedly overbearing maiden sister of one of Cherico's wealthiest families, Mamie had already begun hyperventilating, heaving her ample bosom. Her detractors around town—and there were more than a few—had often conjectured that one of these days she was going to puff herself up so big during one of her tantrums that pricking her with a pin might just send her flying all over Cherico like a deflated Goodyear blimp.

The unassuming and far daintier Marydell Crumpton uncharacteristically joined the attack. "You made that up out of a whole lace tablecloth, Voncille Nettles, and everybody in this room with any knowledge of this town knows it!"

"See?" Mamie added, wagging a bejeweled finger. "You've upset my little sister, and you should know by now how hard that is to do!"

"Neither of you has to get so worked up and take everything so seriously!" Miss Voncille exclaimed, deliberately averting her eyes from her accusers. "This is just par for the course for you, Mamie. You haven't changed in all the years I've known you!"

Maura Beth blinked in disbelief at the heated exchange, realizing she had not been paying close attention to Miss Voncille's latest pronouncement. "Now, everyone, please calm down."

"I have a right to be upset. Armadillos, indeed!" Mamie repeated, practically spitting out the words. "I've never heard such a ridiculous thing in my life. The Crumpton Family has been solvent and respectable from the instant we set foot on these shores. We would never have stooped to the activities you describe. So, once and for all, are you going to retract this incredible fabrication of yours or not? Really, I have no earthly idea what could have gotten into you!"

Miss Voncille folded her arms and turned up her nose at the challenge, just sitting there saying nothing.

"Very well, then. I'll take that as a 'no,' " Mamie declared, rising from the table with all the authority she could muster. "Come along, sister dear, we don't need to be dignifying this with our presence any longer." Whereupon the two of them huffed out of the meeting room, slamming the door behind them and leaving Maura Beth and Locke Linwood sitting in place virtually stupefied.

Miss Voncille finally broke the awkward silence. "Mamie Crumpton always has to have her way. She's so pompous, and there's this morbid side she's had since we were girls in school together. That's an incredible story in itself. Would you like to hear it?"

Maura Beth leaned in with all the poise she could muster. "Another time, perhaps. But I'm afraid I was daydreaming a bit when you revealed whatever it was in your lecture that got the Crumpton sisters so upset. So sorry. Would you mind repeating it?"

Miss Voncille shrugged. "I meant no harm. I just thought we could inject a little fun into one of these outings."

"Well, then, please tell me all about the fun."

"Oh, very well. After I was through talking about the Winchester Family, I said that I'd found an old newspaper article about Hyram Crumpton, their grandfather, opening up a business downtown that specialized in stuffed animals and other novelties like flower baskets made out of armadillo shells. I also said he had to do it because he'd previously gone bankrupt." Miss Voncille was unable to suppress a giggle or two. "And, yes—I made it all up."

"For heaven's sake, why?"

"Maybe I've gotten a little bored with 'Who's Who?' after all these years. The words *deadly dull* come to mind," Miss Voncille confessed with a sigh. But her tone was not particularly contrite, and she even managed to look a trifle smug there at the end.

Locke Linwood straightened his shiny silver tie and noisily cleared his throat to gain the floor. "Miss Voncille, I'd like to tell you something very important and of a personal nature, if you don't mind."

"Go right ahead, Mr. Linwood," Miss Voncille replied, looking intrigued.

"Would you like some privacy?" Maura Beth put in, thinking on her feet.

Locke shook his head of thick gray hair emphatically. "Please stay right where you are, Miz Mayhew. I don't mind you hearing this. It seems to be a night for speaking with abandon."

He appeared to be gathering his thoughts and did not say anything immediately. Maura Beth could not wait to hear what was on his mind, noting the profound lines of displeasure creasing his face. She had never associated frowns with this lanky, distinguished man, as it was well-known to everyone that he and his late wife, Pamela, had been the happiest of married couples for nearly forty years. After her passing, he had surprised everyone by continuing to attend "Who's Who?" by himself, but even then had never exhibited a hint of sorrow in his expressions.

"Miss Voncille," he began at last, "my dear wife and I always enjoyed your diligent efforts to shed light on our family histories here in Cherico. No one could possibly be better researched than you are. We considered you the ultimate authority, and you know we didn't miss many meetings. But I think this so-called joke of yours at the expense of the Crumpton family was in questionable taste, no matter what kind of boredom you say you're going through. It was a complete disappointment to me."

He paused for a moment and swallowed hard. "Not only that, but, well, things have been mighty lonely for me since my wife passed, and I was actually thinking of asking you out, believe it or not. I hope you don't think that's too forward, but there it is. Except that after your behavior tonight and the way you've just shrugged it off as if it was nothing, I realize I don't really know you at all. You're not who I thought you were. There now, I've gotten that off my chest."

Miss Voncille's face dropped noticeably, and she seemed at a loss for words for the longest time. Finally, though, she regained her composure. "Mr. Linwood, I'm not an easy person to surprise, but I have to admit you've just accomplished that." She paused briefly to throw up her hands. "At any rate, it seems that you and Miz Mayhew are in agreement about my behavior. So perhaps I should just go ahead and apologize."

Maura Beth reacted first, but not before finding the polite, formal exchange from the older generation a bit on the endearing side. Was she possibly witnessing the budding of a future romance? "Miss Voncille, I think it's the Crumpton sisters who need your apology. If you lose them as members, you've gotten rid of two thirds of your following."

"Yes, I realize that."

"If you ladies will excuse me, then," Locke said, rising from his chair and squaring his shoulders. "I think I'll call it an evening." He made his way slowly to the door, turning back at the last second with a gentlemanly bow. "But, Miss Voncille, I want you to know that I don't discourage easily. Despite what happened tonight, I fully intend to be here for the next meeting."

"Another surprise! What am I supposed to make of all that?" Miss Voncille exclaimed after Locke had left the room. But Maura Beth could sense the false bravado in her tone.

"We could talk about it, if you like. Would you care to have a heart-to-heart over more punch and cookies?"

Miss Voncille's reply came only after a great deal of fidgeting with the notes she had prepared for the meeting, as if they would somehow acquire some sort of magical powers and tell her what to do. "Oh, why not? Getting things off your chest seems to have worked nicely for Mr. Linwood."

Maura Beth waited as patiently as she could, seeing that Miss Voncille was having some difficulty getting started, but finally broke the ice herself. "I hope you regard me as more than just a librarian by now. I know six years isn't that much history between us in the grand scheme of things, but I've always prided myself on being a good listener. But first, let's keep our energy levels up." So she headed for the refreshment table and poured them each another cup of red punch with maraschino cherries on the bottom, brought back a couple of cookies wrapped in paper napkins, and the exchange began in earnest.

"Locke Linwood was right when he said he didn't really know who I was. He's in good company because very few people know what I'm about to tell you. I can sum it all up in two words, though," Miss Voncille explained after nibbling a cookie and sipping her punch. "Frank Gibbons."

"Frank Gibbons? Who is he?"

"Only the love of my life," Miss Voncille explained. "Today's been rough on me. It's been forty-five years since Frank literally dematerialized. I should have known better than to schedule a meeting of 'Who's Who?' with that so heavy on my mind lately. It comes and goes, of course, but what's worse is that I took it all out on the Crumpton sisters and their money and haughty ways. But I still shouldn't have lashed out at them. I'm bigger than that."

Maura Beth put on her most sympathetic face and lowered her voice accordingly. "So tell me more about this man disappearing into thin air."

"Well, no. You misunderstand. You see, he was a soldier who lived over in Corinth. My parents didn't approve because they said he was from the wrong side of the tracks. It was true that his family didn't have a lot of money or social position, but that didn't mean a thing to me. I was madly in love. Still, very few people here in Cherico even knew this little affair was going on because my parents wanted it like that. From the very beginning, they said they knew it would never last. That would turn out to be the cruelest thing they would ever say to me, and I never forgave them for it." Miss Voncille broke off for a few moments for another swallow of her punch.

"Frank had just introduced me to his family over the Christmas holidays back in 1967. They were as sweet as they could be to me, even though I knew there would be serious in-law problems down the line. Nevertheless, we fully intended to get engaged, no matter what. But in January, Frank was deployed to Vietnam, and we had to put everything on hold. I don't know how well you remember your history, but that was January of 1968. Shortly after he arrived over there, the North Vietnamese launched the Tet Offensive, and Frank's company ended up right in the middle of it."

"As I matter of fact, I do know about the Tet Offensive, even if I wasn't around," Maura Beth explained. "We librarians are always getting refresher courses in everything under the sun when we help students research their school reports. The teachers never stop assigning papers on the Vietnam War, and we're open much later than the school libraries are. Anyway, I know there were a lot of casualties among our troops during that terrible period. So are you telling me Frank was one of those?"

Miss Voncille absent-mindedly snapped her cookie in two, briefly staring down at what she'd done in astonishment. When she looked up, she picked a spot on the wall above Maura Beth's head and spoke to it. "It was the worst thing that can happen. He was officially declared MIA, which doesn't allow for closure. Of course, I never got it. He's still MIA all these many decades later. He was just gone, and no one knew where to find him. I kept in touch with his mother until she died, but there was no further word.

"Of course, there was a memorial service for him over in Corinth, which I sneaked off to when the time came. But it just wasn't the same as putting his actual remains to rest. You might not think that's such a big deal, but, believe me, I'm sure it would have helped me heal. Meanwhile, I busied myself with my school teaching until I retired and then took on all this genealogy research after that and . . . well, here we are sitting side by side, sipping punch and discussing it all as ancient history."

"I'm so sorry about Frank," Maura Beth said, shaking her head slowly.

Miss Voncille brushed away a few cookie crumbs from the palm of her hand with her napkin. "Sometimes, just when I think I'm really over him, something like this bubbles up to remind me I'm not. I mean, like making up a lie about someone skinning armadillos for a living. Of course, those Crumpton sisters have truly annoyed me beyond belief over the years. Mamie, in particular, has managed to make it very clear that my having to earn a living as a schoolteacher practically made me a peasant in her eyes. For that reason alone, I think she had my rude nonsense coming to her. Maybe that will help you understand what I did this evening a little better."

"Just between the two of us," Maura Beth confided, leaning in, "there have been times when Mamie Crumpton has walked into the library and treated me like a servant—ordering me to get a book off the shelf for her without so much as a 'thank you' later."

Miss Voncille started nodding compulsively. "That's Mamie in a nutshell—emphasis on the 'nut.' As far as I can tell, all that money of hers has insulated her from the hard knocks most of us receive in life—such as what happened to me and Frank."

"Well, I haven't experienced your level of pain," Maura Beth said, her voice wavering a bit. "But these lost loves are tough. I got jilted at LSU by a South Louisiana boy named Elphage Alphonse Broussard, Jr. We dated for three years, and I was convinced Al was going to ask me to marry him. Once, he even joked about having a gigantic wedding ceremony on the fifty-yard line of Tiger Stadium with Mike the Tiger in his cage roaring his approval right next to us. Instead, he suddenly made a big deal out of whether or not I'd convert to Catholicism before the ceremony. When I said no, he broke things off very abruptly. It made me suspect there was someone else waiting in the wings, and he was just using that as an excuse. He'd been so indifferent on the subject of religion before. Why, he didn't even like putting on a costume and going to Mardi Gras parades to catch beads and doubloons, which is a complete betrayal of the culture down there. Believe me, college kids live for it. And . . . I've been a little skittish ever since."

"But you haven't remained missing in action like I have, I hope?"

"Oh, my girlfriend, Periwinkle Lattimore, keeps an eye out for me when someone she thinks I might be interested in wanders into The Twinkle. She even takes pictures with her cell phone on the sly and sends them to me. The problem is, we don't exactly have the same taste in men. After all, she's almost forty, and I'll be thirty in two years."

Miss Voncille arched her eyebrows and managed a wry smile. "You say that as if you don't have most of your life ahead of you—although I will admit the pickings are slim here in Cherico."

Maura Beth felt the tension that had filled the room earlier quickly draining away now, and she decided to resume pursuit of her original mission. "Unfortunately, you're right. By the way, I'd like to know what you thought of my Cherico Page Turners. Maybe you could join us? You've probably spotted the sign-up sheet by the front desk. I was thinking that with all these tempers flaring in 'Who's Who?' maybe you could give genealogy a rest for a while and try something a little different while everyone cools off."

Miss Voncille closed her eyes for a brief second trying to remember. "Books and potluck? Was that the gist of it?"

"Essentially. But we thought we would concentrate on Southern female writers in the beginning and maybe bond with each other in the process."

"I don't know if that sort of gaggle would work out for me. I'm used to running the entire show."

"Then what about this?" Maura Beth continued, not willing to let her wiggle off the hook so easily. "Weren't you intrigued by what Mr. Linwood said to you? I mean, the part about asking you out. I'm sure it took us both by surprise."

"At last . . . we get around to that." Miss Voncille let the statement just sit there for a while before moving on. "The truth is, I'm flattered. I had no idea he was thinking along those lines. He was always a man of few words, holding his wife's hand the way he did and letting her do all the talking. As for myself, I've blocked out contemplating male companionship over the years. That's what lack of closure will do for you."

"It's very fortuitous that you've brought up the concept of closure," Maura Beth explained, deciding not to beat around the bush any longer. "Even if I mean closure in an entirely different context." Then she told Miss Voncille everything she had also shared with Connie McShay about the disquieting ultimatum from the City Council. "I realize you have other options besides holding your meetings here, but I wanted you to know what could possibly happen in just a few short months. Does Cherico really want to be without a library?"

Miss Voncille looked and sounded distressed. "I've never cared for the current crop over there at City Hall. Actually, the only one that matters is our very own banana republic hotshot, Durden Sparks. You're originally from Louisiana, aren't you?"

Maura Beth said she was.

"Well, Durden fits the Huey Long model of governance from down your way. Or maybe he's more like Edwin Edwards was with those flashy good looks. I taught Durden in junior high, and he was so conceited and full of himself the way he'd stand up in front of his fellow history students and give an oral report that sounded like he was being nominated for President of the United States at a political convention. It was all I could do to keep from giving him an 'A' in Demagoguery. These days, of course, I can name you scores of silly women who vote for him time after time just because he makes them fantasize and swoon. Not me. My Frank wasn't all that handsome, but he was brave and he stood for something. That's my definition of a man."

"Well, then, there's your incentive. Why don't you sign up and show Councilman Sparks and his cronies that they just can't do whatever they please?" Maura Beth continued, proceeding full speed ahead now. "And not only that, since you're a woman who likes to take charge, why don't you consider inviting Locke Linwood to accompany you to the first meeting? He's already surprised you. Maybe you could surprise him."

Maura Beth saw she had struck a responsive chord when Miss Voncille actually seemed to be blushing. "Very well, then. You've convinced me. I'll become an official Cherico Page Turner." Then she suddenly turned thoughtful. "As for Mr. Linwood . . . I don't want to rush into that one. I think he's looking for a different version of me. I'll have to sleep on it." The next second she was glancing at her watch and rolling her eyes. "It feels like it ought to be later than it is, but then, I ran everybody off tonight, didn't I? It was definitely not my most successful lecture, I can assure you."

Maura Beth reached over and patted her hand warmly. "Oh, I don't know. First, I have to thank you for joining my little club. And then, I think you and I got to know each other a lot better after all this time. Locke Linwood hasn't really gone anywhere, and I'm willing to bet the Crumpton sisters will come back into the fold with a little diplomacy on your part."

"Got a delicious recipe for crow?" Miss Voncille quipped, gathering up her notes and photos and tucking them into the folder she'd brought along.

"Come on," Maura Beth replied, chuckling as she dangled her impressive collection of keys before them. "We'll sign you up and then close down together."

It was just past nine when Maura Beth walked through the door of her cozy one-bedroom apartment on Clover Street and collapsed on the rust-colored living room sofa her parents had shipped to her three Christmases ago from their hometown of Covington, Louisiana. *It'll go with your hair when you sit on it,* her mother had written on the card that had accompanied it.

Actually, it *was* a pretty close match. Auburn, whiskey, or rust—those were the adjectives that had been used most often by the admirers of Maura Beth's hair. But she herself had thought, rather playfully at times, that her mother's sentiments weren't particularly grammatical. Which was she supposed to sit on—the sofa or her hair?

Whatever the case, she sometimes enjoyed entertaining herself with the question for lack of anything better to do after coming home from work. Tonight, she was happily remembering the last thing Miss Voncille had said to her as they were walking under the portico of the library into the steamy July evening air. "Your Cherico Page Turners are no longer missing in action! Miss Voncille Nettles, reporting for duty!"

They had both laughed, waved good-bye, and headed toward their cars down the street.

Back on the sofa where her hair had blended nicely into the fabric of one of the big cushions behind her, Maura Beth suddenly realized that all those cups of fruit punch had coated her throat with sugar. She needed a nice glass of ice water, so she jumped up and headed toward the fridge and the big pitcher she always kept inside on the middle shelf.

The phone rang on the way over, startling her, but she reached the crowded kitchenette counter soon enough. Whoever was on the other end of the line opened the conversation with an enthusiastic, "Guess what?"

Maura Beth immediately played along, easily recognizing Periwinkle's down-home voice. "And hello to you, too. Don't tell me. You have another picture of a person in pants for me. Or is it another set of twin cowboys passing through from Dallas on the way to become country singers in Nashville? One for you, and one for me."

Periwinkle produced her usual hearty laugh. "Even better. Someone signed up for your book club tonight over here. She just left—in fact, we closed the place down together we had so much fun chatting. You won't believe who it is!"

"Enough guessing games," Maura Beth said. "Just tell me."

"Okay, here goes. It's Becca Broccoli!"

Maura Beth frowned immediately. "Who?"

"Surely you've heard of her. Becca Broccoli of radio fame? Haven't you ever listened to her show on WHYY?"

"Periwinkle, I don't listen to the radio or even watch much television," Maura Beth said, growing slightly impatient. "I'm always curled up on my sofa reading the free galleys all the publishers send us librarians. How do you think they get the buzz going for their new writers? We're their foot soldiers in spreading the word."

"Never mind that. This is exciting news. Becca Broccoli has a cooking and recipe show on local radio—how do you think I get some of my best ideas for The Twinkle menu? I listen to her faithfully every morning."

Maura Beth mulled things over, still somewhat puzzled. "Cooking on the radio? Not exactly a visual medium. And what's with the name Broccoli? That can't be real, can it? Is she one of those vegans or vegetarians?"

There was the faint sound of paper rustling, and then Periwinkle explained. "I'm holding the sign-up sheet in my hand right now. I didn't know this before, but Becca's real name is Mrs. Justin B-R-A-C-H-L-E. She told me tonight over her bread pudding that since her name was pronounced like broccoli, she decided to go ahead and capitalize on it. Thus was born *The Becca Broccoli Show*, weekday mornings at seven-thirty. Don't you realize what this means for your club?"

"She can review cookbooks for us?" Maura Beth ventured, unable to resist.

"Seriously, now. Think about the publicity angle, girl. She can mention the club over the radio whenever she has a mind to. She has a huge audience. You're a bit slow on the uptake tonight!"

Maura Beth briefly debated whether to mention all the hoopla at the "Who's Who?" meeting but thought better of it. "Sorry, it's been a long day. But I've got a sign-up myself at this end. Miss Voncille Nettles of 'Who's Who in Cherico?' is on board. So now we'll have at least four people for our organizational meeting next week. And if you could find a way to join us—"

"Like I said before," Periwinkle interrupted, "I just don't have the time, honey. Not to read books and run the restaurant six days a week, too. Just let me hand out flyers here at The Twinkle and talk you up that way. Reading recipes is more my speed. Anyway, you got you a good one in Becca Broccoli, and who knows how many more'll eat at The Twinkle and end up in your club?"

"Thanks, Periwinkle," Maura Beth said. "You really are my eyes and ears, even without your cell phone camera."

• • •

An hour later, Maura Beth was propped up in bed against her purple pillows, smiling down at her wiggling, freshly painted, pink toenails. "You are such a girlie girl sometimes, Maura Beth," she said out loud, pouting her lips playfully.

Anyone surveying her bedroom would have thought so. She had changed the nondescript wallpaper she had inherited to a lavender floral design, and her solid lavender bedspread picked up the theme. What little money she had managed to put aside—with significant help from her parents, of course—had been spent on the brass bed, which was the centerpiece of the room. Altogether, it was an environment that had yet to welcome its first male visitor, and Maura Beth wasn't particularly happy about that.

Before turning out the lights, she decided to open the top drawer of her night stand and retrieve her journal. She had been keeping it off and on since her freshman year at LSU, and whenever she needed a boost of any kind, she would trot it out and turn to page twenty-five. Tonight was one of those nights.

It read:

THREE THINGS TO ACCOMPLISH
BEFORE I'M THIRTY, PLUS A P.S.

1—Become the director of a decent-sized library (city of at least 20,000 people).

2—Get married (but not out of desperation).
3—Have two children, one of each (natural childbirth—ouch!).
P.S.—Hope one of the bambinos has red hair. (We're such a minority!)

Maura Beth gingerly rubbed the tips of her fingers on the page and slowly closed the journal. Then she put it away, sighing resolutely. Would any of those things ever happen, even past thirty?

# 4

# Out of the Mouths of Babes

It was nearly ten after seven on the evening of July 17, but the organizational meeting of The Cherico Page Turners had not yet begun. Maura Beth had decided to disdain the meeting room because of the claustrophobia it never failed to produce. Instead, she was standing behind a podium she had placed in front of the circulation desk in the main lobby, gazing out at the half-circle of folding chairs arranged before her. Connie McShay, Miss Voncille, along with her guest, Locke Linwood, and Councilman Sparks had arrived early and were talking among themselves in their seats. But Mrs. Justin Brachle (aka Becca Broccoli) had not yet made an appearance, and Maura Beth was beginning to worry. Their numbers were paltry enough as it was.

"If Mrs. Brachle doesn't show up within the next five minutes, we'll begin without her," Maura Beth announced.

But no sooner had those words escaped her than the celebrated Becca Broccoli breezed through the front door wearing a summery yellow frock and apologizing profusely as she approached the group. "I know I've kept everyone waiting," she began, "but I had to feed my Stout Fella. That's my husband, Justin, you know. He was trying to wind up one of his real-estate deals over the phone, and he just wouldn't come to the table—" She broke off and flashed a smile. "I guess none of you are really interested in all this. Except, I owe you an introduction, at the very least. I generally go by the name of Becca Broccoli these days, and, again, I'm so sorry I'm late." Finally, she sat down in the open chair next to Connie, who offered her a gracious nod.

Maura Beth couldn't have been more surprised. Not at the tardiness, nor the rambling, breathless monologue, but at Becca's actual appearance. This petite, perfectly accessorized, very attractive blonde did not match the voice on the radio that Maura Beth had taken the time to tune in to the day after Periwinkle had informed her of the sign-up. That next morning, she had envisioned the woman loudly enumerating the ingredients for spicy beef stew as matronly, perhaps even as tall and ungainly as Julia Child had been. Instead, Becca was more like a bouncier, much younger version of Miss Voncille.

"Don't worry," Maura Beth replied, briefly waving her off. "You haven't missed a thing. We've all just been getting better acquainted. So, shall we begin?"

But before she had a chance to mention the first item on her scripted agenda, Councilman Sparks stood up and stole the floor from her. "We're a pretty sparse crowd, aren't we? Is this going to be enough to have a viable book club? I'm just a kibitzer, you know, so don't mind me."

It was Connie, however, who answered his question, turning toward him with a deferential smile. "We started out with seven people for The Music City Page Turners in Nashville, Councilman. It only takes a few dedicated readers to make a book club work."

"Yes, we'll worry about numbers later," Maura Beth added, eager to take back control. "And there's no need for anyone to stand while speaking. We're going to be very casual in our approach."

Councilman Sparks resumed his seat with what amounted to a mock salute. "As you wish."

Maura Beth offered a perfunctory but still civil, "Thank you!" and then moved on immediately. There were a few parliamentary issues to resolve first—such as confirming the head of the club and the necessity of a treasurer. It was decided that Maura Beth would continue to lead and see to it that there were multiple library copies of the books they would reviewing, while Connie would handle the bookkeeping, since she had performed that function so admirably for The Music City Page Turners.

Next came the matter of coordinating the menus for each meeting—something that perhaps only Maura Beth had considered. "After all," she continued, "I think we'd prefer an appetizer, entrée, and dessert for our get-togethers. Someone needs to make sure we have a balance of dishes with a few timely phone calls to the others. Volunteers?"

Becca glanced first one way and then the other, checking for competition. As no one else budged, she said, "I'll be happy to do that since I'm planning menus all the time for my shows."

It was exactly what Maura Beth had hoped to hear. She had even thought about phoning Becca the day before to ask if she would willing to assume the food planning duties. Since the two women had never met, however, she had concluded that it might be too forward and chose to wait until the meeting got under way when they were face-to-face.

"I, for one, would be delighted to have you do that for us," Maura Beth replied, "and I assume that the rest of you feel the same way? Show of hands?"

Councilman Sparks rightfully abstained from voting, but everyone else was on board.

"I'm honored, ladies and gentlemen," Becca stated, while scanning the group with a smile. "But I did have one question. Will we be reviewing cookbooks from time to time? I feel I have special insight into their effectiveness."

Maura Beth was trying her best to conceal her surprise. The flyer had made it quite clear that

Southern literature would be the focus of the club. “To be honest with you, I thought we would sample each other’s dishes and exchange recipes as we saw fit,” Maura Beth explained. “But our discussions would be strictly literary.”

“Didn’t you know that I’m publishing a cookbook next year? I’m calling it *The Best of Becca Broccoli*, and I’ll be transcribing some of my most popular radio shows. Of course, I was hoping it would be the subject of one of our future meetings.”

Maura Beth felt her body tensing up at the wrench that had just been thrown into the works. It was imperative that she think on her feet and strike the right note. “I see no reason why we can’t consider that down the line. You say your cookbook is forthcoming anyway,” she pointed out, proceeding carefully. “For now, though, I believe we need to concentrate on our famous Southern female writers and get firmly established. We can make the rest up as we go along.”

Becca settled back in her chair, offering up a pleasant little nod. “I’ll just keep everyone posted on the progress of my cookbook, then. And I’ll be more than happy to autograph copies when it comes out.”

“Very good. We’ll look forward to that,” Maura Beth continued, returning to her notes with a decided sense of relief. “Now, the next item I have down here is our club name. Are we all in agreement on The Cherico Page Turners? May I have a show of hands?"

Everyone except Councilman Sparks raised their hand briefly, but Connie continued to wave in the studied manner of Queen Elizabeth on the balcony at Buckingham Palace or a newly crowned Miss America walking the runway.

"Yes, Connie? Do you have something to add?"

"Well, I was just thinking, Maura Beth . . . maybe we should consider going with something original instead of copying somebody else."

"But you were the one that told me all about The Music City Page Turners."

"Yes, I know. But if you'll bear with me. Something happened recently that I just have to share with y'all." She took a moment to gather her thoughts, obviously amused by what she was about to reveal.

"Our daughter, Lindy, has been visiting us from Memphis with our little granddaughter, Melissa. We told Lindy we weren't quite ready for visitors yet, but she wanted to come anyway. She said, 'Melissa misses her Gigi and Paw.' That's what the little angel calls my husband, Douglas, and me. Anyway, she's just eight, and she still has trouble with certain words—like Cherico, for instance. So after a few days, she said, 'Gigi and Paw, I just love visitin' with y'all here in Cherry Cola, Mis'sippi!' We just thought it was the cutest thing ever. So I was wondering if we might consider calling ourselves The Cherry Cola Book Club instead of The Cherico Page Turners? What do you think?"

Subdued *oohing, ahhing,* and nodding rippled through the half-circle, and it was Miss Voncille who spoke up first. "I like it. It gets my vote. Locke, you'll go along with it, won't you?"

"Whatever you ladies prefer is fine with me," he said, patting her hand. "I'm only here because of Sadie Hawkins sitting next to me."

"But you didn't say no to me, Locke Linwood!" Miss Voncille exclaimed, looking smug.

Becca then offered her approval, and finally Maura Beth chimed in. "It's highly original, if nothing else. And since I haven't had any logos printed up yet, I don't see why we can't change our minds. Ladies' prerogative, as they say."

All the women were chuckling or rolling their eyes, but it was Maura Beth who truly offered up the exclamation point. "As they also say—out of the mouths of babes. So, many thanks to your precious granddaughter, Connie. Looks like we're now officially The Cherry Cola Book Club. Maybe the name alone will intrigue people enough to join."

"And we could add the cherry cola part to the menus," Becca suggested. "I mean, nothing spruces up a soft drink like dropping a few ice cubes and cherries into a tumbler and then giving it a shake or a stir with a swizzle stick. Add a twist of lime, and you've got a cola to remember—especially in the summer heat."

Connie gave Becca a gentle nudge and chuckled softly. "That sounds marvelously refreshing, of course, but did anyone ever tell you that you talk like a recipe?"

"I'd be in trouble if I didn't, considering the thousands of shows I've produced!" Becca exclaimed. "Oh, yes, my Stout Fella says all the time that I'm very fluent in listing ingredients!"

"What I want to know is how you keep that cute little figure of yours while hanging around the kitchen so much?" Connie continued. "Mine blew up on me years ago. My figure, not my kitchen, of course."

Everyone present enjoyed a good laugh, and Becca said, "No big secret. I do all the cooking, but Stout Fella does all the eating around our house. He's gained about forty-five pounds since we got married ten years ago. I really should put him on a diet for his own good. Last time he went to the doctor, his cholesterol was up in the stratosphere. If I could just stop him from 'islanding' his ice cream, for starters."

Connie's brow furrowed dramatically. "Islanding? You mean scooping?"

"No, I only wish he would scoop. It's when Stout Fella hovers over a half gallon of ice cream with his big spoon. He starts digging around the edges where it's softer, and then he keeps going around and around and deeper and deeper until he's eaten enough to make an island out of the middle."

"What does he do with the middle?" Connie continued, still looking puzzled.

"Oh, he eventually gets around to that, too. Another time, he chips away from the edges until the island has completely disappeared. The point is, he consumes thousands of extra calories at one standing. I've informed him of the existence of bowls, but he won't use them because he knows they would make him commit to a finite amount."

Sensing that she was losing control of the meeting again, Maura Beth stepped in and abruptly switched subjects. "Ladies, this is all very fascinating, but I wanted to get your opinions on when to schedule the next meeting. We need to decide how long it will take us to read our first selection."

"Exactly what is our first selection, by the way?" Miss Voncille wanted to know.

"I planned to go into that, too," Maura Beth explained. "I had one particular classic in mind but thought we'd discuss it first. We might as well do that right now and then worry about the scheduling later. So, to cut to the chase, what does everybody think about getting our feet wet with the very dependable *Gone with the Wind*?"

"I've waded in that pool before with The Music

City Page Turners," Connie explained. "It's been a few years, though."

"So you're less than enthusiastic?" Maura Beth said, sounding slightly disappointed.

Connie shrugged while patting her hair. "I'll go along with the majority, of course, but it's just such familiar territory to me."

"We'll branch out, I assure you," Maura Beth explained. "Harper Lee, Eudora Welty, Ellen Douglas, and Ellen Gilchrist won't be far behind."

"Getting back to *Gone with the Wind*, though," Miss Voncille began. "I'd like to know what could possibly be said about Margaret Mitchell's only contribution to literature after all these decades? Hasn't it been done to death and then some? Because the truth is, I don't know if I can get through all those dialects again. I read the book way back in high school and never deciphered a word Mammy said. Did slaves really talk like that? Lord knows, I don't want to get into that can of worms called political correctness, but I *am* a student of history, and it seemed so exaggerated."

Instead of being discouraged by the negative comments, however, Maura Beth was actually pleased. "But that's exactly the sort of observation I'd like for us to be discussing in the club. We don't have to stick to the same tired angles, as if all criticism has been chiseled in stone. We can explore new and original concepts."

Miss Voncille looked pensive but sounded

placated. “We can bring up anything we want? No matter how outside the box?”

“Absolutely. You can be as revisionist as you like. All writers should be open to interpretation forever, even if we tend to bronze and retire them.”

“On the other hand, you can always rehash the movie,” Councilman Sparks quipped unexpectedly. He was sitting back in his chair with his arms folded and a supreme smirk on his face. “Which would seem to lead to the obvious next question: Will your members fall back on watching Clark Gable and Vivien Leigh instead of taking the time to actually read the book? And how can you prove they didn’t take that DVD shortcut?”

Maura Beth quickly realized that her fears about Councilman Sparks attending the meeting were not groundless. Clearly, he was there to make trouble with his subtle digs, but she was not going to give him the satisfaction of showing her irritation. “If members would like to view the film in addition to reading the book, I would certainly have no objections. That would make an excellent point of comparison for our discussions.”

“Clever girl. You should run for office with that answer,” Councilman Sparks added. “I couldn’t have put it better myself.”

“So, if there’s no further input, shall we vote on my suggestion?” Maura Beth continued, ignoring his comment.

After a few more stray remarks that produced no fireworks, the vote was unanimous in favor of *Gone with the Wind*, even though Becca reminded everyone not to forget about her forthcoming cookbook as an aside. Then it was decided that the group would take a month to read the novel and reconvene on August 17 to discuss it—a straightforward enough proposition.

Councilman Sparks, however, continued to play devil's advocate. "What if someone else enrolls in a few weeks and doesn't have enough time to read the book? Will you allow use of *CliffsNotes*?"

Maura Beth waited for the awkward titters to subside before answering. "This isn't a course, and we're not here to be graded, Councilman. We're here to think, have a good time, and enjoy some good food." Then she decided it would be best to pull the plug. "So, if there are no other questions . . . I think this organizational meeting will come to an end."

"And don't forget, I'll be giving y'all a call to work out who's going to bring what to eat," Becca put in at the last second. "We'll try to make sure everyone whips up one of their best dishes."

Maura Beth did not much care for Councilman Sparks lingering behind after everyone else had left. She did not want to hear what he had to say, knowing quite well that it could not possibly be of a constructive nature. Nevertheless, she resumed her position behind the podium, subconsciously viewing it as a means of protection as much as anything else. Then she plastered a grin on her face and looked directly into his eyes as he spoke.

"I admire your organizational skills, Miz Mayhew," he began. "You run a tight ship just the way I do. But perhaps it's time you faced up to the possibility that your tight ship is also sinking fast. I'm just wondering if all this furious activity of yours isn't much ado about nothing. I hope you realize that a handful of people picnicking in the library is not going to alter the equation here. It may end up amusing a few intellectual types in the community, but I can't see it becoming popular with the masses. I just don't think that dog will hunt in Cherico."

Maura Beth frowned. "We're just getting off the ground. Don't you think you should cut us a little slack?"

"I know you're intelligent enough to understand that even if you doubled the number of people you had in here tonight, it wouldn't be enough to keep the library open when we bear down on the budget," he said, arching his eyebrows.

But she matched his glibness with sturdy body language of her own, leaning toward him with her chin up. "You've made that quite clear. Maybe I have more faith in the public than you do. But never mind that. I still think it's odd that you just don't close me down right now, particularly if you're so sure that nobody will care."

"Are you daring me to do that, Miz Mayhew?"

She cleared her throat and swallowed hard. "Yes."

"Impressive," he answered, turning off his dazzling smile in an instant. "You called my bluff. Chunky and Gopher Joe are way too intimidated to even try something like that. The truth is, if I don't know anything else, I know my politics. And if by some miracle, you should pack every resident of Cherico into your little library five and a half months from now, I don't want to be on the outside looking in. I'll pretend that I knew you'd succeed all the time, and no one will be the wiser. I'll have my attendance at every one of your meetings as my proof, too. So, thank you very much for the invitation to shutter you sooner rather than later, but I think I'll keep all my options open. For the time being, that will be my official position."

Maura Beth took a deep breath, having weathered the latest go-round. "So you'll be dropping in on our review of *Gone with the Wind* next month, I take it?"

"I wouldn't miss it. I've always wanted to observe a literary hen fest."

"We'll do our best to amuse you," Maura Beth replied, matching his sarcastic smile. "And maybe Becca Broccoli can even get someone to cook up an omelet just for you. Perhaps a little cheese added to make you feel right at home."

He leaned over the podium and winked. "Yum, yum!"

As she watched him walk away from her after their perfunctory farewells, Maura Beth steadied herself by grabbing the podium and whispering the phrase she had used earlier in the evening when they'd changed the name of the club. Over and over it came out of her like a soothing mantra: "Out of the mouths of babes . . . out of the mouths of babes . . . out of the mouths of babes . . ."

But when Councilman Sparks reached the front door, turned, and gave her a neat little bow, she couldn't help herself, knowing full well he couldn't hear her at that great distance: ". . . as well as charming rascals up to God-knows-what."

# 5

# I'm Scarlett, You're Melanie!

It was beyond annoying to Maura Beth that Councilman Sparks's snide prediction that the group would end up rehashing the movie version of *Gone with the Wind* stuck in her craw over the next couple of weeks. That, and the lingering feeling that she might have been a bit too heavy-handed with the others at the organizational meeting of what was now to be called The Cherry Cola Book Club. It seemed that no one really wanted to read and review *Gone with the Wind* again except herself, but she had prevailed with authority. Yes, she had promised them that they could explore new angles and ideas regarding the time-honored classic, but she herself had failed to come up with anything viable, despite constant brainstorming. Was anyone else having any better luck?

In fact, she was about to dial Connie McShay's number from her office one slack afternoon when Renette Posey appeared in the doorframe, holding the library's DVD copy of *Gone with the Wind* and looking decidedly puzzled.

"I'd like to ask you a quick question. Don't worry—there's no one waiting at the front desk to check out. Even worse, there's nobody in the library at all. Hasn't been all morning," she explained on the way to Maura Beth's cluttered desk. "It's about this movie I'm returning. I got curious when I read your *Gone with the Wind* flyer."

"Yes?"

"Well, I watched it last night for the first time with a few girlfriends of mine, and we did the slumber party thing in pajamas at my apartment. I know, it sounds lame, like something out of high school. We fooled with each other's hair, talked about boyfriends, popped popcorn, and ate all sorts of junk food. But after the movie was finally over—it went on forever, and thank God for that intermission so we could all take a bathroom break—we sat cross-legged on the floor in a circle and came to the same conclusion."

Maura Beth straightened up in her chair. "And what was that?"

"Well, we decided that every one of us acted in real life like either Scarlett or Melanie, for the most part. We even wondered if every woman might fall into one category or the other. Do you think there's anything to that, or is it just a silly, slumber party idea from a bunch of single girls on a sugar high?"

Maura Beth couldn't help but snap her fingers and smile. "Renette, I'd give you a raise if I had the money!"

"Really, Miz Mayhew?"

"I wish I could, of course. But that's a great idea you and your friends had. By the way, which character were you? Or should I say, are you?"

"Oh, everyone thought I was a Melanie," Renette answered, growing quieter and hanging her head slightly. "I've been called a goody-goody too many times to be anything else. But that's who I am—I like helping people."

"You certainly do!" Maura Beth exclaimed. "You're a star with our scanner, and you tell the patrons about their overdues with honey dripping in your voice. They never get mad—I've gotten so many compliments about you."

Someone calling out, "Hello?" from somewhere in the library broke up their exchange, and Renette turned, dashing toward the front desk to attend to her duties. But Maura Beth made a note to herself to find a way to give her pleasant young clerk a little more in her paycheck, even if she had to juggle a line item or two in the books to get the job done. Landing in her lap from an innocuous slumber party was the perfect angle for the upcoming *Gone with the Wind* outing.

"Declare your allegiance!" would be the challenge she would issue to Miss Voncille, Connie, and Becca over the phone with supreme confidence. "How do you see yourself in today's world—as a Scarlett or a Melanie?"

Suddenly, she could sweep aside the insecurities that had been plaguing her about her leadership style and choice of material. She could even tempt Periwinkle with the ploy, especially since her best girlfriend had already generously agreed to send some sherry custard along from The Twinkle as an extra dessert.

"If things start to go wrong," she had told Maura Beth over the phone just a few days before, "you can at least get you a little buzz off the sherry. Sometimes, when I go home alone, that's all I have to look forward to."

"Now, come on, Periwinkle. Enough of the lonely, sherry custard-eating, sob stories," Maura Beth had returned before signing off with a friendly promise. "I'm going to find a way to get you to take a break from that kitchen and into our book club if it's the last thing I do!"

For the moment, however, she had to run Renette's slumber party angle past her existing membership, and she decided that Connie would be the first she would dial up.

"Are you busy?" Maura Beth said after Connie answered. "You sound out of breath."

"Well, you caught me. I'm out here on the pier grunting in a very unladylike manner with the fish scaler and hoping somebody will rescue me with a cell phone call like you just did."

Maura Beth made a sympathetic noise under her breath. "Douglas isn't pitching in?"

"Nope, he's off to The Marina Bar and Grill for a round or two with his fellow fishermen. He did invite me to join him, but they're all about watching sports on TV and telling off-color jokes out there. Not my style."

Maura Beth changed the subject quickly, launching into the exchange she'd had with Renette. "So what do you think of the Scarlett and Melanie debate?" she concluded.

There was silence at the other end for a while. "Your idea reminds me of something," Connie said finally. "I know. Getting a Girl Scout badge for something that's really a stretch. Only this one would be for adults. You know, who gets the Scarlett badge and who gets the Melanie badge to sew on her blouse."

"I wish I could see your face now," Maura Beth added. "I can't tell whether you like the idea or not from what you just said."

Connie broke the modest tension with a generous laugh. "Of course I like it. Maybe I didn't express myself so well. It's probably these fish fumes poisoning my brain cells."

"You're too much. But thanks for the vote of confidence on my idea."

Next up was Miss Voncille, who seemed to be in an unusually prickly mood. "Do we have to dress up in costume?" she inquired after Maura Beth had explained everything. "What I mean is, if I decide I'm a Scarlett, do I have to rent one of those antebellum dresses complete with hoop-skirts? Actually, I suppose I'd have to do the same if I were a Melanie. And my hair isn't long enough to be done up in ringlets the way they did back then. So that would mean I'd have to buy a wig. I can tell a woman wearing a wig a mile away. And men in bad toupees no matter what the distance."

"This isn't a costume ball, Miss Voncille."

"Thank goodness!"

"So what's your verdict?" Maura Beth continued.

"Fine with me," came the reply, though with little enthusiasm. But a sudden infusion of warmth soon followed. "What I'm more excited about is my friendship with Locke Linwood. We're starting to go out on dinner dates and such. Of course, it's all very innocent at the moment, you understand, and I'm trying very hard to soften my image on these occasions."

"That's lovely to hear, Miss Voncille. You keep at it. We'll expect both you and Mr. Linwood at the meeting in your regular clothes and hair."

Then it was time to speak with Becca. Seemingly not to be outdone by her unpredictable friends, she offered an off-the-wall proposal once Maura Beth had given her all the facts.

"I think it's a really cute idea," she began, "but why don't we make it even more of a theme than that? Everyone could make up a recipe that they think Scarlett or Melanie might have preferred to make or eat, and we could all compare notes."

Maura Beth took a deep breath and tried her best to smile through the phone.

"I'm pretty sure neither Scarlett nor Melanie did much cooking in flush times. And after the Yankees came through and burned up all the crops, recipes were a fond memory for a while. Getting anything at all to eat was the goal. I appreciate your creativity, Becca, but let's just stick with the personality angle this time around."

After they'd hung up, Maura Beth sat frowning at her desk for a few moments. Tricky stuff, this book club business. It was a delicate balancing act once people were in the fold, but it had to be worth the trouble. A kaput library was simply unacceptable.

The next day, Maura Beth decided she would keep Councilman Sparks in the loop, too. Of course, he hardly qualified as either a Scarlett or a Melanie. However, she could easily picture him wandering into the library smelling great, looking spiffy, and smiling from ear to ear to perform his irritating kibitzing act with aplomb to throw her off her game. Well, even though there had been no course at LSU in Dealing with Politicians 101, the truth was that she was living it now, like it or not, and there was no better way to learn her lessons than to face the politician in question without fear. Perhaps she could even throw him off his game.

"We'll be reading and commenting on *Gone with the Wind* from a particular perspective," she began, sitting across from him in his inner office one afternoon. "All our members are women so far, as you know very well from the organizational meeting." Then she explained the Scarlett versus Melanie theme to him and waited for his response.

Councilman Sparks took an awkward amount of time before answering while staring her down, but Maura Beth made a concerted effort not to fidget in her seat or otherwise indulge nervous body language. "Are you going to go feminist with this club, Miz Mayhew?"

"I wouldn't put it that way, no."

"Because I was going to say that you might just be ruling out fifty percent of the population of Cherico with a girlie-girl approach," he continued, flashing one of his dazzling, but completely insincere smiles. "Some men like to read, too."

"Are you a reader, Councilman?"

He produced a peculiar laugh that came off more like an intrusive sound effect. "When it suits my purposes."

"No doubt."

He calculated a moment longer, tightening the muscles of his face further. "You're so full of unexpected visits these days. So, was this one to prepare me to do well at the upcoming book review and 'all you can eat' buffet? Or was it to suggest that I stay away because I couldn't possibly fit in?"

"Oh, I don't think wild horses could keep you away. But I did think it was worth mentioning that

I intend to give this project my all. When I first came here, I promised myself that I would make a success of the Cherico Library, and by that I meant to turn it into the type of facility that people just couldn't do without. I admit that it's been hard, slow going these past six years, but you may have ended up doing me a favor by challenging me the way you have. I trust you'll bring out my best professional instincts."

Councilman Sparks shrugged his shoulders and seemed to relax his posture. "You have a penchant for soapboxing, Miz Mayhew. Maybe you could moonlight in my next election and write speeches for me. That is, in case this library thing of yours doesn't work out."

At that point Maura Beth knew it was time to leave. She had summoned her courage to face her adversary once again and dealt with him aboveboard. Yet, he always had an answer or a clever quip for everything—a master of one-upmanship. She knew his intention was to wear her down, but she just couldn't let that happen.

"Well, if you'll excuse me, Councilman," she said, rising from her chair. "I have a library to run."

He rose across from her without smiling. "But for how long, Miz Mayhew? For how long?"

After what seemed like two months instead of two more weeks, the August 17th inaugural meeting of The Cherry Cola Book Club finally arrived. Once again, Maura Beth had chosen to stage the festivities in the library lobby instead of the meeting room; but she had gone online and ordered some decorative touches to offset the drabness of the premises. As before with the flyers, Connie had been delighted to step up and fund them. Surrounding the refreshments table laden with the various dishes all the women had brought were blown-up movie posters of the stars of *Gone with the Wind*—Vivien Leigh, Clark Gable, Leslie Howard, Olivia de Havilland, and Hattie McDaniel. Maura Beth, Renette, and the Tuesday, Thursday, and Saturday front desk clerk—the amiable, hardworking Mrs. Emma Frost—had reinforced the Technicolor stills with cardboard backing and had spent the previous afternoon standing them up against some of the folding chairs. There in the background, the five Hollywood legends would bear silent witness to the drama that would be unfolding.

At one point Maura Beth had thought about blowing up balloons and tying them to the shelving here and there to add a more festive party accent. She had even gone out and bought a big bag of them with every color of the rainbow showing through the plastic. But she had backed off at the last minute, opting for the gravitas of the library instead. So much better, she had reasoned, that her literary trial balloon not be interpreted so literally.

As for the food, it was a smorgasbord of tempting aromas, colors, and appealing presentation. Becca had done an admirable job of coordinating the menu, keeping egos in check seamlessly. She herself had offered to cook up her chicken spaghetti casserole for the evening's entrée, and everyone was fine with it. Connie had been quite adamant about her contribution: "Assign me anything but fish—nothing with gills and scales, please. If I never cook another fish in my life, it will be too soon!" So the two women readily agreed that a frozen fruit salad would be in order from the McShay household. Miss Voncille thought her jalapeno cornbread would complement Becca's spaghetti and revealed that she would be bringing Locke Linwood as a guest once again; and Maura Beth's chocolate, cherry cola sheet cake in conjunction with Periwinkle's sherry custard would satisfy everyone's sweet tooth there at the end.

"I see you've taken my comment to heart, Miz Mayhew," Councilman Sparks offered after briefly schmoozing the others and surveying the posters and buffet just past seven. He was, in fact, ridiculously overdressed for the occasion, falling just short of black tie apparel, and his cologne announced itself the second he entered the room.

Maura Beth took a sip from her plastic cup, filled to the brim with Becca's summer cola drink recipe swimming with cherries and a tart twist of lime. "And what comment would that be? I don't exactly memorize all your pronouncements."

They walked together past the photo capture of bug-eyed Hattie McDaniel, distancing themselves a bit from the others. "I'm referring to Mammy here," he pointed out. "Looks to me like you're just rehashing the Selznick production with this bigger than life approach. As in 'the movie was so much better than the book.' I believe I mentioned you might end up doing that."

Maura Beth refused to bristle, giving him the most serene of her smiles. "Ah, but I assure you, we'll be exploring uncharted territory tonight with our Scarlett versus Melanie debate—right after we've all enjoyed this delicious repast. So, shall we make our way back to the table and help ourselves? I'm about to tell everyone to dig in. We eat first, then discuss."

At which point she did just that, and a line began to form by the stack of serving trays, paper plates, plastic silverware, and napkins next to Connie's saucers of frozen fruit salad. "I hope you don't mind the informality." Maura Beth continued to the gathering. "I thought we could balance our trays on our laps. The Cherry Cola Book Club won't be about putting on airs."

In fact, no one seemed to mind the balancing act once they had helped themselves and claimed their chairs, and the chatter that bubbled up between bites and sips was natural and friendly.

Even Councilman Sparks was on his best behavior, concentrating on Connie with his banter; then it came to Maura Beth in a flash that the McShays were potential voters now that they had moved to Cherico permanently.

"I was thinking that the City Council ought to consider a Welcome Wagon concept," Councilman Sparks was telling Connie at one point. "Perhaps we could convince a few civic-minded ladies to visit new residents with brochures and flowers—that sort of thing."

Connie nodded in noncommittal fashion as she broke off a piece of jalapeno cornbread. "I'd be more interested in a chapter of Fisherman's Anonymous. You don't have one, do you?" She chuckled and then began explaining her husband's recent addiction to spending most of his time casting his line out on the lake. "I expected my Douglas would be out there now and then, but it's turned into an obsession with him. That, and tossing back a few at The Marina Bar and Grill."

Then Becca joined the conversation with vigor. "Husbands and obsessions—no greater truth exists in the world today. Take my Stout Fella. I don't know if anyone's told you this, Connie, but my Justin single-handedly developed all those home sites out by the lake. I'm sure you bought your lot from him."

"Don't get jealous, but I do remember a big, good-looking man," Connie revealed.

Becca waved her off. "Believe me, anyone who built out on the lake dealt with my husband. His real-estate projects are his oxygen. All he does is eat and talk on his cell phone. Eat and e-mail people. Eat and text, eat and Tweet."

There was polite laughter at the last comment, but Becca's demeanor remained serious. "I wish I could find the humor in it, I really do. I'm sure you all know by now that I do my cooking show weekday mornings, so I'm always in the kitchen trying out new recipes. I suppose you could make a case that I'm obsessed with food. But not the way Justin is. He eats everything I fix him and even wants to lick the spoon. He's insatiable. When we were first married, he was tall and trim—quite the athlete." She hesitated as she blushed. "I know I shouldn't have started calling him Stout Fella, but, well, he's gained so much weight that I couldn't help it. Maybe I thought I could shame him into eating less, but he got to the point where he admitted he actually liked being referred to as Stout Fella. He said it made him feel like he was a big comic book superhero."

Miss Voncille put down her fork and gave Becca an engaging smile. "I haven't had the chance to say this to you yet, but I would have gotten around to it eventually tonight. I've been a huge fan of your *Becca Broccoli Show* since you first came on the radio. I've copied down all your comfort food recipes, and they've turned into staples for me."

She paused for a second and put her hand on Locke Linwood's shoulder. "Why, I fixed your macaroni and cheese with bacon bits just the other evening for myself and my gentleman friend here on one of our dinner dates, didn't I?"

Locke acknowledged her remark by patting his stomach with a contented little smirk on his face. "It was so irresistible I had an extra helping, and I don't normally do that. I like to stay in shape."

Becca rolled her eyes in exasperation. "Oh, I wish I had never invented all those rich, comfort food recipes as my main focus. It's what's really gotten Stout Fella in trouble. That, and the recent explosion of ice-cream flavors!"

"There's so much emphasis on eating smart these days," Miss Voncille added, pausing for a thoughtful frown. "I don't want to tell you how to run your show, but maybe you could put the broccoli back in *The Becca Broccoli Show*. After all, you're in charge of the recipes."

"You're absolutely right," Becca replied, nodding enthusiastically. "I can change the equation if I want. I could put together some episodes that would definitely put the broccoli back and then follow through by fixing the same recipes at home for Justin and myself. Now, let me see, what should I call them? Anyone got any ideas?"

"Calorie-Conscious Comfort Food?" Miss Voncille suggested.

Becca screwed up her face and then smiled diplomatically. "Thanks, but maybe too much of a tongue twister."

"Comfort Food without Calories?" Connie offered.

Becca laughed. "That would be outright fraud. There's no such thing."

"Don't I know it!" Connie exclaimed.

Then Miss Voncille tried again. "Downsizing with Comfort Food?"

Becca perked up immediately. "Oh, I like that. I think it just might work. A clever play on the state of the world today. I'm indebted, Miss Voncille."

"Oh, happy to help out. Perhaps you could keep us informed about these new episodes and let us know when the first one will be broadcast so we can all be sure and tune in. In fact, I'll be upset if I don't hear from you."

The mutual admiration society continued throughout the rest of the meal, and not even Councilman Sparks could disturb the camaraderie that was developing among the group. Then, after everyone had raved about the sheet cake and custard and stacked their trays, it was time for the serious business of The Cherry Cola Book Club to get under way.

"By now, I'm sure all of you have had plenty of time to think about our theme tonight," Maura Beth began, standing behind the podium. "So, who wants to be the first to tackle 'I'm Scarlett, You're Melanie!'?"

Councilman Sparks quickly raised his hand and did not wait to be acknowledged. "I just wanted to assure everyone here that I'm definitely not in the closet, so I'm neither."

"Your contribution to our meeting is very amusing, Councilman," Maura Beth said, as brief, muted laughter broke out. "But now it's time for some real thought."

"I'd like to go first, if you don't mind," Connie said. And as there were no objections, she took the floor but remained seated. "I just wound up a long career as an ICU nurse at a hospital in Nashville. I know I went into that occupation in the first place because I felt I could do all the vital, detailed things that nursing requires. But despite all this moaning I've been doing tonight about my husband and his devotion to fishing, I really do have an empathetic personality. One of the things I did best when our daughter, Lindy, was growing up was to stroke her forehead patiently when she felt bad or had a temperature. It takes that kind of touch and tendency to be a good nurse, I believe. And that's why I think I'm a Melanie. Maybe a somewhat firmer Melanie at times. But still a Melanie."

There was a ripple of polite applause, but Connie held up her hand like a school crossing guard shepherding children. "I had something else to add, though. There's a sequence in *Gone with the Wind* where Scarlett tries to tend to the maimed and dying soldiers at the field hospital. But she just can't stomach it, apologizes to Dr. Mead, turns on her heels, and runs away. She just doesn't have the temperament for it. Reading that passage this time around, I had a frightening vision of a high-tech Scarlett working as a nurse in a modern hospital. I envisioned her going around to all the patients that annoyed her and pulling the plug on them in one of her ongoing hissy fits. I love that expression, by the way—even though I couldn't find it in my dictionary." She waited for the subdued chuckling to subside.

"Maybe you think I'm being too extreme in my observations about Scarlett. But remember, she told Mammy she didn't want to have any more children because of what giving birth to Bonnie Blue had done to her figure. That's not a life-affirming instinct. It's completely self-absorbed. Melanie would never be capable of that kind of behavior—at least not as written by Margaret Mitchell. So, I think you can definitely count me in Melanie's soft, sweep camp, and I'm proud to be there pulling people back from the edge."

More polite applause followed. Then Maura Beth said, "I think we'd all agree with your analysis, Connie. Very thoughtful. So, let's score one for Melanie. Now, who wants to be next?"

It was Becca who volunteered from her seat. "I

don't know about going around pulling the plug on people," she began, "but I have to say that I'm a Scarlett. I suppose I have the sense of entitlement that she always had because she was born at Tara, but mine comes from a different source. I think I've earned mine through hard work. I don't think our culture recognizes merit enough these days. This radio personality of mine, this Becca Broccoli I've become, materialized out of nowhere. I went to bed one night, knowing I had this fifteen-minute radio show to produce after a chance meeting with the program director of WHYY at The Twinkle. We were sitting at adjacent tables, raving about the food to our waitress, and he happened to lean over and say to me, 'I wish there was somebody in Cherico who could teach my wife how to cook like this!' And something inside just egged me on, and I flat out told him I probably could since I loved cooking. One thing led to another, and somehow we came up with the idea of my doing a radio show. Finally—something to do with my degree in communications. Anyway, the very next morning I woke up with a doable gimmick." Becca paused for a coy giggle.

"I liked the possibilities of this character immediately, plus my married name has always been impossible for people to spell. I discovered that Becca Broccoli was a different side of me—she was the take-charge person I'd always wanted to be. Scarlett was like that from the beginning. When she wanted something or someone, such as the incredibly dull Ashley Wilkes, she went all out. What Scarlett wanted to be was mistress of Tara, but she never really achieved it. On the other hand, I wanted to be mistress of the airwaves, and now I have the most popular show on radio station WHYY, The Vibrant Voice of Greater Cherico. That last part always makes me laugh. What are we—maybe five thousand people counting any pregnant women waddling around? Oh, believe me, I know I'll never get a Grammy for being Becca Broccoli. People in the Beltway or out in Hollywood will never hear of me. I live in flyover country. But I'm still proud of what I've done. So perhaps I'm Scarlett, but with a well-adjusted, saner attitude."

After a brief round of applause, Maura Beth put an exclamation point on Becca's testimony. "Now that's the sort of Scarlett I wouldn't be afraid of meeting up with at the top of a dark landing!"

It was Miss Voncille's monologue a few minutes later, however, that had the group riveted to their seats. "I know I started out with Scarlett's fire and headstrong personality," she was explaining. "It was my intention to have it all—a loyal husband from a good family, however many children we decided to have, a fine house with all the trappings. You name it, I didn't see why I couldn't have it if I applied myself. That, of course, was very much the essence of Scarlett. But like Scarlett, I made a crucial error"—she broke off suddenly, putting her hand up—"give me a second, please."

Sensing what Miss Voncille might be about to reveal, Maura Beth spoke up in code. "We value your privacy above everything, Miss Voncille."

"I appreciate that," she resumed, taking time to catch her breath. "But I'm fine. I don't intend to go into a lot of detail here. What I was about to say was that Scarlett made the crucial error of falling in love with the wrong man. Or at least thinking she was in love with him. In my case, I fell in love with a soldier who went missing in action in Vietnam. We were engaged to be married, and when he didn't come back, I found myself embracing Scarlett's rougher edges. It's hard to forget that Margaret Mitchell's first description of Scarlett on the opening page is that she *was not beautiful*. But she ultimately fell back on her strength and the more cunning aspects of her personality. What I fell back on was being a tough, no-nonsense schoolteacher, and lately I've been running 'Who's Who in Cherico?' like a Third World dictator. I know I'd like to try and be more like Melanie, but for the time being, I have to say I'm camped deep behind the front lines in Scarlett Territory."

This time there was no applause. For some in the room it was the first time learning of Miss

Voncille's long-held secret about her lost love. Suddenly, they understood why she was the way she was, and that seemed to have inspired respectful silence with gentle smiles.

"Thank you for sharing that with us," Maura Beth said at last. "That can't have been easy for you."

But Miss Voncille immediately put everyone at ease by chucking Locke Linwood on the shoulder. "Life goes on, people. In fact, he's sitting right next to me in a coat and tie and a twinkle in his eye."

Locke actually seemed to be blushing even as he smiled. "I reserve the right to remain silent."

The laughter that followed cleared the way for Maura Beth's finale, which began with unexpected praise as she remained at the podium. "Before I give my take on this premise of mine, I'd like to thank you, ladies, for being so candid about your lives. You've held nothing of importance back in letting the rest of us know who you are. It occurs to me that maybe we've got something more than a book club going here. I hope this is just the start of our meaningful friendships."

Aside from a skeptical expression from Councilman Sparks, Maura Beth saw nothing but approval reflected in everyone's face as she proceeded. "As for myself, I know that Melanie has always been part of my library personality. In *Gone with the Wind*, she would have been the first to help any lost soul find their way. I grew up thinking it would just be terrific to help people find the right book to read on a stormy evening or locate the perfect source for a report they were doing. As a child, I loved scouring the shelves for something fun to check out, and I can still amuse myself that way as a grown-up and the director of this library." But her easy smile began to fade as she continued.

"There's another side to Melanie that I must mention, however. She was often naïve and a bit too trusting, and I do believe I've been guilty of that here in Cherico. I haven't always stood up for myself the way I should have. A good dose of Scarlett's determination is what I really need. Unfortunately, there are those in this community who feel that a library is a luxury for bored housewives who are too cheap to buy their own copies of best sellers at the nearest bookstore. And that's one of the milder sentiments I could conjure up for public consumption. Those people don't see the library as the educational and job-hunting resource it's always been. But at this juncture of my life, I feel that this little library—corrugated iron siding and all—is my Tara, and I intend to fight for it with every ounce of my strength. So the truth is: I'm in the midst of transforming myself from a Melanie into a Scarlett while trying to retain the best qualities of each. To my way of thinking, both characters ultimately represent what all women should strive to be. The right blend of kindness and ambition never goes out of style."

Amidst muted but genuine applause, Councilman Sparks spoke up loudly. "My goodness, Miz Mayhew—that reminded me of the scene where Scarlett gets down on her knees in the dirt, berates a carrot, and declares that she'll 'never go hungry again!' Why, you left not a dry eye in the house with the intensity of your monologue!"

Maura Beth, however, rose to the occasion. "Maybe it was a bit on the hammy side, but then, I was trained to be a librarian, not an actress. My milieu is shelving, not the stage. Or biographies, not Broadway."

"Touché!" he exclaimed, actually appearing to enjoy the repartee and even blowing her a kiss.

"This was the most fun I've had in ages!" Connie added. "And that includes all those years with The Music City Page Turners up in Nashville. We never mixed our reads with our lives quite like this. It's a different approach, but I like it."

"I have a point to make, though," Locke Linwood put in suddenly. "The food was mighty delicious, but I think the discussion was apparently for ladies only. I mean, nobody asked me if I thought I was a Rhett or an Ashley."

Miss Voncille gave a little gasp as she looked him in the eye. "Now, Locke, you told me you weren't even going to bother to read the book. You said I could do all the yapping, and you were just coming with me for the big spread."

He hung his head, sounding a bit sheepish. "I lied. I'd never read it before. Never saw the movie, either. I guess I wanted to find out what all the hoopla was about."

"Imagine that," Miss Voncille replied, sounding pleased and surprised at the same time. "I thought everyone had seen the movie at least once. It's like admitting you've never seen *The Wizard of Oz* or heard of Judy Garland."

"Well, Miz Mayhew?" Locke asked.

Maura Beth was puzzled. "Well, what, Mr. Linwood?"

"Aren't you going to ask me if I'm a Rhett or an Ashley, or do you have to be a woman to make these important literary connections?"

The request met with laughter throughout the room, after which Maura Beth popped the question. "Okay, by all means. Which are you, then?"

"Of course, I think of myself as a Rhett. My late wife, Pamela, always told me I was her hero."

"You were certainly that," Miss Voncille offered. "Anyone who ever saw the two of you together could confirm it. I saw it at every meeting of 'Who's Who?' that you attended."

"Does this mean that you consider yourself a bona-fide member of The Cherry Cola Book Club,

Mr. Linwood?" Maura Beth said, seizing the opportunity.

"Why not?" he answered quickly. "I agree with Miz McShay over there. This is the most fun I've had in a while."

"Wonderful, and welcome aboard officially!" Maura Beth then glanced over at the front desk clock and decided to test the waters. "I see we've been at this business of dining and discussing for an hour and fifteen minutes now. Does anyone have any other thoughts about the novel? They don't necessarily have to be related to Scarlett and Melanie."

"I'm just curious," Becca said. "What was the final total on that? I mean, how many Melanies and how many Scarletts did we end up with?"

Maura Beth scanned the notes she had scribbled throughout the proceedings and emerged chuckling under her breath. "It's not all that clear, actually. I have Connie down as a Melanie, Becca and Miss Voncille as Scarletts—although with reservations in my estimation—and myself as a work in progress."

"That's hedging," Becca insisted. "Here in the South we always take a stand. It's in the lyrics of 'Dixie,' you know." She began humming the tune until she got to the proper spot in the chorus and then began singing. " '*. . . in Dixie Land I'll take my stand, to live and die in Dixie . . .*' "

"Point well-taken," Maura Beth replied. "Very

*Gone with the Wind*, as a matter of fact. Okay, then, I'll err on the side of Melanie for myself. Just for the time being, though. I have lots of things to accomplish before I'm thirty."

"Tell me everything, girl!" Periwinkle exclaimed after her last customer had left a little past nine. She had just flipped the blue-sequined sign hanging on the front door of The Twinkle from OPEN to CLOSED. "Did anybody get tipsy on my sherry custard? It's actually happened before. Some precious little ole lady had two of 'em one night, and it took a coupla grown men to escort her out the door. Maybe I should put a customer warning on the dessert menu."

Maura Beth laughed as they claimed a table in the middle of the room. "No, I think your custard went down smoothly. No hiccups, just raves. My ooey, gooey, chocolate, cherry cola sheet cake was a winner, too."

Periwinkle settled in, leaning forward with her gum going a mile a minute. "Okay, enough about the food. How did the meeting go? Was Councilman Supremo there throwing off his usual sparks?"

"Oh, yes. Dressed to the nines, too. He looked like he was going to a wedding. Or maybe he was supposed to be the groom. But he behaved, for the most part. Or let's just say, I handled every curve ball he threw me. He even blew me a kiss, believe it or not. He's an odd duck, that one. Anyway, I'm here to tell you that The Cherry Cola Book Club took flight without a hitch this evening. Everyone contributed in a meaningful way, and we ended up with two Scarletts and two Melanies. Oh, and a Rhett!"

"As in Butler?"

"As in Mr. Locke Linwood demanding that I ask him if he was a Rhett or an Ashley. It was so cute, and he's now officially a member."

Periwinkle eyed her intently. "Well, I guess you know I'm in the bunch with Scarlett branded across their foreheads. I'm too feisty to be anything else."

"Scarlett on steroids, perhaps?"

Periwinkle drew back playfully. "Now, sweetie, I'm one of the good guys, remember?"

"Just kidding, of course. I definitely need more of your spine. Anyway, we got a lot accomplished tonight, including all the important decisions for the next meeting. Before we adjourned, we put it to a vote and decided that we'd be reading *To Kill a Mockingbird* this coming month. We'll be getting together on the evening of September 19th, as a matter of fact." Maura Beth gave her friend a hopeful look for emphasis.

"I still don't see how I can swing it, honey," Periwinkle insisted, reacting instantly to the unspoken appeal. "Let's put it this way. If my restaurant bid'ness is going great guns and I've got standing room only all the time, then I simply won't have the time to participate in the club. And if I have so much slack that I can loll around reading and choosing which fictional characters I most resemble, then I'm in deep . . . well, let's just be ladylike about it and settle for the term . . . financial trouble. Does that make sense?"

"Of course. But I was thinking just the other day about your restaurant and my library—particularly about how busy you are. Not to mention that long drive you make round-trip every day to and from The Twinkle. I mean, your house is halfway between Cherico and Corinth. Don't you get bored at times?"

Periwinkle shrugged. "Just part of making a living, honey."

"What if I could spice things up a bit for you?"

"What do you suggest? Cumin, paprika, or something stronger like cayenne pepper? I've got 'em all on the shelf."

They both laughed. Then Maura Beth said, "I was thinking that you could use our audio books to liven up your travel. Our selection is modest due to our budget, but the patrons that use them swear by them. So, what do you say? How about joining the club officially by being a good listener?"

Periwinkle was all smiles. "I think you should recruit for the Army, girl. I'm all ready to sign up under those circumstances."

"Wonderful!" Maura Beth exclaimed, clasping her hands together. "We'll finally get you a card, and we can take it from there."

"And how about if I send over something extra to the buffet this time? Like my aspic."

Maura Beth cut her eyes to the side with a saucy smile. "Can't argue with that."

"Of course, I'll keep handing out your flyers to my customers. I assume you'll be printing up a new one for the *Mockingbird* book?"

"That's the plan."

Then Periwinkle grew serious, briefly stopping her gum and leaning in. "So do you think all this'll be enough to keep those weasels at the City Council from shutting you down?"

Maura Beth sighed plaintively. "Too early to tell. It's very hard to predict Councilman Sparks. All I can do is plug away."

# 6

# Back in the Saddle Again

Miss Voncille's tidy cottage on Painter Street was one of two dozen or so homes in Cherico built around the turn of the twentieth century in the Queen Anne style and had been the only thing of value she had inherited from her parents, Walker and Annis Nettles. It was graced by a small but immaculately manicured front yard featuring a mature fig tree on one side of its brick walkway and a fanciful, green ceramic birdbath on the other.

"Isn't this quaint!" Maura Beth exclaimed, as she and Connie stood in front of it early one humid August morning.

"Exactly the sort of place I would expect Miss Voncille to live," Connie added. "Very spinster schoolteacher-ish."

Just then Miss Voncille spotted them and flung open the front door. "You're right on time, ladies!" she called out. "Come on in. I've got coffee, hot biscuits, and green-pepper jelly waiting for you. We have about fifteen minutes to eat before Becca's show starts!"

Once inside, Maura Beth was surprised to discover a veritable jungle of potted palms set in sturdy ceramic containers. Some were enormous and obviously quite mature, their fronds spreading out like great, spraying fountains. Others were much smaller and newer, but there was hardly a nook or cranny in the front part of the house without them. Nor were they absent in Miss Voncille's bright yellow kitchen, where the three ladies eventually sat down to breakfast in a cozy little nook.

"I've got the station tuned in and everything. All I have to do is turn it on," Miss Voncille explained, as she poured steaming coffee all around. "Please, help yourselves to biscuits. Everything's homemade, including the jelly. I grow the peppers myself in the backyard."

After everyone had sufficiently fussed enough to fix their plates, Maura Beth began making small talk. "I just think it was so generous of you to invite us over here for Becca's first 'Downsizing with Comfort Food' show. She called me up yesterday to tell me how pleased she was that we were all getting together to hear it. She's a bit nervous about it."

"Oh, I know, but it's the least I could do since I put the idea in her head," Miss Voncille said, after swallowing a bite of biscuit. "Besides, she's given me so many great cooking ideas over the years, I want to support her any way I can."

"We all do," Connie added. "From what she's told us, she needs every bit of help she can muster in getting her Stout Fella into shape."

Miss Voncille took a sip of her coffee and drew herself up with great authority. "Ladies, I just love the way we're getting to know each other. I don't have to tell you that I haven't been terribly social over the years. And I don't consider pontificating about genealogy to qualify, either. That's why participating in the club is doing me so much good. It's just what I need, and I thank you again for prodding me to join, Maura Beth. So, I wanted to take the bull by the horns and explain all these potted palms in the house."

The comment took both Maura Beth and Connie by surprise. Neither would have dreamed of bringing up the subject, but it was Maura Beth who found something to say that didn't sound insincere. "Well, if you feel it's necessary."

"Yes, I really do. The house didn't look like this when my parents were still alive. They hated houseplants. But this is my tribute to Frank, my MIA sweetheart. He disappeared in the jungles of Vietnam, as I've explained." She paused, smiling at all the greenery she had strategically placed around the room.

"But the last letter I got from Frank before he went missing was so full of life and his special spirit. You would never have known he was in the middle of a war. He went on and on about how beautiful and exotic all the palm trees were. The line that especially sticks with me after all these years is where he said the entire place would be a wonderful spot for tourists if everybody wasn't shooting at each other. Perhaps he was imagining what it would all look like in peacetime someday. And then he said that before he finally came back to me, he wanted me to go out and buy a bunch of potted palms to welcome him home. How could I not honor his request?"

"They're beautiful," Maura Beth managed, not really knowing what else to say.

"They're also a form of closure for me," Miss Voncille continued. "Since Frank was officially MIA, I wanted to be sure they were always here if he did ever return to me by some miracle. I take care of them year after year and replace them if they die, and all of that gives me great comfort. It may seem nutty, but that's the truth."

"I understand. Whatever works for you," Maura Beth said, while Connie just nodded with a smile.

"Most people who've visited me probably think I'm just a crazy old maid who went gaga for palms. Of course, I gave up worrying what other people thought about me a long time ago."

"Well, this green-pepper jelly of yours is beyond delicious, and so are your biscuits. It all just melts in my mouth," Connie said, trying to lighten the mood a bit.

"How gracious of you!" Miss Voncille exclaimed, her face a study in delight. "I grow the peppers, along with my basil, mint, and rosemary in my backyard plot. And you know, I may have even gotten the jelly recipe from one of Becca's shows." She checked her watch and perked up even further. "Oh, we're just a few seconds away from the debut of the new regime. Now, ladies, you leave everything right where it is. I'll clear the table later. Let's just sit back and give Becca our undivided attention, shall we?"

Then she rose from her chair, headed over to the clunky old radio sitting on the counter, and turned it on just in time for the pre-recorded station ID: *"You're listening to WHYY, The Vibrant Voice of Greater Cherico, Mississippi!"* The theme music that Becca had chosen several years ago—a meandering, nondescript instrumental full of acoustic guitar chords—announced the beginning of yet another episode of *The Becca Broccoli Show*. After another twenty seconds or so of music, Becca's distinctive voice came through loud and clear.

*"Good morning, Chericoans! I'm Becca Broccoli, and welcome once again to my little treasure trove of recipes and cooking tips, coming to you every weekday morning at seven-thirty right here on WHYY. As always, the best fifteen minutes you can spend to get you in and out of the kitchen fast to the applause of your family and friends. Today and over the next few days, however, I'm going to be doing something I've never done before, and that is, put an emphasis on more healthful recipes. We're calling it 'Downsizing with Comfort Food.'*

*As in 'let's go down a size or two and still enjoy our food.'"* Becca paused for a little chuckle. *"Yes, listeners, we're going to be putting the broccoli back in* The Becca Broccoli Show. *Not literally, of course. I don't want you to panic and throw Brussels sprouts at me. More healthful doesn't mean horrendous. Good for you doesn't mean god-awful. Believe me, we're not going to be throwing out the baby back ribs with the bathwater here. . . ."*

The three ladies sitting around Miss Voncille's table laughed out loud, and Connie exclaimed, "Great start! Way to go, Becca!"

"Oh!" Maura Beth added suddenly. "What if we want to write any of this down?"

Miss Voncille shook her head emphatically and made a shushing sound. "Not to worry. Becca told me she'd bring copies of all her new recipes to our *Mockingbird* session next week."

*". . . and you may be asking yourself what the reason for all this is. It's simply that I want my family to get good checkups when they go to the doctor. We all need to be more proactive about our health while we still enjoy our comfort food. So this morning I have for you my new version of tomatoes and okra,"* Becca was saying as the ladies concentrated on the radio broadcast once again. *"Yes, I know some of you think okra is too slimy, and you don't like its texture. But I've got a few good tips for you that'll make it easy to avoid*

*most of that slime. My goodness, this sounds like something out of* Ghostbusters, *doesn't it? Who ya gonna call—Becca Broccoli?!"*

There was more laughter from the ladies. "She's nailing this so far," Maura Beth observed. "Although this is only the second time I've listened to her."

"I want to see what happens when she gets to the actual recipe, though," Connie added. "De-sliming okra is a mighty big promise. I haven't seen it done in my cooking lifetime."

But Becca delivered within a minute or two. *". . . and the key to cutting down on the slime is to sauté your okra quickly on very high heat. Don't let it lie around in the pan because it will end up oozing all those juices some people just don't like. Another tip: Cut your okra on the bias so that you end up with diagonal slices. That way more of the surface has contact with that high heat. Isn't it interesting how the simplest tips can make your life so much easier in the kitchen? Now, we'll be right back to talk about the versatility of tomatoes and okra for your more healthful lifestyle after this message from our sponsor."*

As the latest deals from Harv Eucher's Pre-Owned Vehicles held no interest for the ladies, they began their chatter once again.

"I know Becca has to be telling the truth about the high heat," Miss Voncille commented. "I practically stew my okra on simmer in the pan.

But then, I don't mind the slime. I guess it's an acquired taste."

Connie was shaking her head and wagging a finger at the same time. "I never could get my Lindy to eat it. She always claimed it made her feel like she needed to clear her throat. But my little granddaughter, Melissa, just loves to eat it in gumbo. Of course, she doesn't even know it's in there mixed up with the rice and the onions and the chicken. She's too distracted pushing her spoon around, and she says, 'Gigi, I cain't find the gum in here!' So, I made up a cute little ditty for her, complete with cheerleader-type hand gestures—I forget the tune now—but the lyrics went: 'Who took the gum outta the gumbo, hey? Who took the gum outta the gumbo, hey?' Oh, she danced around and went wild!"

The ladies' laughter erupted just as Harv Eucher's revved-up blather about taking advantage of once-in-a-lifetime trade-ins finally came to an end, and Becca's voice returned for some blessed relief.

*"Welcome back to 'Downsizing with Comfort Food' on* The Becca Broccoli Show. *Next, we want to talk about using tomatoes and okra as a side dish or—as I most often prefer it—as a staple ingredient in my chicken or shrimp gumbo . . ."*

"There you go!" Connie exclaimed.

*". . . and it's my suggestion that your pantry should never be without several jars of what I call*

*my all-purpose gumbo base. Here in the middle of the summer with everything fresh and in season is when you should be putting up that gumbo mix for those cold weather evening suppers looming ahead . . .*" Becca continued.

"I'm not a canner," Connie admitted with a smirk. "I'm from the crowd that thinks Mason jars should be used to serve up humongous cocktails. Why, it's all the rage at certain restaurants up in Nashville."

The others nodded agreeably even as Becca rolled through her script. "*. . . and another tip for lightening up that gumbo base would be to go with about half as much butter when you sauté. Keep your garlic and your salt and pepper for that all-important seasoning. Just take the plunge and use olive oil instead. It's part of the Mediterranean diet that's becoming increasingly popular everywhere. They say a little olive oil and an occasional glass of red wine does wonders for longevity . . . and maybe even your love life. Of course, for those of you out there who are teetotalers, just go with the olive oil and skip the wine . . .*"

Miss Voncille leaned in and raised an eyebrow smartly. "I wonder how these instructions about substituting olive oil will go over with the devout butter believers. I know people from church potluck suppers who think 'Thou Shalt Use Only Butter in Everything' is the eleventh commandment."

"My mother was one of them," Connie added with a wink. "If she had a headache—she'd spread butter on a few aspirin and go about her business."

The ladies couldn't seem to help themselves from that point forward. Whatever Becca said, they had an aside or witticism ready, and they were somehow able to coordinate the two seamlessly in the manner of an old-fashioned television variety show act. It wasn't criticism as much as it was a form of "dishing with the girls," and it made the show's precious minutes fly by with plenty of laughter in the air.

*". . . so be sure and tune in tomorrow at this same time, same station for another installment of* The Becca Broccoli Show,*"* Becca was saying as the show's closing theme came up.

Miss Voncille headed over and shut off the radio, leaned against the counter, and folded her arms. "Well, ladies, what did you think? My opinion is that it went very well, olive oil and all."

Both Maura Beth and Connie agreed that the show had been a success, but then Maura Beth offered up a sheepish grin. "I also think we had a very good time cutting up the way we did. There were even moments when I felt like we were schoolgirls whispering behind the teacher's back. I wonder if we would have said some of the things we said had Becca been here in person."

"Oh, it was all in good fun," Connie insisted.

"I'm sure she wouldn't have minded. I thought Becca's program was full of wit, so it inspired us to react the same way."

"Absolutely!" Miss Voncille exclaimed. "I'm sure that's what Becca was going for—the humor angle to win everyone over to a slightly different point of view." Then Miss Voncille headed over and dramatically plopped herself down in her seat, putting her hands on the table. "Ladies, I have to confess something to you. Of course, I did want you here for breakfast and Becca's show, but I also had an ulterior motive. I thought maybe enjoying the show might bring us together even more than we already are, and I believe it certainly has with the way we've been laughing and talking. But there's something else I had on my mind and, well . . . it's just that . . ."

Maura Beth and Connie exchanged expectant glances, and Maura Beth finally said, "You've come this far, Miss Voncille. Follow through. What is it you wanted to tell us?"

"It's my relationship with Locke Linwood," she began, staring at her hands at first. Then she looked up and caught Maura Beth's gaze. "It's been so long since . . . well, you know what I'm trying to say, don't you?"

Maura Beth reached over and patted her hand with a generous smile. "Since you've been with a man?"

Miss Voncille exhaled and briefly averted her

eyes. “You librarians have good instincts. But, yes, that’s exactly what I wanted to discuss with both of you. Frank and I were intimate, but that was way back in 1967. It seemed so easy then. All you heard from the media was how *free* love was supposed to be, I mean. What a lie! I think love is the dearest thing in the world—in the old-fashioned business sense of that word. What a price you end up paying for it whether you get to keep it or lose it! But now here it is another century. How do I . . . get back in the saddle again after all this time? How do I . . . free myself?"

“Connie, you’re the married woman among us,” Maura Beth said. “Do you want to take this?”

Connie looked briefly uncomfortable but soon drew herself up and patted her big hair—the latter gesture a sure sign that she was ready to tackle anything. “Well, the first thing I’d have to ask you, Miss Voncille, is how far your relationship with Mr. Linwood has progressed. Could you share that with us?”

“It’s been very gentlemanly on his part so far, if you catch my drift,” she explained. “I’m always ready to go out when he arrives. He has reservations at The Twinkle or somewhere else for us, and we talk politely over our dinner and wine. Later, when he walks me to my door, there’s a gentle kiss on the cheek, and there are moments when it seems like something more should happen. But . . . it stops there. Or to be perfectly honest, I stop it there."

"Then you've never asked him in—for a nightcap, as they say?"

"No."

"Why not?"

"I—well, something tugs at me, and I end up thinking it would be disloyal to Frank."

Connie grew pensive, touching an index finger to her lips. "And have you ever ended up at his house?"

"Oh, he says he's not comfortable with that yet. But he insists he is trying his best to accept another woman being in the rooms he shared with his Pamela."

"Well, he is a fairly recent widower," Maura Beth put in. "Maybe it's easier for him to hold on to his memories of his wife and settle for something platonic with you. And maybe that's what he thinks you want—your memories of Frank and a gentlemanly escort."

Miss Voncille looked overwhelmed, putting her fingers to her temples. "Yes, I think you ladies must be right. Neither one of us has been willing to . . . saddle up."

"Do you think you could ever muster up the courage to let Mr. Linwood in for the . . . shank of the evening?" Connie proposed.

"That's such a colorful way of putting it," Miss

Voncille replied, clearly amused. "Reminds me of a big, juicy leg of lamb." Then she grew more resolute, narrowing her eyes. "Maybe if I worked hard at it, I could try to let go. I keep a picture of Frank by the nightstand. It was taken just before he left for Vietnam. You can see the determination in his face, in the way his jaw was set, in the way he refused to smile and still looked contented with where he was about to go and what he was about to do. It's intriguing the way the camera can sometimes capture your soul on film. But in any case, I suppose I should remove it if I invite Locke into my emerald green bedroom . . . and he actually accepts."

"I would if I were in your shoes," Connie offered. "If it gets that far, you need to give the man at least a fighting chance to compete with all those perfect romantic memories of yours."

"And you don't necessarily have to go out of your way to explain the significance of all the potted palms, either," Maura Beth added. "Just go ahead and let him think you've gone a little mad. Lots of women have decorating fetishes. For instance, I've gone a bit crazy in my little apartment with a dozen shades of purple. But in any case, it's better than having Mr. Linwood be reminded of Frank everywhere he turns. It could definitely put a damper on things."

Miss Voncille clasped her hands together with an excitement in her voice that made her sound and seem much younger than her years. "Having girlfriends to talk to after all these years is so much fun. So much better than walking around this empty house talking to my palms while I water them. Therefore, I've decided to try and saddle up after our big *Mockingbird* to-do at the library is over."

"How brave of you!" Connie exclaimed. "And I'm so glad we could help out." Then she turned her head to the side, frowning in contemplation. "Ladies, I've just thought of something brilliant. Why should you be the only one with an escort at these literary outings, Miss Voncille? I need to get Douglas out of that damned boat of his and doing something interesting with me for a change. After all, this is my hard-earned retirement, too. So, I'm going to insist that he come to the *Mockingbird* potluck and book review. If he refuses to go along with such a simple and reasonable request, then I'll refuse to clean his unending stringers of fish. Now that'll put the fear of God in him!"

"Sounds good to me!" Miss Voncille replied. "And you know what else would be lots of fun? Getting Becca to bring her Stout Fella to the meeting. I think we'd all like to meet him since we've heard so much about him. Maura Beth, this would be a surefire way to grow our numbers!"

"Yes, it would," she answered, smiling broadly. "And growing our numbers is the most important thing we can do with this little club of ours. In fact, it's crucial. I only wish I had someone to bring."

Connie then gave Maura Beth one of her famous friendly nudges. "Oh, don't worry. Mr. Right will come along when you least expect it. I met Douglas at a charity auction, and we were bidding for the same piece of antique furniture. Well, he had quite a bankroll from being a successful trial lawyer, so he outbid me and I lost the sideboard. But it was only a temporary defeat because I liked the fact that he had the good taste to spend his money on such fine things. I thought he just might be a keeper, so I snared him in my web, and when I unraveled that big cocoon, the sideboard tumbled out with him, of course. It's sitting in our dining room out at the lake right this minute, and every time I use it for entertaining, I'm reminded of the crusty old adage, 'To the victor belongs the spoils.' "

"Then it's all decided," Maura Beth said. "I'll call up Becca and tell her to work on her Stout Fella, Connie will work on Douglas, and Miss Voncille, you'll show up with Locke Linwood in tow as usual."

Miss Voncille was almost giggling. "Oh, I'm so excited. I never thought I'd let myself feel this way again, and here I am actually considering inviting Locke into my jungle lair. But more as soft, sweet Melanie."

“Men like to think of themselves as the hunters in the game of love,” Connie added, lifting her chin with an air of superiority. “But more often than not, it’s we women who do the trapping.”

# 7

# The Perfect Man

Renette Posey was knocking insistently on Maura Beth's office door. "Gregory Peck has just arrived!" she announced with great enthusiasm, sticking her head in with a girlish smile. It was the good news they had both been anxiously awaiting.

Maura Beth shot up from her chair and clapped half a dozen times in rapid succession. "Well, where is he? I want to get my hot little hands on him right this instant!"

"You and me both!" Renette twisted her head around, looking back briefly. "Here comes the UPS guy in his cute brown shorts with the tubes. Wow! Just under the wire, huh?"

Indeed, it definitely fell into the category of close calls. Here it was the morning of the *Mockingbird* meeting, and the movie poster blow-ups of Gregory Peck as Atticus Finch were just now showing up. This, despite a guarantee from the online company that they would be shipped to The Cherico Library in two to three business days. But more than a week had passed, and there were no posters in sight. Maura Beth hated fooling with tracking numbers, but her sterling organizational skills and note-taking had paid off handsomely for her this time around. The tubes, it turned out, had been mistakenly bundled off to a library in Jericho, Missouri, thus creating the nerve-wracking delay. Murphy's Law, Maura Beth figured.

"Let's pull them out right away and see what we've actually got," Maura Beth instructed, after the UPS man had apologized profusely for the mistake and left quickly. "There were supposed to be three different poses."

Renette began tugging at the tape on one of the tubes, while Maura Beth sat behind her desk and took a pair of scissors to another. A few minutes later, all three black-and-white posters had been retrieved and unfurled. Though the order had gone astray, it was otherwise accurate: There was one pose of Gregory Peck as Atticus Finch in a dramatic courtroom scene; another of him as Atticus with Jem and Scout in her overalls standing in front of the little cottage they all called home; and a third of Peck as himself receiving the Oscar for his performance in *To Kill a Mockingbird*. Maura Beth was certain that these stills would create an ambience similar to the one the *Gone with the Wind* posters had.

"We'll back these with cardboard like we did for the other ones, and no one will be the wiser that they practically traveled all over the country before getting here," Maura Beth added with a sigh of relief. "I want everything to go smoothly this evening. With the two extra men showing up, Councilman Sparks will see that we're building up the club, and we can't be ignored."

"If you have enough food, I'll be happy to show up myself," Renette offered. "I had to read *To Kill a Mockingbird* my senior year in high school, and I still remember it pretty well. Even got an 'A' on my book report. I especially liked the part about the giant ham with the hole in it that saved the little girl's life."

Maura Beth looked especially pleased at the suggestion. "Well, we won't have ham on the menu, but please come, Renette. I know we'll have more than enough to eat."

Then Maura Beth reviewed the menu sitting on her desk. For this second meeting of The Cherry Cola Book Club, Becca would be bringing her healthful version of chicken gumbo with tomatoes and okra; inspired by one of her latest shows, Connie would be throwing together a fresh golden bantam corn and red pepper salad; Miss Voncille was going to bake her delicious biscuits and offer her green-pepper jelly on the side; by popular demand, Maura Beth herself would repeat her chocolate, cherry cola sheet cake; and finally, honorary member Periwinkle had generously agreed to supply another gratis item from The Twinkle—specifically, her knockout tomato aspics with the cream-cheese centers.

"I know a lot of people think men will eat

anything you put in front of them, but I've found that they can sometimes be hard to please," Maura Beth explained. "I think we'll have a good variety on hand tonight, though, and I bet Stout Fella will lead the way."

Renette seemed about to say something several times and finally got it out. "Should I bring a little dish, too? I could . . . thaw something?"

"Just bring yourself, sweetie. I expect a lively and unforgettable debate this evening."

Inside their opulent mansion out in the country, Becca and her Stout Fella were having heated words in their powder blue master bedroom suite around six-thirty that evening. She was applying the finishing touches to her face at her vanity, while he was pacing around the shag carpet in his bare feet, still half-dressed and mumbling things under his breath.

"This is a very important business meeting, Becca," he was saying, refusing to look her straight in the eye as he fumbled with his shirt buttons. "I can't help it if it came up at the last second. I've been trying to pin down Winston Barkeley for the last coupla months, and he wants to get together at The Twinkle tonight while he's in town. Maybe I can even close the deal. This is a premium piece of land for my next plot out at the lake, and it's going to be really high-end."

"As if there are a bunch of paupers out there

now," she replied, briefly eyeing the touch of rouge she had just applied to her right cheekbone. "Sometimes I think all this conspicuous success is the worst possible thing that could have happened to you—Justin Rawlings Brachle. What more do you have to prove to the world?"

He snickered while pulling on his wide-load pants in front of their full-length mirror. "Hey, whatever I need to and with no apologies. There's more to life than winning a football scholarship, you know. Besides, you married me for richer or poorer, and I don't see you turning your back on the richer part."

"Oh, I've done my share as Becca Broccoli. You know as well as I do that I could go it alone if I had to. Not that I want to, of course." She caught her agitated husband's reflection in the vanity mirror as she carefully applied lip gloss, and his steady transformation into Stout Fella came sharply into focus.

She had called him on the weight gain and his eating habits early on. "We're going to have to buy you new clothes the way you're going—at the big, tall, and spiffy store, if it exists," she had said, trying her best to make light of it.

"That's not a bad thing," he had pointed out. "A well-fed husband is good advertising for your cooking show. Your listeners would lose faith in you if I were the gaunt, skinny runt of Cherico." And he had kept right on standing and making more "islands" of his ice cream, while taking second and third helpings of her scrumptious cooking at the dining room table.

"You need to slow down," she had warned on another occasion. "You act like food and time are in limited supply. You're always on that cell phone. I wish the damned thing had never been invented!"

"I sees 'em, and I calls 'em—just like I used to in the huddle," he had answered, making a joke of it.

But he was serious about cornering the real-estate market in Cherico before he was thirty-five, and he had done so with a succession of high-profile lake development projects. After that, his bank balance and his waistline had expanded simultaneously. Yet there were still vestiges in his fleshy face of the rugged, but handsome athlete who had swept bubbly Becca Heflin off her feet and down the aisle to the altar over a decade ago.

"The least you can do is accompany me to the library and have a bite to eat. You don't have to stay and open your big mouth after that. But everyone is expecting you to show up. They've been just dying to meet you," Becca reminded him. "You could end up being the star of the evening."

"And you set all of that up without my permission!" he fired back. "One night, I come home from work, and you tell me that we're going to one of your fussy 'ladies' night out' affairs at the library. You expect me to jump up and down?"

"I expect us to do something together once in a while, Justin. What's the harm in that?"

He didn't answer her, plopping down on the edge of the huge four-poster bed to pull his socks on. "For cripes' sake, these don't match!" he cried out suddenly, dangling the pair in front of his face. "One's navy blue and the other's black. You spend much more time on the radio than you do with our laundry. I told you to hire someone to help you around the house. Why do you object to our having servants? We can easily afford it!"

"I'm well aware of that, but let's argue one thing at a time," she continued as he headed toward his closet. "All I'm asking right now is that you go and at least meet my new friends. Won't you do that much?"

Momentarily, he emerged with a matching pair and then surprisingly gave in, nodding his head grudgingly. "Okay, okay. I'll put in an appearance to keep the peace around here. But after that, I'm off to The Twinkle to meet up with Winston. You can stay and yak about *To Kill a Mockingbird* 'til the cows come home and the early bird gets the worm."

"Now that's original commentary if I ever heard it," Becca remarked, rising from her vanity with a pert little smile firmly in place.

• • •

Connie was standing at one of her great room windows admiring the way the early evening sun played off the slack water of Lake Cherico in the distance. The horizon was tinged with orange and gold, except for wild brush strokes of coral that were doing their best to blot out what remained of the day's blue allotment. It was now quarter to seven, and she had spent the better part of the last hour luring Douglas out of his precious bass boat—which he had named *The Verdict*—and into shaving and showering mode.

"You smell like bait," she had told him, once she had him on the terra firma of the pier's faded planks and he had stowed his stringer of fish in the cooler. "Not that that's anything new. But I don't want everyone at the library to smell you coming. So, please, give yourself a thorough scrubbing."

Once inside, he had good-naturedly fallen to, even to the extent of singing in the shower. She could hear him trying to work his way through "Singin' in the Rain," although he was far from a Gene Kelly in the vocal department. Fishing most of the day had that effect on him, though. In short, he was in paradise. Connie, however, felt she had not yet punched her ticket, and she hoped that this *Mockingbird* evening would be the beginning of a shared retirement experience for them.

"I wouldn't mind seeing ole Justin Brachle again, now that I think about it," Douglas said out of nowhere, emerging from getting dressed at last and heading toward his wife with a snap to his step. He had chosen a silver guayabera shirt and dark slacks for the occasion, complementing the first waves of gray that had invaded his slightly receding hairline. "He did sell us this land seven years ago when we were first thinking of building the lodge."

Connie turned away from the window and the ongoing prelude to the sunset. "I told his wife, Becca, that I thought I remembered him as being quite a catch." Then she took in her own husband's still-trim physique, ending with the devilish smile that never failed to melt her in the bedroom. "Speaking of looking good, I don't think you've been this presentable since we left Nashville. And you smell divine! *To Kill a Mockingbird* be damned! I may have to attack you. What have you got on?"

He inched his sunburned but carefully shaven face closer to hers and lightly kissed her cheek. "Just a splash of Old Spice. I found a bottle in the bedroom closet. It was in one of those boxes we still haven't opened."

She put her arms around his neck and kissed him back. "Weren't you wearing that when we first started dating thirtysomething years ago? That bottle belongs in the Smithsonian."

He pulled away and enjoyed a good laugh. "Not this one. I think Lindy gave it to me for Father's

Day not too long ago. Maybe just before we moved down. She knows her old man's history, that's for sure."

"Not as well as I do," Connie added. "And I've begun to think you've given me up for the fishes. Maybe I should grow scales."

He narrowed his eyes and played at taking offense. "Okay, I haven't been that bad, have I? I even managed to reread five whole chapters of *To Kill a Mockingbird* so I'd be up to snuff and wouldn't embarrass you at the thing tonight. It's been more than a few decades since high school, you know."

"Let's just see how it goes at the library. Then we'll talk," she said, managing a smile as she checked her watch. "We need to get there while the food's still hot. Or before Stout Fella eats it all."

Douglas looked puzzled. "Who?"

"Your Realtor friend, Justin. Oh, I explained everything last week. I'll remind you on the way there."

Miss Voncille got to her feet and smoothed out the wrinkles in her emerald green bedspread. She had been sitting beside her pillow, riveted to her beloved picture of Frank Gibbons on the nightstand for the past five minutes. "I'm going to hide you temporarily in the potpourri," she said out loud to the photo as she cupped it in her hands as if it were an injured baby bird. "The deal is, I may have company tonight, and I don't need you making me nervous standing guard the way you always do. But don't worry, I won't leave you with my scented hankies forever."

For a split second she imagined that her sturdy sentinel might just spring to life and answer her, giving her permission to change things up. But she knew only too well that she could not seek permission from anyone but herself. So she headed toward her chest of drawers, giving the picture a little peck before tucking it away among her many fancy sachets. "There!" she exclaimed, nodding proudly. "That's done. Onward and upward!"

As if staged perfectly by a theater prop crew, the doorbell rang, and Miss Voncille knew that her potential suitor was right on time. She drew in a hopeful, romantic breath and struck a graceful pose. An imaginary photographer would be capturing her at her best and bravest in that moment. After that, the sequence would be a simple one: She and Locke would have something to eat and drink while chatting amiably with the others; then seriously discuss the merits of Harper Lee's work; and finally Locke would escort her to her cozy cottage as usual. Only this time, she would not shrink like a wallflower from her intentions—

Locke Linwood's voice crashed in on her

reverie from the other side of the front door. "Miss Voncille?!" He pushed the doorbell again. "Miss Voncille?!"

"Coming!" she called out, shutting the bottom drawer and rushing out of her bedroom like a teenager on her first date. "I'll be right there!"

From the moment she opened the door, she knew something about Locke had changed, and it wasn't just the single red rose he presented to her right off the bat. "For you, my dear lady," he told her, handing it over with the suggestion of a bow.

"My goodness, Locke!" she exclaimed, taking it and holding it briefly beneath her nose. "You've never brought me flowers before!"

"I still haven't," he said. "This is only one flower. But there could be more where that came from. I think you're getting sweeter every day."

Miss Voncille found herself blushing, and for a few moments she just stood there with her mind a perfect blank. Then she recovered nicely. "Well, I'm honestly trying not to be such a diva anymore. But where are my manners? Come on in, and I'll put this little beauty in a vase. And you can carry the biscuits out to your car for me. Let's head to the kitchen, shall we?"

After she had put the rose in water and pointed out the foil-covered baking sheet full of biscuits that she had prepared, Miss Voncille retrieved an unopened jar of her green pepper jelly and dropped it into her shimmering, emerald green clutch. "Good. It just fits, and the color is a perfect match. I guess that's everything."

"Not quite," Locke said, momentarily putting the biscuits down on the breakfast table and nervously clearing his throat. "I've come to an important decision, and I wanted you to know about it before we headed off to the library."

"I'm intrigued. First a rose, now an important decision."

"Yes, well, I just wanted to say that I think I've finally come to my senses. I haven't let any woman inside my residence on Perry Street since Pamela's wake two years ago. But I know she didn't want the house kept like a museum. So this demeanor of mine has had nothing to do with you. It's all been due to my ridiculous defenses. As if keeping the whole world out could bring Pamela back to me. I have faith that she's gone on to better things." He paused for a big chest full of air. "So, if it's all right with you, I'd like to invite you back to my house after this to-do at the library is over, and we can have a nip of sherry . . . or something."

Miss Voncille could not suppress her laughter, a captivating mixture of delight and surprise. "Forgive me," she managed as she eventually regained control. "You're probably getting the wrong impression. I couldn't be more flattered by what you've just said to me. I've always been a big believer in great minds thinking alike."

Locke looked reassured. “Well, as long as you weren’t laughing *at* me . . .”

“Not even close, believe me. All sorts of images were swirling around my head when you extended your generous invitation to me. Sachets, potpourri, scented handkerchiefs. Don’t ask me to explain, just understand that I’ll be thrilled to extend our evening together. Meanwhile, we need to get these biscuits and jelly to the library and put this party on the front burner.”

Maura Beth was feeling on top of the world as she surveyed her busy lobby. As with the first meeting of The Cherry Cola Book Club a month earlier, the food was going over well, and everyone seemed to be getting along. It also appeared that Miss Voncille and Locke Linwood had chosen to keep largely to themselves, looking as if they were plotting something in a far corner of the room. While the others were either sitting or standing to savor what was on their plates, Stout Fella was living up to his billing and gobbling up his generous servings at what seemed to be a record pace.

“Who woudda thought corn and peppers would go this good together?” he was saying in between hurried bites of Connie’s salad.

Becca gave him a skeptical frown. “For heaven’s sake, Justin, I’ve been serving you Niblets for years. Same thing basically.”

"Oh, yeah, you're right. But it's got something else in it."

Connie stepped up quickly. "It's the herbs. I put dill and rosemary in it. Gives it a little extra zing."

Stout Fella kept right on chowing down as if he were in a competitive eating contest. "Whatever it is, it's mighty good. I'll have another helping, I do believe."

For her part, Maura Beth kept right on circulating to engage her guests. Even Councilman Sparks seemed to be in a fairly sociable mood as she caught up with him near the Academy Award poster of Gregory Peck.

"Very warm, fuzzy shindig, Miz Mayhew. Maybe even award-winning," he told her while pointing to the blow-up. "Your numbers are growing slightly, I see. Emphasis on the slightly. By the way, who's the young lady over by the punch bowl?"

"Oh, that's one of my front desk clerks, Renette Posey. She's also my girl Friday when I need her to be. I didn't ask her to, but she seems to have taken over the ladling duties. She's probably a little nervous, being the youngster here tonight."

"Very sweet girl," he added, looking her over from a distance. "I see you've also gotten the wives to collar their husbands this time out. I never thought Justin Brachle would have the time to darken the doors of this library. He's the all-time wheeler-dealer of Cherico, and we're thankful he works his realty magic so well."

Maura Beth cocked her head. "As in lots more taxes to collect from wealthy homeowners?"

"Precisely."

"But not enough to keep the library open?"

Councilman Sparks gave her one of his most conspiratorial winks. "Don't worry, Miz Mayhew. I fully intend not to underestimate you. That's why I'm here tonight. By the way, I've been meaning to ask you: What shade do you officially call that red hair of yours? It's very unusual—even stunning, if I do say so myself."

"Oh! Well, I guess auburn would be the most traditional way of describing it," she answered, completely caught off guard. "An ex-boyfriend of mine at LSU once told me that I had a head full of good bourbon whiskey, but that always made me sound like the ultimate party girl, which I wasn't."

He wagged his eyebrows and smiled. "I've been noticing the way your hair changes in different kinds of light."

"Yes, it does do that."

"It looks one way in the sun and another way under the fluorescents."

Maura Beth decided to say nothing and nod her head.

"My wife's hair is brunette. It always looks the same everywhere."

They had reached an awkward pause, and

Maura Beth decided she'd had enough. "Maybe you should get a job out at Cherico Tresses, Councilman. I think your comments would be much more appropriate there. So, if you'll excuse me, I'm going to continue to make the rounds."

She walked away without looking back, approaching the McShays and the Brachles. They were in the midst of friendly banter, and it was Connie who was holding forth at the moment. ". . . and I just love the way the light plays off the lake at certain times of the day, particularly around sunset. I could hardly pull myself away this evening." She gave Becca one of her nudges. "We must have you and Justin out for dinner soon around that time so you can see for yourself. I'll try and persuade Douglas to go out in *The Verdict* and catch some fish for us."

"Oh, we'd love to, wouldn't we, Stout Fella?" Becca replied.

He quickly swallowed the last of the corn and pepper salad he was chewing and nodded his head obediently, while Douglas flashed a sarcastic smile at his wife.

Maura Beth glanced at the front desk clock and decided to make an announcement. "Ladies and gentlemen, I think we'll begin our discussion in about fifteen more minutes. Meanwhile, please continue to enjoy this wonderful spread and each other's company."

"I intend to try a piece of your sheet cake next,

Miz Mayhew," Stout Fella explained, stepping up and wiping the edges of his mouth with a napkin. "It looks mighty tempting from here, and Becca raved about it last time she came. Of course, everybody's dish was worth the price of admission. But after my cake, I'm afraid I'll have to make my manners to all you good folks and leave. I have some pressing business to attend to over at The Twinkle. But don't worry, Becca's staying for all this book bid'ness, and I'll be back to pick her up later. And don't let me forget to say again that all a' y'all are fantastic cooks. This was just delicious."

Maura Beth and the others offered up their group thanks and then watched him practically inhale his cake a few moments later. Finally, after guzzling a cup of punch and giving Becca's cheek a perfunctory peck, he headed toward the front door, dialing his cell phone all along the way.

"Isn't he incorrigible?!" Becca exclaimed to Maura Beth and Connie after he'd left. "Never even allows himself time to digest his food. He's the most driven person I've ever known in my life!"

"Connie told me about you nicknaming him Stout Fella," Douglas put in, "but I didn't really get it until he came over and shook hands with me when we first walked in. I did recognize him, of course, but I'm afraid it was a shock all the same. No offense, Becca."

"Oh, none taken. It is what it is. I just don't know what to do about it. He's completely turned up his nose at my new recipes. 'Fix it like you always do,' he complains. 'Stop taking things out. Make it taste like it used to.' I'm afraid he hasn't downsized an ounce."

On that note, Maura Beth decided to put an end to her kibitzing and get the literary portion of The Cherry Cola Book Club under way. "Ladies and gentlemen, shall we put away our plates, freshen up if we need to, and then delve into some Pulitzer Prize–winning prose?"

Maura Beth stood behind the podium ready to tackle the major theme of the evening: namely, "Was *To Kill a Mockingbird* one of the catalysts for the 1964 Civil Rights Act?" She did not, however, intend to open with such a ponderous question. She would lead up to it gradually, soliciting opinions from the members about the consequences of racism described in the novel. She expected the discussion would be far more substantial than the lightweight diversion that was Scarlett versus Melanie of a month ago. Her unspoken motto was: "Start simple, then step it up."

Instead, Councilman Sparks stole the floor right out from under her again. "If I might, Miz Mayhew," he began, "I'd like to pose a question here at the outset to all you good people—but particularly the men." He did not wait for her to acknowledge his request, pressing on like the polished politician he was. "I've been giving this a great deal of thought. Don't you feel that Atticus Finch is unrealistic as a character and a father? For instance, he's raising Jem and Scout by himself and always gives them the right advice and never seems to make any mistakes. He has the moral high ground on everything. I don't know any men like that, do you? Where are the typical male foibles? In fact, he has none."

It took every ounce of Maura Beth's restraint to keep from saying out loud: "I can see why Atticus Finch would be alien to a man like yourself." Instead, she gathered herself and asked for reactions from the others.

Becca was the first to respond. "I wish my Stout Fella was much more like Atticus Finch, even if the character is unrealistic. Justin knows his business and gets things done, but he doesn't leave much time for anything else. For instance, he hasn't made time to slow down and think about us having a family, and we've been married ten years now. If we have children eventually—and I do want to—do I think Justin will be an Atticus Finch? No way. I don't think men are like that in real life. So I suppose Councilman Sparks has a valid point."

Douglas, who had been fidgeting in his chair a bit, entered the discussion with a slight scowl.

"Now, wait just a minute here. I'll admit we men aren't perfect. Neither are our women. But I always took care of my family. I love my wife and daughter and granddaughter. You don't have to be an Atticus Finch to do what you're supposed to do—or the right thing, as the case may be. Have you thought that maybe Atticus Finch is written that way to make us strive to be better men—and lawyers, for that matter?"

"Speaking of which," Councilman Sparks said, "don't you think the law profession has taken a turn for the worse since they allowed billboard and television advertising? Hasn't it cheapened everything?"

Douglas bristled, speaking up quickly. "I don't advertise, Mr. Sparks. Never will."

"But you do admit the existence of high-profile ambulance chasers?"

"Is that what we're here to discuss?" Douglas pointed out, struggling for control.

And then Locke Linwood spoke up while holding Miss Voncille's hand. "I'm not qualified to answer questions about lawyers, but getting back to the subject of the perfection of men, I can tell you for a fact that my Pamela had no complaints about me as a husband. Yes, we both made plenty of mistakes, but we hung in there and raised a family together. I don't know how much more you could ask of any man."

"Seems to me that what all of you are saying

confirms my observation," Councilman Sparks added, his face a study in smugness. "Atticus Finch is the perfect man and lawyer, and the rest of us could never measure up. We all have our profound weaknesses, and I guess we have to try to overcome them. In short, Atticus is unrealistic, and we are real. But we shouldn't be made to feel bad if we can't achieve a fictional ideal for the ages."

Maura Beth realized she must step in soon to rescue the tone of the discussion, but Connie preempted her with an emotional plea. "I think we need to step back a bit. I didn't come here to gang up on the men, and I don't think I would appreciate it if they ganged up on me."

"I agree," Becca added. "Stout Fella drives me crazy, and I don't know how my life with him will turn out in the end, but God knows, I don't expect him to be perfect."

Maura Beth's cell phone vibrated behind the podium, causing her to start noticeably. Her body continued to tense up as she answered the call and listened to the very agitated voice on the other end, while the shocked expression on her face gave no doubt as to the serious nature of the message she was hearing. Then she snapped the phone shut abruptly, as if trying to punish the messenger, and said as calmly as possible: "Becca, I need to speak with you in private, please. If the rest of you will excuse us for a minute."

Becca rose from her seat quickly with a fearful tone in her voice. "What's the matter? What's happened?"

The two of them moved away from the podium and closer to the circulation desk where Maura Beth turned her back to the others for privacy, discreetly lowering her voice and blocking Becca from view. "There's no easy way to say this, but that was Periwinkle Lattimore at The Twinkle. It appears that Justin may be having a heart attack as we speak, and they're rushing him to Cherico Memorial right now—"

Becca lost control before Maura Beth could finish, her face overcome with panic and her voice going shrill. "Oh, my God! Somebody needs to drive me there. Who'll drive me? Who'll take me? He just can't be having a heart attack. That big gorilla is only thirty-nine years old!"

All the others reacted by jumping up and approaching the front desk, with Connie and Douglas being the first to surround Becca. "Stout Fella's having a heart attack!" she cried out, tugging at Connie's sleeve like a frantic child. "Will you drive me there? I don't have the car!"

"Of course we will. Don't worry," Douglas said, taking her gently by the arm. "And we'll stay right by your side."

Everyone in the room offered to do something helpful simultaneously, as the second meeting of The Cherry Cola Book Club dissolved in the face of the crisis. In the end, they all agreed that they would meet up at Cherico Memorial to provide whatever support they could for as long as they were needed. It might end up being a very long night.

# 8

# Balloon Therapy

It was in the crowded, second-floor waiting room of Cherico Memorial Hospital a half hour later that Maura Beth put things in perspective. The Cherry Cola Book Club had switched its focus from snippets of prose to snippets from the ICU, where Stout Fella was being monitored for complications due to acute myocardial infarction. Everyone—including Winston Barkeley and Councilman Sparks, but minus the teenaged Renette Posey—had gathered for the vigil and were variously fidgeting in their seats, blankly turning magazine pages or standing around full of nervous energy.

All except Connie, who had become the liaison between the earnest young cardiologist, Dr. Oberlin, and the others. Each time he ventured out to give the latest update on Stout Fella's condition to a mildly sedated Becca, Connie was there for the helpful translation.

"They've given him a clot-busting drug called streptokinase to stabilize him," she was explaining to the group after the doctor's most recent visit, holding on to Becca's hand all the while. "Fortunately, the blocked artery in question is not the widow maker. The affected area of the heart is on the bottom. Once they're sure he can travel, they'll ambulance him to Centennial Medical Center in Nashville where they specialize in cardiac procedures. I know that facility well. It's one of the best in the country. I would love to have worked there during my career, but I could never quite pull it off."

Becca continued to grip Connie's hand tightly as she spoke. "I need to be there. How will I get up there?"

As he had at the library, Douglas reassured her. "Connie and I will drive you up when the time comes. We know every little nook and cranny of Nashville. We'll both stay with you until he's completely recovered, and we can even drive you and Justin back when the time comes. My brother Paul and his wife live up there and have plenty of room in their Brentwood house. I'll give him a call, and he'll put us all up. No problem."

"And Justin will recover," Connie added. "Dr. Oberlin says there are so many positive signs already. For one thing, Periwinkle's 911 call got him to the ER within minutes. Time is always of the essence with any heart attack. As we speak, I'm sure they've reduced the size of the clot. He has had a slight allergic reaction to the streptokinase, though. They haven't been able to remove the blockage completely, but he's got some blood flow back in the artery and that's the most important thing. He's in no pain at this point, so we can all take a deep breath and think our best, healing thoughts."

"And the rest of the blockage is why they need to take him up to Nashville?" Maura Beth asked.

"This is a very small, rural hospital," Connie continued. "They don't have the equipment or staff to do the next procedure he'll require. It's called a balloon angioplasty. They'll thread a small guide wire with an inflatable balloon from an artery in his leg to his heart. They monitor the whole thing with a camera. Then, once they've inflated the balloon—bam! No more clot!"

Despite her sedation, Becca rambled on a bit. "The doctor said the procedure was safe. But is it really? It sounds so dangerous and complicated. What if I lose him? Just tonight we had this silly argument over nothing and everything. I even told him that I could get along without him. Is this God's way of punishing me for such callous thoughts? Connie, please tell me the truth. Just how safe is this balloon thing?"

"Now, calm down, Becca. I've seen the procedure performed successfully so many times, I can't count," Connie said, stroking the back of Becca's hand. "It's far less intrusive than bypass, and the recovery time is usually a week or less. Some people are back at work in practically no time. This is a maximum recovery situation all around."

It was then that Periwinkle walked off the

elevator with crisp authority, making straight for Becca and extending her hand solicitously. Hugs for Connie and Maura Beth soon followed, and she acknowledged the others with a smile and a nod. "What's the latest?" she asked, catching her breath. "I haven't been able to think about anything else."

Connie brought her up to date with a condensed diagnosis that only a medical professional could manage.

Periwinkle relaxed a bit from head to toe. "Well, I got to close up a little early. Nothing clears a dining room like someone on a stretcher." Then she brought herself up short. "Oh, I didn't mean to make light of the situation. Please forgive me, Becca. I run off at the mouth all the time."

"*Forgive* you?!" Becca exclaimed, her eyes widening in disbelief. "You've got it all wrong. I can't *thank* you enough for what you did, Periwinkle. Dr. Oberlin says the paramedics were there in record time. My Stout Fella probably owes you his life. How did you know what was going on so fast?"

"Call it instinct, I guess," Periwinkle explained, her gum noticeably absent for once. "Your husband called me over to the table and asked if I had some Alka-Seltzer or something for his stomach. He was drinking coffee with his friend over there, but he looked really pale and sweaty to me. I like to keep my restaurant on the chilly side during all this summer heat, so even then I started to wonder what was happening."

The tall, sportily dressed Winston Barkeley stepped up to add his own observations. "Yeah, I could tell something was wrong with him, too. He kept saying he had indigestion from the moment he sat down across from me. Said he'd eaten too much at a party he'd just come from. But I could tell the Alka-Seltzer wasn't helping much by the way he kept rubbing his chest."

Periwinkle nodded and continued, "Then he called me over to the table again and said he was really starting to feel much worse, like there were gears grinding somewhere inside. Well, that did it. I'm never pleased to see indigestion at my restaurant, but this was just way different from the usual drink water and belch, if you'll excuse my language. 'I'm going to call 911 right this instant,' I told him. 'I don't like what's going on here one bit.' So I pulled out my cell phone and the ambulance was at The Twinkle in . . . well, a twinkle, I guess."

Becca squeezed Periwinkle's hand a couple of times. "Bless you, Doctor Periwinkle, bless you. Make all the little jokes you want to."

"Oh, honey, believe me, it's just a part of being out there dealing with the public. You have to be on the lookout for everything and everyone. You're a hero one day—the next day, you're being sued for all you're worth when somebody slips on a piece a' lettuce."

Becca looked incredulous. "Has somebody actually taken you to court for something like that?"

"Not me, knock on wood. But it happened to a nice-looking fella I met at a restaurant supply convention once. Would you believe he ended up spending most of his savings having to defend himself against some spilled Thousand Island dressing that cost someone a broken leg?"

Becca managed to smile for the first time in a good while. "Well, I'm just thankful my Stout Fella was at The Twinkle tonight. That cup of coffee he ordered was the best bargain of his life."

An hour later, only Connie, Douglas, Becca, and Maura Beth were maintaining the vigil in the waiting room. The others had headed home with the understanding that either Connie or Maura Beth would notify them of any change in Stout Fella's status. But the news was as good as it could be for the time being. With all vital signs stable, the doctors had decided that the patient would be ambulanced to Nashville within the hour for an angioplasty early the next morning.

"I know the last thing you want to do is leave this waiting room right now, Becca," Connie was saying. "But if Douglas and I are going to drive you up tomorrow morning, we need to get you home to do some packing, and we need to do the same. Matter of fact, why don't you just spend the night with us after we've picked up your things? Dr. Oberlin assures me there's no immediate danger now. Meanwhile, the three of us have got to get some rest for the trip."

Maura Beth backed her up with authority. "It's best you listen to her, Becca. Connie knows about these things."

But instead of agreeing to their advice, Becca suddenly began to tear up. "I know things are going as well as they can, but I just feel like this is all my fault. I'm the one that put all that weight on him. And then I teased him all the time about it, calling him Stout Fella."

"But you told us he embraced his nickname in the end. Even thought it made him a superhero in his own mind," Maura Beth said. "Don't beat yourself up like this. You pointed out to all of us how driven he's always been. I've never seen anyone eat so much food so fast in my life at the library tonight. No one was shoving it down his throat. You can't be responsible for that kind of behavior."

"You also said you couldn't believe he was having a heart attack at the age of . . . thirty-eight, was it?" Connie added.

"Thirty-nine, actually," came the sniffling reply. "His birthday was last month. I made him a big, fattening devil's food cake, and he ate the whole thing. Of course, if I hadn't baked something homemade, he would have gone out and bought a dozen éclairs from Hanson's Bakery and put candles on every one of them. That big dope and his sweet tooth!"

Connie smiled while once again assuming her medical professional persona. "There you are. But birthday goodies aside, you've got to understand that for someone to be that young and suffer an AMI, there have to be other significant contributing factors. Not just eating habits and weight gain, but issues like management of stress, blood pressure, and cholesterol levels have to be taken into consideration. This is by no means as cut and dried as it seems."

Becca furrowed her brow for a moment. "He's supposed to be taking cholesterol medication, but . . . I can't swear he does. But he does a lot of things he's *not* supposed to. I guess he's paying the price now."

"You can discuss all that with him after the angioplasty in Nashville when he's well on the road to recovery," Connie continued. "Meanwhile, I think we ought to check in with Dr. Oberlin and let him know we intend to join your husband up there."

It was only after she was told her Stout Fella was being prepped for travel and there was no more time for visitors that Becca finally gave in, and the vigil officially came to an end—at least in Cherico.

"What time do you think you'll be leaving

tomorrow?" Maura Beth asked the McShays on the way down in the elevator.

They exchanged glances and then turned toward Becca. "Six-thirty okay with you? We can go up the Natchez Trace Parkway and be in Nashville well before nine," Douglas said. "That's the way we've gone back and forth for our vacation time these past six years."

Becca offered no resistance, nodding slowly while briefly closing her eyes.

"Of course. You have no choice but to get up bright and early," Maura Beth observed. "And you might need something besides a cup or two of coffee to keep you focused on the way up."

Connie looked at her sideways. "What on earth are you talking about? Speed? Douglas and I have never gone there, and I worked many an all-nighter at the hospital to tempt me."

"Oh, don't be silly. It's nothing like that. I've just had this absolutely inspirational idea, and the closer you get to Nashville, the more excited you'll be about it," Maura Beth continued as the elevator doors opened. "I'd like for you to follow me and pop into the library after we leave the hospital. I promise this will only take a few minutes."

Douglas shrugged. "Okay, might as well. Nothing else has gone by the book this evening."

It was Connie who accompanied Maura Beth into the library once Douglas had pulled the car up in front of the portico, idling the engine with a drowsy, emotionally exhausted Becca slumped in the backseat. "I hope you're not going to offer us all the book club leftovers hiding out in your library fridge," Connie remarked. "If not, I can't imagine what you could possibly have up your sleeve."

Maura Beth laughed as she unlocked her office door. "Oh, I assure you, it'll make all of you feel better once you get to Nashville and get to visit with Stout Fella in his hospital room." She walked over to her desk and pulled open the bottom drawer. "Aha, I was right. My memory is not failing. I did put them in here." Then she handed Connie the big bag of balloons she had decided not to use for the *Gone with the Wind* meeting. "I'd hold off on blowing them up now, but they might make a terrific day-brightener when you walk in and say hello to Stout Fella. You can tell him they're from everybody in The Cherry Cola Book Club with their very best wishes for a speedy recovery."

Connie's face lit up as she stared down at the bag. "In honor of his balloon angioplasty, I presume?"

"His successful balloon angioplasty," Maura Beth emphasized.

"There's no other kind in my experience," Connie added. "Maura Beth, you come up with the cleverest ideas. Did they by any chance teach you that in library school?"

"I don't remember the course offering, actually. I think I must have an extracurricular type of brain."

They both laughed, and then Maura Beth leaned down and retrieved a ball of twine from the drawer. "You might also need this to tie the balloons off and string them together. You can make a balloon bouquet of sorts. I think you have to pay a fortune if you order them through one of those delivery services, but I'm going to set you up from scratch real cheap."

Next, she picked up a Magic Marker from a coffee mug atop her desk. "Here's something else you'll need. You can write, 'Get Well!' or whatever you want once you've blown them up. Just be gentle with the marker. I popped one of the balloons pressing down too hard once way back when, and I thought someone had shot me at point-blank range. Other than that, all you and Douglas need is a little carbon dioxide. But don't blow too hard, pass out, and conk yourself on the head. We don't need you in the hospital, too."

Connie gave her a heartfelt hug and pulled back. "I can't believe there's even the slightest possibility that you might be leaving us. Cherico needs more people like you. And I feel so bad that our meeting tonight got sidetracked. You went to so much trouble, and I was looking forward to getting my teeth into *To Kill a Mockingbird* again. Actually, I was proud that Douglas was, too. That sneaky man of mine had been reading chapters in between his beer and fishing expeditions. How about that? Maybe this retirement of ours will turn out to be fun for both of us, after all."

Maura Beth waved her off, smiling pleasantly. "Oh, I'm sure it will. And I can reschedule our *Mockingbird* discussion down the line. In fact, I fully intend to, even though we might have to take Stout Fella's recovery into consideration. I'm sure we'd want Becca to be a part of it."

"I just wish Councilman Sparks would stay out of your business," Connie said. "He found a way to almost get the girls fighting with the boys tonight, and he also went after the lawyers with a vengeance. I saw that exasperated expression on your face at the podium."

Maura Beth exhaled, unable to put that particular mischief out of her head. "I tried my best not to let it show too much. But don't worry about me. I'm not giving up so easily. Scarlett wouldn't have."

Connie turned to get a glimpse of the front desk clock. "Oh, it's almost ten-thirty. We have a lot of packing to do, so I better get going. And I'll give you a call tomorrow morning from the hospital as soon as we know something definite. Then you can phone the others, if you don't mind."

A minute or two later, Maura Beth stood outside the front door, waving to her friends as Douglas pulled away from the curb with a staccato honk.

The prognosis for Stout Fella looked promising, and she was pleased with herself for coming up with the concept of balloon therapy. But as she went back in to turn out the lights before locking up and heading home, she could feel depression spreading over her like the precursor to an oncoming cold.

Recently, she'd read a very interesting and somewhat controversial book in the collection about chaos theory. She hadn't completely understood all of it, but the gist was that random events sometimes coincided to scotch the best-laid plans of the most organized and intelligent minds on the planet. She certainly wasn't about to hold Justin Brachle's heart attack against him, but that unfortunate occurrence, along with Councilman Sparks's concerted attempts at disruption, had effectively rendered the second meeting of The Cherry Cola Book Club less than successful.

It was time to rev things up a notch, to treat the book club more like a political campaign. Somehow, some way, people must cast their votes by walking their warm bodies through the front door of the library to take advantage of its services. Maura Beth's job was at stake, and there were people in Cherico who had stated to her face that they didn't give a flip about that.

# 9

# Four-Letter Words

Miss Voncille and Locke Linwood had been the first to leave the vigil at Cherico Memorial once Stout Fella had been stabilized in the ICU. "I know you'll call us if you hear anything further," Miss Voncille had said to Maura Beth, who assured them that she would.

But after they'd climbed into Locke's Cadillac in the hospital parking lot below, an awkward silence overtook them both. They sat there for a while, listening to the muted sound of the engine and looking straight ahead with emotionless faces.

It was Miss Voncille who finally verbalized what they were both thinking. "Does what just happened change where we're headed?"

He continued to idle the engine and turned her way. "I assume you mean the physical address."

"Yes. Will you be taking me to your house on Perry Street or mine on Painter Street?"

He did not hesitate. "My invitation is still open."

But she posed another question instead. "Do you think we should have stayed longer? I hope the ladies won't think we abandoned them."

"We couldn't have done anything but sit there. The crisis seemed to have cooled by the time we left. We made our manners and showed the proper respect. I know who the Brachles are, but Pamela and I never socialized with them because they're so much younger. They're a different generation." He put the car in gear and started to pull out into the street. "I don't want to do anything tonight that will make you feel uneasy, so tell me which way to head."

"I'm still fine with your invitation," she said finally. "Go ahead and drive us to your house on Perry Street. I was looking forward to seeing it. And also seeing you in it."

They drove through the heart of a mostly deserted downtown, passing the always-spotlighted City Hall, eventually entering the oldest residential neighborhood of Cherico. Tree-lined Perry Street was its crown jewel, featuring a good many more restored Queen Anne cottages than Miss Voncille's fixer-upper on Painter Street on the other side of town. Here was where the Crumpton sisters, Councilman Sparks, and other well-to-do families resided, not necessarily side by side, but well within shouting distance of each other.

"The crepe myrtles are lush this year," Miss Voncille noted, making small talk during the short drive. "Especially the pink ones. Personally, I prefer the whites. I think they named them after Natchez in the southern part of the state."

He nodded enthusiastically. "I think I read that somewhere, too. And as you'll soon see, those are the only kind I have in my yard."

A minute or so later they had pulled into the driveway of 134 Perry Street, and the front porch lights enabled Miss Voncille to appreciate the sprawling, superbly manicured lawn, dotted with the crepe myrtles Locke had described. She had, in fact, driven the length of Perry Street over the years just to admire its perfection but had never had a reason to pay particularly close attention to Locke Linwood's house and grounds. She knew only that he and his wife lived there and religiously attended her genealogical lectures at the library, and that was the extent of her interest. Now, however, the ante had been upped, and the time had come for a sincere compliment.

"If your decorating is anything like your landscaping, I know I'm going to love your house," she said, as he opened the passenger door and helped her out.

"Pamela did all the decorating. Most all the furniture is from her family. She was an Alden from over in the Delta, you know, and they had all that soybean money," he explained as they headed in. "I just sold life insurance for my keep."

The living room they entered was as graciously appointed as Miss Voncille envisioned it would be: It included a spotless wool dhurrie on the hardwood floor, a mahogany linen press against one wall, an English bookcase against the other, a Victorian what-not in the corner, and an Oriental ceramic cat lamp on an end table beside a comfortable contemporary sofa. It was both eclectic and elegant, while at the same time calling to mind the museum-like quality that Locke had confessed to previously.

"Your wife had the touch," Miss Voncille said, her eyes roving around the room in awe. "This is just lovely. Puts my jungle to shame."

Locke shook his head with authority. "Nonsense. *Architectural Digest* is not for everyone." Then he gestured toward the sofa in front of them. "I'll give you the rest of the tour later. But first, why don't you have a seat, and I'll go get us those sherries we talked about?"

While he was gone, Miss Voncille passed the time studying the oil portrait of Pamela hanging beside the bookcase. It had obviously been done when she was very young—perhaps somewhere in her twenties—and it was easy to see why Locke had fallen hard. Here was a gently smiling woman with shoulder-length brunette hair and light brown eyes that suggested a benevolent prescience. They seemed to be looking off in the distance at something wonderful to behold.

"How old was your wife when that was painted?" Miss Voncille asked as soon as Locke had returned and handed over her nightcap.

He settled in beside her and took a sip of his sherry. "That would have been a year or so after we were married, so she was about twenty-five. She wanted one done of me, but I told her I couldn't sit still long enough. The truth is, I didn't want anything in the room to distract from her beauty."

"And nothing does," Miss Voncille remarked. "She aged very well, too, I always thought. I would never have known that—" She broke off, realizing just in time where she was going.

But Locke rubbed her arm gently as he finished her sentence. "That she was so ill there at the end?"

Miss Voncille sipped her drink and nodded.

"My Pamela was a trouper. She spent a fortune on designer scarves to cover up the chemo, and she did it with the same great style she used throughout this house. She wouldn't have made her exit any other way."

He rose from the sofa and headed toward the bookcase, pulling a letter out of a leather-bound journal. "I'd like to take the time to read this out loud to you. I only read it myself the other day, and it was what brought me to my senses regarding our friendship. Pamela wrote it while she was still pretty cogent, and the instructions on the envelope were that it was to be read by myself two years after her death. I kept it in a safety deposit box to avoid temptation, but above all, I wanted to honor her wishes, and I did. So, if you wouldn't mind indulging me?"

"Of course not, Locke. And I have to say again that you are the most constantly surprising man

I've ever known. At my age, that's just so much fun, I can hardly stand it."

He smiled, resumed his seat on the sofa, and began:

> My dearest Locke,
>
> If you are reading this right now, I will assume that two things have happened: 1) You have lived two more years than I did, and 2) you didn't cheat and read this before I asked you to.
>
> That aside, I want you to pay very close attention to what I'm saying. I know you only too well. In our many cherished talks near the end, we both agreed that you should go on with your life as best you could. We agreed that you should continue to attend "Who's Who in Cherico?" at the library; that you should do everything you could to support that sweet young librarian, Maura Beth Mayhew—she's just as darling as she can be, and she'll need all the help she can get with the powers-that-be, believe me; that you should get to know Miss Voncille Nettles better. She's just our age. Ultimately, I think you and she would make excellent companions, but you have to make the effort, Locke, as you did with me many years ago. I'm assuming you've done all those things. If not, just go

ahead and do them now. Take the risk. Try again for love.

I also know that you have not changed anything in our house these past two years. You never were sloppy, so I'm sure you've kept it clean. You could probably charge admission and put our house on tour the way they do during the Pilgrimages in Natchez and Columbus and Holly Springs. But you and I know that won't happen.

It is my belief that I will be very busy with other things during the two years you have been without me. I don't have readily available details at this time, but I want you to stop worrying about me and get on with the rest of your life. I will be very disappointed in you if you don't.

As the song says: I'll be seeing you.

Eternal love,
Your Pamela

Whatever words she had expected to come out of Locke's mouth, Miss Voncille considered these a universe away. She had to take a generous swig of her sherry to steady herself and give herself some time to think of what to say. But another quick glimpse of Pamela's portrait gave her just the inspiration she needed.

"It's almost like your wife was thinking of that

letter when her portrait was painted so long ago," she observed. "Otherwise, I can't think of a thing to add to the sentiments she expressed."

Locke looked consummately pleased with her and himself. "Pamela was like that. She was forward-thinking, even though she wanted to know everything about people here in Cherico. That was why we first started going to 'Who's Who?' meetings. But it was the big picture that really interested her. Not just what came before, but what comes next? That's why having breast cancer never really changed her. She always thought it was part of something that would eventually make sense to her, and when I read her letter the other day after two years had passed, I teared up and laughed at the same time. She really knew me, and I have no choice now but to keep following through on what she's asked me to do."

Miss Voncille exhaled, enjoying the slight buzz from the sherry. "I assume the single rose was your idea, though?"

"That it was. Give me credit for some originality."

"Oh, I do," she said, inching closer to him. "As I've said to you several times, you're a surprising and original man."

The kiss that followed was gentle and brief but held the promise of more to come.

"So, here's a question for you—what's your

opinion of four-letter words?" he said, pulling away slightly.

Her expression was skeptical but amused. "I don't use them. Well . . . not unless I hit my thumb with a hammer putting up a picture. You know how that goes."

"No, I meant the four-letter words that Pamela used in her letter," he explained with a mischievous grin. "She talked about *risk* and she mentioned *love*. Those four-letter words. Here we are getting ready to greet our seventies. Are we willing to take the risk of again losing someone that we love?"

For the first time all night, Frank flashed into Miss Voncille's head. She had put his picture away in a brave attempt at moving forward. If she became further involved with Locke, it would be impossible to predict how many years they might have together.

"It's been a while since I've risked anything in the love department," she answered. "You pose a very pertinent question."

Neither of them said anything for a few minutes, sipping their sherry for courage.

"So, where do we go from here?" he said, finally.

She turned to him with a sweet, reassuring smile. "I'd like to stay here tonight. Is that enough of an answer?"

"More than enough," he replied, matching her

smile. And then they kissed again, this time lingering tenderly.

"Then by all means, show me the rest of the house," she added, pulling away with an expectant sigh. "It's gone unappreciated for too long."

# 10

# All Good Things in Threes

The phone rang at a quarter to ten the next morning in Maura Beth's purple bedroom. The depression she had retired with the night before was still very much hanging over her, and she hadn't yet made a move to throw back the covers and get her day started. It all meant that she was going to be late for work, with Renette holding down the fort until she showed up. As a result, she picked up the receiver trying to make her "Hello?" sound like it wasn't the first word she'd uttered since opening her eyes.

"I didn't wake you up, did I?" said the familiar but discerning voice on the other end of the line.

"Oh, no, I've been up for an hour, Connie," Maura Beth answered, continuing to press the envelope.

"Well, I won't keep you in suspense. All is well. Stout Fella came through beautifully," Connie continued, her voice full of energy and optimism. "There were no complications, whatsoever. The artery was completely cleared, and there was no blockage in any of the others. He's been in his room most of the morning, and Becca is in with him now just beside herself with relief. It's the funniest thing you've ever seen. She alternately kisses him on the cheek and scolds him like a child for putting them both through all this. But he really loved your balloon bouquet! Douglas and I managed to blow up one of each color, and we even wrote a message or two with the marker without popping them. If I still sound a little winded, that's why."

Maura Beth suddenly felt like a schoolgirl waiting for a juicy piece of gossip. "Ooh, what did you write?"

"Well, I wasn't Dorothy Parker, you understand. 'Get well soon' was about it. But we told him it was all your idea, and he said to be sure and tell you what a big kick he got out of it. He also said he hadn't had anyone bring him balloons since he had his tonsils out as a boy. He says when he gets back and into the swing of things, he's going to come to every meeting of The Cherry Cola Book Club with Becca just to show his appreciation."

"That makes my day!" Maura Beth exclaimed. "Frankly, I didn't sleep well last night, worrying about how the procedure would go. And about our little book club, if you want to know the truth."

Connie made a sympathetic noise under her breath. "Well, the procedure part is looking real good now. The doctor predicts a full recovery if Stout Fella will just behave himself. Let's take the rest one step at a time. Meanwhile, you'll let everyone know the latest, won't you?"

"Will do. And you keep these good reports coming!"

After they'd hung up, Maura Beth yawned, stretched, and threw on her bathrobe. Then she trudged into her kitchenette, poured herself a glass of orange juice, and began making phone calls. Miss Voncille was the first person on her short list, but there was no answer at 45 Painter Street—which seemed odd so early in the morning. On the first try, however, she got through to Periwinkle, who was elated with the good news and prognosis, as well as properly supportive of Maura Beth's concerns about the future of the book club.

"All you have to do is reschedule, honey, and I'll help you promote it at The Twinkle, as usual," Periwinkle told her. "And this time, everyone'll show up hale and hearty without so much as a sniffle."

"Hope so," Maura Beth replied, trying her best to sound upbeat.

"Sure they will. I'll talk up your club like nobody's business, especially to all the cute fellas that come in."

Maura Beth ended their conversation with a resigned chuckle. "Yeah, well, I wish there were as many people out there—male or female—who like to read as there are who like to eat. You take care now."

Another call to Miss Voncille still found no one home; then Maura Beth took a deep breath as she dialed Councilman Sparks's office number. She really didn't want to talk to him at all, but temporarily shelved her equivocal feelings for him to do the right thing.

But when she told him the news, she discovered to her surprise that she needn't have bothered.

"Thanks for your call, Miz Mayhew, but I already know he's out of the woods. I phoned up there myself a little while ago and spoke to Becca. We certainly wouldn't want to see anything happen to Mr. Justin Brachle, what with all he's done for Cherico in recent years."

Maura Beth didn't try very hard to prevent a cynical tone from creeping into her reply. "Yes, I'm sure you're glad everything went so well. He'll probably be wheeling and dealing again in no time."

"Maybe not quite wheeling and dealing. His wife was more reserved. Her exact words were, 'He'll go back to work within reason, this time.' She also said he'll have to change some bad old habits of his for good. I imagine she's going to lay down the law to him now. But it's fitting that you called me anyway. If you can work it in, I'd like to talk to you about your future here in Cherico. Would it be possible for you to come to my office around four-thirty this afternoon?"

Maura Beth felt a spurt of adrenaline in her veins and reacted without even consulting her schedule. "I see no reason why I can't do that. But do you mind my being frank with you and sparing myself some anxiety? Will this be good news or bad news for me?"

"That's entirely up to you, Miz Mayhew," came the emotionless reply. "I look forward to seeing you then."

She hung up and closed her eyes. All sorts of paranoid scenarios swirled throughout her brain. Would she soon be looking for another job? Should she have been more proactive in sending out résumés long before the ultimatum because The Cherico Library was basically the dead end she didn't want to face? Four-thirty seemed an eternity away to find out what was actually going to happen, but she would try to make an ordinary day of it until then.

Temporary relief from the uncertainty came through in the form of a third phone call attempt to Miss Voncille, which finally worked like the proverbial charm.

"Oh, I'm so thrilled for him—and Becca, of course!" Miss Voncille exclaimed after Maura Beth had delivered the happy update. "I'll go ahead and call Locke right after we hang up. I know he'll feel the same way." There was an awkward pause highlighted by a sharp intake of breath at the other end, and Maura Beth could sense there was something more to come.

"Do you have a moment?" Miss Voncille added finally.

"For my most loyal library user and the consummate historian and genealogist of Cherico, I always have time."

"Thank God, there's more to me than that now," she began rather breathlessly. "I wanted you to be the first to know—and I want to delay this just the way the kids do these days, so here it comes now . . . wait for it . . . wait for it . . . I'm officially back in the saddle again."

"No!"

"Yes!"

"Was it in your jungle lair?"

"No, in his very formal Perry Street residence, if you please."

They both found themselves laughing like girlfriends, and Maura Beth said, "Oh, I couldn't be happier for you—and Locke, too, of course!"

"I feel so naughty. I was part Melanie, part Scarlett, and I just got home a few minutes ago."

"Scandalous!" Maura Beth exclaimed, picking up on the playfulness. "But it makes sense to me now, since I haven't been able to reach you for the last half hour."

There was another rush of air at the other end. "I guess the next step is for us to become a permanent item. We talked about it seriously, of course, and we're going for it. Can you believe it?"

"Of course I can."

"This is turning out to be quite a day so far," Miss Voncille continued. "Becca's husband on the mend, Locke and myself starting up at our age. I wonder what will happen next?"

Maura Beth sounded more upbeat than she felt. "Well, they say good things come in threes."

The first thing that seemed out of kilter to Maura Beth when she arrived for her four-thirty appointment with Councilman Sparks was the fact that his secretary, Nora Duddney, was missing and unaccounted for. There had never been a time when Maura Beth had entered his office that the blankest, dullest person in the universe had not been at her desk staring at her computer monitor, unable to utter more than two words of passable conversation.

"In case you were wondering, Nora is no longer with me," Councilman Sparks explained the minute Maura Beth walked in, apparently reading her mind. "Please, step into my office and make yourself comfortable." He went in and pulled out her chair and then seated himself behind his desk. "First things first. I think we're both pleased that Justin Brachle is doing so well."

"Yes. We had quite a scare last night, didn't we?" she replied. "But it looks like we're going to have a happy ending. All these advances in modern medicine never cease to amaze me."

"Good choice of words," he continued. "The happy ending part, I mean. We all want that, don't we?"

Maura Beth could only guess where he was going with that but played along as calmly as she could, despite her quickening heartbeat. "We do."

Whatever it was Councilman Sparks had on his mind, he was obviously in no hurry to reveal it. He used the awkward silence that ensued to tap his ball point pen on his desk in erratic, Morse code fashion. It soon became nothing short of annoying to Maura Beth.

"I do think we should be candid with each other today, Miz Mayhew. Or may I call you Maura Beth after all these years?" he said finally.

"Yes, to both," she answered, feeling as if his line of questioning was completely unnecessary. "I mean, yes, we should be candid, and, yes, you may call me Maura Beth."

"Good." He let that rest for an uncomfortable length of time and then resumed. "Maura Beth, we're about three months out from the afternoon I advised you to try and turn your library around. That means you have less than two months left. You've had no increase in your circulation figures, and despite your Herculean efforts, that little book club of yours with the cutesy name has a membership I can count on one hand and a thumb, if I'm not mistaken."

Maura Beth glanced down at the Persian carpet as she spoke. "You're not mistaken. People just haven't signed up like I'd hoped they would. Maybe Cherico really isn't all that interested in literary things. Perhaps I miscalculated, but I don't want to give up yet. Tara wasn't built in a day."

He made a perfunctory effort to smile and then leaned forward, boring into her with his eyes. "Cut out the fiction and try to be realistic. I've always admired your spunk, and I've said as much to you several times. But this just isn't working for you right now. I never thought it would."

Somehow, she found the courage to verbalize her worst fears. "Are you firing me or asking me to resign?"

She was surprised to see him flash that smile of his. "Neither, exactly. I'd like to suggest an alternative to you. I think the library situation is hopeless even though your time is technically not up yet. However, with Nora now gone, I'll have an opening for secretary right here in my office."

Maura Beth slumped in her chair at what she considered to be a lukewarm proposition at best. She couldn't imagine doing anything with her life other than being a librarian. "So my future here in Cherico is to become your secretary and forget all my training?"

"I'm just trying to make the best of a bad situation," he insisted. "You'd be an asset to this office, and, frankly, anyone could see that Nora was not. I owed her father a few favors when I first got elected and was stuck with her up until now. Basically, she has the personality and IQ of a persimmon, but I'm established enough now that I don't have to worry about what her father will say or do about me firing her. But, you, Maura Beth, would make anyone who came through my office door feel welcome and special. I've seen how you handle yourself at these library meetings. But then, that's what I've always found most attractive about you. That glowing innocence of yours, the expectations you arrived with fresh out of school. It flows out of you like your beautiful red hair."

Maura Beth began to feel distinctly uncomfortable. "Aren't you getting a little too personal here again? These odes to my follicles are getting old."

He tapped his pen on the desk again while mulling things over carefully. "I certainly don't mean to offend you, but let me put it this way. I didn't pay that much attention to you when you first came to Cherico. I approved your hire and forgot about it because the library has never been one of our priorities. But you have a way about you, and people took notice. Evie and I had dinner one night with Miss Voncille at The Twinkle, and all she did was rave about how cooperative you were with her 'Who's Who?' organization. I believe her exact words were, 'She's the sweetest thing to ever walk the streets of Cherico.' Of course, we knew she really didn't mean it the way it sounded."

Maura Beth's eyes widened even as she chuckled under her breath. "Thank goodness for small favors."

"My point is that you'd be a vast improvement over the nonentity who greeted my visitors, and with the money we'd save by closing down the library, your salary would take quite a healthy leap. You've worked hard these past six years, and you deserve more money for the effort you've made. But this is practically the only way I can reward you," he concluded.

"Not to mention that you had the time of your life sitting back in your chair and doing your best to keep things stirred up at all my meetings."

He rolled his eyes and screwed up his face for a moment. "Okay, I plead guilty to reading up on the classics to offer extremely literate criticism during sessions of The Cherry Cola Book Club. And by the way, I wasn't kidding when I said that Atticus Finch is the perfect man by any reasonable standard. Anyway, you have to know that Cherico isn't the center of the intellectual universe. The men folk talk college and pro sports all up and down Commerce Street, and the ladies complain about their husbands and children and exchange recipes at all the beauty parlors. I'd say literary criticism is way down the list of their topics to discuss. Do you really think you can ever pull this off?"

She touched her fingertips to her temples for a

few seconds and then leaned in, staring him down. "More to the point, you haven't stamped the budget yet. I still have time to make the book club the talk of the town."

He nodded reluctantly. "Yes."

"Then I choose not to shrink from my ultimate goal. Like Scarlett, I shall valiantly defend my turf."

"You and your never-ending literary conceits!" he declared, cracking a smile. "And there's nothing I can say or do to change your mind at this time?"

"Nothing. I can't see myself putting people on hold for a living."

He stood up slowly, the disappointment clearly showing in his face. "Well, I have to say, it's a damned shame because I think the odds favor Cherico being without a library in the very near future."

"I'll just have to take that chance," she said, standing up and heading for the door.

He moved energetically across the room in time to open it for her. "I guess you will. Meanwhile, for the record, I'll stop trying to louse things up at your meetings. You really don't need any help in that department from what I've seen."

She turned back at the last second and managed to smile anyway. "Thanks for the vote of confidence."

# 11

# Brainstorm in Brentwood

Milepost 327 along the Natchez Trace Parkway found Maura Beth driving across a two-lane bridge high above the Tennessee River, heading slowly northeast toward Nashville. It was now deep into the third week in September, and the first hint of fall color among the leaves of the hardwoods flanking the manicured right of way had begun to appear. Yet the green of the thick stands of pine and cedar still dominated as far as the eye could see. This impulsive escape from Cherico the morning after her showdown with Councilman Sparks was nothing short of liberating for Maura Beth, and she kept breathing in deeply as if she were sampling the bouquet of a fine wine. Occasionally, the fleeting glimpse of a deer or wild turkey at the edge of the woods or near a stone outcropping made her think she had died and gone to heaven. In a very literal sense, it reminded her that she'd had her nose in library books to the exclusion of nearly everything else far too long.

The decision to travel north by northeast for a change of venue came to her shortly after she'd returned to her apartment the evening before, collapsing on her sofa and virtually drenched in self-doubt. She had turned her back on security, which was certainly brave, but was it smart? Her first impulse was to call her parents in Covington—particularly her mother—or Periwinkle at the restaurant, or Miss Voncille wherever she could be found these days, but somehow she resisted. It wasn't so much that she was afraid of failing and going down in flames with the library. It was more that she was putting so much of herself into this ordinary little town of Cherico that had offered her a job straight out of school.

Of course, there were many other library jobs out there—some with far more responsibility, most that paid more money. But by some gradual, inexplicable process, she had gotten hooked on this particular position and this wildly diverse handful of people who had suddenly rallied to her side. They were beginning to mean more and more to her with every passing day, creating one of those alternative definitions of the word *family.* It all meant that making a big hit of The Cherry Cola Book Club was a challenge she fully intended to meet.

Then an idea flashed into her head with a clarity she could not ignore. What would be the harm in simply getting the hell out of Dodge for a day or two? She could put Renette in charge of the library, drive up to Nashville, visit with the McShays and the Brachles, and clear her head. She could run everything past all of them and even go to the hospital to bring Stout Fella another balloon bouquet, this time with something more original than "Get well soon!" to cheer him up.

So she put her doubts and fears aside, and reached Douglas at his brother's house. It did not take very long for her to wangle an invitation after summarizing all the drama that had taken place at City Hall.

"Sounds like you're living right on the edge there," Douglas told her. "But, by all means, come on up for a visit. We'd love to have you. My brother, Paul, and his wife, Susan, are empty nesters with three bedrooms gathering dust now, so they always have room for one more these days. I'll tell Connie and Becca you're coming. I know they'll be thrilled."

And that had sealed the deal. For Maura Beth, it was now Nashville or bust.

All the full-fledged, female members of The Cherry Cola Book Club except Miss Voncille were standing around Stout Fella's room on the fourth floor of Centennial Medical Center, daring him to pick a winner among all the new balloon bouquets they had blown up for him. Of course, the Magic Marker messages were the only criterion that really counted in this impromptu competition. At the moment, Stout Fella was milking it for all it was worth, and everyone looking on was amazed at his outlook and energy.

Not even an AMI and subsequent balloon angioplasty had been able to keep him down for long.

Yes, it was true that his voice was not quite as strong as usual, and he had to pause now and then when he spoke, but there was no doubt in anyone's mind that he would recover completely just as the doctors had said he would.

"Hey . . . I'm sold on Maura Beth's . . . 'Good Health—Check It Out!' motto because it's got that library thing of hers going for it," he began, anchored to his bed by the tangle of lines monitoring his vital signs and the IV drips supplying his meds and nourishment.

"Thanks. And a little birdie told me you wanted to come to all my future Cherry Cola Book Club meetings once you get home," Maura Beth put in quickly. "I'll hold you to that."

He nodded her way and resumed, "On the other hand . . . who wouldn't like Connie's . . . 'No More Ice Cream Islands!' for the humor alone?"

"You do know that means no more standing around the kitchen with a spoon, digging in, don't you?" Connie said.

"Got the message, loud and clear. Nevertheless . . . I'm smart enough to remember who's gonna butter my bread for me . . . or probably not even let me have bread and butter anymore. So the winner is—ta da!—my wife and keeper, Becca Broccoli, for . . . 'I Love You, You Big Lug!' "

Becca leaned down carefully, finding a clear route to his cheek to plant a kiss, while the others laughed and lightly applauded. Then she pulled back and took several quick bows. "Thank you, thank you, one and all. Please, enough applause. This is so unexpected. I never thought I'd win among such fierce competition. And I want to say further that it will be my next goal to turn my Justin into a Medium-Sized Lug once again."

He smiled big and gave the entire room a naughty wink. "I promise to tow the line the best I can . . . but I just wanted to say that I'd like for everyone . . . to keep calling me Stout Fella . . . no matter how much I shape up. I keep telling Becca . . . that it makes me feel solid and sturdy. Hey, there's more than one meaning . . . to the word *stout,* you know."

Becca was rolling her eyes now. "Yes, we know all about that. You're Stout Fella, the Superhero, able to wrap up any real-estate deal with the lightning stroke of a pen."

He gave her a thumbs-up. "Now you're talking!"

"You'll just be writing a bit slower now, kiddo," Becca reminded him. "You'll get a crash course from me in taking your time whether you're eating or buying up all the land on both sides of the Tennessee River."

"But never fear. After you get released and we head home to Cherico, Douglas and I want to make sure you get a glimpse of the Batman Building downtown to honor your ongoing superhero status," Connie explained. "It's really the AT&T Building, but it's got these tall twin spires and a few other contraptions on top that make it look like Batman's mask. It's not quite the landmark Ryman Auditorium is, but it's pretty close. There now, that's a good reason to do what all the doctors ask you to do."

"To the Batmobile, Robin!" Stout Fella replied, enjoying a laugh that turned quickly into a cough, and Becca immediately gave him his water to sip. "By the way . . . where is Douglas right now? No offense to all you beautiful ladies . . . but a man likes to talk to another man now and then."

"Oh, he's spending some time with his brother, Paul, but he'll be back to pick me up soon," Connie said. "Anyhow, don't worry. He'll be stopping by plenty before you get released."

Just then there was a knock at the door, and a mousy female voice announced the single word, "Nutrition." In walked a slight young woman in brown scrubs carrying a tray and smiling deferentially at everyone. "It's almost noon. Time for lunch. It's just a little something to eat—doctor's orders."

"Yeah, but I thought I was getting that . . . through one of these drips," Stout Fella pointed out, narrowing his eyes.

"You are, sir," she answered, nearly in a whisper. "But your doctor wants you to try a little broth, too. And some Jell-O, if you can manage it."

"Hey, I know I need to lose weight . . . but that sounds ridiculous!" he declared. "When do I start back on . . . meat and potatoes?"

"I'll handle him," Becca said, noting the sheepish look on the woman's face. "Here, let me take this from you, please." Whereupon the tray was transferred quickly, the woman scurried out, and Becca gave her husband a stern look.

"You practically scared her to death, you big bully. The poor girl was only doing her job."

"Never mind her. Hoo, boy!" Stout Fella exclaimed. "What have I gotten myself into? From my wife's home cooking to . . . this!"

Becca ignored the remark and uncovered the plate, inhaling the steam from the broth. "I think it's chicken."

He cut his eyes at her and smirked like a mischievous little boy. "I think *I'm* chicken."

"For heaven's sake, don't be such a big baby. If you could watch your artery being unclogged on a TV monitor from start to finish without flinching, you can certainly slurp up a tiny bowl of bland soup. Here, I'll even feed you." And she proceeded to do just that, while her husband made a gallery of ungainly faces even as he swallowed every spoonful guided toward his mouth.

• • •

It was out on the deck overlooking Paul and Susan McShay's vast backyard in the wealthy Nashville suburb of Brentwood that Maura Beth was getting ready to hold a brainstorming session about the future of the book club. That revved-up campaign she had envisioned would start here in earnest. The evening was still young and the air invigorating after a delicious menu in the formal dining room of baked chicken, smashed potatoes, and sautéed green beans that Susan had prepared for all of her guests. Now it was time to get down to business.

"I can only stay for about twenty minutes," Becca told Maura Beth as the gathering seated themselves around a rustic picnic table with their after-dinner drinks in hand. "Stout Fella is expecting me back at the hospital around eight, of course."

Then Douglas chimed in. "I'm going with her, and not just because she doesn't know her way around. Becca says Justin wants to shoot the breeze with me about the NFL, the college game, and other manly topics. So far, he says, they've refused to give him an injection of testosterone."

"You'd think this was just another day at the office, and his heart crisis had never happened," Becca said, waving Douglas off.

Maura Beth smiled as she quietly surveyed the friends she hoped would be sending her back to

Cherico with a successful strategy to keep her library open. Connie, Douglas, and Becca, she had expected to consult, but the Brentwood McShays were an unexpected bonus.

"You might like to know that Susan and Paul are still in The Music City Page Turners," Connie had told Maura Beth at the dinner table. "The three of us were almost half of the founding members, and we all know what it takes to make a success of one of these clubs. Douglas and I brought them up to date on what you're trying to do in Cherico, and they think it's fantastic."

One thing had led to another, and by the time the dessert of chocolate mousse with whipped cream and a cherry on top was served, Susan had committed herself and her husband to the confab out on the deck later on. "That is, unless you'd rather just have your Cherry Cola people only," she had added at the last second.

But Maura Beth had quickly reassured her. "Heavens, no! I need as much brainpower as I can round up!"

The Brentwood McShays certainly appeared to have the right credentials for offering intelligent advice. Paul was a taller, more distinguished-looking version of his brother and had recently retired from teaching psychology at Vanderbilt, while the stylish, model-thin Susan still ran her own crafts boutique at the Cool Springs Galleria south of Brentwood. The most important thing from Maura Beth's point of view, however, was that they were both fans of the printed word and would therefore be sympathetic to her cause.

"Time is growing short," Maura Beth began, officially opening the informal meeting. "The Cherico Library's days may be numbered unless we can drastically increase interest in The Cherry Cola Book Club. And also get more people to use their library cards." Then she offered a blow-by-blow of her most recent encounters with Councilman Sparks, but particularly his offer to take her out of the library business and appoint her his decorative gatekeeper.

"Something about that bothers me," Connie said. "Why doesn't he just shut everything down and let you go your merry way? Or should I say unhappy way?"

Maura Beth decided to hold nothing back. "The truth is, though, I'm not really unhappy. I want to make a go of my job in Cherico because I like the place. There are probably a thousand reasons I shouldn't, but I do. As for why he hasn't shut the library down by now to cut his losses, I don't know. That continues to puzzle me. But these local politicians are a law unto themselves."

"Would you like to have an ex-college professor's opinion?" Paul McShay offered, leaning in her general direction.

"Love to."

"I'm only going by a handful of things that

happened to me during my tenure at Vandy," he began, after a sip of his port. "It doesn't mean that I'm right in my analysis, but what I'm about to tell you may have some merit nonetheless. There were a few young female students in my classes over the years who developed crushes on me." He turned and gave his wife a knowing smile and wink. "And I never kept any of that from Susan. I was determined to nip these things in the bud."

"I'm sure his nipping was effective, too," she put in. "A wife can usually tell if her husband is fooling around."

"Anyway, none of those young ladies ever got anywhere with me, but I got pretty good at picking up on the signals. Sometimes, they'd come up to me after class and tell me what a deep speaking voice I had and 'why didn't I go into broadcasting' and yada, yada, yada. Or other times it was how much they liked the clothes I was wearing—mostly the sweaters and ties that they didn't know Susan had picked out for me. I always thanked them for their compliments but otherwise played dumb, of course."

Maura Beth was frowning now, trying to follow the implications of his story. "What made you bring up the crush angle?"

He finished off his port and said, "Because that's my field of study. Psychology is all about predictable human behavior, and I listened carefully to all the emphasis you put on the comments your councilman kept making about your beautiful red hair. The way he carried on about it, and especially that line about your innocence that you said made you feel uncomfortable. It sounds a lot like my experience in reverse, but at a much higher level of expectation. I think it all probably means the man wants you around at all costs, despite this business about closing the library. It's a roundabout way of setting things up in typical male fashion."

The three other women sitting around the table, all of whom happened to be married, exchanged glances, and it was Becca who finally spoke up for them. "I have to agree with Paul. Regardless of what happens with the library, I think it would be a huge mistake for you to go directly to work for Councilman Sparks. You don't know what kind of pressure he could end up putting on you for—you know what."

Maura Beth bit her lip as she shook her head. "I can be such a naïve girlie-girl at times. The thought had crossed my mind that he might be hitting on me, but I didn't want to believe it."

"Hey, don't be so hard on yourself," Connie said. "You did the right thing. You turned him down and told him you were going for the gold. You have nothing to be ashamed of. The big question now is how to get that gold."

"Right!" Maura Beth exclaimed. "So now it's idea time. First step is to reschedule the *To Kill a*

*Mockingbird* meeting and get into an honest, meaty discussion of Harper Lee's work. No more indulging the war between the sexes. At least Councilman Sparks has promised me he won't be doing that sort of thing anymore—that is, if I can take him at his word. But how do we get more people interested in participating?"

Becca waved her hand in front of her face a few times. "*The Becca Broccoli Show* could go with the downsizing recipes full-time, for starters. And I could keep on pitching *To Kill a Mockingbird* as our upcoming food for thought in the club. Stout Fella could talk about getting his body in shape with my new recipes, and his brain in shape by reading and thinking about Harper Lee's work. I could invite my audience to come to the book club meeting to have a little bite and discuss literature with Becca Broccoli, Stout Fella, and everyone else. Just how far out were you considering scheduling this thing, Maura Beth?"

"A month? Maybe five weeks at the most? We can't wait too long, though, or we'll run up against the budget approval."

Becca nodded enthusiastically. "That should be enough time to get Stout Fella in some sort of reasonable shape—oh, and to get him to read the novel."

Then an inspired Connie stepped in. "I was thinking that Douglas and I could talk things up to all our new neighbors out at the lake. We're just now getting to know some of them. But people are pretty much the same all over. Everybody likes to eat, and you never know who likes to read until you bring up a few pop culture references. That's where you separate the TV watchers and movie-goers from the readers."

Maura Beth's face was suddenly alive with girlish excitement. "And I've just this second thought of something to run past Periwinkle when I get home." Then she took the time to explain The Twinkle and its congenial owner to the Brentwood McShays.

Susan briefly glanced at her husband after the testimonial to the restaurant. "Now that makes my mouth water—and on a full stomach yet. Looks like we're going to have to visit your brother and Connie more often than we'd planned. If nothing else, I want some of that tomato aspic with the cream cheese in the middle. And I bet I'd get so hooked, we'd probably even want to come back another time to take in a certain book review at the library."

Maura Beth clasped her hands together. "Are you saying you'd be willing to come for our *Mockingbird* session?"

"What do you say, Paul?" Susan added, winking smartly.

He thought for a moment and then leaned against his brother. "Let me check first with Doug, here. Think you could return the favor and put us up in Cherico now and then?"

"Done deal. Now that I think about it, I could use a fishing partner on *The Verdict*."

"Wow!" Becca exclaimed, checking her watch. "That was a productive ten or fifteen minutes, wasn't it? Now that all that's decided, I think it's safe to head for the hospital and let Stout Fella know about it."

"And I'll keep him from getting too antsy by predicting who I think will be in the Super Bowl this year," Douglas added, rising from his seat with a wink. "You know—the kind of stuff that only us men like."

Maura Beth took a deep breath as Becca and Douglas headed into the house. "I think I'll head back to Cherico tomorrow. For the first time in a while, I really believe The Cherry Cola Book Club has a chance to make a name for itself."

# 12

# Shaking up the Bottle

When Maura Beth hit the town limits of Cherico upon her return from Nashville the next day, she couldn't believe how much it felt like home to her. It truly mystified her how that could be, since she had spent most of her life growing up in Covington and all of her college years at LSU. Yet there was no question in her mind that she was glad to be back, even after a mere couple of days away.

What was more, she was even happier to see *her* library. Funny, how possessive of it she had become ever since Councilman Sparks had cast it in those terms during the unveiling of his ultimatum several months earlier. She also now knew that she had officially embraced an either/or situation: Either she kept the library open through the book club and other measures, or she left town. As she and her friends had all agreed up in Brentwood in no uncertain terms, there would be no "working under" Councilman Sparks in any capacity whatsoever.

The informal report Renette had prepared for her boss's perusal on her first afternoon back was uneventful for the most part, but a couple of items took a bit of explaining.

"Exactly what is this notation here?" Maura

Beth wanted to know, pointing to the second scribble on the list as they reviewed it in her office. “What does ‘V15 Damage’ mean? Please tell me it doesn’t have anything to do with the one and only Mr. Barnes Putzel.”

Renette looked down at her lap while fidgeting in her seat. “Unfortunately, it does. We ran out of peanut butter crackers, and Mr. Putzel threw Volume Fifteen of the *Encyclopaedia Britannica* all the way across the room and broke the spine. It was actually the only exciting thing that happened all day.”

Maura Beth covered both eyes with the palm of her right hand. “Oh, I knew there was something I forgot to do before I left. I meant to go down to The Cherico Market and buy some more crackers. I had even made a note to myself that we were running low. Well, did he do any more damage, or was it just Volume Fifteen?”

“Just that one. Do we have the money to replace it?”

Maura Beth flashed a sarcastic grin. “We barely have enough money to replace the crackers. I’ll call his sister and tell her to write us a check.” Then she moved down the list with her finger. “And what was this ‘Complaint from Mr. Parker Place’?”

Renette had a guilty expression on her face. “I, uh, was really late putting out the most recent edition of the *Commercial Appeal.*”

Maura Beth shrugged. “Oh, I wouldn’t worry

about it. You put it in the newspaper rack eventually, didn't you?"

"Yes, of course. But Mr. Place told me he comes every day to go through the classifieds looking for a job, and he said he was annoyed that he had to wait three hours. I got sidetracked by some phone calls and stuff. He was polite about it all, but I could tell he was stressed out."

"What does this Mr. Place look like?" Maura Beth wanted to know, reviewing a mental slideshow of their regular patrons.

"Oh, we've both seen him in here a lot recently. He's that handsome black gentleman who's always dressed in a coat and tie. Only he says he's out of work now and comes to the library for job leads in the Memphis paper."

Maura Beth pursed her lips thoughtfully. "I tell you what. Next time he comes in, let me know. I'd like to talk to him. Do you know what kind of work he's looking for?"

"He didn't say."

"Well, you just keep an eye out for him, okay?" Then she ran down the rest of the list, looking up with a smile. "I think I understand the rest of this. All things considered, you did extremely well being in charge. Now, the next thing I want you to do is take some money out of petty cash and run down to The Cherico Market for those crackers. We've got to keep Mr. Putzel from destroying the rest of the encyclopedia."

• • •

For Maura Beth, it had come down to this: The *To Kill a Mockingbird* potluck and review had been rescheduled one week after Halloween, and The Cherry Cola Book Club had two weeks after that to build toward either the ultimate sizzle or a final fizzle. But the momentum that had been rekindled in Brentwood must not be squandered, and Maura Beth was so excited about it all that she was practically hatching schemes in her sleep. One that particularly intrigued her involved meeting Mr. Parker Place and finding out what his story was. Who knew? He just might turn out to be the perfect example of someone successfully using the library for job leads, and that also might impress and sway Councilman Sparks there at the end.

On Maura Beth's second day back from her Nashville trip, in fact, Mr. Place was ushered into her office by a smiling Renette, who had invited him over the minute he had finished with the paper. At close range, Maura Beth found him even more attractive than she had whenever she'd spotted him from a distance. His smooth, ginger-colored skin and generous smile made it easy to linger over his strong, angular features. In addition, there was a maturity about him that was both reassuring and titillating.

"My assistant tells me you're looking for work, Mr. Place," Maura Beth said, after they had exchanged greetings and other pleasantries.

"I am," he told her. "And I never thought I would be at this stage of my life."

"What do you do?"

Discernible pride was clearly evident in his smile and tone of voice. "I'm a pastry chef. And a first-rate one, too. I worked for nearly thirty years at the Grand Shelby Hotel over in Memphis making desserts fit for royalty. Provided the king or queen can practice moderation. What I make is good for your sweet tooth, not necessarily your figure."

Maura Beth chuckled briefly, but then there was a sharp intake of air. "Didn't I read in the *Commercial Appeal* that the Grand Shelby Hotel was torn down about a month ago?"

"Sure was, I'm sorry to say. It went belly-up in this economy, and they couldn't find a buyer for it. So they just tore it down and sold the land off for a parking lot. There's too much of that going on these days. Unfortunately, the hotel was also my home. I had a very nice, spacious suite all to myself on the second floor. So here I am back in my hometown of Cherico after all these years living with my mama until I can get back on track. I check the classifieds every day to see if there's an ad for anything up my alley. I have to say, I wish your library had a computer so I could go online and look for leads that way."

Maura Beth was unable to suppress her frustration at his last comment. "I wish we had one for the patrons, too. More than one, actually. But the City Council keeps turning down my requests for terminals. They're dead set against them, and I've asked for funding every year I've been here. It's just not a priority of theirs."

"That's a shame," Mr. Place answered, scowling momentarily. "If I was still in Memphis, I could use their computers, but down here, I guess I'll have to plunk down for one of my own. I have a little savings to tide me over until I find something that really suits me, though. I left this little town in the first place because there were lots more jobs in Memphis, you know. I'm a native Chericoan, as I said. Born over there at Cherico Memorial in the middle of a hailstorm fifty-four years ago. My mama always said I was a 'hail' of a baby—nine and a half pounds and bouncing all over the place."

Maura Beth leaned in and laughed. "That's cute. Your mother has a delightful sense of humor, and you do, too. I guess it runs in the Place family."

He slowly shook his head, smiling all the while. "Oh, we're not Places. We're Bedloes. I was christened Joe Sam Bedloe, but I changed it legally to Parker Place once I started working for the Grand Shelby Hotel. And yes, I had a good reason for doing that. When I was growing up, Mama gave me a Monopoly game one Christmas, and whenever my aunties would come over with my little cousins, we'd wear that game out. I liked all the names of the streets, particularly Park Place. It sounded so classy, and everybody knew it was where all the imaginary rich folks hung their hats. And if you could buy that deed and Boardwalk and put hotels up, you stood a great chance of winning the game, which I usually did. Made my cousins so mad every time. So here I am—Mis-ter Park-er Place of Cherico, Memphis, and Monopoly fame, pastry chef extraordinaire."

"It all has a nice ring to it, I must say."

"Yep, high-rent district all the way."

Maura Beth then flashed her warmest smile as she decided to tell him all about the book club. "While you're waiting for the right job to come along, maybe you'd consider joining us and coming to our next meeting in about five weeks? And why not bring your mother along with you? I'd love to meet her."

He looked as if he might be seriously considering her invitation. "Yes, I've seen your sign-up sheet. And I have to admit I have a little history with *To Kill a Mockingbird*. So does my mama." He rose from his chair and pointed to the front desk. "Maybe I'll just make my way right over there and sign up now."

Maura Beth could barely contain her delight. "That's fantastic, Mr. Place! And do you have a current library card?"

He told her he didn't as they headed out of her office.

"Well, let's go get you fixed up all around, shall we?"

That evening Maura Beth decided to have a late dinner at The Twinkle to tell Periwinkle all about her impromptu trip to Nashville, as well as the promotional idea that had come to her during the Brentwood brainstorming session with everyone. In fact, the two of them closed the place down, sending Lalie Bevins, the waitress, home to her family, before truly engaging each other.

"So what's this great concept you hinted at when I served you your grilled chicken and pineapple salsa?" Periwinkle began, finally taking a seat at Maura Beth's table after a hard night's work. "By the way, did you like it? It's the first time I've offered it. I don't want to get into a rut, you know. Expanding the menu is something I'd like to do."

"It was delicious, of course. Everything you serve always is." Then Maura Beth briefly outlined all the decisions that had been made in Brentwood before finally getting to Periwinkle's initial question. "Here's my concept. Why don't we cross-promote my library and your restaurant? I've come up with a perfectly brilliant way."

"I'm all ears."

Maura Beth went all girlish and giggly for a few moments. "We use library cards. If one of my patrons presents his or her library card to you when they order, they can get a free drink or dessert."

Periwinkle looked stoic and went silent for a while. "Hmm. I have to think about my margins, you know. What about half-price drinks or desserts?"

Maura Beth felt like negotiating. After all, it would surely be good practice for dealing with Councilman Sparks. "Two-for-one drinks or a half-price dessert?"

"You drive a hard bargain," Periwinkle said, extending her hand to shake on it. "But okay, it's a deal. I have more customers who prefer sweets over liquor anyway."

But Maura Beth kept on pressing. "I figure it makes my library card a more valuable commodity and encourages people to drop by The Twinkle even more than they do now. I'll have some new flyers printed up. I'm sure Connie will go along with it."

Periwinkle was chuckling now. "Okay, girl, you've sold me. You can let up. Besides, I only have two desserts on the menu—my sherry custard and my bread pudding. They're pretty cost-effective."

Then it flashed into Maura Beth's head that she had other work to accomplish at The Twinkle on this autumn evening, and Periwinkle's mention of expanding the menu had triggered it. "You know, I think it's ambitious of you to want to offer more dishes to your customers as time goes by. All successful restaurants do it, and The Twinkle certainly qualifies as successful."

"Yes, I'm doing better than I ever dreamed, and much sooner than I thought," Periwinkle admitted. "It's got my ex-husband, Harlan, green with envy that he let me get away. And what I have to say to him is, 'Tough pork chops!' "

"I love it!" Maura Beth exclaimed, enjoying a big laugh. Then she leaned in and gave Periwinkle her most studied gaze. "I know a way you can expand your menu right now and get raves in the process—no hit or miss dishes, no ifs, ands, or buts."

Periwinkle stopped her gum. "Now this I have to hear."

"No, I'm perfectly serious. Cherico is once again the home of the Memphis Grand Shelby Hotel's former illustrious pastry chef, Mr. Parker Place. The hotel was recently torn down and he's flat out of a job, but more importantly, he's dying to get back to work making his fabulous desserts for some lucky restaurant and its customers."

"And you know this how?"

Maura Beth recanted her morning visit with Mr. Place and went straight for the payoff. "Do you think you can take on a pastry chef? You said yourself you only had two desserts on the menu."

Periwinkle began mulling things over, but Maura Beth could discern the interest in her face.

"I can certainly afford to take on a pastry chef, if that's what you mean," she said finally. "I guess it would just be a question of Mr. Place's salary expectations. I probably can't afford to pay him what the Grand Shelby Hotel was paying him."

"But you'll never know what he'll accept until you ask him."

"That's true. Girl, are you his agent or something?"

They both laughed, and Maura Beth said, "No, it just came to me a few minutes ago. I didn't even think of it this afternoon when he was sitting in my office. So, will you interview him and see what happens? I have his phone number from his book club sign-up today. I'll get it to you tomorrow."

Periwinkle nodded enthusiastically. "Sure, why not? I always like to think I'm at the top of my game."

"Baby, you'll get the job. Don't you worry," Ardenia Bedloe had told her son right before kissing him on the cheek and sending him on his way to the job interview at The Twinkle at nine-thirty in the morning. "That Miz Lattimore is crazy if you don't get it, good as you are. Nobody in Memphis ever fixed desserts as fine as you did!" Then she had drawn herself up as tall as her arthritis and seventy-five years of living would allow and waved good-bye to him at the door.

"Hold your head up and your shoulders back!" she called out at the last minute. "You're a proud Bedloe, no matter what!"

And with that send-off to amuse and embolden him simultaneously, Mr. Parker Place drove from his family home on Big Hill Lane to the restaurant. He was thinking that Maura Beth Mayhew must be some sort of magician, getting back to him just a couple of days after their first meeting to tell him she had talked Periwinkle Lattimore into considering him for a position at The Twinkle. Though his world had come tumbling down around him in Memphis, thanks to the wrecking ball, it appeared he might be on the verge of constructing a new life for himself.

"What were your specialties?" Periwinkle was asking him once they had begun the interview in her cluttered office at precisely nine-thirty. Among the many good work habits he had acquired throughout his career, unerring promptness was near the top of Mr. Parker Place's list.

He took a deep breath and began a tempting recitation. "Crepes of all kinds, both cheese and fruit, Mississippi mud pie, grasshopper pie, carrot cake, red velvet cake, strawberry cake, caramel cake, éclairs, cupcakes of all kinds, macadamia nut cookies, dark chocolate chip cookies—"

Periwinkle held up her hand. "That's more than impressive, Mr. Place. Why don't I take a bite of the samples you brought?" She looked down at the éclair and the slice of grasshopper pie he had placed before her a few minutes earlier and settled on the éclair first. "What on earth have you put in there, Mr. Place?!" she exclaimed as she tasted his creation with ever-widening eyes. "It's heavenly!"

He leaned in smugly. "A little Amaretto in the filling."

"How did you know I love that wedding cake taste?" she continued. "Though why I have no idea. My marriage was a disaster!"

He gently pushed the pie plate toward her with a disarming smile. "Sorry to hear that, but maybe this will make you feel better."

Then she tasted the cool, green grasshopper pie, and he thought she might just swoon. "Ohhh!" Finally, she gathered herself. "My biggest gripe with mint is that it can be so overwhelming that you feel like you don't want to eat anything for another month. How did you manage to tame it like this?"

"Now that," he told her, "is one of my secrets I don't care to reveal."

She nodded enthusiastically. "I can respect that. I keep a few of my best tips hidden away on the pantry shelf myself."

Then it was time to get around to the details of an actual job offer, and Periwinkle predictably led with the issue of compensation. "Can you tell me how much the Grand Shelby Hotel was paying you there at the end?"

He said nothing, preferring to write a figure on a nearby Post-it note and hand it to her.

She looked down at it and smiled. “I must say I think you were worth every penny, judging by what I just tasted.”

“Thank you.”

Then she took another Post-it note and wrote down a figure of her own. “See if this will work for you, Mr. Place,” she said, offering it to him.

He glanced at it quickly and caught her gaze. “Miz Lattimore, I’d love to come work for you whenever you say.” Then he leaned forward, maintaining the intense eye contact. “My mama said you’d give me this job before I left the house. She’s a great judge of character, you know.”

“Tell you what,” Periwinkle added, reaching across her desk to shake his hand. “I want you to bring your mother here for dinner real soon. It’ll be on the house. Just think of it as a sort of signing bonus.”

Miss Voncille glanced at the wall clock in her bright yellow kitchen and made a sour face. It was ten after two in the afternoon, one week exactly before the November *Mockingbird* meeting. “They’re running late,” she said to Locke, who was leaning against the counter nursing a small gin and tonic. “That’s not like them.”

He shrugged and began rummaging through the nearby dish of nuts she intended to set out for their upcoming bridge game with the Crumpton sisters.

"Why do men always do that?" she wanted to know, watching him poking his index finger around and feigning disapproval.

"Do what?"

"Pick out all the cashews and leave all the Brazil nuts."

Locke washed down the nuts with another sip of his drink and smirked. "For the same reason we date the prettiest girls in town if we can get them to go out with us. They're yummier."

"I'm not sure I like the sound of that too much," she added. "But at least it's consistent."

"Yes," he continued. "Also, cashews are compact, and Brazil nuts are . . . well, always the size of Brazil." He decided to take a seat in the breakfast nook, and she joined him, bringing the nuts with her. "Playing bridge with the Crumpton sisters still seems like an extraordinary sacrifice on your part—or on ours, I should say, since I'll have to be in the room except when I'm lucky enough to be dummy. Please see if you can arrange for me to be dummy every deal. Those Crumpton sisters are the world's most acquired taste."

Miss Voncille looked exasperated and went after the last of the cashews herself. "I expect them to be testy if we cut off one of their legs, or even defeat one of their contracts, but if I can maneuver them into coming to the *Mockingbird* meeting in another week, it will help Maura Beth out immeasurably. We're all just trying our best to increase those numbers—day by day, week by week—right up until the last second. Maura Beth and Periwinkle really have that cross-promotional angle going, Connie's doing her thing out at the lake this Sunday with her seafood extravaganza, and Becca's been doing hers on the radio now with Stout Fella as her sidekick. I'm not about to be the only one who doesn't contribute something. And you have to be in on it for the simple reason that it takes four to play bridge."

Locke lifted his glass in tribute and took another swallow. "I must admit I never thought Mamie and Marydell would accept your apology about that crazy armadillo story of yours. Looks like they're back in the genealogy fold. Mind telling me how you managed it?"

"A strange form of flattery, if you must know. I told Mamie that I thought I must be showing the first signs of dementia with all that nonsense I made up. 'Clearly, you're the healthiest, sanest person in our class,' I went on. 'You'll outlive us all!' I laid it on pretty thick because it appeals to that unique morbid streak of hers. That's what we used to call her in high school, you know—Morbid Mamie. I think it started when our journalism teacher, Mrs. Lander, let her write an article for the school paper on poor Preston Durant's tragic death in a wreck. Oh, it was awful! His car stalled on the railroad tracks! After that, it got around that she had asked Mrs. Lander if she could write ‘practice’ obits for some of us. Apparently, something about it got her juices flowing. I only hope she doesn’t drag our senior yearbook out of mothballs again.”

Locke furrowed his brow. “Why? Would that be a bad thing?”

But the doorbell prevented Miss Voncille from answering his question. “Ah, there they are at last! Shall we go greet them and get the afternoon started?”

Unfortunately, Mamie Crumpton bounded through the front door out of the brisk weather with the yearbook of the Cherico High School Class of 1960 and her sister in tow. “This is why we’re late,” she explained, foregoing so much as a hello while brandishing the worn-looking annual over her head like some sort of sports trophy. “We got halfway over here and I realized I had forgotten to bring it. So I said, ‘Marydell, we’ll just have to turn around and go back.’ ”

Somehow Miss Voncille managed a careful, polite smile. “Why, of course you had to.”

“I didn’t know if you knew that two more of us had died last month,” Mamie added, while Locke took the ladies’ coats and hung them up in the hall closet. Then he gestured toward the long green sofa as both Crumpton sisters took their seats and settled in.

Miss Voncille sighed wearily, remaining standing

beside Locke. "Who bought the farm this time?"

Mamie puffed herself up as usual and rattled off all the pertinent information. "It was Dexter Thomas Warrick, Jr. He and his family moved away a long time ago. I believe he was a basketball player back then. But a few weeks ago, he succumbed to a heart attack. I think some of these tall people have trouble with their hearts."

"I vaguely remember him," Miss Voncille said. "It continually amazes me how you keep up with all this. You must have runners all over the country."

Mamie was clearly proud of herself, completely missing the humor. "Oh, I do have my methods."

"So who was the second person to leave us?" Miss Voncille continued. "And then Locke will take your drink orders."

"Well, it was Katherine Anna Wilson. I think she went by Katie, or was it Kathy? I forget which. Anyway, she won Miss Home Ec her senior year. The obit didn't say what did her in—just that she passed away among family and friends. She wasn't in our crowd, though."

Miss Voncille was scowling in a genuine attempt to conjure her up. "Heavy girl?"

"Very much so. She wore dresses that looked like she'd wrapped a fabric bolt around herself. I wouldn't be surprised in the least if she won Miss Home Ec because she ate everything she cooked in class. That always made the teacher look good, you know."

Then it was time for the ritual. Mamie opened the yearbook and gestured to her classmate while locating the senior pictures of the dear departed. Both Locke and Miss Voncille moved around behind the sofa to take them in. "There they are. Both on the same page in the W's. Don't they look young as spring deer? Weren't we all back then? Ah, for the good ole days!"

Miss Voncille couldn't resist. "Yes, indeed! When we were all alive, each and every one of us!"

Locke gave Miss Voncille a playful nudge. "Let's see you, Voncille. Come on, Mamie, find her for me."

Mamie flipped a few pages and zeroed in on the picture with her index finger. "There you have her. Miss Voncille Deloris Nettles. I've always said you were a looker, Voncille."

Locke leaned down for a closer look and wagged his brows. "That you were, my dear. Of course, you still are in my book. Is Deloris a family name with that unusual spelling?"

"I doubt it. My parents just liked to be different. He was Walker Nettles, and she was Annis Favarel, and I have no idea where their first names came from." Miss Voncille finally exhaled dramatically, having survived the ordeal of Morbid Mamie and the yearbook yet another time. "Well, we've paid our proper respects now. Locke, why don't you see what the ladies will have, I'll get out the card table, and we'll play some bridge."

For the first time in their fledgling relationship, Miss Voncille and Locke were having a disagreement over something other than picking through the party nuts or which wine to have with dinner. A somewhat trying two hours of bidding, finessing, and drawing trumps had crawled by, but from Miss Voncille's point of view it had all been worth it. She'd gotten the freshly departed Crumpton sisters to agree to attend the *Mockingbird* meeting and even check out a few books in the interim for lagniappe. Mission more than accomplished.

"You were as obvious as they were clueless," Locke kept insisting. "It's true that I've never been your bridge partner, so I have no point of comparison. But I find it hard to believe that someone could renege, mismanage trumps, and overbid so many times in the same rubber. I wonder if they were wise to you but let you play on like that anyway. A win is a win is a win."

He began imitating her voice and gestures. " 'Oh, my goodness, I thought I had completely drawn trumps. Where did that come from, Mamie, you clever rascal!' And, 'Did I double your contract, Mamie? I wonder what I could have been thinking of with the hand I had?' And my absolute favorite, 'I shouldn't have bid a slam in no-trump without a stopper in spades.' Mamie ran the entire spade suit against us in that one. The only good thing about it was that I was dummy and didn't have to stay in the room to watch all the carnage."

"I had no idea you were such a sore loser," Miss Voncille said, watching him fold her card table and put it away in the hall closet.

He had an impish grin on his face when he emerged from his task. "And I had no idea you would go to such lengths to stay on the good side of your Morbid Mamie and her mousy little sister who only opened her mouth to bid. At least come clean and admit you played like a college student on a drinking binge."

She put her hands on her hips and turned her nose up. "I never drank when I was in college. Besides, what happened here this afternoon was only a game."

"Which you won, despite appearances to the contrary."

She finally gave in. "Very well, then, Locke Linwood. That was indeed the most atrocious rubber of bridge I've ever played in my life. But it got results, didn't it? I know Mamie Crumpton like the back of my hand. She loves nothing more than feeling like she's on top of the world, alive and kicking, while the rest of us are dropping like flies and playing beginner's bridge. This was the perfect afternoon for her—two senior pictures to shed crocodile tears over and two bridge opponents to trounce—with a little help, of course. Besides, it's all just part of my ongoing transformation from semi-curmudgeon to sweet little old lady."

Locke put his hand around Miss Voncille's tidy waist and gently pulled her toward him. "So, do you think they'll keep their word on everything?"

"Oh, I expect so. Even if you and I have to lose another rubber or two of bridge to keep them happy and on track. And I also think explaining to them why they might be without a library soon didn't hurt one bit."

When Maura Beth walked into Connie's seafood extravaganza at her lake house the following Sunday, there was already a respectable crowd milling around, some with drinks, others with plates of grilled catfish and shrimp scampi in hand. In fact, the decibel level of the chatter was so high that Diana Krall's velvety recording of "It Could Happen to You" could barely be recognized.

"What a warm, rustic atmosphere!" Maura Beth exclaimed, as Connie welcomed her into what could only be described as the greatest of great rooms. It occupied the core of the house and sported rustic beams across a shed roof ceiling that was at least twenty feet high. The focal point of one wall was an enormous Tennessee sandstone fireplace, complete with crackling flames on this chilly autumn evening, while the other wall featured at least twenty framed snapshots of the most impressive fish Douglas had caught on Lake Cherico or in the Tennessee River itself. There was no denying that this was the lodge of a sportsman, definitely lacking a woman's touch, and Douglas quickly spirited Maura Beth away for a guided tour of his trophies.

"Now this one here is a thirty-one-pound striped bass I caught on a white spinner," he explained. "White does it for me every time. I just haven't had much luck with the yellow or the blue baits."

"That certainly is a huge fish," Maura Beth said, trying her best to sound interested.

"And this one next to it I caught on a pig 'n' jig," he continued. "Bet you've never heard of a lure like that."

"It sounds like a canapé."

Douglas snickered. "It does, doesn't it? Actually, there is a piece of pork rind on the hook."

"Now, Douglas," Connie said, stepping up to rescue her friend, "let's give Maura Beth a chance at the real canapés, shall we? She can come back and gawk at your fish collection later on. It's not going to swim away. You've seen to that." On the way over to the buffet table, Connie continued her rant. "Believe me, he would have told you how much every single one of those fish weighed and what bait he used to catch them all, if I had let him."

But Maura Beth was in no mood for criticism. "He's just proud of his pastime, that's all. Your husband is a sweetie, and you know it."

"Well, I have to admit, I always know where he is—out on *The Verdict* or at The Marina Bar and Grill every day. Meanwhile, you'll be pleased to hear that we have some of Douglas's family down from Brentwood joining the neighbors. Matter of fact, here comes someone now I'm sure you'll remember."

From across the room, Susan McShay ambled over with a smile and her cocktail in hand. "Surprise!" she exclaimed, giving Maura Beth a quick hug. "Paul and I decided we couldn't miss this. Connie's been talking it up so much."

They were all joined immediately by a robust young man who was in the midst of treating one of the shrimp on his plate as finger food. "You just have to be Maura Beth with that red hair and those blue eyes," he said. "Excuse me while I clean up my act."

She laughed while he found a spot on a nearby coffee table for his plate and wiped his hands on a napkin.

Then Susan made the introductions. "Maura Beth, this is my ravenous son and Connie's nephew, Jeremy. He teaches English at New

Gallatin Academy in Nashville, and he's been dying to meet you."

Jeremy extended his hand and said: "I just missed you when you were up in Brentwood before. I was chaperoning a field trip to the Grand Ole Opry, believe it or not. Nothing ties you up like a busload of eleventh-grade boys ogling rhinestones, big hair, and big—"

Maura Beth grinned at his widening eyes, while she stepped in to rescue him. "Voices?"

He laughed good-naturedly. "Did I mention I teach English and am awfully good at choosing my words carefully?"

"Well, if you'll excuse us, Susan and I will keep on circulating," Connie put in, giving them both a naughty little wink. "Please, you two eat and drink as much as you want."

Once Maura Beth had helped herself to a plate and a drink, and Jeremy had refreshed both of his, they found a couple of seats near the fire and settled in.

"Mom told me what you're trying to do with the book club down here, and I just couldn't pass up the opportunity to meet you. *To Kill a Mockingbird* is my all-time favorite Southern novel," he was saying after a swig of his beer. "I don't think it can ever be reviewed enough, and I make all my students do a term paper on it. It's a rite of passage in my classroom. Sometimes I describe it as a rite of passage for all true Southerners."

Maura Beth was content to let him do most of the talking while she took him in from head to toe. He was tall and dark haired like his father but had more of his mother's softer features, and she liked the fact that he enjoyed his food so much. However, he was no Stout Fella. Her assessment was that he was just about the right size—someone who might have leapt off one of the pages of her cherished journal of wishes.

". . . and it's so unusual for a novel to become an instant classic," Jeremy continued. "But *Mockingbird* was the rare exception. The problem now in teaching it is that we're so far away from that era of turmoil, and so much is taken for granted that was once a great struggle. There are still issues to resolve, of course, and I try to point them out. Getting my students to understand the novel in the context of its time is a tremendous challenge, but it's one I'm determined to meet."

Maura Beth finally put in a word. "Yes, I know what you mean. I think I'd like to make that the focal point of our big meeting in a couple of weeks. I want people to reflect upon the changes in the South since Harper Lee wrote the book. Of course, I wasn't around during all that civil rights turbulence."

"Same here, and I'm afraid my students are far more interested in technology than political history."

Maura Beth rolled her eyes and tilted her head.

"Oh, yes. The cell phone thing, etcetera. It's all we can do to keep patrons from talking up a storm in the library. They hide back in the stacks and think we won't hear them gossiping and carrying on with their friends. It's so distracting. We have signs up everywhere, but they might as well be runes."

"Yep, those ringtones still go off now and then in my classroom despite the threat of detention. I'm afraid it's an addiction for some people."

"Sometimes I wonder what the future of communicating through books will be with all this electronic instant gratification," Maura Beth added. "There are those who feel that some readers will always want to hold a bound copy in their hands—something that they can put on a shelf and hand down to their children as part of our cultural heritage. And then there's the doomsday scenario which always favors books."

"Tell me about it."

"It's the one where if civilization falls apart and there's no technology left, you can still read a book lying in the grass munching berries or sitting up in a tree eating a banana."

"Never heard that one before," he said, tossing his head back as he laughed.

"That's because I just made it up. I have some other scenarios, too."

Now it was his turn to listen to her meanderings, and there was nothing but admiration on his face when she finished. "You really are a dyed-in-the-wool librarian, aren't you?"

"Guilty. I give my mother full credit for encouraging my love affair with books. She took me to the Covington Library when I was six and made me think summer reading was the only way a kid could have fun. That, licking cherry Popsicles to get a red tongue, and playing in the sprinkler to cool off."

The two of them kept probing, tackling various pop culture issues of the day and finding that they were in agreement for the most part. They would have preferred to be left alone entirely, but no matter where they moved throughout the great room, there was someone to hug or a hand to shake and always an introduction to be made.

"Jeremy, I'd like you to meet my friend, Periwinkle Lattimore," Maura Beth began, just as they had grown slightly uncomfortable from the warmth of the fireplace and claimed a couple of chairs farther away. "She runs the most successful restaurant in town, and if you haven't already, you must try her tomato aspic next time you go to the buffet table. They're those round red things that jiggle when you put them on your plate. But believe me, they're beyond delicious."

After a firm handshake, Periwinkle said, "Your Aunt Connie was thoughtful enough to throw this shindig on a Sunday. That's my only day off from The Twinkle." Then she leaned in to Maura Beth.

"Oh, by the way, I've come up with the catchiest new slogan for my advertising, and I'm having it printed on the next batch of flyers, along with announcing Mr. Place as my pastry chef. How does, 'Eat at The Twinkle—The Restaurant of the Stars,' sound to you?"

"Love it. Ties everything up neatly!" Maura Beth exclaimed. "Your decorations, the star quality of your food. It's a winner!"

"Next time I'm down, I'll have to give your restaurant a try," Jeremy added. "Maybe the weekend of the *Mockingbird* review."

Maura Beth's delight was unrestrained. "You'd come all the way from Nashville for that? Of course, I'm sure you'd be a wonderful addition to the discussion with your teaching skills and knowledge of literature."

"Wouldn't miss it, especially now that I've met the moderator."

Periwinkle gave him a thumbs-up and Maura Beth a wink on the sly. "Well, if you kids will excuse me, I'm starving. So I'm headed over to that seafood spread to see what kind of damage I can do."

No sooner had she left, however, than Connie began ushering over some of her neighbors for an introductory chat. Predictably, Maura Beth put the opportunities to good use.

"You and your husband must come and visit me at the library sometime, Mrs. Milner," she advised one couple, mustering every ounce of her charm. "I'm sure we can find you something of interest to put on your card. You do have one, don't you?"

The stylish matron hemmed and hawed. "You know, I—well, I believe I let mine expire. I'll have to check."

Maura Beth continued to press. "No problem, if it did. We'll get you a new one, and you'll show it next time you go to The Twinkle—oh, you do enjoy The Twinkle, don't you?"

"Why, yes, I think it's marvelous. I especially like all those stars spinning around and dangling from the ceiling. And the food is delicious."

"Those mobiles are creative, aren't they? You know, the owner, Periwinkle Lattimore, is here tonight," Maura Beth continued. "Anyway, next time you go there, you can present your library card and get two-for-one drinks or half off your dessert. And with the new pastry chef Periwinkle just hired, you'll have at least a dozen new scrumptious selections to choose from."

Mrs. Milner's eyes widened as she turned to her husband and smiled. "What a clever idea, George. We must take advantage of it!"

When the next couple confessed that they had seen *To Kill a Mockingbird* at the theater many years ago but had never bothered to read the book, Maura Beth was prepared. "Mr. Brimley, I don't know if I'd say that the movie was just as good as Harper Lee's novel, but it did take top honors in

Hollywood. And I have several posters of Gregory Peck as Atticus Finch to remind myself of that illustrious fact. Meanwhile, I'd love to have you and your wife attend our review at the library, have something delicious to eat, and give us your opinions on the subject in general. Connie's left a stack of flyers over by the buffet table with all the information."

During the lull that followed, Jeremy excused himself when he spotted his mother energetically motioning to join her across the way. Meanwhile, Miss Voncille and Locke Linwood showed up, spilling the good news about the Crumpton sisters and the bumbling bridge game that had won them over.

"As Locke has been reminding me constantly," Miss Voncille explained, "I was completely, but I trust not transparently, incompetent in my play. I've never had such a good time losing."

"Excellent work," Maura Beth said, shaking her hand vigorously. "As I keep telling my clerks, nothing less than standing room only will do for The Cherry Cola Book Club this time around."

"Locke and I are getting an awfully good feeling about this," Miss Voncille replied. "Everyone in the club is certainly doing their part." And then they were off to join the crowd at the buffet table.

But it was when Jeremy finally returned from the visit with his mother that Maura Beth realized the evening would end up being about far more than the library's future.

"Mom wanted a blow-by-blow of how it was going with you," he told her. "She said she was getting tired of trying to read our lips and body language from a discreet distance. Typical mother, huh?"

Maura Beth flashed a smile and couldn't help batting her eyelashes coyly. "And what did you tell her?"

"I said that I wanted very much to see you again and that I hoped you felt the same way. And I didn't mean just for the *Mockingbird* review."

At first Maura Beth said nothing, playing at building the suspense, but she couldn't sustain it for long. "When you have a weekend free of field trips, please give me a call. I think I'd like to discuss everything under the sun with you."

Then they both just stood there, locking eyes and letting that and their smiles do all the talking.

Becca's contribution to promoting The Cherry Cola Book Club had been going splendidly in the weeks since the brainstorming in Brentwood, even if it was a constant hassle to keep Stout Fella focused on the over-the-air role he had been assigned. This particular frosty October morning was no exception.

"Just one more week on the air, sweetheart," she was saying to him as they enjoyed their healthful breakfast of cereal, fresh fruit, yogurt, and coffee at the kitchen table.

He glanced at his watch and groaned. "Why couldn't you have gotten you an afternoon radio show? I'm so tired of getting up at six to get to the station on time."

"It's part of the price you have to pay for being a radio personality," she quipped, after swallowing a spoonful of her Cheerios and sliced bananas. "And you, my dear husband—minus all that weight you've lost so far—are helping my program and Maura Beth's library at the same time. You can catch up on your sleep later, and, believe me, I'll see to it that you do."

He leaned back in his chair and briefly glanced down at his significantly reduced girth, the result of the nutrition regimen and exercise program that had been prescribed for him before he'd come home from Nashville over a month ago. "It still seems like apples and oranges to me. I mean, a Pulitzer Prize–winning novel and weight loss don't exactly go together. Unless, you get so caught up in reading it that you forget to eat."

Becca took a sip of her coffee and chuckled softly. "That's a cute idea for a diet. And who knows—it just might work. But you've finished *To Kill a Mockingbird* now, and you said you really enjoyed it."

"Yeah, it's hard to imagine that things were really like that at one time. Kinda opens your eyes."

Becca pointed her index finger in his general direction. "Now you've got it. That's what Maura Beth wants us to concentrate on during the meeting. How much things have changed here in the South since the novel came out. So if one of my listeners comes up to you and compliments you on sticking with my downsizing program, you just shake up the bottle and get all bubbly about The Cherry Cola Book Club." She swallowed more Cheerios and continued, "Now, have you gone over this morning's script yet?"

He dug into his pocket and pulled out a sheet of paper. "Yes, ma'am. If you'd like to rehearse it with me right now, your Stout Fella aims to please."

She put down her cup, glanced at her own copy on the table, and gave him the go-ahead with a nod. "That's more like it. Okay, we'll skip over my intro—yada, yada, yada. 'And how are we feeling this morning, Stout Fella?' "

He began a line reading that was short on enthusiasm but technically correct. "Why, hello there, Miz Becca Broccoli! I'm feeling on top a' the world, mostly due to your downsizing regimen. So, what delicious recipe are we gonna fix up today for all the good folks listening out there in our beloved Greater Cherico?"

"This one's a real crowd pleaser. How does a honey mustard turkey burger strike you?"

His energy level picked up a tad bit, if only

because it was difficult to deliver the next line without sounding excited. "Bam! Pow! It knocks me out! But here's the big question: Is it a lot of trouble to prepare?"

"That's the beauty of it. It's quick and easy and guaranteed to help get and keep you in shape. By the way, Stout Fella, I know our listeners will want to know how many pounds you've dropped since we started you on our 'Downsizing with Comfort Food' regimen."

At last, his sincerity broke through. "Twenty big ones and counting in a little more than five weeks, and I have to say, I don't miss an ounce."

"Wow! That's quite an achievement. But my Stout Fella has also been improving his mind. As I've been telling you, he's been reading *To Kill a Mockingbird* for the November 6th, seven-o'clock meeting of The Cherry Cola Book Club in the library. And now he's finished it and ready to review it with his fellow Chericoans."

"Yes, I am, and I just wanted to say how much fun I've had getting back into reading. You can, too, by using your library card. Let's shake hands, have something good to eat, and talk about it on November 6th, why don't we?"

Becca gave him a thumbs-up for the enthusiasm he was finally showing. "Great suggestion, Stout Fella. But for now, why don't we get those turkey burgers started by listing all the ingredients you'll need? First, of course, you'll want to pick up some lean ground turkey at your supermarket. Be sure it's fresh, and remember to leave time to thaw it if you buy it frozen. You want your meat to be pliable when you form your patties. Next, some seasoned salt, pepper, paprika, bread crumbs, honey mustard—"

Stout Fella's cell phone suddenly buzzed on the kitchen counter, and he jumped up to answer it, cutting short their rehearsal. Despite the early hour, Becca knew it would be pointless to continue. He was talking to whoever was on the line in his real-estate, negotiating voice that had returned full force scarcely a week after his hospitalization.

But at least she had gotten him to take all his medications regularly, chew his food more slowly, get more rest, and go for those thirty-minute walks the doctor had recommended. Leaving nothing to chance or indifference anymore, she had wisely chosen to accompany him so it wouldn't feel so much like work; and she'd dropped a couple of pounds herself in the process.

"I don't care who that was at this ungodly hour or how close you are to a deal," Becca admonished after he had hung up, clearly on one of his negotiating highs. "You and I are still due at the studio in twenty-five minutes."

"Yes, ma'am," he answered. "Can't disappoint my public. And for the record, I'm nowhere close to a deal yet."

She finished her last bite of cereal and gave him a warm smile. “As long as you take your time.”

He returned to the last of his yogurt and then looked up with a quizzical expression. “Do you think all these plugs you’ve been giving the book club will actually work?”

“Judging by the e-mails I’ve been getting, I have to say it looks promising. Some of my listeners say they’ll drop by and see what all this hoopla is about. But one lady said she didn’t know the library was still open. That’s not good. I’m not about to tell Maura Beth about that one. So my opinion is that we can’t plug away at this enough.”

In the weeks leading up to November 6, no one in the club worked harder at promoting the *Mockingbird* event than Maura Beth did. Picking up on her theme of an under-the-radar political campaign, she explored every nook and cranny of Cherico with her flyers and unflagging charm. She was out of the library more than she was in, but the ever-dependable Renette always covered for her beautifully, and the small cadre of loyal patrons never knew the difference.

On one of her appointments at her trendy salon, Cherico Tresses, Maura Beth talked up a storm to her tall, blond stylist with the edgy, geometric cut, Terra Munrow, after getting permission to leave a stack of flyers on the faux-marble front counter.

To be sure, this was not your grandmother's beauty parlor, given over largely to henna and blue rinses. The clients were mostly younger women, many of them single and therefore still searching for a suitable partner. Perhaps, Maura Beth reasoned, a decent percentage of them might also be readers.

"My goodness," Terra told her favorite customer as she applied a towel to her dripping-wet red hair. "I've never seen you so excited before. You haven't talked that much about the library since I started styling you, but now you can't seem to stop. This book club must be a real big deal."

Maura Beth waited for the towel to come off and then kept at it. "Now, Terra, I've heard you say many times that you just love those Wednesday night potluck dinners at the Methodist church. We've got some delicious dishes at our book club, too. But you also told me once that you liked to read romance novels. I remember telling you to check out our selection at the library, but you've never come in."

Terra exhaled and began combing out Maura Beth's hair. "My schedule is so hectic. But, you know what, I think I'll come in on my day off and check something out. You're one of my best tippers. I owe you the courtesy."

"And what about the book club?"

Terra giggled as she took her scissors in hand. "Why not? Truth is, I used to read a lot more than

I do now. Then my grandmother kinda made me feel guilty about reading romance novels all the time. She claimed those covers with the shirtless men and the women spilling out of their bras, as she so graphically put it, were bad news, and they would rot my mind."

"Bodice rippers and lusty busties."

Terra jerked her head and blinked. "What?"

"In the library business that's what we call the books you just described," Maura Beth explained, enjoying herself thoroughly.

"That's news to me. I just liked them for the fantasy of it all."

But by the time Maura Beth had walked out of the salon freshly coiffed, she was reasonably certain that Terra Munrow would resume her career as a reader and maybe even join the book club as a bonus.

On another occasion, Maura Beth was equally effective proselytizing at The Cherico Market, where she already had her flyer tacked to the community bulletin board just inside the automatic sliding doors. But she wanted to go a step further and decided to go all out with the portly but affable manager, James Hannigan, who had special-ordered many holiday food items for her over the years. She also began to wonder if the relatively sparse use of the library might just be on her more than she cared to admit when she realized she had never once invited Mr. Hannigan to patronize her library. Well, it was way past time to do it.

"Mr. Hannigan," she began one afternoon, seated in his office overlooking the aisles filled with shoppers and their carts below. "I wanted to ask you about your P.A. system, if you don't mind."

"Of course I wouldn't mind. What did you want to know? Is the music too loud? I realize it sounds like elevator music," he replied, clearly puzzled.

"Oh, no. The music is just fine. Just wondering if you'd be willing to use the P.A. to help my library," she told him. "You already know about The Cherry Cola Book Club because you've been generous enough to let me post my flyer here. But I'd like to ask you to go a step further. Would it be out of line for me to request that someone in the store read the flyer to the shoppers several times a day over the intercom?"

Mr. Hannigan raised his eyebrows but looked more amused than anything else. "As in, 'Attention, shoppers!' That sort of thing?"

Maura Beth matched his pleasant expression and lighthearted tone of voice. "Any way you wanted to handle it would be fine with me. We're just trying to let everyone know about our next meeting because we need a healthy attendance. Frankly, the future of the library could be at stake."

"I had no idea," he said, his demeanor darkening

considerably. "But let's just put it this way, Miz Mayhew. You're one of my best customers, particularly around holiday time, so if you think these announcements over the P.A. would do you some good, then let's go ahead and start 'em right away."

"That's very generous of you, Mr. Hannigan. I can't tell you how much it means to me," she answered, handing over another of her flyers. But she wasn't finished yet. "And maybe at the tail end of the announcement about the book club meeting, you could mention to the customers that flyers were available at the checkout counters?"

He laughed big, his entire body shaking for a brief moment. "You're as tough-nosed as one of my route salesmen, Miz Mayhew. But in a delightful way. Don't worry, I'd be happy to help you out here."

"I couldn't ask for more than that. Except maybe your attendance, too."

He cut her off with a playful wink. "I'll see what I can do about juggling my schedule. I'll even talk to the wife." Then he pushed a notepad and pen across the desk in front of her. "Meanwhile, as long as you're here, you might as well give me your special-order list for Thanksgiving and Christmas since they're not very far away. I assume you're in the market for another free-range turkey?"

She smiled warmly and began writing. "Among

other things. It's the time of year I like to splurge."

"We'll get everything to you as usual," he added. "I also have something I'd like to share with you. Most everyone here at the store knows you—all the cashiers and the clerks, the deli people, too. You're one of our favorite customers, and we have a special name for you."

She momentarily abandoned her list and caught his impish gaze. "Don't tell me. I bet I can guess."

"Go ahead, then."

"Something to do with crackers?"

"You got it. You're the Peanut Butter Cracker Lady."

They both had a good laugh, and Maura Beth revealed everything about Mr. Putzel and his behavior.

"I'll share that with the store, Miz Mayhew. Maybe everybody that works for The Cherico Market will show up for your book club meeting."

"I've heard rumors from a certain source," Councilman Sparks was saying to Chunky Badham and Gopher Joe Martin, as the three of them gathered in his office for a last-minute strategy session the day before the *Mockingbird* meeting. "Of course, I'll be attending the book club to-do as usual. But I want both of you working that library full-time tomorrow night, too. It shouldn't be a problem for you. There'll be plenty of food to eat and lots of folks to talk to.

What I want you to be on the lookout for is where people are actually from. It should be easy enough to find out if they live here in Cherico or somewhere else. We need to see if these rumors are true that Miz Mayhew may be bringing in out-of-towners to pump up her numbers and give us a false impression of the library's popularity. Not that we'd be fooled."

Chunky frowned. "What about license plates?"

"What about them?"

"Should we inspect all the parked cars and see if there are any from different states?"

Councilman Sparks took a moment and then cleared his throat. "I want you to stay in the library to circulate, Chunky. There's no point in your roaming the streets at night. Someone may think you're about to steal their car. Besides, a license plate is nowhere near as conclusive as a direct question."

"What about if I ask them if that car with the Alabama plate outside belongs to them?" Chunky continued.

Councilman Sparks was unable to keep from rolling his eyes. "Again, not as direct as asking them if they live in Alabama. Or Tennessee, or anywhere else in Mississippi, for that matter. Either they live in Cherico, or they don't. Either they're regular library users, or this is just a bunch of smoke and mirrors on the part of Miz Mayhew and her fellow travelers."

Chunky busied himself writing things down, while Gopher Joe entered the fray. "What kind of rumors you been hearing?"

"Oh, that this book club meeting has gotten to be the talk of the town. All the little people seem to be excited about it. Also, that there might be a bus coming down from Nashville. I have to hand it to Miz Mayhew. She doesn't give up easily, men. She's been out there beating the bushes."

"Can we eat as much as we want?" Chunky said, having finished his note-taking duties.

"Yes, Chunky, you can go for seconds and thirds if you like. Just remember to also use your mouth for a few questions. Listen, I don't want you two going around frightening people or making them think they're being investigated or something. For God's sake, try to be subtle."

"Gotcha!" Gopher Joe exclaimed, while Chunky settled for nodding his head obediently.

Councilman Sparks dismissed his cohorts and then buzzed his new secretary in the outer office. "That'll be all for today, Lottie. See you on Monday morning bright and early."

"Yes, sir," she answered promptly.

He could picture Mrs. Lottie Howard throwing on her warm coat, padding down the hall and out into the chilly weather. She was a pleasant enough woman, certainly more animated than Nora Duddney had ever thought about being, and she had come highly recommended from friends.

But she was also plain, middle-aged, prone to be forgetful, and addicted to abbreviating his messages with cryptic abandon. Above all else, she was a far cry from the first impression that Maura Beth Mayhew and that wild red hair of hers would have made on anyone walking through his office door.

This was a tough one to take on the chin; firing the listless but reasonably efficient Nora Duddney only to end up with someone who had turned out to be quirky, obstinate, and a hundred other adjectives no businessman ever wanted to deal with in his daily routine.

# 13

# Friends of the Library

The weather decided to cooperate on the day that had been so long in coming. To be sure, it was chilly the way early November often is, but there was no threat of rain to give people an excuse for staying inside their homes and not venturing out in "all that stuff." Maura Beth was happy to have at least one given amid so many unknowns. For instance, would all of Connie's lake house neighbors make an appearance as they had said they would? Would the Crumpton sisters renege after their tainted bridge victory? How many of Periwinkle's customers who had taken flyers would be inspired either to get a library card or attend the potluck and review? What about Becca's diligent radio promotion? Or the many businesses Maura Beth had visited personally to stir up interest?

Then there was the New Gallatin Academy field trip that Jeremy had thrown together over the last couple of days. He was still waiting on last-minute approval from the headmaster. There was also some concern on the part of a few of the parents about the overnight expenses they would incur and the matter of the school being willing to share those with them. If the final decision went

Jeremy's way, twenty-one schoolboys from Nashville would be attending the *Mockingbird* event as part of his inspirational "Living the Classics in the Real World" program.

In fact, Maura Beth was a nervous wreck all morning waiting for Jeremy's phone call. She paced around her purple apartment holding her journal in her hand, having already revisited page twenty-five three different times. She truly believed that this was the most important juncture of her life to date.

When the phone finally rang, she jumped like an armadillo in highway traffic and picked up the receiver in the kitchen with great trepidation. "Hello?" she managed, her face looking as if she were tiptoeing around a coiled snake.

But it wasn't the voice she was hoping to hear. "Hey, it's me," Periwinkle said. "I've got good news. Mr. Place is bringing his mother, Ardenia, with him tonight. She's delightful. I treated them both to dinner a few days after I hired him."

"I'll look forward to meeting her, then."

"How are you holding up, honey?"

Maura Beth knew better than to play games with her friend. "I'm about to lose it waiting for Jeremy to call me about the bus trip. I thought you might be him when you called."

"Sorry about that. But you just listen to me. You told me that you were trying to make the transition from a Melanie to a Scarlett right after that first club meeting. So you be strong and don't fade into the wallpaper. That's strictly for wallflowers."

Maura Beth managed a much-needed chuckle. "Thanks for the reminder. You're the best."

Another hour passed and still no call from Jeremy. It was all she could do to keep from dialing him up, but she focused on Periwinkle's advice instead. "If you can't sit still for this little detail, how are you going to manage the entire evening when it rolls around?" she told herself out loud as she stood in front of her full-length mirror.

Then, another phone call, producing another spurt of adrenaline. This time it was Becca.

"You won't believe this. I'm having unexpected trouble with Stout Fella and his wardrobe," she explained, her exasperation flowing through the line.

Maura Beth briefly held the receiver away from her face and then frowned. "What do you mean?"

"He's acting like a prima donna today. I want him to wear the new three-piece suit I just bought him. Of course, all his old clothes just hang on him. Anyway, he wants to wear his old cowboy clothes from back when he went out line dancing three times a week at The Marina Bar and Grill. He had all of them taken in by a seamstress down at Hodge's Department Store without even telling me. He thinks it'll show off his new athletic frame better. I reminded him that he was still very much a married man, and he said he was just doing it to promote our show more effectively. Really, Maura Beth, there's no one like him."

"Look at it this way, Becca. He'll have plenty of opportunities to wear that suit when he negotiates all those big real-estate deals of his. Meanwhile, why not go ahead and let him be Roy Rogers or Tex Ritter for the evening? Just make sure he doesn't bring a horse into my library. I don't have the budget for the cleanup."

Becca's tension immediately dissolved into laughter. "Maura Beth, you always have the right answer for everything. Cowboy shirt, boots, and jeans, it is, then. And I'll make him keep Trigger in the stable."

They both chuckled, said good-bye, and hung up, but Maura Beth stared at the phone for a minute or two with something that felt a lot like resentment. Was Jeremy ever going to call?

Finally, he did, and Maura Beth could tell by the tone of his "Hello, sorry this has taken so long," that the news was not going to be good. "The majority of the parents thought it was too expensive," he continued, "and the headmaster said we just didn't have the money to send one of the buses down there for—his words here—a 'glorified book report.' Translation: *That* kind of travel money is reserved for the football team's road games."

"I'm so disappointed," Maura Beth said. "We're not off to a good start with our attendance."

"Maybe if I'd thought of it a little sooner and had more time to talk to the parents. Anyway, there is a bit of good news in all this. Three of the families want their boys to attend. So they've ponied up for hotel rooms over in Corinth, and I'll be driving down in a few hours with three of my students and one set of parents as chaperones. I know six is a far cry from twenty-one, but it's better than nothing."

There was a hint of relief in Maura Beth's sigh. "You're absolutely right. You went out on a limb with this ambitious project, but we'll have a good time no matter how many people show up."

After Maura Beth hung up, she paced around the apartment for a while, unable to sit still and calm herself. Having a good time was hardly the goal here. That could easily be done at any bar or restaurant. So much more was at stake, and she began to doubt the effectiveness of her untiring campaign with many of the local businesses. True, the first person had yet to walk through the door of the library, but she couldn't help projecting how many actually would. Numbers flew out of her head and swirled before her eyes. Twelve? Too few. Fifteen? Still not enough. Twenty? The beginning of respectability. Thirty? Was that even possible?

No matter what Periwinkle had said, it was hard work becoming a Scarlett.

• • •

The hours leading up to seven o'clock were as unsettling as the original ultimatum from Councilman Sparks had been several months earlier. Maura Beth spent most of the time in the library lobby, arranging tables, chairs, and posters with Renette Posey and Emma Frost, but no configuration seemed to satisfy her.

"Everything has to be just right," she was telling her clerks after the latest round of musical chairs. "And this isn't it."

Renette walked toward the front door and then turned around, making a frame of her hands. "It's the same semicircle we had last time—only a little bigger. It looks just fine when you first walk in."

But Maura Beth was still shaking her head. "I'm going by instinct here, ladies. Something tells me we need to think even bigger tonight. We only have fifteen folding chairs out there right now. Let's double that, okay? If we have empty seats, we have empty seats. But let's don't get caught scrambling if we're lucky enough to have overflow. It won't look professional, and the last thing I want tonight is to come off like I don't know what I'm doing."

So the three of them dragged more chairs out of the storage closet in the back and began making a double row in front of the podium. Finally, everything was laid out so that it passed muster, and Maura Beth sat down in one of the folding chairs beside her cohorts for a breather. "I've already called everyone who's bringing food and reminded them that they need to be here no later than six-thirty." She consulted her checklist. "Let's see, we have Becca and her grilled chicken breasts with avocado and salsa for those watching their weight; Connie with her fish of the day à la Douglas and *The Verdict*, as she calls it; Miss Voncille and her famous biscuits and green-pepper jelly; Susan McShay with her killer potato salad that she swears by; Periwinkle with éclairs, courtesy of the culinary skills of Mr. Place; and I'm bringing my sheet cake again. Plus, we'll have Becca's cherry cola punch with lime. I think we're all set."

Momentarily, Emma Frost excused herself and headed home to her family, but Renette remained, and it was apparent to Maura Beth that she had something on her mind. She kept biting her lip and cutting her eyes this way and that but was still saying nothing.

Finally, Maura Beth decided it was time to put her at ease. "Did you have something you wanted to tell me?"

Renette straightened up a bit and exhaled. "Well . . . yes. Maybe it's not so important now that you've said that the bus isn't going to be coming down from Nashville. But the other day, Councilman Sparks came by while you were at lunch, and he asked me how things were going. I could tell he meant the *Mockingbird* meeting, of course. And I told him that everything was fine and that we were hoping for a big crowd."

"So?"

"It's just that I got a little carried away and let it slip about the field trip that Mr. McShay was working up at the last minute and that there might be a bus full of schoolboys coming down to boost our attendance. Even while I was talking to him, I could hear myself doing that singsongy thing in my head—you know, 'I know something that you don't know.' But it seems I couldn't wait to tell him. Then he got this weird expression on his face, and he goes, 'Interesting.' That's when I felt that maybe I had said too much. And then today when you told me that the bus wasn't coming, I thought I might have had something to do with messing things up."

Maura Beth quickly reassured her with a couple of pats on the shoulder. "Believe me, you had nothing to do with it, Renette. Don't worry too much about our illustrious councilman and his sidekicks. It's always been up to us to keep the doors of this library open, and tonight's the night we can make that happen. But in the future, I'd only offer to check out the councilman's books for him—that is, if he ever comes around for that. Nothing else."

Renette gave her boss a grateful smile. "Yeah,

I'll remember that next time." Then she hesitated as her expression grew slightly more serious. "There was something else I wanted to tell you. It's strictly good news, though. I've talked two of my girlfriends into coming with me tonight. We've all been rereading *To Kill a Mockingbird* to get ready so we don't come off as a bunch of teenaged airheads. So I just wanted you to know that I'm doing my part."

This time Maura Beth gave her a big hug. "You've always done your part, sweetie. You're the best front desk clerk and assistant I've ever had. But don't tell Emma—you might hurt her feelings."

"No, of course not. Emma's a dear. She's just not a reader."

Then Maura Beth sat back and took a deep breath. "Well, we're just a couple of hours away from our defining moment, I think. I'd like nothing better than to clone myself so I could wish us good luck."

Maura Beth had taken it upon herself to greet people inside the front door of the library, playing the gracious hostess starting around a quarter to seven. It was also going to be her way of keeping an accurate head count for the eventual show-down with Councilman Sparks, who was already sampling the buffet. As it happened, it was Renette and her girlfriends, Deborah Benedict and

Liz Trumble, who were the first recipients of her hospitality.

"Help yourself to food and drink over there, young ladies," Maura Beth said after the introductions. "Renette, you'll show them the way, won't you?"

"Of course." Then she leaned in to whisper in Maura Beth's ear. "I see lots of people eating and drinking already."

"Those are all the book club members, a couple of their relatives from Nashville, and the councilmen," Maura Beth whispered back. "Don't get too excited yet."

After another couple of minutes had passed, Jeremy sauntered in with his three New Gallatin Academy students and the parents who were chaperoning.

"Let me introduce these studious young men who would do any teacher proud," he announced. "We have here just champing at the bit to express their literary insights—Mr. Graham Hartley, Mr. Vernon Garner, and Mr. Burke Williams. We also have Burke's parents, Charles and Louise Williams, who are here to enjoy the evening."

Maura Beth made her manners to the contingent, and Jeremy finished all the hoopla with a peck on the cheek for her. "As I told you over the phone, six is better than nothing," he managed out of the corner of his mouth.

She pulled away slightly for her best smile. "You and I will talk later, Mr. Jeremy McShay of New Gallatin Academy."

By five to seven, no one else had appeared, however, and the sweat began to bead across Maura Beth's forehead. Surely the handful of people who had shown up so far were not going to be the extent of the turnout. Perhaps people were caught in traffic. She nearly laughed out loud at that one. What on earth was she thinking? There was no traffic in peaceful little Cherico. Never had been, never would be.

Seven o'clock arrived, and Maura Beth continued to grasp at straws. Maybe the rest were just going to be late. Yes, fashionably late. That had to be the answer.

Then, finally, one minute past seven, more warm bodies. In this case—the Crumpton sisters. They made a grand entrance, indeed, with Mamie leading the way as usual. They were both overdressed for the occasion in floor-length ball gowns and matching clutches—Mamie in gold and Marydell in silver—giving the unmistakable impression that they had shown up principally to preen and be admired lavishly and often.

"Why, look at all this excitement! I had no idea there'd be so many people here," Mamie began, surveying the lobby and striking a dramatic pose just inside the front door. "I thought this would be more like our 'Who's Who?' meetings. Just a few of us hardy souls with a taste for genealogy and the twists and turns of local history. But Marydell and I are pleased to alter our Sunday evening routine to lend a hand, aren't we, sister dear?"

"Oh, yes," came the answer, along with a predictably weak smile.

Even before Maura Beth had a chance to reply, however, Councilman Sparks stepped up to intercept the sisters by executing a pretentious little bow in front of them and then taking each of them by the arm. "May I have the honor of escorting such a delightful pair of ladies?"

"It seems you've assumed the honor before asking," Mamie fired back. "But exactly where are we going?"

"To the buffet table, perhaps?"

Mamie gently pulled her arm away and looked him straight in the eye. "Durden, I believe I'd like to catch my breath first. Perhaps find a nice seat for the proceedings."

"Then let me at least assist you with that," he continued.

"Enjoy yourselves. Thanks so much for coming!" Maura Beth called out, watching them all move away and shaking her head. She knew quite well that Councilman Sparks was nothing if not deferential to money and social position, particularly when it lived on his street and contributed to his former campaigns.

Then, a trio of women whom Maura Beth did not recognize entered with wide eyes and a hint of confusion in their faces. One was young and slim with her brown hair pulled back in a ponytail, while the other two were matronly and somewhat overweight.

The slim woman spoke up immediately. "Hi, there. I'm Donna Gordon, and these are my friends, Paula Newhouse and Bettye Carter. Sorry we're late. First, we couldn't locate the library, and then we had trouble finding a parking space. We had to walk here from two blocks away."

Maura Beth quickly introduced herself, maintaining a smile while her mind raced. Of course. That was probably why people were showing up late. No off-street parking. And Councilman Sparks had turned her down two years ago in no uncertain terms when she had inquired about creating a parking lot next door.

". . . and we found out about your program because we're all fans of *The Becca Broccoli Show*," Donna Gordon was saying when Maura Beth focused in again. "Not a show went by when she didn't mention you. We thought it might be something fun and different to do. We hadn't thought about the library in years."

Maura Beth beamed. "Well, I'm so pleased you decided to come. Meanwhile, if you'd like to meet and chat with Becca, she's the short blonde standing next to the big guy in the cowboy boots over at the buffet table. And, yes, that's her Stout Fella in all his downsized glory."

The trio thanked her and headed over, making all sorts of excited noises under their breath.

Maura Beth began to feel more comfortable. The head count had risen to fourteen, not counting the club members and the councilmen. Could a respectable number be far behind?

In fact, a steady succession began to stream in. Terra Munrow was all possessive smiles introducing her boyfriend with the conspicuous but undecipherable tattoo on his neck. "This is my Ricky I've been telling you about, Maura Beth. Do you have any books he could check out about motorcycles since he's a biker and all?"

"We sure do. I'd be happy to help you locate them any time you come in, Ricky. And by the way, Terra, we probably have a romance novel or two with guys on motorcycles in the plot."

"Doubly righteous!" Ricky exclaimed while raising a fist in the air; then the two of them were off to the buffet table.

But nothing compared with the group of ten led by James Hannigan that showed up next from The Cherico Market. Once again, as Maura Beth had surmised, finding convenient parking spaces had been the culprit for their tardiness.

"We all ended up two streets over. I kept hoping you wouldn't start without us," Mr. Hannigan concluded.

"I wouldn't have dreamed of it."

Then Mr. Hannigan leaned in with another of his friendly winks. "Good. Because we wanted to support our Peanut Butter Cracker Lady at all costs. And it turns out I've got some readers in the store. They just haven't made the time to find their way to the library before. Guess you lit a fire under 'em with your book club to-do."

When The Cherico Market contingent had finally dispersed, Maura Beth realized that the head count was inching toward thirty. They were probably going to need more chairs—and quickly. So she temporarily abandoned her station and hurried across the room to enlist Renette's help.

"Put down your plate for now, sweetie," she told her. "We're going to be scrambling around after all. Quick, think. How many more chairs do we have in the closet?"

Renette squinted for a moment, moving her lips as she counted. "I think six, maybe seven of the folding. Oh, but we have eight more with the soft cushions in the meeting room."

"Good catch!" Maura Beth exclaimed. "I forgot about those."

"If this keeps up, looks like you'll get your standing room only wish," Renette added as they headed toward the closet.

Nor was Maura Beth's urgency unwarranted. At least a dozen more people came through the front door. Among Connie's lakeside neighbors, the Brimleys and the Milners kept their promises to attend. Then Mr. Place walked in with his mother, who was a bit on the fragile side but still had kind, sparkling eyes.

"I'm Ardenia Bedloe," she said to Maura Beth while extending her hand and smiling graciously. "I know you're not confused by that because my son told you all about changing his name, but I just wanted to thank you for introducing him to Miz Lattimore down at The Twinkle."

"Oh, my friend Periwinkle is deliriously happy with all those delicious pastries he makes. His éclairs have been wowing everyone this evening, including myself."

Mr. Place thanked her and then suddenly spotted Miss Voncille across the room. "Mama, I'd like to go speak to someone over by the food table and introduce her to you after all these years. She's the lady standing next to the white-haired gentleman."

Ardenia trained her thick glasses in the direction of his index finger. "Who is she, baby?"

"Miss Voncille Nettles, my history teacher that first year Cherico High was integrated."

"Oh, yes," Ardenia replied, a smile exploding across her face. "I remember now. You liked her best."

"Please go on over and make yourselves at home," Maura Beth added. "I'm sure she'd be delighted to see you both. And help yourselves to the food and drink."

Among the last six or seven people that showed, two more cited Becca's radio program as their inspiration, while the others credited a flyer from such businesses as The Cherico Market, The Twinkle, Cherico Tresses, or the library itself. Happily, The Cherry Cola Book Club was going to be playing to a full house.

Councilman Sparks took a dim view of the party going on full-blast after he had finished schmoozing the Crumpton sisters. Everyone present was eating, chatting, or laughing the way people do on New Year's Eve or some other carefree occasion. It particularly annoyed him that the library suddenly seemed to have discarded its perennial "just growing mold" personality.

Momentarily, Chunky intruded on his leader's pique. "Man, this sure is a helluva lot a' people in here!"

"It doesn't look good from our point of view," Councilman Sparks replied under his breath, making sure that no one was within earshot. "I'd guess there are between forty and fifty people in this room. We've never had a budget hearing when that many people showed up."

Chunky leaned in and responded in a half-whisper. "I know you told me not to, but I checked out the license plates around the library anyway.

Didn't see but a couple from out of state, both from Tennessee. Davidson County, I believe it was. But there was a bunch from other Mississippi counties. I can rattle off the different ones if you want."

"And no bus anywhere to be seen," Gopher Joe added.

"Oh, never mind all that now. Both of you just go get something more to eat and try to mingle."

Something told Councilman Sparks that he had better monitor the situation closely, however, so he kept both of his charges within an approachable radius. As it turned out, his concerns were definitely warranted.

"Hi!" Chunky said, immediately approaching one of Renette's girlfriends even before he'd helped himself to a plate of food. "What's your name and where do you live?"

The ordinarily extroverted Deborah Benedict shrank visibly from his directness, managing an imitation of a smile. "I might ask the same of you."

"Well, I hope you voted for me. I'm E. A. Badham, one of your city councilmen. But folks call me 'Chunky' most of the time," he continued, while patting his bulging belly. "I guess you can see why."

To her credit, Deborah did not pull away further, but neither did she answer his questions. "Well, then, Chunky, I think you should help yourself to more of this delicious food I'm sampling here. I've seen you make several trips already, if I'm not mistaken."

The lurking Councilman Sparks soon intervened, giving Deborah a nod and a perfunctory smile. "If you'll excuse us for a second, young lady." Then he pulled Chunky aside and lowered his voice. "Change of plans. You and Gopher Joe just concentrate on stuffing your faces. Forget the socializing. I don't know what I was thinking."

There was no denying, however, that most everyone else had the knack of socializing down pat. Especially Maura Beth. From afar, Councilman Sparks watched her flitting around the room with such ease that he actually had to turn away at one point. The library was pulsating with an energy it had never possessed before, and it was all due to the outside-the-box efforts of this unusual woman who just refused to go away. More importantly, it would be difficult to shut down her pride and joy with all this to her credit.

"Are you sure you want to do this?" Maura Beth was saying to Becca. They had managed to slip away into the privacy of the meeting room, closing the door behind them shortly before the actual review was about to begin. "Of course I'd be delighted to have you and Stout Fella here doing cooking demonstrations together every month. We need to get as much activity going in the library as possible."

Becca exhaled and thought one more time about what she had just proposed. "I know it'll help you out. And Stout Fella promised even before he got out of the hospital in Nashville that he'd do his part, too."

Maura Beth gave Becca a thoughtful glance. "So what do you think you should call these meetings?"

Becca took her time before a dramatic intake of air. "How about 'Becca Broccoli in the Flesh'—you know, for those who just can't get enough of the radio show?"

"I certainly like your idea of becoming visible after all those years of just being a voice on the radio."

"You know what gave me the idea?" Becca said, smartly raising an eyebrow. "It was all the conversations I've just had at the buffet table with some of my fans. They kept saying over and over how thrilled they were to see me in the flesh. One of them—I believe her name was Donna—said that putting my face with my voice made me seem all the more real. So I thought, 'Why not meet more of my fans in person and help the library at the same time?' "

Maura Beth was nodding enthusiastically now. "I bet it'll work out great. The only thing I'll need to do is make sure you don't conflict with 'Who's

Who?' and Miss Voncille. We don't want to start a turf war, but I have to admit the idea of people fighting over using the library is something I've been wanting for a long time."

Becca smiled pleasantly and then reached over to gently grasp Maura Beth's hand. "There was something else I wanted to say to you. I've been meaning to for a while. You don't know how much it meant to me—and especially Stout Fella—that you came up to Nashville to visit us in the hospital when you did. That entire balloon thing you invented just brightened our days and nights, and we needed something out of the ordinary to get us through it all."

"Oh, it was nothing," Maura Beth insisted, breaking her grip and waving her off. "I think that little trip helped me out as much as it helped you. I needed to clear my head."

"But there was more to it than that," Becca continued. "I was such a mess when Justin had his heart attack and I thought I might lose him. But all of you rallied around me and kept me going. Connie was the reassuring voice of medical authority, and she and Douglas piled me into the backseat of their car and wrapped me up in a blanket of kindness all the way up to Nashville. His brother and sister-in-law in Brentwood were just as soothing to me, and then you inspired all those balloon bouquets. I remember turning to Stout Fella one evening as he was propped up in bed and saying, 'Nothing bad can happen with all these pretty, playful things floating around us. No one's ever sad at a children's party.' "

Then the two women hugged. "That's the sweetest thing anyone's ever said to me," Maura Beth told her. She glanced at her watch and gave a little gasp. "But I think we need to get started. Our big moment has finally arrived."

After Becca had made her initial announcement about the upcoming "In the Flesh" meetings at the library to the delight of her fans, Maura Beth took back the podium and opened the program in earnest.

"I trust all of you have enjoyed plenty of this delicious food, courtesy of various members of The Cherry Cola Book Club," she began after introducing herself. "It's one of the perks you'll enjoy if you join us, which we hope all of you will do. But the time has come for us to tackle our Southern classic novel, *To Kill a Mockingbird*, written by Harper Lee and published in 1960. As everyone surely knows, this was her only work, but it won the Pulitzer Prize for her, and the film version won several Academy Awards, including Best Actor of 1962 for Gregory Peck." She paused to point toward the Gregory Peck posters and waited for a ripple of female sighs and buzzing to dissipate before again consulting her notes.

"For those who are visiting us for the first time,

we do things a bit differently here in The Cherry Cola Book Club," she continued. "Anyone can summarize a plot and express emotions like admiration, disapproval, or even indifference as a result. Such is the subjective nature of literature. But we prefer to relate that plot to our own lives or even wider issues. So I'm going to suggest that we discuss *To Kill a Mockingbird* tonight in the context of the changes that have occurred here in our beloved South since its publication. That said, do I have a volunteer to go first?"

Jeremy's hand went up immediately. "If you don't mind, I'd like to propose that one of my students begins this discussion with a poem he wrote right after reading the novel."

"I think that would be a lovely beginning," Maura Beth replied, stepping aside and smiling at the fresh-faced New Gallatin Academy contingent sitting on the front row in their navy blue blazers and red ties.

"Ladies and gentlemen," Jeremy continued while getting to his feet. "I'd like to introduce to you Mr. Burke Williams of Nashville, Tennessee."

There was polite applause as the lanky young man with big ears and a deferential demeanor rose and took his long strides toward the podium.

"Thank you," he began, after taking his notes out of his pocket. "Before I read my poem, I'd like to say a few words. My teacher, Mr. McShay, told our class all about The Cherry Cola Book Club, and I wanted to be here no matter what. I know I'm only sixteen and don't know much about the real world, but after I'd finished reading *To Kill a Mockingbird*, I felt like I at least knew a little something. I live in the new millennium, not in the 1930s when the novel is supposed to take place, or even in the 1960s when it was published; but *To Kill a Mockingbird* was like a time machine for me. It enabled me to understand what life was like for a wrongly accused black man like Tom Robinson. I understood how things worked back then and how easy it was for justice to be swept under the rug. So, this is my poem in honor of what *To Kill a Mockingbird* did for me."

He cleared his throat and looked up from his prepared speech. "I know this part by heart." The audience laughed gently and he acknowledged them with a grateful smile. "Okay. Here goes: 'On *To Kill a Mockingbird*,' by Burke Williams:

> The Southern town of ancient birth
> Lies prostrate and fervid under summer's
> sun;
> The children of Atticus play in the yard,
> Engrossed in the realms of fantasy and
> fun;
> Then the tranquil streets grow frigid with
> anguish
> As a man of color struggles to live
> Under the wing of Atticus's justice—

Of all the benevolence one man can give;
The wrath of prejudice flows through the
veins
Of those who would try the innocent man;
And here, as o'er earth, life's chances
unjust—
Despite brave attempts to fashion a stand;
But yet as the stars on the face of God's
sky,
Subtly as sweet scents of roses in bloom,
The town slips again into everyday life,
Forgetting the storm and the tears and the
doom."

The polite reception of a few minutes earlier became healthy applause, and the young man blushed, hanging his head at first. But Jeremy's hand signals urging him to lift his chin had an immediate effect, and Mr. Burke Williams accepted his moment in the sun with an ingratiating, boyish smile.

"That was beautifully done, Mr. Williams!" Maura Beth exclaimed, after he had resumed his seat and the reaction had finally died down. "Your insights show a great deal of maturity."

Before Maura Beth could ask for another volunteer, however, Mr. Place stood up, gently waving his hand. "If you don't mind, Miz Mayhew, I have a little something I'd like to contribute. Could I speak next?"

"Of course, come right on up."

Once he was comfortable behind the podium, Mr. Place caught his mother's eye with a smile and began. "Ladies and gentlemen, although Cherico is my hometown, I didn't know what to expect when I left Memphis after losing my job as a pastry chef at the Grand Shelby Hotel. I'd been working at that for decades and would have retired at it up there, too. But you may have read that the hotel went out of business and was torn down recently. So that brought me back home to live with my mama for a while until I could find another job."

He paused to acknowledge first Maura Beth and then Periwinkle with nods and hand gestures. "I found one a lot quicker than I thought I would, thanks to Miz Mayhew here and Miz Lattimore sitting right there on the front row. In case some of you didn't know, I'm now the pastry chef down at The Twinkle. As we like to say here in the South, 'Y'all drop by and see me sometime, ya hear?' "

A spate of warm laughter erupted, and Mr. Place wagged his brows until it tailed off. "So that brings me to our topic tonight—how things have changed here in our South since *To Kill a Mockingbird* appeared. I saw the movie when I was a boy. That's what I want to talk to y'all about next. It played here in Cherico at the old Starbright Theater on Commerce Street, which as we all know, got torn down a while ago. You have to go somewhere else to see movies these days. At the time, my mama made extra money for us by babysitting for white families, and she'd take me with her now and then. I made friends with the son of one of those families. You good folks might remember the Wannamakers over on Painter Street? Since I got back, I found out they don't live here now."

That produced a buzz of recognition among the crowd, and Mr. Place waited for it to die down. "Anyway, I became good friends with Jamie Wannamaker, who was about my age, and we played together out in his yard, doing things that little boys do together like catching fireflies and hide-and-seek. Then, my Mama saw where *To Kill a Mockingbird* was coming to the Starbright. That was back when the *Daily Cherico* was still in business, and she read an article all about it in the paper. She told me, 'Baby, I'm taking you to see that movie. I believe we both need to see it!' "

Mr. Place paused and smiled thoughtfully, shaking his head at the same time. "I didn't understand at the time why she felt that way. Now, of course, I do. But the world is full of strange coincidences, I've found out. Don't know why they happen, but when they do, there's always a lesson to be learned, it seems. Turns out, the very afternoon my mama took me to see *To Kill a Mockingbird* at the Starbright, Miz Wannamaker decided to take Jamie to see it, too. Back then, everybody bought tickets at the booth in front, but only the white people got to go in that way. The coloreds, as they called us back then, went around to the side door to enter the colored section. Some of you might remember that it was much smaller than the white side, but there was a thin wall separating the two."

Again, there was a ripple of noise throughout the audience. "I'll never forget what happened next. Jamie said to his mother right after he'd spied me, 'Oh, this'll be so much fun. We can all sit together.' And she had to tell him that he couldn't sit with me, and I couldn't sit with him, and you could tell she didn't want to go into an explanation of the white and colored thing—just that there'd be a wall between us. Then Jamie started crying, and he wouldn't stop. It was the strangest thing. I was the one who felt real bad for him. I was the one comforting him. You see, I'd been to the Starbright before, and I knew where the coloreds were allowed to sit. So I said, 'Jamie, maybe we can't sit together, but we can be right next to each other. We just have to pretend the wall isn't there.' And he said, 'But how will we know where to sit if we can't see?' And this is what I came up with. I decided that we'd move slowly along either side of the wall, row by row, and make a pounding noise each time. When we'd both found a seat we liked on the edge, we would pound five times. Fortunately, both our mothers didn't make a fuss and let us do it. But I've never forgotten all the trouble we had to go to just to pretend we were together. Today, anyone can go to the movies over in Corinth or up to Memphis, and they don't give a hoot about anything, not even how much noise you make. I sure wish they'd crack down on that—and the prices you have to pay for candy and popcorn."

That produced some much-needed laughter. Then Mr. Place continued, "So it's my belief that *To Kill a Mockingbird* helped tear down that wall in the theater between the whites and the coloreds. Everywhere else, too. That book and that movie helped to make all the fair play we take for granted now possible, and that's pretty much what I had to say here tonight. That, and it's good to be home again in Cherico with my mama and a great job. And don't forget to come by and sample my pastries at The Twinkle. Even if you're on a diet, treat yourself once in a while."

A round of applause even more vigorous than that for Burke Williams erupted, as Mr. Place headed back to his seat, nodding graciously all the way.

"Thank you for that interesting and heartfelt testimony, Mr. Place!" Maura Beth exclaimed. "So much food for thought along with good food to eat."

Then Miss Voncille stood up. "I think all this has inspired me to contribute something, too."

"By all means, step up. We welcome what you have to say."

Miss Voncille approached the podium with gusto as Maura Beth stepped aside. "I had no idea I would be saying anything tonight. I'd made up my mind just to sit and listen. But as young Mr. Williams was talking, I realized that I, too, had a story to tell. It's about my long career as a schoolteacher here at Cherico High. Looking out into the crowd tonight, I can see many familiar faces that I taught. Only, some of the names seem to have changed. When you were my student, Justin Brachle, Stout Fella had yet to see the light of day. And your wife, Becca Heflin, was a few years away from her alter alias of Becca Broccoli on the radio. Then there's Edward Badham, who now goes by the name of 'Chunky,' I believe; and 'Gopher Joe' sitting right next to him is the former Josephus Martin. Of course, I must point out Councilman Durden Sparks, who decided to leave his name alone."

Everyone mentioned was nodding and chuckling, and Miss Voncille paused briefly for a breath. "But let me not forget Mr. Parker Place, who went by the name of Joe Sam Bedloe when I taught him. He was, in fact, a member of my very first integrated classroom, and a very good student he was."

Mr. Place smiled big at his former teacher and gave her a neat little salute. "And you were a great teacher, Miss Voncille. Tough, but great. But I don't remember being all that good a student in your history class. I had trouble remembering dates."

"But you were attentive, and you tried hard. Anyway, none of that is really the main point," she continued, returning his smile. "I wanted to confess something here in public for the first time. I remember the fall Cherico High was getting ready for the first wave of integration. Of course, all of my fellow teachers were white, and some of them were very apprehensive, including myself. Mrs. Johnnie-Dell Crews was the most vocal in the teachers' lounge. 'I don't know what to expect,' she would say all the time while we were having our morning coffee and doughnuts. 'Do you think there'll be any trouble with the coloreds?' "

Miss Voncille seemed a bit hesitant to continue but finally gathered herself. "That was the way people talked back then, and it was definitely on our minds. So I'm here to confess that there were moments when I allowed myself to succumb to my worst fears, and I'm not proud of it. There were those at the time who thought the world would come to an end because Cherico High was going to be integrated. But the world kept on spinning when it finally happened. I found that I had worried needlessly, and when I got students in my class like Joe Sam—I mean, Mr. Place—I felt ashamed that I had doubted myself and my ability to teach even for an instant. Helping him learn was what it was all about—the same goal I'd always had for every student I ever taught."

Mr. Place raised his hand, almost as if he were back in the classroom, but did not wait to be called on to speak. "Miss Voncille, I can tell you what it was like from my point of view, if you'd like to hear it."

"Please tell us, Joe Sam—oops, there I go again. Sorry, I just can't seem to get used to all these name changes."

He waved her off. "Don't worry about it. Anyway, I was just as nervous as you and the other teachers were. My mama sitting right here next to me tonight said to hold my head up high, be calm and respectful no matter what anyone said to me or called me, and to do my best, but I was still scared. There'd been killings and bombings in the state in the years leading up to integrating the school, so that was always in the back of my mind. Nothing terrible like that ever happened to me or my family, thank God, but we had friends in other parts of the South that had some close calls. But the thing I remember most from my first day was the way you smiled at me when you called the roll in homeroom and came to my name, Miss Voncille. There was something about the way you said, 'Joe Sam Bedloe?' that made me feel just like the other students. You pronounced it so it didn't stand out, like I had always been around. Like I belonged there. It made me relax and pay attention from then on to my lessons, not some worst-case scenario running around my head."

Miss Voncille nodded approvingly. "Yes, it was a time for putting out feelers for all of us. But even though my subject was history, I read *To Kill a Mockingbird* when it first came out and Miss Nita Bellows in the English department had recommended it to me so highly. Looking back on it, I'm convinced that reading it before integration actually occurred a few years later helped prepare me for the changes to come. I believe the novel is full of a certain prescience in that way. My final thought is that *To Kill a Mockingbird* seems to be saying to you, 'This might have been the way things were at one time here in the South, but these words will see to it that they don't stay like that much longer.' "

"And I think we would all agree things have changed for the better," Maura Beth pointed out. "Your analysis is certainly well-taken. Does anyone have a further comment or angle to discuss?"

"I like the prescience angle," Jeremy added from his chair. "I've always told my students that the novel was an instant classic when it was released. What that really means is that it tapped into something that had been on a lot of people's minds over the years and verbalized it precisely. I believe it prepared the country for the turmoil to come, as Miss Voncille and Mr. Place have expressed in a very personal way. It was a novel both very much before its time and right on time."

Miss Voncille nodded graciously and said, "I can't top that." Then she stepped away from the podium to generous applause.

Mr. Place rose again briefly once Miss Voncille had resumed her seat. "My mother, Mrs. Ardenia Bedloe, would like to say something at this time."

"By all means," Maura Beth said, gesturing graciously in her direction. "Would you like to take the podium?"

Ardenia shook her head. "I believe I'll stay right here, if you don't mind. My arthritis has been acting up lately."

"Then please go right ahead."

"Well, when I was growing up in this town a long time ago now, I wasn't allowed to check out books in this very library. I wanted to. I wanted to read more fairy tales and look at more picture books after I'd finished with the ones Santa Claus brought me for Christmas, but I couldn't get a library card. Nobody in my family could. That was before Miz Annie Scott came in the sixties and way before *To Kill a Mockingbird*, even. So to be here this evening enjoying the food and the company and feeling so welcome the way I do is the sweetest thing in the world to me. I don't believe I thought things would ever change back when I was a little girl, but they have. They really have."

Maura Beth felt something catching in her throat as she responded. "Thank you, Mrs. Bedloe. I'm sure everyone here appreciates your candor. As for myself, I've been working very hard to make this library an integral part of Cherico for everyone. This book club is my most comprehensive effort yet. I've been library director for six years, and in many respects I now consider myself a Chericoan. But there are things some of you probably don't know. If we still had a newspaper, you likely would have gotten wind of it by now. But since we don't, I feel it's my duty to inform you that this library is in real danger of being closed down at the end of the year. It should come as no surprise to hear that Cherico is not exactly swimming in money, and our City Council will have to make some tough decisions in the years ahead. One of them may be to stop funding the library and use the taxpayers' money elsewhere."

Maura Beth's revelation was creating quite a stir throughout the gathering, causing Councilman Sparks to rise from his seat. "Unfortunately, what Miz Mayhew has just said is correct. The library is a huge drag on our budget, and we'd like to put that money to better use by creating an industrial park to attract new jobs to the community."

"But if I may continue, Councilman," Maura Beth said, careful to keep a pleasant tone in her voice, "what I wanted to emphasize was that this event tonight proves that the library can be a much more valuable community asset than it has been for many decades. If it can regularly accommodate groups like 'Who's Who in Cherico?' and the proposed 'Becca Broccoli in the Flesh,' and, of course, The Cherry Cola Book Club, it is performing a useful service. Over time, that usefulness will expand and become more essential, and the taxpayers will more than get their money's worth. Those who support the library for these and other purposes such as student research after school hours and adults hunting for job leads should make their views known to Councilman Sparks and City Hall as soon as possible."

"What about right now?" Miss Voncille put in quickly, waving her hand energetically.

Knowing better than to cross her, Councilman Sparks deferred. "Go ahead, then, Miss Voncille. Speak your piece to us."

"I will do just that, Durden. You can't brush aside us library users so casually. I've had a wonderful ally in Maura Beth Mayhew for my 'Who's Who?' organization from the day she arrived here in Cherico. Yes, Annie Scott was cooperative, too, but she was never as pleasant about it the way Maura Beth has been. Annie always acted like I was bothering her, intruding on her precious time, whereas Maura Beth has given me the respect a devoted daughter would have."

Surprisingly, Mamie Crumpton was out of her seat. "My sister and I always look forward to coming to the library and hearing what Miss Voncille has to say. We enjoy the sense of continuity. Our parents were big library users. And, Durden, a little birdie told me not too long ago that you were seriously considering this library closure. Of course, I was shocked, and you might as well know that such a move would not be without consequences, I assure you."

Councilman Sparks dropped his trademark smile as he responded. "I understand and respect what you're saying, Mamie, but these club functions can easily be accommodated elsewhere, and, I might add, with more space available in the homes of private citizens, to name at least one alternative. Tonight, this library appears to be bursting at the seams, but it might also be considered something of a dog and pony show. Emphasis on the show. I think we all know very well that the library usually just sits here collecting dust, your genealogy meetings excepted."

Maura Beth intervened, feeling the anger rising in her blood but managing to steady herself. "With all due respect, Councilman, I think what has been discussed here tonight so far has been substantive. We've brought some very diverse elements of the community together to reflect upon their shared history and, by the way, just have an old-fashioned good time together. How many things can you say that about? I think The Cherry Cola Book Club has a promising future, and I trust it will take place right here."

Surprisingly, it was Becca who took the floor next. "If I could just say something. Mrs. Bedloe triggered some pleasant memories for me. I'm so sorry she couldn't come to the library and use it in her day, but I could and did in mine. My mother enrolled me in summer reading every year, and I had a ball. At the time, Miz Scott gave out blue ribbons if we read so many books between the first of June and the end of July. If you fell short, you still got a red ribbon. Let me tell you, I still have every ribbon of every color I won tucked into one of my scrapbooks up in the attic somewhere. It would be a shame not to let Cherico's current crop of children earn those kinds of memories during all the summers ahead of us."

But Councilman Sparks would not back down. "I don't want to come off as the bad guy here, Miz Brachle, but the library is just not an essential service. There are other departments that everyone here would agree we can never do without, such as police, utilities, water, sewage, and fire protection. On the bright side, if our proposed Cherico Industrial Park does bring in industries the way we hope it will, maybe then with more taxes to collect we can consider reopening the library down the road."

"But closing it isn't a done deal, is it?!" Donna Gordon exclaimed out of nowhere. "My friends and I were looking forward to coming to Becca Broccoli's demonstrations, and we were even going to start checking out some cookbooks. We browsed through the stacks before the meeting got started and we really liked the selection."

"Yeah! You can't cut us off just when we're getting started!" Terra Munrow complained. "I spotted some off-the-wall hairstyling books I'd like to read, and my boyfriend found a motorcycle repair manual he wants to check out when he comes back tomorrow to get his library card. Please don't dangle the library in front of us and then snatch it away!"

Locke Linwood got to his feet next. "And I want to say that The Cherico Library and I go back a long way. When I was a little boy, I was hooked on all the Hardy Boys mysteries. I checked out and read every one because at the time I thought I wanted to be a detective when I grew up. Of course, I ended up selling life insurance instead, but I never forgot the sense of wonder and adventure that those books instilled in me. And the library helped sustain me later in life when the sailing got a big rough." Then he sucked in air and lifted his chin with authority. "When my dear wife got terminally ill a few years ago, I checked out as many books as I could find on being a caregiver. I did what I could for her all the way to the end. I'd like to think that the answers I found would always be available to others in their time of need."

Locke's testimony inspired James Hannigan to stand up. "He's right, you know. When my mother passed away, I was having a tough time accepting it. It was so traumatic for me because she died unexpectedly in her sleep. But then my pastor suggested that after I'd finished praying, I go to the library and see if they had any books on dealing with grief." He paused to gesture at Maura Beth. "And Miz Mayhew, you had several for me to choose from. I checked them all out, and as I read them, I began to see that other people had gone through this and come out at the other end ready to get on with their lives. I was able to make my peace, and I accomplished that with a little prayer and my library card. That's another reason I was so eager to help you out."

Maura Beth finally stepped into the respectful lull that followed. "I'm fighting back tears when I say that everything I've just heard from all of you defines what a library is and what it does for a community. All of you are true friends of the library. I'm not sure you can put a price on that, Councilman Sparks."

"Perhaps not," he answered with no trace of his customary arrogance. "But the City Council has to consider the big picture in running this town. Next year's budget will be finalized exactly two weeks from tomorrow. Money is tight, and we're looking for ways to funnel more of it into Cherico. We've had the industrial park on the front burner for some time now, but we'll make our final decision on the library at that time. All of you are welcome to attend."

For a few seconds, Maura Beth felt like she'd lost the battle. This was not the way it was supposed to happen. How could anyone not be impressed with everything that had gone on in the library tonight? She had expected a clear decision in her favor and was temporarily at a loss for words.

But Miss Voncille had no trouble expressing herself. "I'll get a letter and e-mail campaign going, Durden Sparks. I'll rustle up a list of my former pupils and put them on the job. Then you'll have to keep the library open!"

"Miss Voncille," he replied in a tone that was semi-conciliatory, "I have not made my decision yet, and all opinions will be welcomed as the Council reviews the matter. But have you considered that the town of Cherico can do everything a little better with more revenue flowing in? Meanwhile, using library money to pay for movie posters of Gregory Peck seems a bit extravagant to me."

Maura Beth motioned for Miss Voncille to resume her seat and was somehow able to conjure up a smile. "You seem to have covered all bases,

Councilman Sparks. But I want it noted as a matter of public record that Connie McShay, the treasurer of The Cherry Cola Book Club, paid for those posters of Gregory Peck with her own money. They didn't cost the library a cent. So now, if you don't have any objections, I think we'd like to wind up our discussion of *To Kill a Mockingbird*."

"Of course," he answered, turning to head toward the door with Chunky and Gopher Joe. "We're at cross-purposes regarding the library, but I'm sure we both want what's best for Cherico. Now, if you'll excuse us, please."

Maura Beth watched the three of them leave the building, while the Scarlett side of her that she had been cultivating so meticulously seethed with frustration. "Just don't count me out!" she exclaimed finally.

"I never have!" Councilman Sparks returned just before making his exit.

Some of the crowd moved forward to chat with and console Maura Beth, but the words seemed to blend together after a while. One remark stood out, however, when Jeremy said, "I truly wish I could stay a little longer to help you figure out what to do next, but I have to drive the boys over to the hotel in Corinth. Burke Williams wanted to say something to you before we left, though."

The lanky young poet approached Maura Beth shyly, barely able to look her in the eye, but his message struck home. "I hope you don't think this is out of left field, Miz Mayhew, but I keep thinking about the character of Boo Radley in *To Kill a Mockingbird*. How he quietly saved the day there at the end when everything seemed so desperate, I mean. Maybe someone or something like that will happen for you and your library so you'll stay open."

Maura Beth gave him a hug and smiled as he blushed crimson. "Thank you for that, young man." Then she pulled back and turned to Jeremy. "And thank you for bringing these bright young students of yours to The Cherry Cola Book Club. To know that they exist, caring about literature the way they do, gladdens this librarian's heart."

Most of the people left shortly after the unexpected showdown between Councilman Sparks and Maura Beth, but the Brachles, McShays, Locke Linwood, Miss Voncille, and Periwinkle had remained for an impromptu strategy session. Mr. Place wanted to participate as well, but his mother had grown a bit weary, so he understandably drove her home after wishing the core of the book club the best of luck.

"We've got City Hall on the defensive," Maura Beth was explaining to the group gathered around the meeting room table with their serious demeanors in place. "But we can't let up. All of that testimony we heard tonight on the library's behalf was terrific and reassuring, but what we need now is signatures. I say we circulate petitions to keep the library open and then present it to the City Council. Those signatures represent votes, and if I know anything about politicians, they'll pay attention to that when they ignore everything else."

Connie was the first to come on board with enthusiasm. "Absolutely. And we have the perfect starter list, since we asked everyone to write their names, phone numbers, and e-mail addresses on the bulletin board sheet. They can be our first contacts."

Maura Beth smiled and shook her head at the same time. "Well, not quite, Connie. Our patron list will be our first call. But tonight's list won't be far behind."

The suggestion gathered further momentum. "I could put up one petition at The Twinkle," Periwinkle added. "And we could ask the other businesses that have been helping us out with the publicity to do the same."

Maura Beth brightened further. "I bet James Hannigan will make more P.A. announcements for us at The Cherico Market. He's a sweetheart, and he really rounded up his troops tonight. I nearly cried when he told that story about his mother."

"Same here," Becca added. "But we'll publicize the petitions on the show, won't we, Stout Fella?"

"Yes, ma'am," he answered in his most playful tone.

"And I was serious about contacting my former students," Miss Voncille added. "I've kept in touch with some of the ones that never left Cherico."

"Every signature counts," Maura Beth answered.

"Was it just me, or did y'all think that Councilman Sparks might have softened up there at the end?" Douglas wanted to know.

Maura Beth looked amused and caught his gaze, every inch a Scarlett sizing up a formidable situation. "Douglas, that man is a piece of work. I've dealt with him for six years now, and he has agendas coming out the wazoo. We can't go by what he said tonight because the truth is, I've never seen him not get his way. He's hell-bent on creating that industrial park for his greater glory, so it's my opinion that we need to impress him where he lives and breathes. And that, my friends, is with the votes he prizes above everything else. Those signatures are our best shot at keeping this library open."

Locke Linwood pounded his fist on the table for emphasis. "I'm all in. I can contact all my former life insurance customers here in Cherico. You know, I was pretty good at selling policies all those years."

"Go for it, Mr. Linwood!" Maura Beth exclaimed, giving him a wink.

Connie and Douglas exchanged glances, and he said, "We don't know that many people, but we'll keep our neighbors in the loop. They were interested enough to show up tonight, so I don't see why they won't help us out with this. They could certainly network with their friends who care about the library."

"You just design those petitions, and I'll have them printed up for you," Connie added.

Maura Beth took a deep breath while she quickly scanned the room, admiring her very own fearless army of library soldiers. That was yet another course they should have taught in library school—Introduction to Going to War for the Patrons. "I couldn't ask for more support, but we simply can't fail in this. When that budget is approved a couple of weeks from now, the library must not be removed as a line item." There was momentary silence, but then Maura Beth summed it all up. "We're The Cherry Cola Book Club, and we're just not going to let that happen."

# 14

# Two Weeks and Counting

The instant Maura Beth opened the front door of the library the next morning, she found herself entertaining a dark premise. What if all the petitions they were about to circulate failed to excite people or made no difference, no matter what? In that case, this carefully cultivated turf of hers would suddenly become alien terrain. It would no longer be hers to manage and manipulate, to try and improve, or simply to inhabit with professional pride. Six years of hard, mostly thankless work would then be discarded like dead flowers in a vase of stale, discolored water.

But when she plunked herself down at her desk a few minutes later, she chided herself out loud for her pessimistic ramblings. "You, Maura Beth Mayhew, are being most un-Scarlett-like today. Have you no confidence in your ability to pull this out of the fire and keep the enemy at bay?"

Perhaps the long-distance conversation she'd had with her mother when she'd gotten home from the confrontation with Councilman Sparks the evening before had coaxed her doubts out of hiding. "Come on home, honey, just come on home," her mother had said in response to hearing about the possibility of Maura Beth losing her job.

"You can find something better down here where you're closer to your family. We've all missed you so much. Just pack your bags and come back where you belong. You know we'll take care of you."

Maura Beth had long known that William and Cara Lynn Mayhew had never approved of her moving to North Mississippi, especially when she had told them what she would be earning. Apparently, it had never occurred to them that they should be thrilled she had gotten a directorship on the heels of her graduation, applauding her moxie.

Instead, "We'll send you money anytime" had been their initial mantra; followed by the overly dramatic, "Don't worry about getting by. No child of ours is going to clip coupons and go to thrift shops."

Except for the rust-colored sofa—which she had not asked for—and the brass bed—which she had—Maura Beth had resisted financial assistance from her parents. Cherico was her big chance to prove herself, to make a mark on her own. Now she must bear down harder than ever if she intended to achieve the goals on page twenty-five of her college journal.

She had, in fact, just hung up with Connie about the logistics of putting the petition together when Renette knocked at her door and asked to speak with her.

"What's on your mind?" Maura Beth said, once Renette had taken her seat.

"It's what happened last night at the book club meeting," she began, hanging her head. "I never realized politicians could be so scary."

"Dealing with Councilman Sparks in particular is never easy," Maura Beth explained. "Don't let him upset you, although I realize you haven't had as much practice as I have."

But Renette started tearing up anyway. "It's just that if the library does close down—well, I know it will be hard on you. I've seen how much running this library has meant to you. I've seen how hard you've worked at it, and it's inspired me to be the very best front desk clerk Cherico's ever had. Plus, I'll never find a boss as good as you are if I have to get another job."

Maura Beth quickly explained the decision to create the petitions and then moved to Renette to give her a warm hug. "That's sweet of you to worry about me, but you may not even have to do any job hunting. But if the worst happens and you do, you'll probably find a boss that's even better. Now I want you to run to the ladies' room and dry your eyes. After all, we're still up and running, and you're the first impression our patrons get when they walk into the lobby. We don't want them thinking you've been up all night crying. Oh, and get those girlfriends of yours to come in and sign that petition in the next two weeks. And tell them to tell their friends, too."

Renette smiled even as she sniffled. "When are you going to put it up on the bulletin board? Seems like every minute counts."

"Connie McShay is having it printed and copied later today," Maura Beth told her. "She'll be dropping by to tack it up. Then the countdown begins."

After a couple of hours had passed, Maura Beth was pulled away from her petition networking by another knock at her door. "Come in," she announced, wondering if Renette needed further reassurance.

But it was loyal, matronly Emma Frost who appeared instead. "Excuse me, Miz Mayhew. I know I'm prob'ly intruding, but Renette called me up this morning to tell me what went on here last night. I'm sorry I couldn't come, but my husband has a real bad cold, and I don't want it to go into the flu. We just can't afford to have him miss any more workdays. So I had him all bundled up last night, stuffing him with my best home remedies. I know it's not my day to be here, but I just couldn't let this news about the library pass without coming in to say something to you."

"I completely understand. But have a seat for a minute." After Emma had pulled up her chair, Maura Beth continued, "I trust Renette didn't tell you that the library was definitely being closed."

Emma worked her hands into a nervous tangle as she spoke. “Well, I sorta got that impression. And I know we’ve had our share of days without a soul showing up, but I need this job in the worst way to help my family make ends meet. Do you think we really will be shut down?”

Maura Beth gave her an engaging smile, realizing that this was definitely an occasion to bring out the best of both Melanie and Scarlett as she had once promised to do. “You have faith, Emma. We’ll do everything we can over the next two weeks to prevent that from happening with the petitions we’re circulating. Meanwhile, there’s something you can do to help. Tell all your family and friends to come to the library and sign that petition to keep it open. You march straight home and get things started.”

Emma thanked her for the pep talk and left, after which Maura Beth sat back in her chair with a sense of accomplishment. She and her staff must keep it together and plug away at the end game. In fact, every member of The Cherry Cola Book Club must meet that challenge without flinching.

Connie and Douglas McShay were sitting in front of their great room fire discussing their efforts on behalf of the library exactly one week before the budget approval.

“There’s got to be more we can do,” Connie was saying, frustration creeping into her voice.

"We've got everyone we know out here covered, but that's only half a dozen people. Maybe a dozen if the Brimleys, the Milners, and the Paxtons follow up with a few of their friends."

Douglas gave her a little hiccup of a chuckle and wagged his brows. "Surely you're not suggesting we go around badgering strangers at their front doors like Jehovah's Witnesses?"

She punched his arm playfully and snickered. "No, but Maura Beth actually *is* going door-to-door on Commerce Street. I offered to help, but she insisted she had it covered. Meanwhile, Becca and Stout Fella are mentioning the petition every day on the radio show, Miss Voncille and Locke Linwood say they've heard from lots of her students and his customers, and—"

"Okay, okay, I get it," Douglas said, holding his hand up in surrender. "Listen, it's not like we haven't pitched in all along. We've paid for posters and flyers and printing up the petition and that monster seafood party we had out here. I don't think you should be beating yourself up as if you've done nothing."

Connie shrugged with a pleasant smile. "I'm not really. I just want to collect as many signatures as I can for Maura Beth." Suddenly, she snapped her fingers and bore into him with her eyes. "Of course. The Marina Bar and Grill. At last, something useful will come of your haunting that place."

"Haunting? Come on, I go for an occasional beer, that's all," he insisted.

"Do they like you out there?"

He drew back in disbelief. "Uh—yeah. I'm not the Creature from the Black Lagoon. Although I felt like it sometimes in the courtroom."

"I've been thinking about that since we retired here," she began, gently rubbing his arm. "I guess all this fishing really does help you forget some of the legal stunts you had to pull over the years."

Douglas looked suddenly uncomfortable, and he did not answer her for a while. "I suppose you could make a case for that. A guy can put up with only so much stress in his life, you know; and it's not like you didn't have plenty of it in the hospital day and night."

"Yes, I did."

"And you've always had your books to read to keep yourself on an even keel, right?"

She nodded dramatically, widening her eyes. "Going to the library to check out my novels has always been my great escape. I get to explore someone else's mindset for a while. It's a very sane exercise. More people should try it."

"So what do you want me to do out at The Marina Bar and Grill?"

"Ask the owner if you can put up the petition, at the very least," she began. "And then talk it up with your drinking buddies. Well-lubricated people are more apt to listen to what you have to say."

He gave her a little smirk. "Or forget it."

"Never mind that. Don't you guys bond watching football games and other sports out there all the time?"

Douglas laughed out loud. "You make The Marina Bar and Grill sound like one of those tree houses that little boys build where little girls aren't allowed. There are wives and girlfriends on the premises. Women fish, too."

"I can't believe you just said that!" she exclaimed, turning to face him directly now.

"Why? You don't believe me? You don't think women can bait hooks?"

"Don't be absurd. Of course I believe you. It was the perfect segue for something else I wanted to discuss with you. It's about the details of our retirement. I feel like we're leading two separate lives again, just the way we did in Nashville when we put everything we had into our careers. This was supposed to be a new start for us."

"But I think last night at the library went well for us," he pointed out. "Maybe not at the end there for Maura Beth with Councilman Sparks jumping down her throat the way he did, but you and I had a good time together, didn't we?"

"That begs the question. We still spend most of our time apart. You're out there with your beer and your fish, and I'm here inside waiting for you to get your fill. The truth is, the rain brings you in more often than the sound of my voice does. If this is the way it's going to be, I'd rather go back to Nashville where I had Susan and Paul and so many other friends to do things with."

Douglas turned to her with a puzzled expression, briefly shutting one eye. "I thought you considered these Cherry Cola people your friends. You've just finished saying how much helping Maura Beth means to you. Matter of fact, I think we've both made some nice new friends in the book club. Paul and Susan like them, too."

"They are our friends, and I'm thankful for them and the things we've done together. But they can't fill up all of my days or any of my nights. We can only expect so many visits from Lindy and Melissa or Susan and Paul. You and I have to manage the rest of the time together. Since we moved, it's almost like retiring has given us permission to stop working at our marriage."

He folded his arms and made a brief hissing sound. "I don't think I'm such a slouch in bed, if that's what you're implying."

"I'm not talking about that," Connie said, throwing up her arms in frustration. "Your true passion now is fishing, and that wall of photos across the room is proof. Retiring down here has made me realize that I come second."

"Now you're really exaggerating," he said, the annoyance clearly evident in his voice. "But if you truly think that way, then let's talk about what we can do to turn that particular perception around."

Connie straightened up, patted her hair, and surprised him with a pleasant grin on her face. "I thought you'd never ask. Here's what I'm proposing. I know you'll never be a reader the way I am, and two people can't read together anyway, except to sit in the same room and turn pages in silence. So, why don't you teach me how to fish? You've always said you needed a partner out there in *The Verdict*. Why not have a good time with your wife? I'm not too old to learn new tricks."

He jerked to attention, almost as if he had been pricked with a needle. "You're serious? You'd actually be willing to learn about different baits and lures and how and where to cast? You know there's so much more to reading the water than most people think."

"Well, I have to start somewhere. Maybe we'll both be reading together after all. Then we can negotiate what else we can do with our retirement from my point of view."

He put his arm around her shoulder and squeezed it affectionately, followed by a sweet little kiss. "I can handle that. So, being the reader that you are, can you tell me if we're back on the same page again as husband and wife?"

Connie chuckled softly even as she pulled back. "I'm going to say yes, but with an important caveat."

"And what's that?"

"You take over cleaning what we catch and keep

for a while. I'm so over fish guts, it's not funny."

"You got it," he said without a moment's hesitation. Then he extended his hand and they shook on it firmly. "Meanwhile, I'll take one of the petitions out to the lake this afternoon to Harlan Lattimore. Why don't you come with me and make friends with a few of the women? Who knows? Maybe some of them will even be readers, and you can talk best sellers."

Locke Linwood and Miss Voncille were comparing notes, sitting side by side on his living room sofa. It was a mere three days to the budget approval, and they were counting up their successes.

"Okay, that makes a total of sixteen of my life insurance customers with Vince Langham and his wife promising to drop by the library to sign the petition," Locke was saying, puffing himself up proudly. "You have to realize that a lot of my clients have died off, so this is a pretty good response in my estimation."

But Miss Voncille was far less sanguine, disdaining the humor he was trying to inject. "But sixteen is a just a drop in the bucket. Even if you add the twenty-three students who've responded to me positively. That's barely forty people. I wanted to do a lot better for Maura Beth, and frankly, I'm disappointed in my students. Maybe some of them didn't like me as well as I thought."

"You've been in a pessimistic mood all this week

about this, sweetheart. Please don't revert to type and channel that nitpicky schoolmarm of yours again. I thought you'd banished her for good," he contended. "We can only do what we can do."

"I think you're being a little nitpicky with me yourself," she snapped back.

"Perhaps I am. Sorry." Then he rose from the sofa and headed over to the bookcase where he again retrieved Pamela's letter from beyond the grave. "I think we both might be in need of a little inspiration again." He resumed his seat and ran his finger halfway down the paper. "Go ahead and read it out loud starting right there. It shows you just how prescient my Pamela really was—why, she may even have been clairvoyant."

Miss Voncille scanned the page quickly and began:

> "We agreed that you should continue to attend 'Who's Who in Cherico?' at the library; that you should do everything you could to support that sweet young librarian, Maura Beth Mayhew—she's just as darling as she can be, and she'll need all the help she can get with the powers-that-be, believe me—"

"Stop right there. You can't tell me that that doesn't give you goose bumps, knowing how long ago it was written."

Miss Voncille looked up from the letter, staring over at Pamela's mesmerizing portrait. "I have to agree. It's definitely uncanny the way everything has converged to make her words seem as if they were written this morning. Hats off to you and your foresight, Miz Pamela."

"My sentiments exactly. And it's my further opinion that this is a sign we'll succeed with this petition and that this is the right thing to do."

"I'd certainly like to think so."

"I believe there's more to this world than we could ever imagine."

Miss Voncille considered for a moment and then raised an eyebrow. "I know this much. You just can't give up on your life because it gets hard and bad things happen to you. Eventually, something good that you've earned from hanging in there comes along. Like a sweet, chivalrous Southern gentleman fresh from his morning shave."

"I'm happy to resemble that."

They both leaned together in laughter, but she let go of the moment quickly. "I'm still wondering if this petition will sway Durden Sparks in the end, though. I've known him most of his conceited life, and I've never seen him not get his way."

Locke nestled his shoulder against hers again and then shot her a dismissive look. "There's always a first time, and this may very well be it."

Then Miss Voncille sighed dramatically. "Do you think I should call up Morbid Mamie and make sure she's put her John Hancock on our petition yet?"

Locke gave her a thumbs-up. "Not only that, but invite her and her sister over here for what will be our revenge game of bridge. I still have a bad taste in my mouth from last time."

Jeremy McShay's daily phone calls and e-mails from Nashville had kept Maura Beth energized during the two-week petition countdown. Their conversations hadn't lasted all that long but had served to keep their burgeoning emotional connection alive and well, while their e-mails had contained the ordinary details of his life at the school and hers at the library. It particularly pleased Maura Beth that he was always the one to initiate the contact in the old-fashioned manner she had always projected both in her dreams and in her journal. She couldn't get enough of his thoughtful pursuit and made a habit of concluding each and every communication with her very own signature phrase: *Keep those cards and letters comin', folks!*

Finally, though, all the long-distance flirting gave way to the day before the budget approval. Just past three o'clock that afternoon, Maura Beth had set out from the library on what she considered to be the most important journey of her life. The butterflies in her stomach felt more like a swarm of bees as she reached Commerce Street on foot, but she did her best to disguise her anxiety with an unwavering smile as she entered Audra Neely's Antiques to pick up her first petition.

"Here you go," Audra said, smiling brightly while handing it over from behind a counter crowded with everything from music boxes to ceramic figurines. "I talked you up every time someone came in."

"Thank you so much," Maura Beth replied, not particularly surprised by the revelation. She had conjectured that the women who fancied the stylish Audra's cutesy boutique approach to antiquing were among the more sophisticated in Cherico and likely to be sympathetic to the cause.

Then came the surprising downer. "I only wish I could have collected more for you, Miz Mayhew. Business has been a little slow lately. It's the economy, you know."

Maura Beth glanced at the sheet and counted the signatures. "Well, you got fifteen for me, Audra, including your own. That's fifteen I didn't have before I came in. And we'd love to have you make an appearance at City Hall when the final decision on the library is made."

Once she was out on the sidewalk again, Maura Beth drew her overcoat closer to her body against the brisk November breeze. Those fifteen signatures were now registering as a nasty chill at the bone. What if all the petitions turned out to be so disappointing?

The Vernon Dotrice Insurance Agency a few doors down was next. As Maura Beth had discovered, the dynamic and very dashing Vernon had bought the business from Locke Linwood when he had retired a few years back. Furthermore, he had been double-teamed by Locke and Maura Beth herself with e-mails, phone calls, and personal visits, and was now thoroughly behind the valiant attempt to keep the library open.

"Hope this helps," Vernon told her once they were seated inside his office. He handed over two copies of the petition with an impish grin and waited for her reaction.

"You're kidding?!" she exclaimed, scanning the paper with her eyes bugging.

"No, ma'am, I'm not. Seventy-five beauties—signed, sealed, and delivered. Hey, Mr. Linwood sold me a very solvent concern here. I took what he gave me and turned it into an even bigger goldmine." He paused and gently wagged a finger. "Just one caveat. You might want to check my list against Mr. Linwood's to make sure there are no duplicates. I don't think there will be, though. I'm pretty sure all these signatures are customers I've won over since I bought the agency—and their spouses, in many cases. That's what really got the numbers up."

"You must be the only game in town, then," Maura Beth added, still a bit dazed by his results.

"If I ever need life insurance, I promise I'll look you up."

"You do that, Miz Mayhew. You know your way here. And, by the way, I'll make it a point to drop by your library now and then. I don't want to be just a signature on a piece of paper."

"We'd love to see you in the Council Chambers tomorrow, too."

"I'll see what I can do about rounding people up."

An ecstatic Maura Beth felt her marrow warming again as she popped into Cherico Ace Hardware next door to greet the store manager, Harry Weeks. But she could tell by the evasive look on his wide, bearded face that this was probably going to be another Audra Neely's Antiques' outing.

"I'm sorry, Miz Mayhew," he told her, taking the petition down from his bulletin board and handing it to her. "I guess people in the market for a hammer and nails don't go to the library much. Apples and oranges?"

Maura Beth glanced at the six signatures he'd collected for her but was careful to give him her brightest smile. "Thank you for putting it up for me, Mr. Weeks. That's all I could ask. If you get a moment, drop by the Council Chambers tomorrow around nine-thirty."

As Maura Beth made her way one block over to The Cherico Market, she bucked up anyway. Her instincts had told her from the beginning that she wouldn't find much of an audience at the hardware store, but she couldn't imagine that James Hannigan, his employees, and customers wouldn't come through for her.

"There she is!" Mr. Hannigan exclaimed as the automatic doors parted for her, and she walked in eagerly anticipating some good news. The two embraced warmly, and a couple of the cashiers stopped their grocery scanning long enough to smile and wave.

"I hope you're having a special on signatures today," Maura Beth told him, zeroing in on the sheets of paper he was holding in his hand.

"We outdid ourselves," he said, leaning in and presenting three separate petitions to her.

She gasped in delight, feeling as if she'd just received an early Christmas present. Two of the sheets were completely filled, while the third sported only a few empty lines.

"Two-hundred and sixty names, to be exact," he explained. "Count 'em."

She held them against her overcoat and sighed. "I'll take your word. But it's lovely. Just lovely."

"Frankly, I don't think my customers could resist the little announcement I kept making over the P.A. system," he explained, puffing out his chest. "I've still got it memorized. Wanna hear it?"

"Absolutely!"

"Well, first I did the 'Attention, shoppers!' opening because they always perk up when they hear that. 'What's on sale?' they think right away. Then I said, 'If you or your spouse or your children or any other member of your family swears by the library for any reason whatsoever, you'll want to be sure and sign our petitions on the bulletin board to keep it up and running. That's right, your Cherico Library could be closed for good starting the first day of January if you don't stand up to be counted. Books are the only thing about the library that should be shelved! Sign today!' "

Maura Beth gave him another quick hug. "That's so clever, and it obviously worked."

He blushed and gave her a shy smile. "Well, I do write all the copy around here, and it's not bad if I do say so myself."

"As far as I'm concerned, you're the Shakespeare of the supermarket."

Things were definitely looking up, as Maura Beth thanked Mr. Hannigan, reminded him of the time the budget approval would take place, and walked back to the library to complete her rounds—this time in her car. She had to drive over to Cherico Tresses and then out to The Marina Bar and Grill to pick up those petitions. But she would not know the final total until Periwinkle closed her doors that evening. Then she could add the library signatures to those collected at The

Twinkle and by other members of the club such as Locke Linwood and Miss Voncille. That, and continue to solicit warm bodies in the seats for the actual budget approval.

But when all was said and done, would it be enough to force Councilman Sparks to do the right thing tomorrow morning?

# 15

# Standing Room Only

As usual, Councilman Sparks did not know what to make of the latest message Lottie had left in the inbox on his desk. It was a mere fifteen minutes before he was about to head down the hall for the budget approval. “CCBC SAYS SRO”—she had printed in big block letters on his notepad. At the moment, however, further clarification would have to wait until she returned to her post in the outer office—most likely from one of her frequent trips to the ladies’ room.

When she finally showed up a few minutes later, Councilman Sparks was hardly calm and collected as he blocked the door frame while holding her mysterious note in his outstretched hand. “What the hell does this mean, Lottie? You’ve got to give me a break from all these abbreviations. It took me half the afternoon in your absence last week to decipher that we were out of printer solution when you left me a message that read, ‘OOPS—NEED REORDER.’ ”

“I’m sorry, sir,” Lottie replied, although she hardly sounded contrite. “I thought I had mentioned it to you earlier that day. The out of printer solution, OOPS part, I mean.”

"Never mind that. What does this latest hieroglyphic of yours mean?"

He moved aside so she could sit down at her desk, whereupon she started thumbing through some notes she had made to herself that morning in his absence. "Oh. They called around nine before you came in."

He took a deep breath to steady himself. "Who are *they?*"

"The Cherry Cola Book Club," Lottie explained at last. "You've been so involved with them lately, I thought you'd understand my abbreviation."

He was frowning now. "You mean Miz Mayhew—of all people?"

"Yes, it was her."

"Then why didn't you just write—" Once again, he realized he was fighting a losing battle and retreated from this latest argument on her terms. Then he made a mental note to ring in the New Year by advertising for a new secretary. He'd endured this comedy of errors long enough. "I'll settle for SRO. What does that mean?"

Lottie had an almost triumphant look on her face, obviously proud of stumping her boss one more time. "Standing room only. Miz Mayhew said that you should expect a full house for the budget approval. She was on her cell phone and already in her seat waiting, she said."

"Those people never give up," he mumbled as he rolled his eyes. "They've tacked up petitions all over town. But I checked out a couple on Commerce Street like the hardware and the antiques store, and I wasn't impressed with what I saw." He checked his watch while narrowing his eyes. "Anyway, it's time to put all this foolishness to bed, Lottie. You hold down the fort while I give Miz Mayhew and her entourage the bad news."

Maura Beth had not exaggerated when she had spoken to Lottie Howard and told her that there would not be an empty seat in the Council Chambers. All seventy chairs were occupied, and there were at least a dozen more people standing against the wall in the back of the room. As for her Cherry Cola Book Club friends, they were all seated with her on the front row. They had taken no chances and shown up thirty minutes early to ensure maximum physical presence, particularly that all-important eye contact with the councilmen as the budget process unfolded.

There were other friendly faces that Maura Beth was pleased to see among the crowd: James Hannigan, Audra Neely, Vernon Dotrice, Emma Frost, Terra Munrow—even the Crumpton sisters. But there were many others she did not recognize, and she assumed that they were the rank and file of citizens they had managed to reach with their campaign to save the library. That had to be a hopeful sign as the session got under way.

However, Maura Beth noted, as the tall, severe-looking City Clerk, Mrs. Benita Porter, began her robotic reading of each budget item, glaciers had been known to move faster in their trek to the sea.

"This is like listening to a recitation of the phone book," Connie whispered to Maura Beth out of the side of her mouth. Mrs. Porter was taking forever working her way through the Sanitation Department budget, then had hit a snag regarding the question of how much money to allot for road salt during the upcoming year.

"Nobody knows how much snow we'll get," Chunky Badham was pointing out. But he was not about to let up. "Last year, we got three big snows and that ice storm. My wife even had enough to make snow ice cream for me. Plus, I like to have gone off the road and into a ditch during that one we had last January. And it was because we didn't have enough road salt to put out where I live in the Netherfield Community. Now I realize we only have about twelve people out my way . . ."

He kept droning on and on, and neither of the other two councilmen saw fit to interrupt him.

Maura Beth felt her annoyance registering as an adrenaline rush. Here they were going on about how much extra road salt to purchase, while threatening to do away with her library entirely was waiting in the wings. She began playing mind games to calm herself. Which would the good people of Cherico prefer: a sprinkling of salt or books to read? In any case, an extra thousand dollars was finally appropriated for road salt, and there were no objections from the citizens attending, putting the stamp of approval on that specific budget item.

Utilities came next, and Maura Beth caught Councilman Sparks's gaze as Mrs. Porter waded through that particular appropriation. There was an unusual smugness to his handsome features, and her instincts were telling her that he intended to send her packing. But she held inside the folder on her lap the ultimate defense against such a decision—the voice of the people.

Finally, after what seemed like hours, Mrs. Porter announced, "The Cherico Library."

To Maura Beth, those three words felt like bullets penetrating her flesh. She played another game in her head and breathed deeply. Would she end up suffering a fatal wound or live to order and process books for another day? Being in the line of fire was the pits. "Here we go," Maura Beth whispered to Connie, and the two of them gave each other a reassuring smile.

Councilman Sparks rose after Mrs. Porter had reviewed the costs of running the library for another year, line item by line item—a total of $85,000. "It is our intention," he began, "to redirect this money to a new project for Cherico. It is our belief that you, the taxpayers, are not getting your money's worth with our library facility. We further believe that using this money to prepare land just north of town for industrial use will attract new industry and good-paying jobs to Cherico, thus increasing our tax base and improving our infrastructure. At some time in the future, perhaps we will then have collected enough money to improve and reopen the library. But it is the City Council's decision to close the library as of December 31st and begin preparations for the industrial park. We will now entertain feedback from you, the taxpayers."

As other hands and voices were raised all over the room, Maura Beth shot up immediately, brandishing the folder she had been so jealously guarding. "Councilman Sparks!" she exclaimed, taking no chance of being overlooked.

"Miz Mayhew?" he replied, refusing to match her urgent tone and careful to maintain his smile.

"On behalf of many of the taxpayers of Cherico, I would like to present to you today this folder of petitions requesting that the City Council keep The Cherico Library open. I have taken the time to check the names and addresses of all the signatures on these various petitions and have found them to be residents of our town, each and every one. No made-up or dead people, no jokes, no fakes. These are the taxpayers you represent, and as you will see, I have calculated and compiled the total number on all the petitions for you. Eight hundred and three people have expressed their desire to see The Cherico Library stay open. These signatures came mostly from various businesses around town, all of which are well-known to you, as well as the library itself. Those eight hundred and three signatures represent almost half the number of registered voters in this town—one thousand six hundred forty-five, according to public records."

Councilman Sparks was having trouble keeping his smile in place. "That doesn't necessarily mean those eight hundred or so are all actually registered voters. Some of them could even be children or teenagers."

"That might be true," Maura Beth returned. "Although I think the underage signatures would probably be limited to the library. But in any case, children and teenagers grow up to be voters, Councilman. You above all should know that. Surely that's not going to be your argument against these signatures."

His smile had completely disappeared now. "Hand me your folder, please."

She reached over and gave it to him, taking a moment before continuing. Here was Scarlett at her best, daring anyone to take advantage of her.

"Furthermore, I'd like to say that the library's present budget is hardly adequate, even for a town of five thousand. But as the director, I'm not asking for an increase or a raise—only to continue to do my job for the people of Cherico. We've initiated a number of events recently that have this town buzzing about the library. I hardly have to remind you of that since you've attended some of these meetings, such as The Cherry Cola Book Club. I urge you and the other councilmen not to turn your back on what is fast becoming a popular and valuable community resource."

"Listen to her, Durden!" Miss Voncille exclaimed, rising to her feet. "You can postpone that industrial park or find some other way to fund it. My parents always told me that there was some slush fund hanging around from the days the library started up originally. I believe there was some question as to what really happened to some of the money the women of the town donated at the time. Wasn't your father on the Council back then? Being the historian that I am, I'm also quite sure that no one has ever bothered to look into that whole matter. As the saying goes, they just let it ride."

Councilman Sparks had gone from being supremely confident to actually looking uncomfortable for all the chamber to see. "Give me a few minutes, please," he told her, sitting back down and thumbing through the petitions Maura Beth had presented to him. Then the folder was passed around to his cohorts. Finally, after the trio had huddled for a good five minutes with their backs to the crowd, Councilman Sparks turned and rose again, his best campaign smile restored to full glory.

"It is the decision of the City Council to postpone the industrial park for another year and to fund The Cherico Library for the corresponding year—"

Enthusiastic applause and cheering erupted across the room. Maura Beth jumped up, embracing Connie and Miss Voncille, who were sitting on either side of her, and the rest of the book club did the same with one another along the front row.

"If I might continue!" Councilman Sparks cried out, and he had to repeat himself to gain the floor before the commotion died down. "Over the next year, we will be monitoring the library in hopes of seeing increased circulation figures and use of the meeting room facilities by the citizens of this town. It is to be understood that we will be reviewing funding of the library at this same time next year. For the time being, however, we cannot go against the will of the people in this regard."

"Thank you, Councilman," Maura Beth said, nodding his way.

"Please remember that this is a one-year reprieve, Miz Mayhew. There are no guarantees."

"I understand that. Or rather, Scarlett understands that."

She watched him struggling to keep his face from turning sour. Ever the politician, however, he somehow managed. But Maura Beth's smile was genuine and full of the thrill of victory. Above all else, she had played the game and won.

# 16

# A Family Feast

Maura Beth was staring at the clock in her kitchenette and feeling like a million dollars. In less than ten minutes, she would be seeing Jeremy's smiling face at her door, putting an end to their separation of more than two weeks. The time had come to celebrate the library's recent victory over City Hall, and Jeremy was driving down from Nashville on this crisp November Saturday afternoon to help her do just that.

He was on time precisely at three, as she expected a responsible schoolteacher would be. Being late for anything in that profession was a big no-no. When she opened the door to him in her lavender dress, the first words out of his mouth were, "You look amazingly beautiful!" He was standing there dazzled by her with a bouquet of gardenias in his hand.

Maura Beth smiled and took the flowers, briefly inhaling their perfume as she admired his New Gallatin Academy navy blue blazer and red tie. "So do you, and so do these. Come on—I'm going to put them in water."

They headed over to the kitchenette together, and she pulled a large clear vase out of one of her cabinets. "What made you think of gardenias?"

she continued, sticking the vase under the running faucet. "I absolutely love them. They're so delicate."

"A conceit from an English major, I guess," he explained, shrugging his shoulders and looking utterly charming in the process. "Gardenias, like women, bruise easily, but that never takes away their beauty or their fragrance."

She smiled brightly as she finished arranging the flowers and found a spot for them on the counter. "No wonder your students like you so much. I would have loved to have had a teacher like you."

Jeremy pointed to his watch and wagged his brows. "We better scoot. We don't want to be late."

Once they were on their way, Maura Beth shifted into an even more flirtatious gear. "I wanted to tell you just how much all your calls and e-mails have meant to me these past two weeks. I was under such pressure, I don't think I could have made it through without you. Today, I was half expecting you to show up in shining armor."

He drove for another quarter mile or so toward town before turning briefly to snap his fingers. "Darn it! I knew I forgot something!"

She reached over and gently rubbed his arm several times. "Never fear. The flowers did the trick just fine."

They had reached Commerce Street now, and Jeremy began searching for a parking space. “Small town, not much parking,” he observed as they passed The Twinkle. They waved to Becca and Stout Fella as they were walking down the sidewalk toward the restaurant for the grand celebration.

“They obviously found one somewhere around here,” Maura Beth answered. “I don’t mind walking a bit, do you?”

He turned the corner and was immediately rewarded with a space on the right side of the street. “Not at all. We can get a head start on working off this wonderful feast Miz Lattimore has fixed for all of us.”

“This is where it all began a few months back,” Connie was saying as she and Maura Beth were sitting at one of The Twinkle’s corner tables sipping their wine. “I remember dashing in to pick up my aspics that blazing June afternoon and mentioning The Music City Page Turners to you.”

“Ah, yes,” Maura Beth mused. “We almost became The Cherico Page Turners, didn’t we? By the way, you must bring your granddaughter down sometime from Memphis. I’d like very much to meet the little sweetheart, since she ended up changing our name.”

“Lindy almost came down with her for our meeting last Sunday, but Melissa wasn’t feeling well at the last minute. Some bad cough that just wouldn't go away," Connie explained. "But don't worry. We've got plenty of time now for her to shake your hand and take full credit."

Periwinkle headed over to the table with the bottle of good Merlot she was offering to the group, lingering briefly. "Are we all still sufficiently wined up here?"

"I think I'd like another swallow or two," Maura Beth said, feeling on the wild and wooly side.

Periwinkle poured a little more into her glass and wagged her brows. "I see your adorable designated driver not having any over there across the room. Are you and Jeremy definitely becoming an item?"

Maura Beth gave Connie a conspiratorial glance and said, "We're going to be working at it, I think. So you can retire your camera phone."

"No way, Jose. I'm still looking, remember?"

A few minutes later it was time for every member of The Cherry Cola Book Club to take their seats around the big table Periwinkle had configured out of two smaller ones. "Mr. Place and I will join you after we've served the first course," she told them.

Maura Beth perked up and ran her tongue over her lips. "Icepick salad?"

"What else would I serve?"

"Now you're talking!" Douglas exclaimed. "I think we've practically lived on that since we moved down here."

"I can vouch for that," Connie added. "I wish The Twinkle had a delivery service."

"Not a bad suggestion. I'll think about it," Periwinkle said, nudging her gently.

Over Periwinkle's entrée of grilled salmon with dill sauce, the conversation turned toward the next meeting of The Cherry Cola Book Club.

"I don't suppose we've selected our next novel, have we?" Miss Voncille inquired.

Maura Beth's sigh clearly contained a hint of frustration. "How could we? We never seem to be able to finish the one we're reading. Something earthshaking always happens and sends us to the exits. But I think things will settle down now. Anyone got a brilliant suggestion?"

Connie was first up. "Something by Eudora Welty? Or have we put Harper Lee to bed?"

"I think we've had enough of *Mockingbird*," Becca observed. "Not that it wasn't overflowing with drama and portent from the very beginning."

"Sorry about that," Stout Fella added.

"No, no, no," Maura Beth continued, wagging a finger. "Your little incident, if you will, brought us all closer together."

Becca put down her fork and chuckled. "You might even say our friendships ballooned from there."

There was laughter all around; then the subject of the next novel resurfaced quickly. "Seriously, though," Connie offered, "what about Eudora

Welty? We had quite a session up in Nashville with *The Robber Bridegroom.* Specifically, is it or is it not a fairy tale?"

"I definitely like that theme," Maura Beth replied. "What do the rest of you think?"

"Sounds good to me," Locke Linwood put in while Miss Voncille nodded approvingly.

One by one, the others agreed to the choice, and Maura Beth declared that the subject of the January session of The Cherry Cola Book Club had been decided. "And this isn't exactly a prayer, but may we get through it without interruption this time around."

Then slices of one of Mr. Place's scrumptious desserts, Mississippi mud pie, came out to put an exclamation point on the meal.

"I can see myself getting addicted to this," Jeremy was saying after his first bite. "Kudos to you, Mr. Place."

"My pleasure," he returned, smiling graciously.

As everyone was finishing up their pie and coffee, Maura Beth rose from her seat with her wineglass in hand. "I don't know why we didn't do this before the appetizers, but I'd like to make a toast, please." She waited for the group to stand up and hoist their glasses before continuing. "I can't tell you how grateful I will always be to all of you for your generosity of spirit in standing behind me and the library. The thing is, I truly believe that we have already become more than just an ordinary book club. We've gotten involved in each other's lives in ways that we would never have expected—and without even half trying. It just seems to have evolved naturally, as if something we don't fully understand has been driving it and making sure that we all stay connected. You're like a real family to me." She surveyed the table once more and smiled. "I've been told I can go to a long-winded, hammy place at times, and I hope I haven't overstated my case just now. But I think the future looks so much brighter than it did last week, and I want to thank you all again from the bottom of my heart for helping to make it possible."

Everyone leaned this way and that to clink rims and sip, and there were lots of cheerful responses such as, "It was our pleasure," and "I couldn't have said it better myself," to go around.

"And, Periwinkle," Maura Beth continued after all the commotion had finally died down, "you outdid yourself this afternoon with this very special dinner. So, long live both The Cherry Cola Book Club and The Twinkle!"

There was more clinking and sipping; then Periwinkle added the capper, gazing around with great pride at all her fanciful spinning mobiles. "The one and only Restaurant of the Stars!"

"I'm already settled in with Aunt Connie and Uncle Doug at the lodge for tonight, but they told me they weren't coming straight home," Jeremy explained as he and Maura Beth drove through town in the general direction of the lake house. "There were a few logs blazing when I left to pick you up. Would you like to sit and watch them turn to soot together for a while?"

She reached over and patted his knee a few times. "I think I'd like that very much."

"I know that I don't want to rush things," he continued, "but I've always liked telling stories by the fire, ever since I was eleven having a blast at summer camp on Lookout Mountain. It was always chilly after nightfall up there, and it was easy to imagine monsters lurking in the woods as the counselors would try and scare us with their spooky voices and tall tales. I remember everything from deranged farmers on out-of-control tractors to maniacal lumberjacks running around the forests sawing people in half while they were sealed up tight in their sleeping bags. None of us slept a wink after that one. I guess boys grow up with a lot more visceral thoughts in their heads."

Maura Beth had a resigned expression on her face. "I'm afraid my experience at summer camp was a lot tamer. Just us girls allowed, and the most daring thing we ever discussed was makeup and who was being allowed to use it. Or who wasn't and why. The whole summer was an all-out 'my mother is a monster' vent, so in that respect, there was a bit more drama than I first remembered."

They drove on along the two-lane road that wound its way to the lake from the outskirts of town. There was a full moon rising ahead of them, filling up the windshield with such luster and swollen size that it appeared the night had been completely vanquished, difficult to detect even with peripheral vision. There was only the prospect of looking up into the heavens and wanting to drive straight up to eternity immediately. It was all mesmerizing and therefore distracting.

"Oh, my God, here comes Peter Cottontail!" Jeremy suddenly exclaimed, swerving the car slightly to avoid a rabbit scampering across to the safety of the opposite shoulder.

"I'm so glad you missed him," Maura Beth said, smiling gratefully. "If it's a sin to kill a mockingbird, I'm sure I'd feel even worse about being a party to flattening a bunny rabbit."

Jeremy waited for the slight rush of adrenaline his wildlife encounter had produced to subside. "No hint of roadkill here. I'm quick at the wheel. I've even been known to brake for falling leaves."

Maura Beth sighed quite audibly. "Oh, brother!"

"A little too poetic?"

She just smiled and raised her eyebrows, enjoying the ride. He pressed on. "I'd really like to know what you're thinking right now, though."

Once again, she sat there, looking mysterious and utterly irresistible. “We’ll get to the details later on. For now, I’ll just tell you that I was thinking happily about page twenty-five.”

# Recipes for Loyal, Hungry Readers

No trip to Cherico, Mississippi, and the inner workings of The Cherry Cola Book Club would be complete without a few convenient recipes so that readers can duplicate the delicious dishes of some of their favorite characters. For sampling at your leisure, therefore, we present the following pages as lagniappe in hopes that you will enjoy many a satisfying meal with all good wishes in the years to come. Just turn the pages, pick out something you like, and get cooking!

## Becca Broccoli's Easy Peasy Chicken Spaghetti

*Ingredients you will need:*

1 whole chicken
1 package of thin spaghetti
1 stick of butter
1 chopped onion
½ cup chopped green pepper
1 cup chopped celery
1 large can of mushroom soup
1 can of diced pimentos
2 cups grated cheddar cheese
Salt and pepper to taste

Cook chicken in salted water until tender. Remove chicken and dice the meat. Use chicken broth to cook spaghetti until tender. Sauté butter, onion, green pepper, and celery until onions are translucent. Add veggies to pasta; then add large can of mushroom soup, chicken, and pimentos; pour into casserole dish and sprinkle cheese over top. Bake at 350 degrees Fahrenheit until golden bubbly.

—Courtesy Mrs. Rose Williams Turner,
Natchez, Mississippi

## Connie McShay's Frozen Fruit Salad

*Ingredients you will need:*

8 ounces cream cheese
½ cup sugar
1 cup mayo
1 cup white raisins
½ cup chopped nuts (walnuts or pecans)
1 can fruit cocktail (drained)
Poppy seed dressing

Mix cream cheese and sugar; add mayo, raisins, nuts, and fruit cocktail; pour cocktail into twelve lined muffin tins and freeze; package in large Ziploc bag. (For additional flavor, add two tablespoons of poppy seed dressing upon serving.)

—Courtesy Alice Feltus, Lucy Feltus, and Helen Byrnes Jenkins, Natchez, Mississippi

## Periwinkle Lattimore's Baked Sherry Custard

*Ingredients you will need:*

2 tablespoons sugar
1⅓ cups whole milk
Dash of salt
3½ teaspoons sherry
1½ teaspoons vanilla
3 egg whites
1 additional tablespoon of sugar

Combine the two tablespoons of sugar, milk, and salt in a pan; cook on simmer to low heat until sugar dissolves—approximately five minutes; remove and then add sherry and vanilla together.

In a separate bowl, combine the egg whites with the additional tablespoon of sugar; whip or beat into soft-peak stage; and add the milk mixture slowly. Use sieve to strain the entire mixture into a two-cup baking dish; place dish in a baking pan with water bath (usually halfway up the sides) and bake at 325 degrees Fahrenheit for about an hour. If toothpick comes out clean when inserted in middle of mixture, custard is done. Serve warm or cold.

—Courtesy Helen Louise Jenkins Kuehnle,
Natchez, Mississippi

## Becca Broccoli's Cherry Cola/Lime Punch

*Ingredients you will need:*

1 liter any chilled cola beverage (do not use diet variety)
1 liter any chilled ginger ale beverage (do not use diet variety)
1 jar maraschino cherries
3 limes

Pour cola and ginger ale into large punch bowl and stir. Add jar of stemless maraschino cherries and one half the liquid. Cut limes in half and squeeze juice into mixture. Stir everything together and serve.

—Courtesy Lauren R. Good,
Memphis, Tennessee

## Periwinkle Lattimore's Tomato Aspic with Cream Cheese

*Ingredients you will need for tomato aspic liquid:*

2 cups tomato juice (or V8 juice)
½ cup chopped onion
2 chopped celery ribs
1 envelope unflavored gelatin
¼ cup cold water
2 tablespoons lemon juice
Dash of hot pepper sauce
Dash of Worcestershire sauce

Boil tomato juice, onion, and celery for about twenty minutes, or until veggies are tender; drain tomato juice and set aside. Soften gelatin in 1/4 cup cold water and add to tomato juice; then add lemon juice, pepper sauce, and Worcestershire sauce.

*Ingredients you will need for cream cheese filling:*

8 ounces cream cheese
2 tablespoons mayo
1 teaspoon grated onion
Salt and pepper to taste
Paprika (optional)

Make small balls of filling ingredients; put at the bottom of individual molds or at the bottom of a casserole dish and cut into squares. Pour tomato aspic liquid over the cheese balls; after everything has congealed, serve chilled. For additional flavor, top with dollop of mayo and sprinkle paprika over that for color.

—Courtesy Mrs. Rose Williams Turner,
Natchez, Mississippi

## Maura Beth Mayhew's Chocolate, Cherry Cola Sheet Cake

*Ingredients you will need for the batter:*

2 cups flour
Dash of salt
2 cups sugar
1 cup any cola beverage
⅓ cup oil
1 stick butter
3 tablespoons dry cocoa
½ cup buttermilk
1 teaspoon baking soda
2 teaspoons vanilla
3 tablespoons maraschino cherry liquid
1 jar of finely chopped maraschino cherries
2 eggs

Mix flour, salt, and sugar in bowl. In separate pan, bring to a boil the cola drink, oil, butter, and cocoa. Add hot liquid to the bowl and beat heavily; then add buttermilk, baking soda, vanilla, cherry liquid, cherries, and eggs and continue beating. When well mixed, pour into sheet cake pan sprayed with nonstick spray and bake for twenty-five minutes at 350 degrees Fahrenheit.

*Ingredients you will need for the icing:*

1 stick butter
3 tablespoons cocoa
6 tablespoons whole milk
3 tablespoons maraschino cherry liquid
1 pound confectioners' sugar
2 teaspoons vanilla
1 cup finely chopped pecans

Heat the butter, cocoa, and milk until the butter has liquefied; add the remaining ingredients and beat well. Pour icing onto cake while it is hot or still warm for ease of spreading; cut when cake has cooled.

—Courtesy Marion A. Good,
Oxford, Mississippi

## Mr. Parker Place's Lemon/Lime Icebox Pie

*Ingredients you will need for the crust:*

1 7.05-oz box of Carr's Ginger Lemon Creme Tea Cookies
2 tablespoons of butter or margarine

Empty box of Carr's Ginger Lemon Creme Tea Cookies into food processor and pulse until crumb consistency is reached; or, empty box of cookies into Ziploc bag and pound/roll with rolling pin until crumb consistency is reached.

Pour crumb mixture into a 9-inch aluminum-foil pie pan; melt better and then drizzle into crumb mixture; mold mixture into crust, adhering to pie pan; set aside.

*Ingredients you will need for the filling:*

1 can fat-free condensed milk
3 eggs
4 limes or 4 lemons

***Note:*** Using limes will give the pie a tarter taste; using lemons will give it a sweeter taste.

Pour can of condensed milk into large mixing bowl. Crack three medium eggs and separate yolks from whites (if you wish to save whites for omelets, etc., do so; otherwise, discard). Put yolks into condensed milk and stir thoroughly until blended.

Juice four limes or four lemons (do not use reconstituted lemon or lime juice); add juice into condensed milk–egg mixture in small portions and mix in thoroughly each time until all juice has been added and blended.

Pour mixture into pie pan and bake at 350 degrees Fahrenheit for about twenty-five minutes; overbaking will make the texture of the filling mealy. Cool before cutting and serving. Serve at room temperature or chilled. Serves up to six.

—Mr. Parker Place
(Joe Sam Bedloe, Cherico, Mississippi)

## And finally: Stout Fella's Instructions for "Islanding" Ice Cream

*Ingredients you will need:*

1 tablespoon (fresh and hot from being cleaned in the dishwasher, if possible; if not, blow on metal until warm)
1 gallon of previously untouched, unopened ice cream, any flavor

Take ice cream out of freezer, put it on counter, and yell at it to hurry up and soften just a tad bit. Open the hatch or the top and begin testing the edges; start scraping on all four sides; keep going deeper until you have reached the bottom and created an "island," or your wife comes in and screams at you to "Stop, you'll spoil your appetite for dinner!" whichever comes first; repeat, if she goes away, and rinse (the spoon).

—Courtesy Justin Rawlings "Stout Fella" Brachle,
Cherico, Mississippi

## DISCUSSION QUESTIONS

1. Discuss the female character who fascinates you the most, and give the pros and cons of her personality.

2. Discuss the male character who fascinates you the most, and give the pros and cons of his personality.

3. Assign someone to argue for The Cherico Library's existence against someone else who supports the City Council's point of view for its dissolution. Let the group decide who won the argument.

4. Does Cherico reflect some of the economic and cultural realities of your hometown?

5. Which of the couples most resembles your relationship with your spouse or significant other: Becca and Stout Fella; Miss Voncille and Locke Linwood; Douglas and Connie?

6. The character of Pamela Linwood, though deceased, plays an important role in the plot. How do each of you view that role?

7. What has your local library meant to you?

8. Over the long haul, do you think Maura Beth Mayhew is fighting a losing battle?

9. Do you think taxpayers in general have a realistic view of what it takes to keep a library up and running?

10. Do you think library services should fall into the same category for funding as fire-fighting, police protection, streets, water and utilities?

11. Did you ever make the sort of wish/bucket list that Maura Beth Mayhew made on page twenty-five of her journal (Three Things to Accomplish Before I'm Thirty)?

12. Pretend you are a female member of The Cherry Cola Book Club. Do you fall into the Scarlett or the Melanie category as a modern woman?

13. Pretend you are a member (either gender) of The Cherry Cola Book Club. What role do you think *To Kill a Mockingbird* played in the passage of the 1964 Civil Rights Act, if any?

14. There will be a sequel to *The Cherry Cola Book Club*. What do you hope will happen in that book?

15. What is your favorite sequence in *The Cherry Cola Book Club*?

**Center Point Large Print**
600 Brooks Road / PO Box 1
Thorndike ME 04986-0001 USA

**(207) 568-3717**

**US & Canada:**
**1 800 929-9108**
**www.centerpointlargeprint.com**

# DIVISION STREET & OTHER PLAYS

X

# DIVISION STREET
# &
# OTHER PLAYS

STEVE TESICH



PERFORMING ARTS JOURNAL PUBLICATIONS
NEW YORK

First edition


**Library of Congress Cataloging in Publication Data**
Division Street and Other Plays
CONTENTS: *Division Street, Baba Goya, Lake of the Woods, Passing Game.*
Library of Congress Catalog Card No.: 81-83750
ISBN: 0-933826-28-1
ISBN: 0-933826-29-X (paper)





Graphic design: Gautam Dasgupta

Printed in the United States of America

Publication of this book has been made possible in part by grants received from the National Endowment for the Arts, Washington, D.C., a federal agency, and the New York State Council on the Arts.

# Contents

**PAJ PLAYSCRIPT SERIES**

General Editors: Bonnie Marranca and Gautam Dasgupta

OTHER TITLES IN THE SERIES:

THEATRE OF THE RIDICULOUS/Kenneth Bernard, Charles Ludlam, Ronald Tavel

ANIMATIONS: A TRILOGY FOR MABOU MINES/Lee Breuer

THE RED ROBINS/Kenneth Koch

THE WOMEN'S PROJECT/Penelope Gilliatt, Lavonne Mueller, Rose Leiman Goldemberg, Joyce Aaron-Luna Tarlo, Kathleen Collins, Joan Schenkar, Phyllis Purscell

WORDPLAYS: NEW AMERICAN DRAMA/Maria Irene Fornes, Ronald Tavel, Jean-Claude van Itallie, Richard Nelson, William Hauptman, John Wellman

BEELZEBUB SONATA/Stanisław I. Witkiewicz

EVE OF RETIREMENT & THE PRESIDENT/Thomas Bernhard

# Division Street

*Division Street* was first performed on May 22, 1980, by the Mark Taper Forum, Los Angeles. It was directed by Tom Moore. The cast included:

CHRIS . . . . . . . . . . . . . . . . . . . . . . . . . . . . . . *Tim Matheson*
MRS. BRUCHINSKI . . . . . . . . . . . . . . . . . . . . . *Madge Sinclair*
YOVAN . . . . . . . . . . . . . . . . . . . . . . . . . . . . . *Keene Curtis*
BETTY . . . . . . . . . . . . . . . . . . . . . . . . . . . . . . *Justin Lord*
NADJA . . . . . . . . . . . . . . . . . . . . . . . . . . . . . . *Didi Conn*
ROGER . . . . . . . . . . . . . . . . . . . . . . . . . . . . *Joe Regalbuto*
DIANAH . . . . . . . . . . . . . . . . . . . . . . . . . . . *Andrea Akers*
SAL . . . . . . . . . . . . . . . . . . . . . . . . . . . . *Anthony Holland*

Set: Ralph Funicello
Costumes: Robert Blackman
Lighting: Martin Aronstein

The play was subsequently produced on Broadway at the Ambassador Theater where it opened on October 8, 1980. Only the following cast changes were made in the New York production:

CHRIS . . . . . . . . . . . . . . . . . . . . . . . . . . . . . *John Lithgow*
MRS. BRUCHINSKI . . . . . . . . . . . . . . . . . . . . *Theresa Merritt*
NADJA . . . . . . . . . . . . . . . . . . . . . . . . . . . . *Murphy Cross*
DIANAH . . . . . . . . . . . . . . . . . . . . . . . . . . *Christine Lahti*

**Cast:** Chris, an attractive man in his thirties
Mrs. Bruchinski, a Black woman with a Polish accent. Chris's landlady.
Yovan, a powerful Serbian with a Serbian accent.
Dianah, Chris's wife. Very pretty.
Sal, a lawyer. Short and slight.
Nadja, Yovan's daughter. Roger's ex-wife. Beautiful. Sexy.
Roger, Chris's old friend.
Betty, a female cop. Used to be a male.

**Place:** Chicago

**Time:** Present

**Tempo:** Allegro con sentimento

**Set:**

*Mrs. Bruchinski's House:* The entrance to the house is stage right. A stairway leads to Chris Adrian's apartment. Opposite the entrance to his apartment is Mrs. Bruchinski's apartment. All we see of it is her door. Both her door and Chris's door open out. When both doors are opened they just about touch.

*Chris's Apartment:* The apartment is essentially one room. There is a window looking out on the street. A bedroom: all we see is the door. The same is true of the bathroom. There is a kitchen area, a sofa, and boxes containing what's left of Chris's life. The room has been furnished by Mrs. Bruchinski.

*The Street:* . . . surrounds the apartment and is connected organically to the building. It contains a couple of benches, a payphone and perhaps an interesting street sign with the words: DIVISION STREET.

# ACT I

*Lights come up on Chris's apartment. He is asleep on the sofa totally covered by a quilt. The alarm clock rings. He leaps out of bed, rushes to shut it off. Opens the window and yells.*

CHRIS: Hey, you! Paper boy! (*A paper shoots through the window just missing him.*) I told you yesterday, I don't have a subscription, damn it. (*He tries to shut the window. He can't.*) Oh no! Not again! (*Chris tries real hard to shut the window. It won't close.*) MRS. BRUCHINSKI! (*Pause.*) MRS. BRUCHINSKI!

MRS. BRUCHINSKI: (*Offstage.*) YES, VAT IS IT?

CHRIS: COULD YOU PLEASE COME HERE? (*He sits on the window ledge.*)

MRS. BRUCHINSKI: YES, I COULD.

CHRIS: ARE YOU COMING?

MRS. BRUCHINSKI: ARE YOU VAITING?

CHRIS: YES, I AM.

MRS. BRUCHINSKI: I AM COMING. (*Mrs. Bruchinski walks out of her apartment, through the landing, and into Chris's apartment. She is black and speaks with a Polish accent. She carries a newspaper.*) I am here. So vat is big dill.

CHRIS: I don't feel well, and the garbage I smell is upsetting the garbage I ate last night. The window is stuck open again!

MRS. BRUCHINSKI: SHTUCK! DID YOU SAY SHTUCK? (*She slams the door shut and as she does the window comes down. Chris just looks on wondering what to do next.*) Not to worry. I'm Polish. I fix it nothing flat. (*But she is rolling up her sleeves and coming toward him. Chris is desperate. He doesn't want her to open the window.*)

CHRIS: You fixed it already. It's closed. I like it closed.

MRS. BRUCHINSKI: It's shtuck closed. I hate shtuck. I make it unshtuck. (*She pushes Chris out of the way. Speaks to the window.*) Okay, vindow. I make you sorry you ever shtuck you somonabitch. (*She lunges at it and tries to open it. She laughs.*) It's shtuck all right. (*She tries again. Mrs. Bruchinski is upset.*) You somonabitch shtuck vindow, I fix your goose. (*She tries to open it again. She grunts and groans. Chris gives up and walks away. Mrs. Bruchinski opens the window. She is delighted.*) BRAVO FOR ME!

CHRIS: I have a terrible headache.

MRS. BRUCHINSKI: I saw your picture in the *Polish Gazette*. Is is not very cute picture of you, Kris.

CHRIS: It's hard to look cute, Mrs. Bruchinski, when you're throwing up on the streets of Chicago.

MRS. BRUCHINSKI: You get drunk like skunk, no?

CHRIS: I don't drink. I shouldn't eat even. I went to this restaurant–New World Bar and Grill and I ordered the specialty of the house: Stuffed Cabbage a la Serbia.

MRS. BRUCHINSKI: I make very nice stuffed cabbage.

CHRIS: Maybe *you* do. The stuff I had made me sick to my stomach. I ran out in the street and as I was . . . throwing up . . . this photographer recognized me and started taking pictures of me. A.P. and U.P.I. picked it up and now my whole past is splattered on the front page of every newspaper in the country.

MRS. BRUCHINSKI: Yes, I know. I did not know I had such famous big shot radical leader living in my house.

CHRIS: That was during the 60's Mrs. Bruchinski. I don't do that radical stuff anymore. There are no radicals left anywhere. The last few I heard about were into Coors beer and solar power.

MRS. BRUCHINSKI: That I don't know. You come to Chicago to make revolution?

CHRIS: Oh, c'mon. Do I look like a revolutionary?

MRS. BRUCHINSKI: Do I look Polish? There you go. You come to town to make Power to the People.

CHRIS: No. Absolutely, positively no.

MRS. BRUCHINSKI: Why not?

CHRIS: Because I don't want to do that stuff anymore.

MRS. BRUCHINSKI: Too bad. I was hoping to make some kind revolution. Nothing fancy. But nice. You know.

CHRIS: Oh give me a break, Mrs. Bruchinski.

MRS. BRUCHINSKI: We have such fine country, Kris, and it makes me sick nobody gives not one damn anymore. By damn, it is time to give one damn again. Time to march on Washington again and make dream come true.

CHRIS: I came to Chicago with only one dream, Mrs. Bruchinski. To get a job. I don't give a damn about anything else.

MRS. BRUCHINSKI: For shame.

CHRIS: That's how it is. I want to punch the clock and work on my seniority so that I can have a nice pension when the time comes.

MRS. BRUCHINSKI: You don't make march on Washington?

CHRIS: No.

MRS. BRUCHINSKI: Maybe you change your mind?

CHRIS: Mrs. Bruchinski . . . please. I want this job and if I'm going to get it I have to write something very, very important. I need peace and quiet all weekend.

MRS. BRUCHINSKI: It is too peace and quiet for me, Kris.

CHRIS: Mrs. Bruchinski I need your help. You see, the old man Kellogg who lived here before me . . .

MRS. BRUCHINSKI: He's dead. Shtuck in the grave. (*She laughs at her own joke.*) You don't hear such good jokes on TV. Boy, oh boy.

CHRIS: Yes, I know he's dead but his habits live on. He had some weird arrangement with the paper boy. If I don't open the window on the dot the paper goes right through the glass. I've replaced two panes already. And then there's the milk. Somebody keeps delivering milk. And then there's the pimp. Do you know what a pimp is Mrs. Bruchinski?

MRS. BRUCHINSKI: Pimp? I should hope not. But despite everything I still know. I know pimp. I know Spanish fly. I know French tickler. I don't vant to know. But I know. You know what I mean.

CHRIS: This pimp Arnold keeps calling me, Mrs. Bruchinski. He thinks I'm old man Kellogg. I've gathered from our conversations that I've been paid up for a year's worth of whores. One a month. He wants to know which one I want.

MRS. BRUCHINSKI: The Japanese one is nice. If you got yen for Japanese. (*She laughs at her joke.*) Yen for Japanese. Get it.

CHRIS: Mrs. Bruchinski, please. You see I think the crazy old man Kellogg . . .

MRS. BRUCHINSKI: STOP! Old man Kellogg not crazy. He was fine old man. He paid everything year ahead of time. Rent, newspapers, milk, whores. Everything. (*She gets a little sentimental. Tear in her eye.*) Old man and I . . . we did hanky and panky during whores' strike. I even had small baby boy. Old man was not so old then, but he was very forgetful. He took small baby son out for walk and forgot where he left him. I was very angry vith him. I raise his rent. That's last thing I raise for the old man. (*Laughs at joke.*) Now I am all alone. Old woman. All alone. Where is my little baby boy? Ah, Kris, there was a better time for me. I once did "We Shall Overcome." In Washington, District of Columbia. It was so beautiful. So many people . . . marching and singing . . . like big family. And a voice from a man I could not see—saying "I have a dream."

*(She begins to sing "We Shall Overcome" and exits slowly. Chris feels something as she sings. It is not something he wants to feel. When she exits he tries to shut the window by slamming the door shut. It doesn't work. He picks up the newspaper. His actions are ones of a person ready to tear the newspaper to shreds who controls himself. He throws it out of the window. He tries to close the window. He can't. The door opens. Yovan, dark, handsome, dressed like a Mafia tailor, enters. He is carrying a container with several quarts of milk in one hand and newspapers in the other. He looks at Chris. Chris is jumping up and down putting weight on the window, trying to close it.)*

YOVAN: Allo there. (*Chris turns around. Yovan slams the door shut. The window goes down.*) Your milk is getting warm, Mr. Disgusting.

CHRIS: Who're you?

YOVAN: My name is Yovan. I come from the old country and I have a snit to pick with you.

CHRIS: Are you the milk man?

YOVAN: I am man for all seasons. Put milk in fridge.

CHRIS: It's not my milk and my fridge is full of milk as it is. Who the hell . . . (*Yovan pulls gun on Chris.*)

YOVAN: PUT MILK IN FRIDGE BEFORE MILK SPOIL . . . YOU . . . YOU . . . ROTTEN CONSUMER YOU! (*Yovan throws the milk carrier on the ottoman. The gun frightens Chris.*)

CHRIS: Sure. Why not. Yes. Milk in fridge.

YOVAN: Little babies in Peru cry out from hunger in the night and you let milk spoil. You . . . you . . . rotten human being. (*The gun is still on Chris. He takes the milk carefully and starts for the fridge. He has made a big show of putting milk in fridge. There's a lot of milk there already.*)

CHRIS: (*Slams door of fridge closed.*) There. Milk in fridge.

YOVAN: COME HERE! (*Chris comes down to the sofa, arms up, and sits. His stomach and head are acting up again.*) You have seen the newspapers, no?

CHRIS: Yes.

YOVAN: Look at pictures in papers . . . You recognize your ugly self? (*Chris looks at them.*)

CHRIS: Sure do. It's my ugly self all right.

YOVAN: Look at picture one more time again. You see the name of restaurant behind your puking face?

CHRIS: I know the name of restaurant. It's the New World Bar and Grill. Barf and Grill is more like it. (*Chris laughs trying to humor Yovan. Yovan is like a stone wall.*)

YOVAN: You are so hilarious it is going to murder you. I am proud owner of the New World Bar and Grill. (*Chris, despite his fear of the gun, is a little angry now.*)

CHRIS: You should fire your chef, man. He almost killed me.

YOVAN: I am chef, sucker man . . .

CHRIS: Well, Mr. Stuffed Cabbage . . . Do you know what you have done. You've ruined everything. Nobody knew I was in Chicago. Now my wife Dianah knows. Who knows who else knows. And those that knew me in Chicago didn't know who I was. Now they know all about me.

YOVAN: Excellent. I hope your life is in ruins.

CHRIS: My job is, thanks to you. I was supposed to start work today. But oh no . . . My boss saw that picture and read that story about me and now if I want to work for him I have to write a retraction of my Radical Past for the *Chicago Sun-Times,* write it quickly, and write it so he likes it . . . and it's all your fault.

YOVAN: STOP! (*He sticks the gun into Chris's stomach. Chris gets quiet. All is quiet.*) You have just screamed at me. Now I am going to make scream at you. Do you know what you have done. You bring bad publicity on me. Your picture in all the papers of Chicago. (*Goes through the papers, flinging them at Chris.) Polish Sun. Polish Tribune. Lithuanian Gazette. Croatian Times. Polish Times. Polish Gazette.* You make me laughing stock of Chicago nationalities! He, he, he, they all go at me. Ha, ha, ha. I got telephone calls in various languages and they all go: Ho, Ho, Ho.

CHRIS: Sounds like a lot of laughs.

YOVAN: Don't get humorous with me! Your blood, Mr. Rotten Manners, will wash away the insult if you do not make sorry. Make sorry. And make it good and quick. I am not talking about chupped liver . . . Mr. Redical of the Sixties. I am talking proper apple-logy.

CHRIS: Apple-logy! You want *me* to apologize. To *you.* After what *you've* done to *me* . . . Well, I'm not going to apologize. I don't apologize. You have your pride. I have my pride.

YOVAN: I also have a gun. (*He fires the gun in the air and then aims it at Chris. Mrs. Bruchinski runs in. She sees Yovan with the gun.*)

MRS. BRUCHINSKI: Sorry. Did not know you had company, Kris. Bye-Bye. (*She goes out again. The firing of the gun has made Chris settle down a bit. Yovan looks at the door.*)

YOVAN: Funny accent for black lady. Anyways, getting back to brass tacks. Here is offer. You come back to my restaurant.

CHRIS: Never.

YOVAN: Monday. You come back and you sit down at nice table and you eat my food. And you look happy when you eat. You go: Mmmm, yummy, yummy, yummy. In the middle of yumm I take snapshot of you with my Polaroid Pronto. I send picture to all the papers and you write apple-logy with John Hancock on the bottom.

CHRIS: You think I'm crazy.

YOVAN: No. I think I am crazy. I am crazy with anger. I make cement hushpuppies for your feet. Get it.

CHRIS: Hey, give me a break, buddy.

YOVAN: DO NOT GET FAMILIAR. We did not pick walnuts together in our youth.

CHRIS: Look, let's be reasonable, all right?

YOVAN: Okee-dokey.

CHRIS: We've done enough harm to each other already. I've ruined your reputation. You've got me in trouble with my boss, with my wife . . .

YOVAN: At least you have wife.

CHRIS: I don't want wife.

YOVAN: I want wife. My wife, the cook, she died. She left no recipes behind. (*He is getting sentimental. He might even drape his arm around Chris.*) I miss my wife.

CHRIS: I bet all your customers do, too.

YOVAN: Yes, is true. Poof, she died. Then my daughter, Nadja, poof . . .

CHRIS: She died?

YOVAN: No such luck. She run off with some man, Roger, whose hide and hair I never even see. The son I never had I still don't have. A big family is what I always wanted, like Italians and Puerto Ricans and what do I have. Big loneliness is what I have. (*Tears come to his eyes.*) Alone I lie on my waterbed like shipwrecked sailor far from shore of mother country. (*He is weeping. Starts to sing.*) Tamo, daleko . . . Daleko kraj mora . . . Tamo je moja Mama . . . Tamo je Srbija . . . (*He can't sing. Tears choke him. He sobs.*) Ah, Redical of the Sixties. I am so unhappy. I love America but America does not love me.

CHRIS: Sure she does.

YOVAN: No, no, no. There was time . . . Yes. No more. Is every man for himself now.

CHRIS: (*Interrupting.*) Well, you've certainly had a rough time of it. I can't say it's been exactly easy for me either. I guess we just have to be flexible . . . and . . . well, forget the past.

YOVAN: Forget! I forget nothing. Such psychology roll off me like water off the ass of duck.

CHRIS: In that case I suggest you put the ass of duck on your menu. I have already agreed to apologize for having been alive just to keep my job, and I'll be dammed if I'll now apologize for having almost died.

YOVAN: Okee-dokey. I fix your goose, you turkey. Your cork has popped. Your bottle of wine is breathing its last. The telephone is ringing in the house of the man who will be digging your grave. (*Yovan opens the window and starts going out.*)

CHRIS: What the hell you doing now?

YOVAN: Old tradition. We never cross threshold twice of man we threaten to kill. And remember this, Mr. Smartie Panties: sometimes, somehow, somewhere when you least expect it . . . it is not going to be Allen Funt of Candid Camera. Get it! (*Chris picks up the papers. Yovan vanishes through *the window.*)

CHRIS: You just don't shoot people for having an upset stomach. (*Chris throws papers out of the window. He is trying to get a hold of himself. There's not much there. Chris looks out window.*) Hey, you, get away from my car, dammit. (*A shot is heard.*) He shot my car! I don't believe this. He shot my car. (*Another shot—the window slams shut.*) He shot it again. That's it! That does it. You can't shoot my T-Bird and get away with it. (*He staggers to the telephone. Dials.*) Hello, Operator, get me the Police! Hello, Police! This Alien from the New World Bar and Grill where I barfed is threatening to kill me if I don't go "yummy, yummy" and make an apple-logy. And now he just shot my bird. Hello! Hello! (*He hangs up. Mrs. Bruchinski enters.*)

MRS. BRUCHINSKI: Killer man gone?

CHRIS: Yes. He just shot my car. (*She slams door. Crosses to window.*)

MRS. BRUCHINSKI: Sonomogun window shtuck closed again.

CHRIS: (*Goes into bedroom.*) I'm going down to the police station and scream at the cops.

(*Mrs. Bruchinski trying to open window. Just as she opens the window the door opens and Betty, the black cop, who was once a male, enters. She's carrying an armful of newspapers.*)

BETTY: All right, sister. Cool it. I got a complaint from people across the street about a litterbug throwing newspapers out of the window. (*Chris comes out of the bedroom. Betty sees Chris and throws the papers down.*)

CHRIS: Police! God, that was quick.

BETTY: CHRIS! CHRISTOPHER MY MAN! CHRIS BABY! (*She primps a little, wanting to look good for Chris.*)

CHRIS: Who the hell are you?

BETTY: Damn. Been so long. Remember J.B. Kellogg?

CHRIS: No.

BETTY: Remember Bomber Kellogg.

CHRIS: No.

BETTY: You do so.

CHRIS: So what? All right, I do.

BETTY: It's me! J.B.!

CHRIS: J.B. was a man.

BETTY: I was a man.

MRS. BRUCHINSKI: Somonabitch!

BETTY: I got myself a sex change a while ago and . . .

CHRIS: I don't believe any of this.

BETTY: Oh, Chrissie. It's like old times. Give me five!

CHRIS: Give me a break. (*Chris makes it out of the window as Betty comes toward *him. Betty shouts after him.*)

BETTY: Where the hell are you going?

MRS. BRUCHINSKI: Kris is going to make scrims at cops in police station.

BETTY: Give 'em hell, Chris. (*Betty does a long look at Mrs. Bruchinski.*) Hey, Mama, you sure do look like a soul sister but you sure don't sound like no soul sister.

MRS. BRUCHINSKI: You too. You look like soul sister but you make sounds like soul brother. You were a man once.

BETTY: Sister, I was many things once. Chris and I and Roger O'Dwyer and Stokely and Rennie Davis . . . . We were going to change the world, sister.

MRS. BRUCHINSKI: So was I. Such songs we used to sing marching together in the streets of Washington.

BETTY: I marched in Washington when Martin was there. I was just a boy.

MRS. BRUCHINSKI: You were a boy?

BETTY: At one time.

MRS. BRUCHINSKI: I was a mama. At one time.

BETTY: I had a mama. At one time. (*They look at each other. There is something in the air for a split second and then they shoo it away with their hands.*)

MRS. BRUCHINSKI: Now it is all gone. Cute baby boy gone. Rotten old man gone. We shall overcome . . . gone. When will "Overcome" come again?

(*She starts to sing: "We Shall Overcome." She of course weeps when she sings. Betty joins in and Betty weeps a little too. They sing as they exit. Betty slams the door shut. The window goes down again. Mrs. Bruchinski goes into her apartment. Betty goes down the stairs and into the street, singing or humming. Nadja, the slut, is coming onto the street. She stops to peddle. Hitchhike.*)

BETTY: Hey, don't strut that trashy stuff around here, you hear. (Nadja turns around.)

NADJA: Look . . . Hi there, Betty.

BETTY: Hey, Nadja. How's business?

NADJA: I got a new pimp Arnold, and Arnold's got me a gig with this old man Chris. He's paid up for the year. It could mean a steady job.

BETTY: Just saw my man Chris, a former comrade from the days of the barricades. You're too young to know, Nadja, but those were the days. I was a man then and . . . well . . . the times we lived in had balls . . . and I had them too . . . and now . . .

NADJA: I think you look wonderful, Betty. That's the best transsexual operation I've ever seen.

BETTY: Well, thank you, Nadja. Coming from a fellow sister that's quite a compliment.

NADJA: They're going to let you stay on the force?

BETTY: DAMN right. They tried kicking me off but according to the Fed guidelines they have to hire so many minority transsexuals. Girl, I just love your perfume. (*Nadja takes perfume. Sprays Betty.*)

NADJA: It's called "Revenge." It used to drive my husband Roger crazy.

BETTY: Crazy! I like it.

NADJA: Got to go, Betty. Catch you later. (*They kiss.*) I guess your beard's still a problem.

BETTY: That's the least of my problems, Nadja.

NADJA: Bye, Bye.

BETTY: Bye.

(*Nadja strolls off. Betty takes out a battery-operated shaver and shaves her face. Enter Roger. He is an old man dressed in rags. He is carrrying a bunch of newspapers under one arm. He has two bags in the other arm. Slung around his neck is his "box"—a radio-cassette machine. On the cassette we hear: "Those Were the Days." He is walking toward Betty, who is shaving. He is the saddest looking person in the world. As he comes near Betty, he sniffs the air.*)

ROGER: NADJA!

BETTY: The name's Betty, Gramps!

ROGER: That perfume!

BETTY: It's called Revenge.

ROGER: I know it's Revenge. My wife Nadja used to wear it. (*He looks at Betty. He walks toward the entrance to Chris's building. Betty strolls away. She is thinking about something. Roger is thinking about something, too. Both turn around at the same time and look at each other.*) Weren't you . . .

(*Both decide they were wrong about something, or maybe wrong. No, it couldn't be who each of them thought it was. Betty strolls off as Roger walks up the stairs toward Chris's apartment. Mrs. Bruchinski opens the door. Sees Roger. Hears music. Starts to sing. Roger, stunned, joins her. They sing for a bit. Roger breaks into tears and shuts off the cassette.*)

MRS. BRUCHINSKI: Who are you old man and vat is it you vant with me in this terrible don't give a damn times we live in.

ROGER: I want to fall through a time warp. I want to make up for ten wasted years. I want meaning in my life again.

MRS. BRUCHINSKI: Me too old man poopsy. You want revolution maybe.

ROGER: Maybe later.

MRS. BRUCHINSKI: You want cup of tea, maybe now.

ROGER: Now, I just want Chris in my life again.

MRS. BRUCHINSKI: Kris is not home. He went out to scrim at the police.

ROGER: He would! The old rebel! He's still at it.

MRS. BRUCHINSKI: My name is Mrs. Bruchinski.

ROGER: My name is Roger. Roger the Rotten. Roger the Rebel no more.

MRS. BRUCHINSKI: Please to meet you old man poopsy. (*Roger starts going into Chris's place.*) Nice to have old man again. Brings back memories of hanky and panky.

ROGER: Forgive me, Chris!

(*Sirens wail as Dianah and Sal enter. Dianah is carrying a bullhorn and a newspaper. Sal a briefcase.*)

DIANAH: Chris!

ROGER: CHRIS!

DIANAH: OH CHRIS!

ROGER: Oh Chris, oh, Chris! (*Roger sinks back on the floor. Dianah weeps.*)

DIANAH: Chris! Chris! Chris!

SAL: Here we are. This is his address.

DIANAH: This is terrible. Chris Adrian. My husband. Throwing his life away.

SAL: He's throwing more than his life according to that picture.

DIANAH: Hush . . . you . . . You . . . lawyer.

SAL: I may be a lawyer but I'm also a man. You may still be his wife but you're also a woman.

DIANAH: A job. He told me on the telephone that he got a job. A full time middle class job. Oh, Chicago, Chicago, you toddling town, blow my tears away.

SAL: I'll kiss your tears away if you let me.

DIANAH: This isn't the Chris I know. I bet he's been brainwashed. He needs to be de-programmed. I need legal advice. I'll have to get a lawyer.

SAL: I am a lawyer. Remember me. You got me from legal aid. I'm talking to you, Dianah. Can you hear me?

DIANAH: At least I'm here. Close to him.

SAL: You're wasting your time, Dianah.

DIANAH: Let the time go by. I don't really care if I'm . . . on the street where he lives.

SAL: He left you. He didn't even tell you where he was going.

DIANAH: The way his smile just beams. The way he sings off-key. The way he haunts my dream. No, no, they can't take that away from me.

SAL: But, Dianah, he's a bastard. A bum. A puking, no good, sonovabitch. I'm talking to you, Dianah. Can you hear me? Is there something the matter with my voice that you can't hear me?

DIANAH: What a voice he had. He had and he was the voice of his time.

SAL: I am the voice of my time, Dianah. Is it my fault that the times are what they are? (*She doesn't hear him.*)

DIANAH: We met in Chicago. The windy city blew us together. You could say it was Destiny.

SAL: I'll say whatever you want . . . Can you hear me, Dianah? You make me feel very insecure.

DIANAH: And in that troubled and turbulent time I trembled when I saw him on that glorious day in May . . . only yesterday when the world was young. There he was . . . in a crowd . . . and yet alone . . . with a bullhorn in his hand. He stood there like a cross between Che Guevara and Chuck Mangione. And when he put the bullhorn to his lips to speak . . . he didn't speak . . . he played. A born bullhorn player and he seemed to be playing only for me. HO-HO-HO-CHI-MINH! (*She almost sobs.*) I didn't know Ho Chi Minh from Pinnochio at that time, but something in me stirred when I heard his voice. He cared. He cared a lot. He exuded an aroma of Cuban cigars and mimeo ink and his loose fitting army surplus garb could not hide the body of a tango dancer. A woman can tell such things. I swooned. He smiled. I swayed. He played. I died. Oh what a man he was. What a voice he had. An assertive voice without being overbearing. It was the voice of a man who enjoys hearing children laugh.

SAL: I love hearing children laugh. I never laughed as a child. I always meant to but something always came up.

DIANAH: What happened to him? Was it something I did that was his undoing or something I didn't do that did him in? I don't know. All I know is that I feel responsible. I let his spark die . . . The flame of the rebel became a charcoal lighter on the Bar-B-Que Pit of History. (*She falls silent. This is Sal's chance to speak. He jumps at it.*)

SAL: Look at me, Dianah. I'm right here. I'm easy to see. Look at me, please. (*She looks but not really at him, through him and beyond.*) You are looking at a desperate, homeless, friendless creature, Dianah. I just can't seem to make an impression on anyone. Even my parents. I was conceived on a Castro convertible at their friend's house. They never had sex at home. When I was a baby they'd leave me at home with a baby sitter and go and have sex in a motel, or in a hotel, or at a friend's house. They had friends everywhere and they never introduced me to any of them. One day they just didn't come back. They just forgot about me. I was raised by a baby sitter, Dianah, who charged six seventy-five an hour. My old man, Kellogg, that rotten old man of mine, paid her seven years in advance. But when the money ran out she left. I got a job to try and keep her, but I got laid off. I was ten. Out of a job at ten! The older I grew, the more I craved love and friends, the less the world seemed to care. I am nobody's memory. Nobody gets together on a rainy day and wonders: How's Sal Kellogg doing? What's Sal Kellogg up to? Pigeons starving to death will not eat my bread crumbs in the park. Dogs facing certain death in a dog pound will not go home with me. I send letters and checks to the starving of Guatemala but they don't write back. Scientology doesn't want me. Moonies don't want me. I could be had for a song but the world stops humming when Sal goes by. I would become a flasher but who would look. I talk to myself and even I don't listen. Are you listening, Dianah? (*He cries, kneeling to Dianah, sobbing.*) This is the single longest uninterrupted speech I have ever made, Dianah, and I hope it moved you. (*Dianah looks at him.*)

DIANAH: What were you saying?

(*Sal is desperate. He wants to make an impression on her. He flings himself at her, making an amorous attempt.*)

SAL: I love you, Dianah. That's what I'm saying. I love you. Love. Love. Love. (*She doesn't move. Sal screams. Falls on floor.*) Oh, God.

DIANAH: I think my guilt over what I've allowed to happen to Chris has made me frigid.

SAL: Alaska is frigid too! But underneath your frozen tundra there is oil waiting to flow.

DIANAH: I don't think you have the pipeline for the job, Sal.

SAL: Hurt me! I don't care!

(*She clutches the bullhorn to her bosom. Chris enters, carrying what's left of his car—his car top. He looks very upset. He sees Dianah just as she sees him.*)

DIANAH: Chris! Darling!

CHRIS: Dianah! Dammit! (*Sal tries to make an impression on Chris.*)

SAL: Hello, my name is Sal Kellogg. I've been retained by Dianah Adrian in the matter of Adrian vs. Adrian. (*Neither of them seems to hear him.*)

DIANAH: Here we are again, Chris. In the windy city. Only now the crowd is gone and it's just the two of us.

SAL: There's three of us here. Just for the record.

DIANAH: Ah, Chris, the way we were. If we had the chance to do it all again . . . would we . . . could we . . . memories . . . light the corners of my mind.

CHRIS: I think your mind's gone, Dianah. It's over. It's all over.

DIANAH: Why, Chris, why?

CHRIS: Because, Dianah, because.

DIANAH: Was it the women's movement? Did I steal the torch from your hand . . . and you couldn't live with yourself?

CHRIS: I can live with myself. I can't live with you.

SAL: You can't talk to her like this. You hear me? (*Chris doesn't.*)

CHRIS: Dianah, please. I've had a rough day, so don't make it any rougher. The street sharks stripped my Bird. I've never seen anything like it.

They had blow torches and jacks and yankers and pullers. They even had a foreman in charge of the operation. All I could salvage from my whole car was this.

DIANAH: A car! We don't have cars. We don't believe in cars!

CHRIS: We're not we, Dianah. We were we for too long. And while we were we, you were you, but I wasn't me. And I want to be me. I gotta be me . . . Now you got me talking in that way of yours. I'm sick and tired of it all, Dianah. I have O.D.'d on all those causes and issues. I don't care about the boat people, Dianah. (*Dianah lets out a scream of anguish.*) I don't. I don't want to hear about another boat person again. I don't care about nuclear waste. To hell with it. I don't care about oil spills, third world dictators, wilderness preserves, or bi-lingual education. Sugar in kid's cereals. Don't care! I don't give a good goddamn about the ozone layer, the whales, the porpoises . . . the cute little baby seals . . . I don't know who's running Cambodia and I don't care! I don't even care if the Beatles ever get back together again. Anything that I have ever cared about. Anything that you have ever cared about, anything that anyone has ever cared about, I don't care about and I don't care that I don't care.

DIANAH: (*Quietly.*) I understand.

CHRIS: No, you don't. If you understood you wouldn't say "I understand" like that. Don't you understand. I am tired of drinking black coffee out of earthen mugs that you made yourself. I want a cup and saucer and I want sugar in it. I don't care if I never see another mimeo machine or another cruddy leaflet again. Me. That's all I care about. Me. Me. Me. Wonderful, yummy, delicious me! I want a nice condominium without a stitch of macrame in it. I want a TV. A stereo. A toaster oven. Shag rugs. Designer towels. A big fridge. A huge fridge. I want a walk-in fridge. When do I want it? I WANT IT NOW.

DIANAH: Oh, my God, he's gone mad. Chris. Don't do this to yourself.

CHRIS: That's right, Dianah, I'm starting a new life.

DIANAH: He's delirious.

CHRIS: I'm going to be an underwriter in an insurance company. (*Dianah screams. Chris starts to leave.*)

DIANAH: CHRIS! What about me? (*Chris stops.*)

CHRIS: Frankly, Dianah. . . . [I don't give a damn—*optional.*] (*Chris runs off with car top and exits.*)

DIANAH: Oh, my God. Chris! I think it's too late for legal aid. I'll have to get him a psychiatrist.

SAL: He's gove over the edge, Dianah. Anybody that walks around the city with a car top in his arms has made the big plunge. They're playing his song Dianah, and it's looney tunes, you hear me?

DIANAH: I am all alone now.

SAL: You have me.

DIANAH: I can't live alone. I'll throw myself in Lake Michigan.

SAL: Dianah . . . (*She starts to exit. Sal follows her like a puppy. Suddenly Yovan rushes out onto the street running directly toward her. He's carrying in his hand an old-fashioned looking bomb, a round black thing with a long fuse. The fuse is burning. He is heading toward Chris's apartment window with it. But . . . when he sees Dianah, he stops in his tracks. She sees him, she stops in hers. It's love at first sight. Only Sal seems worried but who hears Sal.*) Dianah, the man's got a bomb. (*Nobody hears him.*)

YOVAN: Allo there, stranger lady.

DIANAH: Hello . . . there. (*If Yovan prides himself on being tough, he also prides himself on being suave. The man of many moves. The fuse is burning, but he only has eyes for Dianah. Sal only has eyes for the fuse.*)

YOVAN: Stranger lady, you are beautiful. No, not just beautiful, you are cute.

DIANAH: It takes a very secure man these days to acknowledge beauty in a woman. Most men feel threatened by us.

YOVAN: Most men are chupped liver. Such is not the case in my case. (*In a very sensual gesture, he bites the fuse off just before it is to explode the bomb.*)

DIANAH: Were you going to . . . (*She gestures to the bomb.*)

YOVAN: Yes, I was going to blow up a person's apartment. Maybe blow up person inside.

DIANAH: You're an anarchist?

YOVAN: I am Man. Man is everything.

DIANAH: And woman?

YOVAN: Woman is everything plus something else to boot. This . . . this is a dangerous neighborhood. I do not want to scare the pants off you . . . but you should not be out alone.

SAL: She's not alone. She's with me. (*Nobody, needless to say, hears him.*)

DIANAH: (*Very* triste.) Sometimes, it's best to be alone.

SAL: You're not alone.

DIANAH: We come into this world alone and we got out alone.

SAL: I have nothing more to say on the subject.

YOVAN: Are you, eh, vaiting for somebody or are you, eh, shooting the brizz as they say?

DIANAH: I am mourning. A person I loved died. He died in front of my eyes, so to speak.

YOVAN: It is tough to be lonely. But when the going gets to be tough cookies, my cookies do not crumble, if you know what I mean.

DIANAH: It is clear that you have hot blood in your veins. A woman can tell such things. I, on the other hand, am frigid, so to speak.

YOVAN: Alaska is frigid too. But I tell you this, underknitt your frozen tundra there is oil vating to flow.

SAL: I don't believe this.

DIANAH: Excuse me for asking, but you're not a native of these parts. Your accent . . .

YOVAN: Is true. I am in Chicago only ten years. Originally I am from Cleveland.

DIANAH: I seem to detect a scent of mimeo ink on you.

YOVAN: Your nose is a credit to your brain. I print menus on mimeo machine and I also print Serbian newspaper in my basement. I call it *Serbian Sun.* I write powerful stuff. I write: America, wake up. People need you. My friends. They give up. They go back to the old country. So I write: Fooey on you, you chupped liver patriots. Fooey on your kids. Fooey on your family. Stuff like that I write. Leaflets too.

DIANAH: I used to write leaflets. Oh, those were the days, my friend, we thought they'd never end . . .

YOVAN: Yes, we'd sing and dance forever and a day . . .

DIANAH: We'd lead the life we choose. We'd fight and never lose . . . (*She starts crying.*)

YOVAN: Oh, veep no more my lady. Veep no more today. It is not time to give up. America needs us. We must link up hands and arms and feet and hearts and do big stuff.

DIANAH: Hope stirs in my bosom again.

YOVAN: Something stirs in me, too. My name is Yovan.

DIANAH: My name is Dianah.

SAL: My name is Sal.

YOVAN: My place is not far away.

SAL: That line about the frozen tundra was mine . . . Dianah . . .

(*All go off. Chris enters his apartment, holding the car top. He doesn't know what to do with it. He is tired. He looks around and throws car top in the corner of the room right on top of the pile of rags that is Roger. A groan is heard. Chris is startled. He listens. He hears nothing. He closes the door. Another groan is heard. The car top moves. Chris turns around. He either thinks he is hearing things or there's a prowler in the house.*)

CHRIS: Who's there? Who are you?

(*From underneath the car top the head of the old man emerges. Roger is a little groggy from sleep and a little groggy from the hit in the head with a car top.*)

ROGER: Chris, Chris. It's me. Take me back, Chris.

CHRIS: Hey, who the hell are you? (*There is dead silence. Then Roger softly, very softly and through sobs, begins singing: "All we are saying is . . . "*) Give me a break.

ROGER: It's me, Chris.

CHRIS: Me who?

ROGER: It's me. Roger. You remember Roger O'Dwyer. Your old comrade from the sixties.

CHRIS: I remember Roger. You're not Roger. I know Roger and I don't know you. I don't know how you know me but I do know I don't know you. Who are you?

(*Roger, although hurt by not being remembered, understands. He in effect now has to audition for Chris to show him he is who he says he is.*)

ROGER: Hey, hey, L.B.J. (*Pause.*) Ho, Ho, Ho-Chi-Minh! (*Pause.*) Hi, Hi, Chou-En-Lai!

CHRIS: ROGER!

ROGER: Chris!

(*Chris offers to shake hands, but Roger wants to do "the old hand shake." Chris has forgotten how to do it but they muddle through somehow ending up in an embrace. Roger doesn't want to let go of the embrace. Chris has to peel him off. Although Chris is feeling slightly more in control his feet are hardly on the ground.*)

CHRIS: Roger. It's you, I know . . . but . . . I mean, the last time I saw you . . . you were . . . well . . . frankly, you were my age.

ROGER: I'm still your age, Chris.

CHRIS: Hell, Rog, let's call a spade a spade. You look like an old man, man.

ROGER: Oh, right! I keep forgetting! Underneath all this stuff I look fine. (*He takes wig off. Reveals old Rog.*) Not that I have a right to look fine. But I do.

CHRIS: So, why the disguise, Rog? You hiding from somebody?

ROGER: From "them."

CHRIS: "Them," eh?

ROGER: Yeah, "them."

CHRIS: Do I know any of "them"?

ROGER: You know all of "them." Goddamn women and their goddamn orgasms. So you were down screaming at the cops, eh? Like in the old days, right, Chris?

CHRIS: It was a little different this time.

ROGER: Sure it was. You were by yourself. Alone! But proud! You are alone no more, you majestic son of a bitch, you. I've come to join you. You didn't think I'd remember, did you? (*Chris obviously feels that Roger has lost his mind.*)

CHRIS: Remember what, Rog?

ROGER: Don't tease me, Chris. I'm not that bad. The Big Meeting, Chris. The LAST BIG MEETING before The Big Split.

CHRIS: And . . . eh . . . what happened at the Last Big Meeting?

ROGER: You remember. Everybody was there. Jerry Rubin, Abbie Hoffman, Tom Hayden, Rennie Davis, Mark Rudd, J.B. Kellogg, you, me, and "them." "They" were there too. Remember? The Days of Rage were over. Nobody had any rage left. Nobody had any grass even. The movement was over, we all felt. It was like the last supper. And then Abbie had an idea. The last brillant idea he was to have. Dear Abbie. Remember? He said that we should split up but plan to return. Return to Chicago at the dawn of the new decade, and, if nothing else, as a gesture of our continuing protest, we would march once again and puke on the foul system. Days of Vomit, Abbie called them. Oh Chris! Everybody forgot! Nobody came except for you! When I saw your picture in the papers puking alone, I wanted to kill myself! You! Alone! You did it alone but you did it!

CHRIS: Oh, Rog, Rog, you can't be serious, man.

ROGER: You're all that's left. You're the only one. YOU ARE THE MOVEMENT NOW. (*He falls on his knees.*) Take me back! Forgive me, Chris, for I have sinned, but take me back! PLEASE!

CHRIS: Rog. Rog. Hey . . . I can't take you back . . . You don't understand.

ROGER: NO, YOU DON'T UNDERSTAND! I was going to kill myself. I bought the pills. I wrote my suicide notes. I was going to die and then I saw you puking in the papers, and you gave me hope. If you don't take me back, I'll kill myself.

CHRIS: Rog, I can't. (*Roger opens the bottle of pills. Empties it in his mouth. Chris tries to stop him. Roger throws him back. Chris is frantic.*) ROGER! OH MY GOD! I AM THE MOVEMENT! I TAKE YOU BACK! (*Roger rushes toward him spitting out the pills into Chris's face. Embraces him.*)

ROGER: You saved my life! (*Breaks away from the embrace.*) Why? Why did you save my life? I don't deserve it. You should spit on me! Go ahead, spit on me!

CHRIS: I can't spit, Rog. I am very, very tired. I'll spit on you later, I promise.

ROGER: You'll spit on me when I tell you what I've done.

CHRIS: Don't tell me, Rog.

ROGER: I have to. You have to know the scum that you're taking back.

CHRIS: Give me a break, Rog. Don't tell me.

ROGER: I've done it all, baby. From A to Z, but we'll start in the middle with M for marriage. Married. Me! Yes. Last year, I married this girl named Nadja. I bought a car! Me! A car! A Buick, Chris! Spit on me. Spit at will, Chris. And in my rec room, YES, I HAD A REC ROOM. And in my rec room, I had a letter framed that was printed in the T.V. GUIDE. Concerned viewer writes. I complained because they cancelled my favorite TV show. (*Real anguish, real self-loathing and self-lacerating.*) I HAD A FAVORITE TV SHOW! Hit me! Hurt me! And then my wife left me. The whole middle class shebang, Chris. Do you know why she left me? Because of orgasms. Yes. She wasn't getting enough orgasms. And that's when it hit me! That's when it dawned on me. It's the women that killed the movement! They did it. We never should have told them about orgasms. They didn't know. Why did we tell them. Now they all want them. And not just on May Day, Chris. Every month they want one or two. Yes. Orgasms! And they got us convinced that we should be giving them orgasms! And while we were wondering how to give it to them so they like it they took over the movement. They formed their own movement! Remember J.B. Kellogg? He got a sex change I hear just so he could join the radical wing of NOW. Radical wing, Chris! Are you listening? The women! They've got internal struggles for power. They've got splinter groups. They've got radical wings. They've got all the good shit we used to have! And what are we doing? What are the guys doing? We're wondering why we can't give them orgasms. It's a conspiracy, Chris. They suppress their orgasms on purpose just to confuse us. They've got us shaving twice a day and they're not shaving at all. They've raised our consciousness and lowered our cocks and they want to know why we can't give them an orgasm. They've got us by the balls and they're saying "nuts" to us. Orgasms! Orgasms! IF I HAD AN ORGASM I'D GIVE IT TO THEM JUST SO THEY'D LEAVE ME ALONE! (*He is spent. He falls down on the floor from sheer exhaustion. Chris seems catatonic. Roger speaks again. Slowly now. The hysteria has passed.*) That's why I put on this wig and stuff. I feel safe. Women don't bother me. They don't expect anything from an old man. I'm a sexual incognito. (*Becomes old man. He looks at Chris, at his apartment, at what is left of Chris's car. He is full of admiration.*) But enough about me. You! You're the one! You've remained pure! Look at you. Still the shabby wrinkled clothes. You're probably broke. No job. No wife. Nothing! What's your secret, Chris?! (*Chris is weary of all this.*)

CHRIS: Either you have it or you don't.

(*Roger alludes to the car top.*)

ROGER: That's classic! Walking around the city with that! Mocking our car crazy society. You magnificent son of a bitch. How, Chris, how?

CHRIS: I have to lie down now, Rog.

ROGER: You go right ahead, man. (*Chris flops down on sofa. Roger gives him the power sign.*) Dream on, man!

(*Nadja appears on the street and heads toward Chris's apartment. Roger goes to the window. Looks out. Alarm clock goes off! Chris sits up a little and looks at Roger looking out of the window.*)

CHRIS: Rog. I haven't got the strength to explain but you should move away from the window.
ROGER: Why's that, buddy?

(*Nadja knocks on the door and just as she does a huge rolled up newspaper flies through the window and hits Roger smack in the face. He staggers, falls down, and hits his head. Goes out like a light. Chris gets up slowly to get the door. Nadja knocks. Silence. Nadja knocks again.*)

CHRIS: I'm coming.

(*He opens the door. Nadja is there in a bright halter, shorts and chain belt. She looks at Chris. Chris looks at her. Chris is so exhausted he looks and acts like an old man.*)

NADJA: So, you're old man Chris. You don't look so bad for an old man, pops.
CHRIS: Thank you. It's how you feel that counts. And I feel very old.
NADJA: Don't worry. I'll fix that in no time at all. (*She starts undressing. Chris watches her for a while.*)
CHRIS: Who are you?
NADJA: (*She goes into her act.*) That's up to you, actually. I could be a visiting nurse, no? What about one of those meals on wheels women, huh? I know. A granddaughter? Incest is making a comeback, gramps? But where will I sleep, Grampa. There's only one bed. (*She looks at him.*) You're supposed to chortle now and say: Why don't we sleep together.
CHRIS: Look, kid, I'm too old for this game.
NADJA: No you're not. You, hell, you couldn't be a day over fifty.
CHRIS: I'm thirty-seven, dammit.
NADJA: Sorry, Arnold told me you were touchy about your age.
CHRIS: Who's Arnold?
NADJA: Arnold the pimp.
CHRIS: Oh, the pimp! Oh, I get it. You're one of Arnold's girls.
NADJA: No, Arnold's one of my pimps.
CHRIS: Who cares.
NADJA: I care.
CHRIS: The point is you're a prostitute.
NADJA: No, I'm not. I'm a slut. Prostitutes do it just for the money. I do it as a political statement as well.
CHRIS: Oh, please. No statements. Look, kid, I'm broke. I got no money.
NADJA: That's all right. You're paid up for the year.
CHRIS: I never paid for it.
NADJA: So it was a gift subscription.
CHRIS: Look, the old man who lived here died. (*Nadja sees Roger and screams.*)

NADJA: Is that him?

CHRIS: No, he's not an old man. (*Nadja looks at him again. Then at Chris.*)

NADJA: But he's dead.

CHRIS: No, he's not dead.

NADJA: What's the matter with him. (*Chris has no energy to explain.*)

CHRIS: Would you believe me if I told you the evening news hit him real hard?

NADJA: Is he the old man I was supposed to do it with?

CHRIS: Yeah, sure.

NADJA: We almost had something going at his expense, eh? Too bad. (*She starts putting on her clothes.*)

CHRIS: How old are you?

NADJA: Nineteen.

CHRIS: When I was nineteen . . .

NADJA: I know! I know! You were probably trying to save the world and all.

CHRIS: Well, as a matter of fact . . .

NADJA: Yeah, yeah, I've heard it all before. My husband was a world saver. Where did it get him?

CHRIS: You're married?

NADJA: Divorced.

CHRIS: Where's your husband?

NADJA: I don't know. Lying around somewhere. You married?

CHRIS: I'm getting divorced.

NADJA: It's all crap, isn't it?

CHRIS: Well, it's what it is.

NADJA: Crap. That's what it is.

CHRIS: It's what we make it, right?

NADJA: Right, and we made it crap.

CHRIS: Stop saying "crap."

NADJA: Don't tell me what to do. Nobody tells me what to do.

CHRIS: Nobody's telling you what to do. (*Silence.*)

NADJA: It's crap. That's what life is. A big crap trap.

CHRIS: All right. All right. I get the message. So it's bad.

NADJA: It's not bad. It's nothing. Zero. Pointless. Empty.

CHRIS: You sound like Goldie Hawn in a Bergman movie. You're too damned young to be so cynical.

NADJA: Oh, yeah.

CHRIS: Yeah. Things change.

NADJA: For the worse.

CHRIS: Not necessarily. It's just . . . well . . . it's the times we're in, that's all. Everybody's just thinking about themselves. Me. Me. Me.

NADJA: And what're you thinking about? (*Chris is angry at having no come-*

*back.*)

CHRIS: That's not the point.

NADJA: What is the point?

CHRIS: The point is . . . I'm in my thirties. But you, hell. Nineteen. When I was nineteen . . .

NADJA: Oh yeah, and where did it get you?

CHRIS: Get me? I'll tell you where it got me. Right here. (*Pounds his chest.*) At least I tried. At least I felt something once.

NADJA: I feel for you.

CHRIS: No, I feel for you, kid!

NADJA: I don't want you to feel for me.

CHRIS: That's just too bad, isn't it. Because I feel for you.

NADJA: Feel for yourself, sucker.

CHRIS: I've felt for myself already today. Now I'm going to feel for you. Boy, do I feel for you. (*She swings her purse at him. He ducks. She is ready to cry . . .*)

NADJA: You no good hypocrite. Just because you've done your bit in the past doesn't mean you can feel superior to me. You no good bastard. You're just as bad as my husband, Roger. He wanted me to be his little woman. My father, Yovan, wanted me to be his little girl. A whore, that's all you men want. Well, I will not be a whore. I'm a slut. (*She's bawling. She starts to leave. Chris tries to stop her. She exits, slams door. Window shuts. Chris opens door, goes out into hallway.*)

CHRIS: Wait! What's your name?

(*Roger wakes suddenly.*)

ROGER: Nadja! Revenge! I smell Revenge! (*Nadja is gone. Chris goes back into his apartment.*) Oh, Chris. I had a terrible nightmare. Thank God I'm here. Where is my box? I need my box!

CHRIS: I don't know, Rog. What box?

ROGER: My box, I need my box. I need my song. Oh Chris! (*He leaps for his bag. Pulls out his box. He turns on cassette. "THOSE WERE THE DAYS." Clutches it to his heart like a Bible. Hugs Chris. This time Chris hugs him back.*)

CHRIS: There, there Rog. It's all right.

(*Mrs. Bruchinski enters.*)

MRS. BRUCHINSKI: I got the blues in the night.

ROGER: Oh Chris, remember the old days.

MRS. BRUCHINSKI: I remember. I was young in the old days.

ROGER: And I was a rebel with a cause. I was going to change the world.

MRS. BRUCHINSKI: Instead the world changed us. Oh, so sad.

ROGER: Oh, yes. So sad. (*Roger and Mrs. Bruchinski cry.*)

CHRIS: Oh, my God. C'mon. Don't cry. It's over. When it's over, it's over . . . and it's over.

ROGER: I had a life . . . and it's gone.

MRS. BRUCHINSKI: I had a baby boy . . . and he's gone.

CHRIS: We should all go . . . it's late.

MRS. BRUCHINSKI: Wonderful dreams I remember . . . People in the streets . . . songs in the air.

ROGER: And in the darkest night the burning issues of the day lit up the way for us and we could see the New Dawn. Oh, Chris. Oh, world. Oh, life. (*Roger and Mrs. Bruchinski weep on Chris's shoulder.*)

CHRIS: Oh, Rog.

MRS. BRUCHINSKI: Oh, my gosh.

(*The three of them embrace each other. We hear a heart-rending rendition of "THOSE WERE THE DAYS." Chris breaks away, picks up typewriter and paper, goes out on "stoop" and sits. Lights fade slowly.*)

# ACT II

*Out in the street we hear a loud siren going by and as it starts to fade Sal runs out onto the street. He howls like a young King Lear who's had a vision of his older years and stops. Sal is wearing only a flasher's raincoat. He jumps around like a desperate man "flashing" the city. His efforts, energetic and manic to begin with, depress him. He stops.*

SAL: Just as I thought. Nobody looks. I've bared my soul, and now I've bared by body. The results are in. I don't exist. (*He cries in agony.*) SOMEBODY HELP ME! I'M A MAN IN THE STREET! SOMEBODY INTERVIEW ME! I'M A REAL NICE GUY! YOU DON'T HAVE TO LOVE ME! YOU DON'T EVEN HAVE TO LIKE ME! I'LL TAKE HATE! Today is the worst day of the rest of my life. (*He runs off. Lights come up in the apartment. It's a crack before the crack of dawn. Chris is typing his apology. Roger is asleep on the floor nearby. Chris reads what he has written.*)

CHRIS: Looking back on that time I now feel . . . (*He looks out thinking. He types over what he has written. Writes again.*) That whole period of my life seems like a long nightmare from which I have irrevocably awakened. (*He continues typing.*)

ROGER: (*Singing.*) "All we are saying . . ."

CHRIS: Shut up, Rog.

ROGER: "Is give peace a chance . . ."

CHRIS: Give me a break, Rog. Shut up. (*Chris types. A short silence.*)

ROGER: "All we are saying . . ."

CHRIS: You've said it already, dammit.

ROGER: "Is give peace a chance . . .

(*Chris types "give peace a chance." Realizing his errror he types over it.*)

CHRIS: Shut up. The war is over! It's all over. Even Pete Seeger's winding down. (*Roger snores.*) I'm apologizing for what we did, Rog, so I can keep my job. That's what I'm doing. (*He types. Short silence.*)

ROGER: "All we are saying . . ."

(*Chris can't take it. Jumps up and kicks the rubble on the floor that is Roger.*)

CHRIS: Shut up! Shut up! (*Roger shuts up. Starts snoring. Chris goes back to the typewriter.*)

ROGER: "We shall overcome . . ."

(*Chris drops his head on the typewriter. From across the hall he hears Mrs. Bruchinkski.*)

MRS. BRUCHINSKI: (*Offstage.*) "We shall overcome . . ." (*She opens her door singing and steps into Chris's apartment singing. Roger is asleep singing. She is at the door. A short duet.*)

ROGER & MRS. BRUCHINSKI: "We shall overcome . . . some . . . day . . ."

(*Chris looks at both of them.*)

CHRIS: I live here. This is my place. It's the 80's not the 60's. I insist on that.

(*They stop singing. Roger snores.*)

MRS. BRUCHINSKI: I couldn't sleep. I get blues in the night again. And then I hear song and I come . . . It is song of my heart, Kris. We sing it again.

CHRIS: I don't want to sing anymore . . . I've sung them all, Mrs. Bruchinski . . . peace songs . . . protest songs . . . pollution songs . . . I've sung, I've hummed. I've carried the ball, the poster and the tune . . .

MRS. BRUCHINSKI: (*Jumps in.*) Yes, me too. And it was wonderful. One more time again we sing . . . we climb the mountain, Kris.

CHRIS: There are no mountains in Chicago, Mrs. Bruchinski.

MRS. BRUCHINSKI: Hope is mountain, Kris. Even in Chicago there is hope. We climb the mountain and we sing and together we overcome misery and despair. We overcome trouble and bad life and we overcome disco music too.

CHRIS: That's a helluva lot to overcome.

MRS. BRUCHINSKI: That's right. We better start right away before there's helluva lot more. I stay here and not budge till I hear you sing.

CHRIS: All right. All right. (*Chris escorts Mrs. Bruchinski back to her apartment singing "We Shall Overcome." Roger, in his sleep, joins in. Betty enters on the street and hears them.*)

BETTY: I never thought I'd hear it again!

(*Mrs. Bruchinski walks into her apartment. Chris closes the door and re-enters his apartment, leaning on door frame, singing.*)

CHRIS: "We shall overcome . . . some da-a-a-ay . . ."

(*Betty joins him in singing out in the street, wiping a tear that's making her mascara run. Roger sings in his sleep. It's a trio. The song is even getting to Chris, but when he finishes, in the total silence that follows, he quickly pulls himself out of it and rushes back to his typewriter.*)

MRS. BRUCHINSKI: (*Offstage.*) THANK YOU, KRIS!

CHRIS: (*Softly.*) You're welcome.

MRS. BRUCHINSKI: (*Offstage.*) I SAID "THANK YOU, KRIS!"

CHRIS: I SAID "YOU'RE WELCOME!"

MRS. BRUCHINSKI: (*Offstage.*) DON'T MENTION IT!

(*He tries to go back to the typewriter. Betty stands where she has stood still lost in the emotion of the song. She cries out as if calling the ghosts from the past.*)

BETTY: Stokely! Eldridge!

(*Roger sits up suddenly. He could be awake or asleep.*)

ROGER: Rennie Davis! Tom Hayden! Billy Kunstler! (*Chris, without so much as a thought, slugs him. Betty strolls off, full of nostalgia. Roger's nightmare continues.*) Orgasms! Orgasms! They're everywhere. The women! We thought we had free love in the 60's. It wasn't free. They're sending us the bill in the 80's and we gotta pay!

CHRIS: ROGER. ROGER. Wake up! You're having a nightmare. You're giving me a nightmare!

ROGER: MT. ST. HELENS IS ONE OF THEM! IT'S A WOMAN VOLCANO! The women! The mountains named after guys are doing nothing. Mt. McKinley. Mt. Washington. Pikes Peak. Nothing. They're all dormant and doing zilch, but HELENS . . . is thundering away. The goddamn mountain is having an orgasm! It's a cosmic orgasm, and now they'll expect me to top that if I want to be a man. I can't top that. I can't top that! (*Roger falls, exhausted. Nadja appears on the street and heads straight for Chris's building. She knocks on the door.*)

CHRIS: Go back to sleep, Mrs. Bruchinski. I sang to you once already. What do you want from me? (*Nadja knocks.*) All right. All right. (*Goes toward the door singing rapidly and angrily: "We Shall Overcome." Opens the door. Stops singing when he sees Nadja who is now wearing a skirt.*)

NADJA: Boy, you never give up do you. Once a radical always a radical. (*Chris is a little confused. Goes with it.*)

CHRIS: Yeah, it's in my blood so to speak. Come on in.

NADJA: I couldn't sleep. I've been thinking about what you said. About life.

CHRIS: Yeah, I've been thinking about life too. It's all crap.

NADJA: Don't make fun of me.

CHRIS: I'm not. You were right. It's all crap.

NADJA: Lay off, will you! It's easy for you. You have hopes and dreams and all that stuff and I . . . I don't want to make any excuses for myself but I was just a kid when all that stuff was going on. I didn't know I was missing out on something. So I want the truth. I know it's crap now but was it ever better?

CHRIS: You really want the truth?

NADJA: Hey, what do you think I want: A pair of blue eyes and a smile. I'm a slut. I eat truth for breakfast. I can take it.

CHRIS: It was the worst of times and it was the best of times. (*He pauses.*) That was a joke.

NADJA: I didn't come here for laughs. If you're not going to take me seriously. (*She starts to leave. He stops her.*)

CHRIS: I'll tell you how it was. You knew who the good guys were and you knew who the bad guys were and you knew which one you wanted to be. It was black and white. Now it's gray. People had jobs, they had homes and mortgages and bills to pay, but there was something bigger to worry about and think about that made those small everyday worries bearable. People were not afraid or ashamed to take sides. And both sides went to great extremes to prove a simple point that they loved their country. We were all impatient because we had a feeling, a stupid feeling, that if we could just think of something truly splendid . . . we could make it come true that instant. And I remember going up on a platform . . . I too had a vision . . . a sea of people stood before me . . . My mind went completely blank. I didn't know what to say. So I called out to them . . . almost calling for help . . . CITIZENS OF THE UNITED STATES OF AMERICA . . . And the crowd roared back. I can't remember what I said to them but I do remember that I was there. I spoke my piece. I shared my vision. And I was young. (*Nadja is in tears. Loud crying.*)

NADJA: I was only seven years old, then.

CHRIS: Well, we're both grown up now.

NADJA: Thank God it wasn't all just crap from start to finish. (*She's really crying.*) All right. You've convinced me. That's it. Boy, oh boy, that is it. I don't know what you have in mind but if you want to make things better, I'm with you. Sign me up.

CHRIS: Oh God, now I've done it. (*He sits.*)

NADJA: The only other person who talks like you is my father, Yovan. And I ran away from him. He stays up late at night and types too. Same kind of stuff probably as yours. Full of hope and dreams and stuff like that. Can I read what you've written? (*She heads for the typewriter. Chris jumps up to intercede.*)

CHRIS: No, not that. It's . . . uh . . . uh . . . not finished. (*He hides the typing.*) I'll give you some . . . uh . . . some of my old stuff. (*He runs around looking for it. Nadja looks at Roger. Roger snores.*)

NADJA: Oh! It's so nice to see somebody who still lives with his father.

(*Chris finds an old speech of his. Brings it to her. He feels guilty and trapped. Gives her his old speech.*)

CHRIS: Here, read. (*Nadja settles down with the speech. Chris sits at the typewriter and looks at her. Just as she begins to read Roger lets out a snatch of song in his sleep . . .*)

ROGER: "All we are saying . . ."

NADJA: Like father like son.

(*Chris looks at her across his typewriter. He is falling in love. She is reading. She looks up and sees him looking at her. She then looks down at the pages again. Chris continues staring. Out in the street we hear a howl of loneliness and then we see Sal enter. He is what he is only more so by now. Sal is "flashing" the environs, crying singing.*)

SAL: Sal, Sal, huckleberry Sal
Never knew a sweeter guy
Don't think I ever shall . . .

(*He can't sing anymore. But he can flash. Betty the cop appears. Sees him.*)

BETTY: Hey, you! What the hell you think you're doing!

SAL: I am exposing what's left of myself.

BETTY: And I'm proposing you stop exposing or I'm going to start imposing.

SAL: If you were really there you wouldn't be talking to me.

BETTY: I am talking to you, buddy. (*Sal gets stabbed in the heart by this word.*)

SAL: Buddy! I've always wanted to be somebody's buddy. (*Betty is softening a little.*)

BETTY: You're in a bad way, pal. (*Sal gets stabbed in the heart again.*)

SAL: Don't call me pal, if you don't mean it. Don't tease me, please.

BETTY: Man, I thought I was lonely and insecure.

SAL: Loneliness and insecurity were my happy period. (*Sal cries. Betty goes up to him and starts buttoning his overcoat.*)

BETTY: Has anybody ever told you that you're kind of cute when you cry?

SAL: No never. (*Sal cries.*)

BETTY: You are. You really are. (*Sal cries.*) Oh, come on. It's not your fault that you're suffering.

SAL: It's not. Whose fault is it?

BETTY: It's our fault.

SAL: Thank God.

BETTY: Everybody has let you down. I look at you and I see where we have all failed. You are a living example that the human potential movement didn't work. That the alternate life style movement didn't work. That the cults and the crazes and conscience expanding drugs didn't work. Nothing has worked for you.

SAL: No, not a thing.

BETTY: You know what you are?

SAL: No, tell me!

BETTY: You're the Little Guy. The Republicans, the Democrats, the Socialists . . . they all talk about reaching the little guy and you're him. You're the Little Guy himself. And nobody has reached you.

SAL: Nobody even calls.

BETTY: And yet your lonely suffering is not for naught.

SAL: What's it for?

BETTY: You are a measure of how far we still have to go. You, Little Guy, are the one whose heart and soul we have to reach if we are to realize the dream of humanity. It's up to me . . . up to us . . . The women's movement is your last chance . . . to reach the little guy of history. Reach the little guy. I am reaching out to you. Here is my hand, Little Guy. It's a woman's hand . . . It's black and it's beautiful and it needs you. Take it!

SAL: I'll take it.

BETTY: (*Chants.*) Reach the Little Guy. Reach the Little Guy. (*He crawls to Betty.*)

SAL: Oh, I'm weak with hope. (*Betty picks him up in her arms.*) Oh, My God. I'm being picked up. I've never been picked up before.

BETTY: My place is not far away.

SAL: Wait. I have to tell you something. I think I'm Jewish.

BETTY: All I know is that you're a cute and lonely little guy.

SAL: Wait. I have to tell you something else. I'm a . . . virgin.
BETTY: I just became a virgin myself.

(*They look at each other. She starts carrying him offstage. Yovan runs onto the street. Stops in his tracks when he sees them.*)

YOVAN: Stop! My hat is off to you police woman person. It brings tears to my eyeballs to see black and white get along so nifty. You are a credit to your racial quota. (*Sal mouths "thank you." Betty carries Sal off. Yovan looks after them.*) Only in America!

(*Nadja, having finished reading Chris's speech, clutches it to her bosom and lets out a cry of joy.*)

NADJA: It's so beautiful!

(*Yovan goes to the pay-phone. Looks for a number. He is carrying an attaché case with him, and God only knows what's inside. Chris embraces Nadja.*)

CHRIS: It's an old speech . . . I mean . . . it's kind of dated, don't you think.
NADJA: No, it'll never be dated. You're really something.
CHRIS: Yeah, the question is what? (*Yovan dials. Chris's telephone rings. Chris picks it up.*) Hello.
YOVAN: Allo, buster boy.
CHRIS: Oh, no. It's not you again, is it?
YOVAN: Yes, it is me, Redical of the Sixties. I give you new offer. Since you do not come to the New World, I bring New World to you. I have in my possession two stuffed cabbages à la Serb and one Polaroid Pronto. You can go yummy, yummy in the privacy of your rotten apartment. I shoot you with Polaroid Pronto.
CHRIS: No, you won't.
YOVAN: Then I shoot you with gun. You are not going to make uncle of monkey out of me. Good-bye. Next time you see me you will be dead. (*Yovan hangs up.*)
NADJA: Who was that?
CHRIS: Nobody you'd know.
NADJA: I have to go. I want to find my father and tell him about you.
CHRIS: He doesn't know you're a . . .
NADJA: A slut. No, he'd kill me if he knew. He'd kill you, too.
CHRIS: I already have a guy that wants to kill me.

(*Yovan is pacing down in the street. He is working himself up. Nadja hugs Chris.*

*Nadja kisses Chris.*)

NADJA: Thank you. I'll be back. (*Yovan is coming up the stairs.*) I'll make it up to my father. I've hurt him without even knowing it.

(*She bursts out of the door in a fit of eagerness to start a new life just as Yovan reaches the landing. The door opens and slams him right in the face. He staggers back against the wall as Nadja runs down the stairs and falls out cold on the floor. Chris goes and shuts the door without seeing him. Chris is feeling dreadful. An impostor. He has conned the girl into thinking he is somebody he's not. He's trapped in that role and he doesn't like it. In the end it's all Roger's fault. If it hadn't been for him . . . Roger stirs in his sleep.*)

ROGER: "What do we want?"
CHRIS: I want you out of here!
ROGER: "When do we want it?"
CHRIS: Now! It's all your fault. Why the hell did you have to show up when you did? Why?
ROGER: "All we are saying . . ."

(*Chris screams out in frustration. Can't take it. It's almost the last straw. He starts throwing stuff on top of Roger. Anything he can find. A pillow. Throws the rug on top of him. Puts the remainder of the car on top of him just so he won't hear that song anymore. He is out of breath and shaking with anger by the time he is finished but at least it's silent. He listens. No, he can't hear Roger. He heads for the typewriter. The rubble that is Roger stirs.*)

ROGER: (*Singing.*) "Chicago, Chicago."

(*Chris goes crazy. He jumps on top of the rubble ready to choke him.*)

CHRIS: Shut up! Shut up! Shut up! (*Roger wakes up.*)
ROGER: (*Sees the rubble on top of himself.*) Thanks for tucking me in, Chris. How's the proclamation coming along?
CHRIS: What proclamation!
ROGER: When I went to sleep you were typing the Proclamation of the Second Movement.
CHRIS: ROG! There is no proclamation. There is no second movement. Listen to me, man, and listen well. I've gathered all your sleeping pills and stuff so don't try to pull any of that suicide crap on me. This has gone far enough.
ROGER: I KNEW IT! I KNEW IT WAS TOO GOOD TO BE TRUE! YOU'RE KICKING ME OUT! OUT OF THE MOVEMENT! (*There is movement on the landing. Yovan is reviving a little.*) I'LL KILL MYSELF! (*He scrounges around and pulls

*out something.*)

CHRIS: What's that?

ROGER: Rat poison!

*(Chris throws himself on top of Roger trying to get it away. Yovan manages to get on his feet outside. He staggers a little forward. Just as he does Mrs. Bruchinski opens her door and catches him flat on the face. Yovan goes down again. She goes right past him without seeing him and opens Chris's door. She stands there and sees Chris lying on top of Roger, struggling with him.)*

ROGER: I love you, Chris.

CHRIS: I know. I know.

ROGER: But you don't love me.

CHRIS: I do too. I love you. (*Roger embraces Chris. Chris can't but embrace him back. Yovan is rising slowly. Mrs. Bruchinski just shakes her head at the sight of the two men hugging and starts to leave. Flings the door open. Catches Yovan on the face and plasters him against the wall again. She stands on the landing shaking her head. Looks at Chris's door. She sighs and goes into her place again. Yovan is back on the floor again. Chris is tucking Roger in again.*) Rog, I've got something to tell you. For the sake of the Second Movement, I think we should split up.

ROGER: Split up?

CHRIS: Yes, you should go to Los Angeles and start things out there, while I carry on here in Chicago.

ROGER: And leave you, Chris!

CHRIS: Yes, leave me, Rog. Leave me. Please.

ROGER: I'm scared of L.A., Chris. Look what it did to Tom Hayden.

CHRIS: All the more reason for you to go. They need somebody like you out there.

ROGER: Oh, Chris. I don't even know what the burning issue of the day is anymore.

CHRIS: Sure you do, Rog.

ROGER: I sure don't, Chris. I was hoping you knew. What's the word, Chris? What's the burning issue of the day?

CHRIS: What it's always been, Rog. When the world we envision is better than the one we live in, then we must follow our vision.

ROGER: Because that's the kind of guys we are. Right, Chris?

CHRIS: Right, Rog.

ROGER: All right, I'll go. I'm scared of L.A., but I'll go. Oh, Chris. Wasn't it wonderful when we were young and loved what we did. Wasn't it?

CHRIS: Yes, it was. And now we're older . . .

ROGER: And now we hate ourselves. Why?

CHRIS: Because we quit.

ROGER: I quit. Not you. You didn't quit. That's why I love you . . . you . . . Remember in *Spartacus* . . . when Tony Curtis was dying and he hugged Kirk Douglas. I'm the Tony Curtis here and you're Kirk. I love you Spartacus. Good-bye. (*Roger goes to bedroom to pack up and go. Chris goes to typewriter. Yovan, his bearings lost, staggers up to his feet and goes right for the door. It's Mrs. Bruchinski's door.*)

YOVAN: I fix your goose for good now! (*He charges into her apartment. A scream is heard. Then a loud resounding bang! Then a groan! Chris continues typing. Mrs. Bruchinski's door flings open and Yovan staggers out. Mrs. Bruchinski appears with a rolling pin in her hand.*)

MRS. BRUCHINSKI: Hanky and panky, yes. Rape, no.

YOVAN: Sorry, Black Polish person. I was looking for Kris .

MRS. BRUCHINSKI: You too. Kris already busy with one lover.

YOVAN: Ah, what is the heck. I kill him later. I don't want to frighten innocent girl.

MRS. BRUCHINSKI: What girl?

YOVAN: Kris's girl lover.

MRS. BRUCHINSKI: Kris's girl lover is old man.

YOVAN: What are you saying to my ears?

MRS. BRUCHINSKI: To your ears I am saying this: Kris is into old men.

YOVAN: He has homosexual persuasions!

MRS. BRUCHINSKI: Not the Kris I thought I knew. Kris I thought I knew was not homosexual. Kris I now know is homosexual.

YOVAN: Which is the Kris I know?

MRS. BRUCHINSKI: I don't know.

YOVAN: Which Kris is in there?

MRS. BRUCHINSKI: The Kris I now know. He is into old men like gangbusters.

YOVAN: Alright, you sonuvabitch, Kris—come out with your pants up.

(*Chris hears this and stops typing. He jumps toward Roger.*)

CHRIS: ROGER! ROGER! I got to go. Cover for me, all right. It's, eh, eh . . . It's the F.B.I.

ROGER: The F.B.I. We're right back in the thick of things.

(*Chris rushes for the window. Struggles with it, Yovan goes for Chris's door. He seems hesitant. He knocks. Shouts.*)

YOVAN: PULL UP TROUSERS AND DROP YOUR ACTIVITY! (*Chris manages to open the window. Mrs. Bruchinski goes back to her place. Yovan bursts in and slams the door shut. Chris has just made it out of the window and window drops as the door slams. Roger stands confronting Yovan.*) So, man of no shame, this is what you are now.

ROGER: My name is Chris.

YOVAN: I know your name is Kris. I am no fool. You are into old man disguise. That does not pull wool over my eyeballs. Where is your lover boy?

ROGER: Just drop the accent, man. I know who you are. (*Yovan grabs him.*)

YOVAN: You are not the Kris I know! (*He pulls out gun.*) Where is the Kris I want to kill? (*Roger sees the gun and does not feel very radical.*)

ROGER: I'm not Chris you want to kill!

YOVAN: Where is other Kris?

ROGER: He left, but he'll be back. You can kill him then. (*Yovan lets him go.*)

YOVAN: Oh, I get it. You are old man homosexual loverboy of Kris I want to kill.

ROGER: What? Homosexual?

YOVAN: I call spade a spade. I shoot from hip.

ROGER: Wait a minute. Why do you want to kill Chris?

YOVAN: I have private snit to pick with him.

ROGER: A snit. Chris is into snits.

YOVAN: Into snits and into homosexuals like gang-busters.

ROGER: Oh, Christ, Chris! The women's movement chalks up another casualty! Oh, Chris! (*Roger cries bitter tears. Yovan is a man moved by any tears.*)

YOVAN: Don't cry, old man Kris.

ROGER: My name's not Chris.

YOVAN: I am glad to hear. One less Kris to worry about. Who are you, old man?

ROGER: My name is Roger.

YOVAN: Don't cry old man Roger. So you are homosexual. Big dill! I don't tell anyone.

ROGER: I'm not homosexual. I'm . . . uh . . . uh . . . Chris's father. (*He cries.*)

YOVAN: Ah, now everything falls apart into place. You did not know Kris was homosexual.

ROGER: No, I did not.

YOVAN: I am sorry Papa Roger to be one to bring such news to you. (*He begins crying a litle himself.*) It is tough cookie to be father these days. Our children break our hearts. I never have son, but your name bring to mind the son-in-law I do have but have never laid eyes on. His name Roger too. My wife . . . she died.

ROGER: My wife . . . she left me. The slut.

YOVAN: My daughter left me and some say she slut too. Your son homosexual. My daughter slut. Our wives gone. Life is not a picnic in the park. (*He cries bitter tears himself. He embraces Roger trying to comfort him.*

*Both weep and pat one another on the back. Mrs. Bruchinski enters. Sees two men hugging and weeping and she too starts weeping.*)

MRS. BRUCHINSKI: Men have all the fun!

YOVAN: It is no fun we are having. It is bitter tears we are shedding over children. One is gay for sure. One is slut for maybe.

MRS. BRUCHINSKI: And one is lost for good. Where is my baby boy? (*She cries too. Joins the crowd.*)

YOVAN: This is not American dream come true. I am ready to throw in towel, face cloth and bath mat to boot. Too much tears in America. America used to be plenty laughs. No more. America was land of plenty. Now it's plenty of nothing and nothing is not plenty for me. Two score and one year ago I come to this country. And now what is the score? I am old. I am sad. There is pollution. There is inflation. There is no solution. I warn you, America. I go back to the old country and not think twice about looking back. I quit!! (*He suddenly smiles and cheers up.*) Ah, now I feel much better. I spit bullshit poison out of my system. America, Yovan never gives up on you!

ROGER: I don't know who the hell you are but you're a helluva guy, guy.

YOVAN: That is true. When it is helluva time country needs helluva guy. I am such a man. I go now to kiss Dianah good morning. Tell Kris I kill him later on. Maybe sooner. I don't know. (*He exits.*)

MRS. BRUCHINSKI: We are alone at last, old man poopsy. I don't care you are homosexual. Maybe you try go both ways, no? Acey-deucey?

ROGER: I'm not homosexual . . . although I can see where the road I'm on can lead.

MRS. BRUCHINSKI: You are not homosexual!

ROGER: Not yet.

MRS. BRUCHINSKI: Then it is time to strike while iron is hot. Let us have hanky and panky.

ROGER: Not so fast. I have to know. Are you now or have you ever been a member of the women's movement?

MRS. BRUCHINSKI: Only two movements I have been. We shall overcome movement and Polish Power movement.

ROGER: You are Polish?

MRS. BRUCHINSKI: I was adopted as young baby by Mr. and Mrs. Bruchinski. She give me her name and teach me to speak English.

ROGER: You know what you are?

MRS. BRUCHINSKI: Vat?

ROGER: You're a quadruple minority, sister. You're a woman, you're old, Black and Polish.

MRS. BRUCHINSKI: You betchya.

ROGER: One last question. Do you know what an orgasm is?

MRS. BRUCHINSKI: Never heard of it.

ROGER: YOU'RE THE WOMAN FOR ME, MRS. B.! (*They embrace.*)

MRS. BRUCHINSKI: Wait! We don't want unwanted babies. I have to get my diagram. (*Mrs. Bruchinski exits to primp and get ready.*)

ROGER: She makes me feel like a macho again. Poor Chris, A macho no more.

(*Chris appears at the window again. He tries to open the window. Can't. He knocks on window, Roger sees him. Rushes to open it. Both of them struggle. The window opens. Chris comes in. Roger backs off. Chris looks very gay to him, suddenly.*)

CHRIS: What's the matter with you?

ROGER: It's all right, Chris. I'm O.K. You're O.K., okay?

CHRIS: You're wrong there. I'm not O.K. at all.

ROGER: Yes, you are. You may be what you are . . . but that's okay. In my book you're still who you were.

CHRIS: No, I'm not. People change, Rog.

ROGER: I know.

CHRIS: I've changed. You've changed.

ROGER: I . . . I haven't changed like you're changed. (*Roger backs off from Chris.*) Don't get me wrong. I have changed. But I'm still the same guy.

CHRIS: You can't have it both ways, Rog.

ROGER: I don't want to have it both ways. Chris, I know the truth about you.

CHRIS: I was going to tell you myself. I guess that guy Yovan told you all about it.

ROGER: Yes. I didn't believe him. I mean I . . .

CHRIS: It's true.

ROGER: Oh, God. I better go to L.A. right away. Don't get me wrong. I still love you. LIKE A BROTHER.

CHRIS: I don't know how I love you.

ROGER: I'D PREFER IT LIKE A BROTHER, Chris.

CHRIS: Like a brother it is.

ROGER: Oh, Chris. I understand. What with the way women are, it's a wonder we're all not, you know. I don't want to hurt you, but when it comes to sex . . . I'm on the other side.

CHRIS: Oh, Rog, I didn't know.

ROGER: I didn't think you did.

CHRIS: When did it happen?

ROGER: It never happened. I was always on the other side.

CHRIS: All those years!

ROGER: Yeah, but we were all on the same side for all those years.

CHRIS: No, we weren't. I was always . . .

ROGER: You weren't really, were you, Chris? All those years.

CHRIS: Everybody was, I guess, except for you. All the guys were . . .

ROGER: All the guys! Not all the guys! Jerry, Abbie . . . Billy Kunstler?

CHRIS: Rennie Davis . . . Tom Hayden.

ROGER: TOM TOO! Stop. Stop it, Chris!

CHRIS: It's all right, Rog. There's no right or wrong in this matter. You can be gay. (*Roger clutches his head.*)

ROGER: No, Chris. I can't.

CHRIS: Sure you can. It's fine with me.

ROGER: I know it's fine with you!

CHRIS: What are friends for?

ROGER: Not for that! (*He backs away from Chris. Chris is puzzled.*)

CHRIS: You're acting real queer, Rog.

ROGER: No, I'm not. I am not either. I can't, Chris. I can't. I'm not gay. I don't want to be gay. Please. You can be gay, buy you can't be gay with me.

CHRIS: What are you talking about? I'm not gay.

ROGER: You're not? But that F.B.I. guy . . . (*He slaps his head.*) I fell for it! It was all a cheap F.B.I. trick!

CHRIS: Oh, no. He's not F.B.I.

ROGER: Then he's C.I.A. Crooked bastards tried to make us think we're not straight. We're real guys. Both of us. I love you once again, Chris! (*He flies into Chris's arms and starts kissing him on the cheek. Mrs. Bruchinski walks in and sees the two men hugging. She makes a big gesture of despair and starts to leave. Roger sees her.*) Mrs. Bruchinski, Chris is not gay.

MRS. BRUCHINSKI: And you?

ROGER: Me neither!

MRS. BRUCHINSKI: Praise Jesus! A miracle! Now I am ready to sin like gangbusters.

ROGER: MRS. BRU, I'M READY FOR YOU!

MRS. BRUCHINSKI: I'm time for hanky and panky! (*She grabs Roger and pulls him into Chris's bedroom. They shut the door behind them. Chris just stands there, ossified. He takes his typewriter and paper. Goes to his bedroom door.*)

CHRIS: Since you're using my apartment, Mrs. Bruchinski, I'm going to use yours. Okay?

ROGER/MRS. BRUCHINSKI: OKAY!

(*Nadja appears in the street and is heading toward Chris's building as Chris is heading out of his apartment into Mrs. Bruchinski's apartment. Nadja comes up the stairs just as Chris shuts the door. Nadja enters Chris's apartment. She has a package with her. It's some different clothes she has brought.*)

NADJA: Chris? (*She's almost glad he's not there. She smiles and goes into the bathroom with her package to change. As she shuts the door on the bathroom Yovan appears at the window. He is holding a tear gas cannister in his hand.*)

YOVAN: Allo you in there! This is me out here! This is to make plenty sure you understand I mean beez-wax! (*He throws the grenade inside and vanishes. Smoke starts coming out of the grenade. The door to Chris's bedroom bursts open. Roger stands there without his trousers, the rest of his makeup intact. He sniffs the air.*)

ROGER: IT'S TEAR GAS! OH, MY GOD, IT'S REALLY TEAR GAS! I LOVE IT! I LOVE IT! (*He sniffs the air like a man afflicted with rampaging nostalgia. He picks up the grenade and runs to the window. He throws it out. Fists wave in the air.*) Jerry, Abbie, Rennie, we're back in business! The whole world is watching! The whole world is watching! (*The door to the bathroom opens. Nadja comes out in a different outfit. Roger is at the window.*)

NADJA: What happened in here? (*Roger turns around and lets out a scream.*)

ROGER: NADJA!

NADJA: Oh, Chris told you about me.

ROGER: NADJA!

NADJA: Is something the matter with you?

ROGER: IT'S ME! YOU DID THIS TO ME, YOU! (*He comes toward her. Nadja screams. Roger pursues her. Mrs. Bruchinski comes out. Roger is screaming. Nadja is screaming. Mrs. Bruchinski is looking on. At an opportune moment, she slugs Roger. Roger goes out like a candle.*)

MRS. BRUCHINSKI: He is helluva old man. But he's mine. Okay?

NADJA: Sure. Take him. Where is Chris?

MRS. BRUCHINSKI: Kris is out. You are whore in different clothes, no?

NADJA: No, I'm not going to be a whore anymore.

MRS. BRUCHINSKI: Praise Jesus! Miracle number two! It is a day of conversion!

NADJA: I have to go find my father and tell him the happy news. (*Yovan appears on the street, coughing from the tear gas.*) Tell Chris I'm back.

(*Nadja and Mrs. Bruchinski go out. Nadja goes down the stairs and out into the street and off. Yovan coughing does not see her. Mrs. Bruchinski goes into her apartment. And then Chris comes out of her apartment with his typewriter. Goes into his apartment. Yovan is coming up the stairs. Chris is looking at Roger on the floor. Yovan comes up to the landing. Mrs. Bruchinski flings open her door. Catches Yovan in the face. Marches right on. Opens Chris's door. Goes in as Yovan is recovering a little.*)

MRS. BRUCHINSK: Kris. I forgot to tell you. She will be back.

CHRIS: Who will be back?

MRS. BRUCHINSKI: Whore who is whore no more. (*She swings the door open as she goes out. Catches Yovan in the face again, leaving Chris's door open and goes into her place. Chris sees the open door. Goes to close it. Yovan shook up by the blow falls against the door, slamming it shut. As the door shuts the window falls down. Chris looks at one and then the other. He sniffs the air.*)

CHRIS: I must be losing my mind. Sure, I'm losing my mind. I'm talking to myself and I smell tear gas.

(*Roger is recovering from his blow. He is getting up slowly.*)

ROGER: Where is she?
CHRIS: Where is who? (*Roger sees Chris.*)
ROGER: Chris. My wife was here!
CHRIS: Oh, Rog. Please. She wasn't here. I was the only guy who was here and even I wasn't here. I was next door.
ROGER: She hurled a canister of tear gas in here.
CHRIS: You smell it too? Your mind is gone, Rog. And mine is going. So, I'm going too. (*He starts to leave.*)
ROGER: Where are you going?
CHRIS: If I'm going to go out of my mind, I'd just as soon go out in the street and go out of it there. We're both out of it, anyway. We're out of it, man. I'm leaving. Bye-bye. (*Chris opens the door just as Yovan has recovered and is standing up ready to come at him. Yovan screams. Chris runs back into room and shuts the door, but not fully.*) It's the C.I.A. guy. He wants to kill me. (*He can't shut the door fully because Yovan is pulling on it.*)
ROGER: Then we'll both die. We'll die together.
YOVAN: Open door somonabitch. (*Yovan fires gun at door. He finally triumphs over Chris. He opens the door, bursts in. Shuts the door behind him. Fires gun again.*) Okee-dokey! Now we get down to beez-wax! (*Chris is thinking visibly.*)
CHRIS: Ah, listen. Ah . . . my . . . My father here is very sick. (*Roger doesn't know what he's getting at, but he's trying. There's a plan in the air.*) A bad heart! If you kill me the shock would kill him too! (*Roger gets it.*)
ROGER: He's my only boy. Shoot if you must these gray hairs but spare my boy.
YOVAN: Oh! To find such love between papa and son in these times is a subject worthy of small talk. (*Roger is hugging and kissing Chris.*)
ROGER: He's an angel. The apple of my eye!
YOVAN: He is also the grape of my wrath! But what is the heck. Redical son make apple-logy and I give full pardon and amnesty.
ROGER: Pardon. Amnesty. Apologize! Never! We are radicals and we will die radicals. Shoot us. We don't mind dying. I'd just as soon die as go to Los Angleles anyway. Shoot us!
CHRIS: Shut up, Roger! (*Yovan threatens Chris.*)
YOVAN: YOU! Not to talk to old father in such way. In old country papa gets respect.
ROGER: Blow it out your ear, you C.I.A. stooge. Your old country sucks! (*Yovan is mortified. He is ready to turn his wrath on Roger. Chris realizes things are going badly.*)

CHRIS: Shut your damned mouth, Roger! (*Yovan's wrath switches.*)

YOVAN: YOU! Not to call papa by first name basis. Papa is Papa. (*He pushes Chris into sofa. Confronts Roger.*) Okee-dokey, old papa. Maybe now you tell me which old country makes suck!

ROGER: Which old country are you from?

YOVAN: I no tell you. So there. Ha! Ha! (*He laughs. Roger is furious.*)

ROGER: Poland! Poland sucks.

YOVAN: Poland is no skin off my nose.

ROGER: Czechoslovakia!

YOVAN: Hmmm.

ROGER: Lithuania!

YOVAN: Ha, ha, ha.

ROGER: Estonia! Bulgaria. Rumania! Albania!

YOVAN: You are right. Albania, it is true, sucks.

ROGER: Greece sucks!

YOVAN: You are right.

ROGER: Cyprus, Italy, Spain. They all suck. Turkey sucks!

YOVAN: Do you really think Turkey sucks?

ROGER: Yes, Turkey sucks.

YOVAN: I wasn't sure. I think you are right. Turkey sucks. (*Roger is just about foaming at the mouth.*)

ROGER: That's it! There are no more old countries!

YOVAN: You forget Yugoslavia!

ROGER: YUGOSLAVIA IS THE SUCK CHAMP OF EUROPE!

YOVAN: NOW I KILL YOU! You make apple-logy or I make you dead.

ROGER: Never!

CHRIS: Make apple-logy, Roger.

YOVAN: NOT TO CALL PAPA, ROGER! YOU LET PAPA DIE IN RESPECT! (*He cocks his pistol and points it at Roger.*) Now, either I hear apple-logy or by gosh I shoot you down like son's car.

ROGER: You dumb Yugoslavian. My son doesn't have a car.

YOVAN: You stupid American. Maybe you ask somonabitch son about his car! (*Roger is mildly suspicious. Both eyes turn toward Chris.*)

ROGER: Tell him, son. Tell him you don't have a car.

CHRIS: I, well, I had a car, papa.

ROGER: O—o—o—h!

YOVAN: O—o—o—h!

CHRIS: O—o—o—h!

YOVAN: How come papa not know. Son never give papa ride in car down Michigan Avenue.

ROGER: No, never. Maybe son take papa on different kind of ride. Maybe my boy is not such a good boy after all.

YOVAN: Not to jump to conclusion! Maybe son so upset about divorce he forget.

ROGER: Divorce! My son had a divorce?

YOVAN: You did not know?

ROGER: I did not know son was married. (*Both of them look at Chris.*)

CHRIS: Papa never asked.

YOVAN: Papa not have to ask! What kind cold cut baloney is that. (*To Roger.*) Kids today. My daughter. She is the same way. She stab me in the heart.

ROGER: Yes, but my son stabbed me in the back. He's a bad boy, my son. (*Roger slaps Chris's face.*)

YOVAN: I told you so.

CHRIS: Damn you, Roger! You never gave me a chance. You started raving like a lunatic about your slutty wife . . .

YOVAN: YOU CALL PAPA'S WIFE SLUTTY!

CHRIS: He called her a slut himself.

ROGER: He has no respect.

YOVAN: Papa can call wife slut. Son cannot call mother slut!

CHRIS: His wife is not my mother.

YOVAN: Same applies to step-mother.

CHRIS: Oh, the hell with it. You see, he's not my father.

ROGER: You see. He has no respect.

YOVAN: He's a rotten brat, that much is true. To spill lunch in my place and then say it is the poisoning of the food!

ROGER: Poisoning of the food!

YOVAN: Yes, stuffed cabbage.

ROGER: Days of Vomit was a stuffed cabbage, Chris! ALL THIS WAS A STUFFED CABBAGE! Chris . . . Spartacus . . . you . . . you too.

CHRIS: Me too, Rog. I've done it all, baby, from A to Z, but if you want I'll begin in the middle with M for movement. (*Roger is near tears.*)

ROGER: Oh, no, Chris.

CHRIS: Oh, yes, Rog.

ROGER: The movement?

CHRIS: All gone. (*Roger is in tears. Yovan can't understand what has happened. Roger is weeping.*)

ROGER: Our youth.

CHRIS: All gone too.

ROGER: Oh. Chris. (*Roger goes to him. Embraces him.*) Oh, world. Oh, Life.

CHRIS: Oh, Rog.

YOVAN: Oh, my gosh. (*Roger suddenly knows what he has to do.*)

ROGER: That's it! I don't want to live without hope. Let's die. A double suicide, Chris. Give me the gun. I'll kill myself. (*He runs at Yovan. He wants the gun to shoot himself. Chris tries to stop him. Yovan even tries to stop him. There's a possibility here of a gun going off. The door opens and in walks Dianah with the bullhorn. The fighting continues as she looks on. She puts the bullhorn to her lips.*)

DIANAH: WHAT THE HELL IS GOING ON?

(*The struggle ceases. All eyes turn toward her. She shuts the door. Yovan is glad to see her. She is shocked to see him. Chris is annoyed to see her but glad for the intrusion. Roger is nothing yet. He heads for the window.*)

YOVAN: Dianah!

DIANAH: Yovan!

CHRIS: Dianah!

DIANAH: Chris. (*To Yovan.*) I didn't know you knew Chris.

YOVAN: I knew you knew a Kris but I did not know that the Kris I know is the Kris you know.

DIANAH: It is. I didn't know you knew Yovan, Chris.

CHRIS: I didn't know you knew Yovan either, Dianah.

YOVAN: We all knew each other but I don't know how we all know so much! (*Dianah goes to Chris.*)

DIANAH: Oh, what does it matter. You say tomato, and he says tomahto. You say potato and he says potahto. Potato, potahto, tomato, tomahto . . . Chris, let's call the whole thing off.

CHRIS: Has something happened to you that I should know about?

DIANAH: I'm in love with somebody else.

YOVAN: Who?

DIANAH: You.

YOVAN: Good.

DIANAH: He makes me feel like a woman and I feel like feeling like a woman. I'm sorry, Chris. It was just one of those things, just one of those fabulous flings. A trip to the moon on gossamer wings. But I can't be your wife anymore.

YOVAN: WIFE!

CHRIS: Wonderful.

YOVAN: Not so wonderful so quickly. I did not know you were married.

DIANAH: I was, I am. But I won't be for long.

YOVAN: Ach, somonabitch. I did not know that the woman I find and the wife you lose is the same woman. Gosh, dammit. This takes the cup cake. I come here to offer pardon to Kris and now I have to ask Kris for pardon. Kris, sorry.

CHRIS: Ah, what is the heck. (*They embrace. Nadja appears in the street. She heads for Chris's apartment building.*)

DIANAH: I love this. My past and my future stand before me embracing in the windy city where it all began. I even smell tear gas . . .

ROGER: I smell a rat. I'm going to pack up and leave. (*He goes into the bedroom and shuts the door. The front door opens and in walks Nadja. All eyes are on her.*)

CHRIS: Roger! Nadja!

NADJA: Chris!

YOVAN: Nadja!

NADJA: Daddy!

CHRIS: DADDY!

DIANAH: Daddy!

YOVAN: Nadja my little girl. Oh, I love you like the son I never had. But what the holy heck are you doing here?

NADJA: I'm doing political work with Chris, Daddy.

YOVAN: I didn't know you knew Kris.

NADJA: I didn't know you knew Chris either. (*To Chris*) I didn't know you knew my father.

DIANAH: I didn't know you had a daughter.

YOVAN: I didn't know you had a husband.

NADJA: I love Chris, Daddy.

YOVAN: You love Kris, but you're married.

NADJA: I'm divorced, Daddy.

YOVAN: And where is your husband Roger?

CHRIS: Husband Roger! Oh, no! (*Roger appears with his belongings at the bedroom door. He sees Nadja.*)

ROGER: Revenge! I smell Revenge!

NADJA: I'm glad you're up and at it, Gramps.

ROGER: I'm not up, Nadja.

NADJA: You look up to me.

ROGER: There she goes again. Orgasms, orgasms!

NADJA: He sounds like my husband, Roger.

ROGER: I am your husband Roger. (*He briefly lifts off his wig, then quickly replaces it. Yovan gasps.*)

NADJA: Daddy, I'd like you to meet my ex-husband and your ex-son-in-law, Roger.

YOVAN: By gosh, this takes the cup cake, too. So you are son-in-law Roger! The less names there are the more confusing the people who are left behind. (*All start trying to explain.*) STOP! EVERYBODY MAKE HUSH! (*Silence.*) I have to figure out stuff. (*He begins putting it together. Points at Nadja.*) You are my daughter. I begin with easy stuff first. And you were married to my ex-son-in-law who is the father of the ex-husband of my wife to be. (*Points to Chris.*) You are Kris. Your papa ran off with my daughter. (*Points at Roger.*) You are Roger. Your son Kris, no your stepson, Kris, is the stepson also of my daughter Nadja, your ex-wife. (*Points to Chris again.*) Therefore, you Kris are my step-grandson. No, since my daughter Nadja divorced your papa, you my ex-step-grandson and your ex-wife, your papa's daughter-in-law, will be my daughter's stepmother. Yeah. Now it's all clear. Bravo! At last I have big family. (*He starts hugging one and all.*)

ROGER: What about me? Am I to be left to turn slowly in the wind. What about the movement, Chris?

CHRIS: I told you, Rog. It's over. (*Mrs. Bruchinski enters.*)

ROGER: No, there's still Mrs. Bruchinski. We are the movement now. It's you and me, Mrs. B.

MRS. BRUCHINSKI: We march to Washington. (*A whistle blows. Betty and Sal burst in.*)

BETTY: Everybody freeze! Police! (*Sees Chris.*) Chris.

CHRIS: J.B.

BETTY: Nadja.

NADJA: Betty.

DIANAH: Sal!

SAL: Dianah.

YOVAN: Here we go one more time again, I betcha!

SAL: Oh, my God. So many people. And I know some of them. It's my first reunion.

ROGER: J.B.! I thought I recognized you.

BETTY: And who're you, Gramps?!

ROGER: It's me! Roger. Roger O'Dwyer.

BETTY: Roger!

ROGER: J.B.! (*They do their old time greeting handshake.*)

NADJA: I didn't know you knew Chris and Roger, Betty.

BETTY: I didn't know you knew them either.

NADJA: I was married to one and I love the other.

BETTY: Which is which? (*All try to answer at once.*)

YOVAN: STOP! PLEASE! I AM GETTING A PAIN IN MY HEADACHE! I already explain which is which and who is who and why is for. I beg you on folded legs let us not do it again, Miss!

ROGER: She's not really a Miss. She's a he.

BETTY: The name's Officer Kellogg.

SAL: My last name is Kellogg.

BETTY: Your last name is Kellogg?

MRS. BRUCHINSKI: I had cute baby boy with an old man named Kellogg.

SAL & BETTY: I was a cute baby boy named Kellogg.

MRS. BRUCHINSKI: But old man Kellogg . . . he lost my baby boy on Division Street.

BETTY: I WAS FOUND ON DIVISION STREET!

MRS. BRUCHINSKI: YOU ARE FOUND ONCE AGAIN! MY BOY!

BETTY: MAMA! (*They embrace.*)

SAL: Close, but no cigar.

MRS. BRUCHINSKI: You also have brother somewhere. Old man Kellogg told me he left his first son with a baby sitter.
SAL: I was left with a baby sitter!
MRS. BRUCHINSKI: All paid for?
SAL: All paid for!
MRS. BRUCHINSKI: Then you have a father in common.
SAL: Sister!
BETTY: Brother! (*Sal and Betty embrace.*)
SAL: It was incest! But I didn't know. (*Mrs. Bruchinski embraces both of them.*)
MRS. BRUCHINSKI: My kids!
SAL & BETTY: MAMA! (*She cries tears of joy. Yovan is moved too.*)
YOVAN: ONLY IN AMERICA! Black and white and Polish and Jewish and they kiss and hug like gangbusters. Where else do you find such stuff but in America? I was born in the old country, but my dreams were born in America. The dream . . . it lives!
MRS. BRUCHINSKI: We shall overcome, you crazy man!
YOVAN: Yes, Black Polish person, we shall overcome like gangbusters.
SAL: I am overcome already.
DIANAH: Oh, it brings back the old days to hear you speak like that.
ROGER: Chris! Can you feel it. It's happening again. We're not alone.
CHRIS: C'mon, Rog. It's over.
ROGER: The long night is over. The new dawn of history is at hand. Look . . . look around . . . what do you see?
BETTY: The movement Chris. It moves again.
DIANAH: It does. I can feel it. (*Roger is getting all choked up with emotion.*)
ROGER: It's all here! THE NEW COALITION! IT'S THE NEW COALITON!
ALL: WE'RE THE NEW COALITION!
BETTY: Right on Rog!
SAL: Right on Rog.
MRS. BRUCHINSKI: Bravo for you old man, poopsy!
ROGER: Look. Look around. Men! Women! Black! White! Polish! Jewish! Protestant! Catholic!
DIANAH: Agnostic!
YOVAN: Serbian Orthodox!
BETTY: Trans-sexual!
NADJA: Neo-sexual!
MRS. BRUCHINSKI: Over sexual!
SAL: Under sexual!
ROGER: The lost tribe of the American Dream.
ALL: Yea!
ROGER: It's the new beginning. The new coalition. The new movement!
YOVAN: THE NEW WORLD BAR AND GRILL!
ROGER: Chris. Lead us. Lead us again.
CHRIS: I just want to lead my life and that's all.

DIANAH: Here, Chris. Take the old bullhorn and play it again. Play it again, Chris.

CHRIS: No more playing. I'm sick of playing.

YOVAN: Son, take the bull by horn and speak.

CHRIS: What do you want from me. Nobody gives a damn anymore.

ROGER: I still give a damn.

CHRIS: You're crazy. That's why.

DIANAH: You were crazy once yourself!

ROGER: You were a magnificent crazy sonovabitch!

CHRIS: Oh yeah, and where did it get me.

YOVAN: It got you to Chicago . . . To Division Street . . . to me . . . YOVAN . . . I have mimeo machine. We make leaflets.

DIANAH: And the smell of mimeo ink will be heard throughout the land again.

SAL: The little guy is ready to march.

BETTY: The women's movement throws in its support to the New Movement.

NADJA: The unemployed youth vote is yours, Chris.

MRS. BRUCHINSKI: I give you Black Polish support.

ROGER: We've got them all, baby.

BETTY: Including the crossover vote!

CHRIS: I don't believe this. I don't believe any of this.

ROGER: But wasn't it nice when we believed in it all. America, Chris. Remember.

YOVAN: America! AMERICA! I love it.

CHRIS: You think I don't . . . You're all crazy . . . (*They all begin to talk.*) Look . . . listen to me . . . There were thousands. There were thousands upon thousands . . . there were millions and now . . . look . . . there . . . There's eight of us. What are we going to do with eight people.

ROGER: Look what they did with seven in "The Magnificent Seven." I see the spark, Chris. I see it in your eyes. Don't let it die.

CHRIS: Listen to me. I've done my part. I've warned you. I've told you it's hopeless and that you haven't got a chance. I tried it once and it didn't work. But, I guess there's always a second time. Be a shame to let the new coalition go to waste. Without me you're just the Chicago Seven all over again. So let's do it.

ROGER: What?

CHRIS: Let's do it and do it right this time. (*All cheer.*) There's eight of us. We're eight for the eighties! (*Cheers.*) I've stood by long enough. I think it's time to move again. I don't know where that road is I saw so clearly when I was young, but I know it's there, and I know we can find it if we try. (*He grabs the bullhorn and leaps onto the sofa.*) So let's try. (*Cheers.*) It's not going to be easy. At every step they will tell us that we've had our chance and failed. The voice of despair will tell us that we have had it.

And we will reply: YES. We have had it. We've had it with the Republicans and we've had it with the Democrats. We've had it with the right wing and we've had it with the left wing. (*Cheers, yells, applause.*) This is our manifesto. When the leaders, whoever they are, do not inspire, then we will not follow. When the leaders, whoever they are, try to divide us, we will press all the closer together. (*Roger joins in on this one.*) When the world we envision is better than the one we live in, we will follow our vision. And when they tell us that the frontier is gone we will reply: The frontiers of dreamers is endless and we still have a dream. (*Yovan begins singing "America the Beautiful" and the others join in. Chris's voice rises above their singing.*) It is a time of transition and in those times false prophets and false fears spread throughout the land, but new spirits also arise. New dreams are born and a glorious struggle takes place for the soul of the nation. The struggle is on. Let it be said it began right here on Division Street. CITIZENS OF THE UNITED STATES OF AMERICA . . . (*The group breaks into the chorus of "America."*) It is a new decade and I proclaim in the name of the new decade, the birth of a new movement, the second movement of the great American symphony. The ring of freedom is our tuning fork, hope is our music, America is our song!

(*The group surrounds Chris. Suddenly we hear "America the Beautiful" sung by a huge choir. The company hears it and joins in, marching into the street.*)

CHOIR & COMPANY: (*Singing.*)

O beautiful for spacious skies, for amber waves of grain
For purple mountains majesties, above the fruited plain!
America! America! God shed His grace on thee,
And crown thy good with brotherhood, from sea to shining sea.

O beautiful for pilgrim feet whose stern impassioned stress
A thoroughfare for freedom beat, across the wilderness!
America! America! God mend thine every flaw,
Confirm thy soul in self-control, by liberty in law.

O beautiful for patriot dream, that sees beyond the years
Thine alabaster cities gleam, undimmed by human tears!
America! America! God shed His grace on thee,
And crown thy good with brotherhood, from sea to shining sea.

# Baba Goya

*Baba Goya* was first performed on May 9, 1973, by the American Place Theatre, New York. It was directed by Ed Sherin. The cast included:

GOYA . . . . . . . . . . *Olympia Dukakis*
MARIO . . . . . . . . . . *John Randolph*
OLD MAN . . . . . . . . . . *Lou Gilbert*
BRUNO . . . . . . . . . . *R. A. Dow*
SYLVIA . . . . . . . . . . *Peggy Whitton*
ADOLF . . . . . . . . . . *Ken Tigar*
CRIMINAL . . . . . . . . . . *Randy Kim*
STUDLY . . . . . . . . . . *David A. Butler*
CLIENT . . . . . . . . . . *James Greene*

Set: Karl Eigsti
Lighting: Roger Morgan
Costumes: Whitney Blauser

**Cast:** Goya
Mario
Old Man
Bruno
Sylvia
Adolf
Criminal
Studly
Client

**Set:** All of the action takes place in a large room of an older home. Entrance from the street is through a door on stage left. Next to the door is a window overlooking the street. The window is elevated so that when one looks at the street one looks *down* into the street. On stage right there are two doors. One leads to a bathroom, the other to the room belonging to the old man. The doors are close together with nothing to distinguish one from the other. Stage center we find a large dining room table with three chairs. All three should not match. A little away from the table is an easy chair facing the audience. They also don't match. A kitchen area is in the background. Refrigerator and a stove should suffice. A prominently displayed radiator. A stairway leads to the three rooms upstairs. It's not necessary to have the doors to the rooms seen, but the corridor leading to them should be visible. Other items such as lamps or any other pieces of furniture as deemed fit. The set should look realistic but not cluttered.

# ACT I

## Scene 1

*It's morning. Goya comes down, makes coffee. Mario's coming down the stairway. By the looks of him he's just gotten out of bed. He scratches himself . . . rubs his eyes . . . then when he stops at the foot of the stairway he opens his mouth to yawn but instead of a yawn we hear . . . Sound: A dog howl. Mario grabs his throat. He seems stunned. Sound: The dog howls again. Mario runs over to the window. Looks out. Rubs one eye. Cleans the window. Looks out again.*

MARIO: Can't be. (*Runs to chest of drawers, pulls out telescope, runs back to window.*) Can't be that big. (*Looks through telescope.*) It's bigger. Amazing. Must be a world's record. Must be a hormone imbalance. (*Goya sees Mario staring through window. She wonders what he's looking at.*) Amazing. (*Goya's pondering. Should she ask or shouldn't she. She opens her mouth to say something. Sound: Dog howls.*)

GOYA: All right. I give up. What's going on? (*Without taking his telescope off the window Mario waves to her to come over.*)

MARIO: Would you look at that thing. (*Goya looks.*)

GOYA: It's a dog . . .

MARIO: I know it's a dog but would you look at . . .

GOYA: Oh yes . . .

MARIO: Biggest one I've ever seen.

GOYA: What the . . . what the hell is he doing?

MARIO: Showing off, I think.

GOYA: I wonder whose it is.

(*Sound: Dog howls again.*)

SYLVIA: (*O.S. from upstairs.*) Hush, Dodo, you hear me . . . hush.

(*Goya and Mario look at each other and then look upstairs and then at each other again.*)

GOYA: I should've known. It's Sylvia's dog.
MARIO: Funny name for such a lusty canine . . . Dodo.
GOYA: Last time she came home she brought that kitten with her.
MARIO: Betcha anything this Dodo ate the kitten.
GOYA: The time before that it was a guinea pig.
MARIO: Grandma ate the pig.
GOYA: What are you talking about?
MARIO: Sylvia's guinea pig. Remember . . . I took it to that little old Sicilian lady . . . poor thing, I thought, all alone and everything . . . maybe a pet would cheer her up . . . Well . . . I guess they don't keep pets in the old country . . . Grandma took care of it for one winter and then she ate it. Said it tasted like rabbit.
GOYA: Maybe she'd like a dog. (*She goes back to kitchen area. Comes back carrying a Turkish coffee pot and two demitasse cups. She places coffee and cup on table, sits down. Sound: Loud noise from upstairs. It belongs to Sylvia. Goya's not moved by it.*) I wonder how long she plans to keep that up.
MARIO: It sounds like she's just warming up, to me. I used to be a janitor in an opera house . . . and that's how they did it . . . They'd be there . . . sitting down tying their shoelaces and screaming at the top of their lungs.
GOYA: Your coffee's ready. (*He comes over and sits down.*) Did she say anything to you?
MARIO: Not really . . . I just got back from work last night and there she was standing outside the door. Sylvia, I said. Mario, she says, and starts crying. At first I thought she was crying because she was glad to see me . . . but then she kept it up. Couldn't be that glad, I figured. And then I thought, maybe she found out about my condition . . . you know . . . crying because I was going to die and all . . . but she kept it up. Couldn't be that sorry to see me go, I figured. So I finally asked her. Why are you crying. If you only knew, she says, and erupts with such a barrage of snots and tears that I didn't know whether to offer her sympathy or an antihistamine.
GOYA: She cried all night . . . poor little phony. You think she'd be exhausted.
MARIO: According to an article in *Today's Health* people who cry at night aren't nearly as sick as what they call midday weepers.
GOYA: Taking all that into consideration, Mario, I think we better get our rear in gear and start solving some of these problems. I've let things

slide . . . I feel it . . . things are slipping through my fingers . . . People are running around the house doing all kinds of weird things without so much as a word of explanation . . . You too. Fine time you picked to die.

MARIO: I didn't really choose when . . .

GOYA: We'll get to that later. Now . . . the way I see it, these are the major areas of concern . . .

MARIO: Hold it. (*He takes out a used envelope and a pencil from his pocket.*) Shoot, as Bruno would say.

GOYA: First of all we have to find out why Sylvia came home . . get to the bottom of her chronic "secret sorrow" and then get her out of here.

MARIO: But she's your own daughter, Goya.

GOYA: I can't let family ties interfere with my family affairs. (*Mario writes.*) Next comes Bruno . . . he's been awfully depressed. It takes him half an hour to come down the stairs . . . he gulps his coffee . . . eats fruit cocktail out of a can . . . he took a shower with his socks on the other day.

MARIO: (*Writes.*) I got it.

GOYA: Then there's the old man. He was a nice old man for a while and now, to be blunt, he's rapidly turning into a mean old man. I know . . . I'm partially to blame because I let him linger on under the false assumption that someday . . . well . . . you know . . .

MARIO: (*Writes.*) Yes, I got it.

GOYA: (*Waits for him to finish.*) I think that about does it.

MARIO: What about cheese?

GOYA: What cheese?

MARIO: We're all out of cheese . . . and Sylvia likes cheese.

GOYA: All right, put down cheese. Let's hear what you've got. (*Mario sits up straighter. Coughs. Smooths out envelope.*)

MARIO: Let's see. Things to be done. Soothe Sylvia, brighten Bruno and meliorate the mean old man.

GOYA: Oh, c'mon . . .

MARIO: It's more concise this way. And then there's cheese. (*Sound: Dog howl.*) What about Dodo?

GOYA: The hell with Dodo.

MARIO: Knowing Sylvia she probably didn't feed the poor thing.

GOYA: All right . . . get him some food. (*Mario writes.*) What are you writing down?

MARIO: Just what you said . . . dog food.

GOYA: Let me see. (*Takes envelope.*) Nourish the beast!

MARIO: It's got a nice ring to it. Considering my condition . . . I just might drop dead in the street . . . and it pleases me to think that when they go through my pockets they stumble across this mysterious notation: Nourish the beast.

GOYA: Look here, Mario . . . if you feel the Maker calling you to his bosom then I guess you have to answer the call . . . All I got to say is . . . you picked a helluva time to croak.

MARIO: Who picked the time . . . what . . . I was born and before I knew what was happening I started living . . . I didn't like the way I was living . . . so I started waiting around for things to get better . . . Things, I figured had to get better. Things got worse. Well, I figured, at least they can't get any worse. They got worse. And then they got even worse than that. I was born into a dirty and rotten world and progress being what it is it got dirtier and more rotten. Since yesterday it's got dirtier. In the last half hour . . . (*Looks out of window.*) It wasn't that dirty when I got out of bed . . . now look at it . . . can't find one ripe tomato in the whole city . . . apples are all mealy . . . cucumbers are bitter . . . lettuce is wilted . . . I never have exact change for a bus . . . when I do I can't find a seat . . . the mops they give me at work leave those little strings all over the place . . . they closed down another cafeteria . . . I never run into old friends the way I used to . . . nobody plays dominos any more . . . they left me out of the phone book again . . . I have no idea what Eric Severeid is talking about . . .

GOYA: HOLD IT! DIE IF YOU MUST! (*Silence.*)

MARIO: I just wanted to make sure you understood.

GOYA: I understand. Only . . . I hope you understand . . . that if something does happen to you . . .

MARIO: You mean like death.

GOYA: Yes . . . I hope you realize I'll be sadder than hell.

MARIO: That's understood.

GOYA: I also hope you realize that I can't go around beating my breasts over it . . . It's not in my nature.

MARIO: Believe me, Goya, when I say that breasts like yours were not meant to be beaten.

GOYA: No poetry, please. If you die I'm going to have to get another husband . . . and I'll probably get him the same way I got you . . . I just can't wait around until somebody nice comes along.

MARIO: I already took care of that. I put the ad in the paper myself.

GOYA: You didn't.

MARIO: It should be in this morning's edition.

GOYA: You little sweetheart.

MARIO: No poetry, please.

GOYA: In that case we're all set to kick off the fall schedule. First item on the schedule is Sylvia . . . SYLVIA! COME ON DOWN HERE!

MARIO: Don't you think a subtle approach would work better on her?

GOYA: Fine. I'll be subtle. First I got to get her down here. SYLVIA . . . COME ON DOWN, DEAR . . . If you want some understanding you better get to me before noon . . . SYLVIA!

MARIO: That must be what Dr. Meriweather of the Institute for Family Relations calls the hand grenade approach.

GOYA: SYLVIA! We're waiting . . . (*Old Man comes out of room with note paper; he looks terribly irritated. Both Goya and Mario see him and brace themselves for the inevitable tirade.*)

OLD MAN: What the hell . . . what the hell *is* all this . . . First I hear howling . . . then I hear some madman screaming about a world's record . . . then I hear HUSH, DODO . . . then I hear somebody crying . . . then I start hearing SYLVIA! SYLVIA! I wait . . . and by God it comes again . . . SYLVIA! SYLVIA! Why don't you just come in my room and drop a cannonball down my ears. I'll go deaf if this keeps up, I'm warning you. I'll just sit down and go deaf and then you'll be sorry. You'll come home and ask me if there were any phone calls for you . . . You might feel like talking to me . . . You might even want to know what time it is because your watch stopped . . . and I won't be able to tell you a thing because I won't know what the hell you're talking about because you drove me deaf. Now do you understand!

GOYA: Yes, grandpa. (*This word hits the old man like a slap on the face.*)

OLD MAN: Grampa! (*Takes a threatening step toward Goya.*) How many times do I have to tell you . . . Do I have to get a lawyer . . . I'm not . . . never was . . . and never will be yours or anybody else's grampa. Is that clear? I see it's not. All right. I'll fix you. I'll blast you. You'll see. I'll blast you right out of here. (*He spins around dramatically and goes into the bathroom instead of his room . . . slamming the door. Goya's not looking. Mario is. She looks at Mario. Mario nods. The bathroom door flies open and the old man stomps out. Mario and Goya are looking away from him.*) Don't think I made a mistake. I went in there on purpose . . . there was no mistake. I want that understood. I had business in there. (*Then he stomps away into his room and slams the door shut.*)

GOYA: Got to meliorate that mean old man. (*Mario looks at his notes.*)

MARIO: I got it down. (*Bruno lumbers down stairway. Goya, to make sure Mario notices, does an imitation of Bruno's walk. Mario looks at her, looks at Bruno. Bruno is dressed in a police uniform. Takes the gun from drawer and looks at it.*)

GOYA: Before you shoot yourself I'd like a word with you. (*Bruno puts gun in holster, looks at Goya who shouts.*) Why don't you brighten up, Bruno?

MARIO: You're getting more subtle by the minute.

GOYA: Come here, son. How about some coffee?

BRUNO: All right. (*Goya pours out some coffee into Mario's demitasse cup. Bruno comes over and without sitting down he chugs the coffee in one gulp.*)

GOYA: Care for another shot?

BRUNO: All right. (*Goya pours out another cup. Bruno chugs it in one gulp.*)

GOYA: Bruno, my son, that's Turkish coffee you're annihilating. It costs two fifty a pound; I get it for two ten because I tell this old Turk I hate Greeks. If I can perjure myself the least you can do is enjoy it.

BRUNO: I enjoy it.

GOYA: Don't tell me that . . . You don't drink Turkish coffee standing up . . It's sit down coffee . . . Bend your legs, Bruno . . . You look like you're standing inside a holster. Sit down. (*He sits.*) There . . . doesn't that feel better?

BRUNO: No.

GOYA: (*Leaning over him.*) Bruno . . . I'm not one of those commissions investigating police corruption . . . don't be so defensive . . . This is your little ole mother you're talking to. (*Mario lets out a chortle.*) Did you want to laugh about something, Mario?

MARIO: Yes I did. But I changed my mind.

GOYA: Could you change it a little more quietly? I'm talking to my son, the Fifth Amendment, here. Now where was I?

BRUNO: You were being a little ole mother. (*He and Mario exchange a conspiratory glance.*)

GOYA: What's this . . . you didn't tell me you were taking a stenography course on the sly. Are you listening to this, Mario?

MARIO: Yes, don't you want me to?

GOYA: Of course I do. I need a witness with his kind. Bruno . . . look at me when I talk to you. (*He looks at her.*) Don't look at me like that, Bruno. I'm not a dentist. You know Mario's been very worried about you. (*Mario protests with his hands. Goya ignores him.*) He's got enough to worry about, the poor thing. Look at him, Bruno. (*Bruno looks at Mario and Mario's on the spot.*) He's talking about dying.

BRUNO: I know. I don't want him to die.

GOYA: Well, you're killing him.

MARIO: Let's hold it right there. I wouldn't blame Bruno for . . .

GOYA: Just because you have one foot in the grave is no reason to put the other in your mouth, Mario. Now why don't you go and get me the paper.

BRUNO: I'll get it.

GOYA: I like the way Mario gets it better. Adios Mario. (*Mario exits. Goya lights a cigarette.*) Care for a cigarette?

BRUNO: That's how we treat criminals down at the station. First we offer them a cigarette and then if they refuse we beat them up. I wonder how many people started smoking in police stations.

GOYA: So now your mother is a police station.

BRUNO: No, but we did have a guy down there who was a marvel at getting confessions. He'd hug the suspects and break into tears . . . he'd tell them how he's going to get fired if he doesn't get a conviction soon . . . how his kids are starving . . . his wife dying of scurvy or something . . .

he got more confessions that way. We called him Mother Sarge.

GOYA: How has the word mother come to mean so many unpleasant things?

BRUNO: I think mothers had something to do with it.

GOYA: All any mother wants is for her kids to be happy.

BRUNO: Speaking for the kids . . . all they want is for the mothers to be happy.

GOYA: Mothers can't be happy if their kids aren't happy.

BRUNO: Mothers should try.

GOYA: I'm not going to beg you, Bruno, and I refuse to resort to threats . . . It's not in my nature. Let's just say . . . you're killing your father and you're well on your way to killing me. If that's what you want . . . If that'll make you happy . . . Then you might as well pull out . . .

BRUNO: All right, ma . . . all right . . . don't tell me to pull out my gun and shoot you again. I'll speak. It's the orphanage business . . . it's crept into my mind again.

GOYA: Well, tell it to creep out again. You're not an orphan any more. Do I treat you like an orphan? Haven't I been a real mother to you?

BRUNO: You're the most real mother I've ever seen. Believe me . . . when conversation turns to real mothers I always bring up your name. But I can't get that orphanage business out of my head. It keeps coming back . . . and somehow it's affecting my job now . . . I'm tired of dragging criminals down to the station. I know, for example, that I'll catch some orphaney-looking criminal today . . . I know it . . . and already I'm sweating it . . . what am I going to do with him?

GOYA: Bring him home for coffee if that'll make you happy.

BRUNO: And then there's Sylvia.

GOYA: I knew there was more to it.

BRUNO: I could tell she was coming home again.

GOYA: Did you two get into a fight already?

BRUNO: No. She came home last night and pretended to be crying. I pretended to be asleep but she pretended not to notice and kept right on crying. She's so damned phony.

GOYA: I know. But this is her home and if she wants to come home I can't chase her out right away.

BRUNO: But why does she have to have such phony excuses for coming home? After every election she shows up and starts snotting about the state of the union.

GOYA: That's what phonies cry about.

BRUNO: And another thing . . . how come she doesn't know that I'm an orphan? I mean . . . she thinks I'm her brother and I just don't feel like being a brother to a phony sister like that.

GOYA: I tried to tell her once. I said, you know Bruno's not your real brother. And she said, you can say that again.

BRUNO: Well . . . I'm going to tell her.

GOYA: Go ahead, and if she gives you any lip about being an orphan you can always come back and call her a bastard.

BRUNO: I didn't know that.

GOYA: Well, now you do. But use it sparingly. I never married her father, and for all I know nobody else did either.

BRUNO: How come?

GOYA: Because he was such a phony. You don't think she gets it from me, do you? Now cheer up, son, so mother can move on to other things. (*Bruno gets up, looks at his watch, goes toward door. Goya hugs him. Sound: Dog howl. He looks over his shoulder through window.*)

BRUNO: Would you look at that thing!

GOYA: I already did.

BRUNO: (*As Bruno is going out, Mario comes in carrying newspaper.*) See you this evening.

MARIO: I hope so. (*Bruno exits. Mario shuts the door.*) I see you fixed him up.

GOYA: One down . . . Is it in the paper? I don't want to seem greedy . . . I'm just curious . . . (*Mario leafs through paper.*)

MARIO: Here it is. WANTED: potential husband to assume full duties and responsibilities of the same. Must have a steady job and not hang around the house all day. Apply in person and ask for Goya. And the address.

GOYA: It's a very nice ad . . . and I certainly have no right to complain . . . but you should've put something in there about me not wanting a German . . . I betcha anything Adolf shows up again.

MARIO: Germans are human too.

GOYA: Oh, Mario, I don't want you to die.

MARIO: Don't worry . . . somebody nice'll come along.

GOYA: That's just it . . . what if some Paul Newman answers the ad . . . and I really get the hots for him . . . and you're still alive . . .

MARIO: I think that should be enough to do me in.

GOYA: (*Rises.*) Give me a kiss.

MARIO: Why not. (*They kiss. Cry is heard from Sylvia upstairs.*)

GOYA: There she goes again . . . God forgive me but I just can't face her now . . . any good movies around?

MARIO: No, I don't think so.

GOYA: (*Looks through paper.*) But I'll go anyway. You going to work?

MARIO: Might as well.

GOYA: I'll walk to the subway with you. I hate to say this about anybody who's even part female, but what she needs is a good fuzz bash. (*They start walking out.*)

MARIO: Fuzz bash. (*They walk out. Sylvia appears at top of stairway.*)

SYLVIA: Oh, Mother . . . Mother . . . Mother . . . Mother . . . your little sinner is back . . . your naughty little Sylvia has done it this time . . . No . . . please don't ask me what it is . . . It's horrible . . . It's ghastly . . . if you only knew . . . (*Sylvia lets out a cry. The old man leaps out of his room.*)

OLD MAN: Shut up already.

SYLVIA: Oh . . . I thought . . . where's Mother?

OLD MAN: She went to a movie, you little phony.

SYLVIA: What a mean old man you are. If I wasn't so heartbroken I'd tell you to go to hell.

OLD MAN: So you need a good fuzz bash, do you!

SYLVIA: Even if I did . . . Chances seem slim of getting one here. Are you one of those things Mother took in?

OLD MAN: I am what I am . . . which is more than I can say for you. I heard everything. I'm not deaf yet you know . . . You and that Dodo of yours.

SYLVIA: Poor Dodo . . . animals are so intuitive . . . he senses my grief . . . my burning sense of guilt . . .

OLD MAN: Go burn somewhere else.

SYLVIA: You're probably suffering from inflation . . . People on fixed incomes . . . pensions . . . social security and the like are the ones who suffer the most . . . and I've added to their suffering . . . yours too . . . is that why you hate me . . . You sense the wrong I've done . . . Does it show? . . . I feel that it shows.

OLD MAN: I once ate a rhubarb tart and got sick to my stomach. I vomited in the street and everybody thought I was drunk . . . but I wasn't . . . it was that tart that did me in . . . and that's what *you* remind me of . . . a rhubarb tart.

SYLVIA: Well, you're no birthday cake yourself, handsome. But go ahead . . . hate me . . . I've brought it upon myself . . . It must be hard for you . . . fixed income and all . . . I'm sorry . . . Forgive me, Grampa. (*The Old Man reacts.*)

OLD MAN: Grampa! Somebody's spreading rumors again. Well, if that's how they want to fight. Alright. I'll blast you. You'll see. (*Old Man shakes . . . stomps into bathroom . . . stomps out and goes into bedroom.*)

SYLVIA: That was quick. (*She sits down at the table. Sighs. Drops her head on the newspaper. Looks around, drops her head again. Fade out.*)

## Scene 2

*Fade in. Day—few hours later. Sylvia hasn't moved from her place. Goya is standing behind her. Sylvia is crying and Goya is comforting her.*

GOYA: There .. . . there . . . Mother's here. Mother understands.

SYLVIA: I came down here and nobody was here except this mean old creature . . . My own mother, whom I haven't seen in years, couldn't even wait to comfort me.

GOYA: Well, I waited for a few years for you to come home and then I went to a movie. Some movie. I had a groper on my left and a drunk on my right. So I move and sit down next to this character who's eating popcorn off the floor . . . I want to call the usher and I look again and he is the usher.

SYLVIA: Men are so horrible, aren't they, mother?

GOYA: I wouldn't give you a dime for some women I know either.

SYLVIA: I got a divorce, you know.

GOYA: I didn't know you were married.

SYLVIA: I was.

GOYA: Well, congratulations. I hope you were very happy.

SYLVIA: Happy! You have to be an idiot to be a married woman.

GOYA: I wouldn't give you a dime for some divorcees I know either.

SYLVIA: All he did was wash his car and lie about the miles per gallon he was getting. I married him because he was a liberal and you know what he did . . . He forced me to get pregnant just so I could get an abortion and test the legality of some law or other. So I had an abortion.

GOYA: Haven't we all.

SYLVIA: Then I divorced him and proceeded to do some ghastly things which culminated in an absolute nightmare.

GOYA: You don't have to tell me if you don't want to.

SYLVIA: I was in a pornographic movie.

GOYA: I just came back from one.

SYLVIA: I took drugs; I sold drugs. I rolled drunks . . . I was a shoplifter.

GOYA: Prices being what they are . . . who can blame you.

SYLVIA: I turned my back on morality and decency. I ridiculed honesty and laughed at the ideas of the struggling masses. I lived like an animal.

GOYA: At least you had a good time.

SYLVIA: And then . . . (*She starts sobbing.*)

GOYA: There . . . there . . .

SYLVIA: And then I . . . (*Sobs. Goya mouths the word "phony."*)

GOYA: Mother's here . . . Mother understands.

SYLVIA: And then . . . in the national election . . . I voted for Nixon.

GOYA: You little slut! (*Pushes Sylvia to floor then moves chair close to table. Old Man flies out of his room in a rage with a belt in hand.*)

OLD MAN: Nixon! You little bitch you! And me with fixed income. Let me at her! (*He rushes at Sylvia. Sylvia rolls on ground U.S.R. of radiator. Goya stops him. Sylvia cries.*)

GOYA: I'll handle this.

OLD MAN: Let me at her. I'll blast her.

GOYA: Take it easy, grampa. (*Old Man begins shaking.*)

OLD MAN: Grampa! You're no better than she . . . I'll have to blast both of you . . . I'll . . . I'll do it . . . (*He stomps toward bathroom.*)

GOYA: NOT THAT WAY! (*The Old Man changes his course and stomps away into his room. Sylvia's crying even louder. Sound: Dog howl.*) Shut up, Sylvia. Hush, Dodo! Enough! (*Neither of them do. Goya goes to the window. Opens it and throws magazines at Dodo. Sound: Dog howls—then stops. Sylvia screams. Goya picks up another load of magazines . . . throws it at Old Man's door . . . he just escapes.*) Look, dear, let's not let politics come between us . . . Your rotten voting habits are your own affair.

SYLVIA: I did it to spite my husband . . . Now the whole country hates me . . . it's all my fault.

GOYA: Don't blame yourself, dear. There were other morons who voted the way you did.

SYLVIA: I hate myself.

GOYA: You shouldn't do that . . . that's what mothers are for. Look, honey, I wish I could take the time to soothe you and all . . . but I've got other things on my mind . . . You know Mario's going to die.

SYLVIA: Oh, mother . . . poor mother . . . you're going to be all alone.

GOYA: Never can tell, dear.

SYLVIA: I'll stay with you. The two of us will live together. We're in the same boat, you and I.

GOYA: I don't think we're even in the same sea, dear. But thank you, anyway.

SYLVIA: We'll live together and grow old together. We'll have nothing to do with men. We'll wear dowdy clothes and plant flowers.

GOYA: It's nice of you to paint such a rosy future for me, but . . .

SYLVIA: We'll grieve our lives away like a couple of nuns. I must admit, mother, it did shock me a little the way you didn't grieve for any of your husbands. I mean those newspaper ads . . . no sooner did they die than you'd invite every Tom, Dick and Harry . . .

GOYA: Just for the record, dear . . . their names were Peter, Ferdinand and Marko . . . and Mario of course.

SYLVIA: In any case . . . things'll be different from now on. You and I . . . (*Sees mother's ad—reads same out loud.*) MOTHER! YOU DID IT AGAIN! (*Throws newspaper.*)

GOYA: No I didn't . . . Mario did it. That crazy Mario . . . What'll he think of next? (*Sylvia starts bawling.*)

SYLVIA: You're horrible . . . I can't even have one decent husband and you're working on your fifth.

GOYA: It's really no work, dear, once you get used to it. Don't worry, we'll find you a man.

SYLVIA: I think men are gross.

GOYA: Some are . . . some are downright puny.

SYLVIA: I think you're gross. You have no heart.

GOYA: I gave it away, dear.

SYLVIA: That's not all you gave away. Sex at your age . . . Aren't you ashamed?

GOYA: I am . . . but I've learned to live with it. What can I do, dear, my bed sags on one side . . . I need a man for balance so I don't fall out.

SYLVIA: Then get a new bed.

GOYA: I guess I'm sentimental. I like the old one. (*Sylvia resorts to tears again.*)

SYLVIA: Nobody loves me.

GOYA: There, there, dear . . . (*Sylvia starts towards her.*) . . . somebody must. (*Sylvia stops.*)

SYLVIA: I don't even know why I bothered coming home. (*She runs upstairs.*)

GOYA: Don't worry . . . I'm sure you'll think of something. (*Sylvia breaks into sobs and disappears into her upstairs rooms.*) A phony . . . My God . . . you'd think she went to college and got a degree in it. (*Sound: Doorbell rings. Goya goes to the door. Adolf remains in the doorway out of sight of the audience. She sees him, pushes door shut, then puts on safety chain.*)

ADOLF: Good evening. I'm looking for Goya.

GOYA: What can she do for you?

ADOLF: I happened to be leafing through the *Post* . . . usually I leaf through the New York *Times* . . . but it just so happened that I happened to be leafing through the *Post* . . .

GOYA: Would you mind leafing a little faster?

ADOLF: Why should I mind? You say faster . . . I go faster . . . you say slow . . . I go slow. Whatever you say I do.

GOYA: Why don't you take off your hat or whatever you call that thing? There . . . now why don't you take off your wig? Now what do you want, baldie?

ADOLF: As I was leafing through the *Post* I happened to be struck by an ad . . .

GOYA: You better go home before you get struck by something else. This is a bad neighborhood. Everybody on the block is out on bail.

ADOLF: It says here . . . potential husband to assume . . .

GOYA: Hold it. Don't assume nothing. First of all, I don't like your potential. Secondly, ADOLF, I told you when Peter died I wasn't interested . . . I told you when Ferdinand went that you can go to . . . and I never forgave you for not showing up after Marko's death.

ADOLF: You must have me confused with somebody else.

GOYA: What's there to confuse . . . you're German.

ADOLF: I've told you before and I told you last time that I'm not German.

GOYA: And I told you the last time that you were.

ADOLF: I have changed.

GOYA: You look every bit as German as you ever did. Besides . . . what kind of a man are you . . . have you no pride . . . couldn't you've found a wife in all this time?

ADOLF: I did. I was married but my wife happened to die.

GOYA: Your wife dies and you come looking for another one right away. Ah—you're a cold-hearted man. What's that you got there?

ADOLF: I happened to have a bottle of booze in my possession. (*Goya takes the bottle.*)

GOYA: I'll take it. I'm an alcoholic, you know. Forget the ad, Adolf . . . it was all a mistake . . . My husband, as far as I know, is still alive.

ADOLF: Too bad. Maybe some other time.

GOYA: Sure thing . . . when the last man on earth dies . . . give me a buzz. Guten abend, mein Herr.

ADOLF: Guten abend, Frau Goya. (*Goya shuts the door.*)

GOYA: (*Leaning on door.*) Frau! Ugh! Frau. Frau Goya. Ugh! (*Opens the bottle. Takes a swig.*) It sure doesn't taste like tomato juice. (*Laughs.*) Got to hand it to Adolf. He always brings something to soothe the nasty impression he makes. (*Takes another swig.*) Poor man . . . he had hair when he first came. (*Takes another swig.*) Or maybe it was always a wig. (*Another swig.*) In any case . . . it was a better looking wig than the one he's got now. (*She takes another swig. Sound. A police siren outside. Gun shots. Dodo starts barking. Goya takes a swig and crosses to the door.*) Here we go again . . . What a neighborhood . . . Better lock up the door and get drunk. (*Goya locks door, and goes to the kitchen.*) This is no time to be sober. (*Sound: Footsteps outside the door. They come closer. A noise as if someone is fighting outside Goya's door. Banging on the door.*) I didn't do it, and I don't know who did! (*Goya picks up glass and brings it to table.*)

BRUNO: Ma . . . it's me . . . Open up.

GOYA: Bruno . . . . (*She opens the door. Bruno bursts in carrying an Oriental youth. They are handcuffed, Oriental's got the camera.*)

BRUNO: Can't explain now . . . the cops are out there . . . if they come . . . tell them . . . I don't care . . . just get rid of them . . . (*Sound: Footsteps outside the door. Bruno runs for the john. Drags the Oriental with him inside the john and shuts the door. Sound: Knocking is heard and doorbell rings. Goya heads for the door . . . takes a swig from the bottle on the way. Goya primps. Opens the door and blocks the entrance with her body. Cop remains O.S.*)

GOYA: Good evening, Studly.

STUDLY: Hate to disturb you, ma'am.

GOYA: Oh, that's all right. I'm already disturbed as you can see.

STUDLY: A man just had his camera ripped right off his shoulder . . . we thought we saw the suspect come in here.

GOYA: You've got good eyes . . . no . . . lovely eyes. The suspect did come in here . . or tried . . . But I chased him away . . . A short fellow, right . . . with a scroungy looking wig. Calls everybody and his uncle Frau

. . . killed his wife, I think . . . He went . . . hold on a second . . . I think I have his address. (*Goes to the chest of drawers and produces a card.*) He left his card last time he was here . . . there's his address. (*Gives card to cop.*) It's rough out there, eh?

STUDLY: Happens after every election.

GOYA: Well . . . drop by again . . . during primaries or something.

STUDLY: I just might do that.

GOYA: I just might be here. (*She shuts the door. Deep sigh.*) God, how I love a pair of eyes like that . . . when they're perched on a body like that . . . (*Goes to the bathroom and opens the door. Bruno's head appears.*)

BRUNO: I don't know why I did it . . . I mean . . . I was off duty and I see this guy ripping a camera off this other guy . . . So I nab him . . . Then I start feeling sorry for him . . . what the hell . . . I'm off duty . . . What am I . . . a gung-ho cop or something . . . and then I see these other cops closing in . . . and the guy looks so orphany . . . I don't know.

GOYA: He's welcome. (*Goya shuts door and leans against the wall.*) They're coming at me from all sides . . . two in the bathroom, one next door to the bathroom, Germans, cops, criminals . . . and the day is still young. Hmmm . . . looks Chinese . . . never had a Chinese criminal before . . . at least not such a young one . . . at least not recently. Let me see, got to figure things out. (*Takes a swig.*) Sylvia gets Bruno . . . Adolf gets arrested . . . Mario gets buried . . . and I get the Chinese. I must be tired . . . It's working out too well. (*Takes a swig.*) And who gets Grampa . . . It's not working out at all. (*Fade out.*)

## Scene 3

*Fade in. Late night. The booze bottle is on the table where Goya left it. Sitting in a chair handcuffed to the radiator is the criminal. He's asleep. The front door opens and in comes Mario on his tiptoes . . . he's a little drunk. Sees the bottle of booze on the table and exhales. Does not see the criminal. Goes toward the bottle.*

MARIO: I run away from the bottle and the bottle runs after me . . . It's like in one of them fairy tales. (*He walks toward the bottle.*) According to an article in *Outdoor Life* kids who were bottle fed never outgrow their desire for the bottle . . . or two. The question . . . If I were breast fed would I see a breast sitting on the dining room table. (*Takes bottle. Looks at it. Sniffs it.*) This is German booze . . . Adolf's been here. Goya wouldn't have him if he was the last man on earth. Yes, she would . . . If he was dead last . . . I think she'd like that . . . to have the very last man on earth . . . (*Takes a swig.*) She'd like it even better if she had the last man on earth . . . (*Takes a swig.*) And a whole bunch in between. (*Ready to take another swig . . . sees the criminal handcuffed to the radiator. Stops. Looks at the bottle. Looks at the criminal. Goes over to him.*) Are you here about the ad? Hmmm? Poor soul. Looks exhausted. Probably rushed right over when he read the thing . . . just like I did . . . I couldn't believe I finally saw a position for which I qualified. WANTED—A MAN. That's all. A man. (*Looks at the criminal. Takes another good look at the criminal.*) The thing is . . . he looks Chinese to me . . . or Japanese. Must be Japanese. He has that Japanese look. Plus he's got that camera . . . in short . . . a Japanese. Or a Chinese that looks like a Japanese. He probably carried that camera to make everbody think he's not Chinese. (*To the criminal.*) Not that it matters one bit. Goya likes Chinese men . . . and Japanese men. (*Takes a swig.*) And Arabs . . . and Viet Cong . . . and tall Swedes and short-legged Serbians. (*To the criminal.*) She once told me that Indians make good husbands. And Greeks . . . and Portuguese fishermen. And Montenegrin peasants . . . or was it Lithuanian peasants? Not that it matters. I mean I wouldn't sweat it if you were Lithuanian. You won't believe this . . . (*Takes a swig.*) They had an article in *National Geographic* about this tribe of people that was discovered living in caves . . . living in prehistoric conditions . . . You get the picture . . . prehistoric cavemen . . . and you know what Goya said . . . You guessed it . . . Cavemen, she said, probably make very nice husbands. And the damn thing was that *National Geographic* went on to verify her statement in the next issue . . . I guess they took a poll of prehistoric cave wives and they said they preferred prehistoric cave husbands nine to one. (*Takes a good hard look at the criminal.*) Wait a minute . . . Maybe the poor guy's German . . . That must be it . . . Poor thing . . . He found out Goya hates Germans and he tried to pass himself off as Chinese . . . She'll see right through him. You're wasting your time, buddy. Come clean . . . what is your nationality, Herr Suitor. (*Shakes him.*) Verstehen sie mich? (*Shakes him. Criminal opens his eyes.*)

CRIMINAL: Hey . . .

MARIO: You speak English, I see. Your nationality, my good man, what is your nationality?

CRIMINAL: I'm an American. (*Mario sighs. The criminal shuts his eyes again.*)

MARIO: I find it amazing . . . truly amazing . . . you see some character and you can tell a mile off he's from Hong Kong or some such Kong and he swears to you he's American . . . While this New England dude whose father not only came over on the Mayflower but built the damn thing as well gets his kicks by trying to peddle himself off as a direct descendant of Taras Bulba or some other bulba like that . . . Makes no sense . . . Right? Hmmm? (*He looks at Criminal. Sees the handcuffs.*) She's got him handcuffed. Must want to keep him then and if she wants to keep him he's not German. What the hell is he then? Must be Japanese just as

I thought. (*Walks toward couch.*) Not that it matters. (*Lies down on couch. His head reappears again as he looks at the criminal.*) Oh, it matters to some all right . . . but not to Goya . . . and that's what matters. (*His head disappears from view. A hiccup is heard . . . and then the beginning of a snore and then nothing.*)

## Scene 4

*Fade in. Same as before. It's later on in the night.*

CRIMINAL: Hey . . . (*He looks around room.*) Hey . . . (*Sees bottle next to him.*) Hey . . . (*Rattles handcuffs against radiator. Goya appears at top of stairway. Turns on lights. Walks down in her kimono looking around, looks at Criminal, looks at bottle, picks up bottle.*)

GOYA: You might have left some.

CRIMINAL: Hey . . . I didn't . . . I find this rather pathetic . . . I mean . . . I'm handcuffed to a radiator in a place I've never seen before and all I can do is shout my pathetic hey . . . It's not even a shout . . . it's just a pathetic whine . . . like when the waiter brings me a cheeseburger and I ordered chili . . . what do I do . . . I say, hey . . . and eat the burger . . . the barber butchers my hair . . . I look in the mirror and mutter . . . hey . . . and tip the bastard . . . I see a buddy in the street . . . Hey . . . Hey . . . Hey, man . . . a pretty girl walks by . . . Hey . . . Let me think . . . That's right . . . even when I jumped that moron with the camera . . . what did I say . . . not . . . this is a mugging . . . or . . . stick them up . . . no siree . . . not me . . . I said, hey, let's have that camera. I bet anything that when I'm dying and everybody's gathered around my bed waiting for my last words all I'll have to say is . . . hey . . .

GOYA: It's late . . . where the hell is Mario? He couldn't have died . . . I'd know it . . . Deep down in my heart I know I'm not a widow yet. He's probably hanging around some all night bookstore.

CRIMINAL: Sure beats hanging around a hot radiator. Hey, would somebody mind explaining a few things.

(*Bruno and Sylvia appear at top of stairs.*)

BRUNO: Something the matter, ma?

GOYA: Mario's not home yet.

BRUNO: He's probably hanging around some bookstore.

CRIMINAL: Who's this Mario? (*Nobody looks at him.*) Hey, I'm here too.

(*Bruno and Sylvia come down stairs.*)

SYLVIA: Don't tell me you're worried about him.

GOYA: Of course I'm worried. He should've been home by now.

SYLVIA: Yeah . . . real worried . . . so worried you've already begun replacement procedures.

GOYA: You think I like getting married all these times? I don't. After each untimely departure I swear I'll never do it again . . . But then I think of all those poor lonely men out there . . . and my heart goes out to them . . .

SYLVIA: And your bed as well.

GOYA: Got to have a place to put the heart down, dear.

CRIMINAL: Hey, that's good.

GOYA: I'm going to that bookstore on the corner to see if he's there. (*She goes to closet . . . puts on a man's overcoat over her kimono and goes out. Bruno and Sylvia stand there as if they had never been alone before.*)

CRIMINAL: I find this hard to believe . . . I mean . . .
I mean . . . you'd think I'd be the center of attention here . . . I mean . . . if somebody handcuffed a criminal to the radiator in my house you can be damned sure he'd be the center of attraction . . . But then, my family is overly polite. We're always saying hello to each other . . . All except me . . . I say, hey, Dad . . . Hey, Ma . . . I try to break the ice by being casual but it don't work.

(*Bruno and Sylvia are almost unaware of the criminal's presence. They look at each other . . . then look away . . . like a couple on a first date.*)

We're so polite in my house. Excuse me for being alive. Sorry for being born. Stuff like that. I try to break the ice but my old lady's like one of those automatic ice-makers . . . always a fresh supply . . . yes . . . she's a real modern convenience, my mother . . . that's why I turned to a life of crime . . . I mean . . . it's better than no life at all . . . what I'm trying to say is . . . it's all my mother's fault . . . You should have her handcuffed to this radiator . . . the old ice bag . . . Ah . . . nobody gives a damn about me . . .

(*Sylvia looks at Criminal. Bruno looks at Sylvia looking at Criminal. Criminal looks at Sylvia. Sylvia sits down at the table. Looks at Criminal. Bruno stands frozen.*)

BRUNO: Look here, Sylvia . . . Pretty soon I'm going to start talking . . . It'll be any second now . . . If you don't want me to start say so . . . but once I start I won't be able to stop.

SYLVIA: What is it . . . a speech or something?

BRUNO: Something like that . . . You don't want to hear, right?

SYLVIA: Why not . . . I'll listen.

BRUNO: Because you've got nothing better to do, right?

SYLVIA: No . . . I've got things to do.

BRUNO: Am I keeping you from something?

SYLVIA: I'll listen, alright.

CRIMINAL: Me, too.

BRUNO: You see, Sylvia . . . you're always coming and going . . . I held that against you for a long time . . . because I'd like to be able to come and go myself.

CRIMINAL: That makes two of us.

BRUNO: But I can't. You see this is your home . . . Goya's your mother . . . you take it for granted . . . that you're my sister and that I'm your brother and really nothing's further from the truth . . . I'm an orphan, Sylvia . . .

SYLVIA: Since when.

BRUNO: Ever since they put me in the orphanage and up to the time Goya adopted me . . .

SYLVIA: Adopted?

BRUNO: Yes, I'm an adopted orphan, Sylvia.

SYLVIA: But mother never said . . .

BRUNO: To her it doesn't matter. To Mario it doesn't matter. It shouldn't really matter to me.

SYLVIA: But it does matter.

BRUNO: Yes, it does.

SYLVIA: Don't say another word, Bruno . . . I understand.

BRUNO: I have to say more. I told you before it's a whole speech.

SYLVIA: Oh, Bruno . . . how you must hate me . . . me . . . their real child and you an orphan . . . the envy and jealousy that must have filled your formative years . . . the scars you must carry.

CRIMINAL: Let him speak, eh?

SYLVIA: Is that why you became a cop . . . to get even with the world . . . Oh, Bruno . . . don't say another word.

BRUNO: Hold it, Sylvia! It all sounds good, but hold it. Let me continue . . . I don't know how old I was when they put me in the orphanage . . . not very . . . and the first time I heard the word "orphan" I thought it was this guy's name. Billy Orphan. Then I found out that I was an orphan too. And I figured that Billy and I were related. But then I found out that we were all orphans . . . and I figured . . . hell . . . somebody must be lying . . . we can't all be relatives.

SYLVIA: I'm going to cry.

BRUNO: Later, Sylvia, please . . . let me finish. So we were all orphans but I still didn't know what the word meant except that we talked about everything in terms of that one word . . . the outside world was a non-orphanage . . . those that got placed were de-orphanated . . . those that came back were re-orphanated. For a long time I thought only boys were orphans . . . so when I grew up I wanted to be a girl. Then I found out that there were female orphans too . . . we called them orphenes. But I still didn't know what the word meant. So I asked one of the guards one day . . . what's an orphan? He said it was somebody that nobody liked. But these other orphans liked me . . . Billy liked me . . . so I asked him if that made me a non-orphan. He said no . . . He said being liked by another orphan didn't count.

SYLVIA: The beast! Don't say another . . .

BRUNO: Hold it, Sylvia! So I started thinking that nothing that happened in the orphanage counted. The only things that mattered happened on the outside. For the whole time that I was there some police athletic league kept promising to take us to a ball game. We went to bed every night hoping that tomorrow was the big day when we'd go to a ball game. Hell, we didn't know what a ball game was . . . properly speaking . . . but it was on the outside so we assumed it was something incredible . . something unheard of . . . and finally the big day came and this man took us all to a ball game.

SYLVIA: And what happened?

BRUNO: The Yankees won.

CRIMINAL: There's a shocker for you.

BRUNO: That was it. The Yankees won . . . And all of us orphans sat there scratching our rear thinking . . . You mean this is it . . . this is the real thing . . . That's why I still go to ball games . . . I figure one of these days I'm going to see it the way I thought it would be . . . you know . . . the ball game of the century . . . the ball game of all time . . .

CRIMINAL: Did you catch the Mets against the Cubs . . . there was something.

BRUNO: And you know what? . . . when I go there I see some of those orphans I once knew . . . Billy's there every time . . . They're all grown up and everything but still looking orphany as hell . . . still waiting for the ball game . . . you see, don't you . . . you see how we were tricked into thinking that the outside world was so exciting and full of wonders . . . not that we thought it was all good . . . but we did think it was full of extremes . . . that's it . . . extremes . . . the most beautiful and the ugliest things were on the outside . . . nothing in between . . . and that's why I became a cop.

CRIMINAL: I don't get the connection.

BRUNO: I thought that by being a cop I'd be able to find those extremes . . . and sometimes I think I'm close . . . Sometimes I'd be walking my beat and suddenly I hear this screaming . . . I mean screaming so painful your heart wants to commit suicide . . . and I think to myself . . . Hot dog! This is it! This is the saddest damned thing that ever happened in the world! And I rush to the house . . . I rush upstairs and what do I find . . . This old lady's screaming because her parakeet ate something foul and was vomiting all over the cage.

SYLVIA: (*Laughs.*) It wasn't.

BRUNO: (*Smiles.*) Swear to God, Sylvie . . . that damned parakeet was barfing like a truck driver . . . the old lady screaming her head off . . . for some reason she turned a fan on it . . . there it was . . . bird barf all over the wallpaper . . .

(*Criminal laughs too. Sylvia's laughing . . . doing an imitation of barfing parakeet. She's standing now and in the course of her laughter and imitation she comes to lean on Bruno . . . as if seeking support . . . the leaning turns into a hug but the laughter is still used as an excuse for the contact. Bruno stiffens.*)

SYLVIA: Bruno . . . your story has touched my heart.

BRUNO: Has it, Sylvie . . . has it really?

SYLVIA: It has . . . it's touched it . . .

CRIMINAL: It was a touching story.

SYLVIA: You were forced by circumstances to love me as a sister. How you must have hated me for that.

BRUNO: No, Sylvie . . . I never hated you.

SYLVIA: I hated you because I thought you were my brother. I hate having to love because of traditional family ties. And now that it's too late, I see that I should have loved you all along like a brother I never had. We're in the same boat, you and I. We're brother and sister in spirit. You seek your happiness in the streets . . . I seek mine in the voting booths. . . . Have you ever voted, Bruno?

BRUNO: No.

SYLVIA: You poor baby . . . you've lost faith in the electoral process.

BRUNO: No . . . it's kind of personal.

SYLVIA: Tell me, Bruno.

BRUNO: Something happens every time . . . I register and all . . . I go to vote . . . I wait in line . . . but when my turn comes I always have to go to the bathroom.

SYLVIA: Does that happen just in the national elections?

BRUNO: No . . . state elections . . . city . . . bond issues . . . I don't know what causes it.

SYLVIA: Maybe it's the thrill of being able to participate in a free democracy.

BRUNO: That must be it.

CRIMINAL: That's probably why the parakeet vomited too . . . from the thrill of it.

SYLVIA: How I wish I was in a voting booth right now . . . and I saw your name on the ballot, Bruno . . . I'd vote for you . . . I'd pull that lever for you. Kiss me, Bruno.

CRIMINAL: Hey, now . . .

SYLVIA: Why don't you kiss me?

BRUNO: I'll tell you why not . . .

SYLVIA: Don't tell me . . . Why don't you just do it.

BRUNO: Because . . .

SYLVIA: Don't talk . . . What's there left to say?

BRUNO: One question at a time, Sylvia. My heart is pounding, Sylvia . . . It's going at least eighty-five a minute . . . Is yours pounding?

SYLVIA: It's pounding.

BRUNO: I got to be sure.

CRIMINAL: She said it's pounding.

BRUNO: I couldn't do it if your heart was strolling along at sixty-five beats . . . I've waited too long for something that counted . . . this has to be it.

SYLVIA: This is it.

(*Bruno grabs her, kisses her. Outside the house—Sound: dog howl.*)

CRIMINAL: All I can say is, hey . . .

(*Bruno picks Sylvia up. Sylvia waves to Criminal as Bruno carries her around looking for a place to put her down. Takes her to the couch. Drops her right on top of Mario. Sylvia lets out a scream.*)

SYLVIA: Upstairs, Bruno! Let's go upstairs! (*They run upstairs into room. Sound: another howl. Old Man comes out of his room.*)

OLD MAN: SHUT UP! ALL OF YOU! (*Sees Criminal.*) Who the hell are you?

CRIMINAL: I'm the meter man. How about you, gramps?

OLD MAN: Gramps! (*The Old Man, without even thinking, flies at him, grabs him by the shirt and shakes him.*)

CRIMINAL: I'm handcuffed, dammit. Hey . . .

OLD MAN: You . . . dammit . . . you . . . damn you . . . I'll blast you. (*The Old Man lets go of Criminal's shirt . . . stomps to chest of drawers, opens drawers . . . pulls out a gun.*)

CRIMINAL: Hey . . . (*The Old Man puts gun back, opens another drawer, pulls out a portable typewriter, carries it back to his room.*)

OLD MAN: I'll issue a written statement . . . I'll blast you. (*Goes into room and slams door shut. Mario's head appears above back of couch.*)

MARIO: Jesus . . . It feels like as if somebody sat on my head. (*Gets up. Sound: Typewriter O.S.*) I better go to bed. (*Sees Criminal.*) You still here? (*Criminal is ready to cry.*)

CRIMINAL: Am I still here? No . . . not all here. I don't think anybody here is all here . . . or all there for that matter.

MARIO: Well . . . I'm going to bed. (*Starts going.*)

CRIMINAL: HOLD IT! JUST HOLD IT RIGHT THERE! I want some damned recognition . . . Did you know that I'm a dangerous criminal?

MARIO: Sometimes I feel like a criminal myself. You probably feel like that all the time, eh?

CRIMINAL: It's useless . . .

MARIO: No, don't feel useless. You shouldn't. Criminals have their place in society . . . With all due respect to Bruno . . . I shudder to think what cops would do to decent citizens out of sheer boredom if it wasn't for criminals . . . Keep them busy, my boy . . . I know it's a rotten job but somebody has to do it . . .

CRIMINAL: I'm going to sue somebody. I'll need psychiatric help after all this is over . . . Wait . . . don't go . . . I got news for you . . . Did you know that the cop who lives here is an orphan. Did you know that?

MARIO: Did you know that I'm an orphan, too?

CRIMINAL: No.

MARIO: Well, I am . . . I don't even know what my nationality is. That's why Goya loves me, I think . . . (*Walks upstairs.*) One night I'm a Portuguese fisherman . . . another a prehistoric caveman . . . shortlegged Serbian . . . Fat Fin . . . Greek Orthodox . . . Agnostic Albanian. Catholic . . . Buddhist . . . Monk . . . (*Mutters his way up the stairs and disappears into his room.*)

CRIMINAL: The thing to do is remain casual . . . Agnostic Albanian?. . . All right! And that girl . . . I thought she was giving me the eye, and then she runs off with that orphan. An orphan beats me out . . . A cop orphan! It's sort of like being at home . . . I'm sitting downstairs wondering what the hell I'm doing here.

(*Goya enters, puts coat on rack.*)

GOYA: Well . . . he's not at the bookstore . . . and it looks like rain . . . Where is everybody?

CRIMINAL: Lady . . . I don't even know who everybody is.

GOYA: Mario didn't come while I was gone?

CRIMINAL: Nobody came but a whole bunch of people went. (*Sound: O.S. typing.*)

GOYA: Who's typing?

CRIMINAL: The old man. He said he's going to blast us.

GOYA: What did you do . . . call him gramps or something?

CRIMINAL: Yeah.

GOYA: That was diplomatic of you.

CRIMINAL: I didn't know . . . Good God . . . why am I explaining myself . . . Look . . . I want a lawyer.

GOYA: Can you afford a lawyer?

CRIMINAL: Damn right I can.

GOYA: Then you don't need one. I'm going to bed.

CRIMINAL: Hold it! Don't go. I've got news for you . . . Did you know there are two orphans in this house?

GOYA: Is that counting me or not?

CRIMINAL: No.

GOYA: Then you better make it three.

CRIMINAL: You too . . . you mean nobody here knows who his parents are?

GOYA: No, do you?

CRIMINAL: Of course I do.

GOYA: You criminals think you know everything.

CRIMINAL: I even know who my grandparents are.

GOYA: You must have been adopted when you were very young.

CRIMINAL: I wasn't adopted.

GOYA: I can see why not . . . who would want to adopt a liar like you.

CRIMINAL: I didn't need to be adopted . . . My mother had me and my mother kept me.

GOYA: Sure, sure . . . you criminals are so defensive.

CRIMINAL: If you don't believe me, call her. 555-4598. (*Goya dials number.*) And tell her to come and get me. If a man's voice answers . . . that's my mother.

GOYA: There's no answer.

CRIMINAL: My mother's deaf. Let it ring.

GOYA: Hello . . . hate to wake you up . . . I'm calling from the League of Women Voters and I'm taking a survey . . . Do you have a natural born son who's a criminal? You don't. Thank you. (*Hangs up.*) Now you know the truth.

CRIMINAL: She doesn't know I'm a criminal.

GOYA: I know . . . Bruno knows . . . Sylvia knows . . . and the old man probably knows . . . but your mother doesn't know. C'mon.

CRIMINAL: She doesn't want to know. If she was a real mother . . .

GOYA: Aha . . . if she was a real mother.

CRIMINAL: She's not as real as she could be.

GOYA: I think I see your problem. You think you're not a real son but you have a mother who's not . . . That, my friend, makes you an orphan . . .

CRIMINAL: All I'm trying to say is that she's a cold-hearted witch of a real mother.

GOYA: I don't know about that. I mean . . . I only talked to her once . . . she seemed like a decent woman to me . . .

CRIMINAL: It's useless . . .

GOYA: Don't feel useless. You criminals are our best deterrent to crime . . . I mean . . . look at you . . . You look so miserable in your chosen field . . . But cheer up . . . I've got plans for you . . .

CRIMINAL: I've got plans of my own.

GOYA: Well, change them. I've changed mine often enough. Good night. (*She goes up stairs. At top Criminal speaks.*)

CRIMINAL: Good night.

(*As she disappears, after a beat, the hall lights turn off. After another beat we hear:*)

GOYA: MARIO, YOU BASTARD . . . . WHERE WERE YOU!

CRIMINAL: Oh, so that's Mario. Slowly but surely I'm finding my way around here. It's a club. If you're an orphan, you go upstairs and roll around in bed . . . if you're not . . . they handcuff you to the radiator.

(*Fade out.*)

# ACT II

## Scene 1

*Same as before. It's later on in the night. The Criminal is asleep on the floor. Sylvia appears at the top of the stairway. She's wearing a flimsy dress. She tiptoes carefully down the stairs . . . stops in front of the Criminal. Looks at him from various angles. Coughs, trying to get his attention. He's asleep. She sighs louder. He's still asleep. Sylvia walks past him and kicks on his head.*

SYLVIA: Excuse me. (*A Criminal snore comes as a reply. Sylvia comes back. Stops in front of him. Kicks him again.*) Excuse me. (*Sylvia gets impatient. She stands there and begins kicking his head, timing her kicks to the rhythm of her apologies.*) Excuseme — excuseme — excuseme — (*The Criminal is rudely awakened. Sylvia backs off. Pretends she hardly notices him.*)

CRIMINAL: Oh God! What a nightmare!

SYLVIA: I couldn't sleep.

CRIMINAL: Me neither . . . but that's nothing new to me . . . When you're running from the law you learn to make do without sleep . . . It's like war . . . You develop cat reflexes . . . I could be sound asleep and hear a pin drop and wake up just like that. Like a cat.

SYLVIA: Why did you steal that camera.

CRIMINAL: I wanted to take my mother's picture. Nobody believes me when I say she looks like Johnny Unitas.

SYLVIA: You could have bought it . . . you didn't have to steal.

CRIMINAL: I tried . . . I looked in all the stores but none of them carried my mother's picture.

SYLVIA: I don't think that's funny.

CRIMINAL: Chinese aren't known for their sense of humor.

SYLVIA: Are you Chinese?
CRIMINAL: No . . . but my sense of humor is . . . I'm Japanese.
SYLVIA: I don't think that's funny.
CRIMINAL: What do you expect from a Japanese? With my background . . . family life and gene composition I consider myself lucky to be able to laugh at other people's jokes . . . You know what my mother's favorite game is . . . we play Mt. Rushmore . . . we sit and stare and try to look majestic . . . a majestic Japanese family . . . you could spill a bowl of hot pea soup on my mother's face and if you didn't say excuse me, she wouldn't notice. Every now and then she'd turn to my dad and say . . . did you say something. And he'd whimper, No, should I have.
SYLVIA: I though Japanese were supposed to have a very nice family life.
CRIMINAL: Maybe in Japan they do. Do you realize that my grandparents, on my mother's side, were at Hiroshima when the bomb fell . . . and they survived . . . survived nothing . . . I think the radiation actually perked them up a bit. Taking all this into account can you honestly blame me for becoming a criminal? Don't you want to shake my hand and say well done?
SYLVIA: What kind of a criminal are you?
CRIMINAL: I became a criminal so I wouldn't have to answer questions like that . . . Where do you work . . . How much do you make . . . . . . All right . . . Let's say I'm a freelance criminal . . . Although the part about the free is in doubt right now.

(*Goya appears at the top of the stairway. Sits down and listens, reacting every now and then to something Sylvia says.*)

SYLVIA: Did you ever rape anybody?

(*Goya slaps her forehead.*)

CRIMINAL: Rape? Me? I have my pride, you know . . . I don't have to rape . . . I can pay for it.
SYLVIA: You must have thought about it . . . I mean . . . just in case the opportunity presented itself . . . You must have worked out some plan.
CRIMINAL: All right. Here's my plan . . . I'd pull out my gun and say . . . Hey, this is a rape.
SYLVIA: And then what?
CRIMINAL: And then I'd shoot myself in the head. I have my pride, you know.
SYLVIA: Have you ever thought about reforming?
CRIMINAL: Yeah . . . my mother . . . But I never got anywhere.
SYLVIA: Goya says reformed criminals make good husbands.

CRIMINAL: Not if they're Japanese they don't.

SYLVIA: I saw the way you were looking at me.

CRIMINAL: It's a free country.

SYLVIA: I couldn't sleep. It upset me the way you were looking at me . . . You had the same stinking look my husband had before we were married . . .

CRIMINAL: Oh, I didn't know you . . .

SYLVIA: I'm divorced now . . . Divorced! As if what we had was a marriage in the first place. The first date I had with that beast . . . you know what he told me . . . he said . . . all I have to do is get one of my hands on your breast and I'll have you under my control . . . and that's what you're thinking . . . You men are all alike . . . You think breasts are control panels on a car or something . . . press a button and the heat comes on . . . Well, I've got news for you . . . It doesn't work . . . not on this girl . . . Go ahead . . . try your luck, buster. What's the matter . . . afraid. C'mon . . . I'd like to shatter this myth once and for all.

CRIMINAL: That's not my good hand. I'm a southpaw.

SYLVIA: You want to kiss me. You think that'll do it . . . It won't . . .

CRIMINAL: You've got a helluva way of proving people wrong. What did you do . . . Marry that guy just to prove to him he'd make a rotten husband.

SYLVIA: Don't talk about him . . . I'm trying to forget.

CRIMINAL: How about that huge orphan upstairs . . . Did you forget about him too?

SYLVIA: Bruno . . . dear, gentle Bruno . . . I did think for a minute . . . but no . . . he deserves somebody better than myself.

CRIMINAL: And I don't.

SYLVIA: No.

CRIMINAL: So I don't.

SYLVIA: I'm really no better than you. Sometimes I feel like a criminal myself.

CRIMINAL: I feel like a criminal all the time, I mean . . . I had a steady job and I felt like a criminal . . . I worked for the Department of Welfare . . . If you think I'm a criminal now you should have seen me then . . . so what happens . . . Republicans cut back on Welfare and I lose my job.

SYLVIA: I did it. I brought the Republicans to power . . . and there you stand . . . a victim of my vote . . . How you must hate me.

CRIMINAL: I voted for the Republicans too . . . straight ticket. I did it to spite my mother.

SYLVIA: And I did it to spite my husband.

CRIMINAL: We really showed them, eh?

SYLVIA: We're in the same boat, you and I . . . seeking our happiness in the turbulent sea of forgetfulness . . . All those poor people on fixed incomes . . . How will we ever make it up to them . . . We'll try, won't we? We'll have to try. We'll get a fresh start. You'll get your job back and I'll do charity work. We're still young . . . we have many important elections ahead of us. We can do it.

CRIMINAL: Not handcuffed to the radiator we can't.

SYLVIA: I'll set you free . . . we'll wait till Bruno goes to work.

CRIMINAL: What if he takes me to the station with him?

(*Goya gets up and disappears into her room.*)

SYLVIA: He won't. He says he doesn't know what to do with you. But I do. (*Kisses him.*) You're so warm.

CRIMINAL: That's a funny thing about me. Handcuff me to a radiator for a few hours and I get warm.

SYLVIA: I can see us already . . . We'll have little biracial babies . . . and we'll adopt kids . . . We'll adopt more kids than Goya ever dreamed of adopting . . . and who knows . . . they might even write a story about us in some magazine or something . . . Oh, I'm going back to bed to dream about it all . . . Good night.

CRIMINAL: Good night.

(*Sylvia goes up the strairway . . . blows him a kiss and disappears.*)

CRIMINAL: Biracial babies! Well, I'll be damned . . . I think I'm looking forward to the whole thing . . . I can hear myself already . . . Hey, there, kid . . . I'm your daddy, hey . . .

(*Fade out.*)

## Scene 2

*Fade in: The clock chimes in the darkness. Then morning light comes up. Goya is discovered fixing her hair on the stairs.*

GOYA: Sleep well?

CRIMINAL: Not bad.

GOYA: Glad to hear it . . . "Mr. Southpaw!" So . . . you've got plans of your own, eh? Biracial babies, eh? You want to take my only child away from me?

CRIMINAL: Look, lady, I don't know what Sylvia told you . . .

GOYA: She didn't tell me anything . . . and I can sense things . . .

BRUNO'S VOICE: Hi, Ma.

CRIMINAL: Oh look, lady . . . don't tell Bruno . . .

(*Bruno appears upstairs; he is full dressed and whistles as he comes down the stairs.*)

BRUNO: (*To Criminal.*) Good morning, Charlie.

GOYA: 'Morning, son. You seem cheery.

BRUNO: I feel good, Ma. How's Mario?

GOYA: He thinks he's dead. He'll be terribly disappointed when he wakes up.

BRUNO: I better get going. (*Looks for key in pocket.*) I don't know what I did with my keys. I guess I should take him down to the station.

GOYA: Ah, leave 'im. He's not hurting anybody.

BRUNO: (*To Criminal.*) Be good now. See you, Ma. (*Walks past window, looks at dog.*) Hang in there, Dodo. (*Walks out.*)

CRIMINAL: Look, I've had a rough time of it, lady. It feels like I've been sitting next to this radiator for years. My scalp's all dried out and I'm getting dandruff . . . the transition from my home where we don't even believe in warmth hardly, this heat is too great . . . I'll tell you honestly. I've been trying to get arrested for a few months. I thought prison life would suit me . . . no gas bills . . . no rent . . . no worries . . . I even thought my folks may thaw out a bit if they had to come and visit me . . . I know it sounds absurd . . . I mean . . . I've only talked to Sylvia a few minutes . . . but she seems better than prison . . . as a matter of fact she seems better than most things I've run into.

GOYA: You must have had a rough time of it. Goodness . . . do all you Chinese talk so much?

CRIMINAL: I'm Japanese.

GOYA: That's right. I forgot about the camera.

CRIMINAL: ALL JAPANESE DON'T HAVE CAMERAS!

GOYA: Don't get in a huff . . . Gracious . . .

CRIMINAL: I'm tired of having people think that every Japanese they see is some kind of trained Polaroid bear that knows everything about cameras . . . Perfect strangers stop me in the street and ask my advice about filters . . . why their shutter is getting stuck . . . The only reason I stole this camera is because another Japanese was carrying it . . . I can't stand to see another Japanese with another damned camera . . .

GOYA: I know how you feel . . . They all have them.

CRIMINAL: It's useless . . .

GOYA: Don't feel useless . . . A young man your age. Lord, oh, Lord . . . do you realize that you're going to make me a grandmother? I don't know if I can take it. I'll probably become like that old man over there . . . DON'T CALL ME GRANDMOTHER. I'LL BLAST YOU . . . I just hope I don't start resorting to cosmetics to recapture my youth . . . dying my hair grandmother red . . . plucking my eyebrows and painting on new ones . . . Tell me the truth . . . I don't look like the type to pluck eyebrows, do I?

CRIMINAL: Your own . . . no.

(*Goya laughs.*)

GOYA: Damn you kids . . . you're all criminals. (*Sound: Thunder is heard outside.*) Poor Dodo . . . he's going to get soaked. (*Sound: Doorbell rings. Goya primps ever so slightly and opens the door. A man steps inside, umbrella first . . . A ragged-looking newspaper in the other hand.*)

CLIENT: I'm here about the ad . . . Are you . . .

GOYA: Yes, I'm the ad . . . Shut your umbrella, please . . . It's bad luck inside a house.

(*The Client shuts the umbrella with difficulty. He is nervous. Enters and sees the criminal.*)

CLIENT: Hello.

CRIMINAL: Hey!

GOYA: Sit down. (*Client sits down.*) Coffee? (*Client simply holds out his hands. Goya crosses to kitchen and returns with pot, hot mat and cup and saucer. Client's hands shake so that he spills coffee over himself. He puts empty cup down on the table.*) Want some more?

CLIENT: No . . . not really. (*Client looks at Criminal.*)

GOYA: Well?

CLIENT: Oh . . . am I next?

GOYA: Yes. A German came, but I turned him down.

CLIENT: German?

GOYA: You're not German, are you?

CLIENT: No, not really.

GOYA: Then we're all set.

CLIENT: (*Looking at Criminal.*) I feel a little odd.

GOYA: You look a little wet.

CLIENT: It's raining.

GOYA: Nothing odd about that.

CLIENT: No . . . not really. It always rains when I go out.

GOYA: Good, then you must be used to it.

CLIENT: Yes . . . I suppose . . . (*Looks at Criminal.*) . . . only I still feel a little odd.

GOYA: Oh . . . I see . . . Don't worry, he's handcuffed.

(*Criminal picks up handcuffed hand to show.*)

CLIENT: A relative?

GOYA: No. Not yet . . . he's a criminal.
CLIENT: Nice house. (*Looking at Criminal.*) Steam heat I see.
GOYA: You cold or something?
CLIENT: (*Looks at Criminal.*) Oh no . . . not really.
GOYA: I mean if you're cold . . .
CLIENT: Nein. No I'm not.
GOYA: You're awfully jittery.
CLIENT: Only when I'm warm.
GOYA: Could you cool down a bit?
CLIENT: I'm not sure. Excuse me for asking, but are you the woman who put the ad in the paper?
GOYA: No . . . my husband did.
CLIENT: Where's your husband?
GOYA: Upstairs.
CLIENT: (*Looks at Criminal . . . then at Goya . . . then at ad . . . then full front.*) I don't understand a thing . . . it always happens to me . . . A moment always comes when I don't understand a thing . . . and this is that moment again.
GOYA: What don't you understand?
CLIENT: Not a thing.
GOYA: C'mon, don't be a hog.
CLIENT: Why's the ad in the paper?
GOYA: Because my husband might die any day.
CLIENT: I'm sorry.
GOYA: I'll tell him. So, if he dies I'd like to find somebody to take his place.
CLIENT: That's horrible . . . The man's not even dead and you . . .
GOYA: If he were dead you wouldn't be here talking to me . . . I'd have found somebody by now.
CLIENT: Oh, and I'm supposed to be thrilled to death that I'm here talking with you.
GOYA: Look here . . . it's raining out there . . . it's dry and warm in here . . . there's muggers and killers and rapists out there . . . you could be mugged, killed and raped . . . and wet on top of it . . . be glad you're in here.
CLIENT: Glad? With that criminal sitting over there.
GOYA: We keep our criminals handcuffed.
CLIENT: So what do you want me to say . . . that I'm glad I'm here. All right, I'm glad. It's warm. The coffee smells nice . . . I'm talking with a woman . . . I haven't talked with a woman in years it seems like . . . All right, I'm glad. It's nice. It's lovely. I'm even getting to like that criminal over there. Everything's fantastic . . . and now I'm going to get turned down.

GOYA: Don't be so sure of yourself.

CLIENT: It never fails. If it's nice . . . I get turned down. If it's horrible and I hate it . . . I get an offer. Always has been and always will be. (*The door opens and the old man comes out holding a sheet of paper in his hand. He waits a second and then goes to the bathroom.*) Who's that?

GOYA: An old man . . . he answered the ad some years ago . . . but I couldn't . . I mean he was too old to be my husband . . . so I offered him a nice position . . . to be my grandfather . . . (*Old Man comes out.*) . . . Well . . . he's been thinking it over.

CLIENT: Grandfather?

GOYA: Now you did it.

(*The Old Man was just waiting for this. Takes a few steps forward. Holds out his written statement and half reads from the paper . . . half from his head.*)

OLD MAN: Once and for all I would like to clarify this misunderstanding. I know what you're up to . . . Yes . . . you want me to become your grandfather, which is to say a relative, so that you can treat me like people treat all their relatives . . . which is to say, like dirt. I know all about relatives. You'll pretend you understand me . . . You'll get a fixed idea of my role in the family and forget that I'm a man . . . You'll sneer when I don't do something that grandfathers aren't supposed to do or be disappointed if I don't do something grandfatherly every damned day of the week . . . Well . . . I refuse . . . I couldn't take the pressure. Ever since I can remember I was a man . . . nothing more . . . one of those men you see through the window on the street . . . a man who sometimes pees in the street . . . grandfathers don't do that . . . a man who sometimes looks through his wallet at pictures that have nothing to do with grandchildren or grand anything . . There's nothing grand about me and never will be . . . So I refuse . . . Do you hear me. I spit on your offer. (*Stops. Seems ready to leave.*) BUT . . . and this is only in case of emergency . . . IF . . . and only IF you sometimes wake up in the middle of the night and feel YOU just have to have a grandfather . . . simply have to or your heart will break . . . then . . . I'll think about it. (*Goes back to his room slowly. Goya's touched but does her best not to show it.*)

GOYA: I do believe he's meliorating. Now where were we?

CLIENT: You were about to give me the boot.

GOYA: What's the matter with you. I have all kinds of openings . . . Look . . . if Mario lives . . . that's my husband . . . if he lives . . . husband's out of the question. But you could be my uncle if you want . . . or brother . . . or my brother's distant cousin . . . depending on how close you want to get.

CLIENT: Is your uncle sick?

GOYA: What uncle?

CLIENT: Let's say I want to be your damned uncle. Do I have to wait for him to die too?

GOYA: No . . . we're presently all out of uncles.

(*Client thinks.*)

CLIENT: What else is available?

GOYA: Oh, now you're getting choosy on me.

CLIENT: I hate to jump at the first offer.

GOYA: There's no jumping . . . You walk in or you walk out . . . no jumping.

CLIENT: What about your brother?

GOYA: Don't have one.

CLIENT: Now you do. I'll be your damned brother. Why not. I don't have a sister or nothing . . . I don't have nothing . . .

GOYA: You're a nice looking man, you know.

CLIENT: Thanks, sis.

GOYA: Not too young—mature sort of—the gray in your hair goes well with the gray in mine . . . so you become my brother . . . Well, what happens if Mario dies . . . You know what happens . . . You stay my brother . . . I couldn't take the psychological trauma of marrying my own brother . . . in short . . . as a brother your chances of promotion are nil . . . but as a distant cousin . . .

CLIENT: I'll take it. I got nobody . . . no relatives . . . no friends . . . I'll take it. Please.

GOYA: Look, you don't have to shout, cuz. It's yours. I'll have an empty room shortly . . . bring your things over.

CLIENT: What things . . . I got no things . . . no relatives . . . no friends . . .

GOYA: Good. You can save yourself a trip. Just go upstairs . . . lie down and think about it for a while . . . make sure you know what you're doing . . . SYLVIA! It's the room with a slip hanging on the door knob . . . SYLVIA!

(*Sylvia comes out of the door as the client opens it. They nod at each other. Sylvia's carrying a suitcase. She comes down stairs.*)

SYLVIA: (*Puts suitcase down.*) Oh, mother, have I got things to tell you.

GOYA: Why don't you write me a letter, dear. You never write, you know.

SYLVIA: I will. I'll write you, mother . . . I can't wait to write you how well I'm doing . . . how happy I am.

GOYA: I can't wait to hear. I mean that—(*Rises, crossing to Sylvia—kiss on mouth, then embrace.*) Well . . . you better get started then, eh? Now why don't you unshackle that poor thing before he starts smoking. (*Sylvia takes off the handcuffs from Criminal.*)

CRIMINAL: Hey . . . nice to be free again.

(*Goya opens front door, gets umbrella.*)

GOYA: That's what you think. Bruno comes home for lunch sometimes . . . so the two of you better hurry . . . there . . . take the umbrella . . . Oh, yeah . . . leave the stolen goods here . . . (*She takes the camera from the Criminal. Examines it.*) Well . . . let's have something bordering on a smile. (*Sylvia and Criminal pose—Huge smile.*) Now out into the rain with you. Someday when I'm old and gray and all alone . . . I'll blackmail you with this picture. (*The Criminal wants to say something.*) Sayonara.

(*The two of them leave hurriedly arm in arm. Criminal re-opens the door.*)

CRIMINAL: Hey! (*Exits.*)

GOYA: (*Stands still.*) She took my suitcase. (*Goes to the window.*) Hand in hand . . . I knew it . . . I knew they'd dump that umbrella in the trash can. Just as I thought . . . She left me Dodo. (*Goya crosses to kitchen, starts to make coffee when Bruno comes in with umbrella. He is in civilian clothes. He rests umbrella against sofa.*) You home for lunch?

BRUNO: (*Starting up stairs.*) No . . . not this time. (*Halfway up stairs he stops.*) Some coffee would be nice. (*Sees Mario coming out of his room, then exits into his. Mario descends stairs, sleepy and hung over. Remembers Dodo. Looks through curtain on front door. Sound: Dodo barks greeting. Mario responds to him, sits down at kitchen table. She serves him coffee.*)

## Scene 3

*Same as before. Goya and Mario are sitting at the table drinking coffee. They hear heavy footsteps above them. They look upstairs and continue drinking coffee. More footsteps. Sound of drawers being opened and shut. Bruno appears at top of stairway carrying suitcase. He's dressed in civilian clothes. He comes down stairway, puts suitcase down near door and crosses to kitchen table.*

GOYA: You got everything?

BRUNO: I guess.

GOYA: I wouldn't feel too bad about Sylvia if I were you.

BRUNO: I don't, Ma . . . I was just going to use her as an excuse to leave . . . I get into awful ruts you know . . . When I was an orphan I was a hundred percent orphan . . . and then I became a hundred percent cop. Offhand, I suspect there's a helluva lot more to life than being a cop or an orphan. And I think I've been your son long enough . . . When I come back I'd like to come back as a friend.

GOYA: Now you're talking. I've got all the relatives I can use and not a single friend . . .

BRUNO: How about a kiss?

GOYA: How about a whole bunch? (*She goes up to him and kisses him all over.*) You ought to leave more often. (*Kisses him some more. Mario stands up and coughs. Bruno comes over to him and hugs him. They kiss. Then Bruno gets his suitcase and exits.*) He took my other suitcase. We better pick up a couple.

MARIO: Hold it . . . (*Finds envelope and pencil on table.*) Shoot, as Bruno used to say.

GOYA: We've also got an empty room upstairs. We'll have to fill it. (*Mario does not write, holding pencil.*) What's the matter . . . why so glum?

MARIO: Bruno was my favorite.

GOYA: Well, cheer up . . . he knows that.

MARIO: You think so?

GOYA: Hell, yeah . . . Anything else the matter?

MARIO: Looks like I've got to live in this rotten old world some more. I can't seem to die.

GOYA: Wait it out . . . see who goes first.

MARIO: And I keep worrying . . . what if I live long enough to see the Republicans out of power and the Democrats come back and they're just as bad.

GOYA: The way I see it, Mario, everything that's bothering you is rotten and old and getting older by the minute. The solutions seem to be to outlive them . . . I mean . . . All you've got to do is outlive them. Anything else?

MARIO: I don't think so.

GOYA: Well . . . you'll tell me if something comes up.

MARIO: Roger. You do the same.

GOYA: I'll think about it! You find out anything about the man upstairs?

MARIO: Yeah . . . your cousin says he's Irish.

GOYA: Irish . . . they make good cousins, I hear . . . HEY, SEAN! HEY, COUSIN!

(*Client, hereafter Sean, appears at top of stairs in undershorts.*)

SEAN: My name's not Sean.

GOYA: Don't be so hasty. Try it out for a week and see what you think. Put some clothes on . . . we've got things to do.

SEAN: They're all wet.

GOYA: That's all right. We're not formal around here. (*Sean disappears.*

*Goya turns to Mario.*) I think it's time we made another trip to the orphanage, Mario.

MARIO: I think you're right.

GOYA: I bet you anything they've got some little beauties there . . .

MARIO: And I bet we're going to get one of them.

GOYA: You bet.

MARIO: What'll it be this time . . . boy or a girl?

GOYA: We'll have to put it to a vote. (*Sean comes down the stairs.*) You're just in time to cast your ballot. GRANDPA!

(*Old Man comes out of his room eating an apple.*)

OLD MAN: You don't have to shout . . . I'm not deaf . . . I can still hear . . .

GOYA: Not that way.

OLD MAN: . . . and I say we get a girl.

(*Sean goes up to Old Man.*)

SEAN: Hello . . . my name's . . .

OLD MAN: I know . . . you're Sean.

(*Goya goes to door, opens it, motions to others.*)

GOYA: Fair is fair . . . let's stop at the pound and pick up something for Dodo . . .

MARIO: (*Writing.*) I got it down.

GOYA: After you . . . I love to see men parading past me . . .

(*As they do, they exit. Fade out.*)

# Lake of the Woods

*Lake of the Woods* was first performed on December 8, 1971, by the American Place Theatre, New York. It was directed by Frederick Rolf. The cast included:

WINNEBAGO . . . . . . . . . . . . *Hal Holbrook*
CHRISTO . . . . . . . . . . . . *Armand Assante*
JUANITA . . . . . . . . . . . . *Esther Benson*
FOREST RANGER . . . . . . . . . . . . *Will Hussung*
MUSICIAN . . . . . . . . . . . . *Ron Panvini*

Set and Costumes: Kert Lundell
Lighting: Roger Morgan
Music and Lyrics: Ron Panvini

**Cast:** Winnebago
Juanita, his wife
Christo, their houseboy
Forest Ranger
Musician

**Time:** Now

**Place:** The Great Outdoors

## Scene One

*An apparent desert surrounded by sand dunes. A grill perched on a steel pole. Wooden sign:* LAKE OF THE WOODS. *Enter Winnebago, dressed in pants, wallabies, and a sweaty shirt. He's pulling a long extension cord and chewing on a thick cigar. The cigar stays with him until the end of Scene Two. He pulls the extension cord with slave-like weariness. After a few seconds, Christo follows him on stage carrying all kinds of "picnic" junk: a beach umbrella, canteen, knapsack, chair and stool.*

WINNEBAGO: (*Stops, looks around.*) My God . . . what a hole.
CHRISTO: What's that?
WINNEBAGO: I said . . . what a hole.
CHRISTO: You said the last place was a hole too.
WINNEBAGO: Last place was the Garden of Eden compared to this hole.
CHRISTO: Give it a chance. You're tired.
WINNEBAGO: If it looks this bad when I'm tired, just think what a hole it will look like when I rest up. But, as my poor father said, just before he died, "So what." I thought I'd never get out of all that traffic. Everytime I tried to get off the trailer in front of me slowed down, the one in back of me speeded up, and there I was in the middle like a railroad car. A traffic jam! Out here! Everybody and his uncle must be on vacation. (*Silence. Winnebago looks around.*) My God . . . what a hole.
CHRISTO: I've had it with you Winny . . . I know what you're trying to say.
WINNEBAGO: Do you now?
CHRISTO: Yes I do.
WINNEBAGO: How do you know?

CHRISTO: Cause I know you.

WINNEBAGO: And I know you, too, Christo.

CHRISTO: Well, I know you better, you're trying to say it's all my fault. You have that "Look what Christo's got us into now" look.

WINNEBAGO: You give me too much credit, Christo. I couldn't possibly come up with a complicated look like that. All I can muster is a measly "What a hole" look, or "My God . . . what a hole." No more than that. You don't know what happened to my sunglasses, do you?

CHRISTO: You had them last.

WINNEBAGO: How many times do I have to tell you that I should never be the last one to have anything. I always lose it. Stick that umbrella in the sand, would you . . . I could use some shade.

CHRISTO: I'll be damned if I will. I'll be damned if I'll be ordered about like this. I'm not your servant, you know.

WINNEBAGO: Of course you are.

CHRISTO: So why rub it in.

WINNEBAGO: Stick the thing in, Christo.

CHRISTO: I don't feel like it. (*Starts sticking the umbrella in the sand.*) IT WON'T STICK.

WINNEBAGO: All I expect is a good honest try. That's all right . . . Forget it! We can't stay here. Somebody might see me and spread vile gossip that I had a rotten vacation. I'd be ruined. (*Christo pulls out a map. Looks at it.*)

CHRISTO: I don't know where else we can go today. The nearest place isn't near at all.

WINNEBAGO: What is the nearest place?

CHRISTO: The place we left.

WINNEBAGO: That hole? Anything up ahead?

CHRISTO: There's some kind of national petrified forest. It's got one of those stars by it. That means it's supposed to be an interesting place.

WINNEBAGO: What's this place got by it?

CHRISTO: All kinds of things. A star, a little boat and a tent . . .

WINNEBAGO: Which means?

CHRISTO: Which means that you can go camping, swimming, fishing and boating here. The star, of course, means that it's an interesting place.

WINNEBAGO: (*Looks around.*) Don't you think they're exaggerating a wee bit.

CHRISTO: It's not my fault.

WINNEBAGO: I didn't say it was. I probably turned my directional signals the wrong way. Took the wrong turn again.

CHRISTO: No, we're exactly where we want to be.

WINNEBAGO: Did we want to be here?

CHRISTO: You did.

WINNEBAGO: You wouldn't happen to know why I wanted to be here, would you?

CHRISTO: Yes, you said you wanted to do some fishing.

WINNEBAGO: True, but I didn't know I had to bring my own pond.

CHRISTO: According to the map, there's supposed to be a fishing hole around here.

WINNEBAGO: They're half right . . . the part about the hole.

CHRISTO: You're not even giving this place half a chance . . . You come in here . . . (*Imitates Winny's carriage . . . imaginary cigar.*) What a hole! My God, what a hole! Oh, me oh my I got gypped again . . . Instead you should look around . . . there's beauty everywhere . . .

WINNEBAGO: Wait a minute . . . Let me see if I grasp your meaning. You're saying that it's my fault this place is a hole.

CHRISTO: (*Peeved.*) It's not a hole!

WINNEBAGO: Oh, now I've got it . . . beauty's in the eye of the beholder bit . . . Let's try it. MY GOD . . . IT'S GORGEOUS. (*Looks around, overdoing everything he does.*) . . . what a fantastic spot . . . sun . . . sand . . and solitude . . . I can feel myself becoming one with nature again . . . I'll get a fresh start here . . . I'll buy a little spread . . . raise a few head of cattle . . . It's . . . why, it's the open range . . . it's America as it once was . . . it's . . .

CHRISTO: SHUT UP!

WINNEBAGO: Well?

CHRISTO: You're overdoing it again . . . It's not a hole but it's not the Garden of Eden either.

WINNEBAGO: What is it then?

CHRISTO: It's something in between.

WINNEBAGO: (*Sits down.*) Something in between is always a hole.

CHRISTO: All right . . . it's a hole . . . but it just isn't that bad.

WINNEBAGO: You looked at the Bad Lands and said they weren't that bad.

CHRISTO: You wouldn't even get out to look at them.

WINNEBAGO: I looked at them.

CHRISTO: No, you didn't.

WINNEBAGO: I was saving my enthusiasms for this place. You were right, the Bad Lands weren't that bad after all.

CHRISTO: God you're annoying. If I thought that you really needed me, I'd quit. I might quit anyway. After all, what's a young man of my potential doing hanging around someone like you.

WINNEBAGO: Some rats like a sinking ship.

CHRISTO: You calling me a rat?

WINNEBAGO: You think I'm a sinking ship?

CHRISTO: No. A little dinghy, maybe.

WINNEBAGO: Is it my imagination or arc you mad at me about something?

CHRISTO: Damn right I'm mad at you.

WINNEBAGO: Hmm. Thought so. What did I do?

CHRISTO: It's what you didn't do.

WINNEBAGO: Ahha . . . I didn't pick up those hitchhikers, right?

CHRISTO: That's right.

WINNEBAGO: You know why I didn't pick them up?

CHRISTO: Because they were young. You're jealous.

WINNEBAGO: Jealous . . . I wish I were . . . it's too hot to be jealous . . . maybe tonight . . . when it cools off. I didn't pick them up because they wore "Ban the Car" buttons.

CHRISTO: That's a lie.

WINNEBAGO: The buttons were written all over their faces, . . . made me feel bad . . . I've been driving so long I feel like a car myself . . . and they want to ban me . . .But they want me to ride them around a bit first . . . Give me some water, Christo.

CHRISTO: Get it yourself. (*Tosses him canteen.*)

WINNEBAGO: (*Drinks, stops.*) It's just like tap water. I thought you filled it from that outdoorsy spring.

CHRISTO: I did.

WINNEBAGO: You mean this is it . . . All those signs on the road . . . Natural Outdoor Spring Five Hundred Yards Ahead . . . all those people waiting in line . . . for this . . . It's tap water . . . We've been gypped again, Christo . . . (*Pours out water between legs.*) Listen to it . . . it even sounds like tap water. I'm tired. You have no idea how tired this water makes me.

CHRISTO: You were tired before you left. You should have rested up before you went on vacation.

WINNEBAGO: We went on vacation because of Christine . . . She refused to go out of the house in New York . . . You know that.

CHRISTO: Now she refuses to go out of the trailer.

WINNEBAGO: That's right.

CHRISTO: So all we did was drive her to some more places that she refuses to come out and see.

WINNEBAGO: Right again.

CHRISTO: Is there some other place where she doesn't want to go so we can take her there and let her not see it?

WINNEBAGO: I think if we found a real nice spot . . . you know . . . trees and rivers and some nice kids her own age.

CHRISTO: I'm her age.

WINNEBAGO: You are?

CHRISTO: What the hell do you mean, "You are?" I'm twenty.

WINNEBAGO: You are?

CHRISTO: Damn right I am. I'm not like you. I know how old I am!

WINNEBAGO: It's not that I don't know . . . it's just that I keep hoping I'm wrong . . . it seems too early in life to be so late in life . . . If I'm over the hill, then I'd like to be able to look back and see the damn hill . . . There's the rub . . . no hills in my life . . . nothing but holes . . . Your life any better?

CHRISTO: Not yet . . . But it's going to be . . . I'm going to have a swell life.

CHRISTO: I'm not a corpse.

WINNEBAGO: No, you're not, but your twenty years are . . . dead and gone.

CHRISTO: At least they didn't die for nothing.

WINNEBAGO: What did they die for?

CHRISTO: They died so I can be twenty-one. (*Silence.*) You sure make me uncomfortable today.

WINNEBAGO: Me too. I don't know what's gotten into me. I have this well-furnished middle-aged coffin and I refuse to lie still . . .

CHRISTO: You're just trying to make me feel sorry for you.

WINNEBAGO: Yeah.

CHRISTO: Don't give me that "yeah." I know you. You think by saying "yeah" you'll make me think you mean no. But I know you . . . You want me to feel sorry for you.

WINNEBAGO: Exactly.

CHRISTO: Well, I don't.

WINNEBAGO: Does that mean you do?

CHRISTO: (*Silence.*)Yeah.

WINNEBAGO: Ah . . . Christo . . . You like me after all.

CHRISTO: Of course I like you.

WINNEBAGO: I like you too. If we're so crazy about each other why do we argue?

CHRISTO: Because you refuse to accept the fact that you're getting old.

WINNEBAGO: I thought you told me yesterday that there were no facts, only opinions.

CHRISTO: All right . . . It's everyone's opinion that you're getting old.

WINNEBAGO: What do I care for other people's opinions. Maybe it's just gossip.

CHRISTO: It's not just gossip.

WINNEBAGO: Is that a fact?

CHRISTO: Yes . . . No . . . You're getting old, Winny . . . It's not that horrible to be old.

WINNEBAGO: It's ghastly to be old. It's nauseating. Repulsive. Abominable . . . Well, maybe not abominable.

CHRISTO: Well, think of me. How the hell will I get old gracefully if you make it seem so bad. You should make it look easy.

WINNEBAGO: I am making a big fuss about it, aren't I?

CHRISTO: You sure are. You're scaring me. If I have to go through that, I say to myself, I'll never make it. I'll die young just to keep myself from getting old.

WINNEBAGO: I'll try to be a nice old man, Christo. (*Enter Juanita, carrying a fishing pole.*)

JUANITA: You forgot your fishing things, honey. (*Stops, looks around.*) Is this it?

WINNEBAGO: Now don't panic, but I think it is. Why don't you take a swim while Christo and I take down the boat.

JUANITA: Where's the water?

WINNEBAGO: It was in the canteen but I spilled it.

JUANITA: There was supposed to be a lake here, right? Lake of the Woods?

WINNEBAGO: There probably was. The hole's still here.

JUANITA: Maybe you took the wrong turn again?

WINNEBAGO: No such luck. Tell her Christo.

CHRISTO: I'm just going by the map . . . here it is, LAKE OF THE WOODS. With a star by it. Maybe one of them is a typographical error. In any case, it's not my fault.

JUANITA: Winny. . . .

WINNEBAGO: Did you hear that, Christo . . . the way she said my name . . . I haven't been married for twenty-five years for nothing. Winny, she says, and I know something's up. What's up?

CHRISTO: I'm going to look around the place a bit. If you need something, write it down . . . because you'll forget it if you don't. (*Walks off. After Christo walks off there should be a moment of silence between Winny and Juanita. Winny knows what she's going to say and he tries to prolong the silence.*)

JUANITA: It's Christine, Winny . . .

WINNEBAGO: Yeah . . .

JUANITA: She says she's going to die.

WINNEBAGO: At least she's talking to us again.

JUANITA: Winny, please . . .

WINNEBAGO: How can she die? There's nothing out here . . . What's she going to die of? I'm sorry . . . I'm sorry . . . Listen . . . You were with me when we took her to see that quack in New York. All she needs is some fresh air, he said. There's nothing wrong with her. You remember?

JUANITA: Yes.

WINNEBAGO: Well, here we are. There's nothing but fresh air for miles around.

JUANITA: Then why doesn't she come out?

WINNEBAGO: Probably because she has everything she needs in the trailer. If you didn't spend so much time with her in there she might come out.

JUANITA: I can't help it, Winny. I get so lonely when I'm away from her. I could just sit in there and watch her for hours . . . She looks so much like I did when I was young, don't you think?

WINNEBAGO: Yes . . . there is a resemblance.

JUANITA: Just like me. I keep wanting her to tell me something . . . you know . . . what it's like to be twenty . . . what kind of feelings she has . . . to see if I have any of them left.

WINNEBAGO: You've got plenty left.

JUANITA: I keep thinking that even my eyes were of a different color when I was young.

WINNEBAGO: You had deep and haunting hazel eyes.

JUANITA: What are they now?

WINNEBAGO: Brown. (*Christo appears at the far end of the stage. Coughs to give warning he's coming. He's carrying a torn sheet of paper.*)

JUANITA: She's not going to die, is she, Winny?

WINNEBAGO: Die! Of course not. Whoever heard of anyone dying on a vacation? She's just teasing you. (*Christo gives a whistle and rejoins them.*)

CHRISTO: I looked around . . . no lake anywhere . . . Found this, though. Looks like there is going to be a music festival here . . . (*Reading.*) LAKE OF THE WOODS ROCK FESTIVAL . . . thousands coming . . .

WINNEBAGO: There's no date on it.

CHRISTO: Maybe it's over already . . .

WINNEBAGO: So that's what happened. The kids came and left and took everything with them, including the LAKE OF THE WOODS and the Woods as well. Nice of them to leave us some sand to play in.

CHRISTO: I hope we didn't miss it. I always wanted to go to a music festival.

WINNEBAGO: I always wanted to miss one. (*Silence.*) Well, let's not just stand around and have fun, let's do something.

CHRISTO: If you hate this place so much, why don't we leave?

WINNEBAGO: I can't. I just can't face that traffic again.

JUANITA: No, you shouldn't drive at night.

WINNEBAGO: Is it getting dark? I thought I drove all night. What time is it, Christo?

CHRISTO: Five thirty.

WINNEBAGO: A.M. or P.M.?

CHRISTO: I don't know. I thought you drove all day.

WINNEBAGO: Well, I'm hungry and I don't feel like having bacon and eggs, so it must be evening. Let's call it dusk.

JUANITA: You look tired, whatever it is. Why don't you lie down in the shade and rest?

WINNEBAGO: Shade? If I stuck my cigar in the sand, it'd be the tallest shade tree around here. No, I'm going back to the trailer. Turn on the air conditioner and cry a bit.

CHRISTO: Can't do that. There's no outlets here.

WINNEBAGO: You looked?

CHRISTO: I looked. There aren't any . . .

WINNEBAGO: The kids must have taken the outlets as well. You know what you're telling me, Christo, you're telling me my trailer's full of junk.

CHRISTO: No, I'm not.

WINNEBAGO: Everything in there is electric, except for a box of Kleenex. Without an outlet, it's junk. No outlets, no lake, no nothing. That bastard Fred'll know every rotten thing that happened to us. I'll tell him we had a lovely vacation and he'll give me that smirk . . . (*Stops. Looks at himself sorrowfully.*) I don't even have a tan.

CHRISTO: The back of your neck is nice and red.

WINNEBAGO: That's because I rub the back of my neck. Look at this arm . . . I drove through the length of South Dakota on a sunny day with this arm sticking out the window and would you look at it . . . not a freckle. WHY CAN'T I TAN?

JUANITA: You had a lovely tan when I first met you. He did, Christo. You should have seen him . . . all bronze and sweaty . . .

WINNEBAGO: I could stand under a streetlamp in those days and get a tan. Now I just get hot. I don't even burn. That bastard Fred'll have a tan. (*Picks up something from his leg.*) An ant? Other people run into deer and elk and black and brown bears . . . me . . . I run into ants. (*Examines it.*) I think it's the same one. Followed me all the way from Kansas. I wonder where his two cronies are . . . the fly and the mosquito? (*Throws it away.*)

JUANITA: You look unhappy.

WINNEBAGO: Looks can be deceiving. I'm miserable.

JUANITA: You should rest.

WINNEBAGO: Rest . . . How can I rest when every second I can hear this little man inside my head telling me what a rotten vacation I've had. I feel guilty. Where the hell were all those scenic wonders we were supposed to see. All those falls and buffalos . . . I didn't see one buffalo.

CHRISTO: We should've stayed in Wyoming . . . That ranger said they were expecting some buffalo soon.

WINNEBAGO: Some? Does that mean one or two?

CHRISTO: We could've waited.

WINNEBAGO: You mean just sit there and wait. Hey, what are you folks doing? Waiting for a buffalo. The hell with it. There probably aren't any left anyhow.

CHRISTO: There certainly are. I read . . .

WINNEBAGO: You read. You read there was a lake here.

CHRISTO: It was a typographical error probably.

WINNEBAGO: And so are the buffalos. They are typographical errors too. And so are the falls. And the rivers. There's nothing left but Central Park.

JUANITA: Didn't we see some nice falls . . . Bridal Veil Falls I think they were called.

WINNEBAGO: I don't know. We'll check the pictures when we get home. All I remember seeing is my transmission oil leaking. I'd get out of the car, bend over, and there it was . . . a puddle of oil. I'd look around . . . cars all over the place and nobody's oil leaking but mine.

JUANITA: We should have stayed in one place like we planned instead of driving around so much.

WINNEBAGO: Stay in one place with those goddamned specialists crawling all over . . . Remember that couple from New Jersey . . . They had a notebook and everytime they saw a "forest creature" they put an X in the notebook. Others were x'ing off trees, creeks, geological specimens and picking up turds for pinecones . . . and the camp in Colorado . . . I thought it was a forest fire . . . Screams in the middle of the night . . . flashlights flashing . . horns blowing . . . Mothers dragging their children . . . children crying . . . and what was it . . . a poor deer had wandered into the camp. A deer! Johnny, Johnny, bring the kids, a deer, a deer! They surrounded the poor beast and shot it full of film . . . And those geezers running off to the woods every five minutes to take a pee . . . look at us . . . we're outdoorsy as hell . . . peeing in the woods . . . I saw one old fart standing there with his zipper open for twenty minutes waiting for his pee to come . . . No . . . No more of that . . . No . . . I've had it with nature . . . Oh no, I stepped in some crap. Yeah. It's crap. I must have radar in my feet for this stuff.

CHRISTO: Cheer up . . . it might be buffalo crap.

WINNEBAGO: Is that what I'm down to?

CHRISTO: Well, let's look around . . .

WINNEBAGO: No . . .

CHRISTO: Come on . . . Where there's smoke there's fire.

WINNEBAGO: No . . . I'd just as soon stay here and fish in the sand.

JUANITA: I think I better go and see how she's doing.

WINNEBAGO: You also better tell her to start having some fun. Vacation's just about over.

JUANITA: Give her a chance, Winny.

WINNEBAGO: A chance! I took her all over this crummy country. You think I want to see any of this garbage. No. I thought she might like it, that's all. She won't even look through the window.

JUANITA: She looked at those hitchhikers.

CHRISTO: Winny looked at them too.

WINNEBAGO: Is that what she wants? A hitchhiker? I'll get her one. I'll get her a couple. I'm tired of trying to guess what she wants. I always guess wrong. (*Juanita exits. Winny takes the fishing pole and starts fishing. Casts the line. Reels it in expectantly. Casts it again . . . Slumps over.*) Christo.

CHRISTO: What do you want?

WINNEBAGO: What do we have to eat?

CHRISTO: Cornflakes.

WINNEBAGO: Get me a box.

CHRISTO: There's no milk. (*Gives him a box.*)

WINNEBAGO: That's all right. I can read without milk. (*Reads.*)You ever read the list of ingredients on these things . . . nasty habit . . . You know, there was a time when I read magazines and the New York *Times* and not only read but underlined even . . . kept up with everything . . . a man of learning . . . And then, one fine morning I caught myself sitting on the john reading a box of cornflakes . . . niacin, riboflavin, calcium . . .Then I moved up to candy wrappers, toothpaste tubes and album covers . . . All I'm trying to say, Christo, is that you're looking at a senile man.

CHRISTO: You always act so tough when Juanita's around and as soon as she leaves you start getting corny and pathetic.

WINNEBAGO: Which one do you think I'm better at? Which one is the definitive Winnebago?

CHRISTO: You're horrible at both of them.

WINNEBAGO: Just as I thought.

CHRISTO: I'm going to look around some more. You know . . . I thought I heard music when I was out there.

WINNEBAGO: It's probably our car radio.

CHRISTO: No. We never get any nice music on our radio. (*Leaves. Goes one way. Stops. Goes another way. Winnebago reads the box of cornflakes. Takes a handful of the stuff . . . eats some. Feels the muscles in his arms and legs. Shakes his head and goes back to fishing.*)

WINNEBAGO: Good thing I've got a cigar in my mouth. Makes me look crude . . . A crude flabby man like me can't be all that desperate. (*Looks around.*) What a hole. (*Enter Forest Ranger, a raggedy piece of vegetation crossed with an ancient civil service uniform.*)

RANGER: Howdy? (*Winnebago turns around. Looks at him.*)

WINNEBAGO: What the hell are you?

RANGER: Be careful . . . you could start a fire.

WINNEBAGO: I think somebody beat me to it. (*Looks at him.*) Looks like you've had a worse vacation than I did.

RANGER: I'm the forest ranger.

WINNEBAGO: I'm Winnebago, an up and coming executive from the umpteenth floor of the Crap Building. Now tell me the truth . . . I don't know if it's night or day, so tell me, are you a mirage or a nightmare?

RANGER: I was just making my rounds.

WINNEBAGO: Just as I thought, a nightmare. All right, I was just doing a little fishing.

RANGER: You got a license?

WINNEBAGO: Sure do. What's the limit?

RANGER: Three.

WINNEBAGO: Good thing you told me. I was going to make a hog of myself. (*Looks around as if seeking help.*) You really in charge of this place?

RANGER: That's right.

WINNEBAGO: I like what you did with it. Tell me. How long you been under the sun?

RANGER: Forty years.

WINNEBAGO: You should wear a hat.

RANGER: Never could stand a hat . . . although the regulations say I have to wear one . . . you're supposed to wear the badge on the hat . . . but I wear it on my coat.

WINNEBAGO: A real daredevil, eh? (*Checks out the badge.*) Nice badge . . . Yes, you've got it made . . . nice badge . . . a sweaty job . . .

RANGER: It's not bad if you like to be outdoors.

WINNEBAGO: Kind of hot, though.

RANGER: If you think this is hot you should see my brother's place in New Mexico.

WINNEBAGO: Your brother alive?

RANGER: Sure is. Got himself a wife and everything. Me . . . I'm single. Nobody'd have me.

WINNEBAGO: Can't see why.

RANGER: There's just something nasty about me that don't appeal to women.

WINNEBAGO: I suspect you're not a big hit with men either.

RANGER: Also kids don't like me.

WINNEBAGO: Ever think of going into politics?

RANGER: I already have a job, thanks.

WINNEBAGO: You really are a forest ranger?

RANGER: Why of course. What did you think I was?

WINNEBAGO: I thought you were vacationing here.

RANGER: Here! I'm not that stupid.

WINNEBAGO: Then you're lost.

RANGER: No I'm not. I'm just making my rounds.
WINNEBAGO: If you're a forest ranger then you should be making your rounds in a forest. There's no forest here.
RANGER: No, it's a shame, but there ain't.
WINNEBAGO: Then what the hell you doing here . . . looking for one.
RANGER: It's my territory.
WINNEBAGO: But there's nothing here.
RANGER: If you think there's nothing here you should see my brother's place. He even boarded up his windows cause there was nothing to look at.
WINNEBAGO: Don't you feel a little useless working here?
RANGER: I don't feel much of anything these days. How about you.
WINNEBAGO: Me? I feel fine.
RANGER: You don't look it.
WINNEBAGO: I like to pretend I'm miserable.
RANGER: You don't look like you're pretending.
WINNEBAGO: That's because I'm good at it.
RANGER: (*Laughs.*) You sure are. I could've sworn you were miserable.
WINNEBAGO: That's how much you know. I'm very happy.
RANGER: What are you so happy about?
WINNEBAGO: That I'm not a forest ranger in this place.
RANGER: (*Laughs.*) What's your name again?
WINNEBAGO: Winnebago.
RANGER: Winnebago . . . that's a Jewish name.
WINNEBAGO: The hell it is . . . it's a good old agnostic name.
RANGER: What's a Jew like you doing with a name like that.
WINNEBAGO: I'm not Jewish.
RANGER: You look Jewish.
WINNEBAGO: And how's a Jew supposed to look?
RANGER: Sort of like you.
WINNEBAGO: I just pretend I look like this.
RANGER: Was that your son I saw out there?
WINNEBAGO: Yes . . . No. That's my houseboy.
RANGER: So . . . you don't have a son.
WINNEBAGO: No.
RANGER: I guess you won't be having one either.
WINNEBAGO: I guess not.
RANGER: I know how you feel.
WINNEBAGO: I doubt it.
RANGER: You got a daughter?
WINNEBAGO: What's it to you?
RANGER: I like kids. They don't like me but I like them.
WINNEBAGO: Yes . . . I have a daughter . . . a lovely daughter.

RANGER: I don't see her.
WINNEBAGO: She's inside the trailer.
RANGER: Oh . . . she's sick.
WINNEBAGO: No, dammit, she's not sick.
RANGER: Then why isn't she out here.
WINNEBAGO: It's too hot out here.
RANGER: It's not too hot for me . . . it's not too hot for you.
WINNEBAGO: It's too hot for me.
RANGER: Then why don't you go inside the trailer?
WINNEBAGO: I like to be too hot.
RANGER: How long's she been in there?
WINNEBAGO: About . . . None of your business.
RANGER: You're right. It's not. It's just that I like kids.
WINNEBAGO: You said that already.
RANGER: Yup. Hate to see kids die.
WINNEBAGO: Bully for you.
RANGER: I hear they're dying all over the place, though.
WINNEBAGO: Who?
RANGER: Kids.
WINNEBAGO: I haven't heard anything.
RANGER: Maybe they're keeping it a secret.
WINNEBAGO: WHO?
RANGER: Wouldn't be a secret if I knew who. (*Laughs.*) Sorry . . . but I'm fond of jokes . . . and I don't get a chance to laugh much these days . . . what with all the bad news . . .
WINNEBAGO: What bad news?
RANGER: The kids . . . dying . . . I hear they're dying all over the place.
WINNEBAGO: Listen dammit . . . is there some disease around here?
RANGER: Like you said, there's nothing here.
WINNEBAGO: There must be something.
RANGER: I haven't seen it.
WINNEBAGO: Then what's doing it.
RANGER: Doing what?
WINNEBAGO: Killing the kids.
RANGER: You heard about it too.
WINNEBAGO: I heard about it from you.
RANGER: I'm a blabber mouth. I shouldn't have said anything.
WINNEBAGO: Well, you did.
RANGER: Well, I shouldn't have.
WINNEBAGO: Listen to me old man . . . I'm warning you . . . If you don't tell me what the hell's going on around here I'll report you.
RANGER: For what?
WINNEBAGO: Negligence of duty.

RANGER: You can't do that.

WINNEBAGO: The hell I can't. You're supposed to warn us if there's something going on here so we can leave.

RANGER: You got it all upside down. My job is to keep my mouth shut about anything that might drive the tourists away. If I warned you I'd be neglecting my duty, like you said.

WINNEBAGO: (*Voice of reason.*) Listen . . . we're from New York . . . we don't know this area at all . . . so if there's something we should know . . . you should tell us . . . right?

RANGER: That's what I'm here for. You want a map of the area? It's a pack of lies . . . the map . . . but I'll give you one.

WINNEBAGO: No . . . I have a map.

RANGER: Then you know as much as I do.

WINNEBAGO: About the kids? THE KIDS, DAMMIT . . .

RANGER: Fine people . . . kids. Used to be one myself. Got false teeth now and I swear I can't remember how it happened. One day I was brushing them the next day I was soaking them. (*Laughs.*) Damndest thing, though . . . I can pick up radio waves on my false teeth . . . swear to God I can . . . at night especially . . . I open my mouth and listen . . . the president says . . . well informed sources have it . . . music too . . . I tell you, I never could keep up if it wasn't for my false teeth . . .

WINNEBAGO: Listen, old man, what's your name?

RANGER: Ricky.

WINNEBAGO: Ricky! What kind of name is that for an old corpse like you . . .

RANGER: It's downright inappropriate, ain't it? But that's my name.

WINNEBAGO: Well, listen to me Ricky, you don't mind if I call you Ricky, do you?

RANGER: Don't mind nothing except seeing kids die.

WINNEBAGO: Listen, you old fart, you're trying to scare me for some reason and it isn't going to work.

RANGER: Glad to hear it. Hate scaring people. Don't know what it is about me but it always scares them. Even when I worked in real forests . . . up in Black Hills . . . why I'd come up to some young couple and offer them the map of the area and they'd run off like a couple of scared rabbits.

WINNEBAGO: Well, I'm not some young couple you can scare off, I'll tell you that.

RANGER: No, you're not very young, that's for sure.

WINNEBAGO: Younger than you.

RANGER: (*Laughs.*) The Bible's younger than me.

WINNEBAGO: Why don't you trot along.

RANGER: Can't trot no more. Can you?

WINNEBAGO: Just get the hell out of here.

RANGER: Fine thing. You come to my territory and tell me to get the hell out. You better get back to your territory before it gets dark. It gets awfully dark around here.

WINNEBAGO: I'm staying.

RANGER: Are you now?

WINNEBAGO: I'm staying right here until I'm good and ready to leave.

RANGER: You'll get bored. You've still got enough spunk in you to get bored. Me . . . haven't been bored in years.

WINNEBAGO: Maybe you're stupid.

RANGER: Maybe so, but at least I don't fish in the sand.

WINNEBAGO: I wasn't fishing.

RANGER: I saw you.

WINNEBAGO: I was pretending.

RANGER: Me too. I was pretending I saw you fishing. (*Points to the extension cord.*) What're you going to do with that? Plug it in your armpit? (*Juanita runs in.*)

JUANITA: Winny . . . I wish you'd take a look at Christine . . . (*Sees the Ranger and stops.*) Who's he?

WINNEBAGO: You see him too. I thought I was hallucinating.

RANGER: Is that your trailer over there?

JUANITA: Yes.

WINNEBAGO: No.

RANGER: Your oil's leaking. (*Bending down.*)

WINNEBAGO: I let it leak every now and then.

RANGER: You better get going before it leaks out. The nearest gas station on the map is three hundred miles away and it's no longer there. The nearest one after that is no longer there either.

WINNEBAGO: We're staying. We like it here.

RANGER: (*Laughs.*) You don't look like you like it anywhere. (*To Juanita.*) Is your daughter any better?

JUANITA: No . . . That is . . .

WINNEBAGO: No, she's not any better . . .

RANGER: That's a shame.

WINNEBAGO: And she's not any worse . . .

RANGER: Just hanging on, eh?

WINNEBAGO: She's just fine.

RANGER: Glad to hear it . . . A couple like you . . . well now . . . where would you be without a little daughter . . . If something was to happen to her you'd be as good as dead yourselves.

JUANITA: Winny . . . Who's he?

WINNEBAGO: Don't pay any attention to him.

RANGER: Since you folks are staying for the night, I have to ask you for some money.

WINNEBAGO: What for?
RANGER: For the show tonight.
WINNEBAGO: (*Doesn't want to ask. Does anyway.*) What show.
RANGER: What show! (*Pulls out a leaflet.*) Why it's going to be the biggest show anyone's ever had anywhere and then some. (*Hands leaflet to Winnebago.*)Here . . . you want one . . . they're free . . . If you want a poster, though, it's two fifty . . . Give one to your little girl . . . might cheer her up . . . you know . . . have some young people coming . . .
WINNEBAGO: (*Looks at leaflet.*) Come to the world's largest outdoors for two days and nights of light air and heavy sounds. Sounds like one of Fred's promos. Who's coming? THE MOUNTAIN . . . THE CLOUDS . . . THE RAIN . . . SIX MILLION BUFFALOS . . . FULL MOON AND THE ROLLING PRAIRIE EXPRESS . . . SCENIC WONDERS AND THE HITCHHIKERS . . . and many many more . . . (*To Juanita.*) Is this what she wants?
JUANITA: I don't know . . . she might like it.

(*Christo runs in.*)

CHRISTO: Hey, Winny . . . there's some kids coming . . . One of them's got a guitar . . . The festival's tonight, I think . . . We didn't miss it after all.
RANGER: Darn tootin' you didn't miss it.
CHRISTO: Who's he?
RANGER: If you don't have tickets I can sell you some.
WINNEBAGO: Tickets? Us? You mean you don't recognize us? We're in the show . . . We're MOSES AND THE PROMISED LAND. Let's go, dear . . . Someday we'll come back and put up a little Dairy Queen stand over there. (*Goes offstage with Juanita.*)
CHRISTO: (*Turns to Ranger.*) Who're you?
RANGER: I'm Ricky. (*Laughs a little. Christo exits as lights fade.*)

## Scene Two

*Same as in Scene One. It's night and there's a hint of moon. Winnebago and Christo.*

WINNEBAGO: So . . . How long do we have to wait? When's the music festival supposed to start?
CHRISTO: I don't know . . .
WINNEBAGO: Maybe they only play by appointment, eh?
CHRISTO: Maybe they're waiting for more people to show up.
WINNEBAGO: Maybe we got shafted again.

CHRISTO: I hope not.

WINNEBAGO: I bet there's a guy somewhere right now getting a fat grant from some foundation to study the evolution of the names of Rock Groups . . .

CHRISTO: Yeah, so what?

WINNEBAGO: Nothing. I just think he's a big turd whoever he is. (*Looks up at the moon.*) It must be midnight.

CHRISTO: It looks like two midnights. It's so dark I'm beginning to see things.

WINNEBAGO: If you're scared, why don't you go back to the trailer.

CHRISTO: And listen to Christine crying? No thanks.

WINNEBAGO: She still at it?

CHRISTO: Hasn't stopped since those musicians came.

WINNEBAGO: Can't blame her for crying. It's been a pretty boring vacation.

CHRISTO: Maybe . . . she's crying about something else.

WINNEBAGO: You think she's crying for me . . . that her old man is getting to be an old man.

CHRISTO: The whole world seems old. To her, that is.

WINNEBAGO: But not to you.

CHRISTO: Of course not.

WINNEBAGO: That's good.

CHRISTO: The world seems nice to me . . . and it's going to get nicer . . . you want to know why . . . Because from now on I'm going to do what *I* want to do.

WINNEBAGO: And what's that?

CHRISTO: Wouldn't you like to know?

WINNEBAGO: Yes, I would.

CHRISTO: I don't know what you're going to do but whatever it is it won't be what I have in mind.

WINNEBAGO: You've had it with me, right Christo?

CHRISTO: I've had it with you all right.

WINNEBAGO: If my vacation's this bad just think what the rest of my life is going to be like, right?

CHRISTO: Damn right.

WINNEBAGO: I know what you mean. STOP! WHO GOES THERE?

CHRISTO: Who is it?

WINNEBAGO: It's just me. Trying on a voice. Here we are Christo . . . two centurians standing guard under a full moon . . . youth and age keeping watch through the night.

CHRISTO: Sounds like a singing group . . . Youth and Age.

WINNEBAGO: Let's sing something . . . you and me.

CHRISTO: And wake everyone up?

WINNEBAGO: That's right. This is a music festival, isn't it? And what's everyone doing. The musicians are sleeping and my daughter's crying. Nobody's moving except those cars up there. Look at them Christo, it's midnight and they're crawling along. A traffic jam in the middle of the desert in the middle of the night in the middle of my life. I'm sad as hell, Christo.

CHRISTO: You're sad because you don't know what you want.

WINNEBAGO: I know what I want. (*Pause.*)

CHRISTO: Well?

WINNEBAGO: I want life to be a river and I want to float down that river on my back and look at the sky.

CHRISTO: Life's not a river.

WINNEBAGO: I want life to be an avalanche swooping down mountainsides with a thundering sound . . . with music and singing and strong hands reaching out to shake my hand as we go.

CHRISTO: Life's not like that either.

WINNEBAGO: No, it's not, is it. But it'd be nice if it were, eh?

CHRISTO: Yeah, it'd be O.K. if you like corny things like that.

WINNEBAGO: I've reached the crossroads of my life, Christo, and . . .

CHRISTO: . . . and you're making a fuss again.

WINNEBAGO: It's time someone made a fuss. Here am I aging by the minute and nobody's doing anything about it.

CHRISTO: They're doing something about it. They're sleeping so they don't have to look at you.

WINNEBAGO: Then why don't they look at my wife. She's still pretty. Why don't they flirt with her . . . or make a pass at her . . . She's dying to be unfaithful, the poor thing, and everyone's asleep . . .

CHRISTO: I suppose you're sorry she hasn't found someone.

WINNEBAGO: Sorry isn't the word for it. I'm heartbroken. That's why she went on vacation . . . That's why anyone goes on vacation . . . They want to be unfaithful to their lives back home and find some new life on the road. She's an attractive woman, dammit, and what do those kids do? Sleep. Hey, wake up out there! Wake up!

CHRISTO: (*Backs away from him.*) What the hell's wrong with you?

WINNEBAGO: Everything. Absolutely everything. My soft stomach's all wrong . . . my soft flabby legs are all wrong, my voice is all wrong . . . listen to it . . . no rage in it at all and I should be filled with rage . . . I should howl. I should curse.

CHRISTO: Look Winny, look . . . look at me . . . I'm young and relatively strong and what can I do? Nothing. All I can do is argue. The only exercise I get is being contrary. You tell me to do something and although I know I'll do it, although I might even like to do it, I can still do a better job of arguing why I shouldn't do it than actually do it. Don't make life seem so bad, please. At least don't be so convincing about it. If I can't disagree there's nothing I can do.

WINNEBAGO: Christo . . . you poor orphan, we'll find you a decent life if we have to spend our lives looking for it.

CHRISTO: You think so?

WINNEBAGO: I know it.

CHRISTO: I doubt it. You see? It's horrible . . . I hear something and I got to take the opposite side.

WINNEBAGO: You don't have to.

CHRISTO: Yes I do.

WINNEBAGO: I guess you do.

CHRISTO: Well, I don't have to but I do.

WINNEBAGO: I guess you don't.

CHRISTO: Don't what?

WINNEBAGO: Don't have to but you do.

CHRISTO: I guess so.

WINNEBAGO: See? You don't have to be contrary.

CHRISTO: But I do anyway.

WINNEBAGO: Exactly.

CHRISTO: You win. Now what?

(*In the opposite corner of the stage a figure appears in a white chiffon dress.*)

WINNEBAGO: Christine . . .

CHRISTO: It's about time she came out.

WINNEBAGO: I knew she wasn't sick . . . she was just . . . Oh, Christo, she's beautiful.

CHRISTO: Yes . . . she is.

WINNEBAGO: I give her to you.

CHRISTO: I'll remember that.

WINNEBAGO: The air is so clear . . . I can see her fingers and the ring on her finger I bought her for her birthday . . . and there . . . I can see the comb in her hair and the broken tooth on the comb . . . I was in a cab . . . Manhattan was full of New Jersey air and Long Island people and everything and everyone looked shapeless and deformed like puddles standing upright and suddenly this girl appeared . . . I can't remember her face, maybe it was beautiful . . . maybe not . . . but it's her clarity I remember . . . the lines of her body stood out sharp and clear and everything about her was the thing itself . . . I looked at her hands and it was as if I were seeing human hands for the first time . . . the thing itself . . . and every winedark strand of hair that came undone from her head and floated in the wind was unique and a thing in itself . . . I saw her, Christo . . . a definitive version of mankind in bloom.

CHRISTO: So you jumped out of the cab and into her arms just like in the movies.

WINNEBAGO: No, I stayed in the cab and the cab pushed on toward the Crap Building . . . green lights all the way.

CHRISTO: I think you're making it all up.

WINNEBAGO: Perhaps . . . But if I didn't see her I should have. Now that it's almost over and done with I feel like going back and adding chapters to the definitive biography of my life. There are so many gaps in it . . . so many holes. (*As Christo eases away from him.*) Where are you going?

CHRISTO: A stroll . . . It's a nice night for a stroll . . .

WINNEBAGO: We're leaving tomorrow and you better know where you want to go then.

CHRISTO: I know where I'm going. Don't you worry about me.

WINNEBAGO: Christine . . . Christine honey.

(*Figure hesitates and turns around. It's Juanita, of course.*)

JUANITA: I'm sorry, Winny . . . I just felt like putting on her clothes.

WINNEBAGO: They fit you beautifully.

JUANITA: Tell me the truth, Winny . . . if you were young and you saw me what would you think?

WINNEBAGO: I'd think you were hot to trot. I'd think I was warm for your form . . . and other things along that line. You look lovely . . . as lovely as that night in Tangiers when I slipped you a Spanish flyswatter in your drink.

JUANITA: Don't kid around, Winny . . .

WINNEBAGO: If I didn't kid around I'd hang myself on the nearest tree. (*Looks around.*) Wherever that may be. And what's our daughter doing tonight?

JUANITA: Crying.

WINNEBAGO: Because her old man is so . . . (*Gestures vaguely.*)

JUANITA: No.

WINNEBAGO: Didn't think so.

JUANITA: She saw those musicians and started crying.

WINNEBAGO: I didn't even see them and I'm ready to cry.

JUANITA: Remember when we took her to the circus that one time and those nightingales were singing and singing so lovely . . . remember . . . only it turned out that they were stuffed puppets and that old puppeteer was doing the singing . . . whistling just like a bird . . .

WINNEBAGO: Yes. I remember that old man . . . he was good, wasn't he.

JUANITA: And she cried all the way home . . . not like a spoiled child . . . but like someone betrayed . . . that's how she's crying now and I don't know what to tell her or what to do . . . I put on her clothes thinking I could feel what it was like but I don't think I have those feelings anymore . . . All I remember from my youth is that there seemed to be more of life everywhere . . . living . . . growing . . . moving . . . and I didn't have to pretend that I was alive myself . . . everything told me I was.

WINNEBAGO: Even words were alive then . . . Do you remember, goddamn, do you remember when you said you loved me . . . How did you do it? It had a ring to it . . . It made echos and I could hear the echos without you saying a word . . . Now we have to check to make sure . . . You still love me? Yes, hon. And you still love me? Sure thing, dear. It's a big deal now. It's like we're going for a record. Married for twenty-five years and they still love each other. Think they'll go for thirty?

JUANITA: I don't know how to tell you this but one of those kids . . . one of those musicians, I think . . .

WINNEBAGO: Asked you to slip away with him for some hanky panky in the sand.

JUANITA: Yes . . . he said he wouldn't mind.

WINNEBAGO: Wouldn't mind! Which one is he! Which one. Show him to me . . .

JUANITA: Oh, Winny, you're not jealous . . . so why pretend.

WINNEBAGO: I just want to see him. Wouldn't mind. Where does he get his goddamned nerve. Wouldn't mind. I've spent my life with you and he wouldn't mind spending one night with you. I'll find him . . . I'll tell him exactly what he's getting . . . how you were . . . how I loved you . . . I'll tell him. Here, let me kiss you before I go (*Does.*) . . . I've got to run . . . If I find him I'll tell him about you . . . Good night, wife . . . If I find him I'll tell him about you . . . Good night, wife . . . See you in the morning (*Runs.*) My wife is lonely and my daughter's crying . . . but there's hope in the air . . . (*Listens to the strumming of guitar.*) and music too . . . (*Runs some more. Coughs. Slows down. Stops.*) Where do I think I'm going? (*Feels heart.*) What did I run . . . fifty inches or so . . . ready to spit out my lungs. I wanted to look good in front of her . . . run off like that . . . like those guest stars on the talkie shows when they run on and off the stage . . . the thing is to keep running . . . stay on the stage and run . . . Go out for a pass or something. (*Quarterback stance.*) Sixty eight! Fifty five! Hike! Hike! Hike! (*Begins to throw ball. Sees Ranger sitting on top of the grill and red coals glitter inside.*) What the hell you doing up there?

RANGER: It's cold, the old bones are cold. Tired?

WINNEBAGO: Tired, hell. C'mon, let's have a race. I'll show you who's tired.

RANGER: You've already shown me. Here . . . there's room for two . . . We'll listen to some music. Can you hear it?

WINNEBAGO: Of course I can hear it. It's one of the kids from the music festival . . . I was looking for him . . .

RANGER: Were you now. Well, it's me . . . (*Opens mouth.*) Hear that . . . I'm picking up a folk station . . .

WINNEBAGO: You lie, you old corpse . . . There's a music festival warming up.

RANGER: Is there now? (*Opens mouth.*) Hear that . . . here . . . sit down . . . I'll open my mouth and we'll listen to some songs . . . (*Reaches out for Winny. Winnebago pushes the arm away and Ranger fades.*)

WINNEBAGO: Sleep, why not . . . It's a cold lonely night . . . best thing to do is sleep it off . . . dream it away. Lie down and play dead until it's time to get up and play alive again . . . (*Sergeant's voice.*) Come on, private, wake up. (*His voice.*) What for Sarge? (*Sarge.*) I'll tell you what for, private. You're going up that hill and you're going to take that hill. (*His voice.*) No kidding, Sarge, there still hills left? (*Sarge.*) Damn right, private, and now charge! (*Winny again.*) Where did you say that hill was? (*Sarge.*) No matter. Charge you dogface. Charge now and think later! CHARGE! (*Winnebago charges. Stumbles forward through the night, holding his cigar like a bayonet. Stops.*) I must have missed it. Fantastic . . . Missed the whole hill. There it is again . . . Maybe it's someone serenading Juanita under the stars . . . oh, she'd like that . . . wish I could find him and shake his hand . . . Kid, I'd say, kid . . . you know how to make a woman happy . . . Teach me how . . . (*Somewhere in the dark Christo is heard calling: Winny! Winny!*) Sounds so long ago. Winny, Winny, let's go out and shoot a few . . . let's go out and play . . . let's go and watch Mrs. Fiasco get ready for bed . . . Winny! Winny! (*Christo runs in to join him.*)

CHRISTO: Winny . . . We're being robbed!

WINNEBAGO: Isn't that the truth.

CHRISTO: These characters are taking stuff from the trailer.

WINNEBAGO: Where are they taking it.

CHRISTO: I'm serious, dammit. They're taking everything. They said they wanted money and I told them we had no money.

WINNEBAGO: They wouldn't take a check?

CHRISTO: Your camera . . . suitcases . . .

WINNEBAGO: With all my clothes in them.

CHRISTO: Yes . . .

WINNEBAGO: Tasteless fools. They'll be sorry when they open the suitcase and find that horrible blazer . . . you know the blue one . . . and how about those irridescent trousers . . . Oh, God . . . they shouldn't have to see that . . . Hurry . . . go tell them before it's too late . . . tell them I have a nice sweater under the front seat . . . my favorite sweater . . . Hurry . . .

CHRISTO: Winny . . . you're crazy.

WINNEBAGO: You're right. They wouldn't like the sweater. Sorry Christo but I've got to run . . .

CHRISTO: What am I going to do?

WINNEBAGO: Give my apologies to them . . . Tell them I'm sorry I had nothing better to offer . . . I should have something next time . . . Got to run, Christo . . . Got to run . . . (*Runs off. Seems to be trying to find a running gait more acceptable to his physique.*) I'm doing it all wrong . . . (*Coughs. Slows down. Walks.*) Too bad I can't run in slow motion. Bet I'd look good in slow motion . . . poetic and graceful . . . like a cigarette commercial. (*Talks to Fred.*) I don't know Fred. My life seems empty and boring. (*Fred.*) Maybe it's not your life. Maybe it's your cigarette. Here . . . try one of mine. (*Winnebago does, coughs.*) Yours is worse than mine. Maybe it's not my cigarette . . . Good God, Fred, maybe it is my life! Where to now? (*Stops.*) Let's see . . . what's up ahead? Up periscope! (*Uses cigar as periscope.*) There I am on the umpteenth floor of the Crap Building . . . Must be Friday . . . Everyone's got the Friday *Times* . . . checking out the movies . . . except Fred, of course . . . He's checking out the theatre section in front of everyone . . . Me? I'm showing the pictures of the trip to my secretary . . . doesn't believe I went anywhere . . . no tan . . . now everyone's sipping cold coffee from the coffee break . . . the cleaning lady's early as usual. "You done with the coffee?" Everyone's so friendly to everyone else and no one's got a friend in the whole place. (*Presses torpedo release button.*) Fire one! Fire two! Fire three! All gone. No more Crap. What's left? (*Turns around.*) A desert. There's got to be something else. Where the hell is everybody? There's a man out here. Talk to me for Christ's sake.

A VOICE: Shut up!

WINNEBAGO: Shut up yourself. (*Listens.*) I SAID SHUT UP YOURSELF. (*Listens.*) You don't have to, you know. It's a free country, dammit. Speak! COMPLAIN!

(*Boy with guitar enters.*)

BOY: Will you shut up please?

WINNEBAGO: Hallelujah. Here comes the music festival.

BOY: (*Very drowsy.*) Are you the promoter of this thing?

WINNEBAGO: Not yet. Give me time. Hey, where you going? You just got here.

BOY: So where are the promoters?

WINNEBAGO: On vacation. Didn't you know . . . everyone's on vacation. And who are you?

BOY: I'm the Lost and Found.

WINNEBAGO: That's your name?
BOY: That's my group's name.
WINNEBAGO: Where's your group?
BOY: We split up . . . I'm tired of groups . . . I came here to make it on my own . . . Looks like nobody came . . .
WINNEBAGO: Amazing. We all came here to get away from everyone else . . . and we're all complaining that nobody came.
BOY: (*Drowsier.*) You got any food?
WINNEBAGO: I'm living off nature.
BOY: What's there to eat.
WINNEBAGO: Nothing.
BOY: The promoters said there'd be plenty to eat.
WINNEBAGO: You must have talked to the same promoters I did. (*The Boy getting drowsier.*) What's the matter . . . you look exhausted. What's the matter with all you kids?
BOY: (*Lifts up electric cord of his guitar.*) I got to plug in somewhere . . . I got a song in my head . . . I've already forgotten half of it . . . beautiful song . . .
WINNEBAGO: Sing me the half you know.
BOY: If I don't plug in somewhere, I'll forget the other half . . .
WINNEBAGO: I need to plug in myself . . . me and my family . . . Tell you what . . . let's plug into each other . . . you sing and I'll hum.
BOY: (*Ready to keel over.*) They promised there'd be energy here.
WINNEBAGO: There is. I'm full of energy.
BOY: . . . Got to plug in somewhere.
WINNEBAGO: (*Shakes him.*) Forget the plugs. They're all connected to the promoters. The guitar plug's connected to the radio plug, the radio plug's connected to the business plug. The juice that runs your guitar is the same juice that runs the elevators and the hand dryers in the johns on the umpteenth floor of the Crap Building. You'd be plugging into their washroom. Don't do it . . . Hey, don't go to sleep. (*Shakes him.*) Don't give up . . . Not you . . . Hey, don't do it, kid . . . (*Shakes him, gets no response. Jumps up.*) HELP! A YOUNG MAN'S FALLING ASLEEP OVER HERE! HELP HIM! HE'S ONE OF YOU . . . (*Starts running, not knowing where to go.*) HELP! (*Almost falls.*) Oh . . . Oh God . . . not here . . . I'd hate to die here . . . Tourist Drops Dead in National Park . . . That's all this is . . . a park . . . The promoters call it a wilderness area, but it's only a park . . . nothing wild is left . . . Piss on it . . . Might as well . . . See what it's like . . . (*Unzips and pees.*) Never tried it in the open. No difference . . . same as doing it in the Grand Central john . . . Ahhhh . . . I've sprung a leak and life's trickling out on the sand . . . spilling on my wallabies . . . (*Zips up.*) You can shake and you can dance but the last drop always goes down your pants . . . No the last drop has dropped . . .

(*Looks around.*) I bet some German tourists out there were tàking a picture of me . . . Think I'm some kind of an American animal . . . Morons . . . no more American animals left . . . ants, mosquitoes and flies . . . (*A song is heard. Faintly at first but then louder. It is sung by a soft voice accompanied by a guitar. "Whose garden is this?" Winnebago listens as if spellbound. Breaks out of it and starts running with new energy.*) O how beautiful . . . Oh my God how beautiful . . . They're here . . . The kids are here . . . THEY'RE HERE! . . . THEY'VE COME! . . . (*Runs to figure lying in the sand; tries to get him to stand up.*) Get up! Get up! They're here . . . They're all here . . . The six million buffalos and the mountain . . . the rain and the clouds and all the rest of them . . . Let's go. (*Gets no response and runs himself toward the song; runs into the Ranger.*)

RANGER: I thought you'd be back. . . I'm picking it up loud and clear . . . Here . . . sit down . . . Rest . . .

WINNEBAGO. (*Stumbles backward.*) No . . . not till I drop . . . (*Stumbles backward and falls.*) No sooner said than done . . . (*Keeps crawling.*) It's no picnic . . . going on a vacation . . . (*Keeps crawling, then stops.*) That's it . . . can't go anymore . . . (*Looks up.*) Nothing up there. God's on vacation as well. (*Looks front.*) And the traffic's still crawling along . . . and I'm through . . . just like home . . . Sarge . . . we finally did it . . . we're over the hill at last . . . Here's one for the kids. (*Bites off the end of the cigar as if pulling a grenade pin. Hurls it and falls down.*)

CHRISTO'S VOICE: Winny . . . Winny . . . (*Enters carrying pack on back, canteen around neck, chair, stool and straps.*) Winny. (*Helps him to his knees. Lays pack in sand and helps Winny remove jacket. Winnebago crosses to things in sand.*) I warned you Winny. Remember? By the time I got back to the trailer they were all over the place. Draggin' stuff away like ants. I was going to fight them, but then I figured . . . what the hell . . . if he doesn't care, why should I . . .

WINNEBAGO: Did they leave anything else?

CHRISTO: They cleaned us out.

WINNEBAGO: I've never been cleaned out before . . . must say . . . it feels good . . . to be be cleaned out . . . (*Looks at hands.*) Yes . . . I can see the difference . . . they don't look so hazy anymore. I can do things with them.

CHRISTO: Yeah? And what the hell are you doing?

WINNEBAGO: The best I can, Christo.

CHRISTO: What the hell does that mean?

WINNEBAGO: Getting ready.

CHRISTO: You think you're going to get me to ask you "Getting ready for what?" Eh? Well, I won't. You know why? Because I don't care anymore. I've had it. I'm through with you.

WINNEBAGO: Good. . . . I'm through with me too . . . I could use a bit of rope, though . . . Give me that thing, Christo . . . (*Christo gives him strap.*) Tell me, just to make me happy, tell me what else is gone.

CHRISTO: I told you . . . everything.

WINNEBAGO: Everything? Couldn't you specify?

CHRISTO: All right, I'll specify. They took the hubcaps. They couldn't take the tires, so they punctured them. They ripped out the car radio and broke off the antenna . . . They even took the umbrella.

WINNEBAGO: What industrious kids . . . how nice of them. I never did anything for them. I would have, but I didn't have a chance. And here they come and clean me out . . . God bless them. Anything else gone?

CHRISTO: Yes, to be specific, something else is gone. You know what's gone? Your mind, that's what. You're right out of your tree.

WINNEBAGO: Where is my tree?

CHRISTO: Cut it out, Winny . . . I know what you're doing. Be mushy again . . . or corny . . . I don't care . . . but don't sound like that . . . you're frightening me . . . WHAT ARE YOU MAKING?

WINNEBAGO: A thing.

CHRISTO: What kind of thing?

WINNEBAGO: A thing about so big and so wide. Something to carry our belongings in.

CHRISTO: Didn't you hear me? We don't have any belongings. They took everything.

WINNEBAGO: Not everything.

CHRISTO: Almost everything.

WINNEBAGO: That's good . . . because this thing isn't that big . . . room for a few essentials, that's all . . .

CHRISTO: I don't know you when you're like this.

WINNEBAGO: I don't know you that well either, Christo, but I like you.

CHRISTO: I like you too.

WINNEBAGO: We have perfect communication and a solid basis for a prolonged friendship. We can't go wrong if we like what we don't know about each other. Let's be big about it and like what we don't know about what's up ahead.

CHRISTO: Where up ahead?

WINNEBAGO: Over there . . .

CHRISTO: That's not the way home.

WINNEBAGO: Of course not.

CHRISTO: There's nothing over there.

WINNEBAGO: There's nothing back home either.

CHRISTO: Your whole life's back there.

WINNEBAGO: Good. Let it stay there.

CHRISTO: My whole life's ahead of me . . .

WINNEBAGO: Right you are. It's ahead, not back home.

CHRISTO: You don't know what you're saying.

WINNEBAGO: You might have a point. I think those kids absconded with my vocabulary as well. If this is the Lake of the Woods, then I don't need the following words . . . lake and woods. If there are no buffalos, I don't need the word buffalo. Same goes for the mountains. Let's see . . . what other words don't I need . . .

CHRISTO: Winny . . . poor Winny, you're not kidding . . . You've lost your mind.

WINNEBAGO: Yes, that's the word I was looking for. I don't need it either. We've been tricked . . Someone scribbled some words in the sand and we've been looking for them . . . I'm going to look for the thing from now on, the thing itself, not the words. (*Juanita walks in slowly, dressed as in Scene One.*) Wife . . . you look lovely in the morning . . . It's morning, you know . . . the morning before the day ahead . . .

JUANITA: They played a trick on us just to get you away from the trailer . . . so they could take those things.

WINNEBAGO: So, you spent the night by yourself.

JUANITA: Yes.

WINNEBAGO: So did I. It'll never happen again. And our daughter . . . how is she?

JUANITA: She's sick, Winny . . . very sick.

WINNEBAGO: That's my girl. Takes after her old man.

CHRISTO: Juanita . . . don't listen to him . . . he's mad . . .

JUANITA: You seem so urgent, Christo . . . you're just like Winny used to be . . . hot and urgent and jumping all around.

WINNEBAGO: Was I really . . . hot and urgent?

JUANITA: Yes . . . you were a lovely man.

CHRISTO: Listen to me both of you . . . I hate to sound like this but the two of you . . . you're acting like a couple of kids . . .

WINNEBAGO: And you're acting all grown up. Isn't he Juanita?

JUANITA: Yes, Christo . . . you really are.

WINNEBAGO: No matter. We'll take turns . . . you sound grown-up today and tomorrow I'll try my hand at it again.

CHRISTO: Juanita . . . talk to him . . .

JUANITA: What shall we talk about. Winny.

WINNEBAGO: How about that night in Dubrovnik when we drank red Dalmatian wine in the castle above the sea.

JUANITA: That sounds like one of the loveliest things we never did.

WINNEBAGO: Yes, the wine was dark and dry and the waves were high and in the waves were mermaids for me and young boys for you and we could have gone with them had we been there.

JUANITA: It would have been lovely.

WINNEBAGO: I'm full of stories . . . I'll tell them to you on the way . . .

about the time you didn't and I wouldn't and we easily could have. Remember.

JUANITA: Yes . . . As if it were yesterday.

CHRISTO: Aren't you forgetting something?

WINNEBAGO: Yes, fortunately. All kinds of things.

CHRISTO: You're forgetting about Christine.

WINNEBAGO: Don't you dare tell me that . . . that's all I'm thinking about . . . my lovely child.

CHRISTO: She's sick . . . do you remember that. Winny . . . she needs a doctor.

WINNEBAGO: True.

CHRISTO: Let's take her to one.

WINNEBAGO: Can't. All the doctors are on vacation. The whole country's on vacation. Look . . . look up there . . . everyone's leaving . . .look: cars, trucks, buses, campers, trailers and kids on motorcycles and kids on foot . . . all of them moving . . . trying to find a place to plug into and all of them hooked up like a train playing follow the leader through the desert . . . the 9:05 American Express . . . passing through . . . I don't want to go along anymore . . .

CHRISTO: (*Shouts in the direction of the traffic.*) Help . . . Help . . . we're out of gas . . .

WINNEBAGO: Why do you lie?

CHRISTO: I can't tell them how bad off we are . . . Nobody'd stop then . . . maybe if I told them all we needed was some gas . . . Help!

WINNEBAGO: Can't expect them to help you . . . They're on vacation . . . see . . . they're just passing through . . . they don't look like cars anymore . . . you'd think entire communities had picked up and left . . . churches and institutions . . . everything that seemed solid and stationary is on the move . . . passing through . . . (*Waves.*) Goodbye . . . goodbye countrymen and good luck . . .

CHRISTO: Maybe they could pick us up.

WINNEBAGO: I don't want to be picked up. I want to be rescued. And I can't be rescued until I'm lost . . .

JUANITA: Winny . . . (*Points.*) He's there again.

WINNEBAGO: The old ranger's getting ready too it seems . . . we better get a head start on him . . . You coming, Christo?

CHRISTO: Coming? Isn't there anything left in your head at all . . . look at our trailer . . . look at it . . . we can't go anywhere in it.

WINNEBAGO: We're walking.

CHRISTO: I'm not walking.

WINNEBAGO: You can run if you want, but I can't anymore . . . I'll have to walk.

CHRISTO: And Christine . . . she's going to walk too.

WINNEBAGO: We'll carry her . . . Juanita and I . . .

CHRISTO: I'm not going.

WINNEBAGO: Then you're staying.

CHRISTO: No . . . I'm going back.

WINNEBAGO: You're my houseboy, Christo . . . and I'm taking the house with me . . . you're coming with us. (*Winnebago walks offstage. Christo shouts after him.*)

CHRISTO: The hell I am . . . The hell I am, Winnebago . . . I'm not going anywhere . . . No sir . . . I know where I'm going . . . you hear me, Winny?

JUANITA: You really don't sound very convincing when you shout like that.

CHRISTO: That shows how much you know. I sound very convincing . . . Well . . . I don't know what you'll do without me . . . but you're both old enough . . . this is goodbye.

JUANITA: Have I ever kissed you, Christo?

CHRISTO: You sure as hell haven't. Not once.

JUANITA: Here . . . Let me kiss you now.

CHRISTO: Alright . . . I'll let you . . . but don't think . . . just don't think . . . that you can . . . (*Juanita kisses him. Christo looks . . . Pulls away from her.*) Oh, no . . . (*Enter Winnebago. He's carrying Christine in his arms.*)

WINNEBAGO: It took me forever it seems to find a way to pick her up . . . I tried it this way and that way . . . Am I doing it all right? Can you tell by the way I hold her that I love her . . . Is it clear?

CHRISTO: Is she . . .

WINNEBAGO: Yes, she's alive. Look . . . look how gently life lingers around her . . . she's light and yet very heavy with life . . .

CHRISTO: You can't carry her, Winny.

WINNEBAGO: She's carrying me, Christo . . . Can't you see . . . I'm leaning on her. (*Places her on the thing he made, a stretcher-like thing.*) How unmistakeable life is . . . no arrows . . . no signs . . . no need for them anymore . . .

CHRISTO: This is goodbye, then.

WINNEBAGO: Yes, Goodbye, Goodbye, Goodbye . . . Give a hand, wife. (*Juanita and Winnebago take up the stretcher and start moving. Christo stands his ground. Wavers. Runs after them.*)

CHRISTO: Winny . . . You're going the wrong way . . . according to the map . . .

WINNEBAGO: No . . . this is the way . . . (*Looks around.*) Not a car anywhere. I'd hate to get your hopes all up . . . but I think we're lost . . .

CHRISTO: Let me carry the stretcher for a while . . . Let her rest, at least.

WINNEBAGO: Carry your own youth, Christo. We're carrying ours.

CHRISTO: You promised her to me.

WINNEBAGO: And I'll keep my promise. When I drop you'll have to take my place here . . .

CHRISTO: How long are we going to keep walking . . .

WINNEBAGO: Until Christine says she wants us to stop.

CHRISTO: She hasn't moved for hours . . . she may be dead.

WINNEBAGO: Don't you think I'd know if she were dead . . . don't you think I'd know if I were carrying dead weight . . . Christine . . . Christine, honey . . . you're not dead, are you?

JUANITA: I'm getting tired, Winny.

WINNEBAGO: (*Looks back.*) So's that old ranger . . . I think I see him resting back there . . . he's on his last legs . . . He, ha . . . You better stay close, Christo . . . They say there are sand storms out here and we might get split up . . .

CHRISTO: I can take care of myself . . . I've been in sand storms before . . . (*Takes out map, throws it away. Grabs a hold of the trailing cord.*)

WINNEBAGO: Look . . . look up ahead . . .

CHRISTO: There's nothing up ahead.

WINNEBAGO: We'll camp there tonight. Look . . . you see . . . there are wild animals grazing out there . . . wild beasts in a wild pasture and a whole wilderness of happy people . . . Christine . . . Christine honey . . . look up ahead . . . you'll like it there . . . Oh, Christine, do take a look . . .

JUANITA: Will we ever get there, Winny?

WINNEBAGO: I don't know . . . Cheer up wife . . . we're lost . . . we're sick and tired but we're the thing itself at last.

JUANITA: It's heavy, Winny . . . How much further?

WINNEBAGO: Till we drop.

CHRISTO: The hell we'll drop, Winnebago. Nobody's going to drop. You hear me?

WINNEBAGO: I hear you. You hear me, wife?

JUANITA: Yes, Winny . . .

(*They continue walking, looking ahead, as the lights slowly fade.*)

# Passing Game

*Passing Game* was first performed on November 20, 1977, by the American Place Theatre, New York. It was directed by Peter Yates. The cast included:

DEBBIE .......... *Susan MacDonald*
RANDY .......... *Paul C. O'Keefe*
RICHARD .......... *William Atherton*
JULIE .......... *Margaret Ladd*
ANDREW .......... *Pat McNamara*
HENRY .......... *Howard E. Rollins, Jr.*
RACHEL .......... *Novella Nelson*

Set: Kert Lundell
Costumes: Ruth Morley
Lighting: Neil Peter Jampolis

**Cast:** Richard, actor. Any age.
Julie, his wife. Slightly younger.
Henry, black actor. Richard's age.
Rachel, Henry's wife. Julie's age.
Andrew, night watchman.
Randy, his young nephew.
Debbie, Randy's girlfriend.

**Time:** Present

**Place:** Upstate New York

# ACT I

## Scene 1

*Hennessy cottage. Andrew enters from S.L. He crosses to D.C. on the basketball court. He pauses, loads his shotgun and moves on. The stage is dark. It is night. A shot is heard in the distance. Randy jumps up from the couch. Debbie runs out of the bedroom.*

DEBBIE: What was that?

RANDY: Sounded like Uncle Andrew's shotgun. He goes hunting at night sometimes. (*Light goes on in the Jefferson cottage and Henry steps out.*)

HENRY: I don't see anybody. (*Debbie runs to the window and looks out at him. Randy also looks over at him.*)

DEBBIE: I know him. I mean I've seen him on TV.

RANDY: Uncle says the guy who owns this place's been on TV too. He did some dogfood commercials or something.

HENRY: So what did you want me to do, Rachel? (*Henry goes back inside.*)

RANDY: Want to go to the bedroom?

DEBBIE: Not now.

RANDY: What's the matter? You used to love to break into other people's cottages and goof around. (*Smells the perfume.*)

DEBBIE: Maybe I've changed.

RANDY: What did you do? Steal some of that lady's cologne?

DEBBIE: I did not.

RANDY: You used to love to steal little things.

DEBBIE: I just put some on. And it's perfume. Not cologne. Here smell.

RANDY: Did you do your breasts like you used to? (*He puts his nose in her cleavage.*)

DEBBIE: That's enough. C'mon. Take your damn nose out of there. (*She pushes him away and crosses to sofa and turns on flashlight. Randy stops.*)

RANDY: The only way I ever got anything off you was to force you. A couple of times you even pretended to be drunk.

DEBBIE: I was drunk.

RANDY: No you weren't. I saw you spilling booze out of the car when you thought I wasn't looking.

DEBBIE: Cheat. (*She sits on sofa.*)

RANDY: (*He crosses to sofa and sits.*) I was hoping to get you pregnant. You never would've left for the city had I got you pregnant.

DEBBIE: Maybe not.

RANDY: And you wanted me to get you pregnant. Only it had to be by accident. Like it just happened somehow.

DEBBIE: You had your chance. It's too late now.

RANDY: But you did come back.

DEBBIE: Just to visit. See everyone . . . my parents' house.

RANDY: All the kids are gone. Your parents moved to Florida. I'm the only one left. So maybe you really came back to see me and give me another chance.

DEBBIE: I see you haven't changed at all.

RANDY: (*He takes her hand.*) Hmm. I'm not as sweet as I once was. I was as sweet as baby corn in those days. So, what brings you here if not me?

DEBBIE: (*She rises and crosses to door.*) I told you. Besides . . . it's very hot in the city.

RANDY: Must be hot for everybody. And yet the people who used to come here got scared off.

DEBBIE: So?

RANDY: So, it must be hotter for you in the city than for most. (*He takes flashlight and shines it in her face.*) I mean I get you to come up.

DEBBIE: (*She crosses back toward him.*) Maybe I wanted to see if you still love me. (*She takes the flashlight out of her eyes.*)

RANDY: All you got to do is ask.

DEBBIE: I'm not going to ask.

(*A car is heard pulling up to the cabin. Randy jumps up. Runs to the door and peeks out.*)

RANDY: It's the people. Let's get out of here. (*They exit together. Enter Richard and Julie.*)

RICHARD: WELCOME. (*Julie ignores him. Looks around.*)

JULIE: Quit stalling. You know what you have to do. (*Hands him a flyswatter.*)

RICHARD: I feel silly just thinking about it.

JULIE: All I'm asking for is a little commotion . . . a fair warning to any spiders, june bugs, centipedes and-a-, whoever else might be here . . . that we're back. (*He lifts up the rug, jumps and goes into a tap routine to Forty-Second Street. Getting the beat going, he starts into a little soft-shoe, very corny and self-conscious, from which he moves on to a much more wild free-form choreography . . . a parody of sorts of Gene Kelly. Very show biz, he stops by flopping down on the sofa.*)

RICHARD: How was that?

JULIE: It should be a warning to them . . . to all of us. (*She enters the kitchen and puts the groceries down on the table, and begins to sort through them.*) I don't know why we bought this stuff. We always assume that being in the country will give us an appetite for food we hate in the city. Pork and beans . . . corn meal mush . . . You'd think we were ashamed to bring a bagel into the woods.

RICHARD: Everything looks fine.

JULIE: Yes. The faucets are pouring forth . . . the fridge is fridging . . . the sink is sinking and the lights are lighting . . . your telephone is over there . . .

RICHARD: Yes, but it's not ringing.

JULIE: (*She puts entire bag of groceries in the refrigerator.*) I bet you get something tomorrow. Friday's your lucky day.

RICHARD: Since when?

JULIE: (*Pause.*) That's funny?

RICHARD: What?

JULIE: I thought I smelled that old perfume of mine.

RICHARD: Me too.

JULIE: (*She pulls out a chair and sits.*) Ah, a house in the country. There really should be somebody here to greet us.

RICHARD: Like in a Russian novel.

JULIE: Exactly. Parents . . . or grandparents . . .

RICHARD: (*He sits on the floor and puts his head on her lap.*) And an unmarried daughter who looks after them and says things like: You must tell me all about the city, you really must . . .

JULIE: Something like that . . . Wouldn't you like that, Rich.

RICHARD: I guess I don't have roots like you but, yes, I would like it . . . for your sake.

JULIE: Can I ask you a terrible question? (*Richard gets up and crosses to the suitcase.*)

RICHARD: That in itself is a terrible question.

JULIE: Why are we here?

RICHARD: Why are we here? According to Schopenhauer . . .

JULIE: I'm serious.

RICHARD: So is Schopenhauer. (*He exits to bedroom.*)

JULIE: I bet you expect me to run around and have fun up here.

RICHARD: You don't have to run around.

JULIE: (*She crosses U.L. slowly L. of pillar.*) Then I have to stand on the porch with my hands on my hips taking in huge quantities of "country fresh air" . . . saying things like: And just think . . . it's only a couple of hours from the city.

RICHARD: No.

JULIE: Can I just do nothing?

RICHARD: (*He enters and stands R. of pillar.*) Whatever makes you happy.

JULIE: You make me happy. (*Richard crosses to sofa, pulls off sheet and throws it under sofa. He looks up at her.*) Don't look at me like that?

RICHARD: Like what, Julie?

JULIE: Like you were doing.

RICHARD: But I don't know what I was doing.

JULIE: You were looking at me . . . (*Richard crosses to her. He starts off seriously but gets more playful as he goes on.*)

RICHARD: Yes, but I don't know how I was looking at you. For the last couple of months you've accused me of looking at you a certain way . . . So tell me . . . Do I look at you sneaky with half shut eye. No? Brazenly with bulging pupils? No? Does it begin with a letter "C"? Am I getting warm? Is it bigger than a pine box?

JULIE: Oh forget it. All my problems turn into your showcases. (*He goes and sits on sofa. Once again his look asks the question. She responds. She sits U.S. on sofa.*) I don't know. I just feel so defensive lately. I run into old friends and have to defend myself for having changed . . . I run into recent friends and have to defend myself for not having changed enough. I go to a store to buy lipstick and I just know this checkout girl thinks I've been duped by the latest TV commercial and I just want to scream at her: No, dearie, I haven't been duped . . . I've been buying this same lipstick for years.

RICHARD: I feel the same way when I go to Baskin-Robbins and want a dip of peppermint swirl. Right away you're a fag. So I order chocolate, two scoops like a man.

JULIE: And all of a sudden all of my friends have become Hindus or Buddhists or something . . . Maureen asked me just last week . . . Julie, honey, she said . . . are you still a Christian? You'd think she was accusing me of wearing pleated skirts or something.

RICHARD: You shouldn't listen to Maureen.

JULIE: I didn't. I got real upset and started screaming at her.

RICHARD: That should tell her you're still a Christian. All in all it sounds like a good thing we came up here for a while.

JULIE: You're absolutely right. I think the damn city was getting to us . . . It's nice to be alone and cut off from everybody . . . and I'm going to take advantage of it.

RICHARD: And what does that mean?

JULIE: You'll find out. If you think you're crazy about me now . . . you just wait. I'm going to start exercising . . . blossoming right in front of your eyes. It's time I got my tits back in shape. You should see Maureen's tits. She's got a permanent hardening of the nipples or something. I think mine are beginning to sag.

RICHARD: I read about it in the *Wall Street Journal.* Julie's tits sagged two points in light trading.

JULIE: Just don't sell me short is all I ask. (*She goes to the bathroom. As soon as she's gone there's a change in Richard. His physical "pose" changes. His movements become angular and quick rather than soft and slow. He goes to his brief case, takes out a gun. Julie is heard uttering a cry from the bathroom. Richard returns to his former physical posture. Julie is very upset.*) There was somebody at the window. (*Richard heads for the bathroom. Knock on the back door. Richard stops. Julie seems ready to say something. Stays away from door.*)

RICHARD: It's not who you think it is. They wouldn't knock. (*He opens the back door. Flashlight, shotgun and Andrew, the nightwatchman, appear in that order. Stays in doorway—in darkness.*)

ANDREW: Oh, it's you . . . good evening . . . I didn't know . . .

RICHARD. It's Andrew, honey.

JULIE: (*Her fear now turns to anger for having been afraid of nothing.*) You scared the hell out of me.

ANDREW: Sorry . . . but you should've given me a call to tell me you're coming up . . . I saw a light . . . Could've been anybody . . . Burglars . . . or worse . . .

JULIE: Now what the hell would a burglar be doing in the bathroom?

ANDREW: Just what you were doing, Mrs. . . . We're all human beings. (*Richard gestures to him not to point the shotgun toward him and Andrew moves it aside slowly.*)

RICHARD: I imagine you've got to get going on your rounds. We don't want to keep you.

ANDREW: Feels strange making my rounds. Nobody up here.

RICHARD: Fine, then you can go home. (*Julie crosses and sits on sofa.*)

ANDREW: You know I haven't seen you on those TV commercials lately.

RICHARD: That's because I haven't made any lately.

ANDREW: Oh, moved up to bigger stuff.

RICHARD: No.

ANDREW: That can only mean one thing.

RICHARD: And it does.

ANDREW: Sorry to hear that. I hate to see a man on his way down. (*He steps forward into the light. Julie is a little stunned by his appearance.*) I've fallen apart myself haven't I.

JULIE: No.

RICHARD: We were just going to bed.

ANDREW: Sure I have. I was fine and then all of a sudden I started getting rickety and senile . . . Same thing happened to my father. A fine figure of a man . . . Had a laugh like a thunderstorm . . . And then one morning there he was . . . sitting at a breakfast table and drooling on his French toast . . . My mother burst out crying.

RICHARD: (*Louder.*) WE WERE JUST GOING TO BED.

ANDREW: I'M NOT DEAF YOU KNOW. I HEARD YOU THE FIRST TIME. SOMETIMES WHEN I DON'T PICK UP ON SOMETHING THAT'S BEING SAID IT'S BECAUSE I CHOOSE NOT TO. (*Stops.*) Whew! I'm just starting my rounds and it feels funny doing it without my dog. Poor thing was getting blind. I just shot her a while ago. Maybe you heard the shot?

RICHARD: We didn't hear it.

ANDREW: It's the dampness here . . . The air's so thick it sucks up noise like a sponge. You could scream your head off and nobody'd hear you. I know. Well . . . I suppose you were just getting ready to go to bed . . . (*Starts to leave.*) Oh yes . . . A young couple rented the green cottage across from you. One of them's a man. And the other one's a woman of some kind. Both black as night . . .

RICHARD: (*He interrupts and picks up on the word.*) Good night.

ANDREW: Good night. My nephew's up here with his girl friend. No telling what those kids are doing in my room . . . Enjoy yourselves. (*Andrew leaves.*)

JULIE: I thought you told me last week that you had called Andrew and told him we were coming.

RICHARD: Well I didn't. I knew he'd want to stop by and bring up the whole thing again and I just didn't want him upsetting you.

JULIE: (*Half joke.*) So, ulterior motives after all. Any others?

RICHARD: Nope.

JULIE: Coming to bed?

RICHARD: Yep . . . I'll just lock up. (*She goes into the bedroom. As soon as she does Richard takes the gun out of the briefcase. He looks for a place to hide it . . . he puts it under the sofa. He locks the doors. Turns out the light. There's a shaft of light coming from the bedroom . . . He goes inside the bedroom.*)

## Scene 2

*Morning. Julie opens the refrigerator. Takes out the bag of groceries. Looks inside it unhappily. Takes out a loaf of sliced bread from the bag. Peeks inside bag again.*

JULIE: Is there something you can make with bread and catsup?

RICHARD: (*O.S.*) There is but you shouldn't. Let's skip breakfast.

JULIE: (*She takes out a yogurt for herself and begins to eat it.*) I had such a stupid dream. I dreamt I was living in this country where it's punishable by death to be caught naked. What am I going to do, I kept saying in this absurd voice, I haven't got a thing to wear. (*She waits for some kind of a reply from Richard. None comes. Richard comes out. He is wearing sweatpants . . . sneakers . . . He has been shaving. He is holding his chin. What follows has a ring of a "routine" that Richard and Julie have done before. She looks at his chin.*) What's the matter?

RICHARD: Cut myself shaving.

JULIE: Well . . . put some toilet paper on it.

RICHARD: I did. (*He lets go the hand and a five foot length of toilet paper falls to the floor attached to the nick on his chin at the top. He gets the response he wants from her and then he jauntily swings the toilet paper over his shoulder like a scarf. Pauses. Takes the bottom edge of the T.P. and examines it.*) A message from Iago?

JULIE: I don't like your Iago, my lord. He's such a little turd.

RICHARD: (*He [Othello] reads the message.*) He says you have been unfaithful to me, Desdemona.

JULIE: He would say that . . . horny little runt.

RICHARD: Silence! (*He tears off the end of the toilet paper.*) Is this thy handkerchief, Desdemona?

JULIE: Call me Mona, my lord.

RICHARD: Skipping ahead. Set you down this . . . (*Julie becomes a secretary taking down dictation.*) That in Aleppo once . . .

JULIE: Two P's in Aleppo?

RICHARD: Where a malignant and turbaned Turk beat a Venetian and traduced the State . . . I took by the throat (*Takes himself by the throat.*) the circumcised dog and smote him thus. (*He smites himself over the head with it. Falls on the floor. Julie applauds. He rises.*)

JULIE: You must be feeling good to die so early in the day.

RICHARD: FIRST TIME I slept so well since the last time we were up here.

JULIE: Don't you think you should give Myra a call?

RICHARD: Why?

JULIE: What if something comes up?

RICHARD: Like what?

JULIE: Richard, is there something the matter?

RICHARD: I think Myra and I are slowly parting company.

JULIE: AFTER all these years. Do you have another agent in mind?

RICHARD: (*He crosses into kitchen and pours himself some water.*) I really don't know . . . It's always the same thing . . . You get any agent and the first thing they do is hype up your future . . . just as Myra did . . . She had all these great hopes and plans for my acting career . . . I was supposed to be a star by now . . . so it's kind of awkward for her to call me up for some two bit voice-over spot . . . Both of us have to pretend that we never had those hopes and plans . . . it's painful . . .

JULIE: You're just too good an actor not to be working . . .

RICHARD: You really think so?

JULIE: Of course I do.

RICHARD: I have a shocking new theory why a lot of actors can't find work. It's not because of some conspiracy of producers and directors . . . It's because they're rotten actors.

JULIE: But you're not one of them.

RICHARD: But what if I was?

JULIE: But you're not.

RICHARD: But what if I was?

JULIE: Richard, I don't know what you want me to say.

RICHARD: (*He wants to end the whole thing.*) Ach . . . forget it. I think I'll go out and shoot a few. (*Goes to bedroom.*)

JULIE: You know what . . . I can't remember my mother's telephone number . . . I was going to call her . . .

RICHARD: Oxford something. You always want to call her when we're out of the city.

JULIE: I know. That way she can't ask me to come over.

RICHARD: (*He comes out of closet with basketball.*) I thought you like to visit her.

JULIE: (*He comes back out with sneakers, and stands looking out on basketball court.*) I do . . . but I feel a little guilty because you don't have a mother yourself.

RICHARD: Sometimes I think the only reason you love me is because I'm an orphan.

JULIE: I wonder whatever happened to all those kids you used to tell me about. T-bone and all the rest of them . . . (*Henry comes out of the house and crosses to basketball court, doing warm-up exercises.*) Don't you orphans have reunions or something? What was that thing T-bone used to say? (*Just then we hear a basketball bouncing outside the house. Richard goes to the window and looks out.*)

RICHARD: Well sonovabitch.

JULIE: What's the matter?

RICHARD: You won't believe this. Guess who the black guy is who rented the green house. Just guess.

JULIE: (*She comes over and looks out of the window.*) Oh, I've seen him.

RICHARD: You've seen him! He got the last three commercials I was up for. Mr. Residuals we call him. Bastard. Look at him . . . bouncing his black balls across my court.

JULIE: You sure it's him?

RICHARD: I guess I'll go and find out.

JULIE: Oh Jesus . . . You're not going to carry a grudge are you?
RICHARD: I'd prefer a club.
JULIE: I don't need to start worrying about this . . . I really don't . . .
RICHARD: Nothing to worry about. I can take care of myself. (*Starts going out.*) Maybe we'll just have a friendly little game of one on one. My court. His ball.
JULIE: You're not going to make trouble are you?
RICHARD: Nope. (*Richard drops his ball and goes out. Lights up on the court, fade on the cottage.*)

## Scene 3

*Basketball court. Although the basketball court is near both houses we do not see the houses. The court is a separate area. It feels alien somehow. Stark. There is only one basket and it's attached to a steel pole . . . a red steel pole perhaps . . . and the effect of the basket and the net and the place in general gives it the look of the gallows. Henry is dribbling around and shooting. He's wearing sweatpants . . . sweatshirt . . . sneakers . . . As most solo players would do he seems to be pretending he's in a game . . . he fakes around imaginary opponents . . . drives toward the basket and around and finally shoots. He does not see Richard watching him. Richard waits for the moment when Henry has stopped to shoot. As Henry takes careful aim at the basket Richard comes closer to him from behind and then, just as Henry's about to release the ball, Richard lets go with:*

RICHARD: Hi there!

(*Henry is startled. His shot goes way off the mark. But Henry does not stay startled too long. He recovers . . . both the ball and himself.*)

HENRY: Hi . . . you must be the other people who're up here.
RICHARD: Sounds like you met Andrew already.
HENRY: Oh yeah. Henry Jefferson. (*They shake hands.*)
RICHARD: Richard Hennessy.
HENRY: You look familiar kind of.
RICHARD: You kind of do too.
HENRY: You an actor?
RICHARD: I try to be.
HENRY: Ah . . . it's a rotten business.
RICHARD: For some.
HENRY: I hope you don't mind me using your court.
RICHARD: The court of Richard is honored to have you, Sir Henry. (*Richard crosses D.R.*)

HENRY: You want to shoot a few? (*Henry passes the ball to Richard. Richard looks at it.*)
RICHARD: Hmm . . . man's got a leather ball. Golly. Played college?
HENRY: St. John's. You?
RICHARD: St. Bonaventure. Starter?
HENRY: No. Sub. You?
RICHARD: Same. Guard?
HENRY: Yeap. Too short for that even.
RICHARD: Same here.

(*There's a feeling here that Henry is waiting for Richard to do something with the ball. Either shoot it or give it back to Henry . . . There's also a feeling here that Richard is doing it on purpose. Henry's the kind of man who needs to keep something going. His metabolism does not allow for a pause. If he can't dribble the ball he's got to talk.*)

HENRY: It's a shame, isn't it, what's happening to the Knicks. I mean they were blowing people off the court until that whole default business hit the city . . . and then they just fell apart. It's an interesting connection don't you think . . . the fact that the sport franchises are a barometer of the city's confidence.
RICHARD: (*If Richard were ready to give up the ball and start playing a little Henry's speech makes him pause. He is on to something.*) Yes, it's very interesting. So interesting in fact that somebody even took the trouble to write about that very theory in the New York *Times*. (*Richard throws to Henry.*)
HENRY: I wasn't really pretending that it was mine. (*Henry throws back.*)
RICHARD: Neither was I. (*Richard dribbles up to basket and stops.*) In the same issue, the very same issue in which that theory appeared, there was also another interesting story . . . wasn't there?
HENRY: There were a lot of stories.
RICHARD: Sure . . . but all of them weren't interesting. The one I had in mind was.
HENRY: What story was that?
RICHARD: Well, you see, I was wondering if you remembered it.
HENRY: Maybe I didn't read it.
RICHARD: But it was right next to the article about the Knicks . . . You could hardly miss it . . .
HENRY: Maybe if you refreshed my memory.
RICHARD: Now there's a thought. You see . . . they had a story about this place . . . about those killings that took place in this place . . . about how nobody comes here any more and how this and how that and how among other things they never caught the person or persons who did it and how that's what's keeping people away.
HENRY: Oh yeah . . . I think I do remember now . . .

RICHARD: I bet you do. Well, I just thought it was interesting that you and I were up here. I guess we're not afraid.

(*A woman appears on a wheelchair at this point. Her name is Rachel. She is Henry's wife. Julie also appears in her cottage putting some books away and cleaning up.*)

RACHEL: Henry, could you help?
HENRY: Sure . . . Be right back. (*He pushes her offstage as Richard watches and then Henry returns.*) Oh, I'm sorry . . . that's my wife, Rachel.
RICHARD: (*He picks up on it.*) I'm sorry that's my wife, Julie. Well, Henry . . . you game for a little game?
HENRY: Little one on one?
RICHARD: Yeah.
HENRY: That might be interesting.
RICHARD: Ten point game . . . winner's ball out . . . got to win by two.
HENRY: It's your court, Rich.
RICHARD: It's your ball, Henry. (*Richard takes off his sweatshirt. The way he takes it off hints strongly that he's taking this game seriously. Seeing him take it off Henry responds in kind . . . and in spirit of the gesture as well. Having taken off his sweatshirt Richard reveals a T-shirt with a large "ADIDAS" written on it. Henry reveals a T-shirt with a large "PUMA" written on it. Both of them take in these signs on their chests with cool smiles of acknowledgement. Richard throws the ball to Henry to take out. Henry starts dribbling.*) Here comes Henry, the ball driving man. (*Henry is dribbling slowly, his back to Richard. Richard guards him closely to say the least . . . Too closely . . . Pesters him . . . Pushes him on his ass with his hand??? And then, suddenly, he reaches around in an obvious foul . . . steals the ball from Henry. Henry pauses thinking it was a foul. And while he pauses Richard drives in for an easy layup.*) One zip. Winner's ball out. (*Richard takes the ball out. Henry's a little off balance by the whole thing. But he decides to be cool. He starts guarding Richard. But Richard doesn't seem to be fond of being guarded. He is backing into Henry the whole way . . . pushing him back . . . and then . . . when Henry finally decides to stand his ground Richard really slams into him . . . knocks him down to the ground and goes in to score an easy layup.*) Two zip.
HENRY: (*Still on ground.*) I think we've had a few fouls here.
RICHARD: Oh yeah . . . funny . . . I don't see any referees around here.
HENRY: Oh, I get it. (*Henry fouls Richard in a flagrant manner and takes ball away from Richard and shoots.*) Two to one. (*They start to get into place again, as the lights come up on the Hennessy cottage and down on the court.*)

## Scene 4

*Hennessy cottage. Julie is dressed in a pair of tight and rather revealing leotards. She is doing yoga exercises . . . listening to a record of instructions.*

RECORD: *Sit back on your heels as in Figure 23. Extend arms out over the knees stretching out the fingers for maximum separation. Lean your torso forward and rolling the eyeballs upwards in your sockets stick out the tongue till it reaches the tip of your chin. Hold for fifteen seconds.*

(*There is a knock on the door. Louder. Julie stops the record. Goes to the door. Opens it. It's Andrew. He looks at her and is startled. Then he laughs. Then he stops laughing.*)

ANDREW: I thought you were naked. Took my breath away.
JULIE: No it didn't. (*Allusion to his breath is made.*)
ANDREW: Been drinking a little . . . not much at all . . . Not what you call heavy drinking . . . not your drinking drinking . . .
JULIE: What do you want, Andrew?
ANDREW: Oh, yes . . . I was wondering if you'd seen my dog.
JULIE: You're drunk. You said you shot your dog last night.
ANDREW: Shoot her I did. And I was going to bury her today. Couldn't bury her last night. It's frightening burying things at night. I should've shot her and buried her in daytime, only I couldn't bear to shoot her in daylight . . . She's got eyes . . . they're blind . . . but they're eyes . . . and blind eyes . . .
JULIE: What are you talking about? I don't know what you're talking about.
ANDREW: My dog. I guess I didn't quite kill her. I guess I just wounded her . . . cause she ain't where she was . . . There was a trail of blood . . . but I lost it . . . that's why I was wondering if you'd seen her cause the trail seemed to be heading toward this area . . . (*At this instant Richard appears at the back door. Pushes Andrew aside. Richard is bleeding. His face is covered with blood. He has his head tilted back and is holding his hand to his nose. Henry is following him. Henry looks a little apologetic.*)
RICHARD: I'm alright. Just a little accident. My nose ran into Henry's elbow . . . entirely my nose's fault . . . I'll be fine as soon as I survive. (*He heads toward the bathroom. Goes in.*)
HENRY: (*To Julie.*) I'm really sorry.
ANDREW: I don't care. It's not my nose.
HENRY: I was speaking to Mrs. Hennessy.
ANDREW: It's not her nose either. Doesn't she look nude.
JULIE: You'd better leave now, Andrew.
ANDREW: Oh, I get the picture. (*Starts to leave. Stops. Fiddles with the lock.*) A child could break this lock. And you should peek through the curtains before you let someone in. Enjoy yourselves. (*Laughs and leaves. His*

*departure makes Julie much more self-conscious about her leotards. Henry doesn't hide the way he looks at her.*)

HENRY: This is some way to meet a neighbor! My name's Henry Jefferson.

JULIE: Yes . . . I mean I recognized you. (*Richard appears in the doorway and looks at them. They don't see him.*) You've done some theatre work, haven't you?

HENRY: Just enough to help me break into TV commercials. (*He laughs a little.*)

JULIE: I wish Rich had that attitude. This is going to sound very strange . . . but I wonder if you'd tell me who you have for an agent. (*Richard picks this moment to interrupt.*)

RICHARD: (*He crosses between them.*) The kid's back! Half time's over . . . full speed ahead.

HENRY: I don't think we better play any more.

RICHARD: My nose is fine . . . what's left of it.

HENRY: But my knees are not.

RICHARD: Then we resume tomorrow . . . I never quit when I'm ahead.

HENRY: Tomorrow it is. (*Starts to leave.*) You folks want to drop by tonight for a drink or something?

RICHARD: Sure. I'd love to.

HENRY: Great. Any time . . . And . . . sorry . . . it really was an accident.

RICHARD: Forget it. It's blood under the bridge so to speak. You got me by accident . . . I'll get you back by accident. (*He waves to Henry. Henry leaves. Closes door.*) Accident my ass. Bastard hit me on purpose. I swear . . . if I had a gun I would have shot him . . . shit. It's bleeding again. (*He heads for the bedroom. Julie follows.*)

JULIE: We really don't have to go tonight.

RICHARD: Oh, we'll go, we'll go. (*They both disappear inside the bedroom. Lights fade on the cottage and up on the pier. Blackout.*)

## Scene 5

*Dusk. By the pier. Randy and Debbie. Debbie enters first from the boathouse, followed by Randy, who takes the paint brush she is hiding. He carries a pail.*

RANDY: I can still smell that perfume on you.

DEBBIE: It's very expensive. And it lasts a long time.

RANDY: It smells like you just put it on. You didn't steal it, did you?

DEBBIE: Of course not. Do I look like a thief? (*Debbie sits on pier.*)

RANDY: No, but then those guys don't look like the types to play ball together, either. I hid behind the bushes and watched them play this morning. They stink. Not only that, they don't even know the rules. (*Randy begins to paint rudder and tiller.*)

DEBBIE: Successul people make their own rules.

RANDY: Oh yeah, what's so successful about them?

DEBBIE: If you lived in New York you'd know. I saw both of them on television.

RANDY: I saw Donald Duck on television too.

DEBBIE: It certainly wouldn't hurt to get to know them better. In New York it's who you know . . . that's how you get the good jobs. (*Randy laughs.*) What's so funny?

RANDY: You talking about jobs. When I used to talk about them you made fun of me. I guess I'm making fun of you now.

DEBBIE: It's easy for you. You're living off your uncle.

RANDY: (*He crosses to boathouse.*) Everybody lives off somebody. Uncle will die.

DEBBIE: And then what'll you do?

RANDY: I'll rent the cottages he bought up. I'll be a landlord. (*Re-enters with rag cleaning his hands.*)

DEBBIE: I thought you said everybody got frightened off.

RANDY: They're starting to trickle back.

DEBBIE: The lake is all scummy. The cottages are run down.

RANDY: I've learned something about resorts, Debbie. People go to them to complain. It makes going back home easier to take. I'll do all right. Had you married me, Deb, you wouldn't be worrying about money now.

DEBBIE: Who says I'm worried?

RANDY: I watch you when you eat. You eat a lot, Debbie. Just because it's free.

DEBBIE: You're a nice host.

RANDY: I told you. I'm not as sweet as I used to be. I used to think that seeing your breasts was a treat of a lifetime.

DEBBIE: You'd still like to see them.

RANDY: Sure. You always want the toys you didn't get enough of as a kid.

DEBBIE: (*She begins to walk D.S. on the pier.*) That's a horrible way of putting it.

RANDY: That's just how I felt. I even cried when you left.

DEBBIE: You did not.

RANDY: I tried. And you know what I did last summer. I went to New York. And I saw you, Debbie.

DEBBIE: Saw me where?

RANDY: I called your parents and they told me you weren't doing too well in the city. They said I could visit you. Maybe you told them to say that.

DEBBIE: I did not. You're making it all up.

RANDY: (*He stops painting and walks toward her.*) I got your address from them and I went to see you. There was this little entry way and I saw your little mailbox with your little name on it. I even pushed this little button to buzz you but you weren't at home. So I pushed another little button and whoever it was buzzed back to open the door. And then I pushed another one. And they, too, buzzed back to open the door. The people in your building are dying for visitors, it seems. But I didn't go in. Right outside your building there was this car. The door was open and I sat in the car till you came home. I saw you walking, Debbie. And you weren't skipping along in that breezy way of yours. No, you were sort of plodding home. And I saw you open your little mailbox . . . I saw it all, Debbie.

DEBBIE: You're making it all up. All of it. I was probably very tired when you saw me. If you saw me.

RANDY: That's all I was saying. That you looked tired.

DEBBIE: No, you weren't. You were saying something else. (*He goes back to painting.*)

RANDY: That's all, Debbie. It was a very hot day. It's cool here. Even in summer. Damp but cool. And you're getting to look like your old self again. Breezy Debbie. All those girls in school tried to imitate the way you walked but none could. Do you want to get married?

DEBBIE: Is this a proposal or something?

RANDY: No. It's a question. I already proposed once and you turned me down. It's your turn now.

DEBBIE: So you can say no and get even.

RANDY: Maybe I won't say "no."

DEBBIE: I didn't come here to make decisions, Randy. I've been on my own for two years now and it wears you out. Being the one who's responsible for everything. Making decisions for everything. I just want to rest and have things happen like they used to. (*She gets up suddenly and starts to leave.*) I think I'll go back to the city tomorrow.

RANDY: I'll ask you to stay if you want. (*She exits. He picks up bucket and follows her.*)

## Scene 6

*Richard and Julie enter through Jefferson's cottage. Richard says "goodnight, and thank you." Julie enters their cottage and sits on sofa. Richard follows and turns on the light.*

RICHARD: That was certainly a lovely little get-together. Made you feel good inside . . . nice and warm . . . like open heart surgery.

JULIE: It's just . . . Goddammit, I was looking forward to a little get-together with another woman. If anything, I was worried you and Henry might go at it . . . instead . . . I still don't know what got into her. It's not funny.

RICHARD: Hell, I thought it was hilarious. The way Rachel looked at us when we came in. Even her hair was frowning. And there you were: a bottle of wine in your hand and a smile on your face: Hi, we're the people next door. So what, Rachel says.

JULIE: I couldn't believe it. I was stunned.

RICHARD: So were we all. Things got so silent you could hear a jaw drop. And then you remember the wine. That should break the ice! How about some cold duck, you say. Rachel loves cold duck, Henry says. I hate cold duck, Rachel says.

JULIE: She's got to be crazy.

RICHARD: Damn right she's crazy. That's why I couldn't understand why you kept trying to ingratiate yourself. Poor Henry. He's stuck with that . . . But you, I mean you really tried. You started making plans with Rachel . . . let's all of us get together in the city . . . for a concert . . . for a show . . . for a movie . . . You were going on like a human ticketron.

JULIE: I know. I know. She just made me feel so nervous . . . like the whole thing was my fault.

RICHARD: "The Cold Duck's getting warm," you finally said. "I don't care if the damn duck dies." Rachel snaps back and tries to get away from you. She shifts her wheelchair into overdrive . . . only your shirt gets caught in the damn thing and she's pulling you along with her and you're trying ever so nicely not to embarrass her and free yourself at the same time. And that somehow summed it up. You just tried too hard, honey, that's all.

JULIE: I know I tried too hard. I've been doing that lately and I don't know why. I'm almost desperate to make friends out of strangers.

RICHARD: It's not quite that bad.

JULIE: Sure it is. Especially when you're around. I so much want to have people like me in front of you.

RICHARD: You don't have to prove anything to me, Julie.

JULIE: It's not to prove . . . it's just that . . . you know . . . we all think we have some hidden marvelous side to us . . . and if only the atmosphere were right everybody would see it.

RICHARD: I see enough.

JULIE: But I think there's more to me than you see.

RICHARD: The real Julie Hennessy! Who is she? Does anyone really know?

JULIE: I'm serious, dammit.

RICHARD: We didn't come up here to be serious, dammit.

JULIE: Well, maybe I did.

RICHARD: So-o you're the one with the ulterior motives.

JULIE: I just feel a need to change. I don't know where I fit in today. I remember watching my mother when I was small. Her whole day seemed orchestrated like a fancy waltz and she just danced her way through the day. She knew what was expected of her. She had a framework.

RICHARD: But that world is gone, Julie.

JULIE: That's what everyone keeps saying. It's all gone and we're all so goddamn free to flounder about. I just wish there was something. This will sound silly but if nothing else I wish I believed in sin.

RICHARD: In the orphanage where I grew up this Sister Regina talked about sins all the time. We didn't get along. I kept snickering and making cracks and she kept threatening to curse me for being a heathen. Oh, my head was full of these wonderful Cecil B. DeMille images of what it would be like to be cursed . . . and I kept going after her until finally the poor woman lost all control and jumped to her feet, and mustering all the majesty the moment allowed, she thundered at me: I CURSE YOU! I stood there trembling . . . waiting for the roof and the sky to open up and for God to appear to finish the job . . . but . . . nothing happened. I started crying. The other kids in the room thought it was because I was afraid. It was disappointment. We became good friends. We shared a secret. There was no God. No sin.

JULIE: If there's no God, my mother used to say, then we're all devils.

RICHARD: For once I think your mother is right.

(*A noise makes both of them pause. It's a strange, soft noise . . . a soft whining and then added to it something like scratching on the back door. It is not a sound to make one start or scream . . . but it is the type of noise in the night that the more you listen to it the more uncomfortable it seems. Richard walks slowly toward the door . . . he gestures Julie to stay back, but she follows him. He opens the door. And then he turns the porch light on and as he does, Julie screams.*)

JULIE: What's that? (*Crosses to U.S. and looks out.*) It must be Andrew's dog.

RICHARD: I thought he said he killed it. God . . . it's bleeding all over the place.

JULIE: It's coming in. Don't let it come in, Rich. Oh, it's crying . . . I can't bear it. Do something, Rich.

RICHARD: Do what?

JULIE: Do something. I can't bear it. (*She starts screaming . . . crying.*)

RICHARD: Stop screaming. Stop it. Do you hear me. Stop it.

JULIE: Its stomach is all coming out. Finish it off or something. Finish it off, Richard. I can't bear it. (*She continues screaming as if to cover up any sound the wounded animal might be making.*)

RICHARD: I can't think when you do that. I can't think, damn you. I can't think. Shut up! Shut up!

JULIE: You're just standing there! You're just standing there, Richard.

(*Richard cannot tolerate her screaming. He reaches suddenly for the gun in its hiding place. Pulls it out and without pausing, he steps outside and fires into the dog. It's all very sudden and fast. He shuts the door.*) Is she dead?

RICHARD: Yes.

JULIE: I just couldn't bear to see her suffer like that. Oh, God, she probably came here to hide from Andrew.

RICHARD: Stop saying "she." It's a dog. (*There is a knock on the door and then the door opens. It's Henry. He looks at the dead dog in the doorway and then at the gun in Richard's hand.*)

HENRY: Sorry to burst in like this . . . but I heard the shots. Is everything all right?

RICHARD: Yeah, everything's fine.

HENRY: (*To Julie.*) Some evening, eh? Well . . . good night then.

RICHARD: Good night, Henry. (*Henry leaves. Richard feels awkward with the gun in his hand. Doesn't know where to put it. Sticks it into his jacket pocket.*)

JULIE: You never told me you had a gun.

RICHARD: The subject never came up.

JULIE: What other subjects never came up?

RICHARD: Please, honey. I'm very upset. You seemed so damned afraid of coming up here that some of your fear rubbed off on me. So I bought this stupid thing for protection. I didn't want to tell you. I never thought there would be a reason. I've never killed anything before. (*He sits down, looking shaken by what he has done. Julie comes up to him.*)

JULIE: I'm sorry. I lost my head screaming like that. Let's go to bed.

RICHARD: In a second. I just want to calm down a bit. (*She leaves for the bedroom. As soon as she does there is a change in Richard. He takes the gun from his pocket and looks at it. He stands up. He throws the gun in the air and catches it. Then he pauses. Sees a bright yellow towel draped over the chair. Picks up the towel and wraps the gun into it. And then he pulls off the towel revealing the gun as if he were surprising somebody. Lights dim around him.*)

## Scene 7

*Basketball court. Henry and Debbie. Henry has the ball in his hands.*

HENRY: It all depends. If the comercial runs a long time then I get a lot of residuals. If it doesn't it's just the small flat fee.

DEBBIE: I know a girl in the city. And her sister's a production assistant.

HENRY: Yes?

DEBBIE: Is it hard to get a job like that?

HENRY: It all depends on who you know.

DEBBIE: That's just it. I don't know many people.

HENRY: All it takes is one or two.

DEBBIE: I know one or two . . . but they're not the ones. (*Richard comes toward them, carrying a rolled-up yellow towel. Henry passes him the ball.*)

HENRY: Rich, Debbie here would like to be a production assistant.

RICHARD: That's a good start. Remember that girl, Michele something?

HENRY: Oh, right. We got her a job as a production assistant.

RICHARD: And she went on to bigger and better things. And she wasn't half as pretty as Debbie here.

HENRY: That's right. (*Randy appears at U.R.*)

RANDY: Debbie. Want to go on that walk now?

DEBBIE: Oh, all right. See you guys later. (*She exits with Randy.*)

HENRY: (*Smiles.*) Guy . . . I haven't been called a guy in years.

RICHARD: My wife used to wear the same perfume she had on. (*For a moment he seems lost in the memory and then, quite consciously, he pulls himself out of it. He dribbles the ball. He drives for the basket and then suddenly passes it to Henry.*) West to Baylor. (*Henry dribbles and passes it back to Richard.*)

HENRY: Baylor to West.

RICHARD: Mr. Clutch with the touch. (*Richard dribbles. Stops a la West . . . jumps . . . passes it suddenly to Henry who whips it behind his back and back to Richard, who in turn does the same thing and back to Henry. A frenzy of passing artistry ensues . . . or at least attempted artistry . . . Henry, keeping up the chatter: "Feed me . . . feed me . . . over here . . . feed me . . . " The passing continues until a crescendo is reached and both of them are exhausted, ending up with either of them actually shooting the ball and missing.*)

HENRY: Man, if we could only shoot the way we can pass . . .

RICHARD: We wouldn't be playing the passing game.

HENRY: Sometimes when nobody's around . . . I can hit from anywhere.

RICHARD: No shit. And sometimes when nobody's around I can do King Lear playing all the parts and at the same time being a critic in the audience writing a rave review of my performance AND . . . through a time warp watching all the people I hate reading the raves I got.

HENRY: Oh, man, you're good. Good and warped.

RICHARD: Yes, I am, Henry. (*Something about the way he says this makes Henry want to get back to basketball. He takes the ball.*)

HENRY: I had one ambition when I was a kid.

RICHARD: And I bet it wasn't to grow up to be the best husband there is.

HENRY: It had to do with basketball.

RICHARD: Oh yeah, let me guess . . . Oh, there is such a look in your eye, Sir Henry, as if to hint the ashes of a dream lie there. Was it some lofty goal? To fly perhaps? To soar . . . and then to slam dunk that ball! Woosh!

HENRY: You got it. The ol' stuff shot! (*Richard makes a hoop from his arms and Henry dribbles a few times and then "slam dunks" the ball in the "hoop." As soon as this is done they reverse their roles and Richard does the stuff shot into Henry's arms. Perhaps they have another round . . . perhaps not . . . The crucial element is that Henry is interested in keeping it going but Richard stops suddenly. Fakes Henry out. Just as he's about to dunk the ball into the hoop Richard made out of his arms, Richard pulls his arms aside and stops.*)

RICHARD: I'm thinking, Henry. And you know what I'm thinking. I'm thinking if there's a will, Henry, there's a way, and if there's a way to fulfill our secret ambitions, it must be pursued. (*Henry is holding the ball. Richard picks up the rolled-up towel. Wipes forehead with it and then lets it unroll, but holds on to it.*)

HENRY: What are you getting at, Rich?

RICHARD: I know how we can dunk the ball. (*Henry laughs.*)

HENRY: Sure. Lower this rim. (*His reply was meant to be a joke but he realizes that his joke is Richard's plan. His laugh changes and turns into a comment on such a plan.*) You're kidding. Oh, wow. You got to be kidding. C'mon, we're not that hard up.

RICHARD: Sure we are. Besides, who says it's got to be at that height anyway. Did God put it there? Did we vote on it? Is it a natural phenomenon?

HENRY: No, but . . .

RICHARD: But what?

HENRY: It's real world. You don't mess with that. I mean, what's the point of having standards if you . . .

RICHARD: (*Interrupts.*) We can set our own standards.

HENRY: No.

RICHARD: C'mon. Let's do it.

HENRY: I said "no." (*Richard drops the towel, presses the "gun" into Henry's stomach. We do not see the gun. Henry's back obscures it. Henry reacts to it.*)

RICHARD: Now we're going to do as I say or I'll shoot, dammit.

HENRY: Take it easy, man. Take it easy. Put that thing away.

RICHARD: Standards. You've got a lot of goddamn nerve to use that word after all the ass kissing you've been doing. Tell me. How did you get all those jobs? It sure as hell isn't because of your talent now, is it? You've made life rough for me, you know that.

HENRY: I don't know what you're talking about, man!

RICHARD: Don't give me that "man" stuff. I told you I'd get even. You got me "by accident." Well, now I'm going to get you by accident.

HENRY: Don't do it.

RICHARD: Goodbye, Henry. (*Richard shoots. Henry falls. Only now do we realize that Richard had a transistor radio in his hand. The "blast" of music was the bullet. Both of them are amused by the play. Henry gets up laughing.*)

HENRY: Now why would you want to play a silly game like that?

RICHARD: To see if you'd play along. Now, c'mon. How about the rim?

(*Henry smiles.*)

HENRY: You're rushing me. Maybe tomorrow. I'd like to sleep on it.

RICHARD: Fair enough. Good night.

HENRY: See you in the morning. (*Neither of them leave.*)

RICHARD: (*Yawning.*) 'Morning, Henry. Sleep well?

HENRY: Yes. Fine. (*The words "Yes, Fine" are the go-ahead for the lowering of the rim. Richard picks up on it instantly.*)

RICHARD: Won't take a second. (*Henry holds the ball. Richard gets a bench, climbs up and begins to loosen the rim. Henry is trying to shake some nerves out of himself. Loosen up.*)

HENRY: I can't understand it. I'm getting goosebumps just thinking about it.

RICHARD: Don't worry. Nobody's looking. There's no witnesses.

HENRY: What about you?

RICHARD: I'm a co-conspirator. (*The rim is lowered. Henry is still hesistant.*)

HENRY: Amazing. It feels like we're changing the Constitution or something.

RICHARD: C'mon. Over the rim.

HENRY: Hell with it. Over the rim it is. Feed me. (*He throws the ball to Richard. Richard passes it back to him. Henry catches it on the run. He drives. He cries out loudly as he stuffs the ball down the hole. Blackout.*)

# ACT II

## Scene 1

*The pier by the lake. Julie is sitting on the pier. Her jeans are rolled up above her knees and she's applying suntan lotion to them. Andrew pushes Rachel in her wheelchair onto the pier. He's got his shotgun slung over his shoulder. Julie turns to look at Rachel and then she turns away.*

RACHEL: Sorry. I didn't mean to intrude.

JULIE: It's common property.

ANDREW: Like hell it is. It's my property. I suppose you women want to sunbathe in the nude. Don't mind me if you see me looking at you from afar. I can't see from far but I do enjoy the thought that I'm missing something. Guess I'll go fishing.

JULIE: With a shotgun.

ANDREW: Yes ma'am, this is a foul lake. Any fish that could survive in this lake I wouldn't want to take out alive. Enjoy yourselves. (*He leaves.*)

RACHEL: Isn't that them on the other side?

JULIE: Who?

RACHEL: Richard and Henry. (*Rachel points. Julie looks.*)

JULIE: Yes, I think it is.

RACHEL: Did you come down to keep an eye on them?

JULIE: No, I didn't even know they were there till you . . .

RACHEL: (*Interrupts.*) Look at them. Walking along the shore like a couple of lovers. There they go. Pushing each other in the water. Rambunctious rascals. Certainly strikes me as odd.

JULIE: What's that?

RACHEL: How quickly they became inseparable.

JULIE: I guess men have an easier time making friends.

RACHEL: I bet they're talking about us.

JULIE: We're talking about them.

RACHEL: We're just beginning. They've been at it for a while.

JULIE: I'm sorry but I find it difficult to . . . to chat with you after last night. It seems like one of us should apologize.

RACHEL: It won't be me. You came at a very bad time and I was glad to see you go. God, you danced in there with your cold duck like it was a sorority rush. Oh, it's so nice to have a neighbor. Oh, what a lovely cabin. Oh, we really must get together.

JULIE: I was just trying to be friendly.

RACHEL: The thing is, everybody is trying it all of a sudden. Henry's being friendly as hell. Usually we just sit in silence and all of a sudden . . . well . . . it's like he's trying to entertain me. Diversions.

JULIE: People change.

RACHEL: So do warts and moles.

JULIE: That's a cruel thing to say.

RACHEL: Would you rather we talked about concerts and shows and decorating hints.

JULIE: I didn't prepare an agenda. And I don't like being lectured to by . . . somebody like you.

RACHEL: You mean a cripple?

JULIE: You know damn well that's not what I meant.

RACHEL: But it does make it easier to dismiss what I say. If she's so damn smart why can't she walk?

JULIE: How the hell did you become like that?

RACHEL: You mean a cripple?

JULIE: I mean nothing of the sort. (*Almost without realizing it, Julie is rolling down her jeans.*)

RACHEL: Oh, don't hide your legs on my account. No pity, please.

JULIE: And why not? What is wrong with pity?

RACHEL: I don't need it. It's diverting.

JULIE: It's a fine human feeling.

RACHEL: This is no time to be human.

JULIE: I've heard that before.

RACHEL: Did you know that people were killed up here?

JULIE: Of course, I knew.

RACHEL: Aren't you frightened?

JULIE: Yes, a little.

RACHEL: And still you came?

JULIE: I am here.

RACHEL: And whose idea was it to come here? Yours or Richard's?

JULIE: Mine.

RACHEL: In my case it was Henry's.

JULIE: That's your affair.

RACHEL: No, it's Henry's affair.

JULIE: Then take it up with him.

RACHEL: Since he's taking it up with Richard I thought I'd take it up with you.

JULIE: (*She crosses to Rachel.*) Look . . . you seem to have something on your mind and I'm tired of trying to guess what it is.

RACHEL: If you want I'll tell you. Henry tried to kill me.

JULIE: I suppose you expect me to believe that.

RACHEL: I wasn't always like this.

JULIE: No, of course not. Your husband made you the way you are.

RACHEL: That's right. And now he doesn't like to be reminded of it.

JULIE: Every woman I've met lately has worked out some elaborate excuse for being the way she is. To hear them talk they were all once warm and giving people and then something happened. And it's never their fault. No. It's not that they're now cold and dead and hostile, not at all, it's just a reaction to their environment. Believe me, your excuse, as preposterous as it sounds, is no worse than the others I've heard. The thing is I'm tired of excuses. I'm tired of trying to deal with them. I'm tired of women trying to initiate me into a world I want no part of.

RACHEL: That still doesn't alter the fact that what I said was true. Henry tried to kill me.

JULIE: (*Crosses center.*) You're a liar. Everything you say is a lie. (*She stands up.*)

RACHEL: But why should it upset you that a strange woman you've chanced to meet and never have to see again unless you want to is a liar? Now whose idea was it really to come up here, yours or Richard's? (*Julie begins to walk toward the house as the lights fade to just the rim.*)

## Scene 2

*Hennessy cottage. Evening. Julie and Richard are sitting down at the table, eating dinner.*

JULIE: (*She crosses to table with coffeepot.*) How's the sandwich?

RICHARD: Delicious.

JULIE: (*Crosses back to kitchen.*) My mother's ultimate description of a bad marriage is when you have cold sandwiches for dinner.

RICHARD: Thank God they're cold. Hot sardine sandwiches . . . Mmmm. (*He smiles.*)

JULIE: (*Sits at table.*) When we get back to the city I'm going to take some cooking lessons.

RICHARD: I thought you took some already and didn't like the whole thing.

JULIE: That was the overnight school of cooking. Everything had to be left overnight to do something. Try having a good night's sleep if you're worrying that your meat is not marinating. (*Pause.*) They have schools and lessons for everything now. Seminars for sex. For religion. For married women. For single women. For divorced women. Different age groups. How to relax. How to intimidate. I saw a test you can take to see if you have a true orgasm or a false one. And a book that tells you how to have multiple orgasms. They're the thing to have. What would we all do if we didn't have problems?

RICHARD: I suppose we'd invent some.

JULIE: Poor world.

RICHARD: It's all right.

JULIE: Wouldn't trade it for anything.

RICHARD: What else did Rachel have to say?

JULIE: About what?

RICHARD: I don't know. I saw you two on the pier for quite some time.

JULIE: And we saw you two by the lake.

RICHARD: Henry and I just talked shop.

JULIE: So did Rachel and I. Shop in our case means husbands.

RICHARD: I guess I'm just surprised that after what she said you still stayed there and listened to her.

JULIE: She saved that for the last.

RICHARD: The woman sounds unhinged. Henry tried to kill her?

JULIE: That's what she said.

RICHARD: I think you should stay away from her. Either she's nuts or she's just toying with you.

JULIE: What does Henry have to say about her?

RICHARD: Subject never came up. (*Richard crosses to kitchen; gets juice.*)

JULIE: You just talk shop all this time.

RICHARD: What else?

JULIE: I thought you hated to talk shop.

RICHARD: I guess I've changed.

JULIE: That's what I told Rachel. People change. She thinks you two are seeing an awful lot of each other.

RICHARD: She's just jealous. (*Pours juice in glass and returns it to refrigerator.*)

JULIE: So am I. The way you make friends. I wish I could do it.

RICHARD: It's just that Henry's got a lot of contacts. He's working all the time. I've got to get something going. I feel I owe it to you. (*He sits back down.*)

JULIE: That's a strange thing to say.

RICHARD: You had such high hopes for my career.

JULIE: I thought I was just sharing yours.

RICHARD: When I met you I had none.

JULIE: That's not what you said when we met.

RICHARD: That's not what you wanted to hear.

JULIE: Why does it all keep coming back to me?

RICHARD: Because you made me think I could be better than I was.

JULIE: All I did was love you.

RICHARD: Right. And your kind of love has a way of making a man want to be better.

JULIE: That was never my intent.

RICHARD: But the effect is the same. And I'm grateful.

JULIE: I don't want you to feel grateful.

RICHARD: Why not?

JULIE: Because I don't want it. It has nothing to do with me. It's like your making me into some other person.

RICHARD: You made me into another person. And I am grateful. Your standards are higher. And I need that.

JULIE: Standards of what?

RICHARD: Of success. Of my potential. I would love to be able to live up to that image you had of me.

JULIE: All I've ever done is support your hopes in good faith. I know you don't intend to but lately you've been putting me in a strange position where my support seems to have become a burden to you.

RICHARD: How could such a thing be possible?

JULIE: I don't know. It's just a feeling. It's stupid, isn't it?

RICHARD: Very. I think talking to Rachel has upset you. (*He clears his plate to the sink.*)

JULIE: I think you're right. Can we sleep on the sofa tonight?

RICHARD: Sure.

JULIE: I haven't been sleeping too well. Maybe if we sleep in an unofficial place . . . like in our first apartment. We used to fall asleep on the sofa all the time . . .

RICHARD: And you used to wear that perfume. The one you wore when we met. I miss it. (*He exits to bedroom.*)

JULIE: For some reason it made me uncomfortable a few months ago. Maybe I felt it was time for a change. (*Richard is getting ready to go out. He's putting on his basketball outfit.*) You and Henry going out again? (*He is getting ready, ties his shoes, etc.*)

RICHARD: Yeah, we thought we'd have a game under the lights. See what it's like.

JULIE: I guess we've said everything.

RICHARD: What do you mean?

JULIE: I mean what do you say when you've said everything?

RICHARD: I don't understand.

JULIE: I keep having this insane notion. We've had dinner. We've cleared the dishes. Brushed our teeth . . . put the cap back on the tube and we're ready to say something, only there is nothing left to say. And I don't mean nothing meaningful or crap like that . . . I mean nothing.

RICHARD: And then what?

JULIE: And then we do something terrible just so we can talk about it.

RICHARD: Like what?

JULIE: Oh, all kinds of things. I'll cut my finger with a knife . . . so we can talk about it. And as soon as it's healed I'll whack away at my arm so we can chat about that.

RICHARD: I think that does it. I'm going to take you back to the city.

JULIE: When?

RICHARD: Soon.

JULIE: I'd like that, Rich. Why can't we leave tomorrow? (*Henry enters. He's ready to play ball.*)

HENRY: What's keeping you? You want to forfeit the game or what?

RICHARD: I was just coming out. (*Henry bounce-passes the ball to Richard across the cabin floor. Richard catches it. To Julie.*) We won't be long. (*Richard dribbles the ball across the cabin. Henry half-guards him. Richard dribbles around him and out of the cabin. Henry follows. Julie looks after them. They freeze on the court.*)

## Scene 3

*Basketball court. Night. Lights are on in the court. It's a somewhat chilly evening and the chill is reflected in the dress and physical behavior of Henry and Richard. Henry tends to shudder more. A game of some kind is in progress. Either of them could be dribbling while the other guards. There is a difference in the way they move. It's as if they had been liberated slightly from "classic" basketball moves and are improvising their own. There is something strange about their new moves . . . something frightening. A stranger happening to come upon them would think twice about asking to join the game. One of them shoots. Hit or miss, it doesn't matter, the following dialogue applies.*

HENRY: Hold it. Hold it. I'm lost. What the hell's the score?

RICHARD: Let's see . . . it's nine and a half to seven and three quarters.

HENRY: I think we'd better go over the new scoring system again.

RICHARD: Stuff shot—two points. Regular—one point. Hit the backboard—half point. Hit the rim—three-quarter points. Total miss . . . air ball . . . one quarter.

HENRY: Did you just add that last part?

RICHARD: Sure.

HENRY: No such thing as a miss?

RICHARD: Who needs it? It's our game. (*Henry bounces the ball a couple of times. Squeezes it.*)

HENRY: Ball's getting soft.

RICHARD: It's the cold air. Makes the molecules contract.

HENRY: (*Laughs.*) Molecules! You believe in molecules . . . atoms . . . all that stuff?

RICHARD: Not really.

HENRY: I don't either . . . Then how come we go along with it . . .?

RICHARD: Because there are experts who tell us what exists and what doesn't . . . What's what . . . and what's not. Some jerk comes and reads my meter and sends me a bill and I pay. It's called social trust, Henry.

HENRY: Tell me, Rich. You think you're any good? As an actor? I mean, do you know for sure you're good?

RICHARD: I've been told I am.

HENRY: I've been told I am too.

RICHARD: Got set up to think you were great, eh?

HENRY: Got set up alright.

RICHARD: And you never thought you'd be hustling around for commercials and voice-overs, I bet. It must hurt . . . the comedown.

HENRY: No, you know what hurts? The set-up. The build-up. I never asked for it in the first place. I could have been happy doing what I'm doing . . . I could be happy now.

RICHARD: If there weren't any witnesses of your former glory to remind you that you fell for it.

HENRY: Come on. Let's play. (*He stuffs the ball.*)

RICHARD: So . . . if your past is a crime and you have witnesses to the crime . . . what do you do? You try to get rid of the witnesses. Hmmm. Is that why you tried to kill Rachel?

HENRY: How do you know?

RICHARD: Intuition.

HENRY: Intuition, my ass. Rachel must have said something to Julie. She tells people every now and then, knowing it will get back to me. Just to keep me on my toes. (*Henry passes the ball to Richard. They look at each other.*) I was doing a new play and I was lost from the word go. Didn't know what I was doing, so I asked Rachel to come to the rehearsals.

(*Julie begins to wheel Rachel out onto the pier. The men are not aware of the women and vice versa.*)

RACHEL: He wanted something from me. He'd never let me come to rehearsals before—hardly asked me to come. He seemed lost . . . in need of help.

HENRY: I wanted her to tell me the truth . . . that I was making a fool of myself, but no . . . she tells me I'm doing fine.

RACHEL: You're doing fine, I told him. It was a lie but to tell the truth seemed stupid. The man was drowning. So I threw him a life preserver. Something to hold on to. You're doing fine, Henry . . .

HENRY: You're doing fine, Henry. No, she tells me it's the best she's ever seen me. I start doubting my own lack of talent. Hell, maybe I am good. The play opens and the reviews are terrible. The writer's a moron. The director's worse than the writer. The cast sucks. All except me. They love me. Not only love me but get this . . . they "understood" what I was trying to do. Said stuff like how I reached back . . . way back to some primitive dormant force . . . Yeah . . . and I started falling for it. Maybe, I think, maybe I'm one of those instinctive geniuses . . . one of those "primitives" who doesn't know diddly shit but instinctively makes the right choices . . . Rachel comes to every performance and afterwards feeds me all kinds of goodies . . . Like how she's proud of me . . . In awe of my talent . . .

RACHEL: And he was good. He was great. But he didn't trust it because it wasn't all his . . . Because he was helped and might have to be helped again . . .

HENRY: In awe of my talent! Can you believe that. Over and over again she feeds me that stuff . . . night after night until one evening it hit me. The woman's teasing my ass. I could see it in her eyes . . . she had me. I had fallen for the bait and now she had me. And the more I squirmed . . . the more uncomfortable I felt, the more she poured on the hype and the praise . . .

RACHEL: The more he began to doubt himself the more I tried to reassure him. But that's the last thing he wanted to hear. And yet I couldn't stop. I couldn't. He was like an investment. My little lies had helped create him and damn it all . . . I wasn't lying anymore. I couldn't stop.

HENRY: Inflating me with praise . . . slitting me open and stuffing me full of it . . . telling me what's going to happen to my career . . . star by thirty-five . . . stuff like that. Finally, late one night I couldn't take in any more. I ran out of the house and went down to the garage just to sit in the car and hear the engine run . . .

RACHEL: It was a habit of his. He'd get in the car . . . turn on the engine and pretend he was zooming along on the turnpikes . . . Back to Chicago to visit his old buddies . . . But for once I wouldn't let him . . . we had to resolve it . . . I went after him . . .

HENRY: But she wouldn't let me alone even there . . . No . . . she snuck down there after me . . . and I saw her coming toward me . . . In the rear-view mirror I saw her.

RACHEL: He saw me. And as soon as he did he shifted that car in reverse. The back-up lights flashed on.

HENRY: She seemed to be standing right in my way . . . I floored it like a primitive sonovabitch I was supposed to be.

RACHEL: It all happened in a split second or so . . . the lights . . . the noise of the engine . . . but in that split second I grew so weary . . . the whole game we were playing . . . the thought of going upstairs again . . . waiting for him . . . wondering what we would say to each other . . . it was too much . . . The car was coming toward me . . . It was going to rush past me but I felt so weary . . . and those lights somehow sucked me forward . . . a half step forward . . . no, not so much a step as collapse . . . The car hit me.

HENRY: The car hit her. Unfortunately, she lived to tell about it. She told everybody . . . the cop people . . . the hospital people . . . the insurance people . . . told them all it was an accident. I felt kind of slimy smug about the whole thing. You know . . . Got the bitch and got away with it . . .

RACHEL: It really was an accident but in the days that followed I could tell that he didn't want to look upon it as an accident. Do you understand? He wanted to think that it was all his doing. That for that split second in the darkness he had been totally in charge. He wanted to think that he had tried to kill me, and for his sake, yes, for his sake, I went along with it.

HENRY: But in the weeks that followed, bit by bit, look by look, it became very clear to me that she knew it was no accident. That she had once again fed me the bait and once again I swallowed it. She had tricked me into another lie and she once again had the upper hand. She loved it. She's got me where she wants me. She made grass out of my ass and now she just rolls across it in her chair.

RICHARD: And then, let me guess, and then you read that interesting story in the *Times* about all those killings taking place up here and you thought: Hell, why don't I just take Rachel up there, and maybe the killer will be nice enough to take care of her for me. (*He laughs. Henry laughs too.*)

HENRY: It sounds silly as hell but that's exactly why I came.

RICHARD: I know. I know.

HENRY: You too.

RICHARD: Me too.

HENRY: Don't you think they know?

RACHEL: Of course I know what he has in mind and yet . . . I could have refused to come. You could have too. Nobody really forced us to come here and yet there is something that makes me want to see this thing concluded . . . resolved. And there is something else, too. I enjoy the sensation. It makes me a power to be reckoned with. It makes my life seem of greater consequence if it warrants somebody wanting to end it. It's like being wanted, in a way. (*Rachel turns and exits. Julie stands a moment then follows. Richard and Henry exit.*)

# Scene 4

*The Pier. Day. Debbie is wearing a bikini. She is putting suntan lotion on her body. She undoes her top and lies down. Richard and Henry appear. They seem to have just returned from a stroll around the lake. They see Debbie and pause. She does not see or hear them. Richard and Henry exchange looks. Both of them approach Debbie slowly. On tiptoes almost. They split up. One goes on one side of her. One on the other. They sit down next to her and for a second just watch her.*

RICHARD: Anybody home? (*Debbie is startled. Sits up. Her top is ready to fall. She holds it up.*)

DEBBIE: Oh, it's you. Hi.

HENRY: Hi.

RICHARD: Hi. What's that book you're reading?

DEBBIE: Book? I'm not . . .

RICHARD: Just a joke. That's a line guys usually use with girls on the beach.

DEBBIE: Oh, yeah.

RICHARD: Where's your boy friend?

DEBBIE: You mean Randy? Oh, he's not my boy friend. He's just a boy who's a friend. (*She has Henry tie her top for her.*)

HENRY: You see, Rich. I told you there was nothing between her and Randy.

DEBBIE: God, I should hope not.

RICHARD: Actually, that's what we were hoping, too.

DEBBIE: Nothing at all. Zero. I mean . . . if I can't do better than him.

HENRY: I told you, didn't I? Debbie's not your average girl. I've got an eye for such things.

RICHARD: He does. He really does. He's discovered more people. If Henry says somebody has talent . . . he's seldom wrong.

DEBBIE: Talent. I hardly think I have any talent. I mean, maybe I do. I mean, you never know.

HENRY: That's just it. You never do. But somebody else might. (*Henry takes some lotion from her skin and puts it on his.*)

DEBBIE: I know I could be a production assistant. It's just a feeling . . .

RICHARD: Like the feeling you had when you left for the city. A feeling that you have that "something."

DEBBIE: Yes, exactly. Only . . . you know . . . in the city . . you forget what it is. I mean, it's easy to forget.

RICHARD: Tell me about it. I remember my early years. It's hard as hell to make it in the city on your own. You start worrying about everything.

DEBBIE: I'll say you do. I mean . . . it's amazing. The kind of things a person worries about. (*She laughs.*) This is so silly but like I worry about what if I lose my job and can't find another one. You know. Will I starve to death or what. (*She laughs.*) Nobody starves to death but still. Or what if nobody ever calls me. You know. There's got to be somebody who never gets a call. What if it's me. Real silly. (*Henry lies down.*)

RICHARD: You shouldn't have to worry about stuff like that.

DEBBIE: Oh, I know. I mean, I read somewhere that it's just a phase everybody goes through. That made me feel better. (*Laughs.*) But then I started worrying about how long the phase will last. I mean, what if it's some new phase that lasts forever.

RICHARD: That's a real nice perfume you're wearing.

DEBBIE: Oh, thank you. It's just something . . .

RICHARD: Then she changed and stopped wearing it.

DEBBIE: Maybe she got tired of it.

HENRY: You see what I mean about her voice, Rich?

RICHARD: I think you're right again, Henry. Henry thinks you have a very unusual voice.

DEBBIE: Oh, really. I don't know. I mean, I just open my mouth and there it is.

RICHARD: There are people who would pay a lot of money to use a voice like that.

DEBBIE: To say what?

RICHARD: (*Laughs.*) That you prefer one perfume to another. Commercials, you know. Voice-overs.

DEBBIE: I didn't know they bought voices.

RICHARD: They buy everything, don't they, Henry?

HENRY: They sure do. (*Henry takes her hands, stands her up.*) They buy hands . . . legs . . . they buy hair and lips . . . sometimes they buy a whole person and give him another voice and sometimes they let him keep his voice . . .

RICHARD: You have lovely hair. (*Richard takes her barrette out. He fingers her hair.*) Shampoos. Hair conditioners. Hair dryers. Curlers and rollers and tints and frosts.

HENRY: And your hands. (*He picks them up and examines them.*) You have beautiful long fingers. Firm nails. Smooth skin. Hand lotions. Nail polishes.

RICHARD: And all you have to do is get one foot in . . . you have the kind of legs they want. Long and lean. For stockings and hose. Bath oils. Depilatories. Sandals and things. And all you have to do is get one little foot in and it's another world.

DEBBIE: (*Randy enters D.S. on pier.*) The thing is . . . I mean . . . I wouldn't know what to do. (*Henry takes her down to her knees and leans her back.*)

HENRY: It's an instinct. It's not something you know. It's something you have. You just reach back for it.

RICHARD: Potential, that's all you need. Plus somebody to have faith in you. To support you. To remind you that you're better than you think. Your face alone, Debbie, is enough. (*Richard kisses her. As Henry begins to pull open her legs, Richard gets in between. His finger moves gently across her face.*) Eyebrow liners. Mascara. Make-up foundations. Blushers. Skin cleansers. Facial creams. Lipsticks. All kinds of lipsticks. Perfumes. (*Lights fade as Richard gets on top of Debbie. The last thing we see is Randy looking on.*)

## Scene 5

*Hennessy cottage. Noon. Knocking is heard, as the lights come up. Julie is gathering up pillows and placing the blanket and pillows to sleep. Andrew appears at the back door. Looks through the curtains. Tries to open the door. It's closed. He knocks. Julie peeks through the curtain at Andrew. Not happy to see him. Opens the door.*

JULIE: What can I do for you, Andrew? (*Andrew is amused.*)

ANDREW: That's just what I was going to say. I was going to say . . . Hello, what can I do for you, Mrs. Hennessy. Had it all prepared in my head. It was a toss-up between using, "What can I do for you?" and, "Top of the morning to you," and I opted for, "What can I do for you?" because it seemed more professional and to the point.

JULIE: What is the point, Andrew? Why are you here?

ANDREW: I'm here because you called me on the telephone.

JULIE: But that was last night. You see . . . when I called . . . I thought I saw somebody . . .

ANDREW: Why the hell didn't you say so? I mean . . . you just ring up . . . I pick up and say, "Andrew here" . . . and you just mutter, "Excuse me," and hang up. So I dropped by to see why you called me.

JULIE: I just wanted to make sure . . . (*Stops.*)

ANDREW: (*Picks up.*) Oh, I get it. You thought it was me that was snooping around so you called to check up on me. Well . . . I was at home . . . so it wasn't me . . . which can only mean it was somebody else.

JULIE: I'm really not sure I saw anybody.

ANDREW: If you'd like I could resume making my rounds . . . keep an eye on the place.

JULIE: I didn't know you stopped.

ANDREW: I'm just a private security guard and I take my orders from my clients . . . Your husband said not to come around any more while you're up here. Said I made you nervous.

JULIE: You did.

ANDREW: But I don't anymore?

JULIE: I guess not.

ANDREW: So, shall I resume . . .?

JULIE: Yes. Only don't tell Richard.

ANDREW: Oh, I make him nervous too? Well, I'm glad. I've got a grudge against that man. He's a strange fellow . . . He and that Blackie . . . Saw them swimming in the lake . . . Only reason I can see anybody swimming in that lake is if they want to get dirty. Well . . . Top of the morning to you, Mrs. Hennessy. I know it's not morning but what the hell . . . (*He leaves. Lights go down in the cottage and up on the pier.*)

## Scene 6

*Night. The pier. Richard and Henry have swum and are now "sun-bathing."*

RICHARD: So Henry, want to go for another swim?

HENRY: No. I know why you're a better swimmer than I. They did these tests where it was proven that blacks just don't float as well as whites. In short, we're a race of heavy dudes.

RICHARD: So what do you want to do, Henry?

HENRY: I don't know, Rich. What do you want to do?

RICHARD: I dunno Marty, whaddayou wanna do? Wanna go see a movie or something?

HENRY: What movie?

RICHARD: "The lady in the cottage." We could peek in on the wives and see what they're doing. They do things when they think nobody's looking.

HENRY: I know. I saw Rachel crying once. But then it felt like she knew I was spying on her and did it for my benefit. I can't tell with her. She's got eyes in the back of my head.

RICHARD: I walked into my apartment once and overheard Julie on the telephone . . . she was trying to call up the orphanage where I grew up.

HENRY: Checking up on you.

RICHARD: Yes.

HENRY: I still don't get it. Why would you ever want to make up all that stuff.

RICHARD: Because . . . because, because when I first saw her, Henry, she seemed like some wide-eyed angel who had plopped down from heaven to this cocktail party. There she stood . . . oh, she seemed so spanking sparkling new and unsoiled that I thought I'd love to be like that myself. That it could rub off. I wanted to make a fresh start and share with her something I had never shared with anyone else before. But there was nothing new I could tell her. So I . . . I started making up things . . . a love song to court her with. I created an orphanage where I grew up and populated it with these friends, Aldo and Tee-bone and the rest, who served as mouthpieces for words I was either ashamed or afraid to say on my own. Oh, they were lovely words, Henry. Full of poetry and pathos and unhesitating revelations . . . and I courted her with them. Had she been different she would have caught me at the start. But she was as trusting and openhearted as I made myself out to be . . . and the person she saw in me was far better than the person I really was. It was all based on a lie but in time, I thought, I could recreate myself and become as free and giving as that ghost of the orphanage I had created. It seemed possible. I tried but it got to be so hard. Keeping the ghost alive. Keeping him fed. He turned into a vampire who sucked my soul and imagination dry just to keep going . . . and my life became like some ugly scar that I had to hide. I want to rip off my mask and tell her: Look, Julie, look . . . here I am. But I can't. It would almost be more cruel to do that than . . . I just can't.

HENRY: Oh, man, we've got ourselves in one helluva mess, Rich. So what do we do now?

RICHARD: I don't know, Marty. Whaddayah wanna do? (*He passes the gun to Henry.*)

HENRY: How long have you had this?

RICHARD: A few months.

HENRY: And do you think you could use it?

RICHARD: I already have.

HENRY: But that was on a dog.

RICHARD: Not when I did it it wasn't.

## Scene 7

*Basketball court. Night. Debbie and Randy enter talking.*

DEBBIE: I don't know why you keep asking me to tell you when I've already told you everything. I ran and told you right after it happened. The two of them forced me. They held me down and raped me.

RANDY: And you ran and told me right after it happened.

DEBBIE: No, not right after it happened. I had to think. I was afraid. I didn't know what to do.

RANDY: So you thought and you thought and you thought it all over and decided it was rape.

DEBBIE: Of course it was rape. I didn't have to think or decide about that. Why do you say things like that? Don't you believe me?

RANDY: I'm just trying to understand you, Debbie. It's very important that I understand everything.

DEBBIE: What is there to understand?

RANDY: The way you make decisions, Debbie.

DEBBIE: The only decision I made was telling you what happened.

RANDY: Yes, but you waited. And waiting's a decision. I wonder what you thought while you waited.

DEBBIE: What does it matter? It seems that what really matters is that I was raped by the two of them.

RANDY: I've never seen you so angry.

DEBBIE: Of course I'm angry. A thing like that. The bastards. You'd think you'd be angry too.

RANDY: Oh, I'm getting there, Debbie. And they forced you. They held you down and forced you.

DEBBIE: Of course they forced me. What do you think?

RANDY: I wasn't there, Debbie. I don't know what to think. And you called for help?

DEBBIE: I told you I did.

RANDY: Did you shout: Help! Help! Or did you call my name?

DEBBIE: God, how do you expect me to remember . . . I . . . I called your name, I think.

RANDY: Randy! Randy! Is that how you called?

DEBBIE: Yes.

RANDY: Randy? Randy?

DEBBIE: Yes, Randy, Randy.

RANDY: I wish I'd heard you. Had I only heard you calling my name I would have saved you. But then, maybe it's a good thing I didn't. I would have got real angry. I might have hurt them.

DEBBIE: They should be hurt, dammit. They hurt me. They tricked me.

RANDY: Tricked. Not forced?

DEBBIE: Of course they forced me. But they tricked me. I didn't know what they had in mind when they came there. They lied.

RANDY: If there's one thing I hate it's that. Liars. And so they raped you?

DEBBIE: How many times do I have to tell you? (*Richard enters, takes off his outer clothes and gets under the covers. Julie follows.*)

RANDY: Just a few more so there's no mistake. I mean, each time I made love to you, Debbie, each time it was like a rape. You made it seem like rape. It wasn't like that, was it?

DEBBIE: My God, do I have to repeat everything ten times!?

RANDY: We all have our own way of making decisions, Debbie. You have your way. I have mine. My way is to hear it over and over again. Because each time you tell me how you were raped, I get a little meaner . . . and when I get mean enough, then I will decide what to do.

DEBBIE: It certainly is taking you a long time.

RANDY: I'm almost there, Debbie. Almost there. (*Randy exits.*)

DEBBIE: Randy, Randy. (*She calls after him, and exits.*)

## Scene 8

*Everything is the same except that time has passed. It is nearly morning. Richard and Julie seem to be asleep. Richard's arm is hanging off the bed toward the floor. Julie sits up slowly. She looks at Richard.*

JULIE: Richard . . . are you awake? (*We see his eyes open and his hand, neither of which she can see, move as a signal that he is awake. The rest of him does not move. She waits a second for a reply.*) I think you are awake but you don't have to say anything. You can pretend you're asleep . . . You can pretend, if you want, that I am a dream you are having . . . it might be better that way because I seem to be unable to say what I want to say when you are looking at me . . . your eyes squint ever so slightly when you look at me . . . as if you were taking aim at my words . . . and all I can do is squirm under your stare and camouflage myself. It's exhausting me, Richard. There is a beautiful lie dying inside both of us and it is not in my power to counteract what's happening. It takes energy to break out of this pattern and I just don't have it on my own, Richard. All I seem to want now, my one desire, is to compress all of it . . . all the meals I'll have . . . all the periods, all the lovemaking and the baths and the looks out of the window . . . just compress all of them and get them over with . . . I try. Every morning I want to start anew. I open my eyes and it feels within my power to do so . . . and then I see my slip draped over a chair . . . something sticking out of a drawer . . . my wrist watch is waiting for my wrist, and by the time I put it on it's too late. All these thoughts I am told are not real. I am told there is no soul. I am told there is no God. There are only glands secreting . . . and even the little shred of unhappiness that I thought I could claim as my own . . . even that . . . I am told is nothing more than a case of glands . . . and hormones . . . secreting or undersecreting. I am more than fluids, Richard . . . more . . . I am wounded, I feel, and life is trickling out of me and your lies . . . yes, I know about them . . . your lies will not let the wound heal. I could be a glorious woman. There is so much that is beautiful in me. I beg you, don't keep killing me like this. Let me live. Richard? (*There is only so much as a split second pause and then the alarm clock rings. Richard sits up as if startled from his sleep. Shuts off the alarm clock. He begins to get dressed.*)

RICHARD: Sleep well, Honey. (*He exits to the basketball court.*)

## Scene 9

*Basketball court. Day. Henry is standing at the free throw line. He's taking careful aim. Shoots. Hit or miss, the ball finally lands on the court and hardly bounces at all. It needs air. Richard appears. He walks toward Henry. Henry is a little nervous. Half whisper.*

HENRY: Morning, Rich.

RICHARD: Good morning, Henry.

HENRY: Rachel's been in the window for the last hour. She just looks out at me. Look at her.

RICHARD: You don't have to whisper. They can't hear us.

HENRY: I have a feeling they can hear every word.

RICHARD: Just your imagination.

HENRY: I have a feeling they can hear that too.

RICHARD: (*Picks up the ball and "palms" it.*) I have stuffed the ball . . . and I have palmed it . . . my life is full. (*Holding the ball in one hand, he fake-throws it to Henry.*) It's got to be done soon.

HENRY: I know.

RICHARD: The set-up is getting set up again. Julie will undermine my resolve if it's not done soon.

HENRY: I know. Rachel's at it too. She's telling me how we can make a fresh start . . . forget the past . . . Julie saying that?

RICHARD: Yes.

HENRY: And do you think it's possible?

RICHARD: No.

HENRY: You sure?

RICHARD: Yes.

HENRY: I need you to keep talking.

RICHARD: I just see more lies ahead. Mine. Hers. Ours. I see myself getting older and the more shuffle-stepped I get . . . the more stooped-shouldered and weak-kneed I become, the more she'll tell me, because she knows I'll want to hear it, the more she'll tell me that I'm as vital as ever, no, even more so, that I've improved with age, and wanting to hear such words from a beautiful woman, the more I'll pretend that she too is what she's pretending I am. And we will slosh in that dirty tub of lies until I die and I'll never know . . . not once . . . what it is to be a naked homeless animal . . . free . . . on its own . . .

HENRY: But what happens . . . I mean . . . what do we do after we do it?

RICHARD: I don't know. It's a blank space . . . empty . . . All I know is I yearn for it . . . nobody there in that space to remind me of my potential . . . that goddamned potential . . .

HENRY: Keep talking, Richie, keep feeding me, Baby.

RICHARD: The gun is clean.
HENRY: That's funny. Like we're trying to be near.
RICHARD: We wipe off the prints . . . throw it somewhere near Andrew's place . . . People have been killed up here before.
HENRY: Is that a legal precedent or something?
RICHARD: You and I were not here when it happened.
HENRY: That's right, Richie, you just keep feeding me.
RICHARD: There's a bar down the road. We were there.
HENRY: Is that it?
RICHARD: No.
HENRY: Good. I want to hear more.
RICHARD: I don't think you can shoot Rachel, Henry. I don't think you can do it.
HENRY: And what am I supposed to say: Yes, I can. I'll show you?
RICHARD: Neither of us can. Not our own. We've lost too many times in front of them.
HENRY: Home court jinx, eh, Richie. So what do we do? (*A slight pause. Henry doesn't like it.*) No silence, please.
RICHARD: That's one up on wife swapping, isn't it? Oh, wow! That's ugly but it sounds better. It sounds like it will be done. It has that sound to it. And so . . . and so . . . who goes first?
RICHARD: We have one last game. Loser goes first.
HENRY: The ball's dead.
RICHARD: No matter. No dribbling. Just shooting. Strictly stuffball. How you get there is your own business.
HENRY: We keep it going. (*Richard throws the ball to Henry. It's a weird game they play. Henry carries the ball. No dribbling. It's almost like football except there is no tackling. There is pushing and body checking. Henry runs around trying to fake Richard out of position so he can stuff dunk. They talk while they play. We can see as much of the game as we want as long as it "plays." They make noises at each other in between the chit chat in order to throw each other off guard. Crowd noises and organ music is heard. Lights fade as the game gets more violent.*)

## Scene 10

*Hennessy cottage. Night. The place seems empty. Julie is on the phone as the lights come up.*

JULIE: Rachel . . . I feel funny calling you like this . . . You think I could . . . (*She seems to want to say "come over," but she stops.*) I was just wondering if you knew where the men were . . . I thought maybe. Oh, they're not. (*Rachel seems to have hung up. Julie puts the phone down. Once again, a certain *paralysis seems to be setting into her. She picks up the alarm clock again and plays with the knob until she flicks it in place. The alarm clock rings in her hand until it stops. She turns and sees Henry.*) Henry. What're you doing there? (*Henry appears in view almost on all fours indicating that he had been either lying or sitting there and is now trying to arise.*)

HENRY: Just resting. (*He enters the cottage uninvited. He seems nervous. His face is bruised, his hand is behind his back.*) It was a rough game.

JULIE: Where is Richard?

HENRY: He won. I mean it was a draw. Ten to ten. Eleven to eleven . . . and so on . . . twenty-three all. So we decided to have a sudden death. Free throw wins it. Richie shoots. Richie makes it. Henry gets the ball. And I'm not good at free throws. You see . . . I just don't have the follow-through . . . it should be natural . . . You just go . . . (*Demonstrates.*) And it's swish . . . but no . . . I could never do it . . . You know . . . just stand there . . . there's no interaction . . . no interplay . . . no pick and roll and give and go, no . . . you just stand there . . . Everything stops. And I don't like that. I like to have some kind of rhythm to carry me through . . . somebody to feed me, you know . . . like guys in my business do one-man shows and things and I just never could . . . I need to have stuff come at me . . . you know . . .

JULIE: Would you like a drink or something?

HENRY: That's the stuff. (*She starts putting ice from a container into a glass. Pours in booze.*)

JULIE: Is Richard out there or what?

HENRY: I don't know. He said . . . What the hell did he say . . . (*Julie is bringing the drink to Henry. As she turns she sees the gun.*)

JULIE: Isn't that Richard's? (*He stands poised.*)

HENRY: Come on . . . come on, come on . . . say something. You got to speak. I can't do it all. (*Henry seems like a junkie who needs a fix.*) What kind of goddamned set-up is this? What is this, eh . . . another free throw . . . It doesn't have to be eloquent, you know. Just a couple of lines to play off . . . Shit . . . I know. Phone rings and I play off the ring. Phone rings and I shoot. (*A second or two wait for the phone to ring. Both of them are frozen, Julie crouching with glass of ice cubes in her hand. Henry standing and looking.*) You got a radio? Stereo? Some music or something? (*Henry is really getting frantic. He stops suddenly.*) That was just preparation. Here it comes. Score's all tied up. In bounds pass. The clock doesn't start till he gets the ball. In bounds pass to Henry . . . (*He "dribbles" towards the exit.*) He dribbles . . . he drives . . . he stops . . . shoots. (*He shoots twice and then exits. Julie stands.*)

## Scene 11

*Richard is waiting at the pier. Henry runs out of the cottage. He stumbles past the basketball court, gun in hand. He seems out of control. Richard is tense and excited at the same time. Henry staggers toward him.*

RICHARD: I heard the shots.

HENRY: How'd they sound?

RICHARD: Well?

HENRY: Yes?

RICHARD: Did you do it?

HENRY: What do you think?

RICHARD: You did it?

HENRY: Is that what you think?

RICHARD: C'mon. C'mon. Did-you-do-it!?

HENRY: You heard the shots.

RICHARD: C'mon.

HENRY: Not unless she keeled over from a heart attack.

RICHARD: HENRY. This is no time for games, dammit.

HENRY: Black man speak with dry tongue. (*Richard is getting frantic.*)

RICHARD: HENRY! (*Gestures as if to come after him with his hands. Henry counters by pointing the pistol at him.*)

HENRY: You better watch it. I've missed with this baby once and I can miss again. (*Laughs at his own despair. Richard realizes.*)

RICHARD: You didn't kill her.

HENRY: Kill her! I couldn't strike up a conversation with her.

RICHARD: Oh, Christ.

HENRY: A clutch shot at the buzzer. And I blew it. We're into overtime.

RICHARD: Shut up with that stuff.

HENRY: But there's no such thing as a miss, right? I get a quarter point.

RICHARD: Will you drop that stuff. I'm trying to think. I got to do something.

HENRY: It was terrible. She killed the scene. She said nothing. Nothing. She just played with these ice cubes. I got nervous and started chattering. It was like a blind date. You'd think I was trying to get a good night kiss from her.

RICHARD: WHAT THE HELL DID YOU SHOOT FOR THEN?

HENRY: TO END THE SCENE. TO GET MYSELF TO SHUT UP. It was terrible. It's like she knew I couldn't do it and felt sorry for me.

RICHARD: Why couldn't you do it?

HENRY: Because I was by myself. You should've sent me in there with that transistor radio. We could've listened to some music. Had some potato chips.

RICHARD: Listen to me. Listen. Nothing's lost. There's just a change of plans.

HENRY: I can't take no more plans. Let's raise the rim, Rich. The damned thing feels like it's around my neck. I can't think straight with that thing . . .

RICHARD: Calm down. Just calm down. It's not too late. Do you understand?

HENRY: Let's raise it so high, so damned high, that we don't even consider it. Oh, God, it's like she knew I couldn't do it and felt sorry for me.

RICHARD: She tricked you. Do you understand? She tricked you.

HENRY: It was some trick. She had an ice cube. I had a gun. She won.

RICHARD: All right. Forget everything, Henry. You stay here. Just give me the gun.

HENRY: I'm staying nowhere by myself.

RICHARD: Give me the gun.

HENRY: If you could've done it you would have by now.

RICHARD: I killed that dog, didn't I? (*Henry cracks up.*)

HENRY: Killed the dog. Oh, that's Rich, all right. Well, I've drowned a few goldfish in my time too. (*He can't keep his eyes off the cottage.*) Look. Her lights are still off. Hey, maybe she went to bed. Eh, wouldn't that be something. Goes to bed. Leaves you a note. Rich: Dinner's in the oven. (*Richard switches tactics in mid-course. It does no good to assault Henry. So he tries something else.*)

RICHARD: That would be like her.

HENRY: They got our number, Rich.

RICHARD: They sure do, Henry.

HENRY: Tomorrow morning it'll be like nothing happened. It'll be sleep well dear.

RICHARD: I guess you're right. (*He tries to be casual but his eagerness is showing.*) Might as well give me that thing.

HENRY: What do you want the "thing" for.

RICHARD: Well, it's my "thing" isn't it? (*The strain is showing on Richard.*)

HENRY: We're getting a divorce, eh? Well, I'll let you visit the little rascals on weekends.

RICHARD: Please, Henry. Eh? C'mon. Give me the gun.

HENRY: Let's throw it away.

RICHARD: Listen to me, Henry. Listen to me, please. I can't go back to her. She'll forgive me. I can't take to be forgiven. It nullifies you. She'll understand me and I can't take to be understood anymore. I feel I can do it. And I know myself well enough to know that the feeling won't last. It will go away and another feeling will take its place. I have to hurry. I have to do it now.

HENRY: What about me?

RICHARD: You're free to do what you want.

HENRY: I'm not asking for permission. I'm asking for an answer. (*Richard loses control.*)

RICHARD: Give me the gun, damn you.

HENRY: You can't kill her.

RICHARD: I can do it.

HENRY: Well I can't! So I'd like to think nobody can. I got to have company in this world. I'm throwing the damned thing in the lake.

RICHARD: You can't! (*Henry tries to go to the pier to hurl the gun in the lake. Richard intercepts him and goes for the gun. They struggle. As they do Randy appears behind them with a rifle. Henry and Richard's physical struggle becomes Randy's internal struggle. He's not sure he can do it. For a second or two he seems ready to give up and leave. At this moment Richard overpowers Henry. Takes the gun from him. Henry's still clinging to him. Richard tries to free himself and as he does the gun in his hand seems to swing toward Randy's direction. Randy plays off their action. Fires once. Fires twice. Henry and Richard fall into the boathouse.*)

## Scene 12

*Basketball court. Night. Rachel is U.C. on the court. Andrew talks to Rachel. Randy and Debbie are D.R.*

ANDREW: Randy said they had a gun and were going to force his girl to do something. I don't see why he'd lie. He hardly knew them. So that's what I'll tell the police unless there's something you know that I don't know that you'd like me to know.

RACHEL: It's a terrible shock to both of us.

ANDREW: That I know. You want me to arrange for some transportation for you.

RACHEL: No, thank you. My friend here will drive me.

ANDREW: Fine. Good night. (*He crosses D.S. to Randy and takes his gun.*) If the police asks why you had the gun you tell them you were making the rounds for me. Hear?

RANDY: Yes, Uncle. (*Andrew walks on.*)

DEBBIE: You said you were just going to frighten them. You swore you wouldn't shoot.

RANDY: But I did. And you brought me the gun.

DEBBIE: You asked me to do it.

RANDY: And you asked me to do it.

DEBBIE: Not to kill.

RANDY: Did you say that?

DEBBIE: No, but it was understood.

RANDY: You brought me the gun, Debbie.

DEBBIE: You asked me to do it.

RANDY: You didn't have to, Debbie.

DEBBIE: You said you were just going to scare them. Teach them a lesson.

RANDY: Yes, but then I remembered how they raped you. How they forced you. How you called my name. Randy. Randy. And I lost control.

DEBBIE: I don't believe you.

RANDY: I believe everything you tell me.

DEBBIE: Why does it all keep coming back to me.

RANDY: I did it because of you. Because of what they did to you. And you brought me the gun, Debbie.

DEBBIE: Stop saying that.

RANDY: I said you'll have to bring me the gun, Debbie. I said, Uncle keeps it in his room and he won't let me into his room. But he'll let you. I said, pretend you're going into his room to use the big mirror and then lower the gun through the window. And you did. While Uncle and I talked in the living room you went in there and lowered the gun and then you came out. Both of us saw you. Uncle knows what you did. But you don't have to worry about anything, Debbie. We'll cover up for you. I was making the rounds. I came upon them trying to rape you and I shot them. You're in the clear.

DEBBIE: Oh. That's right. You see . . . you had me worried the way you talked . . .

RANDY: You have absolutely nothing to worry about.

DEBBIE: Yes, and I'll go home in a few days. I mean as soon as . . .

RANDY: You are home, Debbie.

DEBBIE: What are you talking about.

RANDY: You can't leave me now. You have to stand by your man.

DEBBIE: You couldn't be more wrong.

RANDY: I could be more of everything, Debbie.

DEBBIE: I'm going to leave tonight. (*Debbie moves away.*)

RANDY: Then I might have to tell the police about the gun.

DEBBIE: Please Randy . . . please let me go.

RANDY: But you don't want to go, Debbie. You've tried it once already. (*He leads her away by the arm. She is too weak to resist. Julie enters from the house.*)

RACHEL: How are you feeling?

JULIE: I don't know. It's like I don't dare feel anything.

RACHEL: Of course. It's a terrible shock. Losing your husband like that. At least you're not alone. I'll stay with you as long as you need me.

JULIE: Nobody ever wanted to hurt me like that. I turned around and there he was with a gun in his hand. I still remember the way he looked at me.

RACHEL: Forget about Henry.

JULIE: It was Richard.

RACHEL: You must calm down. You're getting all confused.

JULIE: I saw him.

RACHEL: You saw Henry.

JULIE: I saw Henry come in and then when I turned around I saw Richard standing in front of me with a gun in his hand. I was paralyzed. Now they're dead!

RACHEL: It had nothing to do with us. Nobody forced them to do anything.

JULIE: (*Crosses D.R.*) But we followed along and by doing that we forced them to lead.

RACHEL: You want to take all the blame.

JULIE: No, just my share. (*Sits.*)

RACHEL: Nobody has to know about this. About us . . . It can be our little secret.

JULIE: I've kept too many secrets. I don't want to do it anymore.

RACHEL: (*She wheels D.S.*) Listen to me, Julie. We all have those women in us . . . tender little things . . . and we all want to let them out for the world to see . . . but the world kills them, Julie. Men smell the victim on you. Hide the scent. Change before it's too late.

JULIE: I think I've changed too much already and left something essential behind. I feel so transparent. I can see all my joints and seams but the framework is there. I can almost touch it.

RACHEL: Aren't we going back together?

JULIE: There is a way out of this pattern and I must find it on my own.

(*Blackout.*)

# ANYONE CAN WHISTLE

❀❀❀

*A Musical Fable*

*Book by*

*Arthur Laurents*

*Music and Lyrics by*

*Stephen Sondheim*

*A Carl Peek Book*
LEON AMIEL PUBLISHER
New York, New York

Photographs by courtesy of Joseph Abeles

Published by arrangement with Random House
and copyright holders
MANUFACTURED IN THE UNITED STATES OF AMERICA

## A NOTE FROM THE PUBLISHER

Publishing trade editions of Broadway shows is a precarious business at best; reissuing *Anyone Can Whistle* after 12 years and only 9 performances is downright crazy (or so I've been told). But there are some things worth saving: *Anyone Can Whistle* is one—a modern classic from the American musical stage. So a note of thanks to those people who made this edition possible: Mike Stapleton, whose idea it was; Herman Krawitz of Yale University who located the seemingly only extant copy of the original edition; C. V. Wimpfheimer of Random House; Nancy Stark of Doubleday's Fireside Theatre; Charles Schlessiger of Brandt & Brandt; Flora Roberts; Lee Snider of Chappell Music; Terry Hammond, who first played me the score; Joseph Abeles; Bill Konecky, Curtis Holsapple, Roy Jensen and David Smith, all of whom contributed to the final product. And special thanks to Leon Amiel whose concern for artistic achievement in all fields made the republication of this book a reality.

—*Carl Peek*

## *Introduction*

When *Anyone Can Whistle* opened on Broadway on April 4, 1964, Whitney Bolton of the *Morning Telegraph* prophesied:

"If *Anyone Can Whistle* is a success, the American musical theatre will have advanced itself and prepared the way for further breakdown of now old and worn techniques and points of view. If it is not a success, we sink back into the old formula method and must wait for the breakthrough.

"Arthur Laurents takes a scalpel to a flourish of our illusions and cuts away the fat. He puts before us the credo that in this day to be mad is to be sane, to be insane is to be healthy and in proper mental frame for this day. We live, in short, in crazy times and it is better for the individual to be somewhat daft and, thus, meet craze with craze.

"To all concerned, top and bottom, a thank you for trying, a thank you for wanting to elevate the American musical theatre to new standards of intellect. Let no one concerned be discouraged.

"The American musical theatre is less ponderous and ridiculous today because of *Anyone Can Whistle,* no matter what its fate."

Its fate was not a bright one. For despite the efforts of a few particularly insightful critics, the majority were outraged at the violation of traditional musical comedy forms. With the wrath of the Broadway establishment raining upon its head, *Anyone Can Whistle* succumbed to a premature demise after but nine performances at a loss of its entire $350,000 investment (including financial backing by four musical theatre greats: Irving Berlin, Frank Loesser, Richard Rodgers, and Jule Styne, who had faith in the project).

Here, at last, was a truly new musical, in a theatre full of so-called new musicals, which were, in actuality, musical adaptations of other sources usually best left unmusicalized; a musical that incorporated scathing satire with sly subtlety; a lively but literate libretto with a wise and witty score. *Anyone Can Whistle* was the marriage of musical comedy with theatre of the absurd, consummated cleverly and exhilaratingly executed.

Martin Gottfried of *Women's Wear Daily* exulted:

"It's not simply that *Anyone Can Whistle* is a brilliantly inventive musical . . . It is a ringingly bright shout for individuality and because it is so individual itself, it is whole, it is fresh, it is new, and it is perfectly wonderful.

"Thank heavens that there still are adults in the theatre. And that they are willing to assume that their audience is adult, too. Mr. Laurents has written a book that fairly glitters with fey wit and mature insight . . . His humor does not condescend with cheap broadness, his characters do not insult with nice-guy, sweet girl superficiality. He has not written a simple story geared for handy songs and dances. Nor has Mr. Sondheim provided simpleminded music for it. Here are songs that combine musical sophistication with theatrical flair. At once melodic and interesting, they easily represent the finest Broadway composing in years.

"This is—you must know by now—a real original, and that is just what it is asking us to be if we want to be alive at all.

"*Anyone Can Whistle* is as alive as it is telling everybody to be and that makes it both important and exciting."

Although *Anyone Can Whistle* was short-lived on Broadway, it has had more influence on the development of the contemporary musical theatre than dozens of more commercially successful shows. It helped sow the seeds of discontent with a once fresh and vital art form that had begun to atrophy with convention, to shine a light through a glut of tuneful but essentially mindless mediocrities that littered the musical stages of the 1960's. It posed new challenges to librettists who made money by stringing songs to one-liners and writing caricatures instead of characters. And it began to establish a criterion on which a musical score should be based: Is a good score just something you can hum on your way out of the theatre? Or shouldn't it accomplish some development of tone, or characterization?

Many of these dilemmas were confronted and conquered in the later concept musicals devised by Stephen Sondheim and producer, Harold Prince; landmarks that include *Company* (1970), *Follies* (1971), *A Little Night Music* (1973), and *Pacific Overtures* (1976). Certainly, *Anyone Can Whistle* definitively marks the turning point in Mr. Sondheim's musical direction.

Mr. Laurents' and Mr. Sondheim's contributions notwithstanding, *Anyone Can Whistle* had other assets, including remarkable sets by William and Jean Eckart, clever costumes by Theoni V. Aldredge and evocative lighting by Jules Fisher. Arthur Laurents directed the production himself, a particularly uncommon accomplishment in the incorporation of the creative and interpretative artist, with Herbert Ross supplying truly memorable and undeniably innovative dance numbers. The show was also blessed with performances of pin-point accuracy and sincerity by Lee Remick as Nurse Fay Apple, and Harry Guardino as J. Bowden Hapgood. Angela Lansbury made her musical comedy debut as Cora Hoover Hooper, an important first step toward a brilliantly successful career in that medium which would include a third Tony Award as star of the 1974 revival of the Arthur Laurents-Stephen Sondheim-Jule Styne musical, *Gypsy*.

Although *Anyone Can Whistle* did not win popular acclaim, or even acceptance during its brief lifetime, it has endured to become that rare phenomenon, a cult musical (By definition, a musical of distinguished merit which enjoys continued, albeit limited popularity despite an abbreviated commercial run. *Candide* is another example, unique in that the perseverance of its cult inspired a major revival.), whose devotees can savor this little known masterpiece on the original cast album (recorded posthumously, following the show's closing on April 11, 1964) and now in this new published edition.

—*David Smith*

## MUSICAL NUMBERS

### Act One

| | |
|---|---|
| "I'M LIKE THE BLUEBIRD" | Cookies |
| "ME AND MY TOWN" | Cora and The Boys |
| "MIRACLE SONG" | Cora, Cooley, Townspeople, Tourists, and Pilgrims |
| "SIMPLE" | Hapgood and Company |

### Act Two

| | |
|---|---|
| "A-1 MARCH" | Company |
| "COME PLAY WITH ME" | Fay, Hapgood and The Boys |
| "ANYONE CAN WHISTLE" | Fay |
| "A PARADE IN TOWN" | Cora |
| "EVERYBODY SAYS DON'T" | Hapgood |

### Act Three

| | |
|---|---|
| "I'VE GOT YOU TO LEAN ON" | Cora, Schub, Cooley, Magruder and The Boys |
| "SEE WHAT IT GETS YOU" | Fay |
| "THE COOKIE CHASE" | Cora, Fay and Company |
| "WITH SO LITTLE TO BE SURE OF" | Fay and Hapgood |

ANYONE CAN WHISTLE *was first presented by Kermit Bloomgarden and Diana Krasny at the Majestic Theatre, New York City, on April 4, 1964, with the following cast:*

*(In order of appearance)*

| | |
|---|---|
| SANDWICH MAN | Jeff Killion |
| BABY JOAN | Jeanne Tanzy |
| MRS. SCHROEDER | Peg Murray |
| TREASURER COOLEY | Arnold Soboloff |
| CHIEF MAGRUDER | James Frawley |
| COMPTROLLER SCHUB | Gabriel Dell |
| CORA HOOVER HOOPER | Angela Lansbury |
| THE BOYS | Sterling Clark, Harvey Evans, Larry Roquemore, Tucker Smith |
| FAY APPLE | Lee Remick |
| J. BOWDEN HAPGOOD | Harry Guardino |
| DR. DETMOLD | Don Doherty |
| GEORGE | Larry Roquemore |
| JUNE | Janet Hayes |
| JOHN | Harvey Evans |
| MARTIN | Lester Wilson |
| OLD LADY | Eleonore Treiber |
| TELEGRAPH BOY | Alan Johnson |
| OSGOOD | Georgia Creighton |

*and*

Susan Borree, Georgia Creighton, Janet Hayes, Bettye Jenkins, Patricia Kelly, Barbara Lang, Paula Lloyd, Barbara Monte, Odette Phillips, Hanne-Marie Reiner, Eleonore Treiber, Sterling Clark, Eugene Edwards, Harvey Evans, Dick Ensslen, Loren Hightower, Alan Johnson, Jeff Killion, Jack Murray, William Reilly, Larry Roquemore, Tucker Smith, Don Stewart, Lester Wilson *as*

Cookies, Nurses, Deputies, Townspeople, Pilgrims and Tourists.

*Directed by* Arthur Laurents
*Dances and Musical Numbers Staged by* Herbert Ross
*Scenery designed by* William and Jean Eckart
*Costumes by* Theoni V. Aldredge
*Lighting by* Jules Fisher
*Orchestrations by* Don Walker
*Vocal Arrangements and Musical Direction by*
Herbert Green
*Dance Arrangements by* Betty Walberg
*Associate Producer:* Arlene Sellers

# ACT ONE

*The curtain rises to a burst of circus-like music on the main square of a town. The colors are gay, exaggerated; the look is rather Pop Art cockeyed. At one side is the entrance to City Hall; at the other, the entrance to the Hotel Superbe. As the music softens to a jazzy pulse underneath, from offstage comes a humorously folksy voice.*

NARRATOR

This is our setting: the main square of a town. This town manufactured a product that never wore out. This is what happened. (*Immediately, a building falls down; a crack appears in the facade of City Hall; the Hotel Superbe's sign teeters at an angle; and signs fly in reading* CLOSED, VACANCY *and* HELP!) These are some of the citizens of the town. (*A group of people in stylized rags and clown wigs lope on and glare at the audience*) Believe it or not, they once looked as good as you. Maybe better. It'll take a miracle to make them human again—but we may be able to produce one.

(*The music changes and a group of pleasantly dressed, smiling people enters, led by a slightly tipsy nurse. These people are* COOKIES *and they sing*)

COOKIES

I'm like the bluebird.
I should worry, I should care.
I should be a millionaire.
I'm like the blue—

(*In mid-phrase, they cut off and freeze with smiles on their faces*)

NARRATOR

There *is* one place in this town that's still doing business: that's The Cookie Jar: a sanitarium for the socially pressured. Those Cookies look as good as you. Maybe better. (*The* COOKIES *wave*) Our heroine is the head nurse. No, not that nurse. (*She hiccups silently*) She drinks. Our girl won't be along for eleven minutes. Run along, Cookies. (*They exit to the "Bluebird March"*) Now to return to this broken-down town.

(*The music takes on a strong jazz rhythm as the* TOWNSPEOPLE *do vaudeville-like dance movements and chant with great glee*)

TOWNSPEOPLE

Help! Help!
Hungry! Hungry!
Poor! Poor!
RESIGN!

(*On this last, they turn to City Hall and freeze with upraised fists*)

NARRATOR

Where is all the town's money? Where it usually is: in City Hall.

(*A burst of music and out of City Hall snakes a thin man with a fistful of money. He leers at the money and freezes as one of the townsmen who has been carrying a sandwich board reading* DOWN WITH THE ADMINISTRATION *flips over a card so that the sign now reads* DOWN WITH TREASURER COOLEY)

SANDWICH MAN

Down With Treasurer Cooley!

NARRATOR

That snoop's got some of it.

*(The* TOWNSPEOPLE *hiss as there is another burst of music and a hulking, uniformed man comes out of City Hall. He has a stupid grin on his face which changes to a pout as he holds out his hand for money and* COOLEY *merely gives him one bill. Everyone freezes but the* SANDWICH MAN *who flips his card over to read)*

SANDWICH MAN

Down With Chief of Police Magruder!

NARRATOR

That moron's got some of it.

*(The people growl angrily as there is another burst of music and a foppish Edwardian-looking man comes out of City Hall. He takes all the money from both* COOLEY *and* MAGRUDER *as, again, everybody freezes except the* SANDWICH MAN *for)*

SANDWICH MAN

Down With Comptroller Schub!

NARRATOR

That operator's got some of it—but his eye is on the main chunk. And there it is! *(An enormous fanfare: the crowd boos;* SCHUB, COOLEY *and* MAGRUDER *move to one side; and on comes an attractive lady, glittering madly with too many diamonds. Her name is* CORA HOOVER HOOPER *and she is carried Cleopatra-like on a litter, by four* PAGE BOYS*)* Cora Hoover Hooper: the Mayoress. They ought to throw rocks at her.

*(And the people do! They snarl, boo, shout curses; the* SANDWICH MAN *flips his sign to read* DOWN WITH THE MAYORESS. *But none of this disturbs* CORA *who descends from her litter with great hauteur. The* BOYS *carry the litter off, the columned facade of City Hall slides on behind her and, midst the last of the flying rocks, she sings)*

CORA

Everyone hates me—yes, yes—
Being the Mayor—ess, yes.
All of the peasants
Throw rocks in my presence
Which causes me nervous distress, yes.
Oooh Oooooooooh, Oooh-ooh Ooooooooh.

*(During this rather torch-singer-like moan, the last peasant straggles off)*

Me and my town, battered about,
Everyone in it would like to get out.
Me and my town,
We just wanna be loved!
Stores are for rent, theatres are dark,
Grass on the sidewalks but not in the park,
Me and my town—me and my town—
We just wanna be loved!

*(Behind her now some of the people appear doing a shuffling dance step)*

The people are starving,
So they sleep the day through.
My poor little people,
What can they do?

TOWNSPEOPLE

Boo!

CORA

Who asked you?
*(She glares at them; they run off)*
Come on the train, come on the bus,
Somebody please buy a ticket to us.
Hurry on down—
We need a little renown.
Love me,
Love my
Town!
Ooohhh—ooooohhhhh—ooooooooooooohhhhhhhhhhhh!
*(Four* BOYS *appear suddenly out of nowhere. The number becomes a jazzy parody of a night-club number)*

BOYS

Hi there, Cora. What's new?

CORA

The bank went bust and I'm feeling blue.

BOYS

And who took over the bankruptcy?

CORA

Me, boys, me!

BOYS

*Si, si!*

CORA

Me, boys, me!

BOYS

Tell us, Cora, how you are.

CORA

I just got back from the reservoir.

BOYS

And what's the state of the water supply?

CORA

Dry, boys, dry!

BOYS

My, my!

CORA

Dry, boys, dry!

BOYS

Ay, ay!

*(The music stops and they begin a clapping accompaniment)*

CORA

A lady has responsibilities . . .

BOYS

Responsibilities . . .

CORA

And civic pride.

BOYS

Civic pride!

CORA

Well, I look around and what do I see? I see *no* crops.

BOYS

No crops.

CORA

I see *no* business.

BOYS

No business.

CORA

To the North, to the South,
Only hoof-and-mouth!
To the East, to the West,
No Community Chest!

CORA *and* BOYS

I see a terrible depression all over the town—
Oh, a terrible depression,
Yes, a terrible depression,

CORA

What a terrible depression
And I'm so depressed I can hardly talk on the phone.
I feel all alone.

CORA *and* BOYS

But a lady has responsibilities—

BOYS

Responsibilities—

CORA

To all my poor! starving! miserable! dirty! dreary!
depressing!
Peasants!

ALL

Peasants! Ugh!

CORA

But a lady has responsibilities—

BOYS

Responsibilities—

CORA

To try to be
Popular with the populace.

BOYS

She's unpopular with the populace!

CORA *and* BOYS

Unpopular with the populace, unpopular with the populace . . .

(*Music sneaks back in under* CORA)

CORA

Last week a flood, this week a drought,
Even the locusts want to get out,
But me and my town, we never pout,
We just wanna be loved!

BOYS

A friendship is lovely
And a courtship sublime,
But give her a township

CORA

Township!
Every time!

CORA *and* BOYS

What'll we do, me and my town?
Gotta do something or we're gonna drown!

(*In a strut*)

Give me my coat,
Give me my crown,
Give me your vote
And hurry on down.

CORA

Show me how much you think *of* me!

ALL

Love me,
Love my
Town!

*(On the last close-harmony held note, they are strutting across the stage towards an exit.* CORA *gives the last boy a playful little shove so that she can take the bow for the number alone—which she does. She then beckons them to return with her litter as* SCHUB *enters)*

SCHUB

My dear Madam Mayor—

CORA

I'm in the depths of positive despair.

*(She sinks onto the litter)*

SCHUB

Ah now, Cora, you need to relax.

CORA

I need a miracle, that's what I need.

SCHUB

Why don't we dine together this evening? *(The* BOYS *glare at him and lift* CORA *and the litter into the air)* My house at eight. Or your house. It makes no difference. I'll be at your house at seven.

CORA

You will not! You'll just try to talk me into re-opening my

great big enormous factory. I know that's why you got me elected, you and Magruder and Cooley–where is that little snoop?

COOLEY

(*Who has sneaked on and been listening under the litter*)
At your service, Sister Hoover Hooper.

CORA

A fine City Treasurer you are!

COOLEY

I thank you.

CORA

My desk is littered with bills. Pay them.

COOLEY

With what, Sister?

CORA

Ingenuity, Brother, ingenuity.

COOLEY

By the day after tomorrow, this town will be bankrupt!

SCHUB

We had thought of selling it–

COOLEY

But only you, Sister, could afford to buy it.

CORA

Count–me–out–and–(*To her* BOYS) Put–me–down!

SCHUB

Now Cora, I have conjured up a plan to save your town.

CORA

(*To the* BOYS)

Home! (*They leave with the litter; to* SCHUB) You and your plans! Another World's Fair? Another Peer Gynt Festival? Why can't you think of a plan that will work?

SCHUB

This one will: it's unethical.

COOLEY

Highly.

CORA

(*Suddenly singing* a capella)

*I didn't hear it! Don't tell me!* (*She speaks sharply*) *But* do it! Now: how much is it going to cost?

SCHUB

Nothing.

CORA

I love it.

SCHUB

All it needs is Baby Joan.

CORA

Baby Joan? Baby Joan Schroeder??

COOLEY

Don't worry. I'll get her.
(*He goes*)

CORA

Get her for what? Schub, you genius, what *is* this plan?

SCHUB

(*Fondling her*)
Let me surprise you, dear lady.

CORA

Oh, I adore surprises!

SCHUB

Then prepare for prosperity and meet me at The Rock as soon as you can.

CORA

I'll change and be there in no time! (SCHUB *kisses her hand and exits. Music strikes up and the four* BOYS *dance on with a change of costume and jewelry for* CORA. *At the same time, the scenery is changing: City Hall is sliding off as a great rock slides on. But before everything can be set in place,* CORA, *who has been struggling to get a glove on, holds up her hand for everything to stop. And it does, both music and scenery. She hums cheerfully until she gets the glove on, then beckons with her hand for the music and scene change to resume.*

*They do, speedily; the lights come up and she looks around, singing* a capella) *Schub! Comptroller Schub!*

*(At the same time, there is yelling from offstage and a rather mad-looking woman in rags enters)*

MRS. SCHROEDER

Baby Joan! Baby Joan!

CORA

SCHUB!

MRS. SCHROEDER

BABY JOAN!

CORA

Schroeder, have you lost that child of yours again? I thought I told you to put a bell around her neck.

MRS. SCHROEDER

You take care of your town, I'll take care of my kid. BABY JOAN!

CORA

SCHUB! COMPTROLLER–

*(Both ladies stop dead. A weird looking little brat of 7 or 8–*BABY JOAN*–has been shoved on by* COOLEY *who then scurries behind the rock.* BABY JOAN *shuts her eyes, extends her hands, begins to head for the rock, uttering strange moans)*

MRS. SCHROEDER

*(In disgust)*

Oh, Baby Joan!

CORA

Is she in some sort of a trance?

MRS. SCHROEDER

No. (BABY JOAN *now nestles down and begins to lick the rock*) She's thirsty.

CORA

*And* in a trance.

MRS. SCHROEDER

Have it your way.

CORA

Don't you tell me this town is even out of water! If you were any kind of a decent mother, you'd take that child home!

MRS. SCHROEDER

Why? All she needs is a good belt in the—

(*But suddenly there is an enormous spurt of water from the rock and a spurt of music from the orchestra*)

CORA

(*A whisper*)

Schroeder—

MRS. SCHROEDER

Your Honor—

CORA

*(Clutching her)*

Schroeder!

MRS. SCHROEDER

Your Honor! It's—it's a miracle!

CORA

It's a what?

MRS. SCHROEDER

A miracle! It's a miracle!

CORA

*(Looks at the water, then back at* MRS. SCHROEDER*)*

You know, you're absolutely right! It's a miracle! I'm saved!

*(At this,* BABY JOAN *runs to the footlights, curtseys modestly, then returns to the rock where she stands in an angelic pose as religious music starts.* TOWNSPEOPLE *come running on, and* COOLEY *appears from behind the rock to make sure the "miracle" is working and* BABY JOAN *is behaving)*

TOWNSPEOPLE

*(Chanting)*

Ah! Ah!

MRS. SCHROEDER

*(Sings)*

It's a sign! It's a sign!

CORA

And it's mine!

MRS. SCHROEDER

It's a shrine ! It's a shrine!

CORA

And it's mine!
It's a gold mine!
And it's all mine!

TOWNSPEOPLE

It's a sign!
It's a shrine!
See it shine!

CORA

And it's holier than thine!

CORA, COOLEY, MRS. SCHROEDER, TOWNSPEOPLE

There's water in a lake,
Water in a river,
Water in the deep blue sea.
But water in a rock–Lord! That's a miracle!

CORA *and* COOLEY

Who's got the miracle? We!

ALL

There's water that you part,
Water that you walk on,

Water that you turn to wine!
But water from a rock—Lord! What a miracle!
This is a miracle that's divine,
Truly divine!

CORA

Really *divine!*

CORA, COOLEY, MRS. SCHROEDER

The Lord said, "Let there be water,"
The Lord said, "Turn on the font!"
Lord said, "Let there be pilgrims
And let 'em all think whatever they want."

ALL

Blessed be the child,
Blessed be the tourist,
Blessed is its own reward.

COOLEY

Water is a boon, we'll soon be in clover!

CORA

Better issue stock, my rock runneth over!

ALL

Glory Hallelu,
You finally came through,
And thank you, Lord!
Our faith is restored!
Thank you, Lord!

(*And now* PILGRIMS *enter—all types from all over*)

CORA

Come all ye pilgrims!

TOWNSPEOPLE

Hail the miracle!

CORA

See ye the wondrous sight!

TOWNSPEOPLE

Hail the miracle, praise the miracle!

CORA

Take ye the bus tonight.

TOWNSPEOPLE

There's a miracle that's happening in this town.

CORA

If you want to see a miracle, then hurry on down!

COOLEY

Come all ye pilgrims!

TOWNSPEOPLE

Hail the miracle.

COOLEY

Hear ye the joyful bells!

TOWNSPEOPLE

Hail the miracle.

COOLEY

Fill ye the new motels!

TOWNSPEOPLE

It's a miracle that's going to change your life.

COOLEY

Come along and see the miracle and bring the wife!

TOWNSPEOPLE

There's a miracle that's happening in this town
And you'll never have to worry if you hurry on down.
There's a miracle that's going to change your life!
Come along and see the miracle and bring the wife!

CORA

(*Like a revival meeting leader, to the* PILGRIMS)
Are you looking for hope?

TOWNSPEOPLE

Looking for hope . . .

CORA

Hoping for an answer?

TOWNSPEOPLE

Hoping for an answer . . .

CORA

New life.

TOWNSPEOPLE

New life . . .

CORA

True happiness.

TOWNSPEOPLE

True happiness . . .

CORA

Come.

*(There is a murmuring babble from the* PILGRIMS, *not unlike that heard in crowd-filled cathedrals, which culminates in a single distinct word)*

PILGRIMS

*(Murmur)*

Help.

CORA

Come and take the waters for a modest fee.
Come and take the waters and feel new.
Come and take the waters and with luck you'll be
Anything whatever except you.

*(During this, the* PILGRIMS *take offerings to* BABY JOAN *on the rock: jewelry, wrist watches, cameras, money, suitcases, anything. And anything, particularly money, is solemnly accepted and raked in by* COOLEY. *Then the* PILGRIMS *extend their hands and murmur)*

PILGRIMS

Comfort.

TOWNSPEOPLE

Come and take the waters with humility.
Come and take the waters and feel new.

CORA

Come and take the waters and with luck you'll be
Happy and successful!

PILGRIMS *and* TOWNSPEOPLE

Happy and successful!

CORA

Liked and loved and beautiful and perfect!

PILGRIMS *and* TOWNSPEOPLE

Beautiful and perfect!

CORA

Healthy, rich, handsome, independent,
Wise, adjusted and secure and athletic!

PILGRIMS

(*With wild excitement, they babble, rush to the rock, and call out, pointing in different directions:*)

Rainbow; rainbow; rainbow; rainbow! (*And now they all rush forward and pointing here, there, everywhere, all scream in one burst of ecstasy*) RAINBOW! ! !

(*The music roars over them as they go really wild: dashing up the rock to the water, throwing water over each other, kissing the rock, rolling on the ground, kissing* BABY JOAN'*s feet. This last is a bit disconcerting to* CORA *who, with* MRS. SCHROEDER, *is trying to get* BABY JOAN *into one of her better nightgowns. At the same time flowers appear, buildings straighten and the town gets a look of prosperity*)

ALL

The Lord said, "Let there be water!"
The Lord said, "Turn on the font!"
Lord said, "Let ye be what ye want!"
Our troubles are over!
OUR TROUBLES ARE OVER! ! !
Look upon the gift and lift up your chin now!

CORA *and* COOLEY

Look upon the boom—no room at the Inn now!

ALL

Glory Hallelu,
Our problems are through,
And thank you, Lord!
Thank you, Lord!

(CORA *is hoisted on the shoulders of admirers and over the final note, shrieks*)

CORA

THEY LOVE ME! ! !

(*Jubilant music and singing resume as the rock revolves and we see what is behind it: a cave in the interior in which* MAGRUDER *is enthusiastically working a long-handled water pump.* COOLEY *and* SCHUB *rush in;* SCHUB *begins to fiddle with some electrical wires*)

COOLEY

More and more pilgrims!

SCHUB

It's an absolute gold rush!

COOLEY

As long as the flock is happy, Brethren—they spend.
(*Helps* MAGRUDER *pump*)

SCHUB

Which reminds me: I got Madam Schroeder to sign three exclusive contracts for the manufacture of Baby Joan statuettes: small, medium and life-size.

COOLEY

To be sold, Brother Schub—

SCHUB

Exclusively in Cooley stores—

MAGRUDER

Providing a license is obtained—

SCHUB

From the Chief of Police. Subject to the approval of the Comptroller and payable to the Treasurer.

COOLEY

(*Hands to heaven*)
Sing out the truth!

SCHUB

Keep pumping. If either of you cretins knew anything about electricity, I'd have had this working automatically ages—

CORA

(*Off—singing* a capella)
*Schub! Comptroller Schub!*

MAGRUDER

We're lost!

SCHUB

Keep pumping!

CORA

(*Off*)
*Schub! Comptroller—(They freeze as she bursts in the door, carrying an armful of roses)*—Schub . . .

SCHUB

It's a nonsectarian miracle, Cora.

CORA

(A capella)
*I didn't hear it! Don't tell me!* (*Then speaks sharply*) But do it. (*The pumping resumes*) And keep doing it.

SCHUB

You are a mayor and a lady. Seven-thirty, my house.

CORA

*(Sadly)*

Ah me. On my wedding day, the late Harvey Hoover Hooper gave me a triple strand of pearls. The next morning—it was my fourteenth birthday—I took them to a jeweler.

SCHUB

For safekeeping.

CORA

No, for appraisal. My pearls were cultured. (*Dumps the roses on* SCHUB) I keep hoping for something real.

SCHUB

Madame, a little while ago, they wanted to run you out of town. Now they want to run you for governor. If that isn't a real miracle, nothing is.

CORA

*Ha ha ha ha!* You're right. (*Yanks the roses back*) I shall proceed with my plan to re-open my factory as a bottling plant for Miracle Water. Keep pumping. And don't get tired.

SCHUB

One brilliant moment, dear lady. I'm about ready to hook up the electricity.

CORA

Electricity! Oh, Schub-chen! It's like the opening of the Suez Canal and I'm Queen Whatever-her-name-was! I knight all of you! (*A rose to each of them*) A miracle is a miracle if it works like a miracle! All those poor sweet pilgrims standing in line: I never knew so many would pay so much for new lives. And I never dreamed it would all happen in my reign!

SCHUB

Dinner, your Highness?

CORA

Seven-thirty, my house.

*(A last rose to him, and she exits)*

MAGRUDER

Ten to one, she's not gonna cut us in on her water.

COOLEY

Feareth not, Brother. We shall sell tickets to ours!

SCHUB

Stop pumping! . . . Stand back! . . . And pray. *(He goes to a switch)* If this works, it *will* be a miracle.

*(He throws the switch. Nothing happens. In disgust, he removes a rose stuck in the pump. A moment, then the handle starts pumping, slowly, awkwardly to music, faster, then cheerfully and happily.* COOLEY *and* MAGRUDER *yell ecstatically and begin to dance in time to the pumping as the rock revolves again, and we see the "miracle" and a longer line of* PILGRIMS *waiting for it.* BABY JOAN *is sitting on top of the rock, extending her hand for* PILGRIMS *to kiss—and then opening it for a fee which they pay her and which she puts in a tin can.* COOLEY *now has a fat roll of red movie-theatre tickets which he is selling)*

COOLEY

Step up, brethren and sistren! Get your tickets!

MAGRUDER

Buy your blessings!

COOLEY

*Count* your blessings, buy your tickets.

MAGRUDER

Yeah, step right up! Only one blessing per pilgrim per ticket!

COOLEY

Step up! Special discount for minority groups!

*(As they continue, the music changes and the "Bluebird Song" is heard as a line of* COOKIES *marches on, led by their young, pretty head nurse,* FAY APPLE. *The music stops as she stops, leaving her* COOKIES *in a line behind her, downstage of and parallel to the line of* PILGRIMS. FAY *takes a step and looks coldly at the rock)*

FAY

So that's it.

COOLEY

Yes, ma'am, Sister Nurse Apple!

FAY

Forty-nine tickets, please.

COOLEY

Forty-nine?

FAY

We have forty-nine patients in Dr. Detmold's Cookie Jar! I want a ticket for each and every Cookie.

COOKIES

Hooray!

COOLEY

Sing out the truth!

FAY

Baby Joan Schroeder, you come right down off that wet rock!

BABY JOAN

Goodie!

(*Scrambles down*)

FAY

Really, Mr. Cooley, as the father of eleven natural children, you should know that child will catch her death of cold sitting in all that damp. Baby Joan—home and change those panties.

BABY JOAN

I gotta sell blessings.

FAY

After you change.

BABY JOAN

(*Threatening*)

I'll go into a trance.

FAY

After you change. Scoot!

(BABY JOAN *stalks off as* SCHUB *enters opposite*)

COOLEY

(*To* FAY)

Forty-nine tickets for your forty-nine Cookies reckons up to—

SCHUB

Treasurer, a word with you? Magruder, hold the line. A brief moment, my dear Head-nursie. (*Takes* COOLEY *to one side*) Cooley, you are stupid beyond the dreams of man. Don't you know those loonies from Dr. Detmold's sanitarium will be just as looney *after* they take the waters as they were before?

COOLEY

So what, Brother? Forty-nine full-rate tickets—

SCHUB

If forty-nine people partake of that miracle in one fell group, and nothing happens, don't you think someone is going to be suspicious of something?

COOLEY

Sister Apple, we're fresh out of tickets.

FAY

*(Advancing on them)*

No, Mr. Cooley.

SCHUB

My dear up-dated Nightingale—

FAY

No, Mr. Schub.

SCHUB

Now, Nursie, why do you want your Cookies to take the waters? They're well-fed, well-housed, well-clothed; they're happy—

FAY

Are they? Oh, they smile according to their schedules, but they're in limbo while they're in The Jar. I want them out and free to be happy or unhappy any way *they* want.

SCHUB

And do you think our miracle can do anything for them?

FAY

If it can do anything for anyone.

SCHUB

My dear devoted Whitenurse, you're a woman of science: age of reason, ego and id, order and control. Do you honestly believe in people being healed by mere faith?

FAY

Faith in dirty water from a slimy old rock? No.

SCHUB

Aha! Exposed!

FAY

Who?

SCHUB

You, you anarchist! You can't believe in anything that can't be proved in your laboratory of a head! All miracles are fake to you, Nurse Apple. You're in love with science, Nurse Apple; you sleep with discipline, Nurse Apple; you have a core of stone, Nurse Apple. Let these happy hopeful Pilgrims be lost and miserable, again, eh? Let this boom town be a ghost town again, eh? Let those forty-nine loonies—

FAY

NOT—THAT—WORD! (*Fast vamp under*) Nor any word like it! Cookies, Schub, that's what my charges are: Cookies from The Cookie Jar. Patients from Dr. Detmold's Asylum for the Socially Pressured. Quarantined out of fear their disease may be contagious, they are people who made other people nervous by leading individual lives. They suffer from contact with groups and systems, I won't specify who or what. But if the shoe fits, boys, you put your foot in it. NOW—POINT—ONE! (*Music up a key and faster*) I *am* in love with reason and against any balderdash superstition that holds up progress, and those dripping waters of yours not only hold it up, they flood and drown it. My name is Apple, A-Double P-L-E, a fruit well-mentioned in the Bible, that best seller of many miracles. I cite the Ten Commandments and the Burning Bush, to mention only two. Or eleven—depending on your arithmetic. Mine makes them add up to zero because I personally am for the miracles of man such as the wheel, the alphabet and The Pyramids of Egypt! NOW—POINT—TWO! (*Music, as above*) If that exposed sewer system *is* a miracle, I freely admit I will take a running jump in the origin of that water. What is more, if it can make any of those lazy pilgrims—yes they're lazy, trying to get a new life quick—if it can make any of them permanently happy, I will take three running jumps and only come up twice. But I will bet you that the same thing will happen that happens everytime you sell people a myth. Those water works will turn out *not* to be a miracle and those pilgrims are going to end up pounding on our doors! Well, we have no room, Schub. Every bed is full and they are sleeping in shifts! There is no more room in The Jar! NOW—POINT—THREE!!! (*Music, as above*) If these are my beliefs, and they are, why do I want my Cookies to take your waters? I'll tell you why. Because my Cookies are people, Schub, they are human beings and they are to be treated as such and have the same rights as everyone else! You let them sit in your movies, Schub, although you make them sit in a segregated section. You let them charge in your stores, Cooley—although you make them pay on the ninth and not the tenth of the month. So you both can bloody well let them dip into that leaking drain pipe. If you don't I'm not saying I'll go to the police because I am no fool. Nor will I go to the Mayoress because she is. But this is a free town in a free county in a free state in a free country and I am a free woman with a free mouth and if you say No to my Cookies, I will open up that mouth and talk and I am telling you here and now that when I talk, I talk *LONG-AND-LOUD!!!*

(*Music finishes with a crash*)

COOLEY

Mercy!

SCHUB

Apple, you will be rotting in the cellar at the bottom of the jail unless your people are conducted back—*(He stops. He,* FAY *and* COOLEY *have been on one side. On the other, the line of* COOKIES *has unobtrusively blended right into the line of* PILGRIMS*)* Where are they?

FAY

There.

SCHUB

Where?

FAY

There.

SCHUB

But *where* are they there?

*(Slowly, she smiles sweetly at him. He forces a smile back)*

MAGRUDER

All right, now. Who's who?

SCHUB

Shut up. *(To the line)* My dear citizens, will all those who are pilgrims kindly take one short step forward?

*(They all do)*

FAY

Dear friends, will all those who believe in miracles, clap your hands!

(*Everybody does*)

COOLEY

Hear me, Brethren. Everybody who bought one of these red tickets to the miracle, raise it up—high! (*Slowly, one by one, each person on line raises a red ticket*) She stole 'em!

SCHUB

Are you going to say which is which?

FAY

Are you going to let everyone take that water?

SCHUB

No!

FAY

Then No to you!

SCHUB

Then to jail with you!

FAY

You can put me in jail—when you catch me!

(*She starts to run. Instantly, some of the* COOKIES *move to block* SCHUB, COOLEY *and* MAGRUDER. PILGRIMS *on the line move in confusion. This movement is very quick, for all the lights go out except a spot on*

FAY; *everyone else freezes in an attitude of chasing or protecting her. The angry music from her earlier speech begins underneath and she sings)*

FAY

Those smug little men with their smug little schemes,
They forgot one thing:
The play isn't over by a long shot yet!
There are heroes in the world,
Princes and heroes in the world,
And one of them will save me.
Wait and see!
Wait and see!

There won't be trumpets or bolts of fire
To say he's coming.
No Roman candles, no angels' choir,
No sound of distant drumming.
He may not be the cavalier,
Tall and graceful, fair and strong.
Doesn't matter,
Just as long as he comes along!
But not with trumpets or lightning flashing
Or shining armor.
He may be daring, he may be dashing,
Or maybe he's a farmer.
I can wait—what's another day?
He has lots of hills to climb.
And a hero
Doesn't come till the nick of time!
Don't look for trumpets or whistles tooting
To guarantee him!
There won't be trumpets, but sure as shooting
I'll know him when I see him!

Don't know when, don't know where,
And I can't even say that I care!
All I know is, the minute I turn and he's suddenly there
I won't need trumpets!
There are no trumpets!
Who needs trumpets?

*(After the song, the lights return. The freeze is broken by* FAY *who breaks through the crowd and dashes behind the rock as:)*

SCHUB

Don't let her get away! Police!

MAGRUDER

Police!

SCHUB

Idiot! *(To* COOLEY*)* Go to The Cookie Jar and get Dr. Detmold. *(To* MAGRUDER*)* You fool, arrest her at once!

MAGRUDER

*(Grabs the sexy teen-ager he is standing next to)*
Thank you.

SCHUB

Not her, you sex fiend! The nurse! The nurse!

MAGRUDER

Oh, the nurse, the nurse!

*(Runs off)*

SCHUB

*(To the crowd)*

My dear idiots, excuse my friends. I mean—my dear friends, I must ask you to refrain, for the moment, from taking the waters. *(But the crowd now re-forms its line)* While it is true that it is a miracle—

*(Suddenly, there is a great clap of thunder, several flashes of lightning, trumpet calls—which nobody notices—and on walks a very personable man, dressed casually and carrying a small, oblong case:* J. BOWDEN HAPGOOD. *Behind him is a nondescript man carrying a large suitcase)*

HAPGOOD

Excuse me, but could you direct me to The Cookie Jar?

SCHUB

What for?! There's nobody there, they're all here.

HAPGOOD

Where?

SCHUB

There.

HAPGOOD

*(Smiling)*

They don't look it.

SCHUB

Of course they don't look it because all of them aren't!

HAPGOOD

Well, which ones are?

SCHUB

You're asking me?!

HAPGOOD

Not really.

SCHUB

You can't tell by looking anyway! Do I look it?

HAPGOOD

Actually, no.

SCHUB

There you are!

HAPGOOD

Then why aren't you there?

SCHUB

Why should I be?

HAPGOOD

Oh, you mean they allow you to wander around.

SCHUB

I mean I'm here because I belong here! I'm in charge!

HAPGOOD

You can't be Dr. Detmold!

SCHUB

Of course I'm not Dr. Detmold! He isn't here; he's at The Cookie Jar.

HAPGOOD

Ah! And—which way *is* The Cookie Jar?

SCHUB.

That way.

HAPGOOD

(*To his companion*)

No wonder it takes so long to get anywhere. (*To* SCHUB, *indicating the waters*) By the way, what is that?

SCHUB

It's perfectly obvious what that is. That's a miracle, that's what that is.

HAPGOOD

Thank you. See you at The Cookie Jar.

(*And he exits with his companion*)

SCHUB

Where was I? Where *am* I?

CORA

(*Off—singing* a capella)

*Schub! Comptroller Schub!*

SCHUB

O, Father in Heaven—(*As* CORA *enters*) My dear Madam Mayor, I regret—

CORA

(A capella)

*I don't want to hear it! Don't tell me!* (*Speaks, in disgust*) You blew it. Well, I absolutely refuse to be hated again. Where's Dr. Detmold?

(*On this, a fussy, businesslike-looking man with gray hair enters:* DR. DETMOLD)

DETMOLD

In a temper (*He laughs*) Schub, I am in the midst of writing an extremely revolutionary paper for our *Quarterly Monthly*—

SCHUB

Who in that line is a patient of yours?

DETMOLD

You interrupt me and progress to ask that? My new assistant will help you. He is younger but less eminent.

(*He laughs again*)

CORA

Ah! And where is he?

DETMOLD

He knows, I don't.

SCHUB

Doctor, it is a simple matter for you to point out who on that line you know and who—

DETMOLD

It is *not* simple! Psychiatrists do not fraternize with patients so how can we recognize them? We see them only during the analytic hour—when they are lying down. I can do nothing.

(*He starts to go*)

CORA

*Detmold.* We are not amused.

DETMOLD

(*Cringing*)

Your Honor, we doctors are underworked and overpaid. Surely you can wait for my new assistant? He was due several patients ago but I'm—

(*Behind them the drunken* NURSE *enters, cozily hanging on* HAPGOOD'S *arm. He carries both cases now*)

NURSE

Ahoy, Doctor . . .

DETMOLD

(*Joyously*)

Doctor!

(*He extends his hand*)

HAPGOOD

(*Shaking hands*)

Doctor.

DETMOLD

Detmold, L. Sidney.

HAPGOOD

Hapgood, J. Bowden.

DETMOLD

Of course! I may be terrible on faces but I never remember a name. Mayor Schub, Comptroller Hoover Hooper, my new assistant, Dr. Jay.

HAPGOOD *and* SCHUB

(*Simultaneously*)

Doctor–

CORA

He's Schub, you're Hapgood and I'm delighted.

DETMOLD

So am I. Doctor, take care of these good people. Nurse, take the doctor's luggage to the hotel.

HAPGOOD

Just a minute–

DETMOLD

If you need help, bring your dreams to The Cookie Jar and my new assistant will take care of you.

(*He laughs and goes*)

CORA

(*Leering*)

Hello . . .

HAPGOOD

Hello . . .

CORA

So *you* are going to take care of *me*.

SCHUB

First he's going to take care of us. Now Doctor, here's our problem in a nutshell.

CORA

Oh Schub! Ha ha ha ha!

HAPGOOD

(*Aside to* SCHUB)

She's the Mayor . . . ?

SCHUB

Yes: *I'm* the Comptroller. You know about our miracle.

HAPGOOD

Oh yes.

(*He winks at* CORA)

SCHUB

Why are you winking?

HAPGOOD

I wasn't winking. It's just a tic.

SCHUB

It *is* a miracle.

HAPGOOD

Oh yes, so you said. And so I've heard. I think I heard everything from that alcoholic nurse.

SCHUB

Then you realize that we must know immediately which of the people on that line are bona fide pilgrims, entitled to take our miracle waters, and which are—

HAPGOOD

Cookies.

SCHUB

Yes.

HAPGOOD

*(Shakes his hand, then* CORA'S*)*

Good-bye. Good-bye.

CORA

Doctor!

HAPGOOD

*(Leaving)*

You've got the wrong man.

SCHUB

Stop him!

(COOLEY *and a deputy, holding guns, appear and block* HAPGOOD. *He turns and* MAGRUDER *runs on from the other side, a* DEPUTY *behind him*)

MAGRUDER

Your Honor, we can't find a trace of Nurse Apple! She's completely disappeared!

SCHUB

Set up road blocks—get out the police dogs—

CORA

You can borrow mine.

SCHUB

But—Hunt—Her—Down! (DEPUTY *runs off*) Now Doctor, you're an eminent psychiatrist, aren't you?

HAPGOOD

No.

SCHUB

I loathe modesty.

HAPGOOD

Even if I were Freud, I've just arrived here! How can I tell you like that who's a pilgrim and who's a Cookie?

CORA

I'm sure you can.

HAPGOOD

Your Honor—

CORA

Dear Doctor—

HAPGOOD

Dear Mayor—

CORA

—ess.

HAPGOOD

That—is obvious.

CORA

You know, you're divine!

HAPGOOD

Shall we dance?

CORA

Your place or mine?

HAPGOOD

Here and now!

*(Tosses his hat away, the orchestra strikes up and they dance)*

SCHUB

What the hell is this?

HAPGOOD

I have to think and I think best on my feet.

SCHUB

Dancing??

HAPGOOD

Well, usually, I walk. But when I don't want to get anywhere, I dance.

SCHUB

My dear Doctor, it is very urgent we all get somewhere—*fast.*

*(Yanks him out of the dance, ending the music)*

HAPGOOD

. . . Are you cutting in, Schub? Because I don't like—

CORA

Dr. Hapgood, it's *Comptroller* Schub. He is *my* comptroller; this is *my* town; that is *my* miracle. Dr. Detmold, of course, is *your* superior, but he is just another of *my* tax payers. And like all tax payers he is, of course, behind in his taxes. Which means that he—and therefore, *you*—are at *my* disposal. Like garbage. Which means that oh my God, when I look into your eyes, I wish I'd lost that election.

HAPGOOD

I see your problem. And mine. Yesterday mine would have upset me. But today—I'll have fun solving it!

SCHUB

Fun? I'm not following.

HAPGOOD

No, you're leading. That is you were. But now I shall. May I have this dance?

SCHUB

Sir?!

HAPGOOD

With Her Honor. I really do think best on my feet, Comptroller. And I must think out a quick way to discover who is who, what is what and make everybody—

SCHUB

Yes . . . ?

HAPGOOD

Happy. (*Holding out his arms*) Mayor?

CORA

You may.
(*A deep curtsey*)

SCHUB

Then on with the dance! (*Orchestra blast, and they're off! Motioning them toward the line*) No, no. They're over here.

CORA

(*To* HAPGOOD)
Oh, I could think all night!

SCHUB

We haven't got all night. Can't you pick up the tempo?

HAPGOOD

No: Give me a fanfare!

CORA

*While* we're dancing?

HAPGOOD

To announce I'm going to sing to you.

CORA

Brilliant! Dear man, sing it all! (*A fanfare*) But how are you going to separate them?

HAPGOOD

I'm going to examine them according to the principles of logic.

CORA

Logic?

HAPGOOD

It's quick and easy.

(*Sings*)

Grass is green,
Sky is blue,
False is false and
True is true.
Who is who?

You are you,
I'm me!
Simple? Simple? Simple?
Simple as ABC.
Simple as one-two-three!

SCHUB

But who on that line is what?

HAPGOOD

*(Sings)*

One is one,
Two is two,
Who is what and
Which is who?
No one's always what they seem to be.

CORA

*(A crack at* SCHUB*)*

That's certainly true.

HAPGOOD

*(Sings)*

Simple? Simple? Simple?
Simple as A-B-C.
Simple as one-two three.

*(Music continues under. He speaks to a young man on the line)*

For example—you, sir, with the manly good looks. Would you come forward please, Mr. Hapgood?

SCHUB

I thought you were Hapgood.

HAPGOOD

Calling the patient by my name, he identifies with me immediately, we have an instant transference and thereby save five years of psychoanalysis.

CORA

Brilliant! What happens if I call you Hoover Hooper?

HAPGOOD

Shall we dance? No, we have. Now then, Mr. Hapgood—

GEORGE (The YOUNG MAN)

Call me Happy, Sir. Or George.

HAPGOOD

All right, Georgie.

GEORGE

Thank you, George.

HAPGOOD

Thank *you*. Now when we were a child, that is, when you were a child, a boy—you *were* a boy?

GEORGE

I was a manly little fellow, sir.

HAPGOOD

Then I'm sure there was a saying you learned that you have used ever since to govern your life. A motto, a watchcry.

GEORGE

A watchcry. Yes, sir. (*He sings*) "I am the master of my fate and the captain of my soul."

HAPGOOD

Good, Hapgood! Now then: (*Following is spoken rhythmically to orchestral vamp*) Married?

GEORGE

Yes, sir.

HAPGOOD

Two children?

GEORGE

Yes, sir.

HAPGOOD

Two TV sets?

GEORGE

Yes, sir.

HAPGOOD

Two martinis?

GEORGE

Yes, sir.

HAPGOOD

Bank on Friday?

GEORGE

Yes, sir.

HAPGOOD

Golf on Saturday?

GEORGE

Yes, sir.

HAPGOOD

Church on Sunday?

GEORGE

Yes, sir.

HAPGOOD

Do you vote?

GEORGE

Only for the man who wins.
Only for the man who wins.
Only for the man who—

HAPGOOD

*(Holds up his hand)*
All right. Headaches?

GEORGE

No, sir.

HAPGOOD

Backaches?

GEORGE

No, sir.

HAPGOOD

Heartaches?

GEORGE

No, sir.

HAPGOOD

Thank you, Hapgood. (*Music out*) Group A. Over there, please.

SCHUB

(*To* CORA)

What's Group A?

CORA

Obviously mad as a hatter.

SCHUB

Magruder! Place that Cookie under arrest.

HAPGOOD

Just a moment. (*To* GEORGE) George—do you ever wonder whether you're real?

GEORGE

No, sir. I know I'm not.

HAPGOOD

Group One. Over *there*, please.

(*As* GEORGE *crosses to the opposite side, the music returns and* HAPGOOD *sings*)

Grass is green,
Sky is blue
Safe is sane and
Tried is true.
You be you and me to some degree.
Simple? Simple? Simple as A-B-C,
Simple as one-two-three.

CORA

Well, is he safe or sane, Doctor? Darling.

SCHUB

Safe *is* sane.

HAPGOOD

Not always.

(*He sings*)

The opposite of safe is out.
The opposite of out is in.
So anyone who's safe is "in."

GEORGE

(*He sings*)

That I've always been!

CORA

Shh!

(*She sings, joined by* SCHUB, COOLEY *and* MAGRUDER)

The opposite of safe is out.
The opposite of out is in.
So anyone who's safe is "in."

HAPGOOD

Right!

(*He sings*)

That's how groups begin!

CORA, *et al*

When you're in, you win!

HAPGOOD

Simple? Simple? Simple?
Simple as A-B-C.

CORA, *et al*

Simple? Simple? Simple?

HAPGOOD

Simple as do you do like me?

CORA

(*Cooing*)

I do indeed like you. The question is—

SCHUB

(*Overriding impatiently*)

The question is—(*To a* MAN *who has been sneaking over to* GEORGE) Just a moment there—

MAN

(*Sings*)

"I am the master of my fate and the captain of my soul." (*He speaks*) But my name isn't George, Doctor.

HAPGOOD

What is it?

MAN

Hapgood.

HAPGOOD

Group A. Over there, please.

(CORA *and* SCHUB *look at each other*)

SCHUB

What *is* this?

CORA

I don't know, but it's brilliant.

SCHUB

But which group is what?

HAPGOOD

It's very simple.
(*He sings*)
Grass is green,
Sky is blue,
A is one group,
One is too,
One is One or one is A, you see . . .

CORA

(*Nodding brightly, sings*)
Grass is green,
Sky is blue,
One is one and
A is two.

SCHUB

(*Sings*)
No, A is one and
One is, too.

SIMULTANEOUSLY

| CORA | COOLEY | MAGRUDER | SCHUB |
|---|---|---|---|
| No, one and one | | | |
| Is always two | No, One is green, | | |
| To me! | A is blue. | No, A is green, | |
| | One can be | One is blue! | No, One is One, |
| I don't agree! | In A, you see. | A is "out" and | A is one group, |
| A is you and | A is crazy! | One is "in"! | Too. |
| Me! | Maybe. | I agree. | See? |

(*They are interrupted by a* WOMAN *who sings in a strong contralto and comes forward at* HAPGOOD'S *beckoning*)

WOMAN

*(Very loud)*

Aaaaaaaaaaaaaaaa—

*(She is joined by a* MAN; *she is in a very feminine dress, he in a threadbare suit; she keeps dropping a handkerchief for him to pick up, he has a tin cup she keeps dropping coins into)*

MAN *and* WOMAN

*(Singing, a nervous accompaniment underneath)*

A woman's place is in the home,
A woman's place is in the house.
And home is where you hang your hat,
And that is where you hang your spouse.

HAPGOOD

*(Speaks, as music contines)*

Dear Mr. and Mrs. Hapgood.

JUNE (The WOMAN)

Oh, we're not married, Doctor. He's June and I'm John. I mean she's John and he's June.

JOHN

June and John are engaged.

JUNE

John's my secretary.

JOHN

June used to be my secretary but his corporation went bust.

JUNE

And her syndicate took over.

HAPGOOD

Well, it would all be in the family if you got married.

JOHN

But John can't support June.

JUNE

Every cent John makes goes to pay for June's dinners.

HAPGOOD

Why doesn't June give John a raise?

JUNE

He's not worth it.

HAPGOOD

I see. And neither of you wants John to stay home and do the housekeeping because—

HAPGOOD, JUNE, JOHN

*(Sing)*

A woman's place is in the home,
A woman's place is on the shelf.
And home is where he hangs her hat,
And that is where she hangs himself.

CORA *and* SCHUB

*(Expectantly)*

Group—

*(Music stops)*

HAPGOOD

*(To* JUNE*)*

A.

SCHUB

Magruder!

HAPGOOD

*(To* JOHN*)*

One.

*(Music resumes.* HAPGOOD *steers him away from* JUNE *as* ANOTHER COUPLE *and* JUNE *and* JOHN *again sing "A Woman's Place is in the Home" while* GEORGE *and the* SNEAKING MAN *sing "I am the Master of my Fate."* HAPGOOD *directs the* WOMAN *to One and the* MAN *to A. Everybody stares; there is more singing of watchcries, during which* HAPGOOD *splits the singers into one or the other of the Groups and during which* PEOPLE *from each Group—or the line—cross to the other side)*

PEOPLE

*(Sing, simultaneously)*

"A woman's place is in the home, a woman's place is in the house."

"I am the master of my fate and the captain of my soul."

"If at first you don't succeed, try, try again."

"Beauty is only skin deep."

SCHUB

Stop the music! (*It does*) A man crossed over.

HAPGOOD

That was a woman.

SCHUB

Oh.

CORA

(*Pushing* SCHUB)
Group One. (*Music re-enters under*) *Ha ha ha ha ha!*

SCHUB

Now wait! Are they *all* Cookies? If you could produce someone who is sane, present company excluded, of course—
(*A Negro steps forward as* HAPGOOD *beckons*)

HAPGOOD

Ah—good lad, Hapgood. Watchcry!

MARTIN (The NEGRO)

(*Sings*)
You can't judge a book by its cover.
You can't judge a book by its cover.
You can't judge a book
By how literate it look,
No, you can't judge a book by its cubber.
(*Music continues under*)

HAPGOOD

Occupation?

MARTIN

Going to schools, riding in buses, eating in restaurants.

HAPGOOD

Isn't that line of work getting rather easy?

MARTIN

Not for me. I'm Jewish . . . Group A, would you say?

HAPGOOD

Group One's more fun.

MARTIN

Crazy.

CORA

Group A . . .

SCHUB

Group One . . .

CORA

It's maddening!

SCHUB

What's the difference between them?

HAPGOOD

It's obvious:
(*Sings*)
The opposite of dark is bright,

The opposite of bright is dumb.
So anything that's dark is dumb—

MARTIN

But they sure can hum.

(HAPGOOD *and* TWO MEN—*one each from Groups A and One—hum a close-harmony counterpoint to* MARTIN)

The opposite of dark is bright,
The opposite of bright is dumb.

HAPGOOD, MARTIN, TWO MEN

So anything that's dark is dumb.

HAPGOOD, TWO MEN

That's the rule of thumb.

MARTIN

Depends where you're from.

HAPGOOD

(*As* MARTIN *shuffles over to One, Uncle Tom style*)

Simple? Simple? Simple?
Simple as A-B-C.
Simple as NAACP!

(*Music continues under*)

MAN

I get the point, Comptroller Hapgood.

SCHUB

Oh, shut up and get in Group A.

CORA

Who's that?

SCHUB

My brother-in-law.

CORA

But he's not a Pilgrim . . . and he's not a Cookie—Hapgood . . .

HAPGOOD

*(Grins and starts to sing; the music takes on a slightly sinister tone; slowly the line and the rock begin to move upstage)*

Who is what?
Which is who?
That is that and
How are you?
I feel fine, what else is new?

CORA

*(During the above)*

What was he doing on the line?

SCHUB

Oh . . . every fool wants a miracle. Hapgood—

CORA

Who *is* on that line? . . .

SCHUB

Doctor, you are not doing what we want you to!

CORA

You're right! Look here, Hapgood—*(But he holds out his arms to her)*—darling—

*(They dance as she sings; the music becomes a gay waltz)*

Grass is green,
Sky is blue,
I'd join any Group with you.
Schub's a boob and you belong to me!
Simple? Simple? Simple?
Simple as one-two-three, one-two-three, one-two-three . . .

*(Some of the* PEOPLE *on the line pick up the refrain with delight. A few crowd around* HAPGOOD*)*

PEOPLE

Doctor, what Group am I in? Where do I belong? Where am I? Tell me where I am? Where am I?!

*(*HAPGOOD *directs them to one or the other of the Groups until there is no one left on the line)*

SCHUB

*(Pushing through)*

Get back! Your Honor! Cora! He's taking over! They're turning to *him!* Stop it! *(Music suddenly becomes low and sinister; little scenery is left; upstage area darkens)* Doctor—Group A: Cookies? Or Group One: Cookies? The truth now—*Which—is—what?*

HAPGOOD

*(Suddenly, to Group A)*

Watchcry!

GROUP A

*(Singing simultaneously)*
"I am the master of my fate and—"
"A woman's place is in the—"
"If at first you don't succeed—"
(HAPGOOD *cuts them off suddenly and sharply)*

HAPGOOD

Rub your stomachs!
*(They do)*
Goo-ood. Goo-ood.
*(To Group One)*
Watchcry!

GROUP ONE

*(Singing simultaneously)*
"I am the master of my fate and—"
"A woman's place is in the—"
"Beauty is only skin—"
(HAPGOOD *cuts them off)*

HAPGOOD

Pat your heads. *(They do)* Hello. Hello . . . Goo-ood . . . Hello. Hello . . . Reverse! Good. Hello. Hello. That's goo-ood, goo-ood, goo-ood, goo-ood, Comptroller.

SCHUB

*(Who has started doing it)*
Dammit!

CORA

I adore games!

HAPGOOD

Watchcry!

CORA

Hello.

SCHUB

He's boring from within!

HAPGOOD

(*To* SCHUB)

Watchcry!

SCHUB

Communist!

HAPGOOD

You would say that.

(*Sings*)

The opposite of Left is right,
The opposite of right is wrong,
So anyone who's Left is wrong, right?

CROWD

Goo-ood! Goo-ood!

HAPGOOD

Hello!

CROWD

Hello!

HAPGOOD

(*Sings, to* SCHUB)
Simple? Simple? Simple?
Simple as you tell me!
Simple as one-two-three
Cheers for the Red, White and Blue . . .
(*To* MAGRUDER, *as he instinctively straightens to attention*)
Watchcry!

MAGRUDER

Look here: I'm the Chief of—

HAPGOOD

Watchcry!
(*The music, still sinister, becomes martial*)

MAGRUDER

(*Sings*)
"Ours not to reason why, ours but to do or die."
(*Speaks*)
Sergeant Magruder reporting, sir.

HAPGOOD

Occupation?

MAGRUDER

Fighting the enemy.

HAPGOOD

What enemy?

MAGRUDER

What year?

HAPGOOD

Yesterday:

MAGRUDER

(*Angrily*)

The Germans: *Heil!*

HAPGOOD

The day before:

MAGRUDER

(*Angrily*)

The Germans: *Heil!*

HAPGOOD

Today:

MAGRUDER

(*Beaming*)

The Germans: Hail!

HAPGOOD

Tomorrow:

MAGRUDER

(*Beaming*)

Hail!

(*Angrily*)

*Heil!*

(*Puzzled*)

Hail? . . . *Heil?* . . . Hail?

HAPGOOD

Group A.

MAGRUDER

*Heil?*

HAPGOOD

Group One.

MAGRUDER

Hail?

(*He is marching back and forth*)

COOLEY

You're just making him *seem* crazy, but he's twisted. I mean—he's been twisted.

HAPGOOD

(*Sings*)

Grass is blue,
Sky is green,
Change of time is change of scene.
What you meant is what you mean!

(*Wheeling on* COOLEY)

Watchcry!

COOLEY

Hallelujah! Now listen, Brother—

HAPGOOD

Occupation:

COOLEY

Preacher—er, Treasurer.

HAPGOOD

Oh, you *were* a preacher, Hapgood.

COOLEY

I'm a treasurer, Cooley—I mean—

HAPGOOD

They threw you out of your pulpit—

COOLEY

(*To* SCHUB)

Brother!

HAPGOOD

Because you were crazy!

COOLEY

Because I believed!

HAPGOOD

In being treasurer.

COOLEY

In God, and they only believed in religion.

HAPGOOD

And *that* made you crazy, Hapgood.

COOLEY

I am *not* crazy, Cooley!

HAPGOOD

No, you're Crazy Hapgood.

COOLEY

I am not Cooley, I mean I am not crazy, I'm Hapgood!

HAPGOOD

Are you sure?

COOLEY

I am completely Schub!

SCHUB

He's crazy!

HAPGOOD

Thank you.
(*To* COOLEY)
Group A.
(*To Group One*)
Watchcry!
(*They respond automatically; immediately, to Group A*)
Watchcry!
(*They respond; to* SCHUB)
Watchcry!

SCHUB

I don't have one, Cooley!

HAPGOOD

Ah ha!

(*The chanting stops; the music drops to a single spaced beat under*)

SCHUB

Hapgood, we are going to end all this right here and now, my dear Treasurer, I mean Doctor, dammit! Right now: which group is—

HAPGOOD

Two questions.

SCHUB

One answer.

HAPGOOD

Just two little questions, Schub, and you'll *know* which group is what. (*Percussion starts low, under*) Where does most of your money go?

SCHUB

I hardly—

HAPGOOD

Where does most of your money go, Hapgood?

SCHUB

In taxes.

HAPGOOD

*(Motioning to Group One to start gesture)*
Goo-od. *(To* SCHUB*)* What do you think of someone who makes a product and doesn't use it?

SCHUB

He's crazy.

HAPGOOD

*(To second Group)*
Hello, hello. *(They continue as he turns to* SCHUB*)* Most of your money goes to the government in taxes. What does the government do with most of the money? Makes bombs. *(To the Groups)* Reverse! Goo-od. Hello, hello. *(To* SCHUB*)* But you say to make a product and not to use it is crazy. Isn't that what you said, Comptroller Cooley? And doesn't that make you crazy for letting them waste your money, Treasurer Schub? *(To the Groups)* Reverse! *(To* SCHUB*)* But perhaps the government is making bombs because it means to use the product. Which means everyone will be killed, Hapgood. Including you, Schub. *(To the Groups)* Both together now! *(They do both gestures. To* SCHUB*)* Which means you are paying most of your money to have yourself killed. Which means, my dear Doctor Comptroller Mayor Schub, you are the maddest of all! Watchcry!

SCHUB

HELP!!
*(He runs off)*

HAPGOOD

WATCHCRY!

CORA

BRILLIANT!!

HAPGOOD

WATCHCRY!

*(And now everybody on stage begins a chant, led by a wild, cheering, jeering* HAPGOOD. CORA, *at first amused, picks up the chant but then gets more and more frightened as the two Groups form a circle, at* HAPGOOD's *direction, which gets smaller until it closes in on her completely)*

GROUPS

Grass is green.
Sky is blue.
The opposite of left is right.
The opposite of right is wrong.
Simple? Simple? Simple?
Simple as A-B-three,
Simple as one-two-C,
As grass is green
As sky is blue;
As simple as the opposite of left is right
Is wrong Is right Is A Is One
Is A Is One Hello! Hello! Goo-od! Goo-od!
A is One! One is A!
Grass is who is opposite of what is green is safe is opposite
Of dark is opposite of simple which is
Watchcry! Watchcry! Watchcry! Watchcry!

*(The Groups have now crushed* CORA *in their center;* HAPGOOD *is sitting at the footlights. There is a loud furious drum break as* CORA *is tossed in the air like a broken puppet. The light goes almost black except for*

*a weird glow from the footlights. The two Groups run down to the footlights and, in a straight line right across the stage, chant fast and shrill, with mounting intensity)*

Who is what? Which is who?
Who is what? Which is who?
Who is what? Which is WHO is WHO?

*(Silence and blackout except for a light on* HAPGOOD. *He looks at the audience with a smile and says, quietly)*

HAPGOOD

You are all mad.

*(There is a burst of gay, wild circus music. A row of lights resembling the balcony rail of a theatre has been lowered and it now begins to burn brighter and brighter with pink, blue, yellow lights, flooding the theatre audience. At the same time, the real balcony rail lights in the theatre are coming on and lighting up the stage. And there we see the company sitting in theatre seats and laughing and applauding louder and louder as*

*The Curtain Falls*

# ACT TWO

*The theatre seats are now in the town square. A center aisle separates them so that they look like bleachers. One side has pennants and placards reading Group A; the other side has similar signs reading Group One. As the two Groups sing the following march,* HAPGOOD *is carried on by two members of each Group on* CORA*'s litter and is cheered and besieged for autographs.*

GROUP A

Hooray for A, the Group that's well-adjusted,
Everyone can be trusted in Group A.

GROUP ONE

Have fun with One, the Group that's not neurotic,
Everyone's patriotic in Group One.

BOTH

Dignity, integrity and so on,
We haven't much to go on,
Still we go on.
We've a platform strong enough to grow on:

GROUP A

Whenever they cheer, we're incensed!

GROUP ONE

Whatever they're for, we're against!
(HAPGOOD *enters*)

GROUP A

Hooray for Hapgood,
Hapgood can be trusted,
Friend of the well-adjusted in Group A!

GROUP ONE

Hooray for Hapgood
Hapgood's patriotic,
Friend of the un-neurotic in Group One!

BOTH

Hapgood has no answers or suggestions,
Only a lot of questions—
We like questions.
What's the use of answers or suggestions?
As long as we're told where to go,
There isn't a thing we need to know!

*(The march never really ends; it fades off as both Groups leave their seats and march out after* HAPGOOD, *aloft on his litter. As the last marchers clear, a flamboyantly sexy-looking creature is revealed sitting in one of the theatre seats, glancing through a program. She wears an extravagant red coat trimmed with feathers, dark glasses and a red wig.* SCHUB *enters, sees her, preens and takes a seat near her. He doesn't recognize her but we do. Or we will. It is* FAY APPLE *who speaks with one of the thickest French accents in captivity)*

FAY

*Bon—jour.*

SCHUB

A very *bonjour* to you, my dear, dear Madame.

FAY

*Mademoiselle*—unfortunately. (*She and* SCHUB *get out of the seats which slide off, revealing a small red traveling case*) I am—(*A hot chord blasts from the orchestra*) Colette—(*Chord*)—Antoinette—(*Chord*)—Alouette—(*Chord*)—Mistinguette—(*Chord*)—Alfabette—(*Chord*)—de—la—Val—lere: Ze lady from Lourdes!

(*Instantly, music;* CORA'S *four* BOYS *pop out and with* FAY *sing à la "The Lady in Red"*)

FAY *and* BOYS

Ze Lady from Lourdes,
Ze boys are all crazy bout ze
Lady from Lourdes!
Ooh, la la!

(*The* BOYS *exit*)

SCHUB

Lourdes is in France, I gather.

FAY

*Oui, monsieur.*

SCHUB

You must be very weary after your journey. Why don't we have an *apéritif* this evening? My place, seven-thirty. Better make that six-thirty. Your place. Or mine. It makes no difference. Your place at six. Sharp.

FAY

I have ze work to do first, *monsieur*.

SCHUB

Work?

FAY

*Certainement*. I am from Lourdes.

SCHUB

So you sang . . . What are you looking at?

(*Across the stage,* HAPGOOD *appears on the balcony of the Hotel Superbe with cigar and champagne.* SCHUB'S *back is to him, but he and* FAY *are facing each other*)

FAY

Zat *docteur*. He is ze most important man in town, no?

SCHUB

No. I'm the most important man in town—next to the Mayor-ess.

FAY

Zen you are ze man to 'elp me! *Monsieur* knows that which Lourdes she is famous for, no?

SCHUB

*L'amour?*

FAY

No, no, *monsieur*.

SCHUB

*La sexe?*

FAY

Ah, you make ze funny of me. (*She and* HAPGOOD *leer at each other. She beckons to him; he leans closer; she beckons again and the scenery obliges: the whole balcony moves to her. During this, she continues to* SCHUB) Ze whole world, she know that which Lourdes she is famous for, is—*la miracle! Et moi*—me—I am sent 'ere to investigate your miracle.

SCHUB

To investigate—my—miracle.

FAY

*Oui.* Since Lourdes, she is ze mama of all ze miracles, so we ladies from Lourdes, we go all over ze globe to see if ze new little baby miracles are 'ow you say—legitimate.

SCHUB

If you'll excuse me, dear *mademoiselle,* I think I must go home and faint.

(*He exits*)

FAY

*Au'voir, monsieur.*

(*She tosses her dark glasses away, and she and* HAPGOOD *smile at each other. During their conversation subtitles are flashed on, indicated here by parentheses. Everything is spoken as though they were in an old French sex film*)

FAY

*Il est fou.* (He's mad.)

HAPGOOD

*Tout le monde est fou, sauf vous et moi.* (The whole world's mad—except you and me.)

FAY

*Et bien—bonjour!* (Well, then—hello!)

HAPGOOD

*Comment ça va?* (How are you?)

FAY

*Bien. Êtes-vous marié?* (Well. Are you married?)

HAPGOOD

*Quatre fois.* (Four times.)

FAY

*Au'voir.* (Good-bye.)
(*She starts to go*)

HAPGOOD

*Mais, je suis divorcé!* (But I'm divorced!)

FAY

*Combien de fois?* (How many times?)

HAPGOOD

*Quatre.* (Four.)

From left to right, James Frawley as CHIEF MAGRUDER, Arnold Soboloff as TREASURER COOLEY, and Gabriel Dell as CONTROLLER SCHUB inside the miraculous rock. *Jos. Abeles Studio*

Lee Remick and Harry Guardino. *Jos. Abeles Studio*

Angela Lansbury as CORA HOOVER HOOPER celebrates the miracle. *Jos. Abeles Studio*

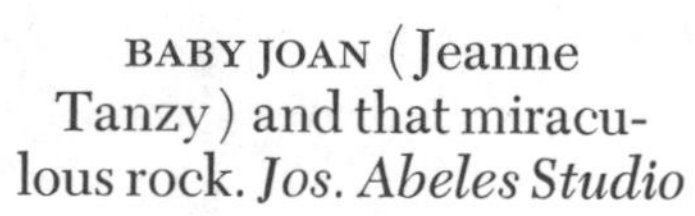

BABY JOAN (Jeanne Tanzy) and that miraculous rock. *Jos. Abeles Studio*

FAY

*Bonjour.* (Hello.)
(*She returns*)

HAPGOOD

*Voulez-vous monter?* (Would you like to come up?)

FAY

*Comment?* (What?)

HAPGOOD

*Monter, monter?* (Come up, come up?)
(FAY *frowns, then steps back to look up at the translation*)

FAY

*Ah, oui, oui—monter! Oui, oui.* (Ah, yes, yes—come up. Yes, yes.)

HAPGOOD

*Pardon: parlez-vous français?* (Excuse me: do you speak French?)

FAY

*Un peu.* (A little.)

HAPGOOD

*Anglais?* (English?)

FAY

*Parfaitement.* (Perfectly.)

HAPGOOD

*Et puis, vous êtes Américaine.* (Then you're an American.)

FAY

*Qui n'est pas?* (Who isn't?)

HAPGOOD

*Et vos cheveux, en votre famille qui a des cheveux rouges?* (And your hair, who in your family has red hair?)

FAY

*Personne.* (Nobody.)

HAPGOOD

*Même pas vous?* (Not even you?)

FAY

*Même pas moi. C'est une*—how do you say? Wig? (Not even me. It's a—)

HAPGOOD

Wig.

FAY

Do you mind?

HAPGOOD

Not a bit.

FAY

I didn't think you would. (*She sings*) *Docteur, docteur, vous êtes charmant.* (Doctor, doctor, you're charming.)

HAPGOOD

(*Sings*)
*Mademoiselle, vous, aussi.* (Mademoiselle, you too.)

FAY

(*Sings, keeping French accent*)
You like my hair, yes? My lips, yes?
Ze sway of my—how you say?—of my hips, yes?
You wish to play wiz me?
Okay wiz me,
Come out and play wiz me.
(*She leaves the balcony*)

HAPGOOD

(*Following*)
*Mademoiselle, vous êtes jolie.* (Mademoiselle, you're pretty.)

FAY

*Docteur, docteur, si gentil.* (Doctor, doctor, you're too kind.)
You like my style, yes? My brand, yes?
Ze lay of my—how say?—of my land, yes?
You wish to pray wiz me?
To stray wiz me?
Come out and play wiz me.

HAPGOOD

*Mademoiselle, vous êtes timide.* (Mademoiselle, you're shy.)

FAY

*Docteur, docteur,* you're so right.
I like your—how you say—
Imperturbable perspicacity.
It's never how you say, it's what you see!

We have ze lark, yes? Ze fling, yes?
Ze play is ze—how you say?—is ze thing, yes?
If you will play wiz me,
*Mon chéri,*
Though we may not agree
Today
In time—
*Mais oui!*
We may.

*Docteur, docteur,* ze English it fails me.
Ah, but, *docteur,* you're good for what ails me.

HAPGOOD

I like your hair—

FAY

Yes?

HAPGOOD

Your lips—

FAY

Yes?

HAPGOOD

Ze sway of your—how you say?—of your hips—

FAY

Yes?

HAPGOOD

Come up and play wiz me.

FAY

Come out and play wiz me.

BOTH

Come on and play wiz me.

FAY

*(Not coming up)*
*Docteur, docteur,* let's play *docteur* . . .

HAPGOOD

*Mademoiselle,* you're not well!
But I like your style—

FAY

Yes?

HAPGOOD

Your brand—

FAY

Yes?

HAPGOOD

Ze lay of your—*qu'est-ce que c'est*—of your land—

FAY

Yes?

HAPGOOD

Come up and play wiz me.

FAY

Come out and play wiz me.

BOTH

Come on and play wiz me!

HAPGOOD

(*Gesturing her up*)

*Mademoiselle,* doctor's orders . . .

FAY

(*Climbing up*)

You're ze *docteur,* I'm impatient . . .

HAPGOOD

You have such—how you say?—unmistakable authen-
ticity!
It isn't how you say, it's what I see!

FAY

We have ze lark—yes? Ze fling—yes?
Ze play is ze—how you say?—is ze thing—yes?

*(During this, she strips off her gloves and her red coat so that she is down to a very skimpy, alluring dress. Now, she leans back against the proscenium, the music becomes satirically seductive, and four gloved hands steal out and begin to caress her body.* HAPGOOD *gapes and makes a dive for her; she eludes him and the owners of the hands appear:* CORA*'s four* BOYS. *During the dance that follows, they keep preventing* HAPGOOD *from getting to* FAY *who keeps luring him on. At last, he does get rid of them and he and* FAY *end together, singing)*

FAY *and* HAPGOOD

Come on and play wiz me,
*Mon ami,*
Come have your way wiz me
Today!
You play
Wiz me—

HAPGOOD

My way—

FAY

Maybe—

HAPGOOD

*Bé-bé—*

FAY

*Mais oui!*

BOTH

We play!

*(After the song, the music resumes softly as* HAPGOOD *leads* FAY *up onto the balcony and through a door, presumably leading to the room inside. The balcony revolves as they come out. He reaches up to the flowered wall panel revealed—and pulls down a short, thin, impractical Murphy bed.* FAY *tries to sit on it seductively but it is hard wood.* HAPGOOD *is trying to get on the bed with her when the telephone rings)*

HAPGOOD

Hello? . . . That is none of your business . . . Well, send up another. *(He hangs up)* It was the management. They wanted to know if you were staying in my room, so I told them to send up—ah! Here it comes now!

*(And another room is riding on; an enormous bed, with glass flowers on the headboard which can light up like a pinball machine when the activity warrants)*

FAY

*(French accent)*

What splendor! A living room—and a loving room!

HAPGOOD

How come you still have the accent?

FAY

It came wiz ze wig.

*(He lies on the big bed, which is very luxurious)*

HAPGOOD

Ah! You know where *you* are? In the living room.

FAY

*Bon.* Zat is good for discussing ze first reason I am 'ere. Doctor, I 'ave need of your 'elp.

HAPGOOD

*(Cooing)*

It's here: in the loving room.

FAY

Ze loving room . . .

HAPGOOD

Cozy . . .

FAY

Comfortable . . .

HAPGOOD

Come on.

FAY

Chase me.

HAPGOOD

Uh-uh.

FAY

You can catch me.

HAPGOOD

I chased four women in my life—and every one of 'em caught me (*He gets up*) and tried to change me.

FAY

(*Going to him*)

I would not.

HAPGOOD

You're a woman—I adore women.

(*Suddenly, he throws her on the bed in a wild embrace and the flowers light up*)

FAY

And I adore *docteurs.*

HAPGOOD

*Médecins.* You adore *médecins.*

FAY

*Oui. J'adore des médecins parce que je suis une*—How do you say "nurse"?

HAPGOOD

You're no nurse—

FAY

I am. (*He laughs. She jumps up*) *Mais oui!* And you are ze *un* doctor who can help me!

HAPGOOD

Come back to the operating table.

FAY

I am *sérieuse!*

HAPGOOD

I'll take you seriously!

FAY

But I am a monster as a nurse! Now—Point—*Une!* (*Music as earlier. She parodies herself*) My name is Apple A-double P-L-E, Fay Apple, qualified head nurse in charge of forty-nine patients in Dr. Detmold's Asylum for the Socially Pressured!

(*Music holds for*)

HAPGOOD

Oh no, not you!

FAY

Now—Point—*Deux!* (*Music up as before*) Zere is an urgent matter of duty and responsibility and I can never shirk either as I am a dedicated woman of science, control, and—

HAPGOOD

Come here.

FAY

—and order—and—

HAPGOOD

Here.

(*Music becomes a* beguine)

FAY

In order not to identify my beloved Cookies, I am done up in zis outlandish dress and zis ridiculous wig—

HAPGOOD

Lovely dress, lovely wig—

FAY

And zis lovely wig.

(*She returns to the bed. He begins making love to her as*)

HAPGOOD

Why the Lady from Lourdes?

FAY

I 'ave come from someplace French.

HAPGOOD

*Oui.*

FAY

*Eh bien!* I sink if Madame 'oover 'ooper et Monsieur Schub, if zey sink I am from Lourdes, per'aps I can frighten zem into letting my forty-nine Cookies take ze miracle waters.

*(A long kiss; it satisfies both of them; they start to undress)*

HAPGOOD

Why?

FAY

To expose zat miracle as ze fake.

HAPGOOD

What happens if zey find your Cookies first?

FAY

Zey won't. I 'ave stolen ze records which are in my 'andbag. Which is in ze living room—which is where we better go zis minute or I will never get you to help me.

HAPGOOD

'Elp.

FAY

'Elp.

HAPGOOD

'Elp you do what?

*(He kisses her)*

FAY

I forgot.

HAPGOOD

I'll do it. Do you believe in miracles?

FAY

No.

HAPGOOD

I do. *One* miracle, anyway.

FAY

Me.

HAPGOOD

*(Starting to unzip her dress)*

Uh-uh.

FAY

Us.

HAPGOOD

Uh-uh.

FAY

Ow!

*(His hand which has been going up her back, pulls at her hair. She shrieks and rolls off the bed)*

HAPGOOD

I'm just helping you take your things off.

FAY

(*No accent*)

Not my *hair!*

HAPGOOD

It's not your hair, it's a wig.

FAY

How do you know?

HAPGOOD

You told me!

FAY

I was lying!

HAPGOOD

You're mad!

FAY

It's staying on!

HAPGOOD

I *couldn't* with that thing on!

FAY

(*Scrambling to her feet*)

I couldn't with it off!

HAPGOOD

You probably want the lights off!

FAY

Lights on, wig on!

HAPGOOD

You think if I see you without that damn-fool wig, I won't want to—

FAY

NO! I won't!!!

HAPGOOD

*(After a moment)*

*You* won't?? . . . Oh, nonsense.

*(He moves to her)*

FAY

*(Backing away)*

I'm warning you—

HAPGOOD

Nonsense.

*(He grabs her, snatches the wig off and kisses her violently. But she is like a rag doll in his arms. He lets go; then tests one of her arms; it is rigid. A pause)*

FAY

Are you angry?

HAPGOOD

Baffled. Absolutely baffled. Damnedest thing.

FAY

(*Goes to the other room for her red handbag, comb and mirror*)

Eight years ago, at the hospital where I was training, we put on a graduation play. I was what I still am—control and order—so everyone thought it would be funny to make me be a French *soubrette*. This was the dress; zis was ze accent; and (*She holds up the wig*) I put it on; I wore it to the party afterwards. A week later I woke up in a hotel room in Cleveland with an interne.

HAPGOOD

(*Has been dressing*)

A week in a wig—and woe.

FAY

Yes. The wig was off. I was me again and I was shocked.

HAPGOOD

At what?

FAY

Me! Control and order; out the window of that hotel room! Well, I packed that dress *and* that wig *and* that accent; and ever since, wherever I've gone, they've been in a box under my bed. You know how people in AA keep a bottle of whiskey around as a reminder?

HAPGOOD

Think less, enjoy more

FAY

I try. But I just can't let go. Even with that damn wig, it's a struggle. And you can't leave it on. You've got to wash your hair *some*time. And *its* hair.

HAPGOOD

I didn't know you wash a wig.

FAY

Oh sure. I do try! I even had myself psychoanalyzed. By Dr. Detmold.

HAPGOOD

What did you expect?

FAY

A miracle.

(*A moment. She forces a giggle*)

HAPGOOD

Woman of science?

FAY

I didn't say—

HAPGOOD

(*Laughs*)

YOU'RE A FAKE! You really *want* your Cookies to take those waters! You hope it really is a miracle!

FAY

Merely because I try to keep an open mind—

HAPGOOD

*Merde, mademoiselle!* I'll bet you'd like to bathe in those waters yourself!

FAY

All right: yes; I would! For God's sake, I *need* a miracle!

HAPGOOD

Well, there aren't any.

FAY

You said there was one.

HAPGOOD

One you're too complicated to enjoy.

FAY

Oh, am I? What is it?

HAPGOOD

Being alive.

FAY

Oh that.

HAPGOOD

"Oh that." You don't think "that's" a miracle because you don't understand human nature. We are all out to do each other in, and if we're not celebrating victory tomorrow, it'll be Miracle Number Two. "Oh that." We're never present at the end of "oh that" so we never know what it means—if anything. All we *do* know about "oh that," Nurse A-double P-L-E, is we have it; and the only thing we can do is enjoy it—*now!*

FAY

Wait; I'll put on the wig!

HAPGOOD

That'd be like taking advantage of a drunk.

FAY

Take advantage!

HAPGOOD

Go home to your asylum.

FAY

No!—Listen, I'll get drunk!

HAPGOOD

I'll bet you can't.

FAY

I can't . . . I can't be hypnotized. I can't laugh—not really. I can't whistle—

HAPGOOD

Nonsense.

FAY

No, true. I can't sing at parties. I can't play the piano by ear. When I was little, my, how I wanted to! My girl friend could. Once I walked into a music store, sat down at a big, shiny grand piano—and I played. (*Terrible sounds from pit piano*) Well, you can take piano lessons. Use a metronome; learn control and order. (*Scales on pit piano, turning into lead-in for the song*) But . . . you can't take lessons in whistling. So—your woman of science; every walk I take, every street, every year, I wait. My mouth waits. But—(*Her mouth puckers*) I can't.

(*She sings*)

Anyone can whistle,
That's what they say—
Easy.
Anyone can whistle
Any old day—
Easy.
It's all so simple:
Relax, let go, let fly.
So someone tell me why
Can't I?
I can dance a tango,
I can read Greek—
Easy.
I can slay a dragon
Any old week—
Easy.
What's hard is simple,
What's natural comes hard.
Maybe you could show me
How to let go,
Lower my guard,
Learn to be free.

Maybe if you whistle,
Whistle for me.
*(The music continues softly as* HAPGOOD *goes to her and kisses her gently. Even though she tries to respond, she goes rigid again, and he moves away)*

HAPGOOD

I thought perhaps that week in Cleveland—

FAY

*(Sadly)*

It was a helluva week in Cleveland . . . But I was wearing that wig and—

HAPGOOD

I know.
*(He smiles nicely at her, turns away and goes back to the bed as she reprises the last half of the song. At the end, they are apart from each other. The lights dim out and both beds slide off into the darkness. A moment, then the march from the opening of the act strikes up and the lights come up on the town square. The two Groups are parading, carrying their placards and singing lustily. During their marching, the reverse side of their signs is shown and all are exactly the same: all bear the one word* YES *on the same colored background)*

GROUP A

Hooray for Hapgood,
Hapgood can be trusted,
Friend of the well-adjusted in Group A!

GROUP ONE

Hooray for Hapgood,
Play a part with Hapgood,
Miracles start with Hapgood,
Gladden your heart with Hapgood!

BOTH

Join the parade with Hapgood!
No one's afraid with Hapgood!

Follow your star with Hapgood!
Know who you are with Hapgood!

Throw in your lot for Hapgood!
Everyone's hot for Hapgood!

(CORA *emerges through the singing marchers waving a chiffon handkerchief. She gets shoved around a bit and sings out to them, as they march by, ignoring her*)

CORA

Hi! . . . Hey! . . . Wait! . . . Voters . . .

(*They are gone; she is alone, and she sings quietly*)

I see flags, I hear bells,
There's a parade in town.
I see crowds, I hear yells,
There's a parade in town!

I hear drums in the air,
I see clowns in the square,
I see marchers marching,
Tossing hats at the sky.

Did you hear? Did you see?
Is a parade in town?
Are there drums without me?
Is a parade in town?
Well, they're out of step, the flutes are squeaky, the banners are frayed.
Any parade in town without me
Must be a second class parade!

So! . . . Ha! . . .

*(But the marchers storm on again, singing loudly and paying no attention to her)*

BOTH GROUPS

Hapgood has no answers or suggestions,
Only a lot of questions.
We like questions!
What's the use of answers or suggestions?
As long as we're told where to go,
There isn't a thing we need to know.

*(They start to repeat their original refrains, but* CORA *claps her hands over her ears, shutting them out as she sings until they have marched off and she is alone)*

CORA

Did you hear? Did you see?
Was a parade in town?
Were there drums without me?
Was a parade in town?
Cause I'm dressed at last, at my best, and my banners are high
Tell me, while I was getting ready
Did a parade go by?

*(She stands bewildered, forlorn:* SCHUB *enters)*

SCHUB

I know: they hate you.

CORA

And they love him!

SCHUB

Oh, everybody loves a pretty face. And the rabble worships anyone who tells 'em they belong to anything.

CORA

*(Pacing)*

They belong to *me*—and they were carrying him on *my* litter.

SCHUB

*(He too paces furiously)*

If he weren't a psychiatrist, I'd swear he knew what he was doing.

CORA

*I* should be on their backs!

SCHUB

He's turned the whole town into a madhouse! We're on the brink of a disaster!

CORA

It's *my* disaster!

SCHUB

Madam, will you forget yourself for the moment?

CORA

I only live for the moment.

SCHUB

Well, at this moment we must stop every single person from taking those waters until those damn Cookies are locked up.

CORA

Why?

SCHUB

Otherwise Hapgood or some other anarchist will say an epidemic of lunacy was caused by our miracle.

CORA

Oh my God! We'll be ruined by our saviour! Quick!

SCHUB

What?

CORA

Here!

SCHUB

Where?

CORA

Somewhere, something, somebody! *SCHUB! COMPTROL—*

SCHUB

I'm here.

CORA

Don't panic.

SCHUB

Don't you panic.

CORA

But we must do something!

SCHUB

Of course, we must do something!

CORA

I am doing something.

SCHUB

What?

CORA

I'm panicking.

SCHUB

So am I.

BOTH

*(A shriek)*

*POLICE!*

CORA

Ah, There's nothing like a good scream.

SCHUB

Yes, I feel much better. Now: a quick way to destroy that damn doctor's popularity.

CORA

Is that absolutely necessary?

SCHUB

My dear girl—

CORA

*(A deep breath)*

All right, Schub.

SCHUB

All right what?

CORA

I'll marry him. *(He looks at her. Weakly)* Just a—tiny bit of humor.

SCHUB

*(Wistfully)*

Not everybody loves a pretty face.

CORA

*(Gently)*

You have charm, Schub.

SCHUB

(*Sweetly*)

Your place or mine?

CORA

Mine. I'm getting a massage.

MAGRUDER

(*Runs on with* COOLEY)

Your honor!

SCHUB

I told you to guard the miracle!

MAGRUDER

I got a posse of special deputies around the rock.

COOLEY

Brother, it'll take more than deputies to keep that crowd from taking the waters.

CORA

(*Sings* a capella)

*Schub! Comptroller Schub!*

SCHUB

No need to panic, dear lady. I'll think of a plan to save us.

CORA

(*Charming steel*)

Of course you will. After all, a man who is capable of inventing a miracle is capable of anything. (*He kisses her hand)* Seven-thirty. My house. *(She starts off, then turns back)* All of you.

*(She exits)*

SCHUB

By God, gentlemen, there's a woman who can handle a crowd!

*(And the crowd of marchers returns, singing away as* SCHUB, COOLEY *and* MAGRUDER *stride off. As the marchers parade around and off, the "living room" and the "loving room" come back on.* HAPGOOD *is lying across the big bed, watching* FAY *put her wig back on. The contents of her red traveling bag are strewn around her—including the stolen records)*

HAPGOOD

It's damn depressing: watching a woman get dressed after you didn't.

FAY

It's time to charge City Hall.

HAPGOOD

Where's the accent?

FAY

No point in wasting it here. Are you coming?

HAPGOOD

You know, with or without that wig, you're almost beautiful.

FAY

I'm not a real beauty and I'm glad.

HAPGOOD

Why?

FAY

Because I never have to worry about becoming an ex-beauty.

HAPGOOD

*Bonjour.*

FAY

Hello; and come on.

HAPGOOD

I said *Bonjour.*

FAY

And I said Hello. (*She look at him; then*) Oh, Hell!! (*She hurls herself into his arms*) *Bon-jour!*

(*A wild kiss*)

HAPGOOD

It's that nurse who gets in the way.

FAY

*Oui.*

HAPGOOD

What're we going to do about her?

FAY

Kiss her.

HAPGOOD

Are these her records?

FAY

*Oui.*

HAPGOOD

Tear 'em up.

FAY

What??

HAPGOOD

What's the easiest way to get rid of a nurse? Get rid of her patients. Tear 'em up!

FAY

That's tearing up people.

HAPGOOD

Most people'd like to be torn up and set free. You'd love it!

FAY

I would not!

(*She starts gathering up records frantically*)

HAPGOOD

And your Cookies would, too! They could stop pretending

to be like everybody else and go back to living the way they want; they could enjoy!

FAY

And end up right back in the asylum again!

HAPGOOD

So what? We're all going to end up dead; why lie down and fold up now?! (*Stopping her*) Fay, the world made those Cookies, you didn't. Fix the world, not them! Come on, lady: tear 'em up! (*He grabs a record*) Let 'em go! Let yourself go!

FAY

I couldn't.

HAPGOOD

It's easy.

FAY

No.

HAPGOOD

I'll show you how.

(*He holds up record to rip it*)

FAY

Don't!

HAPGOOD

Are you protesting or do you mean it?

FAY

I mean it. Don't.

HAPGOOD

*(Contemptuously drops record on bed as music starts. He sings low, with tight anger at first, then with mounting passion)*

Everybody says don't,
Everybody says don't,
Everybody says don't—it isn't right,
Don't—it isn't nice!

Everybody says don't,
Everybody says don't,
Everybody says don't walk on the grass,
Don't disturb the peace,
Don't skate on the ice.

Well, I
Say
Do.
I say
Walk on the grass, it was meant to feel!
I
Say
Sail!
Tilt at the windmill,
And if you fail, you fail.

Everybody says don't,
Everybody says don't,
Everybody says don't get out of line
When they say that, then,
Lady, that's a sign:

Nine times out of ten,
Lady, you are doing just fine!

Make just a ripple.
Come on, be brave.
This time a ripple,
Next time a wave.
Sometimes you have to start small,
Climbing the tiniest wall,
Maybe you're going to fall—
But it's better than not starting at all!

Everybody says no,
Everybody says stop,
Everybody says mustn't rock the boat!
Mustn't touch a thing!

Everybody says don't,
Everybody says wait,
Everybody says can't fight City Hall,
Can't upset the cart,
Can't laugh at the King!

Well, I
Say
Try!
I
Say
Laugh at the kings, or they'll make you cry.
Lose
Your
Poise!
Fall if you have to,
But, lady, make a noise!

Everybody says don't.
Everybody says can't.
Everybody says wait around for miracles,
That's the way the world is made!
I insist on
Miracles, if *you* do them,
Miracles—nothing to them!
I say don't:
Don't be afraid!

*(He holds up the record and reads)*

"Engels, David J."

*(A moment. He starts to rip it; she snatches it from him)*

FAY

I don't know what kind of a doctor you are but I'm a registered nurse and I cannot allow you to tear up my patients.

HAPGOOD

I'm no kind of doctor.

FAY

*(Putting record away)*

That's right: pout.

HAPGOOD

I'm not pouting, I am merely telling you I am not a doctor.

FAY

What do you mean you're not a doctor?

HAPGOOD

I mean I'm not a doctor.

FAY

You certainly are a doctor. You're Dr. J. Bowden Hapgood.

HAPGOOD

I am J. Bowden Hapgood but I am not now, nor have I ever been a member of the medical profession. I've never even been sick.

FAY

But everybody knows—

HAPGOOD

Everybody knows whatever they're told.

FAY

But you said—

HAPGOOD

*(Goes for his coat)*

I said? I said "Doctor," that's all. I came here by train, escorted by a very charming if slightly overly-attached gentleman. Before we got to the asylum, we were met by a very amiable if slightly alcoholic nurse. She in turn escorted me to your very gracious if slightly befuddled boss. *She* said "Doctor"—*he* said "Doctor"—*(He extends his hand)* *I* said "Doctor"—*(He extends his other hand)* And there I was: Dr. J. Bowden Hapgood.

*(He shakes hands with himself)*

FAY

Then you're—

HAPGOOD

Dear Nurse Apple—
*(He reaches into the coat pocket)*

FAY

Oh no.

HAPGOOD

*(Pulls out a record identical to the others and presents it)*
—I am your fiftieth Cookie.

FAY

You're crazy!

HAPGOOD

*(Beams)*
And you have to take care of me. Read it. But don't tear *me* up because I love being a Cookie and I want to stay in your lovely Jar.

FAY

*(Reading from the record)*
"Hapgood, J. Bowden. Professor of Statistical Philosophy." Four, no, five degrees! Adviser to the President"!

HAPGOOD

Until late one recession when it dawned on me you can use any figures to prove any side of any question.

FAY

What'd you do?

HAPGOOD

Quit.

FAY

And then?

HAPGOOD

Then? . . . I followed the seasons around the world.

FAY

*(Softly)*

Oh my Hapgood!

HAPGOOD

Not quite so fast. *(He points to the record)* I've been arrested.

FAY

*(Admiringly)*

Seventeen times!

HAPGOOD

A hundred and seventeen. Machines are getting to be as bad as people.

FAY

Why were you arrested?

HAPGOOD

For trying to keep the miracle going.

FAY

How?

HAPGOOD

In a hundred and seventeen different ways. Once I held an aquacade off a testing island. That was my hundredth arrest. Then day before yesterday, I went to the UN—and played "Auld Lang Syne" on my horn.

FAY

What horn?

HAPGOOD

My trumpet. (*He produces it from the small oblong case he arrived with*) I thought it was loud enough to waken the dying. Turns out I'm only the Pied Piper for lunatics. So that trumpet goes under *my* bed.

FAY

How can they say you're crazy! You're a musician!

HAPGOOD

I only play by ear.

FAY

Oh, darling!

HAPGOOD

But they're right! Until this morning, I was probably the

craziest man in the world. Because I was not only an idealist, I was a practising idealist! Now *that is mad;* it's thankless; and it's absolutely exhausting! (*He looks at her, smiles*) Smile: it's finished. I'm free now!

FAY

Free? (*Holds up his record*) You lunatic, you've been certified! You've been committed!

HAPGOOD

Yes, isn't it marvelous! I'm not responsible to or for any thing or anyone. I'm a retired Don Quixote!

FAY

. . . Then why have you been trying to help me?

HAPGOOD

Oh—for fun . . . (*She keeps staring*) Habit. And a bad one . . . A hangover from yesterday . . . Well, I can't just turn it off in one day!

FAY

I don't think you can turn it off at all!

HAPGOOD

But I'm mad, I'm crazy, I'm insane!

(*On this, he grabs his coat, jumps over the beds and ends in a madman-like pose with the coat over his head.* FAY *looks at him with loving admiration and says softly*)

FAY

You're marvelous. (*A moment; then he removes the coat,*

*straightens up and stares at this girl who believes in him. She goes for her records and holds up the one he started to tear)*
"Engels, David J."
*(Holds it out to him)*

HAPGOOD

It's on your head.

FAY

It's your miracle.

HAPGOOD

It's anybody's.

FAY

. . . Even–mine?

HAPGOOD

Could be.

FAY

"Engels, David J."
*(Music, and a spotlight picks out Engels who stands quite still with the "Cookie" grin on his face, waiting to be freed. The two rooms begin to disappear,* HAPGOOD *riding off with them as he urges:)*

HAPGOOD

Well, come on! Do it!
*(*FAY *hesitates and then with a surge of music, rips the record, setting Engels free. He stops his grin and begins to dance. This is the beginning of a ballet in*

*which* FAY *rips up the records of the* COOKIES, *setting them free, in dance, to be what they want. As each gets free, he infects other people who pick up what he is doing. Until, at last,* FAY *herself is infected and begins to dance freely and happily. At the climax,* HAPGOOD *appears on the balcony of the hotel. Everyone clears but* FAY *who is across the stage from him. A brief moment, then she slowly begins to walk across the stage to him, with her hands outstretched to him as*

*The Curtain Falls*

## ACT THREE

(CORA *is stretched out on a massage table in her solarium getting a massage from one of the four* BOYS. *She sings out,* a capella, *as usual*)

*Schub! Comptroller Schub!*

(COOLEY *enters: his eyebrows and hands go up at the spectacle of her body on the table*)

COOLEY

He isn't here yet.

CORA

I know he isn't here yet. It comforts me to call him.

COOLEY

Good for you, Sister!

(*He starts to massage her. The masseur gets resentful and works harder;* CORA *remains oblivious*)

CORA

But where is he? Where is his plan to save me? Oh, I'm depressed! NO! (COOLEY *removes his hands*) Cora Hoover Hooper will not be depressed!

COOLEY

Right you are, Sister!

(*Back go his hands*)

CORA

It's out of character. My newspaper always comments on my joy, my gaiety, my God! To think of Hapgood and that Lady from Lourdes joining forces in adjoining rooms! Oh, Cooley, pray she's too religious!

COOLEY

What's the good of praying? She's French.

MAGRUDER

*(Hurrying in)*

Reporting in, Your Honor.

*(His mouth drops open at the sight of the double massage)*

CORA

*(Salutes him, then)*

Where's Schub? Where's his plan? Magruder, will you shut your mouth and answer me?

MAGRUDER

The comptroller's on his way over.

*(Now he begins to massage Cora: all three masseurs are working in the same rhythm. She appears not to notice)*

CORA

Heaven! Schub will save me; he's brilliant. I'm attracted to brilliant men. The late Harvey Hoover Hooper was brilliant —in a rather stupid way, of course.

SCHUB

(*He enters*)

Dear Mayor-ess–

CORA

Dear Comptroller–(*She holds out her free hand for him to kiss. He does and begins to massage her arm. Now all four men are massaging her in rhythm*) You're here!

SCHUB

I am!

CORA

And the plan?

SCHUB

I have it.

CORA

What is it?

SCHUB

You resign.

CORA

I resign. (*Now realizing what it means*) I resign?! EVERY-BODY–OFF! (*On this, she pushes out with hands and feet, shoving the four masseurs away from her. Another of the four* BOYS *enters with negligee and shoes which she puts on while she screams at* SCHUB *and the others*) I resign? I resign?

SCHUB

Well, it *is* your administration that's in trouble—

CORA

My administration—you're putting the shoe on the wrong foot, you poop! I don't resign for one minute, Comptroller Schub! But you're fired. You're all fired. No, no, you're demoted. To Dog Catcher. Dog Catcher Schub, that's the job for a man like you. Man? (*She is dressed and raging about like a tigress now. The massage table and the two* BOYS *have gone*) Harvey Hoover Hooper was a man but his breed died with him! No wonder you have a lady mayor, you male impersonators! Well, guard the governor's mansion! Guard the White House! You're finished and I'm taking over! STOP THE MIRACLE!

COOLEY

Now, Sister—

CORA

Don't "sister" me, Sister! I said Stop the Miracle!

MAGRUDER

How?

CORA

By turning off the water, you nymphomaniac! The three of you have got exactly fifteen minutes in which to do it and to get that machinery out of the pumphouse or you go to jail. I am not going to have a scandal in my administration because when I run for Governor—

COOLEY

But Sister, Your Honor—

CORA

*And* President—

COOLEY

But you have just saved us!

CORA

. . . What?

COOLEY

If there is no water, there's no miracle. And if there's no miracle, there's nothing for that Lady from Lourdes to investigate!

MAGRUDER

She'll go home!

COOLEY

Right!

CORA

—*I'm brilliant!* But that still leaves Dr. Hapgood—

MAGRUDER

And the town.

COOLEY

Oh Sistren and Brethren, if we can just show the people

the evil of Dr. Hapgood's ways, they'll be normal and frightened—like they used to be—

CORA

And they'll do as I say. Cooley, *you're* brilliant. Now: how do we get them to turn against Hapgood? (COOLEY's *happy face falls; she pushes him away*) Washout. (*She turns and sees* SCHUB. *A little girl smile comes over her face and very sweetly, she croons*) Schub? *Comptroller* Schub?

(*He turns and looks at her. She lowers herself into a deep curtsey. Gallantly, he takes her hand, raises her and holds her in an embrace*)

SCHUB

All right: now.

CORA

Now?

COOLEY

(*Firmly*)

Now.

(*They all begin to pace, music enters and continues throughout the scene which is part rhythmic dialogue, part song*)

MAGRUDER

Now what?

SCHUB

(*Sings*)

Now why did the miracle go dry?

MAGRUDER

(*Sings*)

'Cause we turned the water off, is why.

CORA

Idiot!

SCHUB

Fool!

COOLEY

Oaf!

SCHUB

Moron!

CORA

Idiot!

SCHUB

Dolt!

CORA

IDIOT!

SCHUB

(*Sings*)

We didn't turn it off, you see,
'Cause we didn't turn it on, not *we* . . .

MAGRUDER

Who did?

SCHUB

(*After a moment, beaming*)

He did.

CORA

Who did?

COOLEY

He did?

MAGRUDER

You did?

SCHUB

(*Points upward*)

*He* did.

OTHERS

(*The light dawns; singing*)

*He* did!
Just what we just what we just what we needed!

SCHUB

(*Sings*)

Now why did He turn it off so quick?
A sign that our little town is sick.

CORA

Brilliant!

MAGRUDER

Good.

COOLEY

Clever.

CORA

(*Shoots him a look*)

*Brilliant.*

COOLEY

Brilliant.

SCHUB

(*Sings*)

Sick people running wild, no less.
And who is responsible?
(*Smiling slowly*)
One guess.

MAGRUDER

Who is?

CORA

(*Catching on, slowly*)

Doctor Hapgood.

COOLEY

*(Faster)*

Doctor Hapgood.

MAGRUDER

*(Faster)*

Doctor Hapgood!

ALL

*(Singing joyfully)*

Doctor Hapgood! Doctor Hapgood! Doctor Hapgood!
Hallelujah, Brother, cheers and acclaim!
Hallelujah, we've got someone to blame!
Hallelujah, Praise the Lord and Amen!

CORA

Schub, you've done it again.
*(The clinging vine)*
Whenever my world falls apart,
I never lose hope or lose heart.
Whatever the form
Of the storm
That may brew,
I've got you to lean on.
When everything's hopelessly gray,
You'll notice I'm youthfully gay!
There isn't a sing-
Le great thing
I can't do,
Not with you to lean on,
Darling you!

With you to depend on, I'll never quit.

There isn't a murder I couldn't commit.
I look like a love-
Ly girl of
Twenty-two!
I've got you to lean on!

SCHUB

*(Leaning on* COOLEY*)*
I've got you to lean on!

COOLEY

*(Leaning on* MAGRUDER*)*
I've got you to lean on!
(MAGRUDER *looks around in vain, starts to open his mouth, but* SCHUB *resumes pacing)*

SCHUB

*(Sings)*
Now how do we educate the mass?

MAGRUDER

*(Sings)*
With hoses and tommy-guns and gas.

CORA

Idiot!

SCHUB

Fool!

COOLEY

Oaf!

SCHUB

Moron!

CORA

Idiot!

SCHUB

Dolt!

CORA

IDIOT!

SCHUB

*(Sings)*

Can't tear a hero down by force.
So how do we educate—
*(Beaming, slowly)*
Of course—

MAGRUDER

How?

SCHUB

Smear him.

CORA

Smear him?

COOLEY

Smear him . . .

MAGRUDER

Spear him?

SCHUB

*Smear* him.

OTHERS

(*Singing*)

Smear him!
No one'll no one'll no one'll hear him!

SCHUB

(*Sings*)

Now what can we label him, my friends?
A phrase that the rabble comprehends . . .

COOLEY

"Religious pervert."

MAGRUDER

Brilliant!

CORA

Terrible!

MAGRUDER

(*Hastily*)

Terrible!

CORA

Idiot.

SCHUB

*(Sings)*

A phrase with a little more finesse . . .
Obscene but inspiring—
*(Smiling, slowly)*
Ah, yes—

MAGRUDER

Yes?

SCHUB

"Enemy of Heaven."

CORA

"—Heaven . . ."

COOLEY

"—Heaven . . ."

MAGRUDER

"—Heaven . . ."

CORA

*Heaven!*

MEN

*(Sing)*

Enemy of God,
Enemy of the Church,
Enemy of Heaven!

CORA

(*Sings*)

I didn't hear it,
But spread it.
I never said it,
But spread it!

ALL

(*Sing*)

Hallelujah, all our problems are through!
Hallelujah, that's what teamwork can do!
Hallelujah, Brothers, pull on the oars!

CORA

Schub, my kingdom is yours.
(*Clinging, as before*)
Whenever my world turns to dust,
I've always got someone to trust.
Whatever the sort
Of support
That I need,
I've got you to lean on.

MEN

When everything's hollow and black,
You'll always have us at your back.
(CORA *does a take*)
No matter how hollow,
We'll follow
Your lead—
And with us to lean on,
You'll succeed!

CORA

What comfort it is to have always known
That if they should catch me, I won't go alone.
I'll always give credit
Where credit
Is due—
I've got you to lean on!

MEN

We've got you to lean on!

CORA

*(Shakes her head, lovingly)*
*I've* got *you* to lean on—
*(They all start a vaudeville exit, music continuing under)*

SCHUB

Once *he's* out of the way . . .

CORA

And *she's* out of the way . . .

SCHUB

Our miracle is working again . . .
*(He exits)*

COOLEY

We're back in business . . .
*(He exits)*

MAGRUDER

(*Pointing up*)

And *he* turns off the water.

(*He exits*)

CORA

Idiot.

(CORA *doublecrosses the men by not exiting with them. Instead, joined by the four* BOYS *who come sneaking on from the opposite side, she goes into a joyful tap dance with them which ends with them throwing her on the massage table and wheeling her off madly but triumphantly. Blackout.*
*When the lights come up, they are rather dim. We are in the town square and the rock is slowly sliding on.* SCHUB, COOLEY *and* MAGRUDER *enter quietly.* SCHUB *looks up at the water, gives* MAGRUDER *a pat on the back and* MAGRUDER *disappears behind the rock. Music has begun a slow beat under this and continues as a* TOWNSMAN *enters.* SCHUB *begins to whisper to him and then points to the water—which suddenly has stopped.* SCHUB *wanders off as the* TOWNSMAN *stares and runs off.* COOLEY *has begun to impart the same news to a woman. Other people come on; the news is passed along; the first* TOWNSMAN *returns with some others. More and more people run on, look at the place where the water used to be; whisper to each other. Then, against the steadily building music, they begin to chant*)

CROWD

Hapgood. Hapgood! HAPGOOD! HAPGOOD! *HAPGOOD!!*

*(At the peak of the chant, the music cuts off and there is dead silence as* HAPGOOD *and* FAY *come out of the hotel. The smile leaves* HAPGOOD*'s face as he realizes this is not the admiring crowd who cheered him before.* MRS. SCHROEDER *makes her way forward to him)*

MRS. SCHROEDER

All right, Doctor . . . who's loony?

HAPGOOD

*(Charm)*

All of us.

MRS. SCHROEDER

*(Patient but hard)*

Doctor—*which* are the loonies?

FAY

Now—hear—this!

HAPGOOD

*(Stopping her)*

Mademoiselle feels that inasmuch as we are all children of heaven—

MAN

Shut up. We know about you.

HAPGOOD

You know what about—

MRS. SCHROEDER

Blasphemer! Which are your loony patients?

HAPGOOD

They're all gone.

MRS. SCHROEDER

Then where's our miracle? (*Percussion starts*) Name your patients, Doctor.

HAPGOOD

(*Charm*)

I never had any. I'm not even a doctor.

MAN

Come on! We want those loonies back in the bin.

MRS. SCHROEDER

We want our miracle!

HAPGOOD

Look–

MRS. SCHROEDER

Are you going to tell us?

MAN

We'll make him tell!

(*Interrogation music starts, darkly*)

HAPGOOD

(*To* SCHROEDER)

Watchcry!

MRS. SCHROEDER

(*Pointing at him*)

Enemy of the church!

HAPGOOD

(*Wheeling*)

Watchcry!

MAN

(*Pointing*)

Enemy of Heaven!

HAPGOOD

Watchcry!

SECOND MAN

(*Pointing*)

Enemy of God! *Get him!*

(*The crowd has slowly been edging closer. Now, as the music breaks out, they break out and go for* HAPGOOD *and* FAY. *The only escape is over the rock and* HAPGOOD *takes* FAY'*s hand and drags her up onto the rock which begins to revolve as the lights go down and the music gets louder. When the lights come up full, the rock has revolved and* FAY *and* HAPGOOD *are running into the cave. The pump and the hoseline for the water have been covered with old burlap.* HAPGOOD *starts to peer around as* FAY *rages*)

FAY

Ingrates. Traitors. Turncoats. Turntails. Rats. Finks!

HAPGOOD

(*Grins*)

Apostates

FAY

And after the way they worshipped you!

HAPGOOD

That's par for people. What is this place?

FAY

A cave left over from the Peer Gynt Festival. I don't understand you. You expect the worst and you hope for the best.

HAPGOOD

It's protection. And sometimes (*He takes her in his arms*) I get the best.

FAY

Blushing doesn't suit this wig.

HAPGOOD

Well, you'd better leave it on or you'll be recognized and arrested—and you'll have to identify your Cookies.

FAY

Never!

HAPGOOD

Never say that until you've—

*(He has been following the trail of a wire which has led him to the pump switch. He flicks it and now the burlap covering the pump begins to jiggle crazily. Bells peal out. As* HAPGOOD *yanks down the burlap and he and* FAY *see what the cave has been used for, there are cries and joyful yells from offstage. The door to the cave opens and* CORA *enters. She turns and calls out)*

CORA

Hold that mob at bay! *(Then, seeing* HAPGOOD *with* FAY *in his arms)* Doctor! What's been going on in here?

SCHUB

*(Enters)*

What's been going on in here?

CORA

Oh, stop asking damn fool questions. (SCHUB *shuts the cave door)* It's perfectly obvious what's been going on in here.

HAPGOOD

It certainly is.

SCHUB

Our miracles, my dear *mademoiselle*—*(He rips wires out: pump stops; noise outside stops)*—are a bit different from yours.

CORA

Oh, Schub!

SCHUB

This one is not going to work again until our dear doctor is run out of town.

FAY

*(To* CORA *and* SCHUB, *with the accent)*
You miserable, low, dirty—

MAGRUDER

*(Runs in)*
Your Honor, they're getting restless! Should we open fire?

CORA

Yes—on France!

MAGRUDER

Right!

*(He turns and crashes into a* TELEGRAPH BOY *with a long white beard who runs in)*

TELEGRAPH BOY

Telegram for Her Honor, the Mayor-ess!

CORA

*(To* MAGRUDER*)*
Clumsy! Have you no respect for the aged?

*(*MAGRUDER *goes as* CORA *passes the telegram to* SCHUB *who reads it)*

TELEGRAPH BOY

*(Nudging* CORA*)*
It's from the Governor.

CORA

(*Proudly*)

Ah!

SCHUB

Not exactly. (*Reading*) "Mayor-ess Cora Hoover Hooper: unless your quota of forty-nine patients is behind bars by sundown, you will be impeached."

CORA

(A capella)

*Schub!*

SCHUB

I'm here.

CORA

I'm finished.

SCHUB

Never say die.

CORA

I'd rather die than be dumped!

SCHUB

Dear lady, use my head. Forty-nine patients are as good as behind bars right this minute.

CORA

They are?! Where are they?

SCHUB

We can pick and choose from anybody in town—thanks to you, dear Doctor.

HAPGOOD

At your service, dear Comptroller. What have I done?

SCHUB

Group A? Group One? No difference between them; all mad as hatters? You've already certified them. All we need do is commit them.

CORA

Brilliant!

HAPGOOD

*Touché!*

FAY

No!

CORA

No?????

FAY

You cannot just pick people up off ze streets and lock zem up!

CORA

*I can do anything I want! (To* SCHUB*)* What do we need? A mere forty-nine patients! That's twenty head of males—no, *ten* head of males and thirty-nine head of females!

SCHUB

We'll just round them up and lock them up.

CORA

What a sweet ring that has to it! Schub-chen, you're a genius!

HAPGOOD

I salute you! Both of you! King and Queen of Madmen!

CORA

No: President and First Gentleman. *En garde, mademoiselle.* You have seventeen minutes to leave town—or I'll lock *you* up as an unregistered foreign agent. Schub!

SCHUB

Your Honor—

CORA

*Allez-y!*

(*And they exit grandly as* HAPGOOD *bows like a courtier*)

FAY

You salute them?

HAPGOOD

Sure

FAY

They're mad.

HAPGOOD

Very. But they were driven into a corner.

FAY

Who hasn't been?

HAPGOOD

And look at you, with that wig. Look at me! How else do you get out of corners? Either you die slowly or you have the strength to go crazy.

FAY

But what that pair of madmen is going to do is frightening! And we can stop them so easily by telling the town about that pump.

HAPGOOD

You might as well tell them there is no God.

FAY

But we *know* that miracle is a fake.

HAPGOOD

But it *works,* Fay. It works like any miracle!

FAY

For the moment!

HAPGOOD

That's all they want it for! They need it! You can lead

them by the hand into this cave, show them that electric pump, and they will still say: it's a miracle!

FAY

SO SALUTE! So do nothing!

HAPGOOD

Why not?

FAY

You can't die slowly!

HAPGOOD

Maybe not, but I can vegetate! Look, I was granted your asylum and I intend to enjoy it. Until the staff returns, I am going back to my hotel, sit on my balcony and watch life in the square.

FAY

You can't. I won't let you!

HAPGOOD

Fay, I AM NO DOCTOR FOR THIS COCKEYED WORLD!

FAY

But you're *my* doctor!

HAPGOOD

Then, I'm a bad doctor for you—because you've become as crazy as I *was*.

FAY

*So to hell with me!*

*(She slaps him across the face and rushes away from him furiously. All the lights go out except a spot on her as she sings angrily)*

Take one step
And see what it gets you,
See what it gets you,
See what it gets you!
One step up
And see how it gets you
Down.
Give yourself,
If somebody lets you—
See what it gets you,
See what it gets you!
Give yourself
And somebody lets you
Down.

Here's how to crawl
Now run, lady!
Here's how to walk
Now fly!
Here's how to feel—have fun, lady,
And a fond goodbye!

Reach out your hand
And see what it gets you,
See what it gets you,
See what it gets you!
Trouble is, whatever it gets,
You find
That once you see, you can't stay blind.

What do I do now,
Now that my eyes are wide?
Well, when the world goes mad, then they've got to be shown,
And when the hero quits then you're left on your own,
And when you want things done, you have to do them yourself alone!
And if I'm not ready
And light-headed,
I can't stand here dumb.
So, ready or not, here—I hope—I come!

Anyone can whistle, that's what they say—easy.
Anyone can whistle any old day—easy.
It's all so simple: relax, let go, let fly.
And someone tell me why can't I?
Whistle at a dragon: down it'll fall—easy.
Whistle at a hero, trumpets and all—easy.
Just once I'll do it,
Just once before I die.
Lead me to the battle,
What does it take?
Over the top!
Joan at the stake!
Anyone can whistle—

*(She tries, unsuccessfully)*

Well, no one can say
I didn't try!

*(There is a blackout. In the darkness, the sound of a police whistle and the lights come up on the town square where police* DEPUTIES *are rushing back and forth with small machine guns, getting in each other's way and upsetting* MAGRUDER *who is directing others as they wheel on a large animal cage. Over all this, we hear* CORA*'s voice enormously amplified:)*

CORA (*Off*)

PLACES, EVERYONE! IT'S LOCK UP TIME! SYNCHRONIZE YOUR WATCHES! SURROUND THE SQUARE!

(DR. DETMOLD *has come on and stands by the door to the cage with a hospital clipboard in his hand. Another "civilian" has wandered on: an* OLD LADY *with a shopping bag full of vegetables. She is watching the activities with a touch of interest and pleasure when:*)

CORA (*Off*)

ARREST THAT CRAZY LADY! (MRS. SCHROEDER *wanders on; the* DEPUTIES *make a dive for her*) NO, NOT MRS. SCHROEDER! THE OTHER CRAZY LADY! SHE'S A FUGITIVE FROM THE COOKIE JAR!

(*The* OLD LADY *has been looking around for the "other crazy lady" when the* DEPUTIES *descend on her, surround her and shove her into a pastel-colored straitjacket. There is dead silence, and then* CORA *sweeps on in a chic but bizarre version of a deputy's uniform*)

CORA

Well done, gentlemen! From now, I expect every man among you to be—*on—your—toes!*

(*And as the lights brighten and the music starts, that is precisely where the* DEPUTIES *get: every one of them stands on point! Even the* OLD LADY *is up on point, for this is the beginning of the Cookie Chase, a sequence wherein* CORA, *her cohorts and the* DEPUTIES *lock up anybody in town they can get their hands on. It is all done to waltz music in the style of classical ballet short variations, punctuated by someone being thrown into or released from the cage*)

CORA

(*Sings, as* DEPUTIES *promenade with the* OLD LADY)
Lock 'em up! Put 'em away
In The Jar!
Time to start getting the nets out!
Lock 'em up
Into the cage!
Quietly: no one must know.
Cart 'em off into the bin;
Turn the key
Quick before anyone gets out!
Turn the key, throw it away,
There we are: forty-eight to go!

(*On this last, she points to the* OLD LADY *who has been captured in an arabesque by two* DEPUTIES. *The music continues as*)

CORA

Detmold.

DETMOLD

Yes, Your Honor.

CORA

Check in your patients.

DETMOLD

(*To* OLD LADY)
Your name, Madame?

OLD LADY

This doesn't fit. It's much too big. I wear a size eleven, *maybe a* twelve—

DETMOLD

Did you always hate your father?

CORA

Convict her later, arrest her now! There's only one question that needs answering.

(*She sings*)

Are they breathing? Then they're Cookies.
Are they moving? Then they're Cookies.
Are they living? Then they're Cookies.
So get on with it! Quick, get on with it!
Are they human? Then they're Cookies.
So shut up, my dear Doctor, and shut her up too!

(*The waltz ends with a flourish as the* OLD LADY *is clapped into the cage and the cage and the door slammed shut. A new waltz, a gentle one, begins and on dances—on point, of course—a* PILGRIM *we have seen before*)

CORA

(*Sings*)

Lookie, lookie, here comes Cookie
Now.
Naughty Cookie, playing hookey—
That, we don't allow.

(*Three* DEPUTIES *dance a* pas de quatre *with the* PILGRIM *who also is tossed into the cage at the end. Then other people are captured—waltz variations—and locked up in the cage: a wildly weeping widow; a pair of young lovers; a "Blanche Du Bois." Finally, the activity is a bit too much for* CORA *who takes the key to the cage and hands it to* SCHUB*—who has just entered executing a* tour jeté*—as she sings*)

CORA

You take the key, my love,
I'm too exhausted to move!
Music, I must have music,
A moment's music or my head will burst!

(DEPUTIES *bring on her litter; a* QUARTET OF DEPUTIES *stands by it, ready to sing for her*)

I know you'll meet the test—
You've been well rehearsed.
Do your best
(Meaning do your worst),
Let me rest
And remember, Schub-chen:
Women and children first!

(*She collapses on the litter. The* QUARTET *reprises "Lock 'Em Up" while* SCHUB *does a variation with three different girls—whom he locks up. Now* FAY *appears in her red wig and her red feather-trimmed coat*)

SCHUB

(*Speaks, to music*)

Not yet gone back to Lourdes yet?

FAY

*Non*

SCHUB

*Pourquoi pas?*

FAY

*Pourquoi* you hold ze key to my heart.

(*She whips out a feather fan and proceeds to do a

*wild ballroom waltz with* SCHUB *during which she vamps him and gets the key out of his pocket. A* LADY DEPUTY *appears like an operatic soprano complete with chiffon handkerchief and trills madly while* FAY *pursues her task and gets rid of* SCHUB. FAY *then unlocks the cage and lets out the captured victims.* CORA *awakens from her little nap on the litter and is livid to find her victims gone. This inspires a furioso chase with* DEPUTIES *rounding up people wildly and dumping them in the cage.* CORA *goes off—Tally-Ho-ing for the hunt—at the moment when the* DEPUTIES *have captured a particularly fierce looking woman. They throw her in the cage but she escapes and proceeds to knock them out with a balletic series of spins, kicks and uppercuts. She stalks off and they are just coming to when* FAY *returns and sings frantically)*

FAY

Fire!
Hurricane!
Everyone off of ze streets!
Run for your lives! Run for your lives!
Ze dam has burst!
Run for your lives, run for your lives!
Ze lion's loose!
Fire, bubonic plague, air raid warning—
Hurry, run! Run! Run!

*(The clarion call is picked up by the frightened* DEPUTIES *who run about and off as* FAY *opens the cage and lets out the captured people. This time, they dance out like the swans in* Swan Lake. *The* DEPUTIES *return as the hunters in that ballet and a winding line of fleeing "Swans" led by* FAY *and following*

*"Hunters" led by* CORA *and* SCHUB *is dancing about the stage as the music builds to a big Tschaikovskian climax. The chase ends with a ballet tableau:* FAY *is downstage, stretched out in the arms of three* DEPUTIES; CORA *is to one side,* SCHUB *to the other.* DR. DETMOLD *ambles forward, looks down at* FAY *exactly as an analyst looks down on his patient)*

DETMOLD

Why, there you are, Nurse Apple! Have you been acting out your dreams?

CORA

Nurse Apple?? (*She reaches over and snatches off* FAY'S *wig which she then hands to* SCHUB, *saying*) It's that Lady from Lourdes! I always knew she dyed her hair.

(*The* DEPUTIES *release* FAY *as* SCHUB *hands the wig to* MAGRUDER. *Other* DEPUTIES *roll the cage off and* HAPGOOD *appears on the balcony of the Hotel*)

SCHUB

(*To* FAY)

Dear lady, take defeat like a gentleman and hand over the records.

FAY

I don't have them.

CORA

(*Indicating* HAPGOOD)

Then he has!

FAY

No one has them.

CORA

How can no one have something that exists?

FAY

They don't exist. I destroyed them.

CORA

(*Indicating* FAY'S *feather-trimmed coat*)

Magruder! Get out the tar! You can use her own feathers.

SCHUB

Haste makes waste, Madame President. (*To* FAY) The names will do. I'm sure you know them.

DETMOLD

By heart! She may never forget a face but she always remembers a name.

FAY

Oh, Dr. Detmold . . .

CORA

Front and center, missy.

(*Slowly,* FAY *comes forward*)

HAPGOOD

(*Softly, in French*)

*Courage, mademoiselle.*

CORA

Never mind the *courage;* just the names.

FAY

I . . . I'll begin with the names of the people who faked the miracle.

SCHUB

What?!

FAY

Comptroller Schub and Mayor—

SCHUB

Anarchist!

COOLEY

Atheist!

CORA

Suffragette!

FAY

They invented the miracle! There's a pump in the old cave—

CROWD

Communist! Fascist! Red! Pink! Cheat! Liar! Fraud! Foreigner! Stoolpigeon! Embezzler! Capitalist! Egghead! Etc.

*(They go for her but* HAPGOOD *leaps over the Hotel balcony and pulls* FAY *to one side, protecting her from*

*the mob as* SCHUB *orders the* DEPUTIES *to hold them back)*

CORA

At ease . . . It's an old game for the fox to cry "wolf" when she's really a rat. The names, Miss Apple, in alphabetical order. Dr. Detmold, stand by to check in your homing pigeons.

(FAY *stands alone. There is a slight movement from the crowd, as though some* COOKIES *are trying to hide)*

SCHUB

*(Softly)*

We are going to lock up forty-nine people, Nurse Apple. Whether that includes the innocent—depends on a lady who claims she fights for justice.

FAY

*(After a moment)*

Anthony, Susie B.

*(A woman slowly comes forward)*

Brecht, Herman.

*(A young man comes forward and stands next to the woman. During the following, others step out slowly and sadly, forming a column in two lines)*

FAY

Chaplin, Rodney . . . Dillinger, Myrna . . . Engels, Dave . . . Freud, Harriet . . . Gandhi, Salvatore . . .

*(Now she pauses a fraction longer.* HAPGOOD *looks at her, then steps forward and joins the column.* FAY *sees this and speaks hastily:)*

Ibsen, Selma . . .

*(At this,* HAPGOOD *leaves the line and walks up to* FAY. *But she turns away and continues to call other names as the lights dim and the "Bluebird" music begins softly)*

Jorgenson, Otto . . . Kierkegaard, Mac . . . Lafitte, Roger . . . Mozart, Miriam . . .

*(The stage is quite dim now. The brightest light is on the column of* COOKIES *as the grin breaks over their faces and they sing "The Bluebird Song" as they march off in the direction of Dr. Detmold's Cookie Jar.*

*When the last note has trailed off, the stage is empty except for* FAY *and* HAPGOOD. *Everyone else has disappeared into the darkness. She cannot face him, and his tone to her is cold)*

HAPGOOD

Why didn't you turn me in?

FAY

Why didn't you turn yourself in?

HAPGOOD

I can't stop being crazy. But that's my own affair.

FAY

No, it isn't. You're the hope of the world.

HAPGOOD

I don't think you can possibly repeat that sentence without laughing.

FAY

You're the hope of the world. You and all the crazy people like you.

HAPGOOD

From the first moment, you've been trying to put me on a white horse! Now stop it!

FAY

*(Turning to him, angrily)*

Then why don't you go turn yourself in now?!

*(A long moment; then)*

HAPGOOD

. . . I can't. And you know it. *(Then, with a smile)* Well, you might at least look pleased.

FAY

But now you'll go away.

HAPGOOD

You know, you confuse issues: you get too personal.

FAY

It's a problem ladies have.

HAPGOOOD

*(Goes to her)*

Come with me, Fay.

FAY

My Cookies need someone to take care of them.

HAPGOOD

That's an excuse. Come with me.

FAY

I'm too unmusical.

HAPGOOD

I'll teach you.

FAY

You tried that. You saw a minute ago how easily I crumble.

HAPGOOD

. . . Where's your wig?

FAY

You wouldn't want me like that. Not really. You see, you're marvelous and crazy. I'm competent and practical—and that's what *I'm* stuck with . . . But I'm very important here.

(*Music begins softly*)

HAPGOOD

Four wives: they all tried to change me. The girls who don't . . . are the girls you don't marry.

(*He reaches out, almost touches her, then turns and slowly starts off. But he stops as she begins to sing very quietly*)

FAY

You like my hair, yes? My lips, yes?
Ze sway of my, how you say? of my hips . . .
Yes? . . .

(*Music continues under; after a moment, she speaks*)
You don't leave me with anything.

HAPGOOD

I'm sorry. For me, it was marvelous.

FAY

Marvelous?

HAPGOOD

(*Sings*)
With so little to be sure of,
If there's anything at all,
If there's anything at all,
I'm sure of her and now and us together.
All I'll ever be I owe you,
If there's anything to be.
Being sure enough of you
Makes me sure enough of me.
Thanks for everything we did,
Everything that's past,
Everything that's over too fast.
None of it was wasted,
All of it will last:
Everything that's here and now and us together!
It was marvelous to know you
And it isn't really through.
Crazy business this, this life we live in—
Don't complain about the time we're given—
With so little to be sure of in this world,
We had a moment!
A marvelous moment!

FAY

(*Sings, quietly*)

A marvelous moment.
A beautiful time.
I need you more than I can say.
I need you more than just today.
I guess I need you more than you need me,
And yet I'm happy.
All I'll ever be I owe you,
If there's anything to be.
Being sure enough of you
Made me sure enough of me.

HAPGOOD

(*Simultaneously with the above*)

The more I memorize your face,
The more I never want to leave.
Come with me, Fay.

FAY

(*Shakes her head*)

Thanks for everything we did,
Everything that's past,
Everything that's over too fast.

HAPGOOD

(*Simultaneously*)

There's more of love in me right now
Than all the little bits of love
I've known before.

BOTH

None of it was wasted,
All of it will last:

Everything that's here and now and us together!
It was marvelous to know you
And it's never really through.
Crazy business this, this life we live in—
Can't complain about the time we're given—
With so little to be sure of in this world—

FAY

*(To herself)*

Hold me.
Hold me.

*(Softly, the music ends and they walk off in opposite directions, she toward the asylum, he toward the outside world. The lights come up slowly on the town square and with them, comes the sound of bells pealing faintly in the distance. As the bells get louder and louder, first one, then another and another* PILGRIM *hurries excitedly across the square. Then a* TOWNSPERSON; *a* PILGRIM; *more* TOWNSPEOPLE; *all hurrying, excited, beckoning, all rushing elatedly toward the sound of the bells. During this,* CORA *rushes out of City Hall and tries to stop one of the running people)*

CORA

Where are you running? I asked you a question. You there, with the blue pants with the pleats in front: WHERE ARE YOU RUNNING? *(Calling into the doorway of City Hall)* Cooley! Stop tampering with those books and find out what that ringing is and what is—WHERE ARE YOU RUNNING? I am your Mayor-ess, Cora Hoover Hooper, and I demand to know where—

COOLEY

(*Outside now, beckons to one of the runners*)
Ho there! Ho there!

CORA

"Ho there." Don't *ask*, you coward. Stop them; grab one of them; make one of them—(MAGRUDER *is racing by with a sexy young girl*) Magruder! MAGRUDER, STOP!

MAGRUDER

Excuse me, Y'r Honor—Brother Cooley—

CORA

Where are you running?

MAGRUDER

The town beyond the valley—they've got a miracle!

CORA

How dare they!

COOLEY

What's *their* water coming out of?

MAGRUDER

It ain't water. It's a miracle.

COOLEY

What do you mean, it's a miracle?

MAGRUDER

It's this statue—in the middle of the square—nothing and no one near it—and suddenly—it got a warm heart!

CORA

Oh, that can happen to anyone.

MAGRUDER

But this statue is made of marble! And they say a man who was born without sight just touched the heart of that statue and—

VELMA (The sexy girl)

(*To* Magruder)

Sam, are you coming? I wanna see that miracle today!

MAGRUDER

Okay, little lady. Excuse me, Y'r Honor, but maybe what ails me—

(*Backing away*)

VELMA

SAM!

MAGRUDER

Comin'!

(*He runs off with her*)

CORA

Magruder, you're disgusting and you're fired! (*To others fleeing*) You're all disgusting, and I'm going to fine everyone of you. Cooley! Cooley, where are you sneaking, you little sneak? Now don't tell me that you, of all people—

COOLEY

It could be a miracle.

CORA

It could not!

COOLEY

(*Hurrying off*)

I want to see for myself!

CORA

But if you've seen one, you've seen them all! Cooley! Cooley, you're fired! You there! I appoint *you* Treasurer! (*To another*) I appoint you Chief of Police! (*To another*) I appoint you (*But now her four* BOYS *come tapping across in an Off-to-Buffalo; and after them comes the rock as though even it wants to go to the new miracle.* CORA *calls desperately:*) SCHUB! COMPTROLLER SCHUB! Where are you? I need you! (*Silence. Everything stops. No more running, no more bells, and the rock is still behind her as* SCHUB *comes quietly out of City Hall. A moment*) Is it really you?

SCHUB

There is no reasonable facsimile of me.

CORA

And you're not running with the others?

SCHUB

My dear lady, running is for the herd. Come now, Cora: you can't win 'em all. You need to relax. Let's dine together this evening. My house at eight. Or your house. It makes no difference. I'll be at your house at seven.

CORA

*(Shakes her head)*

My lovely town. They'll be poor again and they'll hate me again.

SCHUB

True.

CORA

I don't like economics, Schub. That's the trouble with making history. You come down from the mount or the hills: the leader, the saviour. The peasants cheer and parade: "Off with the old! On with the new!" It's all glamorous and exciting—and then you have to get down to the dreary business of getting money in the till . . . Oh Schub, if only we could think of a new miracle!

SCHUB

It isn't miracles we need, Cora. It's to be in step. Where's everybody going? Mad.

*(He stops; she looks at him. Slowly, music comes in under)*

CORA

*(Hushed)*

Schub—

SCHUB

Your Honor—

CORA

There's no more room at The Cookie Jar—

SCHUB

Your factories are empty—

CORA

Your houses are empty—

SCHUB

The stores are empty—

CORA

City Hall is empty—

SCHUB

Your Honor—

CORA

Schub—

SCHUB

We'll turn the whole damn town into a Cookie Jar!!!!

CORA

AND THEY'LL LOVE ME! (*Music: "I've Got You to Lean On." Very gay*) Schub, you *are* brilliant! If I'm not careful, I'll marry you.

SCHUB

It's your life or mine.

CORA

*Mine.* It's later than I thought.
(*She sings*)
With you to depend on, I'll never quit.
There isn't a murder I couldn't commit.
Whenever I falter, Gibraltar comes through.
I've got you to lean on—
(*A dance break*)

SCHUB

I've got you to lean on—
(*A dance break*)

BOTH

I've got you to lean on—
(*And on comes an official-looking woman in a severe suit, carrying a small black case. Her name is* OSGOOD)

OSGOOD

Excuse me, but could you direct me to The Cookie Jar?

CORA

Certainly! Right this way!
(*And she and* SCHUB *dance off into City Hall.* OSGOOD *gapes at them as the music ends; and from across the square comes a small group of* COOKIES *led by* FAY *who is once again in her nurse's uniform*)

OSGOOD

Just a moment, nurse. Are you from Dr. Detmold's Asylum?

FAY

Yes, I'm the head nurse.

OSGOOD

Good, I'm Dr. Detmold's new assistant: Dr. Jane Borden Osgood.

FAY

I'm glad you're late.

OSGOOD

My train was delayed at the town beyond the valley. They have what they think is a miracle there.

FAY

Yes; we just heard.

OSGOOD

Well—hear—this! (*And the same music as for* FAY'S *speech in the beginning comes in angrily*) Now—Point—One! I am a woman of science: control and order, reason and logic.

(*Slowly,* FAY *turns and stares at* OSGOOD *in horror*)

FAY

Oh, no!

OSGOOD

(*Simultaneously*)

I shall take these beings who are human on a quick march to that miracle, real or imaginary. If anyone of any race, creed, or color tries to stop you from taking that miracle, wait until you see the whites of their eyes and then spit—and spit *hard!* (*Music stops*) Human beings! Atten-shun! Forward—march! Hut-two-three-four! Hut-two-three-four!

(*"The Bluebird Song" has come in as a loud, lusty march. Led by* OSGOOD, *the* COOKIES *march off to the new miracle, leaving* FAY *alone on the stage. She looks after them desolately, then murmurs*)

FAY

Oh, Hapgood . . . (*She moves, looking to where he last went off*) Hapgood? (*Frantically now, she climbs up the rock and calls desperately*) HAPGOOD! (*No answer, no sign*) HAPGOOD!!

(*Nothing. She tries to whistle for him: not a sound. Then, she cups her hands around her mouth as though to shout for him but in one last, desperate effort, she shoves two fingers in her mouth and blows with all her strength and hope. And out comes a whistle: a shrill, piercing, ugly whistle—but it's a whistle! It even startles her but a great smile breaks over her face. A moment, then* HAPGOOD *saunters on*)

HAPGOOD

(*Laughing*)

That's good enough.

(*The music of "With So Little to Be Sure Of" comes in strong as he lifts her down off the rock into his arms. They look at each other and kiss; and as they do, there is a surge of music from the orchestra and again, a great surge of water from the rock. But this time, it is an enormous spout of water which is every color of the rainbow and which drenches them like a shower as*

*The Curtain Falls*

When ANYONE CAN WHISTLE opened on Broadway on April 4, 1964, Whitney Bolton of the *Morning Telegraph* prophesied:

"If *Anyone Can Whistle* is a success, the American musical theatre will have advanced itself and prepared the way for further breakdown of now old and worn techniques and points of view. If it is not a success, we sink back into the old formula method and must wait for the breakthrough.

"Arthur Laurents takes a scalpel to a flourish of our illusions and cuts away the fat. He puts before us the credo that in this day to be mad is to be sane, to be insane is to be healthy and in proper mental frame for this day. We live, in short, in crazy times and it is better for the individual to be somewhat daft and, thus, meet craze with craze.

"To all concerned, top and bottom, a thank you for trying, a thank you for wanting to elevate the American musical theatre to new standards of intellect. Let no one concerned be discouraged.

"The American musical theatre is less ponderous and ridiculous today because of *Anyone Can Whistle*, no matter what its fate."

Its fate was not a bright one. For despite the efforts of a few particularly insightful critics, the majority were outraged at the violation of traditional musical comedy forms. With the wrath of the Broadway establishment raining upon its head, *Anyone Can Whistle* succumbed to a premature demise after but nine performances at a loss of its entire $350,000 investment (including financial backing by four musical theatre greats: Irving Berlin, Frank Loesser, Richard Rodgers, and Jule Styne, who had faith in the project).

Here, at last, was a truly new musical, in a theatre full of so-called new musicals, which were, in actuality, musical adaptations of other sources usually best left unmusicalized; a musical that incorporated scathing satire with sly subtlety; a lively but literate libretto with a wise and witty score. *Anyone Can Whistle* was the marriage of musical comedy with theatre of the absurd, consummated cleverly and exhilaratingly executed.